Robert Barr (16 September 1849 – 21 October 1912) was a Scottish-Canadian short story writer and novelist. Robert Barr was born in Barony, Lanark, Scotland to Robert Barr and Jane Watson. In 1854, he emigrated with his parents to Upper Canada at the age of four years old. His family settled on a farm near the village of Muirkirk. Barr assisted his father with his job as a carpenter, and developed a sound work ethic. Robert Barr then worked as a steel smelter for a number of years before he was educated at Toronto Normal School in 1873 to train as a teacher. After graduating Toronto Normal School, Barr became a teacher, and eventually headmaster/principal of the Central School of Windsor, Ontario in 1874. While Barr worked as head master of the Central School of Windsor, Ontario, he began to contribute short stories—often based on personal experiences, and recorded his work. On August 1876, when he was 27, Robert Barr married Ontario-born Eva Bennett, who was 21. (Source: Wikipedia)

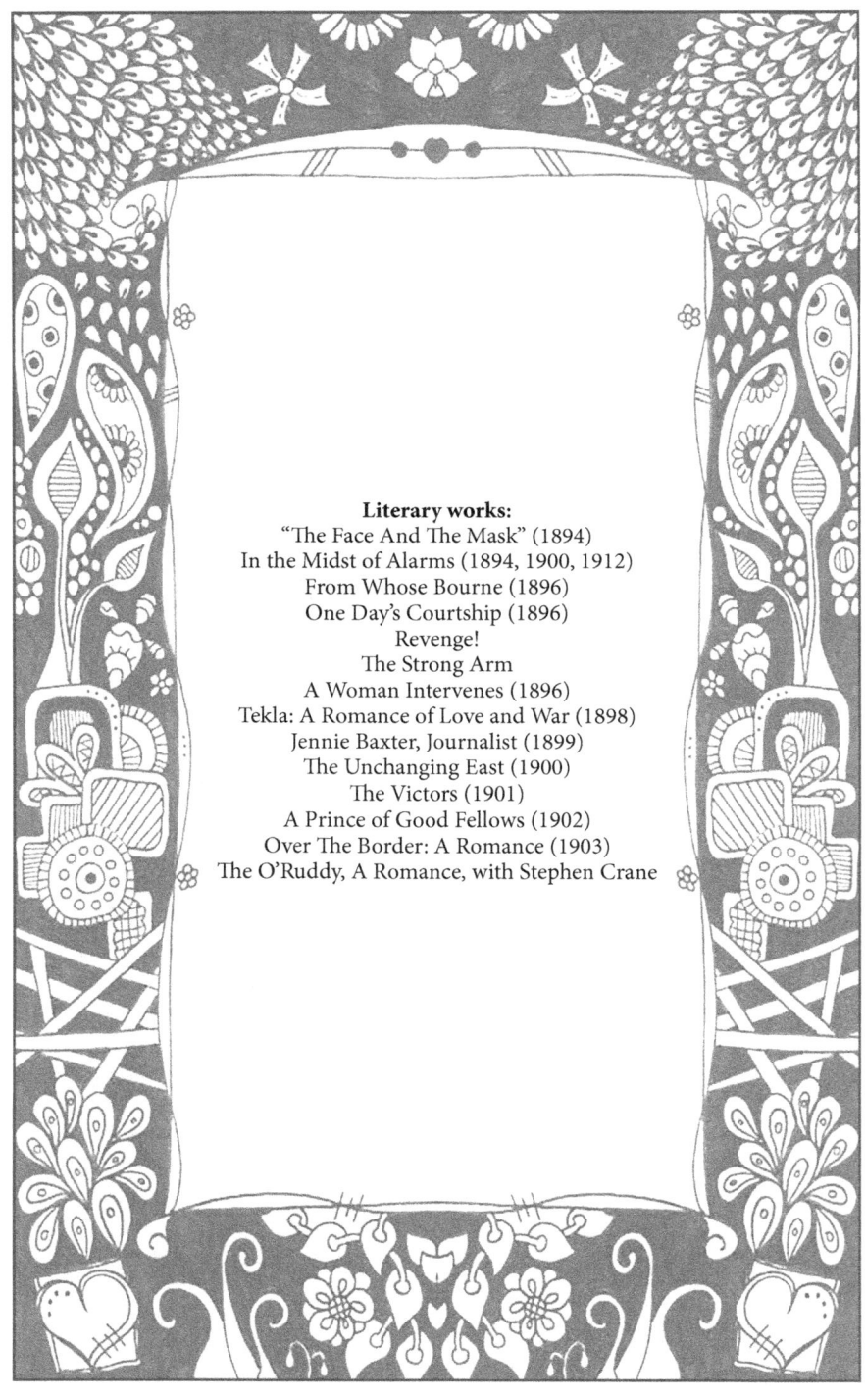

Literary works:
"The Face And The Mask" (1894)
In the Midst of Alarms (1894, 1900, 1912)
From Whose Bourne (1896)
One Day's Courtship (1896)
Revenge!
The Strong Arm
A Woman Intervenes (1896)
Tekla: A Romance of Love and War (1898)
Jennie Baxter, Journalist (1899)
The Unchanging East (1900)
The Victors (1901)
A Prince of Good Fellows (1902)
Over The Border: A Romance (1903)
The O'Ruddy, A Romance, with Stephen Crane

THRONE CLASSICS

In a Steamer Chair
and Other Stories,

A Woman Intervenes
&
The Sword Maker
ROBERT BARR

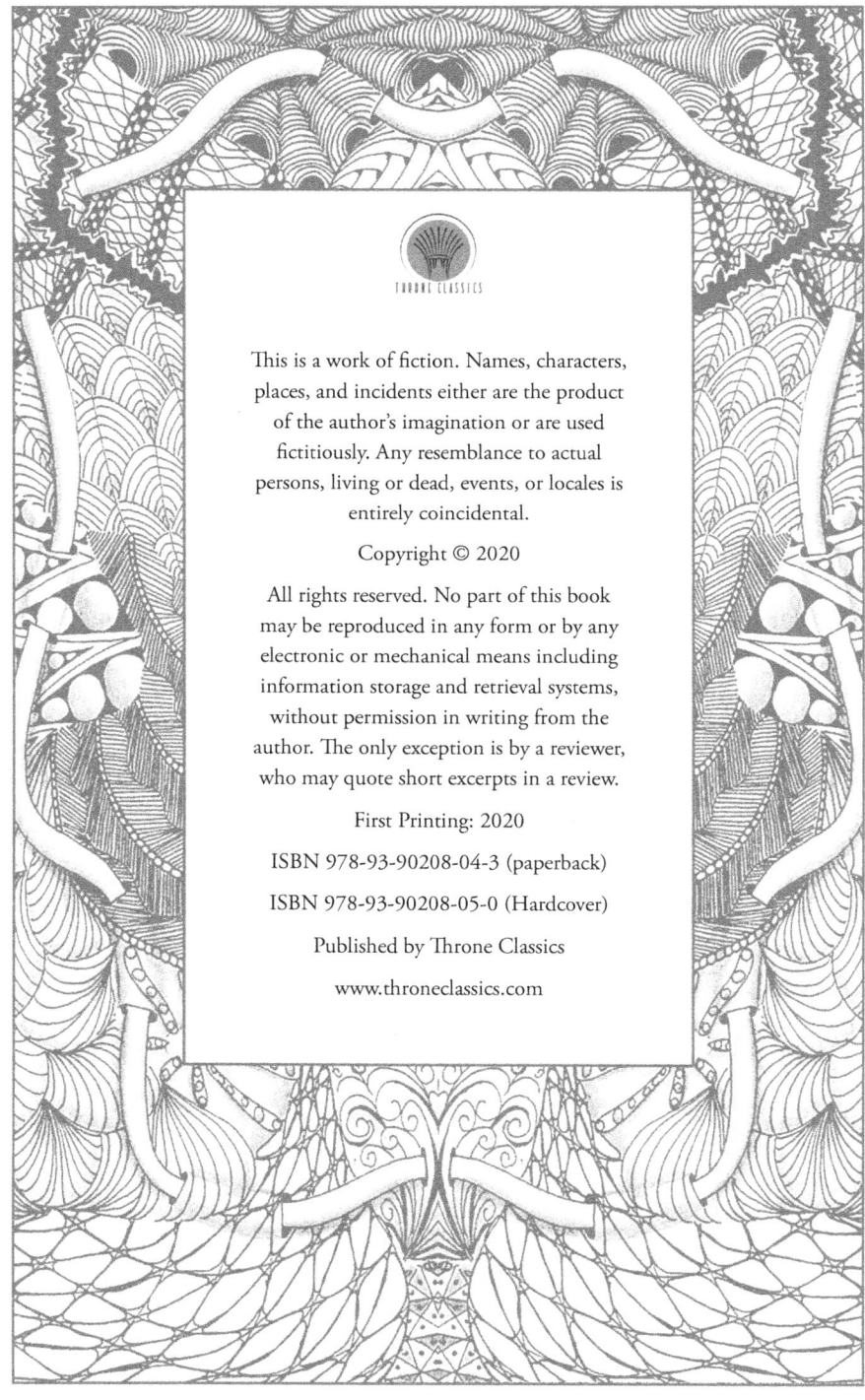

THRONE CLASSICS

First Printing: 2020

ISBN 978-93-90208-04-3 (paperback)

ISBN 978-93-90208-05-0 (Hardcover)

Published by Throne Classics

www.throneclassics.com

Contents

In a Steamer Chair
and Other Stories,

A Woman Intervenes
&
The Sword Maker

IN A STEAMER CHAIR, AND
OTHER STORIES

As the incidents related herein took place during voyages between England and America, I dedicate this book to the Vagabond Club of London, and the Witenagemote Club of Detroit, in the hope that, if any one charges me with telling a previously told tale, the fifty members of each club will rise as one man and testify that they were called upon to endure the story in question from my own lips prior to the alleged original appearance of the same.

R. B.

In a Steamer Chair

The First Day

Mr. George Morris stood with his arms folded on the bulwarks of the steamship City of Buffalo, and gazed down into the water. All around him was the bustle and hurry of passengers embarking, with friends bidding good-bye. Among the throng, here and there, the hardworking men of the steamer were getting things in order for the coming voyage. Trunks were piled up in great heaps ready to be lowered into the hold; portmanteaux, satchels, and hand-bags, with tags tied to them, were placed in a row waiting to be claimed by the passengers, or taken down into the state-rooms. To all this bustle and confusion George Morris paid no heed. He was thinking deeply, and his thoughts did not seem to be very pleasant. There was nobody to see him off, and he had evidently very little interest in either those who were going or those who were staying behind. Other passengers who had no friends to bid them farewell appeared to take a lively interest in watching the hurry and scurry, and in picking out the voyagers from those who came merely to say good-bye.

At last the rapid ringing of a bell warned all lingerers that the time for the final parting had come. There were final hand-shakings, many embraces, and not a few tears, while men in uniform with stentorian voices cried, "All ashore." The second clanging of the bell, and the preparations for pulling up the gang-planks hurried the laggards to the pier. After the third ringing the gang-plank was hauled away, the inevitable last man sprang to the wharf, the equally inevitable last passenger, who had just dashed up in a cab, flung his valises to the steward, was helped on board the ship, and then began the low pulsating stroke, like the beating of a heart, that would not cease until the vessel had sighted land on the other side. George Morris's eyes were fixed on the water, yet apparently he was not looking at it, for when it began to spin away from the sides of the ship he took no notice, but still gazed at the mass of seething foam that the steamer threw off from her as she moved through the bay. It was evident that the sights of New York harbour were very familiar to the young man, for he paid no attention to them, and the vessel was beyond Sandy Hook before he changed his position. It is doubtful if he would have changed it then, had not a steward touched him on the elbow, and said— had not a steward touched him on the elbow, and said—

"Any letters, sir?"

"Any what?" cried Morris, suddenly waking up from his reverie.

"Any letters, sir, to go ashore with the pilot?"

"Oh, letters. No, no, I haven't any. You have a regular post-office on

board, have you? Mail leaves every day?"

"No, sir," replied the steward with a smile, "not every day, sir. We

send letters ashore for passengers when the pilot leaves the ship. The next mail, sir, will leave at Queenstown."

The steward seemed uncertain as to whether the passenger was trying to joke with him or was really ignorant of the ways of steamships. However, his tone was very deferential and explanatory, not knowing but that this particular passenger might come to his lot at the table, and stewards take very good care to offend nobody. Future fees must not be jeopardized.

Being aroused, Mr. Morris now took a look around him. It seemed wonderful how soon order had been restored from the chaos of the starting. The trunks had disappeared down the hold; the portmanteaux were nowhere to be seen. Most of the passengers apparently were in their state-rooms exploring their new quarters, getting out their wraps, Tam-o-Shanters, fore-and-aft caps, steamer chairs, rugs, and copies of paper-covered novels. The deck was almost deserted, yet here and there a steamer chair had already been placed, and one or two were occupied. The voyage had commenced. The engine had settled down to its regular low thud, thud; the vessel's head rose gracefully with the long swell of the ocean, and, to make everything complete, several passengers already felt that inward qualm—the accompaniment of so many ocean voyages. George Morris yawned, and seemed the very picture of ennui. He put his hands deeply into his coat pockets, and sauntered across the deck. Then he took a stroll up the one side and down the other. As he lounged along it was very evident that he was tired of the voyage, even before it began. Judging from his listless manner nothing on earth could arouse the interest of the young man. The gong sounded faintly in the inner depths of the ship somewhere announcing dinner. Then, as the steward appeared up the companion way, the sonorous whang, whang became louder, and the hatless official, with the gong in hand, beat that instrument several final strokes, after which he disappeared into the regions below.

"I may as well go down," said Morris to himself, "and see where they have placed me at table. But I haven't much interest in dinner."

As he walked to the companion-way an elderly gentleman and a young lady appeared at the opposite door, ready to descend the stairs. Neither of them saw the young man. But if they had, one of them at least would have doubted the young man's sanity. He stared at the couple for a moment with a look of grotesque horror on his face that was absolutely comical. Then he turned, and ran the length of the deck, with a speed unconscious of all obstacles.

"Say," he cried to the captain, "I want to go ashore. I must go ashore. I want to go ashore with the pilot."

The captain smiled, and said, "I shall be very happy to put you ashore, sir, but it will have to be at Queenstown. The pilot has gone."

"Why, it was only a moment ago that the steward asked me if I had any letters to post. Surely he cannot have gone yet?"

"It is longer than that, I am afraid," said the captain. "The pilot left the ship half an hour ago."

"Is there no way I can get ashore? I don't mind what I pay for it."

"Unless we break a shaft and have to turn back there is no way that I know of. I am afraid you will have to make the best of it until we reach Queenstown."

"Can't you signal a boat and let me get off on her?"

"Well, I suppose we could. It is a very unusual thing to do. But that would delay us for some time, and unless the business is of the utmost necessity, I would not feel justified in delaying the steamer, or in other words delaying several hundred passengers for the convenience of one. If you tell me what the trouble is I shall tell you at once whether I can promise to signal a boat if I get the opportunity of doing so."

Morris thought for a moment. It would sound very absurd to the captain for him to say that there was a passenger on the ship whom he desired very much not to meet, and yet, after all, that was what made the thought of the voyage so distasteful to him.

He merely said, "Thank you," and turned away, muttering to himself something in condemnation of his luck in general. As he walked slowly down the deck up which he had rushed with such headlong speed a few moments before, he noticed a lady trying to set together her steamer chair, which had seemingly given way—a habit of steamer chairs. She looked up appealing at Mr. Morris, but that gentleman was too preoccupied with his own situation to be gallant. As he passed her, the lady said—

"Would you be kind enough to see if you can put my steamer chair together?"

Mr. Morris looked astonished at this very simple request. He had resolved to make this particular voyage without becoming acquainted with anybody, more especially a lady.

"Madam," he said, "I shall be pleased to call to your assistance the deck steward if you wish."

"If I had wished that," replied the lady, with some asperity, "I would have asked you to do so. As it is, I asked you to fix it yourself."

"I do not understand you," said Mr. Morris, with some haughtiness. "I do not see that it matters who mends the steamer chair so long as the steamer chair is mended. I am not a deck steward." Then, thinking he had spoken rather harshly, he added, "I am not a deck steward, and don't understand the construction of steamer chairs as well as they do, you see."

The lady rose. There was a certain amount of indignation in her voice as she said—

"Then pray allow me to present you with this steamer chair."

"I—I—really, madam, I do not understand you," stammered the young man, astonished at the turn the unsought conversation had taken.

"I think," replied the lady, "that what I said was plain enough. I beg you to accept this steamer chair as your own. It is of no further use to me."

Saying this, the young woman, with some dignity, turned her back upon him, and disappeared down the companion-way, leaving Morris in a state of utter bewilderment as he looked down at the broken steamer chair, wondering if the lady was insane. All at once he noticed a rent in his trousers, between the knee and the instep.

"Good heavens, how have I done this? My best pair of trousers, too. Gracious!" he cried, as a bewildered look stole over his face, "it isn't possible that in racing up this deck I ran against this steamer chair and knocked it to flinders, and possibly upset the lady at the same time? By George! that's just what the trouble is."

Looking at the back of the flimsy chair he noticed a tag tied to it, and on the tag he saw the name, "Miss Katherine Earle, New York." Passing to the other side he called the deck steward.

"Steward," he said, "there is a chair somewhere among your pile with the name 'Geo. Morris' on it. Will you get it for me?"

"Certainly, sir," answered the steward, and very shortly the other steamer chair, which, by the way, was a much more elegant, expensive, and stable affair than the one that belonged to Miss Katherine Earle, was brought to him. Then he untied the tag from his own chair and tied it to the flimsy structure that had just been offered to him; next he untied the tag from the lady's chair and put it on his own.

"Now, steward," he said, "do you know the lady who sat in this chair?"

"No, sir," said the steward, "I do not. You see, we are only a few hours out, sir."

"Very well, you will have no trouble finding her. When she comes on deck again, please tell her that this chair is hers, with the apologies of the gentleman who broke her own, and see if you can mend this other chair for me."

"Oh yes," said the steward, "there will be no trouble about that. They are rather rickety things at best, sir."

"Very well, if you do this for me nicely you will not be a financial sufferer."

"Thank you, sir. The dinner gong rang some time ago, sir."

"Yes, I heard it," answered Morris.

Placing his hands behind him he walked up and down the deck, keeping an anxious eye now and then on the companion way. Finally, the young lady whom he had seen going down with the elderly gentleman appeared alone on deck. Then Morris acted very strangely. With the stealthy demeanour of an Indian avoiding his deadly enemy, he slunk behind the different structures on the deck until he reached the other door of the companion-way, and then, with a sigh of relief, ran down the steps. There were still quite a number of people in the saloon, and seated at the side of one of the smaller tables he noticed the lady whose name he imagined was Miss Katherine Earle.

"My name is Morris," said that gentleman to the head steward. "Where have you placed me?"

The steward took him down the long table, looking at the cards beside the row of plates.

"Here you are, sir," said the steward. "We are rather crowded this voyage, sir."

Morris did not answer him, for opposite he noticed the old gentleman, who had been the companion of the young lady, lingering over his wine.

"Isn't there any other place vacant? At one of the smaller tables, for instance? I don't like to sit at the long table," said Morris, placing his finger and thumb significantly in his waistcoat pocket.

"I think that can be arranged, sir," answered the steward, with a smile.

"Is there a place vacant at the table where that young lady is sitting alone?" said Morris, nodding in the direction.

"Well, sir, all the places are taken there; but the gentleman who has been placed at the head of the table has not come down, sir, and if you like I will change his card for yours at the long table."

"I wish you would."

So with that he took his place at the head of the small table, and had the indignant young lady at his right hand.

"There ought to be a master of ceremonies," began Morris with some hesitation, "to introduce people to each other on board a steamship. As it is, however, people have to get acquainted as best they may. My name is Morris, and, unless I am mistaken, you are Miss Katherine Earle. Am I right?"

"You are right about my name," answered the young lady, "I presume you ought to be about your own."

"Oh, I can prove that," said Morris, with a smile. "I have letters to show, and cards and things like that."

Then he seemed to catch his breath as he remembered there was also a young woman on board who could vouch that his name was George Morris This took him aback for a moment, and he was silent. Miss Earle made no reply to his offer of identification.

"Miss Earle," he said hesitatingly at last, "I wish you would permit me to apologise to you if I am as culpable as I imagine. Did I run against your chair and break it?"

"Do you mean to say," replied the young lady, looking at him steadily, "that you do not know whether you did or not?"

"Well, it's a pretty hard thing to ask a person to believe, and yet I assure you that is the fact. I have only the dimmest remembrance of the disaster, as of something I might have done in a dream. To tell you the truth, I did not even suspect I had done so until I noticed I had torn a portion of my clothing by the collision. After you left, it just dawned upon me that I was the one who smashed the chair. I therefore desire to apologise very humbly, and hope you will permit me to do so."

"For what do you intend to apologise, Mr. Morris? For breaking the chair, or refusing to mend it when I asked you?"

"For both. I was really in a good deal of trouble just the moment before I ran against your chair, Miss Earle, and I hope you will excuse me on the ground of temporary insanity. Why, you know, they even let off murderers on that plea, so I hope to be forgiven for being careless in the first place, and boorish in the second."

"You are freely forgiven, Mr. Morris. In fact, now that I think more calmly about the incident, it was really a very trivial affair to get angry over, and I must confess I was angry."

"You were perfectly justified."

"In getting angry, perhaps; but in showing my anger, no—as some one says in a play. Meanwhile, we'll forget all about it," and with that the young lady rose, bidding her new acquaintance good night.

George Morris found he had more appetite for dinner than he expected to have.

Second Day

Mr. George Morris did not sleep well his first night on the City of Buffalo. He dreamt that he was being chased around the deck by a couple of young ladies, one a very pronounced blonde, and the other an equally pronounced brunette, and he suffered a great deal because of the uncertainty as to which of the two pursuers he desired the most to avoid. It seemed to him that at last he was cornered, and the fiendish young ladies began literally, as the slang phrase is, to mop the deck with him. He felt himself being slowly pushed back and forward across the deck, and he wondered how long he would last if this treatment were kept up. By and by he found himself lying still in his bunk, and the swish, swish above him of the men scrubbing the deck in the early morning showed him his dream had merged into reality. He remembered then that it was the custom of the smoking-room steward to bring a large silver pot of fragrant coffee early every morning and place it on the table of the smoking-room. Morris also recollected that on former voyages that early morning coffee had always tasted particularly good. It was grateful and comforting, as the advertisement has it. Shortly after, Mr. Morris was on the wet deck, which the men were still scrubbing with the slow, measured swish, swish of the brush he had heard earlier in the morning. No rain was falling, but everything had a rainy look. At first he could see only a short distance from the ship. The clouds appeared to have come down on the water, where they hung, lowering. There was no evidence that such a thing as a sun existed. The waves rolled out of this watery mist with an oily look, and the air was so damp and chilly that it made Morris shiver as he looked out on the dreary prospect. He thrust his hands deep into his coat pockets, which seemed to be an indolent habit of his, and walked along the slippery deck to search for the smoking-room. He was thinking of his curious and troublesome dream, when around the corner came the brunette, wrapped in a long cloak that covered her from head to foot. The cloak had a couple of side pockets set angleways in front, after the manner of the pockets in ulsters. In these pockets Miss Earle's hands were placed, and she walked the deck with a certain independent manner which Mr. Morris remembered that he disliked. She seemed to be about to pass him without recognition, when the young man took off his cap and said pleasantly, "Good morning, Miss Earle. You are a very early riser."

"The habit of years," answered that young lady, "is not broken by merely coming on board ship."

Mr. Morris changed step and walked beside her.

"The habit of years?" he said. "Why, you speak as if you were an old woman."

"I am an old woman," replied the girl, "in everything but one particular."

23

"And that particular," said her companion, "is the very important one, I imagine, of years."

"I don't know why that is so very important."

"Oh, you will think so in after life, I assure you. I speak as a veteran myself."

The young lady gave him a quick side glance with her black eyes from under the hood that almost concealed her face.

"You say you are a veteran," she answered, "but you don't think so. It would offend you very deeply to be called old."

"Oh, I don't know about that. I think such a remark is offensive only when there is truth in it. A young fellow slaps his companion on the shoulder and calls him 'old man.' The grey-haired veteran always addresses his elderly friend as 'my boy.'"

"Under which category do you think you come, then?"

"Well, I don't come under either exactly. I am sort of on the middle ground. I sometimes feel very old. In fact, to confess to you, I never felt older in my life than I did yesterday. Today I am a great deal younger."

"Dear me," replied the young lady, "I am sorry to hear that."

"Sorry!" echoed her companion; "I don't see why you should be sorry. It is said that every one rejoices in the misfortunes of others, but it is rather unusual to hear them admit it."

"It is because of my sympathy for others that I am sorry to hear you are younger today than you were yesterday. If you take to running along the deck today then the results will be disastrous and I think you owe it to your fellow passengers to send the steward with his gong ahead of you so as to give people in steamer chairs warning."

"Miss Earle," said the young man, "I thought you had forgiven me for yesterday. I am sure I apologised very humbly, and am willing to apologise again to-day."

"Did I forgive you? I had forgotten?"

"But you remembered the fault. I am afraid that is misplaced forgetfulness. The truth is, I imagine, you are very unforgiving."

"My friends do not think so."

"Then I suppose you rank me among your enemies?"

"You forget that I have known you for a day only."

"That is true, chronologically speaking. But you must remember a day on shipboard is very much longer than a day on shore. In fact, I look on you now as an old acquaintance, and I should be sorry to think you looked on me as an enemy."

"You are mistaken. I do not. I look on you now as you do on your own age—sort of between the two."

"And which way do you think I shall drift? Towards the enemy line, or towards the line of friendship?"

"I am sure I cannot tell."

"Well, Miss Earle, I am going to use my best endeavours to reach the friendship line, which I shall make unless the current is too strong for me. I hope you are not so prejudiced against me that the pleasant effort will be fruitless."

"Oh, I am strictly neutral," said the young lady. "Besides, it really amounts to nothing. Steamer friendships are the most evanescent things on earth."

"Not on earth, surely, Miss Earle. You must mean on sea."

"Well, the earth includes the sea, you know."

"Have you had experience with steamer friendships? I thought, somehow, this was your first voyage."

"What made you think so?"

"Well, I don't know. I thought it was, that's all."

"I hope there is nothing in my manner that would induce a stranger to think I am a verdant traveller."

"Oh, not at all. You know, a person somehow classifies a person's fellow-passengers. Some appear to have been crossing the ocean all their lives, whereas, in fact, they are probably on shipboard for the first time. Have you crossed the ocean before?"

"Yes."

"Now, tell me whether you think I ever crossed before?"

"Why, of course you have. I should say that you cross probably once a year. Maybe oftener."

"Really? For business or pleasure?"

"Oh, business, entirely. You did not look yesterday as if you ever had any pleasure in your life."

"Oh, yesterday! Don't let us talk about yesterday. It's to-day now, you know. You seem to be a mind-reader. Perhaps you could tell my occupation?"

"Certainly. Your occupation is doubtless that of a junior partner in a prosperous New York house. You go over to Europe every year—perhaps twice a year, to look after the interests of your business."

"You think I am a sort of commercial traveller, then?"

"Well, practically, yes. The older members of the firm, I should imagine, are too comfortably situated, and care too little for the pleasures of foreign travel, to devote much of their time to it. So what foreign travel there is to be done falls on the shoulders of the younger partner. Am I correct?"

"Well, I don't quite class myself as a commercial traveller, you know, but in the main you are—in fact, you are remarkably near right. I think you must be something of a mind-reader, as I said before, Miss Earle, or is it possible that I carry my business so plainly in my demeanour as all that?"

Miss Earle laughed. It was a very bright, pleasant, cheerful laugh.

"Still, I must correct you where you are wrong, for fear you become too conceited altogether about your powers of observation. I have not crossed the ocean as often as you seem to think. In the future I shall perhaps do so frequently. I am the junior partner, as you say, but have not been a partner long. In fact I am now on my first voyage in connection with the new partnership. Now, Miss Earle, let me try a guess at your occupation."

"You are quite at liberty to guess at it."

"But will you tell me if I guess correctly?"

"Yes. I have no desire to conceal it."

"Then, I should say off-hand that you are a teacher, and are now taking a vacation in Europe. Am I right?"

"Tell me first why you think so?"

"I am afraid to tell you. I do not want to drift towards the line of enmity."

"You need have no fear. I have every respect for a man who tells the truth when he has to."

"Well, I think a school teacher is very apt to get into a certain dictatorial habit of speech. School teachers are something like military men. They are accustomed to implicit obedience without question, and this, I think, affects their manner with other people."

"You think I am dictatorial, then?"

"Well, I shouldn't say that you were dictatorial exactly. But there is a certain confidence—I don't know just how to express it, but it seems to me, you know—well, I am going deeper and deeper into trouble by what I am saying, so really I shall not say any more. I do not know just how to express it."

"I think you express it very nicely. Go on, please."

"Oh, you are laughing at me now."

"Not at all, I assure you. You were trying to say that I was very dictatorial."

"No, I was trying to say nothing of the kind. I was merely trying to say that you have a certain confidence in yourself and a certain belief that everything you say is perfectly correct, and is not to be questioned. Now, do as you promised, and tell me how near right I am."

"You are entirely wrong. I never taught school."

"Well, Miss Earle, I confessed to my occupation without citing any mitigating circumstances. So now, would you think me impertinent if I asked you to be equally frank?"

"Oh, not at all! But I may say at once that I wouldn't answer you."

"But you will tell me if I guess?"

"Yes, I promise that."

"Well, I am certainly right in saying that you are crossing the ocean for pleasure."

"No, you are entirely wrong. I am crossing for business."

"Then, perhaps you cross very often, too?"

"No; I crossed only once before, and that was coming the other way."

"Really, this is very mysterious. When are you coming back?"

"I am not coming back."

"Oh, well," said Morris, "I give it up. I think I have scored the unusual triumph of managing to be wrong in everything that I have said. Have I not?"

"I think you have."

"And you refuse to put me right?"

"Certainly."

"I don't think you are quite fair, Miss Earle."

"I don't think I ever claimed to be, Mr. Morris. But I am tired of walking now. You see, I have been walking the deck for considerably longer than you have. I think I shall sit down for a while."

"Let me take you to your chair."

Miss Earle smiled. "It would be very little use," she said.

The deck steward was not to be seen, and Morris, diving into a dark and cluttered-up apartment, in which the chairs were piled, speedily picked out his own, brought it to where the young lady was standing, spread it out in its proper position, and said—

"Now let me get you a rug or two."

"You have made a mistake. That is not my chair."

"Oh yes, it is. I looked at the tag. This is your name, is it not?"

"Yes, that is my name; but this is not my chair."

"Well, I beg that you will use it until the owner calls for it."

"But who is the owner? Is this your chair?"

"It was mine until after I smashed up yours."

"Oh, but I cannot accept your chair, Mr. Morris."

"You surely wouldn't refuse to do what you desired, in fact, commanded, another to do. You know you practically ordered me to take your chair. Well, I have accepted it. It is going to be put right to-day. So, you see, you cannot refuse mine."

Miss Earle looked at him for a moment.

"This is hardly what I would call a fair exchange," she said. "My chair was really a very cheap and flimsy one. This chair is much more expensive. You see, I know the price of them. I think you are trying to arrange your revenge, Mr. Morris. I think you want to bring things about so that I shall have to apologise to you in relation to that chair-breaking incident. However, I see that this chair is very comfortable, so I will take it. Wait a moment till I get my rugs."

"No, no," cried Morris, "tell me where you left them. I will get them for you."

"Thank you. I left them on the seat at the head of the companion-way. One is red, the other is more variegated; I cannot describe it, but they are the only two rugs there, I think."

A moment afterwards the young man appeared with the rugs on his arm, and arranged them around the young lady after the manner of deck stewards and gallant young men who are in the habit of crossing the ocean.

"Would you like to have a cup of coffee?"

"I would, if it can be had."

"Well, I will let you into a shipboard secret. Every morning on this vessel the smoking-room steward brings up a pot of very delicious coffee, which he leaves on the table of the smoking-room. He also brings a few biscuits—not the biscuit of American fame, but the biscuit of English manufacture, the cracker, as we call it—and those who frequent the smoking-room are in the habit sometimes of rising early, and, after a walk on deck, pouring out a cup of coffee for themselves."

"But I do not expert to be a habitué of the smoking-room," said Miss Earle.

"Nevertheless, you have a friend who will be, and so in that way, you see, you will enjoy the advantages of belonging to the smoking club."

A few moments afterwards, Morris appeared with a camp-stool under his arm, and two cups of coffee in his hands. Miss Earle noticed the smile suddenly fade from his face, and a look of annoyance, even of terror, succeed it. His hands trembled, so that the coffee spilled from the cup into the saucer.

"Excuse my awkwardness," he said huskily; then, handing her the cup, he added, "I shall have to go now. I will see you at breakfast-time. Good morning." With the other cup still in his hand, he made his way to the stair.

Miss Earle looked around and saw, coming up the deck, a very handsome young lady with blonde hair.

Third Day

On the morning of the third day, Mr. George Morris woke up after a sound and dreamless sleep. He woke up feeling very dissatisfied with himself, indeed. He said he was a fool, which was probably true enough, but even the calling himself so did not seem to make matters any better. He reviewed in his mind the events of the day before. He remembered his very pleasant walk and talk with Miss Earle. He knew the talk had been rather purposeless, being merely that sort of preliminary conversation which two people who do not yet know each other indulge in, as a forerunner to future friendship. Then, he thought of his awkward leave-taking of Miss Earle when he presented her with the cup of coffee, and for the first time he remembered with a pang that he had under his arm a camp-stool. It must have been evident to Miss Earle that he had intended to sit down and have a cup of coffee with her, and continue the acquaintance begun so auspiciously that morning. He wondered if she had noticed that his precipitate retreat had taken place the moment there appeared on the deck a very handsome and stylishly dressed young lady. He began to fear that Miss Earle must have thought him suddenly taken with insanity, or, worse still, sea-sickness. The more Morris thought about the matter the more dissatisfied he was with himself and his actions. At breakfast—he had arrived very late, almost as Miss Earle was leaving—he felt he had preserved a glum, reticent demeanour, and that he had the general manner of a fugitive anxious to escape justice. He wondered what Miss Earle must have thought of him after his eager conversation of the morning. The rest of the day he had spent gloomily in the smoking-room, and had not seen the young lady again. The more he thought of the day the worse he felt about it. However, he was philosopher enough to know that all the thinking he could do would not change a single item in the sum of the day's doing. So he slipped back the curtain on its brass rod and looked out into his state-room. The valise which he had left carelessly on the floor the night before was now making an excursion backwards and forwards from the bunk to the sofa, and the books that had been piled up on the sofa were scattered all over the room. It was evident that dressing was going to be an acrobatic performance.

The deck, when he reached it, was wet, but not with the moisture of the scrubbing. The outlook was clear enough, but a strong head-wind was blowing that whistled through the cordage of the vessel, and caused the black smoke of the funnels to float back like huge sombre streamers. The prow of the big ship rose now into the sky and then sank down into the bosom of the sea, and every time it descended a white cloud of spray drenched everything forward and sent a drizzly salt rain along the whole length of the steamer.

"There will be no ladies on deck this morning," said Morris to himself, as he held his cap on with both hands and looked around at the threatening sky. At this moment one wave struck the steamer with more than usual force and raised its crest amidship over the decks. Morris had just time to escape into the companion-way when it fell with a crash on the deck, flooding the promenade, and then rushing out through the scuppers into the sea.

"By George!" said Morris. "I guess there won't be many at breakfast either, if this sort of thing keeps up. I think the other side of the ship is the best."

Coming out on the other side of the deck, he was astonished to see, sitting in her steamer chair, snugly wrapped up in her rugs, Miss Katherine Earle, balancing a cup of steaming coffee in her hand. The steamer chair had been tightly tied to the brass stanchion, or hand-rail, that ran along the side of the housed-in portion of the companion-way, and although the steamer swayed to and fro, as well as up and down, the chair was immovable. An awning had been put up over the place where the chair was fastened, and every now and then on that dripping piece of canvas the salt rain fell, the result of the waves that dashed in on the other side of the steamer.

"Good morning, Mr. Morris!" said the young lady, brightly. "I am very glad you have come. I will let you into a shipboard secret. The steward of the smoking-room brings up every morning a pot of very fragrant coffee. Now, if you will speak to him, I am sure he will be very glad to give you a cup."

"You do like to make fun of me, don't you?" answered the young man.

"Oh, dear no," said Miss Earle, "I shouldn't think of making fun of anything so serious. Is it making fun of a person who looks half frozen to offer him a cup of warm coffee? I think there is more philanthropy than fun about that."

"Well, I don't know but you are right. At any rate, I prefer to take it as philanthropy rather than fun. I shall go and get a cup of coffee for myself, if you will permit me to place a chair beside yours?"

"Oh, I beg you not to go for the coffee yourself. You certainly will never reach here with it. You see the remains of that cup down by the side of the vessel. The steward himself slipped and fell with that piece of crockery in his hands. I am sure he hurt himself, although he said he didn't."

"Did you give him an extra fee on that account?" asked Morris, cynically.

"Of course I did. I am like the Government in that respect. I take care of those who are injured in my service."

"Perhaps, that's why he went down. They are a sly set, those stewards. He knew that a man would simply laugh at him, or perhaps utter some maledictions if he were not feeling in very good humour. In all my ocean voyages I have never had the good fortune to see a steward fall. He knew, also, the rascal, that a lady would sympathise with him, and that he wouldn't lose anything by it, except the cup, which is not his loss."

"Oh yes, it is," replied the young lady, "he tells me they charge all breakages against him."

"He didn't tell you what method they had of keeping track of the breakages, did he? Suppose he told the chief steward that you broke the cup, which is likely he did. What then?"

"Oh, you are too cynical this morning, and it would serve you just right if you go and get some coffee for yourself, and meet with the same disaster that overtook the unfortunate steward. Only you are forewarned that you shall have neither sympathy nor fee."

"Well, in that case," said the young man, "I shall not take the risk. I shall sacrifice the steward rather. Oh, here he is. I say, steward, will you bring me a cup of coffee, please?"

"Yes, sir. Any biscuit, sir?"

"No, no biscuit. Just a cup of coffee and a couple of lumps of sugar, please; and if you can first get me a chair, and strap it to this rod in the manner you do so well, I shall be very much obliged."

"Yes, sir. I shall call the deck steward, sir."

"Now, notice that. You see the rascals never interfere with each other. The deck steward wants a fee, and the smoking-room steward wants a fee, and each one attends strictly to his own business, and doesn't interfere with the possible fees of anybody else."

"Well," said Miss Earle, "is not that the correct way? If things are to be well done, that is how they should be done. Now, just notice how much more artistically the deck steward arranged these rugs than you did yesterday morning. I think it is worth a good fee to be wrapped up so comfortably as that."

"I guess I'll take lessons from the deck steward then, and even if I do not get a fee, I may perhaps get some gratitude at least."

"Gratitude? Why, you should think it a privilege."

"Well, Miss Earle, to tell the truth, I do. It is a privilege that—I hope you will not think I am trying to flatter you when I say—any man might be proud of."

"Oh, dear," replied the young lady, laughing, "I did not mean it in that way at all. I meant that it was a privilege to be allowed to practise on those particular rugs. Now, a man should remember that he undertakes a very great responsibility when he volunteers to place the rugs around a lady on a steamer chair. He may make her look very neat and even pretty by a nice disposal of the rugs, or he may make her look like a horrible bundle."

"Well, then, I think I was not such a failure after all yesterday morning, for you certainly looked very neat and pretty."

"Then, if I did, Mr. Morris, do not flatter yourself it was at all on account of your disposal of the rugs, for the moment you had left a very handsome young lady came along, and, looking at me, said, with such a pleasant smile, 'Why, what a pretty rug you have there; but how the steward has bungled it about you! Let me fix it,' and with that she gave it a touch here and a smooth down there, and the result was really so nice that I hated to go down to breakfast. It is a pity you went away so quickly yesterday morning. You might have had an opportunity of becoming acquainted with the lady, who is, I think, the prettiest girl on board this ship."

"Do you?" said Mr. Morris, shortly.

"Yes, I do. Have you noticed her? She sits over there at the long table near the centre. You must have seen her; she is so very, very pretty, that you cannot help noticing her."

"I am not looking after pretty women this voyage," said Morris, savagely.

"Oh, are you not? Well, I must thank you for that. That is evidently a very sincere compliment. No, I can't call it a compliment, but a sincere remark, I think the first sincere one you have made to-day."

"Why, what do you mean?" said Morris, looking at her in a bewildered sort of way.

"You have been looking after me this morning, have you not, and yesterday morning? And taking ever so much pains to be helpful and entertaining, and now, all at once you say—Well, you know what you said just now."

"Oh yes. Well, you see—"

"Oh, you can't get out of it, Mr. Morris. It was said, and with evident sincerity."

"Then you really think you are pretty?" said Mr. Morris, looking at his companion, who flushed under the remark.

"Ah, now," she said, "you imagine you are carrying the war into the enemy's country. But I don't at all appreciate a remark like that. I don't know but I dislike it even more than I do your compliments, which is saying a good deal."

"I assure you," said Morris, stiffly, "that I have not intended to pay any compliments. I am not a man who pays compliments."

"Not even left-handed ones?"

"Not even any kind, that I know of. I try as a general thing to speak the truth."

"Ah, and shame your hearers?"

"Well, I don't care who I shame as long as I succeed in speaking the truth."

"Very well, then; tell me the truth. Have you noticed this handsome young lady I speak of?"

"Yes, I have seen her."

"Don't you think she is very pretty?"

"Yes, I think she is."

"Don't you think she is the prettiest woman on the ship?"

"Yes, I think she is."

"Are you afraid of pretty women?"

"No, I don't think I am."

"Then, tell me why, the moment she appeared on the deck yesterday morning, you were so much agitated that you spilled most of my coffee in the saucer?"

"Did I appear agitated?" asked Morris, with some hesitation.

"Now, I consider that sort of thing worse than a direct prevarication."

"What sort of thing?"

"Why, a disingenuous answer. You know you appeared agitated. You know you were agitated. You know you had a camp-stool, and that you intended to sit down here and drink your coffee. All at once you changed your mind, and that change was coincident with the appearance on deck of the handsome young lady I speak of. I merely ask why?"

"Now, look here, Miss Earle, even the worst malefactor is not expected to incriminate himself. I can refuse to answer, can I not?"

"Certainly you may. You may refuse to answer anything, if you like. It was only because you were boasting about speaking the truth that I thought I should test your truth-telling qualities. I have been expecting every moment that you would say to me I was very impertinent, and that it was no business of mine, which would have been quite true. There, you see, you had a beautiful chance of speaking the truth which you let slip entirely unnoticed. But there is the breakfast gong. Now, I must confess to being very hungry indeed. I think I shall go down into the saloon."

"Please take my arm, Miss Earle," said the young man.

"Oh, not at all," replied that young lady; "I want something infinitely more stable. I shall work my way along this brass rod until I can make a bolt for the door. If you want to make yourself real useful, go and stand on the stairway, or the companion-way I think you call it, and if I come through the door with too great force you'll prevent me from going down the stairs."

"'Who ran to help me when I fell,'" quoted Mr. Morris, as he walked along ahead of her, having some difficulty in maintaining his equilibrium.

"I wouldn't mind the falling," replied the young lady, "if you only would some pretty story tell; but you are very prosaic, Mr. Morris. Do you ever read anything at all?"

"I never read when I have somebody more interesting than a book to talk to."

"Oh, thank you. Now, if you will get into position on the stairway, I shall make my attempts at getting to the door."

"I feel like a base-ball catcher," said Morris, taking up a position

37

somewhat similar to that of the useful man behind the bat.

Miss Earle, however, waited until the ship was on an even keel, then walked to the top of the companion-way, and, deftly catching up the train of her dress with as much composure as if she were in a ballroom, stepped lightly down the stairway. Looking smilingly over her shoulder at the astonished baseball catcher, she said—

"I wish you would not stand in that ridiculous attitude, but come and accompany me to the breakfast table. As I told you, I am very hungry."

The steamer gave a lurch that nearly precipitated Morris down the stairway, and the next moment he was by her side.

"Are you fond of base-ball?" she said to him.

"You should see me in the park when our side makes a home run. Do you like the game?"

"I never saw a game in my life."

"What! you an American girl, and never saw a game of base-ball? Why, I am astonished."

"I did not say that I was an American girl."

"Oh, that's a fact. I took you for one, however."

They were both of them so intent on their conversation in walking up the narrow way between the long table and the short ones, that neither of them noticed the handsome blonde young lady standing beside her chair looking at them. It was only when that young lady said, "Why, Mr. Morris, is this you?" and when that gentleman jumped as if a cannon had been fired beside him, that either of them noticed their fair fellow-traveller.

"Y—es," stammered Morris, "it is!"

The young lady smiled sweetly and held out her hand, which Morris took in an awkward way.

"I was just going to ask you," she said, "when you came aboard. How ridiculous that would have been. Of course, you have been here all the time. Isn't it curious that we have not met each other?—we of all persons in the world."

Morris, who had somewhat recovered his breath, looked steadily at her as she said this, and her eyes, after encountering his gaze for a moment, sank to the floor.

Miss Earle, who had waited for a moment expecting that Morris would introduce her, but seeing that he had for the time being apparently forgotten everything on earth, quietly left them, and took her place at the breakfast table. The blonde young lady looked up again at Mr. Morris, and said—

"I am afraid I am keeping you from breakfast."

"Oh, that doesn't matter."

"I am afraid, then," she continued sweetly, "that I am keeping you from your very interesting table companion."

"Yes, that does matter," said Morris, looking at her. "I wish you good morning, madam." And with that he left her and took his place at the head of the small table.

There was a vindictive look in the blonde young lady's pretty eyes as she sank into her own seat at the breakfast table.

Miss Earle had noticed the depressing effect which even the sight of the blonde lady exercised on Morris the day before, and she looked forward, therefore, to rather an uncompanionable breakfast. She was surprised, however, to see that Morris had an air of jaunty joviality, which she could not help thinking was rather forced.

"Now," he said, as he sat down on the sofa at the head of the table, "I think it's about time for us to begin our chutney fight."

"Our what?" asked the young lady, looking up at him with open eyes.

"Is it possible," he said, "that you have crossed the ocean and never engaged in the chutney fight? I always have it on this line."

"I am sorry to appear so ignorant," said Miss Earle, "but I have to confess I do not know what chutney is."

"I am glad of that," returned the young man. "It delights me to find in your nature certain desert spots—certain irreclaimable lands, I might say—of ignorance."

"I do not see why a person should rejoice in the misfortunes of another person," replied the young lady.

"Oh, don't you? Why, it is the most natural thing in the world. There is nothing that we so thoroughly dislike as a person, either lady or gentleman, who is perfect. I suspect you rather have the advantage of me in the reading of books, but I certainly have the advantage of you on chutney, and I intend to make the most of it."

"I am sure I shall be very glad to be enlightened, and to confess my ignorance whenever it is necessary, and that, I fear, will be rather often. So, if our acquaintance continues until the end of the voyage, you will be in a state of perpetual delight."

"Well, that's encouraging. You will be pleased to learn that chutney is a sauce, an Indian sauce, and on this line somehow or other they never have more than one or two bottles. I do not know whether it is very expensive. I presume it is. Perhaps it is because there is very little demand for it, a great number of people not knowing what chutney is."

"Thank you," said the young lady, "I am glad to find that I am in the majority, at least, even in the matter of ignorance."

"Well, as I was saying, chutney is rather a seductive sauce. You may not like it at first, but it grows on you. You acquire, as it were, the chutney habit. An old Indian traveller, whom I had the pleasure of crossing with once, and who sat at the same table with me, demanded chutney. He initiated me into the mysteries of chutney, and he had a chutney fight all the way across."

"I still have to confess that I do not see what there is to fight about in the matter of chutney."

"Don't you? Well, you shall soon have a practical illustration of the terrors of a chutney fight. Steward," called Morris, "just bring me a bottle of chutney, will you?"

"Chutney, air?" asked the steward, as if he had never heard the word before.

"Yes, chutney. Chutney sauce."

"I am afraid, sir," said the steward, "that we haven't any chutney sauce."

"Oh yes, you have. I see a bottle there on the captain's table. I think there is a second bottle at the smaller table. Just two doors up the street. Have the kindness to bring it to me."

The steward left for the chutney, and Morris looking after him, saw that there was some discussion between him and the steward of the other table. Finally, Morris's steward came back and said, "I am very sorry, sir, but they are using the chutney at that table."

"Now look here, steward," said Morris, "you know that you are here to take care of us, and that at the end of the voyage I will take care of you. Don't make any mistake about that. You understand me?"

"Yes, sir, I do," said the steward. "Thank you, sir."

"All right," replied Morris. "Now you understand that I want chutney, and chutney I am going to have."

Steward number one waited until steward number two had disappeared after another order, and then he deftly reached over, took the chutney sauce, and placed it before Mr. Morris.

"Now, Miss Earle, I hope that you will like this chutney sauce. You see there is some difficulty in getting it, and that of itself ought to be a strong recommendation for it."

"It is a little too hot to suit me," answered the young lady, trying the Indian sauce, "still, there is a pleasant flavour about it that I like."

"Oh, you are all right," said Morris, jauntily; "you will be a victim of the

41

chutney habit before two days. People who dislike it at first are its warmest advocates afterwards. I use the word warmest without any allusion to the sauce itself, you know. I shall now try some myself."

As he looked round the table for the large bottle, he saw that it had been whisked away by steward number two, and now stood on the other table. Miss Earle laughed.

"Oh, I shall have it in a moment," said the young man.

"Do you think it is worth while?"

"Worth while? Why, that is the excitement of a chutney fight. It is not that we care for chutney at all, but that we simply are bound to have it. If there were a bottle of chutney at every table, the delights of chutney would be gone. Steward," said Morris, as that functionary appeared, "the chutney, please."

The steward cast a rapid glance at the other table, and waited until steward number two had disappeared. Then Morris had his chutney. Steward number two, seeing his precious bottle gone, tried a second time to stealthily obtain possession of it, but Morris said to him in a pleasant voice, "That's all right, steward, we are through with the chutney. Take it along, please. So that," continued Mr. Morris, as Miss Earle rose from the table, "that is your first experience of a chutney fight—one of the delights of ocean travel."

Fourth Day

Mr. George Morris began to find his "early coffees," as he called them, very delightful. It was charming to meet a pretty and entertaining young lady every morning early when they had the deck practically to themselves. The fourth day was bright and clear, and the sea was reasonably calm. For the first time he was up earlier than Miss Earle, and he paced the deck with great impatience, waiting for her appearance. He wondered who and what she was. He had a dim, hazy idea that some time before in his life, he had met her, and probably had been acquainted with her. What an embarrassing thing it would be, he thought, if he had really known her years before, and had forgotten her, while she knew who he was, and had remembered him.

He thought of how accurately she had guessed his position in life—if it was a guess. He remembered that often, when he looked at her, he felt certain he had known her and spoken to her before. He placed the two steamer chairs in position, so that Miss Earle's chair would be ready for her when she did appear, and then, as he walked up and down the deck waiting for her, he began to wonder at himself. If any one had told him when he left New York that, within three or four days he could feel such an interest in a person who previous to that time had been an utter stranger to him, he would have laughed scornfully and bitterly at the idea. As it was, when he thought of all the peculiar circumstances of the case, he laughed aloud, but neither scornfully nor bitterly.

"You must be having very pleasant thoughts, Mr. Morris," said Miss Earle, as she appeared with a bright shawl thrown over her shoulders, instead of the long cloak that had encased her before, and with a Tam o' Shanter set jauntily on her black, curly hair.

"You are right," said Morris, taking off his cap, "I was thinking of you."

"Oh, indeed," replied the young lady, "that's why you laughed, was it? I may say that I do not relish being laughed at in my absence, or in my presence either, for that matter."

"Oh, I assure you I wasn't laughing at you. I laughed with pleasure to see you come on deck. I have been waiting for you."

"Now, Mr. Morris, that from a man who boasts of his truthfulness is a little too much. You did not see me at all until I spoke; and if, as you say, you were thinking of me, you will have to explain that laugh."

"I will explain it before the voyage is over, Miss Earle. I can't explain it just now."

"Ah, then you admit you were untruthful when you said you laughed because you saw me?"

"I may as well admit it. You seem to know things intuitively. I am not nearly as truthful a person as I thought I was until I met you. You seem the very embodiment of truth. If I had not met you, I imagine I should have gone through life thinking myself one of the most truthful men in New York."

"Perhaps that would not be saying very much for yourself," replied the young lady, as she took her place in the steamer chair.

"I am sorry you have such a poor opinion of us New Yorkers," said the young man. "Why are you so late this morning?"

"I am not late; it is you who are early. This is my usual time. I have been a very punctual person all my life."

"There you go again, speaking as if you were ever so old."

"I am."

"Well, I don't believe it. I wish, however, that you had confidence enough in me to tell me something about yourself. Do you know, I was thinking this morning that I had met you before somewhere? I feel almost certain I have."

"Well, that is quite possible, you know. You are a New Yorker, and I have lived in New York for a great number of years, much as you seem to dislike that phrase."

"New York! Oh, that is like saying you have lived in America and I have lived in America. We might live for hundreds of years in New York and never meet one another!"

"That is very true, except that the time is a little long."

"Then won't you tell me something about yourself?"

"No, I will not."

"Why?"

"Why? Well, if you will tell me why you have the right to ask such a question, I shall answer why."

"Oh, if you talk of rights, I suppose I haven't the right. But I am willing to tell you anything about myself. Now, a fair exchange, you know—"

"But I don't wish to know anything about you."

"Oh, thank you."

George Morris's face clouded, and he sat silent for a few moments.

"I presume," he said again, "that you think me very impertinent?"

"Well, frankly, I do."

Morris gazed out at the sea, and Miss Earle opened the book which she had brought with her, and began to read. After a while her companion said—

"I think that you are a little too harsh with me, Miss Earle."

The young lady placed her finger between the leaves of the book and closed it, looking up at him with a frank, calm expression in her dark eyes, but said nothing.

"You see, it's like this. I said to you a little while since that I seem to have known you before. Now, I'll tell you what I was thinking of when you met me this morning. I was thinking what a curious thing it would be if I had been acquainted with you some time during my past life, and had forgotten you, while you had remembered me."

"That was very flattering to me," said the young lady; "I don't wonder you laughed."

"That is why I did not wish to tell you what I had been thinking of—just for fear that you would put a wrong construction on it—as you have done. But now you can't say anything much harsher to me than you have said, and so I tell you frankly just what I thought, and why I asked you those questions which you seem to think are so impertinent. Besides this, you know, a sea acquaintance is different from any other acquaintance. As I said, the first time I spoke to you—or the second—there is no one here to introduce us. On land, when a person is introduced to another person, he does not say, 'Miss Earle, this is Mr. Morris, who is a younger partner in the house of So-and-so.' He merely says, 'Miss Earle, Mr. Morris,' and there it is. If you want to find anything out about him you can ask your introducer or ask your friends, and you can find out. Now, on shipboard it is entirely different. Suppose, for instance, that I did not tell you who I am, and—if you will pardon me for suggesting such an absurd supposition—-imagine that you wanted to find out, how could you do it?"

Miss Earle looked at him for a moment, and then she answered—

"I would ask that blonde young lady."

This reply was so utterly unexpected by Morris that he looked at her with wide eyes, the picture of a man dumbfounded. At that moment the smoking-room steward came up to them and said—

"Will you have your coffee now, sir?"

"Coffee!" cried Morris, as if he had never heard the word before. "Coffee!"

"Yes," answered Miss Earle, sweetly, "we will have the coffee now, if you please. You will have a cup with me, will you not, Mr. Morris?"

"Yes, I will, if it is not too much trouble."

"Oh, it is no trouble to me," said, the young lady; "some trouble to the steward, but I believe even for him that it is not a trouble that cannot be recompensed."

Morris sipped his coffee in silence. Every now and then Miss Earle stole a quiet look at him, and apparently was waiting for him to again resume the conversation. This he did not seem in a hurry to do. At last she said—

"Mr. Morris, suppose we were on shipboard and that we had become acquainted without the friendly intervention of an introducer, and suppose, if such a supposition is at all within the bounds of probability, that you wanted to find out something about me, how would you go about it?"

"How would I go about it?"

"Yes. How?"

"I would go about it in what would be the worst possible way. I would frankly ask you, and you would as frankly snub me.

"

"Suppose, then, while declining to tell you anything about myself I were to refer you to somebody who would give you the information you desire, would you take the opportunity of learning?"

"I would prefer to hear from yourself anything I desired to learn."

"Now, that is very nicely said, Mr. Morris, and you make me feel almost sorry, for having spoken to you as I did. Still, if you really want to find out something about me, I shall tell you some one whom you can ask, and who will doubtless answer you."

"Who is that? The captain?"

"No. It is the same person to whom I should go if I wished to have information of you—the blonde young lady."

"Do you mean to say you know her?" asked the astonished young man.

"I said nothing of the sort."

"Well, do you know her?"

"No, I do not."

"Do you know her name?"

"No, I do not even know her name."

"Have you ever met her before you came on board this ship?"

"Yes, I have."

"Well, if that isn't the most astonishing thing I ever heard!"

"I don't see why it is. You say you thought you had met me before. As you are a man no doubt you have forgotten it. I say I think I have met that young lady before. As she is a woman I don't think she will have forgotten. If you have any interest in the matter at all you might inquire."

"I shall do nothing of the sort."

"Well, of course, I said I thought you hadn't very much interest. I only supposed the case."

"It is not that I have not the interest, but it is that I prefer to go to the person who can best answer my question if she chooses to do so. If she doesn't choose to answer me, then I don't choose to learn."

"Now, I like that ever so much," said the young lady; "if you will get me another cup of coffee I shall be exceedingly obliged to you. My excuse is that these cups are very small, and the coffee is very good."

"I am sure you don't need any excuse," replied Morris, springing to his feet, "and I am only too happy to be your steward without the hope of the fee at the end of the voyage."

When he returned she said, "I think we had better stop the personal conversation into which we have drifted. It isn't at all pleasant to me, and I don't think it is very agreeable to you. Now, I intended this morning to give you a lesson on American literature. I feel that you need enlightening on the subject, and that you have neglected your opportunities, as most New York men do, and so I thought you would be glad of a lesson or two."

"I shall be very glad of it indeed. I don't know what our opportunities are, but if most New York men are like me I imagine a great many of them are in the same fix. We have very little time for the study of the literature of any country."

"And perhaps very little inclination."

"Well, you know, Miss Earle, there is some excuse for a busy man. Don't you think there is?"

"I don't think there is very much. Who in America is a busier man than Mr. Gladstone? Yet he reads nearly everything, and is familiar with almost any subject you can mention."

"Oh, Gladstone! Well, he is a man of a million. But you take the average

New York man. He is worried in business, and kept on the keen jump all the year round. Then he has a vacation, say for a couple of weeks or a month, in summer, and he goes off into the woods with his fishing kit, or canoeing outfit, or his amateur photographic set, or whatever the tools of his particular fad may be. He goes to a book-store and buys up a lot of paper-covered novels. There is no use of buying an expensive book, because he would spoil it before he gets back, and he would be sure to leave it in some shanty. So he takes those paper-covered abominations, and you will find torn copies of them scattered all through the Adirondacks, and down the St. Lawrence, and everywhere else that tourists congregate. I always tell the book-store man to give me the worst lot of trash he has got, and he does. Now, what is that book you have with you?"

"This is one of Mr. Howells' novels. You will admit, at least, that you have heard of Howells, I suppose?"

"Heard of him? Oh yes; I have read some of Howells' books. I am not as ignorant as you seem to think."

"What have you read of Mr. Howells'?"

"Well, I read The American, I don't remember the others."

"The American! That is by Henry James."

"Is it? Well, I knew that it was by either Howells or James, I forgot which. They didn't write a book together, did they?"

"Well, not that I know of. Why, the depth of your ignorance about American literature is something appalling. You talk of it so jauntily that you evidently have no idea of it yourself."

"I wish you would take me in hand, Miss Earle. Isn't there any sort of condensed version that a person could get hold of? Couldn't you give me a synopsis of what is written, so that I might post myself up in literature without going to the trouble of reading the books?"

"The trouble! Oh, if that is the way you speak, then your case is hopeless! I suspected it for some time, but now I am certain. The trouble! The delight of reading a new novel by Howells is something that you evidently have not the remotest idea of. Why, I don't know what I would give to have with me a novel of Howells' that I had not read."

"Goodness gracious! You don't mean to say that you have read everything he has written?"

"Certainly I have, and I am reading one now that is coming out in the magazine; and I don't know what I shall do if I am not able to get the magazine when I go to Europe."

"Oh, you can get them over there right enough, and cheaper than you can in America. They publish them over there."

"Do they? Well, I am glad to hear it."

"You see, there is something about American literature that you are not acquainted with, the publication of our magazines in England, for instance. Ah, there is the breakfast gong. Well, we will have to postpone our lesson in literature until afterwards. Will you be up here after breakfast?"

"Yes, I think so."

"Well, we will leave our chairs and rugs just where they are. I will take your book down for you. Books have the habit of disappearing if they are left around on shipboard."

After breakfast Mr. Morris went to the smoking-room to enjoy his cigar, and there was challenged to a game of cards. He played one game; but his mind was evidently not on his amusement, so he excused himself from any further dissipation in that line, and walked out on deck. The promise of the morning had been more than fulfilled in the day, and the warm sunlight and mild air had brought on deck many who had not been visible up to that time. There was a long row of muffled up figures on steamer chairs, and the deck steward was kept busy hurrying here and there attending to the wants of the passengers. Nearly every one had a book, but many of the books were turned face downwards on the steamer rugs, while the owners either talked to those next them, or gazed idly out at the blue ocean. In the long and narrow open space between the chairs and the bulwarks of the ship, the energetic pedestrians were walking up and down.

At this stage of the voyage most of the passengers had found congenial companions, and nearly everybody was acquainted with everybody else. Morris walked along in front of the reclining passengers, scanning each one eagerly to find the person he wanted, but she was not there. Remembering then that the chairs had been on the other side of the ship, he continued his walk around the wheel-house, and there he saw Miss Earle, and sitting beside her was the blonde young lady talking vivaciously, while Miss Earle listened.

Morris hesitated for a moment, but before he could turn back the young lady sprang to her feet, and said—"Oh, Mr. Morris, am I sitting in your chair?"

"What makes you think it is my chair?" asked that gentleman, not in the most genial tone of voice.

"I thought so," replied the young lady, with a laugh, "because it was near Miss Earle."

Miss Earle did not look at all pleased at this remark. She coloured slightly, and, taking the open book from her lap, began to read.

"You are quite welcome to the chair," replied Morris, and the moment the words were spoken he felt that somehow it was one of those things he would rather have left unsaid, as far as Miss Earle was concerned. "I beg that you will not disturb yourself," he continued; and, raising his hat to the lady, he continued his walk.

A chance acquaintance joined him, changing his step to suit that of Morris, and talked with him on the prospects of the next year being a good business season in the United States. Morris answered rather absent-mindedly, and it was nearly lunch-time before he had an opportunity of going back to see whether or not Miss Earle's companion had left. When he reached the spot where they had been sitting he found things the very reverse of what he had hoped. Miss Earle's chair was vacant, but her companion sat there, idly turning over the leaves of the book that Miss Earle had been reading. "Won't you sit down, Mr. Morris?" said the young woman, looking up at him with a winning smile. "Miss Earle has gone to dress for lunch. I should do the same thing, but, alas! I am too indolent."

Morris hesitated for a moment, and then sat down beside her.

"Why do you act so perfectly horrid to me?" asked the young lady, closing the book sharply.

"I was not aware that I acted horridly to anybody," answered Morris.

"You know well enough that you have been trying your very best to avoid me."

"I think you are mistaken. I seldom try to avoid any one, and I see no reason why I should try to avoid you. Do you know of any reason?"

The young lady blushed and looked down at her book, whose leaves she again began to turn.

"I thought," she said at last, "that you might have some feeling against me, and I have no doubt you judge me very harshly. You never did make any allowances."

Morris gave a little laugh that was half a sneer.

"Allowances?" he said.

"Yes, allowances. You know you always were harsh with me, George, always." And as she looked up at him her blue eyes were filled with tears, and there was a quiver at the corner of her mouth. "What a splendid actress you would make, Blanche," said the young man, calling her by her name for the first time.

She gave him a quick look as he did so. "Actress!" she cried. "No one was ever less an actress than I am, and you know that."

"Oh, well, what's the use of us talking? It's all right. We made a little mistake, that's all, and people often make mistakes in this life, don't they, Blanche?"

"Yes," sobbed that young lady, putting her dainty silk handkerchief to her eyes.

"Now, for goodness sake," said the young man, "don't do that. People will think I am scolding you, and certainly there is no one in this world who has less right to scold you than I have."

"I thought," murmured the young lady, from behind her handkerchief, "that we might at least be friends. I didn't think you could ever act so harshly towards me as you have done for the past few days."

"Act?" cried the young man. "Bless me, I haven't acted one way or the other. I simply haven't had the pleasure of meeting you till the other evening, or morning, which ever it was. I have said nothing, and done nothing. I don't see how I could be accused of acting, or of anything else."

"I think," sobbed the young lady, "that you might at least have spoken kindly to me."

"Good gracious!" cried Morris, starting up, "here comes Miss Earle. For heaven's sake put up that handkerchief."

But Blanche merely sank her face lower in it, while silent sobs shook her somewhat slender form.

Miss Earle stood for a moment amazed as she looked at Morris's flushed face, and at the bowed head of the young lady beside him; then, without a word, she turned and walked away.

"I wish to goodness," said Morris, harshly, "that if you are going to have a fit of crying you would not have it on deck, and where people can see you."

The young woman at once straightened up and flashed a look at him in which there were no traces of her former emotion.

"People!" she said, scornfully. "Much you care about people. It is because Miss Katherine Earle saw me that you are annoyed. You are afraid that it will interfere with your flirtation with her."

"Flirtation?"

"Yes, flirtation. Surely it can't be anything more serious?"

"Why should it not be something more serious?" asked Morris, very coldly. The blue eyes opened wide in apparent astonishment.

"Would you marry her?" she said, with telling emphasis upon the word.

"Why not?" he answered. "Any man might be proud to marry a lady like Miss Earle."

"A lady! Much of a lady she is! Why, she is one of your own shop-girls. You know it."

"Shop-girls?" cried Morris, in astonishment.

"Yes, shop-girls. You don't mean to say that she has concealed that fact from you, or that you didn't know it by seeing her in the store?"

"A shop-girl in my store?" he murmured, bewildered. "I knew I had seen her somewhere."

Blanche laughed a little irritating laugh.

"What a splendid item it would make for the society papers," she said. "The junior partner marries one of his own shop-girls, or, worse still, the junior partner and one of his shop-girls leave New York on the City of Buffalo, and are married in England. I hope that the reporters will not get the particulars of the affair." Then, rising, she left the amazed young man to his thoughts.

George Morris saw nothing more of Miss Katherine Earle that day.

"I wonder what that vixen has said to her," he thought, as he turned in for the night.

Fifth Day

In the early morning of the fifth day out, George Morris paced the deck alone.

"Shop-girl or not," he had said to himself, "Miss Katherine Earle is much more of a lady than the other ever was." But as he paced the deck, and as Miss Earle did not appear, he began to wonder more and more what had been said to her in the long talk of yesterday forenoon. Meanwhile Miss Earle sat in her own state-room thinking over the same subject. Blanche had sweetly asked her for permission to sit down beside her.

"I know no ladies on board," she said, "and I think I have met you before."

"Yes," answered Miss Earle, "I think we have met before."

"How good of you to have remembered me," said Blanche, kindly.

"I think," replied Miss Earle, "that it is more remarkable that you should remember me than that I should remember you. Ladies very rarely notice the shop-girls who wait upon them."

"You seemed so superior to your station," said Blanche, "that I could not help remembering you, and could not help thinking what a pity it was you had to be there."

"I do not think that there is anything either superior or inferior about the station. It is quite as honourable, or dishonourable, which ever it may be, as any other branch of business. I cannot see, for instance, why my station, selling ribbons at retail, should be any more dishonourable than the station of the head of the firm, who merely does on a very large scale what I was trying to do for him on a very limited scale."

"Still," said Blanche, with a yawn, "people do not all look upon it in exactly that light."

"Hardly any two persons look on any one thing in the same light. I hope you have enjoyed your voyage so far?"

"I have not enjoyed it very much," replied the young lady with a sigh.

"I am sorry to hear that. I presume your father has been ill most of the way?"

"My father?" cried the other, looking at her questioner.

"Yes, I did not see him at the table since the first day."

"Oh, he has had to keep his room almost since we left. He is a very poor sailor."

"Then that must make your voyage rather unpleasant?"

The blonde young lady made no reply, but, taking up the book which Miss Earle was reading, said, "You don't find Mr. Morris much of a reader, I presume? He used not to be."

"I know very little about Mr. Morris," said Miss Earle, freezingly.

"Why, you knew him before you came on board, did you not?" questioned the other, raising her eyebrows.

"No, I did not."

"You certainly know he is junior partner in the establishment where you work?"

"I know that, yes, but I had never spoken to him before I met him on board this steamer."

"Is that possible? Might I ask you if there is any probability of your becoming interested in Mr. Morris?"

"Interested! What do you mean?"

"Oh, you know well enough what I mean. We girls do not need to be humbugs with each other, whatever we may be before the men. When a young woman meets a young man in the early morning, and has coffee with him, and when she reads to him, and tries to cultivate his literary tastes, whatever they may be, she certainly shows some interest in the young man, don't you think so?"

Miss Earle looked for a moment indignantly at her questioner. "I do not recognise your right," she said, "to ask me such a question."

"No? Then let me tell you that I have every right to ask it. I assure you that I have thought over the matter deeply before I spoke. It seemed to me there was one chance in a thousand—only one chance in a thousand, remember—that you were acting honestly, and on that one chance I took the liberty of speaking to you. The right I have to ask such a question is this—Mr. George Morris has been engaged to me for several years."

"Engaged to you?"

"Yes. If you don't believe it, ask him."

"It is the very last question in the world I would ask anybody."

"Well, then, you will have to take my word for it. I hope you are not very shocked, Miss Earle, to hear what I have had to tell you."

"Shocked? Oh dear, no. Why should I be? It is really a matter of no interest to me, I assure you."

"Well, I am very glad to hear you say so. I did not know but you might have become more interested in Mr. Morris than you would care to own. I think myself that he is quite a fascinating young gentleman; but I thought it only just to you that you should know exactly how matters stood."

"I am sure I am very much obliged to you."

This much of the conversation Miss Earle had thought over in her own room that morning. "Did it make a difference to her or not?" that was the question she was asking herself. The information had certainly affected her opinion of Mr. Morris, and she smiled to herself rather bitterly as she thought of his claiming to be so exceedingly truthful. Miss Earle did not, however, go up on deck until the breakfast gong had rung.

"Good morning," said Morris, as he took his place at the little table. "I was like the boy on the burning deck this morning, when all but he had fled. I was very much disappointed that you did not come up, and have your usual cup of coffee."

"I am sorry to hear that," said Miss Earle; "if I had known I was disappointing anybody I should have been here."

"Miss Katherine," he said, "you are a humbug. You knew very well that I would be disappointed if you did not come."

The young lady looked up at him, and for a moment she thought of telling him that her name was Miss Earle, but for some reason she did not do so.

"I want you to promise now," he continued, "that to-morrow morning you will be on deck as usual."

"Has it become a usual thing, then?"

"Well, that's what I am trying to make it," he answered. "Will you promise?"

"Yes, I promise."

"Very well, then, I look on that as settled. Now, about to-day. What are you going to do with yourself after breakfast?"

"Oh, the usual thing, I suppose. I shall sit in my steamer chair and read an interesting book."

"And what is the interesting book for to-day?"

"It is a little volume by Henry James, entitled The Siege of London."

"Why, I never knew that London had been besieged. When did that happen?"

"Well, I haven't got very far in the book yet, but it seems to have happened quite recently, within a year or two, I think. It is one of the latest of Mr. James's short stories. I have not read it yet."

"Ah, then the siege is not historical?"

"Not historical further than Mr. James is the historian."

"Now, Miss Earle, are you good at reading out loud?"

"No, I am not."

"Why, how decisively you say that. I couldn't answer like that, because I don't know whether I am or not. I have never tried any of it. But if you will allow me, I will read that book out to you. I should like to have the good points indicated to me, and also the defects."

"There are not likely to be many defects," said the young lady. "Mr. James is a very correct writer. But I do not care either to read aloud or have a book read to me. Besides, we disturb the conversation or the reading of any one else who happens to sit near us. I prefer to enjoy a book by reading it myself."

"Ah, I see you are resolved cruelly to shut me out of all participation in your enjoyment."

"Oh, not at all. I shall be very happy to discuss the book with you afterwards. You should read it for yourself. Then, when you have done so, we might have a talk on its merits or demerits, if you think, after you have read it, that it has any."

"Any what? merits or demerits?"

"Well, any either."

"No; I will tell you a better plan than that. I am not going to waste my time reading it."

"Waste, indeed!"

"Certainly waste. Not when I have a much better plan of finding out what is in the book. I am going to get you to tell me the story after you have read it."

"Oh, indeed, and suppose I refuse?"

"Will you?"

"Well, I don't know. I only said suppose."

"Then I shall spend the rest of the voyage trying to persuade you."

"I am not very easily persuaded, Mr. Morris."

"I believe that," said the young man. "I presume I may sit beside you while you are reading your book?"

"You certainly may, if you wish to. The deck is not mine, only that portion of it, I suppose, which I occupy with the steamer chair. I have no authority over any of the rest."

"Now, is that a refusal or an acceptance?"

"It is which ever you choose to think."

"Well, if it is a refusal, it is probably softening down the No, but if it is an acceptance it is rather an ungracious one, it seems to me."

"Well, then, I shall be frank with you. I am very much interested in this book. I should a great deal rather read it than talk to you."

"Oh, thank you, Miss Earle. There can be no possible doubt about your meaning now."

"Well, I am glad of that, Mr. Morris. I am always pleased to think that I can speak in such a way as not to be misunderstood."

"I don't see any possible way of misunderstanding that. I wish I did."

"And then, after lunch," said the young lady, "I think I shall finish the book before that time;—if you care to sit beside me or to walk the deck with me, I shall be very glad to tell you the story."

"Now, that is perfectly delightful," cried the young man. "You throw a person down into the depths, so that he will appreciate all the more being brought up into the light again."

"Oh, not at all. I have no such dramatic ideas in speaking frankly with you. I merely mean that this forenoon I wish to have to myself, because I am interested in my book. At the end of the forenoon I shall probably be tired of my book and will prefer a talk with you. I don't see why you should think it odd that a person should say exactly what a person means."

"And then I suppose in the evening you will be tired of talking with me, and will want to take up your book again."

"Possibly."

"And if you are, you won't hesitate a moment about saying so?"

"Certainly not."

"Well, you are a decidedly frank young lady, Miss Earle; and, after all, I don't know but what I like that sort of thing best. I think if all the world were honest we would all have a better time of it here."

"Do you really think so?"

"Yes, I do."

"You believe in honesty, then?"

"Why, certainly. Have you seen anything in my conduct or bearing that would induce you to think that I did not believe in honesty?"

"No, I can't say I have. Still, honesty is such a rare quality that a person naturally is surprised when one comes unexpectedly upon it."

George Morris found the forenoon rather tedious and lonesome. He sat in the smoking room, and once or twice he ventured near where Miss Earle sat engrossed in her book, in the hope that the volume might have been put aside for the time, and that he would have some excuse for sitting down and talking with her. Once as he passed she looked up with a bright smile and nodded to him.

"Nearly through?" he asked dolefully.

"Of The Siege of London?" she asked.

"Yes."

"Oh, I am through that long ago, and have begun another story."

"Now, that is not according to contract," claimed Morris. "The contract was that when you got through with The Siege of London you were to let me talk with you, and that you were to tell me the story."

"That was not my interpretation of it. Our bargain, as I understood it, was that I was to have this forenoon to myself, and that I was to use the forenoon for reading. I believe my engagement with you began in the afternoon."

"I wish it did," said the young man, with a wistful look.

"You wish what?" she said, glancing up at him sharply.

He blushed as he bent over towards her and whispered, "That our engagement, Miss Katherine, began in the afternoon."

The colour mounted rapidly into her cheeks, and for a moment George Morris thought he had gone too far. It seemed as if a sharp reply was ready on her lips; but, as on another occasion, she checked it and said nothing. Then she opened her book and began to read. He waited for a moment and said—

"Miss Earle, have I offended you?"

"Did you mean to give offence?" she asked.

"No, certainly, I did not."

"Then why should you think you had offended me?"

"Well, I don't know, I—" he stammered.

Miss Earle looked at him with such clear, innocent, and unwavering eyes that the young man felt that he could neither apologise nor make an explanation.

"I'm afraid," he said, "that I am encroaching on your time."

"Yes, I think you are: that is, if you intend to live up to your contract, and let me live up to mine. You have no idea how much more interesting this book is than you are."

"Why, you are not a bit flattering, Miss Earle, are you?"

"No, I don't think I am. Do you try to be?"

"I'm afraid that in my lifetime I have tried to be, but I assure you, Miss Earle, that I don't try to be flattering, or try to be anything but what I really am when I am in your company. To tell the truth, I am too much afraid of you."

Miss Earle smiled and went on with her reading, while Morris went once more back into the smoking-room.

"Now then," said George Morris, when lunch was over, "which is it to be? The luxurious languor of the steamer chair or the energetic exercise of the deck? Take your choice."

"Well," answered the young lady, "as I have been enjoying the luxurious languor all the forenoon, I prefer the energetic exercise, if it is agreeable to you, for a while, at least."

"It is very agreeable to me. I am all energy this afternoon. In fact, now that you have consented to allow me to talk with you, I feel as if I were imbued with a new life."

"Dear me," said she, "and all because of the privilege of talking to me?"

"All."

"How nice that is. You are sure that it is not the effect of the sea air?"

"Quite certain. I had the sea air this forenoon, you know."

"Oh, yes, I had forgotten that."

"Well, which side of the deck then?"

"Oh, which ever is the least popular side. I dislike a crowd."

"I think, Miss Earle, that we will have this side pretty much to ourselves. The madd'ing crowd seems to have a preference for the sunny part of the ship. Now, then, for the siege of London. Who besieged it?"

"A lady."

"Did she succeed?"

"She did."

"Well, I am very glad to hear it, indeed. What was she besieging it for?"

"For social position, I presume.

"Then, as we say out West, I suppose she had a pretty hard row to hoe?"

"Yes, she had."

"Well, I never can get at the story by cross-questioning. Now, supposing that you tell it to me."

"I think that you had better take the book and read it. I am not a good story-teller."

"Why, I thought we Americans were considered excellent story-tellers.'

"We Americans?"

"Oh, I remember now, you do not lay claim to being an American. You are English, I think you said?"

"I said nothing of the kind. I merely said I lay no claims to being an American."

"Yes, that was it."

"Well, you will be pleased to know that this lady in the siege of London was an American. You seem so anxious to establish a person's nationality that I am glad to be able to tell you at the very first that she was an American, and, what is more, seemed to be a Western American."

"Seemed? Oh, there we get into uncertainties again. If I like to know whether persons are Americans or not, it naturally follows that I am anxious to know whether they were Western or Eastern Americans. Aren't you sure she was a Westerner?"

"The story, unfortunately, leaves that a little vague, so if it displeases you I shall be glad to stop the telling of it."

"Oh no, don't do that. I am quite satisfied to take her as an American citizen; whether she is East or West, or North or South, does not make the slightest difference to me. Please go on with the story."

"Well, the other characters, I am happy to be able to say, are not at all indefinite in the matter of nationality. One is an Englishman; he is even more than that, he is an English nobleman. The other is an American. Then there is the English nobleman's mother, who, of course, is an English woman; and the American's sister, married to an Englishman, and she, of course, is English-American. Does that satisfy you?"

"Perfectly. Go on."

"It seems that the besieger, the heroine of the story if you may call her so, had a past."

"Has not everybody had a past?"

"Oh no. This past is known to the American and is unknown to the English nobleman."

"Ah, I see; and the American is in love with her in spite of her past?"

"Not in Mr. James's story."

"Oh, I beg pardon. Well, go on; I shall not interrupt again."

"It is the English nobleman who is in love with her in spite of his absence of knowledge about her past. The English nobleman's mother is very much against the match. She tries to get the American to tell what the past of this woman is. The American refuses to do so. In fact, in Paris he has half promised the besieger not to say anything about her past. She is besieging London, and she wishes the American to remain neutral. But the nobleman's mother at last gets the American to promise that he will tell her son what he knows of this woman's past. The American informs the woman what he has promised the nobleman's mother to do, and at this moment the nobleman enters the room. The besieger of London, feeling that her game is up, leaves them together. The American says to the nobleman, who stands rather stiffly before him, 'If you wish to ask me any questions regarding the lady who has gone out I shall be happy to tell you.' Those are not the words of the book, but they are in substance what he said. The nobleman looked at him for a moment with that hauteur which, we presume, belongs to noblemen, and said quietly, 'I wish to know nothing.' Now, that strikes me as a very dramatic point in the story."

"But didn't he wish to know anything of the woman whom he was going to marry?"

"I presume that, naturally, he did."

"And yet he did not take the opportunity of finding out when he had the chance?"

"No, he did not."

"Well, what do you think of that?"

"What do I think of it? I think it's a very dramatic point in the story."

"Yes, but what do you think of his wisdom in refusing to find out what sort of a woman he was going to marry? Was he a fool or was he a very noble man?"

"Why, I thought I said at the first that he was a nobleman, an Englishman."

"Miss Katherine, you are dodging the question. I asked your opinion of that man's wisdom. Was he wise, or was he a fool?"

"What do you think about it? Do you think he was a fool, or a wise man?"

"Well, I asked you for your opinion first. However, I have very little hesitation in saying, that a man who marries a woman of whom he knows nothing, is a fool."

"Oh, but he was well acquainted with this woman. It was only her past that he knew nothing about."

"Well, I think you must admit that a woman's past and a man's past are very important parts of their lives. Don't you agree with me?"

"I agree with you so seldom that I should hesitate to say I did on this occasion. But I have told the story very badly. You will have to read it for yourself to thoroughly appreciate the different situations, and then we can discuss the matter intelligently."

"You evidently think the man was very noble in refusing to hear anything about the past of the lady he was interested in."

"I confess I do. He was noble, at least, in refusing to let a third party tell him. If he wished any information he should have asked the lady himself."

"Yes, but supposing she refused to answer him?"

"Then, I think he should either have declined to have anything more to do with her, or, if he kept up his acquaintance, he should have taken her just as she was, without any reference to her past."

"I suppose you are right. Still, it is a very serious thing for two people to marry without knowing something of each other's lives."

"I am tired of walking," said Miss Earle, "I am now going to seek comfort in the luxuriousness, as you call it, of my steamer chair."

"And may I go with you?" asked the young man.

"If you also are tired of walking."

"You know," he said, "you promised the whole afternoon. You took the forenoon with The Siege, and now I don't wish to be cheated out of my half of the day."

"Very well, I am rather interested in another story, and if you will take The Siege of London, and read it, you'll find how much better the book is than my telling of the story."

George Morris had, of course, to content himself with this proposition, and they walked together to the steamer chairs, over which the gaily coloured rugs were spread.

"Shall I get your book for you?" asked the young man, as he picked up the rugs.

"Thank you," answered Miss Earle, with a laugh, "you have already done so," for, as he shook out the rugs, the two books, which were small handy volumes, fell out on the deck.

"I see you won't accept my hint about not leaving the books around. You will lose some precious volume one of these days."

"Oh, I fold them in the rugs, and they are all right. Now, here is your volume. Sit down there and read it." "That means also, 'and keep quiet,' I suppose?"

"I don't imagine you are versatile enough to read and talk at the same time. Are you?"

"I should be very tempted to try it this afternoon."

Miss Earle went on with her reading, and Morris pretended to go on with his. He soon found, however, that he could not concentrate his attention on the little volume in his hand, and so quickly abandoned the attempt, and spent his time in meditation and in casting furtive glances at his fair companion over the top of his book. He thought the steamer chair a perfectly delightful invention. It was an easy, comfortable, and adjustable apparatus, that allowed a person to sit up or to recline at almost any angle. He pushed his chair back a little, so that he could watch the profile of Miss Katherine Earle, and the dark tresses that formed a frame for it, without risking the chance of having his espionage discovered.

"Aren't you comfortable?" asked the young lady, as he shoved back his chair.

"I am very, very comfortable," replied the young man.

"I am glad of that," she said, as she resumed her reading.

George Morris watched her turn leaf after leaf as he reclined lazily in his chair, with half-closed eyes, and said to himself, "Shop-girl or not, past or not, I'm going to propose to that young lady the first good opportunity I get. I wonder what she will say?"

"How do you like it?" cried the young lady he was thinking of, with a suddenness that made Morris jump in his chair.

"Like it?" he cried; "oh, I like it immensely."

"How far have you got?" she continued.

"How far? Oh, a great distance. Very much further than I would have thought it possible when I began this voyage."

Miss Earle turned and looked at him with wide-open eyes, as he made this strange reply.

"What are you speaking of?" she said.

"Oh, of everything—of the book, of the voyage, of the day.'"

"I was speaking of the book," she replied quietly. "Are you sure you have not fallen asleep and been dreaming?"

"Fallen asleep? No. Dreaming? Yes."

"Well, I hope your dreams have been pleasant ones."

"They have."

Miss Earle, who seemed to think it best not to follow her investigations any further, turned once more to her own book, and read it until it was time to dress for dinner. When that important meal was over, Morris said to Miss Earle: "Do you know you still owe me part of the day?"

"I thought you said you had a very pleasant afternoon."

"So I had. So pleasant, you see, that I want to have the pleasure prolonged. I want you to come out and have a walk on the deck now in the starlight. It is a lovely night, and, besides, you are now halfway across the ocean, and yet I don't think you have been out once to see the phosphorescence. That is one of the standard sights of an ocean voyage. Will you come?"

Although the words were commonplace enough, there was a tremor in his voice which gave a meaning to them that could not be misunderstood. Miss Earle looked at him with serene composure, and yet with a touch of reproachfulness in her glance. "He talks like this to me," she said to herself, "while he is engaged to another woman."

"Yes," she answered aloud, with more firmness in her voice than might have seemed necessary, "I will be happy to walk on the deck with you to see the phosphorescence."

He helped to hinder her for a moment in adjusting her wraps, and they went out in the starlit night together.

"Now," he said, "if we are fortunate enough to find the place behind the after-wheel house vacant we can have a splendid view of the phosphorescence."

"Is it so much in demand that the place is generally crowded?" she asked.

"I may tell you in confidence," replied Mr. Morris, "that this particular portion of the boat is always very popular. Soon as the evening shades prevail the place is apt to be pre-empted by couples that are very fond of—"

"Phosphorescence," interjected the young lady.

"Yes," he said, with a smile that she could not see in the darkness, "of phosphorescence."

"I should think," said she, as they walked towards the stern of the boat, "that in scientific researches of that sort, the more people who were there, the more interesting the discussion would be, and the more chance a person would have to improve his mind on the subject of phosphorescence, or other matters pertaining to the sea."

"Yes," replied Morris. "A person naturally would think that, and yet, strange as it may appear, if there ever was a time when two is company and three is a crowd, it is when looking at the phosphorescence that follows the wake of an ocean steamer."

"Really?" observed the young lady, archly. "I remember you told me that you had crossed the ocean several times."

The young man laughed joyously at this repartee, and his companion joined him with a laugh that was low and musical.

"He seems very sure of his ground," she said to herself. "Well, we shall see."

As they came to the end of the boat and passed behind the temporary wheel-house erected there, filled with debris of various sorts, blocks and tackle and old steamer chairs, Morris noticed that two others were there before them standing close together with arms upon the bulwarks. They were standing very close together, so close in fact, that in the darkness, it seemed like one person. But as Morris stumbled over some chains, the dark, united shadow dissolved itself quickly into two distinct separate shadows. A flagpole stood at the extreme end of the ship, inclining backwards from the centre of the bulwarks, and leaning over the troubled, luminous sea beneath. The two who had taken their position first were on one side of the flag-pole and Morris and Miss Earle on the other. Their coming had evidently broken the spell for the others. After waiting for a few moments, the lady took the arm of the gentleman and walked forward. "Now," said Morris, with a sigh, "we have the phosphorescence to ourselves."

"It is very, very strange," remarked the lady in a low voice. "It seems as if a person could see weird shapes arising in the air, as if in torment."

The young man said nothing for a few moments. He cleared his throat several times as if to speak, but still remained silent. Miss Earle gazed down at the restless, luminous water. The throb, throb of the great ship made the bulwarks on which their arms rested tremble and quiver.

Finally Morris seemed to muster up courage enough to begin, and he said one word—

"Katherine." As he said this he placed his hand on hers as it lay white before him in the darkness upon the trembling bulwark. It seemed to him that she made a motion to withdraw her hand, and then allowed it to remain where it was.

"Katherine," he continued, in a voice that he hardly recognised as his own, "we have known each other only a very short time comparatively; but, as I think I said to you once before, a day on shipboard may be as long as a

71

month on shore. Katherine, I want to ask you a question, and yet I do not know—I cannot find—I—I don't know what words to use."

The young lady turned her face towards him, and he saw her clear-cut profile sharply outlined against the glowing water as he looked down at her. Although the young man struggled against the emotion, which is usually experienced by any man in his position, yet he felt reasonably sure of the answer to his question. She had come with him out into the night. She had allowed her hand to remain in his. He was, therefore, stricken dumb with amazement when she replied, in a soft and musical voice—

"You do not know what to say? What do you usually say on such an occasion?"

"Usually say?" he gasped in dismay. "I do not understand you. What do you mean?"

"Isn't my meaning plain enough? Am I the first young lady to whom you have not known exactly what to say?"

Mr. Morris straightened up, and folded his arms across his breast; then, ridiculously enough, this struck him as a heroic attitude, and altogether unsuitable for an American, so he thrust his hands deep in his coat pockets.

"Miss Earle," he said, "I knew that you could be cruel, but I did not think it possible that you could be so cruel as this."

"Is the cruelty all on my side, Mr. Morris?" she answered. "Have you been perfectly honest and frank with me? You know you have not. Now, I shall be perfectly honest and frank with you. I like you very much indeed. I have not the slightest hesitation in saying this, because it is true, and I don't care whether you know it, or whether anybody else knows it or not."

As she said this the hope which Morris had felt at first, and which had been dashed so rudely to the ground, now returned, and he attempted to put his arm about her and draw her to him; but the young lady quickly eluded his grasp, stepping to the other side of the flag-pole, and putting her hand upon it.

"Mr. Morris," she said, "there is no use of your saying anything further. There is a barrier between us; you know it as well as I. I would like us to be friends as usual; but, if we are to be, you will have to remember the barrier, and keep to your own side of it."

"I know of no barrier," cried Morris, vehemently, attempting to come over to her side.

"There is the barrier," she said, placing her hand on the flag-pole. "My place is on this side of that barrier; your place is on the other. If you come on this side of that flag-pole, I shall leave you. If you remain on your own side, I shall be very glad to talk with you."

Morris sullenly took his place on the other side of the flag-pole. "Has there been anything in my actions," said the young lady, "during the time we have been acquainted that would lead you to expect a different answer?"

"Yes. You have treated me outrageously at times, and that gave me some hope."

Miss Earle laughed her low, musical laugh at this remark.

"Oh, you may laugh," said Morris, savagely; "but it is no laughing matter to me, I assure you."

"Oh, it will be, Mr. Morris, when you come to think of this episode after you get on shore. It will seem to you very, very funny indeed; and when you speak to the next young lady on the same subject, perhaps you will think of how outrageously I have treated your remarks to-night, and be glad that there are so few young women in the world who would act as I have done."

"Where did you get the notion," inquired George Morris, "that I am in the habit of proposing to young ladies? It is a most ridiculous idea. I have been engaged once, I confess it. I made a mistake, and I am sorry for it. There is surely nothing criminal in that."

"It depends."

"Depends on what?"

"It depends on how the other party feels about it. It takes two to make an engagement, and it should take two to break it."

"Well, it didn't in my case," said the young man.

"So I understand," replied Miss Earle. "Mr. Morris, I wish you a very good evening." And before he could say a word she had disappeared in the darkness, leaving him to ponder bitterly over the events of the evening.

Sixth Day

In the vague hope of meeting Miss Earle, Morris rose early, and for a while paced the deck alone; but she did not appear. Neither did he have the pleasure of her company at breakfast. The more the young man thought of their interview of the previous evening, the more puzzled he was.

Miss Earle had frankly confessed that she thought a great deal of him, and yet she had treated him with an unfeelingness which left him sore and bitter. She might have refused him; that was her right, of course. But she need not have done it so sarcastically. He walked the deck after breakfast, but saw nothing of Miss Earle. As he paced up and down, he met the very person of all others whom he did not wish to meet. "Good morning, Mr. Morris," she said lightly, holding out her hand.

"Good morning," he answered, taking it without much warmth.

"You are walking the deck all alone, I see. May I accompany you?"

"Certainly," said the young man, and with that she put her hand on his arm and they walked together the first two rounds without saying anything to each other. Then she looked up at him, with a bright smile, and said, "So she refused you?"

"How do you know?" answered the young man, reddening and turning a quick look at her.

"How do I know?" laughed the other. "How should I know?"

For a moment it flashed across his mind that Miss Katherine Earle had spoken of their interview of last night; but a moment later he dismissed the suspicion as unworthy.

"How do you know?" he repeated.

"Because I was told so on very good authority."

"I don't believe it."

"Ha, ha! now you are very rude. It is very rude to say to a lady that she doesn't speak the truth."

"Well, rude or not, you are not speaking the truth. Nobody told you such a thing."

"My dear George, how impolite you are. What a perfect bear you have grown to be. Do you want to know who told me?"

"I don't care to know anything about it."

"Well, nevertheless, I shall tell you. You told me."

"I did? Nonsense, I never said anything about it."

"Yes, you did. Your walk showed it. The dejected look showed it, and when I spoke to you, your actions, your tone, and your words told it to me plainer than if you had said, 'I proposed to Miss Earle last night and I was rejected.' You poor, dear innocent, if you don't brighten up you will tell it to the whole ship."

"I am sure, Blanche, that I am very much obliged to you for the interest you take in me. Very much obliged, indeed."

"Oh no, you are not; and now, don't try to be sarcastic, it really doesn't suit your manner at all. I was very anxious to know how your little flirtation had turned out. I really was. You know I have an interest in you, George, and always will have, and I wouldn't like that spiteful little black-haired minx to have got you, and I am very glad she refused you, although why she did so I cannot for the life of me imagine."

"It must be hard for you to comprehend why she refused me, now that I am a partner in the firm." Blanche looked down upon the deck, and did not answer.

"I am glad," she said finally, looking up brightly at him with her innocent blue eyes, "that you did not put off your proposal until to-night. We expect to be at Queenstown to-night some time, and we leave there and go on through by the Lakes of Killarney. So, you see, if you hadn't proposed last night I should have known nothing at all about how the matter turned out, and I should have died of curiosity and anxiety to know."

"Oh, I would have written to you," said Morris. "Leave me your address now, and I'll write and let you know how it turns out."

"Oh," she cried quickly, "then it isn't ended yet? I didn't think you were a man who would need to be refused twice or thrice."

"I should be glad to be refused by Miss Earle five hundred times."

"Indeed?"

"Yes, five hundred times, if on the five hundredth and first time she accepted."

"Is it really so serious as that?"

"It is just exactly that serious."

"Then your talk to me after all was only pretence?"

"No, only a mistake."

"What an escape I have had!"

"You have, indeed."

"Ah, here comes Miss Earle. Really, for a lady who has rejected a gentleman, she does not look as supremely happy as she might. I must go and have a talk with her."

"Look here, Blanche," cried the young man, angrily, "if you say a word to her about what we have been speaking of, I'll—"

"What will you do?" said the young lady, sweetly.

Morris stood looking at her. He didn't himself know what he would do; and Blanche, bowing to him, walked along the deck, and sat down in the steamer chair beside Miss Earle, who gave her a very scant recognition.

"Now, you needn't be so cool and dignified," said the lady. "George and I have been talking over the matter, and I told him he wasn't to feel discouraged at a first refusal, if he is resolved to have a shop-girl for his wife."

"What! Mr. Morris and you have been discussing me, have you?"

"Is there anything forbidden in that, Miss Earle? You must remember that George and I are very, very old friends, old and dear friends. Did you refuse him on my account? I know you like him."

"Like him?" said Miss Earle, with a fierce light in her eyes, as she looked at her tormentor. "Yes, I like him, and I'll tell you more than that;" she bent over and added in an intense whisper, "I love him, and if you say another word to me about him, or if you dare to discuss me with him, I shall go up to him where he stands now and accept him. I shall say to him, 'George Morris, I love you.' Now if you doubt I shall do that, just continue in your present style of conversation."

Blanche leaned back in the steamer chair and turned a trifle pale. Then she laughed, that irritating little laugh of hers, and said, "Really I did not think it had gone so far as that. I'll bid you good morning."

The moment the chair was vacated, George Morris strolled up and sat down on it.

"What has that vixen been saying to you?" he asked.

"That vixen," said Miss Earle, quietly, "has been telling me that you and she were discussing me this morning, and discussing the conversation that took place last night."

"It is a lie," said Morris.

"What is? What I say, or what she said, or what she says you said?"

"That we were discussing you, or discussing our conversation, is not true. Forgive me for using the coarser word. This was how it was; she came up to me—"

"My dear Mr. Morris, don't say a word. I know well enough that you would not discuss the matter with anybody. I, perhaps, may go so far as to say, least of all with her. Still, Mr. Morris, you must remember this, that even if you do not like her now—"

"Like her?" cried Morris; "I hate her."

"As I was going to say, and it is very hard for me to say it, Mr. Morris, you have a duty towards her as you—we all have our duties to perform," said Miss Earle, with a broken voice. "You must do yours, and I must do mine. It may be hard, but it is settled. I cannot talk this morning. Excuse me." And she rose and left him sitting there.

"What in the world does the girl mean? I am glad that witch gets off at Queenstown. I believe it is she who has mixed everything up. I wish I knew what she has been saying."

Miss Earle kept very closely to her room that day, and in the evening, as they approached the Fastnet Light, George Morris was not able to find her to tell her of the fact that they had sighted land. He took the liberty, however, of scribbling a little note to her, which the stewardess promised to deliver. He waited around the foot of the companion-way for an answer. The answer came in the person of Miss Katherine herself.

If refusing a man was any satisfaction, it seemed as if Miss Katherine Earle had obtained very little gratification from it. She looked weary and sad as she took the young man's arm, and her smile as she looked up at him had something very pathetic in it, as if a word might bring the tears. They sat in the chairs and watched the Irish coast. Morris pointed out objects here and there, and told her what they were. At last, when they went down to supper together, he said—

"We will be at Queenstown some time to-night. It will be quite a curious sight in the moonlight. Wouldn't you like to stay up and see it?"

"I think I would," she answered. "I take so few ocean voyages that I wish to get all the nautical experiences possible."

The young man looked at her sharply, then he said—

"Well, the stop at Queenstown is one of the experiences. May I send the steward to rap at your door when the engine stops?"

"Oh, I shall stay up in the saloon until that time?"

"It may be a little late. It may be as late as one or two o'clock in the morning. We can't tell. I should think the best thing for you to do would be to take a rest until the time comes. I think, Miss Earle, you need it."

It was a little after twelve o'clock when the engine stopped. The saloon was dimly lighted, and porters were hurrying to and fro, getting up the baggage which belonged to those who were going to get off at Queenstown. The night was very still, and rather cold. The lights of Queenstown could be seen here and there along the semi-circular range of hills on which the town stood. Passengers who were to land stood around the deck well muffled up, and others who had come to bid them good-bye were talking sleepily with them. Morris was about to send the steward to Miss Earle's room, when that young lady herself appeared. There was something spirit-like about her, wrapped in her long cloak, as she walked through the half-darkness to meet George Morris.

"I was just going to send for you," he said.

"I did not sleep any," was the answer, "and the moment the engine stopped I knew we were there. Shall we go on deck?"

"Yes," he said, "but come away from the crowd," and with that he led her towards the stern of the boat. For a moment Miss Earle seemed to hold back, but finally she walked along by his side firmly to where they had stood the night before. With seeming intention Morris tried to take his place beside her, but Miss Earle, quietly folding her cloak around her, stood on the opposite side of the flagpole, and, as if there should be no forgetfulness on his part, she reached up her hand and laid it against the staff.

"She evidently meant what she said," thought Morris to himself, with a sigh, as he watched the low, dim outlines of the hills around Queenstown Harbour, and the twinkling lights here and there.

"That is the tender coming now," he said, pointing to the red and green lights of the approaching boat. "How small it looks beside our monster steamship."

Miss Earle shivered.

"I pity the poor folks who have to get up at this hour of the night and go ashore. I should a great deal rather go back to my state-room."

"Well, there is one passenger I am not sorry for," said Morris, "and that is the young woman who has, I am afraid, been saying something to you which has made you deal more harshly with me than perhaps you might otherwise have done. I wish you would tell me what she said?"

"She has said nothing," murmured Miss Earle, with a sigh, "but what you yourself have confirmed. I do not pay much attention to what she says."

"Well, you don't pay much attention to what I say either," he replied. "However, as I say, there is one person I am not sorry for; I even wish it were raining. I am very revengeful, you see."

"I do not know that I am very sorry for her myself," replied Miss Earle, frankly; "but I am sorry for her poor old father, who hasn't appeared in the saloon a single day except the first. He has been sick the entire voyage."

"Her father?" cried Morris, with a rising inflection in his voice.

"Certainly."

"Why, bless my soul! Her father has been dead for ages and ages."

"Then who is the old man she is with?"

"Old man! It would do me good to have her hear you call him the old man. Why, that is her husband."

"Her husband!" echoed Miss Earle, with wide open eyes, "I thought he was her father."

"Oh, not at all. It is true, as you know, that I was engaged to the young lady, and I presume if I had become a partner in our firm sooner we would have been married. But that was a longer time coming than suited my young lady's convenience, and so she threw me over with as little ceremony as you would toss a penny to a beggar, and she married this old man for his wealth, I presume. I don't see exactly why she should take a fancy to him otherwise. I felt very cut up about it, of course, and I thought if I took this voyage I would at least be rid for a while of the thought of her. They are now on their wedding trip. That is the reason your steamer chair was broken, Miss Earle. Here I came on board an ocean steamer to get rid of the sight or thought of a certain woman, and to find that I was penned up with that woman, even if her aged husband was with her, for eight or nine days, was too much for me. So I raced up the deck and tried to get ashore. I didn't succeed in that, but I did succeed in breaking your chair."

Miss Earle was evidently very much astonished at this revelation, but she said nothing. After waiting in vain for her to speak, Morris gazed off at the dim shore. When he looked around he noticed that Miss Earle was standing on his side of the flagstaff. There was no longer a barrier between them.

Seventh Day

If George Morris were asked to say which day of all his life had been the most thoroughly enjoyable, he would probably have answered that the seventh of his voyage from New York to Liverpool was the red-letter day of his life. The sea was as calm as it was possible for a sea to be. The sun shone bright and warm. Towards the latter part of the day they saw the mountains of Wales, which, from the steamer's deck, seemed but a low range of hills. It did not detract from Morris's enjoyment to know that Mrs. Blanche was now on the troubleless island of Ireland, and that he was sailing over this summer sea with the lady who, the night before, had promised to be his wife.

During the day Morris and Katherine sat together on the sunny side of the ship looking at the Welsh coast. Their books lay unread on the rug, and there were long periods of silences between them.

"I don't believe," said Morris, "that anything could be more perfectly delightful than this. I wish the shaft would break."

"I hope it won't," answered the young lady; "the chances are you would be as cross as a bear before two days had gone past, and would want to go off in a small boat."

"Oh, I should be quite willing to go off in a small boat if you would come with me. I would do that now."

"I am very comfortable where I am," answered Miss Katherine. "I know when to let well enough alone."

"And I don't, I suppose you mean?"

"Well, if you wanted to change this perfectly delightful day for any other day, or this perfectly luxurious and comfortable mode of travel for any other method, I should suspect you of not letting well enough alone."

"I have to admit," said George, "that I am completely and serenely happy. The only thing that bothers me is that to-night we shall be in Liverpool. I wish this hazy and dreamy weather could last for ever, and I am sure I could stand two extra days of it going just as we are now. I think with regret of how much of this voyage we have wasted."

"Oh, you think it was wasted, do you?"

"Well, wasted as compared with this sort of life. This seems to me like a rest after a long chase."

"Up the deck?" asked the young lady, smiling at him.

"Now, see here," said Morris, "we may as well understand this first as last, that unfortunate up-the-deck chase has to be left out of our future life. I am not going to be twitted about that race every time a certain young lady takes a notion to have a sort of joke upon me."

"That was no joke, George. It was the most serious race you ever ran in your life. You were running away from one woman, and, poor blind young man, you ran right in the arms of another. The danger you have run into is ever so much greater than the one you were running away from."

"Oh, I realise that," said the young man, lightly; "that's what makes me so solemn to-day, you know." His hand stole under the steamer rugs and imprisoned her own.

"I am afraid people will notice that," she said quietly.

"Well, let them; I don't care. I don't know anybody on board this ship, anyhow, except you, and if you realised how very little I care for their opinions you would not try to withdraw your hand."

"I am not trying very hard," answered the young woman; and then there was another long silence. Finally she continued—

"I am going to take the steamer chair and do it up in ribbons when I get ashore."

"I am afraid it will not be a very substantial chair, no matter what you do with it. It will be a trap for those who sit in it."

"Are you speaking of your own experience?"

"No, of yours."

"George," she said, after a long pause, "did you like her very much?"

"Her?" exclaimed the young man, surprised. "Who?"

"Why, the young lady you ran away from. You know very well whom I mean."

"Like her? Why, I hate her."

"Yes, perhaps you do now. But I am asking of former years. How long were you engaged to her?"

"Engaged? Let me see, I have been engaged just about—well, not twenty-four hours yet. I was never engaged before. I thought I was, but I wasn't really."

Miss Earle shook her head. "You must have liked her very much," she said, "or you never would have proposed marriage to her. You would never have been engaged to her. You never would have felt so badly when she—"

"Oh, say it out," said George, "jilted me, that is the word."

"No, that is not the phrase I wanted to use. She didn't really jilt you, you know. It was because you didn't have, or thought you didn't have, money enough. She would like to be married to you to-day."

George shuddered.

"I wish," he said, "that you wouldn't mar a perfect day by a horrible suggestion."

"The suggestion would not have been so horrible a month ago."

"My dear girl," said Morris, rousing himself up, "it's a subject that I do not care much to talk about, but all young men, or reasonably young men, make mistakes in their lives. That was my mistake. My great luck was that it was discovered in time. As a general thing, affairs in this world are admirably planned, but it does seem to me a great mistake that young people have to choose companions for life at an age when they really haven't the judgment to choose a house and lot. Now, confess yourself, I am not your first lover, am I?"

Miss Earle looked at him for a moment before replying.

"You remember," she said, "that once you spoke of not having to incriminate yourself. You refused to answer a question I asked you on that ground. Now, I think this is a case in which I would be quite justified in refusing to answer. If I told you that you were my first lover, you would perhaps be manlike enough to think that after all you had only taken what nobody else had expressed a desire for. A man does not seem to value anything unless some one else is struggling for it."

"Why, what sage and valuable ideas you have about men, haven't you, my dear?"

"Well, you can't deny but what there is truth in them."

"I not only can, but I do. On behalf of my fellow men, and on behalf of myself, I deny it."

"Then, on the other hand," she continued, "if I confessed to you that

I did have half a score or half a dozen of lovers, you would perhaps think I had been jilting somebody or had been jilted. So you see, taking it all in, and thinking the matter over, I shall refuse to answer your question."

"Then you will not confess?"

"Yes, I shall confess. I have been wanting to confess to you for some little time, and have felt guilty because I did not do so."

"I am prepared to receive the confession," replied the young man, lazily, "and to grant absolution."

"Well, you talk a great deal about America and about Americans, and talk as if you were proud of the country, and of its ways, and of its people."

"Why, I am," answered the young man.

"Very well, then; according to your creed one person is just as good as another."

"Oh, I don't say that, I don't hold that for a moment. I don't think I am as good as you, for instance."

"But what I mean is this, that one's occupation does not necessarily give one a lower station than another. If that is not your belief then you are not a true American, that is all."

"Well, yes, that is my belief. I will admit I believe all that. What of it?"

"What of it? There is this of it. You are the junior partner of a large establishment in New York?"

"Nothing criminal in that, is there?"

"Oh, I don't put it as an accusation, I am merely stating the fact. You admit the fact, of course?"

"Yes. The fact is admitted, and marked Exhibit A, and placed in evidence. Now, what next?"

"In the same establishment there was a young woman who sold ribbons to all comers?"

"Yes, I admit that also, and the young lady's name was Miss Katherine Earle."

"Oh, you knew it, then?"

"Why, certainly I did."

"You knew it before you proposed to me."

"Oh, I seem to have known that fact for years and years."

"She told it to you."

"She? What she?"

"You know very well who I mean, George. She told it to you, didn't she?"

"Why, don't you think I remembered you—remembered seeing you there?"

"I know very well you did not. You may have seen me there, but you did not remember me. The moment I spoke to you on the deck that day in the broken chair, I saw at once you did not remember me, and there is very little use of your trying to pretend you thought of it afterwards. She told it to you, didn't she?"

"Now, look here, Katherine, it isn't I who am making a confession, it is you. It is not customary for a penitent to cross-examine the father confessor in that style."

"It does not make any difference whether you confess or not, George; I shall always know she told you that. After all, I wish she had left it for me to tell. I believe I dislike that woman very much."

"Shake hands, Kate, over that. So do I. Now, my dear, tell me what she told you."

"Then she did tell you that, did she?"

"Why, if you are so sure of it without my admitting it, why do you ask again?"

"I suppose because I wanted to make doubly sure."

"Well, then, assurance is doubly sure. I admit she did."

"And you listened to her, George?" said Katherine, reproachfully.

"Listened? Why, of course I did. I couldn't help myself. She said it before I knew what she was going to say. She didn't give me the chance that your man had in that story you were speaking of. I said something that irritated her and she out with it at once as if it had been a crime on your part. I did not look on it in that light, and don't now. Anyhow, you are not going back to the ribbon counter."

"No," answered the young lady, with a sigh, looking dreamily out into the hazy distance. "No, I am not."

"At least, not that side of the counter," said George.

She looked at him for a moment, as if she did not understand him; then she laughed lightly.

"Now," said Morris, "I have done most of the confession on this confession of yours. Supposing I make a confession, and ask you to tell me what she told you."

"Well, she told me that you were a very fascinating young man," answered Katherine, with a sigh.

"Really. And did after-acquaintance corroborate that statement?"

"I never had occasion to tell her she was mistaken."

"What else did she say? Didn't mention anything about my prospects or financial standing in any way?"

"No; we did not touch on that subject."

"Come, now, you cannot evade the question. What else did she say to you about me?"

"I don't know that it is quite right to tell you, but I suppose I may. She said that you were engaged to her."

"Had been."

"No, were."

"Oh, that's it. She did not tell you she was on her wedding tour?"

"No, she did not."

"And didn't you speak to her about her father being on board?"

Katherine laughed her low, enjoyable laugh.

"Yes," she said, "I did, and I did not think till this moment of how flustered she looked. But she recovered her lost ground with a great deal of dexterity."

"By George, I should like to have heard that! I am avenged!"

"Well, so is she," was the answer.

"How is that?"

"You are engaged to me, are you not?"

Before George could make any suitable reply to this bit of humbug, one of the officers of the ship stopped before them.

"Well," he said, "I am afraid we shall not see Liverpool to-night."

"Really. Why?" asked George.

"This haze is settling down into a fog. It will be as thick as pea-soup before an hour. I expect there will be a good deal of grumbling among the passengers."

As he walked on, George said to Katherine, "There are two passengers who won't grumble any, will they, my dear?"

"I know one who won't," she answered.

The fog grew thicker and thicker; the vessel slowed down, and finally stopped, sounding every now and then its mournful, timber-shaking whistle.

Eighth Day

On the afternoon of the eighth day George Morris and Katherine Earle stood together on the deck of the tender, looking back at the huge steamship which they had just left.

"When we return," he said, "I think we shall choose this ship."

"Return?" she answered, looking at him.

"Why, certainly; we are going back, are we not?"

"Dear me," she replied, "I had not thought of that. You see, when I left America I did not intend to go back."

"Did you not? I thought you were only over here for the trip."

"Oh no. I told you I came on business, not on pleasure."

"And did you intend to stay over here?"

"Certainly."

"Why, that's strange; I never thought of that."

"It is strange, too," said Katherine, "that I never thought of going back."

"And—and," said the young man, "won't you go?"

She pressed his arm, and stood motionless.

"Where thou goest, I will go. Thy people shall be my people."

"That's a quotation, I suppose?" said George.

"It is," answered Katherine.

"Well, you see, as I told you, I am not very well read up on the books of the day."

"I don't know whether you would call that one of the books of the day or not," said Katherine; "it is from the Bible."

"Oh," answered the other. "I believe, Kate, you will spend the rest of your life laughing at me."

"Oh no," said the young lady, "I always thought I was fitted for missionary life. Now, look what a chance I have."

"You have taken a big contract, I admit."

They had very little trouble with their luggage. It is true that the English officials looked rather searchingly in Katherine's trunk for dynamite, but, their fears being allayed in that direction, the trunks were soon chalked and on the back of a stout porter, who transferred them to the top of a cab.

"I tell you what it is," said George, "it takes an American Custom-house official to make the average American feel ashamed of his country."

"Why, I did not think there was anything over there that could make you feel ashamed of your country. You are such a thorough-going American."

"Well, the Customs officials in New York have a knack of making a person feel that he belongs to no place on earth."

They drove to the big Liverpool hotel which is usually frequented by Americans who land in that city, and George spent the afternoon in attending to business in Liverpool, which he said he did not expect to have to look after when he left America, but which he desired very much to get some information about.

Katherine innocently asked if she could be of any assistance to him, and he replied that she might later on, but not at the present state of proceedings.

In the evening they went to a theatre together, and took a long route back to the hotel.

"It isn't a very pretty city," said Miss Earle.

"Oh, I think you are mistaken," replied her lover. "To me it is the most beautiful city in the world."

"Do you really mean that?" she said, looking at him with surprise.

"Yes, I do. It is the first city through which I have walked with the lady who is to be my wife."

"Oh, indeed," remarked the lady who was to be his wife, "and have you never walked with—"

"Now, see here," said Morris, "that subject is barred out. We left all those allusions on the steamer. I say I am walking now with the lady who is to be my wife. I think that statement of the case is perfectly correct, is it not?"

"I believe it is rather more accurate than the average statement of the average American."

"Now, Katherine," he said, "do you know what information I have been looking up since I have been in Liverpool?"

"I haven't the slightest idea," she said. "Property?"

"No, not property."

"Looking after your baggage, probably?"

"Well, I think you have got it this time. I was looking after my baggage. I was trying to find out how and when we could get married."

"Oh!"

"Yes, oh! Does that shock you? I find they have some idiotic arrangement by which a person has to live here three months before he can be married, although I was given some hope that, by paying for it, a person could get a special licence. If that is the case, I am going to have a special licence to-morrow."

"Indeed?"

"Yes, indeed. Then we can be married at the hotel."

"And don't you think, George, that I might have something to say about that?"

"Oh, certainly! I intended to talk with you about it. Of course I am talking with you now on that subject. You admitted the possibility of our getting married. I believe I had better get you to put it down in writing, or have you say it before witnesses, or something of that sort."

"Well, I shouldn't like to be married in a hotel."

"In a church, then? I suppose I can make arrangements that will include a church. A parson will marry us. That parson, if he is the right sort, will have a church. It stands to reason, therefore, that if we give him the contract he will give us the use of his church, quid pro quo, you know."

"Don't talk flippantly, please. I think it better to wait until to-morrow, George, before you do anything rash. I want to see something of the country. I want us to take a little journey together to-morrow, and then, out in the country, not in this grimy, sooty city, we will make arrangements for our marriage."

"All right, my dear. Where do you intend to go?"

"While you have been wasting your time in getting information relating to matrimony, I have been examining time-tables. Where I want to go is two or three hours' ride from here. We can take one of the morning trains, and when we get to the place I will allow you to hire a conveyance, and we will have a real country drive. Will you go with me?"

"Will I? You better believe I will. But you see, Katherine, I want to get married as soon as possible. Then we can take a little trip on the Continent before it is time for us to go back to America. You have never been on the Continent, have you?"

"Never."

"Well, I am very glad of that. I shall be your guide, philosopher, and friend, and, added to that, your husband."

"Very well, we will arrange all that on our little excursion to-morrow."

Ninth Day

Spring in England—and one of those perfect spring days in which all rural England looks like a garden. The landscape was especially beautiful to American eyes, after the more rugged views of Transatlantic scenery. The hedges were closely clipped, the fields of the deepest green, and the hills far away were blue and hazy in the distance.

"There is no getting over the fact," said Morris, "that this is the prettiest country in the whole world."

During most of the journey Katherine Earle sat back in her corner of the first-class compartment, and gazed silently out of the flying windows. She seemed too deeply impressed with the beauty of the scene to care for conversation even with the man she was to marry. At last they stopped at a pretty little rural station, with the name of the place done in flowers of vivid colour that stood out against the brown of the earth around, them and the green turf which formed the sloping bank.

"Now," said George, as they stood on the platform, "whither away? Which direction?"

"I want to see," said she, "a real, genuine, old English country home."

"A castle?"

"No, not a castle."

"Oh, I know what you want. Something like Haddon Hall, or that sort of thing. An old manor house. Well, wait a minute, and I'll talk to the station master, and find out all there is about this part of the country."

And before she could stop him, he had gone to make his inquiry of that official. Shortly after he came back with a list of places that were worth seeing, which he named.

"Holmwood House," she repeated. "Let us see that. How far is it?"

George again made inquiries, and found that it was about eight miles away. The station-master assured him that the road thither was one of the prettiest drives in the whole country.

"Now, what kind of a conveyance will you have? There are four-wheeled cabs, and there is even a hansom to be had. Will you have two horses or one, and will you have a coachman?"

"None of these," she said, "if you can get something you can drive yourself—I suppose you are a driver?"

"Oh, I have driven a buggy."

"Well, get some sort of conveyance that we can both sit in while you drive."

"But don't you think we will get lost?"

"We can inquire the way," she said, "and if we do get lost, it won't matter. I want to have a long talk with you before we reach the place."

They crossed the railway by a bridge over the line, and descended into a valley along which the road wound.

The outfit which George had secured was a neat little cart made of wood in the natural colour and varnished, and a trim little pony, which looked ridiculously small for two grown people, and yet was, as George afterwards said, "as tough as a pine knot."

The pony trotted merrily along, and needed no urging. George doubtless was a good driver, but whatever talents he had in that line were not brought into play. The pony was a treasure that had apparently no bad qualities. For a long time the two in the cart rode along the smooth highway silently, until at last Morris broke out with—

"Oh, see here! This is not according to contract. You said you wanted a long talk, and now you are complacently saying nothing."

"I do not know exactly how to begin."

"Is it so serious as all that?"

"It is not serious exactly—it is merely, as it were, a continuation of the confession."

"I thought we were through with that long ago. Are there any more horrible revelations?"

She looked at him with something like reproach in her eyes.

"If you are going to talk flippantly, I think I will postpone what I have to say until another time."

"My dear Kate, give a man a chance. He can't reform in a moment. I never had my flippancy checked before. Now then, I am serious again. What appalling—I mean—you see how difficult it is, Katherine—I mean, what serious subject shall we discuss?"

"Some other time."

"No—now. I insist on it. Otherwise I will know I am unforgiven."

"There is nothing to forgive. I merely wanted to tell you something more than you know about my own history."

"I know more now than that man in the story."

"He did not object to the knowledge, you know. He objected to receiving it from a third person. Now I am not a third person, am I?"

"Indeed, you are not. You are first person singular—at present—the first person to me at least. There, I am afraid I have dropped into flippancy again."

"That is not flippancy. That is very nice." The interval shall be unreported.

At last Katherine said quietly, "My mother came from this part of England."

"Ah! That is why you wanted to come here."

"That is why I wanted to come here. She was her father's only daughter, and, strange to say, he was very fond of her, and proud of her."

"Why strange?"

"Strange from his action for years after. She married against his will. He never forgave her. My father did not seem to have the knack of getting along in the world, and he moved to America in the hope of bettering his condition. He did not better it. My father died ten years ago, a prematurely broken down man, and my mother and I struggled along as best we could until she died two years ago. My grandfather returned her letter unopened when mother wrote to him ten years ago, although the letter had a black border around it. When I think of her I find it hard to forgive him, so I suppose some of his nature has been transmitted to me."

"Find it hard? Katherine, if you were not an angel you would find it impossible."

"Well, there is nothing more to tell, or at least, not much. I thought you should know this. I intended to tell you that last day on shipboard, but it seemed to me that here was where it should be told—among the hills and valleys that she saw when she was my age."

"Katherine, my dear, do not think about it any more than you can help. It will only uselessly depress you. Here is a man coming. Let us find out now whether we have lost our way or not."

They had.

Even after that they managed to get up some wrong lanes and byways, and took several wrong turnings; but by means of inquiry from every one they met, they succeeded at last in reaching the place they were in search of.

There was an old and grey porter's lodge, and an old and grey gateway, with two tall, moss-grown stone pillars, and an iron gate between them. On the top of the pillars were crumbled stone shields, seemingly held in place by a lion on each pillar.

"Is this Holmwood House?" asked Morris of the old and grey man who came out of the porter's lodge.

"Yes, sir, it be," replied the man.

"Are visitors permitted to see the house and the grounds?"

"No, they be'ant," was the answer. "Visitors were allowed on Saturdays in the old Squire's time, but since he died they tell me the estate is in the courts, and we have orders from the London lawyers to let nobody in."

"I can make it worth your while," said George, feeling in his vest pocket; "this lady would like to see the house."

The old man shook his head, even although George showed him a gold piece between his finger and thumb. Morris was astonished at this, for he had the mistaken belief which all Americans have, that a tip in Europe, if it is only large enough, will accomplish anything.

"I think perhaps I can get permission," said Katherine, "if you will let me talk a while to the old man."

"All right. Go ahead," said George. "I believe you could wheedle anybody into doing what he shouldn't do."

"Now, after saying that, I shall not allow you to listen. I shall step down and talk with him a moment and you can drive on for a little distance, and come back."

"Oh, that's all right," said George, "I know how it is. You don't want to give away the secret of your power. Be careful, now, in stepping down. This is not an American buggy," but before he had finished the warning, Katherine had jumped lightly on the gravel, and stood waiting for him to drive on. When he came back he found the iron gates open.

"I shall not get in again," she said. "You may leave the pony with this man, George, he will take care of it. We can walk up the avenue to the house."

After a short walk under the spreading old oaks they came in sight of the house, which was of red brick and of the Elizabethan style of architecture.

"I am rather disappointed with that," said George, "I always thought old English homesteads were of stone."

"Well, this one at least is of brick, and I imagine you will find a great many of them are of the same material."

They met with further opposition from the housekeeper who came to the door which the servant had opened after the bell was rung.

She would allow nobody in the house, she said. As for Giles, if he allowed people on the grounds that was his own look-out, but she had been forbidden by the lawyers to allow anybody in the house, and she had let nobody in, and she wasn't going to let anybody in.

"Shall I offer her a tip?" asked George, in a whisper.

"No, don't do that."

"You can't wheedle her like you did the old man, you know. A woman may do a great deal with a man, but when she meets another woman she meets her match. You women know each other, you know."

Meanwhile the housekeeper, who had been about to shut the door, seemed to pause and regard the young lady with a good deal of curiosity. Her attention had before that time been taken up with the gentleman.

"Well, I shall walk to the end of the terrace, and give you a chance to try your wiles. But I am ready to bet ten dollars that you don't succeed."

"I'll take you," answered the young lady.

"Yes, you said you would that night on the steamer."

"Oh, that's a very good way of getting out of a hopeless bet."

"I am ready to make the bet all right enough, but I know you haven't a ten-dollar bill about you."

"Well, that is very true, for I have changed all my money to English currency; but I am willing to bet its equivalent."

Morris walked to the end of the terrace. When he got back he found that the door of the house was as wide open as the gates of the park had been.

"There is something uncanny about all this," he said. "I am just beginning to see that you have a most dangerous power of fascination. I could understand it with old Giles, but I must admit that I thought the stern housekeeper would—"

"My dear George," interrupted Katherine, "almost anything can be accomplished with people, if you only go about it the right way."

"Now, what is there to be seen in this house?"

"All that there is to be seen about any old English house. I thought, perhaps, you might be interested in it."

"Oh, I am. But I mean, isn't there any notable things? For instance, I was in Haddon Hall once, and they showed me the back stairway where a fair lady had eloped with her lover. Have they anything of that kind to show here?"

Miss Earle was silent for a few moments. "Yes," she said, "I am afraid they have."

"Afraid? Why, that is perfectly delightful. Did the young lady of the house elope with her lover?"

"Oh, don't talk in that way, George," she said. "Please don't."

"Well, I won't, if you say so. I admit those little episodes generally turn out badly. Still you must acknowledge that they add a great interest to an old house of the Elizabethan age like this?"

Miss Earle was silent. They had, by this time, gone up the polished stairway, which was dimly lighted by a large window of stained glass.

"Here we are in the portrait hall," said Miss Earle. "There is a picture here that I have never seen, although I have heard of it, and I want to see it. Where is it?" she asked, turning to the housekeeper, who had been following them up the stairs.

"This way, my lady," answered the housekeeper, as she brought them before a painting completely concealed by a dark covering of cloth.

"Why is it covered in that way? To keep the dust from it?"

The housekeeper hesitated for a moment; then she said—

"The old Squire, my lady, put that on when she left, and it has never been taken off since."

"Then take it off at once," demanded Katherine Earle, in a tone that astonished Morris.

The housekeeper, who was too dignified to take down the covering herself, went to find the servant, but Miss Earle, with a gesture of impatience, grasped the cloth and tore it from its place, revealing the full-length portrait of a young lady.

Morris looked at the portrait in astonishment, and then at the girl by his side.

"Why, Katherine," he cried, "it is your picture!"

The young lady was standing with her hands tightly clenched and her lips quivering with nervous excitement. There were tears in her eyes, and she did not answer her lover for a moment; then she said—

"No, it is not my picture. This is a portrait of my mother."

Mrs. Tremain

"And Woman, wit a flaming torch

Sings heedless, in a powder—

Her careless smiles they warp and scorch

Man's heart, as fire the pine

Cuts keener than the thrust of lance

Her glance"

The trouble about this story is that it really has no ending. Taking an ocean voyage is something like picking up an interesting novel, and reading a chapter in the middle of it. The passenger on a big steamer gets glimpses of other people's lives, but he doesn't know what the beginning was, nor what the ending will be.

The last time I saw Mrs. Tremain she was looking over her shoulder and smiling at Glendenning as she walked up the gangway plank at Liverpool, hanging affectionately on the arm of her husband. I said to myself at the time, "You silly little handsome idiot, Lord only knows what trouble you will cause before flirting has lost its charm for you." Personally I would like to have shoved Glendenning off the gangway plank into the dark Mersey; but that would have been against the laws of the country on which we were then landing.

Mrs. Tremain was a woman whom other women did not like, and whom men did. Glendenning was a man that the average man detested, but he was a great favourite with the ladies.

I shall never forget the sensation Mrs. Tremain caused when she first entered the saloon of our steamer. I wish I were able to describe accurately just how she was dressed; for her dress, of course, had a great deal to do with her appearance, notwithstanding the fact that she was one of the loveliest women

I ever saw in my life. But it would require a woman to describe her dress with accuracy, and I am afraid any woman who was on board the steamer that trip would decline to help me. Women were in the habit of sniffing when Mrs. Tremain's name was mentioned. Much can be expressed by a woman's sniff. All that I can say about Mrs. Tremain's dress is that it was of some dark material, brightly shot with threads of gold, and that she had looped in some way over her shoulders and around her waist a very startlingly coloured silken scarf, while over her hair was thrown a black lace arrangement that reached down nearly to her feet, giving her a half-Spanish appearance. A military-looking gentleman, at least twice her age, was walking beside her. He was as grave and sober as she appeared light and frivolous, and she walked by his side with a peculiar elastic step, that seemed hardly to touch the carpet, laughing and talking to him just as if fifty pair of eyes were not riveted upon her as the pair entered. Everybody thought her a Spanish woman; but, as it turned out afterward, she was of Spanish-Mexican-American origin, and whatever beauty there is in those three nationalities seemed to be blended in some subtle, perfectly indescribable way in the face and figure of Mrs. Tremain.

The grave military-looking gentleman at her side was Captain Tremain, her husband, although in reality he was old enough to be her father. He was a captain in the United States army, and had been stationed at some fort near the Mexican border where he met the young girl whom he made his wife. She had seen absolutely nothing of the world, and they were now on their wedding trip to Europe, the first holiday he had taken for many a year.

In an incredibly short space of time Mrs. Tremain was the acknowledged belle of the ship. She could not have been more than nineteen or twenty years of age, yet she was as perfectly at her ease, and as thoroughly a lady as if she had been accustomed to palaces and castles for years. It was astonishing to see how naturally she took to it. She had lived all her life in a rough village in the wilds of the South-West, yet she had the bearing of a duchess or a queen.

The second day out she walked the deck with the captain, which, as everybody knows, is a very great honour. She always had a crowd of men around her, and apparently did not care the snap of her pretty fingers whether a woman on board spoke to her or not. Her husband was one of those slow-going, sterling men whom you meet now and again, with no nonsense about him, and with a perfect trust in his young wife. He was delighted to see her enjoying her voyage so well, and proud of the universal court that was paid to her. It was quite evident to everybody on board but himself that Mrs. Tremain was a born coquette, and the way she could use those dark, languishing, Spanish-Mexican eyes of hers was a lesson to flirts all the world over. It didn't, apparently, so much matter as long as her smiles were distributed pretty evenly over the whole masculine portion of the ship. But by-and-by things began to simmer down until the smiles were concentrated on the most utterly objectionable man on board—Glendenning. She walked the deck with him, she sat in cozy corners of the saloon with him, when there were not many people there, and at night they placed their chairs in a little corner of the deck where the electric light did not shine. One by one the other admirers dropped off, and left her almost entirely to Glendenning.

Of all those of us who were deserted by Mrs. Tremain none took it so hard as young Howard of Brooklyn. I liked Howard, for he was so palpably and irretrievably young, through no fault of his own, and so thoroughly ashamed of it. He wished to be considered a man of the world, and he had grave opinions on great questions, and his opinions were ever so much more settled and firm than those of us older people.

Young Howard confided a good deal in me, and even went so far one time as to ask if I thought he appeared very young, and if I would believe he was really as old as he stated.

I told him frankly I had taken him to be a very much older man than that, and the only thing about him I didn't like was a certain cynicism and knowledge of the world which didn't look well in a man who ought to be thinking about the serious things of life. After this young Howard confided in me even more than before. He said that he didn't care for Mrs. Tremain in that sort of way at all. She was simply an innocent child, with no knowledge of the world whatever, such as he and I possessed. Her husband—and in this I quite agreed with him—had two bad qualities: in the first place he was too easy going at the present, and in the second place he was one of those quiet men who would do something terrible if once he were aroused.

One day, as young Howard and I walked the deck together, he burst out with this extraordinary sentiment—

"All women," he said, "are canting hypocrites."

"When a man says that," I answered, "he means some particular woman. What woman have you in your eye, Howard?"

"No, I mean all women. All the women on board this boat, for instance."

"Except one, of course," I said.

"Yes," he answered, "except one. Look at the generality of women," he cried bitterly; "especially those who are what they call philanthropic and good. They will fuss and mourn over some drunken wretch who cannot be reclaimed, and would be no use if he could, and they will spend their time and sympathy over some creature bedraggled in the slums, whose only hope can be death, and that as soon as possible, yet not one of them will lift a finger to save a fellow creature from going over the brink of ruin. They will turn their noses in the air when a word from them would do some good, and then they will spend their time fussing and weeping over somebody that nothing on earth can help."

"Now, Howard," I said, "that's your cynicism which I've so often deplored. Come down to plain language, and tell me what you mean?"

"Look at the women on board this steamer," he cried indignantly. "There's pretty little Mrs. Tremain, who seems to have become fascinated by that scoundrel Glendenning. Any person can see what kind of a man he is—any one but an innocent child, such as Mrs. Tremain is. Now, no man can help. What she needs is some good kindly woman to take her by the hand and give her a word of warning. Is there a woman on board of this steamer who will do it? Not one. They see as plainly as any one else how things are drifting; but it takes a man who has murdered his wife to get sympathy and flowers from the modern so-called lady."

"Didn't you ever hear of the man, Howard, who made a large sum of money, I forget at the moment exactly how much, by minding his own business?"

"Oh yes, it's all very well to talk like that; but I would like to pitch Glendenning overboard."

"I admit that it would be a desirable thing to do, but if anybody is to do it, it is Captain Tremain and not you. Are you a married man, Howard?"

"No," answered Howard, evidently very much flattered by the question.

"Well, you see, a person never can tell on board ship; but, if you happen to be, it seems to me that you wouldn't care for any outsider to interfere in a matter such as we are discussing. At any rate Mrs. Tremain is a married woman, and I can't see what interest you should have in her. Take my advice and leave her alone, and if you want to start a reforming crusade among women, try to convert the rest of the ladies of the ship to be more charitable and speak the proper word in time."

"You may sneer as much as you like," answered young Howard, "but I will tell you what I am going to do. Two is company, and three is none; I'm going to make the third, as far as Mrs. Tremain and Glendenning are concerned."

"Supposing she objects to that?"

"Very likely she will; I don't care. The voyage lasts only a few days longer, and I am going to make the third party at any tête-à-tête."

"Dangerous business, Howard; first thing, you know, Glendenning will be wanting to throw you overboard."

"I would like to see him try it," said the young fellow, clenching his fist.

And young Howard was as good as his word. It was very interesting to an onlooker to see the way the different parties took it. Mrs. Tremain seemed to be partly amused with the boy, and think it all rather good fun. Glendenning scowled somewhat, and tried to be silent; but, finding that made no particular difference, began to make allusions to the extreme youth of young Howard, and seemed to try to provoke him, which laudable intention, to young Howard's great credit, did not succeed.

One evening I came down the forward narrow staircase, that leads to the long corridor running from the saloon, and met, under the electric light at the foot, Mrs. Tremain, young Howard, and Glendenning. They were evidently about to ascend the stairway; but, seeing me come down, they paused, and I stopped for a moment to have a chat with them, and see how things were going on.

Glendenning said, addressing me, "Don't you think it's time for children to be in bed?"

"If you mean me," I answered, "I am just on my way there."

Mrs. Tremain and young Howard laughed, and Glendenning after that ignored both Howard and myself.

He said to Mrs. Tremain, "I never noticed you wearing that ring before. It is a very strange ornament."

"Yes," answered Mrs. Tremain, turning it round and round. "This is a Mexican charmed ring. There is a secret about it, see if you can find it out." And with that she pulled off the ring, and handed it to Glendenning.

"You ought to give it to him as a keepsake," said young Howard, aggressively. "The ring, I notice, is a couple of snakes twisted together."

"Little boys," said Mrs. Tremain, laughing, "shouldn't make remarks like that. They lead to trouble."

Young Howard flushed angrily as Mrs. Tremain said this. He did not seem to mind it when Glendenning accused him of his youth, but he didn't like it coming from her.

Meanwhile Glendenning was examining the ring, and suddenly it came apart in his hand. The coils of the snake were still linked together, but instead of composing one solid ring they could now be spread several inches apart like the links of a golden chain. Mrs. Tremain turned pale, and gave a little shriek, as she saw this.

"Put it together again," she cried; "put it together quickly."

"What is the matter?" said Glendenning, looking up at her. She was standing two or three steps above him; Glendenning was at the bottom of the stair; young Howard stood on the same step as Mrs. Tremain, and I was a step or two above them.

"Put it together," cried Mrs. Tremain again. "I am trying to," said Glendenning, "is there a spring somewhere?"

"Oh, I cannot tell you," she answered, nervously clasping and unclasping her hands; "but if you do not put it together without help, that means very great ill-luck for both you and me."

"Does it?" said Glendenning, looking up at her with a peculiar glance, quite ignoring our presence.

"Yes, it does," she said; "try your best to put that ring together as you found it." It was quite evident that Mrs. Tremain had all the superstition of Mexico.

Glendenning fumbled with the ring one way and another, and finally said, "I cannot put it together."

"Let me try," said young Howard.

"No, no, that will do no good." Saying which Mrs. Tremain snatched the links from Glendenning, slipped them into one ring again, put it on her finger, and dashed quickly up the stairs without saying a word of good night to any of us.

Glendenning was about to proceed up the stair after her, when young Howard very ostentatiously placed himself directly in his path. Glendenning seemed to hesitate for a moment, then thought better of it, turned on his heel and walked down the passage towards the saloon.

"Look here, Howard," I said, "you are going to get yourself into trouble. There's sure to be a fuss on board this steamer before we reach Liverpool."

"I wouldn't be at all surprised," answered young Howard.

"Well, do you think it will be quite fair to Mrs. Tremain?"

"Oh, I shan't bring her name into the matter."

"The trouble will be to keep her name out. It may not be in your power to do that. A person who interferes in other people's affairs must do so with tact and caution."

Young Howard looked up at me with a trace of resentment in his face. "Aren't you interfering now?" he said.

"You are quite right, I am. Good night." And I went up the stairway. Howard shouted after me, but I did not see him again that night.

Next day we were nearing Queenstown, and, as I had letters to write, I saw nothing of young Howard till the evening. I found him unreasonably contrite for what he had said to me the night before; and when I told him he had merely spoken the truth, and was quite justified in doing so, he seemed more miserable than ever.

"Come," he said, "let us have a walk on the deck."

It was between nine and ten o'clock; and when we got out on the deck, I said to him, "Without wishing to interfere any further—"

"Now, don't say that," he cried; "it is cruel."

"Well, I merely wanted to know where your two charges are."

"I don't know," he answered, in a husky whisper; "they are not in the usual corner to-night, and I don't know where they are."

"She is probably with her husband," I suggested.

"No, he is down in the saloon reading."

As young Howard was somewhat prone to get emphatic when he began to talk upon this subject, and as there was always a danger of other people overhearing what he said, I drew him away to a more secluded part of the ship. On this particular boat there was a wheelhouse aft unused, and generally filled up with old steamer chairs. A narrow passage led around this at the curving stern, seldom used by promenaders because of certain obstructions which, in the dark, were apt to trip a person up. Chains or something went from this wheelhouse to the sides of the ship, and, being covered up by boxes of plank, made this part of the deck hard to travel on in the dark. As we went around this narrow passage young Howard was the first to stop. He clutched my arm, but said nothing. There in the dark was the faint outline of two persons, with their backs towards us, leaning over the stern of the ship. The vibration at this part of the boat, from the throbbing of the screw, made it impossible for them to hear our approach. They doubtless thought they were completely in the dark; but they were deluded in that idea, because the turmoil of the water left a brilliant phosphorescent belt far in the rear of the ship, and against this bright, faintly yellow luminous track their forms were distinctly outlined. It needed no second glance to see that the two were Glendenning and Mrs. Tremain. Her head rested on his shoulder, and his arm was around her waist.

"Let us get back," I said in a whisper; and, somewhat to my surprise, young Howard turned back with me. I felt his hand trembling on my arm, but he said nothing. Before we could say a word to each other a sudden and unexpected complication arose. We met Captain Tremain, with a shawl on his arm, coming towards us.

"Good evening, captain," I said; "have a turn on the deck with us?"

"No, thanks," he replied, "I am looking for my wife. I want to give her this shawl to put over her shoulders. She is not accustomed to such chilly weather as we are now running into, and I am afraid she may take cold."

All this time young Howard stood looking at him with a startled expression in his eyes, and his lower jaw dropped. I was afraid Captain Tremain would see him, and wonder what was the matter with the boy. I tried to bring him to himself by stamping my heel—not too gently—on his toes, but he turned his face in the semi-darkness toward me without changing its expression. The one idea that had taken possession of my mind was that Captain Tremain must not be allowed to go further aft than he was, and I tried by looks and nudges to tell young Howard to go back and give her warning, but the boy seemed to be completely dazed with the unexpected horror of the situation. To have this calm, stern, unsuspecting man come suddenly upon what we had seen at the stern of the boat was simply appalling to think of. He certainly would have killed Glendenning where he stood, and very likely Mrs. Tremain as well. As Captain Tremain essayed to pass us I collected my wits as well as I could, and said—

"Oh, by the way, captain, I wanted to speak to you about Mexico. Do you—do you—think that it is a good—er—place for investment?"

"Well," said Captain Tremain, pausing, "I am not so sure about that. You see, their Government is so very unstable. The country itself is rich enough in mineral wealth, if that is what you mean." All the while Howard stood there with his mouth agape, and I felt like shoving my fist into it.

"Here, Howard," I said, "I want to speak to Captain Tremain for a moment. Take this shawl and find Mrs. Tremain, and give it to her." Saying this, I took the shawl from the captain's arm and threw it at young Howard. He appeared then to realise, for the first time, what was expected of him, and, giving me a grateful look, disappeared toward the stern.

"What I wanted more particularly to know about Mexico," I said to the captain, who made no objection to this move, "was whether there would be any more—well, likely to have trouble—whether we would have trouble with them in a military way, you know—that's more in your line."

"Oh, I think not," said the captain. "Of course, on the boundary where we were, there was always more or less trouble with border ruffians, sometimes on one side of the line and sometimes on the other. There is a possibility always that complications may arise from that sort of thing. Our officers might go over into the Mexican territory and seize a desperado there, or they might come over into ours. Still, I don't think anything will happen to bring on a war such as we had once or twice with Mexico."

At this moment I was appalled to hear Glendenning's voice ring out above the noise of the vibration of the vessel.

"What do you mean by that, you scoundrel," he said.

"Hallo," exclaimed the captain, "there seems to be a row back there. I wonder what it is?"

"Oh, nothing serious, I imagine. Probably some steerage passengers have come on the cabin deck. I heard them having a row with some one to-day on that score. Let's walk away from it."

The captain took my arm, and we strolled along the deck while he gave me a great deal of valuable information about Mexico and the state of things along the border line, which I regret to say I cannot remember a word of. The impressions of a man who has been on the spot are always worth hearing, but my ears were strained to catch a repetition of the angry cry I had heard, or the continuation of the quarrel which it certainly seemed to be the beginning of. As we came up the deck again we met young Howard with the shawl still on his arm and Mrs. Tremain walking beside him. She was laughing in a somewhat hysterical manner, and his face was as pale as ashes with a drawn look about the corners of his lips, but the captain's eyes were only on his wife.

"Why don't you put on the shawl, my dear?" he said to her affectionately. "The shawl?" she answered. Then, seeing it on young Howard's arm, she laughed, and said, "He never offered it to me."

Young Howard made haste to place the shawl on her shoulders, which she arranged around herself in a very coquettish and charming way. Then she took her husband's arm.

"Good night," she said to me; "good night, and thanks, Mr. Howard."

"Good night," said the captain; "I will tell you more about that mine to-morrow."

We watched them disappear towards the companion-way. I drew young Howard towards the side of the boat.

"What happened?" I asked eagerly. "Did you have trouble?"

"Very nearly, I made a slip of the tongue. I called her Mrs. Glendenning."

"You called her what?"

"I said, 'Mrs. Glendenning, your husband is looking for you.' I had come right up behind them, and they hadn't heard me, and of course both were very much startled. Glendenning turned round and shouted, 'What do you mean by that, you scoundrel?' and caught me by the throat. She instantly sprang between us, pushing him toward the stern of the boat, and me against the wheelhouse. "'Hush, hush,' she whispered; 'you mean, Mr. Howard, that my husband is there, do you not?'

"'Yes,' I answered, 'and he will be here in a moment unless you come with me.' With that she said 'Good night, Mr. Glendenning,' and took my arm, and he, like a thief, slunk away round the other side of the wheelhouse. I was very much agitated. I suppose I acted like a fool when we met the captain, didn't I?"

"You did," I answered; "go on."

"Well, Mrs. Tremain saw that, and she laughed at me, although I could see she was rather disturbed herself."

Some time that night we touched at Queenstown, and next evening we were in Liverpool. When the inevitable explosion came, I have no means of knowing, and this, as I have said before, is a story without a conclusion.

Mrs. Tremain the next day was as bright and jolly as ever, and the last time I saw her, she was smiling over her shoulder at Glendenning, and not paying the slightest attention to either her husband on whose arm she hung, or to young Howard, who was hovering near.

Share and Share Alike

"The quick must haste to vengeance taste,

For time is on his head;

But he can wait at the door of fate,

Though the stay be long and the hour be late—

The dead."

Melville Hardlock stood in the centre of the room with his feet wide apart and his hands in his trousers pockets, a characteristic attitude of his. He gave a quick glance at the door, and saw with relief that the key was in the lock, and that the bolt prevented anybody coming in unexpectedly. Then he gazed once more at the body of his friend, which lay in such a helpless-looking attitude upon the floor. He looked at the body with a feeling of mild curiosity, and wondered what there was about the lines of the figure on the floor that so certainly betokened death rather than sleep, even though the face was turned away from him. He thought, perhaps, it might be the hand with its back to the floor and its palm towards the ceiling; there was a certain look of hopelessness about that. He resolved to investigate the subject some time when he had leisure. Then his thoughts turned towards the subject of murder. It was so easy to kill, he felt no pride in having been able to accomplish that much. But it was not everybody who could escape the consequences of his crime. It required an acute brain to plan after events so that shrewd detectives would be baffled. There was a complacent conceit about Melville Hardlock, which was as much a part of him as his intense selfishness, and this conceit led him to believe that the future path he had outlined for himself would not be followed by justice.

With a sigh Melville suddenly seemed to realise that while there was no necessity for undue haste, yet it was not wise to be too leisurely in some things, so he took his hands from his pockets and drew to the middle of the floor a large Saratoga trunk. He threw the heavy lid open, and in doing so showed that the trunk was empty. Picking up the body of his friend, which he was surprised to note was so heavy and troublesome to handle, he with some difficulty doubled it up so that it slipped into the trunk. He piled on top of it some old coats, vests, newspapers, and other miscellaneous articles until the space above the body was filled. Then he pressed down the lid and locked it, fastening the catches at each end. Two stout straps were now placed around the trunk and firmly buckled after he had drawn them as tight as possible. Finally he damped the gum side of a paper label, and when he had pasted it on the end of the trunk, it showed the words in red letters, "S.S. Platonic, cabin, wanted." This done, Melville threw open the window to allow the fumes of chloroform to dissipate themselves in the outside air. He placed a closed, packed and labelled portmanteau beside the trunk, and a valise beside that again, which, with a couple of handbags, made up his luggage. Then he unlocked the door, threw back the bolt, and, having turned the key again from the outside, strode down the thickly-carpeted stairs of the hotel into the large pillared and marble-floored vestibule where the clerk's office was. Strolling up to the counter behind which stood the clerk of the hotel, he shoved his key across to that functionary, who placed it in the pigeon-hole marked by the number of his room.

"Did my friend leave for the West last night, do you know?"

"Yes," answered the clerk, "he paid his bill and left. Haven't you seen him since?"

"No," replied Hardlock.

"Well, he'll be disappointed about that, because he told me he expected to see you before he left, and would call up at your room later. I suppose he didn't have time. By the way, he said you were going back to England to-morrow. Is that so?"

"Yes, I sail on the Platonic. I suppose I can have my luggage sent to the steamer from here without further trouble?"

"Oh, certainly," answered the clerk; "how many pieces are there? It will be fifty cents each."

114

"Very well; just put that down in my bill with the rest of the expenses, and let me have it to-night. I will settle when I come in. Five pieces of luggage altogether."

"Very good. You'll have breakfast to-morrow, I suppose?"

"Yes, the boat does not leave till nine o'clock."

"Very well; better call you about seven, Mr. Hardlock. Will you have a carriage?"

"No, I shall walk down to the boat. You will be sure, of course, to have my things there in time."

"Oh, no fear of that. They will be on the steamer by half-past eight."

"Thank you."

As Mr. Hardlock walked down to the boat next morning he thought he had done rather a clever thing in sending his trunk in the ordinary way to the steamer. "Most people," he said to himself, "would have made the mistake of being too careful about it. It goes along in the ordinary course of business. If anything should go wrong it will seem incredible that a sane man would send such a package in an ordinary express waggon to be dumped about, as they do dump luggage about in New York."

He stood by the gangway on the steamer watching the trunks, valises, and portmanteaus come on board.

"Stop!" he cried to the man, "that is not to go down in the hold; I want it. Don't you see it's marked 'wanted?'"

"It is very large, sir," said the man; "it will fill up a state-room by itself."

"I have the captain's room," was the answer.

So the man flung the trunk down on the deck with a crash that made even the cool Mr. Hardlock shudder.

"Did you say you had the captain's room, sir?" asked the steward standing near.

"Yes."

"Then I am your bedroom steward," was the answer; "I will see that the trunk is put in all right."

The first day out was rainy but not rough; the second day was fair and the sea smooth. The second night Hardlock remained in the smoking-room until the last man had left. Then, when the lights were extinguished, he went out on the upper deck, where his room was, and walked up and down smoking his cigar. There was another man also walking the deck, and the red glow of his cigar, dim and bright alternately, shone in the darkness like a glow-worm.

Hardlock wished that he would turn in, whoever he was. Finally the man flung his cigar overboard and went down the stairway. Hartlock had now the dark deck to himself. He pushed open the door of his room and turned out the electric light. It was only a few steps from his door to the rail of the vessel high above the water. Dimly on the bridge he saw the shadowy figure of an officer walking back and forth. Hardlock looked over the side at the phosphorescent glitter of the water which made the black ocean seem blacker still. The sharp ring of the bell betokening midnight made Melville start as if a hand had touched him, and the quick beating of his heart took some moments to subside. "I've been smoking too much to-day," he said to himself. Then looking quickly up and down the deck, he walked on tip toe to his room, took the trunk by its stout leather handle and pulled it over the ledge in the doorway. There were small wheels at the bottom of the trunk, but although they made the pulling of it easy, they seemed to creak with appalling loudness. He realised the fearful weight of the trunk as he lifted the end of it up on the rail. He balanced it there for a moment, and glanced sharply around him, but there was nothing to alarm him. In spite of his natural coolness, he felt a strange, haunting dread of some undefinable disaster, a dread which had been completely absent from him at the time he committed the murder. He shoved off the trunk before he had quite intended to do so, and the next instant he nearly bit through his tongue to suppress a groan of agony. There passed half a dozen moments of supreme pain and fear before he realised what had happened. His wrist had caught in the strap handle of the trunk, and his shoulder was dislocated. His right arm was stretched taut and helpless, like a rope holding up the frightful and ever-increasing weight that hung between him and the sea. His breast was pressed against the rail and his left hand gripped the iron stanchion to keep himself from going over. He felt that his feet were slipping, and he set his teeth and gripped the iron with a grasp that was itself like iron. He hoped the trunk would slip from his useless wrist, but it rested against the side of the vessel, and the longer it hung the more it pressed the hard strap handle into his nerveless flesh. He had realised from the first that he dare not cry for help, and his breath came hard through his clenched teeth as the weight grew heavier and heavier. Then, with his eyes strained by the fearful pressure, and perhaps dazzled by the glittering phosphorescence running so swiftly by the side of the steamer far below, he seemed to see from out the trunk something in the form and semblance of his dead friend quivering like summer heat below him. Sometimes it was the shimmering phosphorescence, then again it was the wraith hovering over the trunk. Hardlock, in spite of his agony, wondered which it really was; but he wondered no longer when it spoke to him.

"Old Friend," it said, "you remember our compact when we left England. It was to be share and share alike, my boy—share and share alike. I have had my share. Come!"

Then on the still night air came the belated cry for help, but it was after the foot had slipped and the hand had been wrenched from the iron stanchion.

An International Row

"A simple child

That lightly draws its breath,

And feels its life in every limb,

What should it know of—kicking up a row

(Note.—Only the last four words of the above poem are claimed as original.)

"Then America declared war on England."—*History of 1812*

Lady, not feeling particularly well, reclining in a steamer chair, covered up with rags. Little girl beside her, who wants to know. Gentleman in an adjoining steamer chair. The little girl begins to speak.

"And do you have to pay to go in, mamma?"

"Yes, dear."

"How much do you have to pay? As much as at a theatre?"

"Oh, you need not pay anything particular—no set sum, you know. You pay just what you can afford."

"Then it's like a collection at church, mamma?"

"Yes, dear."

"And does the captain get the money, mamma?"

"No, dear; the money goes to the poor orphans, I think."

"Where are the orphans, mamma?"

"I don't know, dear, I think they are in Liverpool."

"Whose orphans are they, mamma?"

"They are the orphans of sailors, dear."

"What kind of sailors, mamma?"

"British sailors, darling."

"Aren't there any sailors in America, mamma?"

"Oh yes, dear, lots of them."

"And do they have any orphans?"

"Yes, dear, I suppose there are orphans there too."

"And don't they get any of the money, mamma?"

"I am sure I do not know, dear. By the way, Mr. Daveling, how is that? Do they give any of the money to American orphans?"

"I believe not, madam. Subscriptions at concerts given on board British steamers are of course donated entirely to the Seamen's Hospital or Orphanage of Liverpool."

"Well, that doesn't seem to be quite fair, does it? A great deal of the money is subscribed by Americans."

"Yes, madam, that is perfectly true."

"I should think that ten Americans cross on these lines for every one Englishman."

"I am sure I do not know, madam, what the proportion is. The Americans are great travellers, so are the English too, for that matter."

"Yes; but I saw in one of the papers that this year alone over a hundred thousand persons had taken their passage from New York to England. It seems to me, that as all of them contribute to the receipts of the concerts, some sort of a division should be made."

"Oh, I have no doubt if the case were presented to the captain, he would be quite willing to have part of the proceeds at least go to some American seamen's charity."

"I think that would be only fair."

Two young ladies, arm in arm, approach, and ask Mrs. Pengo how she is feeling to-day.

Mrs. Pengo replies that she doesn't suppose she will feel any better as long as this rolling of the ship continues.

They claim, standing there, endeavouring to keep as perpendicular as possible, that the rolling is something simply awful.

Then the lady says to them, "Do you know, girls, that all the money subscribed at the concerts goes to England?"

"Why, no; I thought it went to some charity."

"Oh, it does go to a charity. It goes to the Liverpool Seamen's Hospital."

"Well, isn't that all right?"

"Yes, it's all right enough; but, as Sadie was just suggesting now, it doesn't seem quite fair, when there are orphans of sailors belonging to America, and as long as such large sums are subscribed by Americans, that the money should not be divided and part of it at least given to an American charity."

"Why, that seems perfectly fair, doesn't it, Mr. Daveling?"

"Yes, it is perfectly fair. I was just suggesting that perhaps if the state of things was presented to the captain, he would doubtless give a portion at least of the proceeds to an American Seamen's Home—if such an institution exists."

"Then," remarked the other girl, "I propose we form a committee, and interview the captain. I think that if Americans subscribe the bulk of the money, which they certainly do, they should have a voice in the disposal of it."

This was agreed to on all hands, and so began one of the biggest rows that ever occurred on board an Atlantic liner. Possibly, if the captain had had any tact, and if he had not been so thoroughly impressed with his own tremendous importance, what happened later on would not have happened.

The lady in the steamer chair took little part in the matter, in fact it was not at that time assumed to be of any importance whatever; but the two young American girls were enthusiastic, and they spoke to several of the passengers about it, both American and English. The English passengers all recognised the justice of the proposed plan, so a committee of five young ladies, and one young gentleman as spokesman, waited upon the captain. The young ladies at first had asked the doctor of the ship to be the spokesman; but when the doctor heard what the proposal was, he looked somewhat alarmed, and stroked his moustache thoughtfully.

"I don't know about that," he said; "it is a little unusual. The money has always gone to the Liverpool Seamen's Hospital, and—well, you see, we are a conservative people. We do a thing in one way for a number of years, and then keep on doing it because we have always done it in that way."

"Yes," burst out one of the young ladies, "that is no reason why an unjust thing should be perpetuated. Merely because a wrong has been done is no reason why it should be done again."

"True," said the doctor, "true," for he did not wish to fall out with the young lady, who was very pretty; "but, you see, in England we think a great deal of precedent."

And so the result of it all was that the doctor demurred at going to see the captain in relation to the matter. He said it wouldn't be the thing, as he was an official, and that it would be better to get one of the passengers.

I was not present at the interview, and of course know only what was told me by those who were there. It seems that the captain was highly offended at being approached on such a subject at all. A captain of an ocean liner, as I have endeavoured to show, is a very great personage indeed. And sometimes I imagine the passengers are not fully aware of this fact, or at least they do not show it as plainly as they ought to. Anyhow, the committee thought the captain had been exceedingly gruff with them, as well as just a trifle impolite. He told them that the money from the concerts had always gone to the Liverpool Seamen's Hospital, and always would while he was commanding a ship. He seemed to infer that the permission given them to hold a concert on board the ship was a very great concession, and that people should be thankful for the privilege of contributing to such a worthy object.

So, beginning with the little girl who wanted to know, and ending with the captain who commanded the ship, the conflagration was started.

Such is British deference to authority that, as soon as the captain's decision was known, those who had hitherto shown an open mind on the subject, and even those who had expressed themselves as favouring the dividing of the money, claimed that the captain's dictum had settled the matter. Then it was that every passenger had to declare himself. "Those who are not with us," said the young women, "are against us." The ship was almost immediately divided into two camps. It was determined to form a committee of Americans to take the money received from the second concert; for it was soon resolved to hold two concerts, one for the American Seamen's Orphans' Home and the other for that at Liverpool.

One comical thing about the row was, that nobody on board knew whether an American Seamen's Orphans' Home existed or not. When this problem was placed before the committee of young people, they pooh-poohed the matter. They said it didn't make any difference at all; if there was no Seamen's Hospital in America, it was quite time there should be one; and so they proposed that the money should be given to the future hospital, if it did not already exist.

When everything was prepared for the second concert there came a bolt from the blue. It was rumoured round the ship that the captain had refused his permission for the second concert to be held. The American men, who had up to date looked with a certain amused indifference on the efforts of the ladies, now rallied and held a meeting in the smoking-room. Every one felt that a crisis had come, and that the time to let loose the dogs of war— sea-dogs in this instance—had arrived. A committee was appointed to wait upon the captain next day. The following morning the excitement was at its highest pitch. It was not safe for an American to be seen conversing with an

Englishman, or vice versâ

Rumour had it at first—in fact all sorts of wild rumours were flying around the whole forenoon—that the captain refused to see the delegation of gentlemen who had requested audience with him. This rumour, however, turned out to be incorrect. He received the delegation in his room with one or two of the officers standing beside him. The spokesman said—

"Captain, we are informed that you have concluded not to grant permission to the Americans to hold a concert in aid of the American Seamen's Orphans' Home. We wish to know if this is true?"

"You have been correctly informed," replied the captain.

"We are sorry to hear that," answered the spokesman. "Perhaps you will not object to tell us on what grounds you have refused your permission?"

"Gentlemen," said the captain, "I have received you in my room because you requested an interview. I may say, however, that I am not in the habit of giving reasons for anything I do, to the passengers who honour this ship with their company."

"Then," said the spokesman, endeavouring to keep calm, but succeeding only indifferently, "it is but right that we should tell you that we regard such a proceeding on your part as a high handed outrage; that we will appeal against your decision to the owners of this steamship, and that, unless an apology is tendered, we will never cross on this line again, and we will advise all our compatriots never to patronise a line where such injustice is allowed."

"Might I ask you," said the captain very suavely, "of what injustice you complain?"

"It seems to us," said the spokesman, "that it is a very unjust thing to allow one class of passengers to hold a concert, and to refuse permission to another class to do the same thing."

"If that is all you complain of," said the captain, "I quite agree with you. I think that would be an exceedingly unjust proceeding."

"Is not that what you are about to do?"

123

"Not that I am aware of."

"You have prohibited the American concert?"

"Certainly. But I have prohibited the English concert as well."

The American delegates looked rather blankly at each other, and then the spokesman smiled. "Oh, well," he said, "if you have prohibited both of them, I don't see that we have anything to grumble at."

"Neither do I," said the captain.

The delegation then withdrew; and the passengers had the unusual pleasure of making one ocean voyage without having to attend the generally inevitable amateur concert.

A Ladies Man

"Jest w'en we guess we've covered the trail

So's no one can't foller, w'y then we fail

W'en we feel safe hid. Nemesis, the cuss,

Waltzes up with nary a warnin' nor fuss.

Grins quiet like, and says, 'How d'y do,

So glad we've met, I'm a-lookin' fer you'"

I do not wish to particularise any of the steamers on which the incidents given in this book occurred, so the boat of which I now write I shall call The Tub. This does not sound very flattering to the steamer, but I must say The Tub was a comfortable old boat, as everybody will testify who has ever taken a voyage in her. I know a very rich man who can well afford to take the best room in the best steamer if he wants to, but his preference always is for a slow boat like The Tub. He says that if you are not in a hurry, a slow boat is preferable to one of the new fast liners, because you have more individuality there, you get more attention, the officers are flattered by your preference for their ship, and you are not merely one of a great mob of passengers as in a crowded fast liner. The officers on a popular big and swift boat are prone to be a trifle snobbish. This is especially the case on the particular liner which for the moment stands at the top—a steamer that has broken the record, and is considered the best boat in the Atlantic service for the time being. If you get a word from the captain of such a boat you may consider yourself a peculiarly honoured individual, and even the purser is apt to answer you very shortly, and make you feel you are but a worm of the dust, even though you have paid a very large price for your state-room. On The Tub there was nothing of this. The officers were genial good fellows who admitted their boat was not the fastest on the Atlantic, although at one time she had been; but if The Tub never broke the record, on the other hand, she never broke a shaft, and so things were evened up. She wallowed her way across the Atlantic in a leisurely manner, and there was no feverish anxiety among the passengers when they reached Queenstown, to find whether the rival boat had got in ahead of us or not.

Everybody on board The Tub knew that any vessel which started from New York the same day would reach Queenstown before us. In fact, a good smart sailing vessel, with a fair wind, might have made it lively for us in an ocean race. The Tub was a broad slow boat, whose great speciality was freight, and her very broadness, which kept her from being a racer, even if her engines had had the power, made her particularly comfortable in a storm. She rolled but little; and as the state-rooms were large and airy, every passenger on board The Tub was sure of a reasonably pleasant voyage.

It was always amusing to hear the reasons each of the passengers gave for being on board The Tub. A fast and splendid liner of an opposition company left New York the next day, and many of our passengers explained to me they had come to New York with the intention of going by that boat, but they found all the rooms taken, that is, all the desirable rooms. Of course they might have had a room down on the third deck; but they were accustomed in travelling to have the best rooms, and if they couldn't be had, why it didn't much matter what was given them, so that was the reason they took passage on The Tub. Others were on the boat because they remembered the time when she was one of the fastest on the ocean, and they didn't like changing ships. Others again were particular friends of the captain, and he would have been annoyed if they had taken any other steamer. Everybody had some particularly valid reason for choosing The Tub, that is, every reason except economy, for it was well known that The Tub was one of the cheapest boats crossing the ocean. For my own part I crossed on her, because the purser was a particular friend of mine, and knew how to amalgamate fluids and different solid substances in a manner that produced a very palatable refreshment. He has himself deserted The Tub long ago, and is now purser on one of the new boats of the same line.

When the gong rang for the first meal on hoard The Tub after leaving New York, we filed down from the smoking-room to the great saloon to take our places at the table. There were never enough passengers on board

The Tub to cause a great rush for places at the table; but on this particular occasion, when we reached the foot of the stairway, two or three of us stood for a moment both appalled and entranced. Sitting at the captain's right hand was a somewhat sour and unattractive elderly woman, who was talking to that smiling and urbane official. Down the long table from where she sat, in the next fifteen seats were fifteen young and pretty girls, most of them looking smilingly and expectantly toward the stairway down which we were descending. The elderly woman paused for a moment in her conversation with the captain, glanced along the line of beauty, said sharply, 'Girls!' and instantly every face was turned demurely toward the plate that was in front of it, and then we, who had hesitated for a moment on the stairway, at once made a break, not for our seats at the table, but for the purser.

"It's all right, gentlemen," said that charming man, before we could speak; "it's all right. I've arranged your places down the table on the opposite side. You don't need to say a word, and those of you who want to change from the small tables to the large one, will find your names on the long table as well as at the small tables, where you have already chosen your places. So, you see, I knew just how you wished things arranged; but," he continued, lowering his voice, "boys, there's a dragon in charge. I know her. She has crossed with us two or three times. She wanted me to arrange it so that fifteen ladies should sit opposite her fifteen girls; but, of course, we couldn't do that, because there aren't fifteen other ladies on board, and there had to be one or two ladies placed next the girls at the foot of the table, so that no girl should have a young man sitting beside her. I have done the best I could, gentlemen, and, if you want the seats rearranged, I think we can manage it for you. Individual preferences may crop up, you know." And the purser smiled gently, for he had crossed the ocean very, very often.

We all took our places, sternly scrutinised by the lady, whom the purser had flatteringly termed the "dragon." She evidently didn't think very much of us as a crowd, and I am sure in my own heart I cannot blame her. We were principally students going over to German colleges on the cheap, some commercial travellers, and a crowd generally who could not afford to take a better boat, although we had all just missed the fast liner that had left a few

127

days before, or had for some reason not succeeded in securing a berth on the fast boat, which was to leave the day after.

If any of the fifteen young ladies were aware of our presence, they did not show it by glancing toward us. They seemed to confine their conversation to whispers among themselves, and now and then a little suppressed giggle arose from one part of the line or the other, upon which the "dragon" looked along the row, and said severely, "Girls!" whereupon everything was quiet again, although some independent young lady generally broke the silence by another giggle just at the time the stillness was becoming most impressive.

After dinner, in the smoking-room, there was a great deal of discussion about the fifteen pretty girls and about the "dragon." As the officers on board The Tub were gentlemen whom an ordinary person might speak to, a delegation of one was deputed to go to the purser's room and find out all that could be learned in relation to the young and lovely passengers.

The purser said that the dragon's name was Mrs. Scrivener-Yapling, with a hyphen. The hyphen was a very important part of the name, and Mrs. Scrivener-Yapling always insisted upon it. Any one who ignored that hyphen speedily fell from the good graces of Mrs. Scrivener-Yapling. I regret to say, however, in spite of the hyphen, the lady was very generally known as the "dragon" during that voyage. The purser told us further, that Mrs. Scrivener-Yapling was in the habit of coming over once a year with a party of girls whom she trotted around Europe. The idea was that they learnt a great deal of geography, a good deal of French and German, and received in a general way a polish which Europe is supposed to give.

The circular which Mrs. Scrivener-Yapling issued was shown to me once by one of the girls, and it represented that all travelling was first-class, that nothing but the very best accommodations on steamers and in hotels were provided, and on account of Mrs. S. Y.'s intimate knowledge of Europe, and the different languages spoken there, she managed the excursion in a way which any one else would find impossible to emulate, and the advantages accruing from such a trip could not be obtained in any other manner without a very much larger expenditure of money. The girls had the advantage of motherly care during all the time they were abroad, and as the party was strictly limited in number, and the greatest care taken to select members only from the very best families in America, Mrs. Scrivener-Yapling was certain that all her patrons would realise that this was an opportunity of a lifetime, etc., etc.

Even if The Tub were not the finest boat on the Atlantic, she certainly belonged to one of the best lines, and as the circular mentioned the line and not the particular vessel on which the excursion was to go, the whole thing had a very high-class appearance.

The first morning out, shortly after, breakfast, the "dragon" and her girls appeared on deck. The girls walked two and two together, and kept their eyes pretty much on the planks beneath them. The fifteenth girl walked with the "dragon," and thus the eight pairs paced slowly up and down the deck under the "dragon's" eye. When this morning promenade was over the young ladies were marshalled into the ladies' saloon, where no masculine foot was allowed to tread. Shortly before lunch an indignation meeting was held in the smoking-room. Stewart Montague, a commercial traveller from Milwaukee, said that he had crossed the ocean many times, but had never seen such a state of things before. This young ladies' seminary business (he alluded to the two and two walk along the deck) ought not to be permitted on any well regulated ship. Here were a number of young ladies, ranging in age from eighteen upwards, and there lay ahead of us a long and possibly dreary voyage, yet the "dragon" evidently expected that not one of the young ladies was to be allowed to speak to one of the young gentlemen on board, much less walk the deck with him. Now, for his part, said Stewart Montague, he was going to take off his hat the next morning to the young lady who sat opposite him at the dinner-table and boldly ask her to walk the deck with him. If the "dragon" interfered, he proposed that we all mutiny, seize the vessel, put the captain in irons, imprison the "dragon" in the hold, and then take to pirating on the high seas. One of the others pointed out to him an objection to this plan, claiming that The Tub could not overtake anything but a sailing-vessel, while even that was doubtful. Montague explained that the mutiny was only to be resorted to as a last desperate chance. He believed the officers of the boat would give us every assistance possible, and so it was only in case of everything else failing that we should seize the ship.

In a moment of temporary aberration I suggested that the "dragon" might not be, after all, such an objectionable person as she appeared, and that perhaps she could be won over by kindness. Instantly a motion was put, and carried unanimously, appointing me a committee to try the effect of kindness on the "dragon." It was further resolved that the meeting should be adjourned, and I should report progress at the next conclave.

I respectfully declined this mission. I said it was none of my affair. I didn't wish to talk to any of the fifteen girls, or even walk the deck with them. I was perfectly satisfied as I was. I saw no reason why I should sacrifice myself for the good of others. I suggested that the name of Stewart Montague be substituted for mine, and that he should face the "dragon" and report progress.

Mr. Montague said it had been my suggestion, not his, that the "dragon" might be overcome by kindness. He did not believe she could, but he was quite willing to suspend hostilities until my plan had been tried and the result reported to the meeting. It was only when they brought in a motion to expel me from the smoking-room that I succumbed to the pressure. The voyage was just beginning, and what is a voyage to a smoker who dare not set foot in the smoking-room?

I do not care to dwell on the painful interview I had with the "dragon." I put my foot in it at the very first by pretending that I thought she came from New York, whereas she had really come from Boston. To take a New York person for a Bostonian is flattery, but to reverse the order of things, especially with a woman of the uncertain temper of Mrs. Scrivener-Yapling, was really a deadly insult, and I fear this helped to shipwreck my mission, although I presume it would have been shipwrecked in any case. Mrs. Scrivener-Yapling gave me to understand that if there was one thing more than another she excelled in it was the reading of character. She knew at a glance whether a man could be trusted or not; most men were not, I gathered from her conversation. It seems she had taken a great many voyages across the Atlantic, and never in the whole course of her experience had she seen such an objectionable body of young men as on this present occasion. She accused me of being a married man, and I surmised that there were other iniquities of which she strongly suspected me.

The mission was not a success, and I reported at the adjourned meeting accordingly.

Mr. Stewart Montague gave it as his opinion that the mission was hopeless from the first, and in this I quite agreed with him. He said he would try his plan at dinner, but what it was he refused to state. We asked if he would report on the success or failure, and he answered that we would all see whether it was a success or failure for ourselves. So there was a good deal of interest centring around the meal, an interest not altogether called forth by the pangs of hunger.

Dinner had hardly commenced when Mr. Stewart Montague leaned over the table and said, in quite an audible voice, to the young lady opposite him, "I understand you have never been over the ocean before?"

The young lady looked just a trifle frightened, blushed very prettily, and answered in a low voice that she had not.

Then he said, "I envy you the first impressions you will have of Europe. It is a charming country. Where do you go after leaving England?"

"We are going across to Paris first," she replied, still in a low voice.

Most of us, however, were looking at the "dragon." That lady sat bolt upright in her chair as if she could not believe her ears. Then she said, in an acid voice, "Miss Fleming."

"Yes, Mrs. Scrivener-Yapling," answered that young lady.

"Will you oblige me by coming here for a moment?"

Miss Fleming slowly revolved in her circular chair, then rose and walked up to the head of the table.

"Miss Strong," said the "dragon" calmly, to the young lady who sat beside her, "will you oblige me by taking Miss Fleming's place at the centre of the table?"

Miss Strong rose and took Miss Fleming's place.

"Sit down beside me, please?" said the "dragon" to Miss Fleming; and that unfortunate young woman, now as red as a rose, sat down beside the "dragon."

Stewart Montague bit his lip. The rest of us said nothing, and appeared not to notice what had occurred. Conversation went on among ourselves. The incident seemed ended; but, when the fish was brought, and placed before Miss Fleming, she did not touch it. Her eyes were still upon the table. Then, apparently unable to struggle any longer with her emotions, she rose gracefully, and, bowing to the captain, said, "Excuse me, please." She walked down the long saloon with a firm step, and disappeared. The "dragon" tried to resume conversation with the captain as if nothing had happened; but that official answered only in monosyllables, and a gloom seemed to have settled down upon the dinner party.

Very soon the captain rose and excused himself. There was something to attend to on deck, he said, and he left us.

As soon as we had reassembled in the smoking-room, and the steward had brought in our cups of black coffee, Stewart Montague arose and said, "Gentlemen, I know just what you are going to say to me. It was brutal. Of course I didn't think the 'dragon' would do such a thing. My plan was a complete failure. I expected that conversation would take place across the table all along the line, if I broke the ice."

Whatever opinions were held, none found expression, and that evening in the smoking-room was as gloomy as the hour at the dinner-table.

Towards the shank of the evening a gentleman, who had never been in the smoking-room before, entered very quietly. We recognised him as the man who sat to the left of the captain opposite the "dragon." He was a man of middle age and of somewhat severe aspect. He spoke with deliberation when he did speak, and evidently, weighed his words. All we knew of him was that the chair beside his at meal-times had been empty since the voyage began, and it was said that his wife took her meals in her state-room. She had appeared once on deck with him, very closely veiled, and hung upon his arm in a way that showed she was not standing the voyage very well, pleasant as it had been.

"Gentlemen," began the man suavely, "I would like to say a few words to you if I were certain that my remarks would be taken in the spirit in which they are given, and that you would not think me intrusive or impertinent."

"Go ahead," said Montague, gloomily, who evidently felt a premonition of coming trouble.

The serious individual waited until the steward had left the room, then he closed the door. "Gentlemen," he continued, "I will not recur to the painful incident which happened at the dinner-table to-night further than by asking you, as honourable men, to think of Mrs. Scrivener-Yapling's position of great responsibility. She stands in the place of a mother to a number of young ladies who, for the first time in their lives, have left their homes."

"Lord pity them," said somebody, who was sitting in the corner.

The gentleman paid no attention to the remark.

"Now what I wish to ask of you is that you will not make Mrs. Scrivener-Yapling's position any harder by futile endeavours to form the acquaintance of the young ladies."

At this point Stewart Montague broke out. "Who the devil are you, sir, and who gave you the right to interfere?"

"As to who I am," said the gentleman, quietly, "my name is Kensington, and—"

"West or South?" asked the man in the corner.

At this there was a titter of laughter.

"My name is Kensington," repeated the gentleman, "and I have been asked by Mrs. Scrivener-Yapling to interfere, which I do very reluctantly.

As I said at the beginning, I hope you will not think my interference is impertinent. I only do so at the earnest request of the lady I have mentioned, because I am a family man myself, and I understand and sympathise with the lady in the responsibility which she has assumed."

"It seems to me," said the man in the corner, "that if the 'dragon' has assumed responsibilities and they have not been thrust upon her, which I understand they have not, then she must take the responsibility of the responsibilities which she has assumed. Do I make myself clear?"

"Gentlemen," said Mr. Kensington, "it is very painful for me to speak with you upon this subject. I feel that what I have so clumsily expressed may not be correctly understood; but I appeal to your honour as gentlemen, and I am sure I will not appeal in vain when I ask you not to make further effort towards the acquaintance of the young ladies, because all that you can succeed in doing will be to render their voyage unpleasant to themselves, and interrupt, if not seriously endanger, the good feeling which I understand has always existed between Mrs. Scrivener-Yapling and her protégées."

"All right," said the man in the corner. "Have a drink, Mr. Kensington?"

"Thank you, I never drink," answered Mr. Kensington.

"Have a smoke, then?"

"I do not smoke either, thank you all the same for your offer. I hope, gentlemen, you will forgive my intrusion on you this evening. Good night."

"Impudent puppy," said Stewart Montague, as he closed the door behind him.

But in this we did not agree with him, not even the man in the corner.

"He is perfectly right," said that individual, "and I believe that we ought to be ashamed of ourselves. It will only make trouble, and I for one am going to give up the hunt."

So, from that time forward, the smoking-room collectively made no effort towards the acquaintance of the young ladies. The ladies' seminary walk, as it was called, took place every morning punctually, and sometimes Mr. Kensington accompanied the walkers. Nevertheless, individual friendships, in spite of everything that either Mr. Kensington or the "dragon" could do, sprang up between some of the young men and some of the girls, but the "dragon" had an invaluable ally in Mr. Kensington. The moment any of the young ladies began walking with any of the young gentlemen on deck, or the moment they seated themselves in steamer chairs together, the urbane, always polite Mr. Kensington appeared on the scene and said, "Miss So-and-So, Mrs. Scrivener-Yapling would like to speak with you."

Then the young lady would go with Mr. Kensington, while the young gentleman was apt to use strong language and gnash his teeth.

Mr. Kensington seemed lynx-eyed. There was no escaping him. Many in the smoking-room no doubt would have liked to have picked a flaw in his character if they could. One even spoke of the old chestnut about a man who had no small vices being certain to have some very large ones; but even the speakers themselves did not believe this, and any one could see at a glance that Mr. Kensington was a man of sterling character. Some hinted that his wife was the victim of his cruelty, and kept her state-room only because she knew that he was so fond of the "dragon's" company, and possibly that of some of the young ladies as well. But this grotesque sentiment did not pass current even in the smoking-room. Nevertheless, although he was evidently so good a man, he was certainly the most unpopular individual on board The Tub. The hatred that Stewart Montague felt for him ever since that episode in the smoking-room was almost grotesque.

Montague had somehow managed to get a contrite note of apology and distress to Miss Fleming, and several times the alert Mr. Kensington had caught them together, and asked Miss Fleming with the utmost respect to come down and see Mrs. Scrivener-Yapling.

All in all the "dragon" did not have a very easy time of it. She fussed around like any other old hen who had in charge a brood of ducks.

Once I thought there was going to be a row between Montague and Kensington. He met that gentleman in a secluded part of the deck, and,

135

going up to him, said—

"You old wife deserter, why can't you attend to your own affairs?"

Kensington turned deadly pale at this insult, and his fists clinched—

"What do you mean?" he said huskily.

"I mean what I say. Why don't you take your own wife walking on the deck, and leave the young ladies alone. It's none of your business with whom they walk."

Kensington seemed about to reply; but he thought better of it, turned on his heel, and left Montague standing there.

The old Tub worried her way across the ocean, and reached the bar at Liverpool just in time to be too late to cross it that night. Word was passed along that a tender would come out from Liverpool for us, which was not a very cheering prospect, as we would have two hours' sail at least in what was practically an open boat.

Finally the tender came alongside, and the baggage was dumped down upon it. All of us gathered together ready to leave The Tub. Mr. Kensington, with his closely-veiled wife hanging on his arm, was receiving the thanks and congratulations of the "dragon." The fifteen girls were all around her. Before any one started down the sloping gangway plank, however, two policemen, accompanied by a woman, hurried up on board The Tub.

"Now, madam," said the policeman, "is he here?"

We saw that trouble was coming, and everybody looked at everybody else.

"Is he here?" cried the woman excitedly; "there he stands, the villain. Oh, you villain, you scoundrel, you mean rascal, to leave me, as you thought, penniless in New York, and desert your own wife and family for that—that creature!" We all looked at Kensington, and his face was greenish-pale. The heavily veiled woman shrunk behind him and the policeman tried to make the true wife keep quiet.

"Is your name Braughton?"

Kensington did not answer. His eyes were riveted on his wife. "In the name of God," he cried aghast, "how did you come here?"

"How did I come here," she shrieked. "Oh, you thought you slipped away nicely, didn't you? But you forgot that the Clipper left the next day, and I've been here two days waiting for you. You little thought when you deserted me and my children in New York that we would be here to confront you at Liverpool."

"Come, come." said the policeman, "there's no use of this. I am afraid you will have to come with us, sir."

They took him in charge, and the irate wife then turned like a tigress on the heavily veiled woman who was with him.

"No wonder you are ashamed to show your face," she cried.

"Come, come," said the policeman, "come, come." And they managed to induce her to say no more.

"Madam," said young Montague to the speechless 'dragon,' "I want to ask your permission to allow me to carry Miss Fleming's hand- baggage ashore."

"How dare you speak to me, sir?" she answered.

"Because," he said, in a low voice, "I thought perhaps you wouldn't like an account of this affair to go to the Boston newspapers. I'm a newspaper man, you see," he added, with unblushing mendacity. Then, turning to Miss Fleming, he said, "Won't you allow me to carry this for you?"

Miss Fleming surrendered the natty little handbag she had with her, and smiled. The "dragon" made no objection.

A Society For The Reformation Of Poker Players.

"O Unseen Hand that ever makes and deals us,

And plays our game!

That now obscures and then to light reveals us,

Serves blanks of fame

How vain our shuffling, bluff and weak pretending!

Tis Thou alone can name the final ending"

The seductive game of poker is one that I do not understand. I do not care to understand it, because it cannot be played without the putting up of a good deal of the coin of the realm, and although I have nothing to say against betting, my own theory of conduct in the matter is this, that I want no man's money which I do not earn, and I do not want any man to get my money unless he earns it. So it happens, in the matter of cards, I content myself with euchre and other games which do not require the wagering of money.

On board the Atlantic steamers there is always more or less gambling. I have heard it said that men make trips to and fro merely for the purpose of fleecing their fellow-passengers; but, except in one instance, I never had any experience with this sort of thing.

Our little society for the reformation of poker players, or to speak more correctly, for the reformation of one particular poker player, was formed one bright starlight night, latitude such a number, and longitude something else, as four of us sat on a seat at the extreme rear end of the great steamer. We four, with one other, sat at a small table in the saloon. One of the small tables on a Transatlantic steamer is very pleasant if you have a nice crowd with you. A seat at a small table compares with a seat at the large table as living in a village compares with living in a city. You have some individuality at the short table; you are merely one of a crowd at the long table. Our small table was not quite full. I had the honour of sitting at the head of it, and on each side of me were two young fellows, making five altogether. We all rather prided ourselves on the fact that there were no ladies at our little table.

The young Englishman who sat at my right hand at the corner of the table was going out to America to learn farming. I could, myself, have taught him a good deal about it, but I refrained from throwing cold water on his enthusiastic ideas about American agriculture. His notion was that it was an occupation mostly made up of hunting and fishing, and having a good time generally. The profits, he thought, were large and easily acquired. He had guns with him, and beautiful fishing-rods, and things of that sort. He even had a vague idea that he might be able to introduce fox-hunting in the rural district to which he was going. He understood, and regretted the fact, that we in the United States were rather behind-hand in the matter of fox-hunting. He had a good deal of money with him, I understood, and he had already paid a hundred pounds to a firm in England that had agreed to place him on a farm in America. Of course, now that the money had been paid, there was no use in telling the young man he had been a fool. He would find that out soon enough when he got to America. Henry Storm was his name, and a milder mannered man with a more unsuitable name could hardly be found. The first two or three days out he was the life of our party. We all liked him, in fact, nobody could help liking him; but, as the voyage progressed, he grew more and more melancholy, and, what was really serious, took little food, which is not natural in an Englishman. I thought somebody had been telling him what a fool he had been to pay away his hundred pounds before leaving England, but young Smith of Rochester, who sat at my left, told me what the trouble was one day as we walked the deck. "Do you know," he began, "that Henry Storm is being robbed?"

"Being robbed?" I answered; "you mean he has been robbed."

"Well, has been, and is being, too. The thing is going on yet. He is playing altogether too much poker in the smoking-room, and has lost a pile of money—more, I imagine, than he can well afford."

"That's what's the trouble with him, is it? Well, he ought to know better than to play for bigger stakes than he can afford to lose."

"Oh, it's easy to say that; but he's in the hands of a swindler, of a professional gambler. You see that man?" He lowered his voice as he spoke, and I looked in the direction of his glance. By this time we knew, in a way, everybody on board the ship. The particular man Smith pointed out was a fellow I had noticed a good deal, who was very quiet and gentlemanly, interfering with nobody, and talking with few. I had spoken to him once, but he had answered rather shortly, and, apparently to his relief, and certainly to my own, our acquaintance ceased where it began. He had jet black beard and hair, both rather closely clipped; and he wore a fore and aft cap, which never improves a man's appearance very much.

"That man," continued Smith, as he passed us, "was practically under arrest for gambling on the steamer in which I came over. It seems that he is a regular professional gambler, who does nothing but go across the ocean and back again, fleecing young fellows like Storm."

"Does he cheat?" I asked.

"He doesn't need to. He plays poker. An old hand, and a cool one, has no occasion to cheat at that game to get a young one's money away from him."

"Then why doesn't some one warn young Storm?"

"Well, that's just what I wanted to speak to you about. I think it ought to be done. I think we should call a meeting of our table, somewhere out here in the quiet, and have a talk over it, and make up our mind what is to be done. It's a delicate matter, you know, and I am afraid we are a little late as it is. I do believe young Storm has lost nearly all his money to that fellow."

"Can't he be made to disgorge?"

"How? The money has been won fairly enough, as that sort of thing goes. Other fellows have played with them. It isn't as if he had been caught cheating—he hasn't, and won't be. He doesn't cheat—he doesn't need to, as I said before. Now that gambler pretends he is a commercial traveller from Buffalo. I know Buffalo down to the ground, so I took him aside yesterday and said plumply to him, 'What firm in Buffalo do you represent?' He answered shortly that his business was his own affair. I said, 'Certainly it is, and you are quite right in keeping it dark. When I was coming over to Europe, I saw a man in your line of business who looked very much like you, practically put under arrest by the purser for gambling. You were travelling for a St. Louis house then.'"

"What did he say to that?"

"Nothing; he just gave me one of those sly, sinister looks of his, turned on his heel, and left me."

The result of this conversation was the inauguration of the Society for the Reforming of a Poker Player. It was agreed between us that if young Storm had lost all his money we would subscribe enough as a loan to take care of him until he got a remittance from home. Of course we knew that any young fellow who goes out to America to begin farming, does not, as a general rule, leave people in England exceedingly well off, and probably this fact, more than any other, accounted for the remorse visible on Storm's countenance. We knew quite well that the offering of money to him would be a very delicate matter, but it was agreed that Smith should take this in hand if we saw the offer was necessary. Then I, as the man who sat at the head of the table, was selected to speak to young Storm, and, if possible, get him to abandon poker. I knew this was a somewhat impudent piece of business on my part, and so I took that evening to determine how best to perform the task set for me. I resolved to walk the deck with him in the morning, and have a frank talk over the matter.

When the morning came, I took young Storm's arm and walked two or three turns up and down the deck, but all the while I could not get up courage enough to speak with him in relation to gambling. When he left me, I again thought over the matter. I concluded to go into the smoking-room myself, sit down beside him, see him lose some money and use that fact as a test for my coming discourse on the evils of gambling. After luncheon I strolled into the smoking-room, and there sat this dark-faced man with his half-closed eyes opposite young Storm, while two others made up the four-handed game of poker.

141

Storm's face was very pale, and his lips seemed dry, for he moistened them every now and then as the game went on. He was sitting on the sofa, and I sat down beside him, paying no heed to the dark gambler's look of annoyance. However, the alleged Buffalo man said nothing, for he was not a person who did much talking. Storm paid no attention to me as I sat down beside him. The gambler had just dealt. It was very interesting to see the way he looked at his hand. He allowed merely the edges of the cards to show over each other, and then closed up his hand and seemed to know just what he had. When young Storm looked at his hand he gave a sort of gasp, and for the first time cast his eyes upon me. I had seen his hand, but did not know whether it was a good one or not. I imagined it was not very good, because all the cards were of a low denomination. Threes or fours I think, but four of the cards had a like number of spots. There was some money in the centre of the table. Storm pushed a half-crown in front of him, and the next man did the same. The gambler put down a half-sovereign, and the man at his left, after a moment's hesitation, shoved out an equal amount from the pile of gold in front of him.

Young Storm pushed out a sovereign.

"I'm out," said the man whose next bet it was, throwing down his cards.

The gambler raised it a sovereign, and the man at his left dropped out. It now rested between Storm and the gambler. Storm increased the bet a sovereign. The gambler then put on a five-pound note.

Storm said to me huskily, "Have you any money?"

"Yes," I answered him.

"Lend me five pounds if you can."

Now, the object of my being there was to stop gambling, not to encourage it. I was the president pro tem, of the Society for the Reformation of Poker Players, yet I dived into my pocket, pulled out my purse under the table and slipped a five-pound note into his hand. He put that on the table as if he had just taken it from his own pocket.

"I call you," he said.

"What have you got?" asked the gambler.

"Four fours," said Storm, putting down his hand.

The gambler closed up his and threw the cards over to the man who was to deal. Storm paused a moment and then pulled towards him the money in the centre of the table and handed me my five-pound note.

When the cards were next dealt, Storm seemed to have rather an ordinary hand, so apparently had all the rest, and there was not much money in the pile. But, poor as Storm's hand was, the rest appeared to be poorer, and he raked in the cash. This went on for two or three deals, and finding that, as Storm was winning all the time, although not heavily, I was not getting an object lesson against gambling, I made a move to go.

"Stay where you are," whispered Storm to me, pinching my knee with his hand so hard that I almost cried out.

Then it came to the gambler's turn to deal again. All the time he deftly shuffled the cards he watched the players with that furtive glance of his from out his half-shut eyes.

Storm's hand was a remarkable one, after he had drawn two cards, but I did not know whether it had any special value or not. The other players drew three cards each, and the gambler took one.

"How much money have you got?" whispered Storm to me.

"I don't know," I said, "perhaps a hundred pounds."

"Be prepared to lend me every penny of it," he whispered.

I said nothing; but I never knew the president of a society for the suppression of gambling to be in such a predicament.

Storm bet a sovereign. The player to his left threw down his hand. The gambler pushed out two sovereigns. The other player went out.

Storm said, "I see your bet, and raise you another sovereign." The gambler, without saying a word, shoved forward some more gold.

"Get your money ready," whispered Storm to I did not quite like his tone, but I made allowance for the excitement under which he was evidently labouring.

He threw on a five-pound note. The gambler put down another five-pound note, and then, as if it were the slightest thing possible, put a ten-pound note on top of that, which made the side players gasp. Storm had won sufficient to cover the bet and raise it. After that I had to feed in to him five-pound notes, keeping count of their number on my fingers as I did so. The first to begin to hesitate about putting money forward was the gambler. He shot a glance now and again from under his eyebrows at the young man opposite. Finally, when my last five-pound note had been thrown on the pile, the gambler spoke for the first time.

"I call you," he said.

"Put down another five-pound note," cried the young man.

"I have called you," said the gambler.

Henry Storm half rose from his seat in his excitement. "Put down another five-pound note, if you dare."

"That isn't poker," said the gambler. "I have called you. What have you got?"

"Put down another five-pound note, and I'll put a ten-pound note on top of it."

"I say that isn't poker. You have been called. What have you got?"

"I'll bet you twenty pounds against your five-pound note, if you dare put it down."

By this time Storm was standing up, quivering with excitement, his cards tightly clenched in his hand. The gambler sat opposite him calm and imperturbable.

"What have you got?" said Storm.

"I called you," said the gambler, "show your hand."

"Yes; but when I called you, you asked me what I had, and I told you. What have you got?"

"I am not afraid to show my hand," said the gambler, and he put down on the table four aces.

"There's the king of hearts," said Storm, putting it down on the table. "There's the queen of hearts, there's the knave of hearts, there's the ten of hearts. Now," he cried, waving his other card in the air, "can you tell me what this card is?"

"I am sure I don't know," answered the gambler, quietly, "probably the nine of hearts."

"It is the nine of hearts," shouted Storm, placing it down beside the others.

The gambler quietly picked up the cards, and handed them to the man who was to deal. Storm's hands were trembling with excitement as he pulled the pile of bank notes and gold towards him. He counted out what I had given him, and passed it to me under the table. The rest he thrust into his pocket.

"Come," I said, "it is time to go. Don't strain your luck."

"Another five pounds," he whispered; "sit where you are."

"Nonsense," I said, "another five pounds will certainly mean that you lose, everything you have won. Come away, I want to talk with you."

"Another five pounds, I have sworn it."

"Very well, I shall not stay here any longer."

"No, no," he cried eagerly; "sit where you are, sit where you are."

There was a grim thin smile on the lips of the gambler as this whispered conversation took place.

When the next hand was dealt around and Storm looked at his cards, he gave another gasp of delight. I thought that a poker player should not be so free with his emotions; but of course I said nothing. When it came his time to bet, he planked down a five-pound note on the table. The other two, as was usual, put down their cards. They were evidently very timorous players. The gambler hesitated for a second, then he put a ten-pound note on Storm's five-pounds. Storm at once saw him, and raised him ten. The gambler hesitated longer this time, but at last he said, "I shall not bet. What have you got?"

"Do you call me?" asked Storm. "Put up your money if you do."

"No, I do not call you."

Storm laughed and threw his cards face up on the table. "I have nothing," he said, "I have bluffed you for once."

"It is very often done," answered the gambler, quietly, as Storm drew in his pile of money, stuffing it again in his coat pocket. "Your deal, Storm."

"No, sir," said the young man, rising up; "I'll never touch a poker hand again. I have got my own money back and five or ten pounds over. I know when I've had enough."

Although it was Storm's deal, the gambler had the pack of cards in his hand idly shuffling them to and fro.

"I have often heard," he said slowly without raising his eyes, "that when one fool sits down beside another fool at poker, the player has the luck of two fools—but I never believed it before."

The Man Who was Not on the Passenger List.

"The well-sworn Lie, franked to the world with all

The circumstance of proof,

Cringes abashed, and sneaks along the wall

At the first sight of Truth."

The Gibrontus of the Hot Cross Bun Line was at one time the best ship of that justly celebrated fleet. All steamships have, of course, their turn at the head of the fleet until a better boat is built, but the Gibrontus is even now a reasonably fast and popular boat. An accident happened on board the Gibrontus some years ago which was of small importance to the general public, but of some moment to Richard Keeling—for it killed him. The poor man got only a line or two in the papers when the steamer arrived at New York, and then they spelled his name wrong. It had happened something like this: Keeling was wandering around very late at night, when he should have been in his bunk, and he stepped on a dark place that he thought was solid. As it happened, there was nothing between him and the bottom of the hold but space. They buried Keeling at sea, and the officers knew absolutely nothing about the matter when inquisitive passengers, hearing rumours, questioned them. This state of things very often exists both on sea and land, as far as officials are concerned. Mrs. Keeling, who had been left in England while her husband went to America to make his fortune, and tumbled down a hole instead, felt aggrieved at the company. The company said that Keeling had no business to be nosing around dark places on the deck at that time of night, and doubtless their contention was just. Mrs. Keeling, on the other hand, held that a steamer had no right to have such mantraps open at any time, night or day, without having them properly guarded, and in that she was also probably correct. The company was very sorry, of course, that the thing had occurred; but they refused to pay for Keeling unless compelled to do so by the law of the land, and there matters stood. No one can tell what the law of the land will do when it is put in motion, although many people thought that if Mrs. Keeling had brought a suit against the Hot Cross Bun Company she would have won it. But Mrs. Keeling was a poor woman, and you have to put a penny in the slot when you want the figures of justice to work, so the unfortunate creature signed something which the lawyer of the company had written out, and accepted the few pounds which Keeling had paid for Room 18 on the Gibrontus. It would seem that this ought to have settled the matter, for the lawyer told Mrs. Keeling he thought the company acted very generously in refunding the passage money; but it didn't settle the matter. Within a year from that time, the company voluntarily paid Mrs. Keeling £2100 for her husband. Now that the occurrence is called to your mind, you will perhaps remember the editorial one of the leading London dailies had on the extraordinary circumstance, in which it was very ably shown that the old saying about corporations having no souls to be condemned or bodies to be kicked did not apply in these days of commercial honour and integrity. It was a very touching editorial, and it caused tears to be shed on the Stock Exchange, the members having had no idea, before reading it, that they were so noble and generous.

How, then, was it that the Hot Cross Bun Company did this commendable act when their lawyer took such pains to clear them of all legal liability? The purser of the Gibrontus, who is now old and superannuated, could probably tell you if he liked.

When the negotiations with Mrs. Keeling had been brought to a satisfactory conclusion by the lawyer of the company, and when that gentleman was rubbing his hands over his easy victory, the good ship Gibrontus was steaming out of the Mersey on her way to New York. The stewards in the grand saloon were busy getting things in order for dinner, when a wan and gaunt passenger spoke to one of them.

"Where have you placed me at table?" he asked.

"What name, sir?" asked the steward.

"Keeling."

The steward looked along the main tables, up one side and down the other, reading the cards, but nowhere did he find the name he was in search of. Then he looked at the small tables, but also without success.

"How do you spell it, sir?" he asked the patient passenger.

"K-double-e-l-i-n-g."

"Thank you, sir."

Then he looked up and down the four rows of names on the passenger list he held in his hand, but finally shook his head.

"I can't find your name on the passenger list," he said. "I'll speak to the purser, sir."

"I wish you would," replied the passenger in a listless way, as if he had not much interest in the matter. The passenger, whose name was not on the list, waited until the steward returned. "Would you mind stepping into the purser's room for a moment, sir? I'll show you the way, sir."

When the passenger was shown into the purser's room that official said to him, in the urbane manner of pursers—

"Might I look at your ticket, sir?"

The passenger pulled a long pocket-book from the inside of his coat, opened it, and handed the purser the document it contained. The purser scrutinized it sharply, and then referred to a list he had on the desk before him.

"This is very strange," he said at last. "I never knew such a thing to occur before, although, of course, it is always possible. The people on shore have in some unaccountable manner left your name out of my list. I am sorry you have been put to any inconvenience, sir."

"There has been no inconvenience so far," said the passenger, "and I trust there will be none. You find the ticket regular, I presume?"

"Quite so—quite so," replied the purser. Then, to the waiting steward, "Give Mr. Keeling any place he prefers at the table which is not already taken.

You have Room 18."

"That was what I bought at Liverpool."

"Well, I see you have the room to yourself, and I hope you will find it comfortable. Have you ever crossed with us before, sir? I seem to recollect your face."

"I have never been in America."

"Ah! I see so many faces, of course, that I sometimes fancy I know a man when I don't. Well, I hope you will have a pleasant voyage, sir."

"Thank you."

No. 18 was not a popular passenger. People seemed instinctively to shrink from him, although it must be admitted that he made no advances. All went well until the Gibrontus was about half-way over. One forenoon the chief officer entered the captain's room with a pale face, and, shutting the door after him, said—

"I am very sorry to have to report, sir, that one of the passengers has fallen into the hold."

"Good heavens!" cried the captain. "Is he hurt?"

"He is killed, sir."

The captain stared aghast at his subordinate.

"How did it happen? I gave the strictest orders those places were on no account to be left unguarded."

Although the company had held to Mrs. Keeling that the captain was not to blame, their talk with that gentleman was of an entirely different tone.

"That is the strange part of it, sir. The hatch has not been opened this voyage, sir, and was securely bolted down."

"Nonsense! Nobody will believe such a story! Some one has been careless! Ask the purser to come here, please."

When the purser saw the body, he recollected, and came as near fainting as a purser can.

They dropped Keeling overboard in the night, and the whole affair was managed so quietly that nobody suspected anything, and, what is the most incredible thing in this story, the New York papers did not have a word about it. What the Liverpool office said about the matter nobody knows, but it must have stirred up something like a breeze in that strictly business locality. It is likely they pooh-poohed the whole affair, for, strange to say, when the purser tried to corroborate the story with the dead man's ticket the document was nowhere to be found.

The Gibrontus started out on her next voyage from Liverpool with all her colours flying, but some of her officers had a vague feeling of unrest within them which reminded them of the time they first sailed on the heaving seas. The purser was seated in his room, busy, as pursers always are at the beginning of a voyage, when there was a rap at the door.

"Come in!" shouted the important official, and there entered unto him a stranger, who said—"Are you the purser?"

"Yes, sir. What can I do for you?"

"I have room No. 18."

"What!" cried the purser, with a gasp, almost jumping from his chair. Then he looked at the robust man before him, and sank back with a sigh of relief. It was not Keeling.

"I have room No. 18," continued the passenger, "and the arrangement I made with your people in Liverpool was that I was to have the room to myself. I do a great deal of shipping over your—"

"Yes, my dear sir," said the purser, after having looked rapidly over his list, "you have No. 18 to yourself."

"So I told the man who is unpacking his luggage there; but he showed me his ticket, and it was issued before mine. I can't quite understand why your people should—"

"What kind of a looking man is he?"

"A thin, unhealthy, cadaverous man, who doesn't look as if he would last till the voyage ends. I don't want him for a room mate, if I have to have one. I think you ought—"

"I will, sir. I will make it all right. I suppose, if it should happen that a mistake has been made, and he has the prior claim to the room, you would not mind taking No. 24—it is a larger and better room."

"That will suit me exactly."

So the purser locked his door and went down to No. 18.

"Well?" he said to its occupant.

"Well," answered Mr. Keeling, looking up at him with his cold and fishy eyes.

"You're here again, are you?"

"I'm here again, and I will be here again. And again and again, and again and again."

"Now, what the—" Then the purser hesitated a moment, and thought perhaps he had better not swear, with that icy, clammy gaze fixed upon him. "What object have you in all this?"

"Object? The very simple one of making your company live up to its contract. From Liverpool to New York, my ticket reads. I paid for being landed in the United States, not for being dumped overboard in mid-ocean. Do you think you can take me over? You have had two tries at it and have not succeeded. Yours is a big and powerful company too."

"If you know we can't do it, then why do you—?" The purser hesitated.

"Pester you with my presence?" suggested Mr. Keeling. "Because I want you to do justice. Two thousand pounds is the price, and I will raise it one hundred pounds every trip." This time the New York papers got hold of the incident, but not of its peculiar features. They spoke of the extraordinary carelessness of the officers in allowing practically the same accident to occur twice on the same boat. When the Gibrontus reached Liverpool all the officers, from the captain down, sent in their resignations. Most of the sailors did not take the trouble to resign, but cut for it. The managing director was annoyed at the newspaper comments, but laughed at the rest of the story. He was invited to come over and interview Keeling for his own satisfaction, most of the officers promising to remain on the ship if he did so. He took Room 18 himself. What happened I do not know, for the purser refused to sail again on the Gibrontus, and was given another ship.

But this much is certain. When the managing director got back, the company generously paid Mrs. Keeling £2100.

The Terrible Experience of Plodkins

"Which—life or death? Tis a gambler's chance!

Yet, unconcerned, we spin and dance,

On the brittle thread of circumstance."

I understand that Plodkins is in the habit of referring sceptical listeners to me, and telling them that I will substantiate every word of his story. Now this is hardly fair of Plodkins. I can certainly corroborate part of what he says, and I can bear witness to the condition in which I found him after his ordeal was over. So I have thought it best, in order to set myself right with the public, to put down exactly what occurred. If I were asked whether or not I believe Plodkins' story myself, I would have to answer that sometimes I believe it, and sometimes I do not. Of course Plodkins will be offended when he reads this, but there are other things that I have to say about him which will perhaps enrage him still more; still they are the truth. For instance, Plodkins can hardly deny, and yet probably he will deny, that he was one of the most talented drinkers in America. I venture to say that every time he set foot in Liverpool coming East, or in New York going West, he was just on the verge of delirium tremens, because, being necessarily idle during the voyage, he did little else but drink and smoke. I never knew a man who could take so much liquor and show such small results. The fact was, that in the morning Plodkins was never at his best, because he was nearer sober then than at any other part of the day; but, after dinner, a more entertaining, genial, generous, kind-hearted man than Hiram Plodkins could not be found anywhere.

I want to speak of Plodkins' story with the calm, dispassionate manner of a judge, rather than with the partisanship of a favourable witness; and although my allusion to Plodkins' habits of intoxication may seem to him defamatory in character, and unnecessary, yet I mention them only to show that something terrible must have occurred in the bath-room to make him stop short. The extraordinary thing is, from that day to this Plodkins has not touched a drop of intoxicating liquor, which fact in itself strikes me as more wonderful than the story he tells.

Plodkins was a frequent crosser on the Atlantic steamers. He was connected with commercial houses on both sides of the ocean; selling in America for an English house, and buying in England for an American establishment. I presume it was his experiences in selling goods that led to his terrible habits of drinking. I understood from him that out West, if you are selling goods you have to do a great deal of treating, and every time you treat another man to a glass of wine, or a whiskey cocktail, you have, of course, to drink with him. But this has nothing to do with Plodkins' story.

On an Atlantic liner, when there is a large list of passengers, especially of English passengers, it is difficult to get a convenient hour in the morning at which to take a bath. This being the case, the purser usually takes down the names of applicants and assigns each a particular hour. Your hour may be, say seven o'clock in the morning. The next man comes on at half-past seven, and the third man at eight, and so on. The bedroom steward raps at your door when the proper time arrives, and informs you that the bath is ready. You wrap a dressing-gown or a cloak around you, and go along the silent corridors to the bath-room, coming back, generally before your half hour is up, like a giant refreshed.

Plodkins' bath hour was seven o'clock in the morning. Mine was half-past seven. On the particular morning in question the steward did not call me, and I thought he had forgotten, so I passed along the dark corridor and tried the bath-room door. I found it unbolted, and as everything was quiet inside, I entered. I thought nobody was there, so I shoved the bolt in the door, and went over to see if the water had been turned on. The light was a little dim even at that time of the morning, and I must say I was horror-stricken to see, lying in the bottom of the bath-tub, with his eyes fixed on the ceiling, Plodkins. I am quite willing to admit that I was never so startled in my life. I thought at first Plodkins was dead, notwithstanding his open eyes staring at the ceiling; but he murmured, in a sort of husky far-away whisper, "Thank God," and then closed his eyes.

"What's the matter, Plodkins?" I said. "Are you ill? What's the matter

155

with you? Shall I call for help?"

There was a feeble negative motion of the head. Then he said, in a whisper, "Is the door bolted?"

"Yes," I answered.

After another moment's pause, I said—

"Shall I ring, and get you some whiskey or brandy?"

Again he shook his head.

"Help me to get up," he said feebly.

He was very much shaken, and I had some trouble in getting him on his feet, and seating him on the one chair in the room.

"You had better come to my state-room," I said; "it is nearer than yours. What has happened to you?"

He replied, "I will go in a moment. Wait a minute." And I waited.

"Now," he continued, when he had apparently pulled himself together a bit, "just turn on the electric light, will you?"

I reached up to the peg of the electric light and turned it on. A shudder passed over Plodkins' frame, but he said nothing. He seemed puzzled, and once more I asked him to let me take him to my stateroom, but he shook his head.

"Turn on the water." I did so.

"Turn out the electric light." I did that also.

"Now," he added, "put your hand in the water and turn on the electric light."

I was convinced Plodkins had become insane, but I recollected I was there alone with him, shaky as he was, in a room with a bolted door, so I put my fingers in the water and attempted to turn on the electric light. I got a shock that was very much greater than that which I received when I saw

Plodkins lying at the bottom of the bath-tub. I gave a yell and a groan, and staggered backwards. Then Plodkins laughed a feeble laugh.

"Now," he said, "I will go with you to your state-room."

The laugh seemed to have braced up Plodkins like a glass of liquor would have done, and when we got to my state-room he was able to tell me what had happened. As a sort of preface to his remarks, I would like to say a word or two about that bath-tub. It was similar to bath-tubs on board other steamers; a great and very deep receptacle of solid marble. There were different nickel-plated taps for letting in hot or cold water, or fresh water or salt water as was desired; and the escape-pipe instead of being at the end, as it is in most bath-tubs, was in the centre. It was the custom of the bath-room steward to fill it about half full of water at whatever temperature you desired. Then, placing a couple of towels on the rack, he would go and call the man whose hour it was to bathe.

Plodkins said, "When I went in there everything appeared as usual, except that the morning was very dark. I stood in the bath-tub, the water coming nearly to my knees, and reached up to turn on the electric light. The moment I touched the brass key I received a shock that simply paralyzed me. I think liquor has something to do with the awful effect the electricity had upon me, because I had taken too much the night before, and was feeling very shaky indeed; but the result was that I simply fell full length in the bath-tub just as you found me. I was unable to move anything except my fingers and toes. I did not appear to be hurt in the least, and my senses, instead of being dulled by the shock, seemed to be preternaturally sharp, and I realized in a moment that if this inability to move remained with me for five minutes I was a dead man—dead, not from the shock, but by drowning. I gazed up through that clear green water, and I could see the ripples on the surface slowly subsiding after my plunge into the tub. It reminded me of looking into an aquarium. You know how you see up through the water to the surface with the bubbles rising to the top. I knew that nobody would come in for at least half an hour, and even then I couldn't remember whether I had bolted the door or not. Sometimes I bolt it, and sometimes I don't. I didn't this morning, as it happens. All the time I felt that strength was slowly returning to me, for I continually worked my fingers and toes, and now feeling seemed to be coming up to my wrists and arms. Then I remembered that the vent was in the middle of the bath-tub; so, wriggling my fingers around, I got hold of the ring, and pulled up the plug. In the dense silence that was around me, I could not tell whether the water was running out or not; but gazing up towards the ceiling I thought I saw the surface gradually sinking down and down and down. Of course it couldn't have been more than a few seconds, but it seemed to be years and years and years. I knew that if once I let my breath go I would be drowned, merely by the spasmodic action of my lungs trying to recover air. I felt as if I should burst. It was a match against time, with life or death as the stake. At first, as I said, my senses were abnormally sharp, but, by and by, I began to notice that they were wavering. I thought the glassy surface of the water, which I could see above me, was in reality a great sheet of crystal that somebody was pressing down upon me, and I began to think that the moment it reached my face I would smother. I tried to struggle, but was held with a grip of steel. Finally, this slab of crystal came down to my nose, and seemed to split apart. I could hold on no longer, and with a mighty expiration blew the water up towards the ceiling, and drew in a frightful smothering breath of salt water, that I blew in turn upwards, and the next breath I took in had some air with the water. I felt the water tickling the corners of my mouth, and receding slower and slower down my face and neck. Then I think I must have become insensible until just before you entered the room. Of course there is something wrong with the electric fittings, and there is a leak of electricity; but I think liquor is at the bottom of all this. I don't believe it would have affected me like this if I had not been soaked in whiskey."

"If I were you," I said, "I would leave whiskey alone."

"I intend to," he answered solemnly, "and baths too."

A Case Of Fever

"O, underneath the blood red sun,

No bloodier deed was ever done!

Nor fiercer retribution sought

The hand that first red ruin wrought."

This is the doctor's story—

The doctors on board the Atlantic liners are usually young men. They are good-looking and entertaining as well, and generally they can play the violin or some other instrument that is of great use at the inevitable concert which takes place about the middle of the Atlantic. They are urbane, polite young men, and they chat pleasantly and nicely to the ladies on board. I believe that the doctor on the Transatlantic steamer has to be there on account of the steerage passengers. Of course the doctor goes to the steerage; but I imagine, as a general thing, he does not spend any more time there than the rules of the service compel him to. The ladies, at least, would be unanimous in saying that the doctor is one of the most charming officials on board the ship.

This doctor, who tells the story I am about to relate, was not like the usual Atlantic physician. He was older than the average, and, to judge by his somewhat haggard, rugged face, had seen hard times and rough usage in different parts of the world. Why he came to settle down on an Atlantic steamer—a berth which is a starting-point rather than a terminus—I have no means of knowing. He never told us; but there he was, and one night, as he smoked his pipe with us in the smoking-room, we closed the door, and compelled him to tell us a story.

As a preliminary, he took out of his inside pocket a book, from which he selected a slip of creased paper, which had been there so long that it was rather the worse for wear, and had to be tenderly handled.

"As a beginning," said the doctor, "I will read you what this slip of paper says. It is an extract from one of the United States Government Reports in the Indian department, and it relates to a case of fever, which caused the death of the celebrated Indian chief Wolf Tusk.

"I am not sure that I am doing quite right in telling this story. There may be some risk for myself in relating it, and I don't know exactly what the United States Government might have in store for me if the truth came to be known. In fact, I am not able to say whether I acted rightly or wrongly in the matter I have to tell you about. You shall be the best judges of that. There is no question but Wolf Tusk was an old monster, and there is no question either that the men who dealt with him had been grievously—but, then, there is no use in my giving you too many preliminaries; each one will say for himself whether he would have acted as I did or not. I will make my excuses at the end of the story." Then he read the slip of paper. I have not a copy of it, and have to quote from memory. It was the report of the physician who saw Wolf Tusk die, and it went on to say that about nine o'clock in the morning a heavy and unusual fever set in on that chief. He had been wounded in the battle of the day before, when he was captured, and the fever attacked all parts of his body. Although the doctor had made every effort in his power to relieve the Indian, nothing could stop the ravages of the fever. At four o'clock in the afternoon, having been in great pain, and, during the latter part, delirious, he died, and was buried near the spot where he had taken ill. This was signed by the doctor.

"What I have read you," said the physician, folding up the paper again, and placing it in his pocket-book, "is strictly and accurately true, otherwise, of course, I would not have so reported to the Government. Wolf Tusk was the chief of a band of irreconcilables, who were now in one part of the West and now in another, giving a great deal of trouble to the authorities. Wolf Tusk and his band had splendid horses, and they never attacked a force that outnumbered their own. In fact, they never attacked anything where the chances were not twenty to one in their favour, but that, of course, is Indian warfare; and in this, Wolf Tusk was no different from his fellows.

"On one occasion Wolf Tusk and his band swooped down on a settlement where they knew that all the defenders were away, and no one but women and children were left to meet them. Here one of the most atrocious massacres of the West took place. Every woman and child in the settlement was killed under circumstances of inconceivable brutality. The buildings, such as they were, were burnt down, and, when the men returned, they found nothing but heaps of smouldering ruin.

"Wolf Tusk and his band, knowing there would be trouble about this, had made for the broken ground where they could so well defend themselves. The alarm, however, was speedily given, and a company of cavalry from the nearest fort started in hot pursuit.

"I was the physician who accompanied the troops. The men whose families had been massacred, and who were all mounted on swift horses, begged permission to go with the soldiers, and that permission was granted, because it was known that their leader would take them after Wolf Tusk on his own account, and it was thought better to have every one engaged in the pursuit under the direct command of the chief officer.

"He divided his troop into three parts, one following slowly after Wolf Tusk, and the other two taking roundabout ways to head off the savages from the broken ground and foothills from which no number of United States troops could have dislodged them. These flanking parties were partly successful. They did not succeed in heading off the Indians entirely, but one succeeded in changing their course, and throwing the Indians unexpectedly into the way of the other flanking party, when a sharp battle took place, and, during its progress, we in the rear came up. When the Indians saw our reinforcing party come towards them each man broke away for himself and made for the wilderness. Wolf Tusk, who had been wounded, and had his horse shot under him, did not succeed in escaping. The two flanking parties now having reunited with the main body, it was decided to keep the Indians on the run for a day or two at least, and so a question arose as to the disposal of the wounded chief. He could not be taken with the fighting party; there were no soldiers to spare to take him back, and so the leader of the settlers said that as they had had enough of war, they would convey him to the fort. Why the commander allowed this to be done, I do not know. He must have realized the feelings of the settlers towards the man who massacred their wives and children. However, the request of the settlers was acceded to, and I was ordered back also, as I had been slightly wounded. You can see the mark here on my cheek, nothing serious; but the commander thought I had better get back into the fort, as he was certain there would be no more need of my services. The Indians were on the run, and would make no further stand.

"It was about three days' march from where the engagement had taken place to the fort. Wolf Tusk was given one of the captured Indian horses. I attended to the wound in his leg, and he was strapped on the horse, so that there could be no possibility of his escaping.

"We camped the first night in a little belt of timber that bordered a small stream, now nearly dry. In the morning I was somewhat rudely awakened, and found myself tied hand and foot, with two or three of the settlers standing over me. They helped me to my feet, then half carried and half led me to a tree, where they tied me securely to the trunk.

"'What are you going to do? What is the meaning of this?' I said to them in astonishment.

"'Nothing,' was the answer of the leader; 'that is, nothing, if you will sign a certain medical report which is to go to the Government. You will see, from where you are, everything that is going to happen, and we expect you to report truthfully; but we will take the liberty of writing the report for you.

"Then I noticed that Wolf Tusk was tied to a tree in a manner similar to myself, and around him had been collected a quantity of firewood. This firewood, was not piled up to his feet, but formed a circle at some distance from him, so that the Indian would be slowly roasted.

"There is no use in my describing what took place. When I tell you that they lit the fire at nine o'clock, and that it was not until four in the afternoon that Wolf Tusk died, you will understand the peculiar horror of it.

"'Now,' said the leader to me when everything was over,' here is the report I have written out,' and he read to me the report which I have read to you.

"'This dead villain has murdered our wives and our children. If I could have made his torture last for two weeks I would have done so. You have made every effort to save him by trying to break loose, and you have not succeeded. We are not going to harm you, even though you refuse to sign this report. You cannot bring him to life again, thank God, and all you can do is to put more trouble on the heads of men who have already, through red devils like this, had more trouble than they can well stand and keep sane. Will you sign the report?'

"I said I would, and I did."

How The Captain Got His Steamer Out

"On his own perticular well-wrought row,

That he's straddled for ages—

Learnt its lay and its gages—

His style may seem queer, but permit him to know,

The likeliest, sprightliest, manner to hoe."

"There is nothing more certain than that some day we may have to record a terrible disaster directly traceable to ocean racing.

"The vivid account which one of our reporters gives in another column of how the captain of the Arrowic went blundering across the bar yesterday in one of the densest fogs of the season is very interesting reading. Of course the account does not pretend to be anything more than imaginary, for, until the Arrowic reaches Queenstown, if she ever does under her present captain, no one can tell how much of luck was mixed with the recklessness which took this steamer out into the Atlantic in the midst of the thickest fog we have had this year. All that can be known at present is, that, when the fog lifted, the splendid steamer Dartonia was lying at anchor in the bay, having missed the tide, while the Arrowic was nowhere to be seen. If the fog was too thick for the Dartonia to cross the bar, how, then, did the captain of the Arrowic get his boat out? The captain of the Arrowic should be taught to remember that there are other things to be thought of beside the defeating of a rival steamer. He should be made to understand that he has under his charge a steamer worth a million and a half of dollars, and a cargo probably nearly as valuable. Still, he might have lost his ship and cargo, and we would have had no word to say. That concerns the steamship company and the owners of the cargo; but he had also in his care nearly a thousand human lives, and these he should not be allowed to juggle with in order to beat all the rival steamers in the world."

The above editorial is taken from the columns of the New York Daily

Mentor. The substance of it had been cabled across to London and it made pleasant reading for the captain of the Arrowic at Queenstown. The captain didn't say anything about it; he was not a talkative man. Probably he explained to his chief, if the captain of an ocean liner can possibly have a chief, how he got his vessel out of New York harbour in a fog; but, if he did, the explanation was never made public, and so here's an account of it published for the first time, and it may give a pointer to the captain of the rival liner Dartonia. I may say, however, that the purser was not as silent as the captain. He was very indignant at what he called the outrage of the New York paper, and said a great many unjustifiable things about newspaper men. He knew I was a newspaper man myself, and probably that is the reason he launched his maledictions against the fraternity at my head.

"Just listen to that wretched penny-a-liner," he said, rapping savagely on the paper with the back of his hand.

I intimated mildly that they paid more than a penny a line for newspaper work in New York, but he said that wasn't the point. In fact the purser was too angry to argue calmly. He was angry the whole way from Queenstown to Liverpool.

"Here," he said, "is some young fellow, who probably never saw the inside of a ship in his life, and yet he thinks he can tell the captain of a great ocean liner what should be done and what shouldn't. Just think of the cheek of it."

"I don't see any cheek in it," I said, as soothingly as possible. "You don't mean to pretend to argue, at this time of day that a newspaper man does not know how to conduct every other business as well as his own."

But the purser did make that very contention, although of course he must be excused, for, as I said, he was not in a good temper.

"Newspaper men," he continued, "act as if they did know everything. They pretend in their papers that every man thinks he knows how to run a newspaper or a hotel. But look at their own case. See the advice they give to statesmen. See how they would govern Germany, or England, or any other country under the sun. Does a big bank get into trouble, the newspaper man at once informs the financiers how they should have conducted their business. Is there a great railway smash-up, the newspaper man shows exactly how it could have been avoided if he had had the management of the railway. Is there a big strike, the newspaper man steps in. He tells both sides what they should do. If every man thinks he can run a hotel, or a newspaper—and I am sure most men could run a newspaper as well as the newspapers are conducted now—the conceit of the ordinary man is nothing to the conceit of the newspaper man. He not only thinks he can run a newspaper and a hotel, but every other business under the sun."

"And how do you know he can't," I asked.

But the purser would not listen to reason. He contended that a captain who had crossed the ocean hundreds of times and for years and years had worked his way up, had just as big a sense of responsibility for his passengers and his ship and his cargo as any newspaper man in New York could have, and this palpably absurd contention he maintained all the way to Liverpool.

When a great ocean racer is making ready to put out to sea, there can hardly be imagined a more bustling scene than that which presents itself on the deck and on the wharf. There is the rush of passengers, the banging about of luggage, the hurrying to and fro on the decks, the roar of escaping steam, the working of immense steam cranes hoisting and lowering great bales of merchandise and luggage from the wharf to the hold, and here and there in quiet corners, away from the rush, are tearful people bidding good-bye to one another.

The Arrowic and the Dartonia left on the same day and within the same hour, from wharfs that were almost adjoining each other. We on board the Arrowic could see the same bustle and stir on board the Dartonia that we ourselves were in the midst of.

The Dartonia was timed to leave about half an hour ahead of us, and we heard the frantic ringing of her last bell warning everybody to get on shore who were not going to cross the ocean. Then the great steamer backed slowly out from her wharf.

166

Of course all of us who were going on the Arrowic were warm champions of that ship as the crack ocean racer; but, as the Dartonia moved backwards with slow stately majesty, all her colours flying, and her decks black with passengers crowding to the rail and gazing towards us, we could not deny that she was a splendid vessel, and "even the ranks of Tuscany could scarce forbear a cheer." Once out in the stream her twin screws enabled her to turn around almost without the help of tugs, and just as our last bell was ringing she moved off down the bay. Then we backed slowly out in the same fashion, and, although we had not the advantage of seeing ourselves, we saw a great sight on the wharf, which was covered with people, ringing with cheers, and white with the flutter of handkerchiefs.

As we headed down stream the day began to get rather thick. It had been gloomy all morning, and by the time we reached the Statue of Liberty it was so foggy that one could hardly see three boats' length ahead or behind. All eyes were strained to catch a glimpse of the Dartonia, but nothing of her was visible. Shortly after, the fog came down in earnest and blotted out everything. There was a strong wind blowing, and the vapour, which was cold and piercing, swept the deck with dripping moisture. Then we came to a standstill. The ship's bell was rung continually forward and somebody was whanging on the gong towards the stern. Everybody knew that, if this sort of thing lasted long, we would not get over the bar that tide, and consequently everybody felt annoyed, for this delay would lengthen the trip, and people, as a general thing, do not take passage on an ocean racer with the idea of getting in a day late. Suddenly the fog lifted clear from shore to shore. Then we saw something that was not calculated to put our minds at ease. A big three-masted vessel, with full sail, dashed past us only a very few yards behind the stern of the mammoth steamer.

"Look at that blundering idiot," said the purser to me, "rushing full speed over crowded New York Bay in a fog as thick as pea-soup. A captain who would do a thing like that ought to be hanged."

Before the fog settled down again we saw the Dartonia with her anchor chain out a few hundred yards to our left, and, farther on, one of the big German steamers, also at anchor.

167

In the short time that the fog was lifted our own vessel made some progress towards the bar. Then the thickness came down again. A nautical passenger, who had crossed many times, came aft to where I was standing, and said—

"Do you notice what the captain is trying to do?"

"Well," I answered, "I don't see how anybody can do anything in weather like this."

"There is a strong wind blowing," continued the nautical passenger, "and the fog is liable to lift for a few minutes at a time. If it lifts often enough our captain is going to get us over the bar. It will be rather a sharp bit of work if he succeeds. You notice that the Dartonia has thrown out her anchor. She is evidently going to wait where she is until the fog clears away entirely."

So with that we two went forward to see what was being done. The captain stood on the bridge and beside him the pilot, but the fog was now so thick we could hardly see them, although we stood close by, on the piece of deck in front of the wheelhouse. The almost incessant clanging of the bell was kept up, and in the pauses we heard answering bells from different points in the thick fog. Then, for a second time, and with equal suddenness, the fog lifted ahead of us. Behind we could not see either the Dartonia or the German steamer. Our own boat, however, went full speed ahead and kept up the pace till the fog shut down again. The captain now, in pacing the bridge, had his chronometer in his hand, and those of us who were at the front frequently looked at our watches, for of course the nautical passenger knew just how late it was possible for us to cross the bar.

"I am afraid," said the passenger, "he is not going to succeed." But, as he said this, the fog lifted for the third time, and again the mammoth steamer forged ahead.

"If this clearance will only last for ten minutes," said the nautical passenger, "we are all right." But the fog, as if it had heard him, closed down on us again damper and thicker than ever.

"We are just at the bar," said the nautical passenger, "and if this doesn't clear up pretty soon the vessel will have to go back."

The captain kept his eyes fixed on the chronometer in his hand. The pilot tried to peer ahead, but everything was a thick white blank.

"Ten minutes more and it is too late," said the nautical passenger.

There was a sudden rift in the fog that gave a moment's hope, but it closed down again. A minute afterwards, with a suddenness that was strange, the whole blue ocean lay before us. Then full steam ahead. The fog still was thick behind us in New York Bay. We saw it far ahead coming in from the ocean. All at once the captain closed his chronometer with a snap. We were over the bar and into the Atlantic, and that is how the captain got the Arrowic out of New York Bay.

My Stowaway

"Ye can play yer jokes on Nature,

An' play 'em slick,

She'll grin a grin, but, landsakes, friend,

Look out fer the kick!"

One night about eleven o'clock I stood at the stern of that fine Atlantic steamship, the City of Venice, which was ploughing its way through the darkness towards America. I leaned on the rounded bulwark and enjoyed a smoke as I gazed on the luminous trail the wheel was making in the quiet sea. Some one touched me on the shoulder, saying, "Beg pardon, sir;" and, on straightening up, I saw in the dim light a man whom at first I took to be one of the steerage passengers. I thought he wanted to get past me, for the room was rather restricted in the passage between the aft wheelhouse and the stern, and I moved aside. The man looked hurriedly to one side and then the other and, approaching, said in a whisper, "I'm starving, sir!"

"Why don't you go and get something to eat, then? Don't they give you plenty forward?"

"I suppose they do, sir; but I'm a stowaway. I got on at Liverpool. What little I took with me is gone, and for two days I've had nothing."

"Come with me. I'll take you to the steward, he'll fix you all right."

"Oh, no, no, no," he cried, trembling with excitement. "If you speak to any of the officers or crew I'm lost. I assure you, sir, I'm an honest man, I am indeed, sir. It's the old story—nothing but starvation at home, so my only chance seemed to be to get this way to America. If I'm caught I shall get dreadful usage and will be taken back and put in jail."

"Oh, you're mistaken. The officers are all courteous gentlemen."

"Yes, to you cabin passengers they are. But to a stowaway—that's a different matter. If you can't help me, sir, please don't inform on me."

"How can I help you but by speaking to the captain or purser?"

"Get me a morsel to eat."

"Where were you hid?"

"Right here, sir, in this place," and he put his hand on the square deck-edifice beside us. This seemed to be a spare wheel-house, used if anything went wrong with the one in front. It had a door on each side and there were windows all round it. At present it was piled full of cane folding steamer chairs and other odds and ends.

"I crawl in between the chairs and the wall and get under that piece of tarpaulin."

"Well, you're sure of being caught, for the first fine day all these chairs will be taken out and the deck steward can't miss you."

The man sighed as I said this and admitted the chances were much against him. Then, starting up, he cried, "Poverty is the great crime. If I had stolen some one else's money I would have been able to take cabin passage instead of—"

"If you weren't caught."

"Well, if I were caught, what then? I would be well fed and taken care of."

"Oh, they'd take care of you."

"The waste food in this great ship would feed a hundred hungry wretches like me. Does my presence keep the steamer back a moment of time? No. Well, who is harmed by my trying to better myself in a new world? No one. I am begging for a crust from the lavish plenty, all because I am struggling to be honest. It is only when I become a thief that I am out of danger of starvation—caught or free."

"There, there; now, don't speak so loud or you'll have some one here.

171

You hang round and I'll bring you some provender. What would you like to have? Poached eggs on toast, roast turkey, or—"

The wretch sank down at my feet as I said this, and, recognising the cruelty of it, I hurried down into the saloon and hunted up a steward who had not yet turned in. "Steward," I said, "can you get me a few sandwiches or anything to eat at this late hour?"

"Yessir, certainly, sir; beef or 'am, sir?"

"Both, and a cup of coffee, please."

"Well, sir, I'm afraid there's no coffee, sir; but I could make you a pot of tea in a moment, sir."

"All right, and bring them to my room, please?"

"Yessir."

In a very short time there was that faint steward rap at the state-room door and a most appetising tray-load was respectfully placed at my service.

When the waiter had gone I hurried up the companion-way with much the air of a man who is stealing fowls, and I found my stowaway just in the position I had left him.

"Now, pitch in," I said. "I'll stand guard forward here, and, if you hear me cough, strike for cover. I'll explain the tray matter if it's found."

He simply said, "Thank you, sir," and I went forward. When I came back the tray had been swept clean and the teapot emptied. My stowaway was making for his den when I said, "How about to-morrow?"

He answered, "This'll do me for a couple of days."

"Nonsense. I'll have a square meal for you here in the corner of this wheel-house, so that you can get at it without trouble. I'll leave it about this time to-morrow night."

"You won't tell any one, any one at all, sir?"

"No. At least, I'll think over the matter, and if I see a way out I'll let you know."

"God bless you, sir."

I turned the incident over in my mind a good deal that night, and I almost made a resolution to take Cupples into my confidence. Roger Cupples, a lawyer of San Francisco, sat next me at table, and with the freedom of wild Westerners we were already well acquainted, although only a few days out. Then I thought of putting a supposititious case to the captain—he was a thorough gentleman—and if he spoke generously about the supposititious case I would spring the real one on him. The stowaway had impressed me by his language as being a man worth doing something for.

Nest day I was glad to see that it was rainy. There would be no demand for ship chairs that day. I felt that real sunshiny weather would certainly unearth, or unchair, my stowaway. I met Cupples on deck, and we walked a few rounds together.

At last, Cupples, who had been telling me some stories of court trials in San Francisco, said, "Let's sit down and wrap up. This deck's too wet to walk on."

"All the seats are damp," I said.

"I'll get out my steamer chair. Steward," he cried to the deck steward who was shoving a mop back and forth, "get me my chair. There's a tag on it, 'Berth 96.'"

"No, no," I cried hastily; "let's go into the cabin. It's raining."

"Only a drizzle. Won't hurt you at sea, you know."

By this time the deck steward was hauling down chairs trying to find No. 96, which I felt sure would be near the bottom. I could not control my anxiety as the steward got nearer and nearer the tarpaulin. At last I cried—

"Steward, never mind that chair; take the first two that come handy."

Cupples looked astonished, and, as we sat down, I said—

"I have something to tell you, and I trust you will say nothing about it to any one else. There's a man under those chairs."

The look that came into the lawyer's face showed that he thought me demented; but, when I told him the whole story, the judicial expression came on, and he said, shaking his head—

"That's bad business."

"I know it."

"Yes, but it's worse than you have any idea of. I presume that you don't know what section 4738 of the Revised Statutes says?"

"No; I don't."

"Well, it is to the effect that any person or persons, who wilfully or with malice aforethought or otherwise, shall aid, abet, succor or cherish, either directly or indirectly or by implication, any person who feloniously or secretly conceals himself on any vessel, barge, brig, schooner, bark, clipper, steamship or other craft touching at or coming within the jurisdiction of these United States, the said person's purpose being the defrauding of the revenue of, or the escaping any or all of the just legal dues exacted by such vessel, barge, etc., the person so aiding or abetting, shall in the eye of the law be considered as accomplice before, during and after the illegal act, and shall in such case be subject to the penalties accruing thereunto, to wit—a fine of not more than five thousand dollars, or imprisonment of not more than two years—or both at the option of the judge before whom the party so accused is convicted."

"Great heavens! is that really so?"

"Well, it isn't word for word, but that is the purport. Of course, if I had my books here, I—why, you've doubtless heard of the case of the Pacific Steamship Company versus Cumberland. I was retained on behalf of the company. Now all Cumberland did was to allow the man—he was sent up for two years—to carry his valise on board, but we proved the intent. Like a fool, he boasted of it, but the steamer brought back the man, and Cumberland got off with four thousand dollars and costs. Never got out of that scrape less than ten thousand dollars. Then again, the steamship Peruvian versus McNish;

that is even more to the—"

"See here, Cupples. Come with me to-night and see the man. If you heard him talk you would see the inhumanity—"

"Tush. I'm not fool enough to mix up in such a matter, and look here, you'll have to work it pretty slick if you get yourself out. The man will be caught as sure as fate; then knowingly or through fright he'll incriminate you."

"What would you do if you were in my place?"

"My dear sir, don't put it that way. It's a reflection on both my judgment and my legal knowledge. I couldn't be in such a scrape. But, as a lawyer—minus the fee—I'll tell you what you should do. You should give the man up before witnesses—before witnesses. I'll be one of them myself. Get as many of the cabin passengers as you like out here, to-day, and let the officers search. If he charges you with what the law terms support, deny it, and call attention to the fact that you have given information. By the way, I would give written information and keep a copy."

"I gave the man my word not to inform on him and so I can't do it to-day, but I'll tell him of it to-night."

"And have him commit suicide or give himself up first and incriminate you? Nonsense. Just release yourself from your promise. That's all. He'll trust you."

"Yes, poor wretch, I'm afraid he will."

About ten o'clock that night I resolved to make another appeal to Roger Cupples to at least stand off and hear the man talk. Cupples' state-room, No. 96, was in the forward part of the steamer, down a long passage and off a short side passage. Mine was aft the cabin. The door of 96 was partly open, and inside an astonishing sight met my gaze.

There stood my stowaway.

He was evidently admiring himself in the glass, and with a brush was touching up his face with dark paint here and there. When he put on a woe-begone look he was the stowaway; when he chuckled to himself he was Roger Cupples, Esq.

The moment the thing dawned on me I quietly withdrew and went up the forward companion way. Soon Cupples came cautiously up and seeing the way clear scudded along in the darkness and hid in the aft wheelhouse. I saw the whole thing now. It was a scheme to get me to make a fool of myself some fine day before the rest of the passengers and have a standing joke on me. I walked forward. The first officer was on duty.

"I have reason to believe," I said, "that there is a stowaway in the aft wheelhouse."

Quicker than it takes me to tell it a detachment of sailors were sent aft under the guidance of the third mate. I went through the saloon and smoking room, and said to the gentlemen who were playing cards and reading— "There's a row upstairs of some kind."

We were all on deck before the crew had surrounded the wheelhouse. There was a rattle of steamer folded chairs, a pounce by the third mate, and out came the unfortunate Cupples, dragged by the collar.

"Hold on; let go. This is a mistake."

"You can't both hold on and let go," said Stalker, of Indiana.

"Come out o' this," cried the mate, jerking him forward.

With a wrench the stowaway tore himself free and made a dash for the companion way. A couple of sailors instantly tripped him up.

"Let go of me; I'm a cabin passenger," cried Cupples.

"Bless me!" I cried in astonishment. "This isn't you, Cupples? Why, I acted on your own advice and that of Revised Statutes, No. what ever-they-were."

"Well, act on my advice again," cried the infuriated Cupples, "and go to—the hold."

However, he was better in humour the next day, and stood treat all round. We found, subsequently, that Cupples was a New York actor, and at the entertainment given for the benefit of the sailors' orphans, a few nights after, he recited a piece in costume that just melted the ladies. It was voted a wonderfully touching performance, and he called it "The Stowaway."

The Purser's Story

"O Mother-nature, kind in touch and tone.

Act as we may, thou clearest to thine own"

I don't know that I should tell this story.

When the purser related it to me I know it was his intention to write it out for a magazine. In fact he had written it, and I understand that a noted American magazine had offered to publish it, but I have watched that magazine for over three years and I have not yet seen the purser's story in it. I am sorry that I did not write the story at the time; then perhaps I should have caught the exquisite peculiarities of the purser's way of telling it. I find myself gradually forgetting the story and I write it now in case I shall forget it, and then be harassed all through after life by the remembrance of the forgetting.

There is no position more painful and tormenting than the consciousness of having had something worth the telling, which, in spite of all mental effort, just eludes the memory. It hovers nebulously beyond the outstretched finger-ends of recollection, and, like the fish that gets off the hook, becomes more and more important as the years fade.

Perhaps, when you read this story, you will say there is nothing in it after all. Well, that will be my fault, then, and I can only regret I did not write down the story when it was told to me, for as I sat in the purser's room that day it seemed to me I had never heard anything more graphic.

The purser's room was well forward on the Atlantic steamship. From one of the little red-curtained windows you could look down to where the steerage passengers were gathered on the deck. When the bow of the great vessel plunged down into the big Atlantic waves, the smother of foam that shot upwards would be borne along with the wind, and spatter like rain against the purser's window. Something about this intermittent patter on the pane reminded the purser of the story, and so he told it to me.

There were a great many steerage passengers coming on at Queenstown, he said, and there was quite a hurry getting them aboard. Two officers stood at each side of the gangway and took the tickets as the people crowded forward. They generally had their tickets in their hands and there was usually no trouble. I stood there and watched them coming aboard. Suddenly there was a fuss and a jam. "What is it?" I asked the officer.

"Two girls, sir, say they have lost their tickets."

I took the girls aside and the stream of humanity poured in. One was about fourteen and the other, perhaps, eight years old. The little one had a firm grip of the elder's hand and she was crying. The larger girl looked me straight in the eye as I questioned her.

"Where's your tickets?"

"We lost thim, sur."

"Where?"

"I dunno, sur."

"Do you think you have them about you or in your luggage?"

"We've no luggage, sur."

"Is this your sister?"

"She is, sur."

"Are your parents aboard?"

"They are not, sur."

"Are you all alone?"

"We are, sur."

"You can't go without your tickets."

The younger one began to cry the more, and the elder answered, "Mabbe we can foind thim, sur."

They were bright-looking, intelligent children, and the larger girl gave me such quick, straightforward answers, and it seemed so impossible that children so young should attempt to cross the ocean without tickets that I concluded to let them come, and resolved to get at the truth on the way over.

Next day I told the deck steward to bring the children to my room.

They came in just as I saw them the day before, the elder with a tight grip on the hand of the younger, whose eyes I never caught sight of. She kept them resolutely on the floor, while the other looked straight at me with her big, blue eyes.

"Well, have you found your tickets?"

"No, sur."

"What is your name?"

"Bridget, sur."

"Bridget what?"

"Bridget Mulligan, sur."

"Where did you live?"

"In Kildormey, sur."

"Where did you get your tickets?"

"From Mr. O'Grady, sur."

Now, I knew Kildormey as well as I know this ship, and I knew O'Grady was our agent there. I would have given a good deal at that moment for a few words with him. But I knew of no Mulligans in Kildormey, although, of course, there might be. I was born myself only a few miles from the place. Now, thinks I to myself, if these two children can baffle a purser who has been twenty years on the Atlantic when they say they came from his own town almost, by the powers they deserve their passage over the ocean. I had often seen grown people try to cheat their way across, and I may say none of them succeeded on my ships.

"Where's your father and mother?"

"Both dead, sur."

"Who was your father?"

"He was a pinshoner, sur."

"Where did he draw his pension?"

"I donno, sur."

"Where did you get the money to buy your tickets?"

"The neighbors, sur, and Mr. O'Grady helped, sur."

"What neighbours? Name them."

She unhesitatingly named a number, many of whom I knew; and as that had frequently been done before, I saw no reason to doubt the girl's word.

"Now," I said, "I want to speak with your sister. You may go."

The little one held on to her sister's hand and cried bitterly.

When the other was gone, I drew the child towards me and questioned her, but could not get a word in reply.

For the next day or two I was bothered somewhat by a big Irishman named O'Donnell, who was a fire-brand among the steerage passengers. He would harangue them at all hours on the wrongs of Ireland, and the desirability of blowing England out of the water; and as we had many English and German passengers, as well as many peaceable Irishmen, who complained of the constant ructions O'Donnell was kicking up, I was forced to ask him to keep quiet. He became very abusive one day and tried to strike me. I had him locked up until he came to his senses.

While I was in my room, after this little excitement, Mrs. O'Donnell came to me and pleaded for her rascally husband. I had noticed her before. She was a poor, weak, broken-hearted woman whom her husband made a slave of, and I have no doubt beat her when he had the chance. She was evidently mortally afraid of him, and a look from him seemed enough to take the life out of her. He was a worse tyrant, in his own small way, than England had ever been.

"Well, Mrs. O'Donnell," I said, "I'll let your husband go, but he will have to keep a civil tongue in his head and keep his hands off people. I've seen men, for less, put in irons during a voyage and handed over to the authorities when they landed. And now I want you to do me a favour. There are two children on board without tickets. I don't believe they ever had tickets, and I want to find out. You're a kind-hearted woman, Mrs. O'Donnell, and perhaps the children will answer you." I had the two called in, and they came hand in hand as usual. The elder looked at me as if she couldn't take her eyes off my face.

"Look at this woman," I said to her; "she wants to speak to you. Ask her some questions about herself," I whispered to Mrs. O'Donnell.

"Acushla," said Mrs. O'Donnell with infinite tenderness, taking the disengaged hand of the elder girl. "Tell me, darlint, where yees are from."

I suppose I had spoken rather harshly to them before, although I had not intended to do so, but however that may be, at the first words of kindness from the lips of their countrywoman both girls broke down and cried as if their hearts would break. The poor woman drew them towards her, and, stroking the fair hair of the elder girl, tried to comfort her while the tears streamed down her own cheeks. "Hush, acushla; hush, darlints, shure the gentlemin's not goin' to be hard wid two poor childher going to a strange country."

Of course it would never do to admit that the company could carry emigrants free through sympathy, and I must have appeared rather hard-hearted when I told Mrs. O'Donnell that I would have to take them back with me to Cork. I sent the children away, and then arranged with Mrs. O'Donnell to see after them during the voyage, to which she agreed if her husband would let her. I could get nothing from the girl except that she had lost her ticket; and when we sighted New York, I took them through the steerage and asked the passengers if any one would assume charge of the children and pay their passage. No one would do so.

"Then," I said, "these children will go back with me to Cork; and if I find they never bought tickets, they will have to go to jail."

There were groans and hisses at that, and I gave the children in charge of the cabin stewardess, with orders to see that they did not leave the ship. I was at last convinced that they had no friends among the steerage passengers. I intended to take them ashore myself before we sailed; and I knew of good friends in New York who would see to the little waifs, although I did not propose that any of the emigrants should know that an old bachelor purser was fool enough to pay for the passage of a couple of unknown Irish children.

We landed our cabin passengers, and the tender came alongside to take the steerage passengers to Castle Garden. I got the stewardess to bring out the children, and the two stood and watched every one get aboard the tender.

Just as the tender moved away, there was a wild shriek among the crowded passengers, and Mrs. O'Donnell flung her arms above her head and cried in the most heart-rending tone I ever heard—"Oh, my babies, my babies."

"Kape quiet, ye divil," hissed O'Donnell, grasping her by the arm. The terrible ten days' strain had been broken at last, and the poor woman sank in a heap at his feet.

"Bring back that boat," I shouted, and the tender came back.

"Come aboard here, O'Donnell."

"I'll not!" he yelled, shaking his fist at me.

"Bring that man aboard."

They soon brought him back, and I gave his wife over to the care of the stewardess. She speedily rallied, and hugged and kissed her children as if she would never part with them.

"So, O'Donnell, these are your children?"

"Yis, they are; an' I'd have ye know I'm in a frae country, bedad, and I dare ye to lay a finger on me."

"Don't dare too much," I said, "or I'll show you what can be done in a free country. Now, if I let the children go, will you send their passage money to the company when you get it?"

"I will," he answered, although I knew he lied.

"Well," I said, "for Mrs. O'Donnell's sake, I'll let them go; and I must congratulate any free country that gets a citizen like you."

Of course I never heard from O'Donnell again.

Miss McMillan

"Come hop, come skip, fair children all,

Old Father Time is in the hall.

He'll take you on his knee, and stroke

Your golden hair to silver bright,

Your rosy cheeks to wrinkles white"

In the saloon of the fine Transatlantic liner the Climatus, two long tables extend from the piano at one end to the bookcase at the other end of the ample dining-room.

On each side of this main saloon are four small tables intended to accommodate six or seven persons. At one of these tables sat a pleasant party of four ladies and three gentlemen. Three ladies were from Detroit, and one from Kent, in England. At the head of the table sat Mr. Blair, the frosts of many American winters in his hair and beard, while the lines of care in his ragged, cheerful Scottish face told of a life of business crowned with generous success.

Mr. Waters, a younger merchant, had all the alert vivacity of the pushing American. He had the distinguished honour of sitting opposite me at the small table. Blair and Waters occupied the same room, No. 27. The one had crossed the Atlantic more than fifty times, the other nearly thirty. Those figures show the relative proportion of their business experience.

The presence of Mr. Blair gave to our table a sort of patriarchal dignity that we all appreciated. If a louder burst of laughter than usual came from where we sat and the other passengers looked inquiringly our way the sedate and self-possessed face of Mr. Blair kept us in countenance, and we, who had given way to undue levity, felt ourselves enshrouded by an atmosphere of genial seriousness. This prevented our table from getting the reputation of being funny or frivolous.

Some remark that Blair made brought forth the following extraordinary statement from Waters, who told it with the air of a man exposing the pretensions of a whited sepulchre.

"Now, before this voyage goes any further," he began, "I have a serious duty to perform which I can shirk no longer, unpleasant though it be. Mr. Blair and myself occupy the same state-room. Into that state-room has been sent a most lovely basket of flowers. It is not an ordinary basket of flowers, I assure you, ladies. There is a beautiful floral arch over a bed of colour, and I believe there is some tender sentiment connected with the display;—Bon Voyage, Auf Wiedersehen, or some such motto marked out in red buds. Now those flowers are not for me. I think, therefore, that Mr. Blair owes it to this company, which has so unanimously placed him at the head of the table, to explain how it comes that an elderly gentleman gets such a handsome floral tribute sent him from some unknown person in New York."

We all looked at Mr. Blair, who gazed with imperturbability at Waters.

"If you had all crossed with Waters as often as I have you would know that he is subject to attacks like that. He means well, but occasionally he gives way in the deplorable manner you have just witnessed. Now all there is of it consists in this—a basket of flowers has been sent (no doubt by mistake) to our state-room. There is nothing but a card on it which says 'Room 27.' Steward," he cried, "would you go to room 27, bring that basket of flowers, and set it on this table. We may as well all have the benefit of them."

The steward soon returned with a large and lovely basket of flowers, which he set on the table, shoving the caster and other things aside to make room for it.

We all admired it very much, and the handsome young lady on my left asked Mr. Blair's permission to take one of the roses for her own. "Now, mind you," said Blair, "I cannot grant a flower from the basket, for you see it is as much the property of Waters as of myself, for all of his virtuous indignation. It was sent to the room, and he is one of the occupants. The flowers have evidently been misdirected."

The lady referred to took it upon herself to purloin the flower she wanted.

As she did so a card came in view with the words written in a masculine hand—

To Miss McMillan, With the loving regards of Edwin J—

"Miss McMillan!" cried the lady; "I wonder if she is on board? I'd give anything to know."

"We'll have a glance at the passenger list," said Waters.

Down among the M's on the long list of cabin passengers appeared the name "Miss McMillan."

"Now," said I, "it seems to me that the duty devolves on both Blair and Waters to spare no pains in delicately returning those flowers to their proper owner. I think that both have been very remiss in not doing so long ago. They should apologise publicly to the young lady for having deprived her of the offering for a day and a half, and then I think they owe an apology to this table for the mere pretence that any sane person in New York or elsewhere would go to the trouble of sending either of them a single flower."

"There will be no apology from me," said Waters. "If I do not receive the thanks of Miss McMillan, it will be because good deeds are rarely recognised in this world. I think it must be evident, even to the limited intelligence of my journalistic friend across the table, that Mr. Blair intended to keep those flowers in his state-room, and—of course I make no direct charges—the concealment of that card certainly looks bad. It may have been concealed by the sender of the flowers, but to me it looks bad."

"Of course," said Blair dryly, "to you it looks bad. To the pure, etc."

"Now," said the sentimental lady on my left, "while you gentlemen are wasting the time in useless talk the lady is without her roses. There is one thing that you all seem to miss. It is not the mere value of the bouquet. There is a subtle perfume about an offering like this more delicate than that which Nature gave the flowers—"

"Hear, hear," broke in Waters.

"I told you," said Blair aside, "the kind of fellow Waters is. He thinks nothing of interrupting a lady."

"Order, both of you!" I cried, rapping on the table; "the lady from England has the floor."

"What I was going to say—"

"When Waters interrupted you."

"When Mr. Waters interrupted me I was going to say that there seems to me a romantic tinge to this incident that you old married men cannot be expected to appreciate."

I looked with surprise at Waters, while he sank back in his seat with the resigned air of a man in the hands of his enemies. We had both been carefully concealing the fact that we were married men, and the blunt announcement of the lady was a painful shock. Waters gave a side nod at Blair, as much as to say, "He's given it away." I looked reproachfully at my old friend at the head of the table, but he seemed to be absorbed in what our sentimental lady was saying.

"It is this," she continued. "Here is a young lady. Her lover sends her a basket. There may be some hidden meaning that she alone will understand in the very flowers chosen, or in the arrangement of them. The flowers, let us suppose, never reach their destination. The message is unspoken, or, rather, spoken, but unheard. The young lady grieves at the apparent neglect, and then, in her pride, resents it. She does not write, and he knows not why. The mistake may be discovered too late, and all because a basket of flowers has been missent."

"Now, Blair," said Waters, "if anything can make you do the square thing surely that appeal will."

"I shall not so far forget what is due to myself and to the dignity of this table as to reply to our erratic friend. Here is what I propose to do—first catch our hare. Steward, can you find out for me at what table and at what seat Miss McMillan is?"

While the steward was gone on his errand Mr. Blair proceeded.

"I will become acquainted with her. McMillan is a good Scotch name and Blair is another. On that as a basis I think we can speedily form an acquaintance. I shall then in a casual manner ask her if she knows a young man by the name of Edwin J., and I shall tell you what effect the mention of the name has on her."

"Now, as part owner in the flowers up to date, I protest against that. I insist that Miss McMillan be brought to this table, and that we all hear exactly what is said to her," put in Mr. Waters.

Nevertheless we agreed that Mr. Blair's proposal was a good one and the majority sanctioned it.

Meanwhile our sentimental lady had been looking among the crowd for the unconscious Miss McMillan.

"I think I have found her," she whispered to me. "Do you see that handsome girl at the captain's table. Really the handsomest girl on board."

"I thought that distinction rested with our own table."

"Now, please pay attention. Do you see how pensive she is, with her cheek resting on her hand? I am sure she is thinking of Edwin."

"I wouldn't bet on that," I replied. "There is considerable motion just now, and indications of a storm. The pensiveness may have other causes."

Here the steward returned and reported that Miss McMillan had not yet appeared at table, but had her meals taken to her room by the stewardess.

Blair called to the good-natured, portly stewardess of the Climatus, who at that moment was passing through the saloon.

"Is Miss McMillan ill?" he asked.

"No, not ill," replied Mrs. Kay; "but she seems very much depressed at leaving home, and she has not left her room since we started."

"There!" said our sentimental lady, triumphantly.

"I would like very much to see her," said Mr. Blair; "I have some good news for her."

"I will ask her to come out. It will do her good," said the stewardess, as she went away.

In a few moments she appeared, and, following her, came an old woman, with white hair, and her eyes concealed by a pair of spectacles.

"Miss McMillan," said the stewardess, "this is Mr. Blair, who wanted to speak to you."

Although Mr. Blair was, as we all were, astonished to see our mythical young lady changed into a real old woman, he did not lose his equanimity, nor did his kindly face show any surprise, but he evidently forgot the part he had intended to play.

"You will pardon me for troubling you, Miss McMillan," he said, "but this basket of flowers was evidently intended for you, and was sent to my room by mistake."

Miss McMillan did not look at the flowers, but gazed long at the card with the writing on it, and as she did so one tear and then another stole down the wrinkled face from behind the glasses.

"There is no mistake, is there?" asked Mr. Blair. "You know the writer."

"There is no mistake—no mistake," replied Miss McMillan in a low voice, "he is a very dear and kind friend." Then, as if unable to trust herself further, she took the flowers and hurriedly said, "Thank you," and left us.

"There," I said to the lady on my left, "your romance turns out to be nothing after all."

"No, sir," she cried with emphasis; "the romance is there, and very much more of a romance than if Miss McMillan was a young and silly girl of twenty."

Perhaps she was right.

A WOMAN INTERVENES

TO

MY FRIEND

HORACE HART

CHAPTER I.

The managing editor of the New York Argus sat at his desk with a deep frown on his face, looking out from under his shaggy eyebrows at the young man who had just thrown a huge fur overcoat on the back of one chair, while he sat down himself on another.

'I got your telegram,' began the editor. 'Am I to understand from it that you have failed?'

'Yes, sir,' answered the young man, without the slightest hesitation.

'Completely?'

'Utterly.'

'Didn't you even get a synopsis of the documents?'

'Not a hanged synop.'

The editor's frown grew deeper. The ends of his fingers drummed nervously on the desk.

'You take failure rather jauntily, it strikes me,' he said at last.

'What's the use of taking it any other way? I have the consciousness of knowing that I did my best.'

'Um, yes. It's a great consolation, no doubt, but it doesn't count in the newspaper business. What did you do?'

'I received your telegram at Montreal, and at once left for Burnt Pine—most outlandish spot on earth. I found that Kenyon and Wentworth were staying at the only hotel in the place. Tried to worm out of them what their reports were to be. They were very polite, but I didn't succeed. Then I tried to bribe them, and they ordered me out of the room.'

'Perhaps you didn't offer them enough.'

'I offered double what the London Syndicate was to pay them for making the report, taking their own word for the amount. I couldn't offer more, because at that point they closed the discussion by ordering me out of the room. I tried to get the papers that night, on the quiet, out of Wentworth's valise, but was unfortunately interrupted. The young men were suspicious, and next morning they left for Ottawa to post the reports, as I gathered afterwards, to England. I succeeded in getting hold of the reports, but I couldn't hang on. There are too many police in Ottawa to suit me.'

'Do you mean to tell me,' said the editor, 'that you actually had the reports in your hands, and that they were taken from you?'

'Certainly I had; and as to their being taken from me, it was either that or gaol. They don't mince matters in Canada as they do in the United States, you know.'

'But I should think a man of your shrewdness would have been able to get at least a synopsis of the reports before letting them out of his possession.'

'My dear sir,' said the reporter, rather angry, 'the whole thing covered I forget how many pages of foolscap paper, and was the most mixed-up matter I ever saw in my life. I tried—I sat in my room at the hotel, and did my best to master the details. It was full of technicalities, and I couldn't make it out. It required a mining expert to get the hang of their phrases and figures, so I thought the best thing to do was to telegraph it all straight through to New York. I knew it would cost a lot of money, but I knew, also, you didn't mind that; and I thought, perhaps, somebody here could make sense out of what baffled me; besides, I wanted to get the documents out of my possession just as quickly as possible.'

'Hem!' said the editor. 'You took no notes whatever?'

'No, I did not. I had no time. I knew the moment they missed the documents they would have the detectives on my track. As it was, I was arrested when I entered the telegraph-office.'

'Well, it seems to me,' said the managing editor, 'if I had once had the papers in my hand, I should not have let them go until I had got the gist of what was in them.'

'Oh, it's all very well for you to say so,' replied the reporter, with the free and easy manner in which an American newspaper man talks to his employer; 'but I can tell you, with a Canadian gaol facing a man, it is hard to decide what is best to do. I couldn't get out of the town for three hours, and before the end of that time they would have had my description in the hands of every policeman in the place. They knew well enough who took the papers, so my only hope lay in getting the thing telegraphed through; and if that had been accomplished, everything would have been all right. I would have gone to gaol with pleasure if I had got the particulars through to New York.'

'Well, what are we to do now?' asked the editor.

'I'm sure I don't know. The two men will be in New York very shortly. They sail, I understand, on the Caloric, which leaves in a week. If you think you have a reporter who can get the particulars out of these men, I should be very pleased to see you set him on. I tell you it isn't so easy to discover what an Englishman doesn't want you to know.'

'Well,' said the editor, 'perhaps that's true. I will think about it. Of course you did your best, and I appreciate your efforts; but I am sorry you failed.'

'You are not half so sorry as I am,' said Rivers, as he picked up his big Canadian fur coat and took his leave.

The editor did think about it. He thought for fully two minutes. Then he dashed off a note on a sheet of paper, pulled down the little knob that rang the District Messenger alarm, and when the uniformed boy appeared, gave him the note, saying:

'Deliver this as quickly as you can.'

The boy disappeared, and the result of his trip was soon apparent in the arrival of a very natty young woman in the editorial rooms. She was dressed in a neatly-fitting tailor-made costume, and was a very pretty girl, who looked about nineteen, but was, in reality, somewhat older. She had large, appealing blue eyes, with a tender, trustful expression in them, which made the ordinary man say: 'What a sweet, innocent look that girl has!' yet, what the young woman didn't know about New York was not worth knowing. She boasted that she could get State secrets from dignified members of the Cabinet, and an ordinary Senator or Congressman she looked upon as her lawful prey. That which had been told her in the strictest confidence had often become the sensation of the next day in the paper she represented. She wrote over a nom de guerre, and had tried her hand at nearly everything. She had answered advertisements, exposed rogues and swindlers, and had gone to a hotel as chambermaid, in order to write her experiences. She had been arrested and locked up, so that she might write a three-column account, for the Sunday edition of the Argus, of 'How Women are Treated at Police Headquarters.' The editor looked upon her as one of the most valuable members of his staff, and she was paid accordingly.

She came into the room with the self-possessed air of the owner of the building, took a seat, after nodding to the editor, and said, 'Well?'

'Look here, Jennie,' began that austere individual, 'do you wish to take a trip to Europe?'

'That depends,' said Jennie; 'this is not just the time of year that people go to Europe for pleasure, you know.'

'Well, this is not exactly a pleasure trip. The truth of the matter is, Rivers has been on a job and has bungled it fearfully, besides nearly getting himself arrested.'

The young woman's eyes twinkled. She liked anything with a spice of danger in it, and did not object to hear that she was expected to succeed where a mere masculine reporter had failed.

The editor continued:

'Two young men are going across to England on the Caloric. It sails in a week. I want you to take a ticket for Liverpool by that boat, and obtain from either of those two men the particulars—the full particulars—of reports they have made on some mining properties in Canada. Then you must land at Queenstown and cable a complete account to the Argus.'

'Mining isn't much in my line,' said Miss Jennie, with a frown on her pretty brow. 'What sort of mines were they dealing with—gold, silver, copper, or what?'

'They are certain mines on the Ottawa River.'

'That's rather indefinite.'

'I know it is. I can't give you much information about the matter. I don't know myself, to tell the truth, but I know it is vitally important that we should get a synopsis of what the reports of these young men are to be. A company, called the London Syndicate, has been formed in England. This syndicate is to acquire a large number of mines in Canada, if the accounts given by the present owners are anything like correct. Two men, Kenyon and Wentworth—the first a mining engineer, and the second an experienced accountant—have been sent from London to Canada, one to examine the mines, the other to examine the books of the various corporations. Whether the mines are bought or not will depend a good deal on the reports these two men have in their possession. The reports, when published, will make a big difference, one way or the other, on the Stock Exchange. I want to have the gist of them before the London Syndicate sees them. It will be a big thing for the Argus if it is the first in the field, and I am willing to spend a pile of hard cash to succeed. So, don't economize on your cable expenses.'

'Very well; have you a book on Canadian mines?'

'I don't know that we have; but there is a book here, "The Mining Resources of Canada;" will that be of any use?'

'I shall need something of that sort. I want to be a little familiar with the subject, you know.'

'Quite so,' said the editor; 'I will see what can be got in that line. You can read it before you start, and on the way over.'

'All right,' said Miss Jennie; 'and am I to take my pick of the two young men?'

'Certainly,' answered the editor. 'You will see them both, and can easily make up your mind which will the sooner fall a victim.'

'The Caloric sails in a week, does it?'

'Yes.'

'Then I shall need at least five hundred dollars to get new dresses with.'

'Good gracious!' cried the editor.

'There is no "good gracious" about it. I'm going to travel as a millionaire's daughter, and it isn't likely that one or two dresses will do me all the way over.'

'But you can't get new dresses made in a week,' said the editor.

'Can't I? Well, you just get me the five hundred dollars, and I'll see about the making.'

The editor jotted the amount down.

'You don't think four hundred dollars would do?' he said.

'No, I don't. And, say, am I to get a trip to Paris after this is over, or must I come directly back?'

'Oh, I guess we can throw in the trip to Paris,' said the editor.

'What did you say the names of the young men are?—or are they not young? Probably they are old fogies, if they are in the mining business.'

'No; they are young, they are shrewd, and they are English. So you see your work is cut out for you. Their names are George Wentworth and John Kenyon.'

'Oh, Wentworth is my man,' said the young woman breezily. 'John Kenyon! I know just what sort of a person he is—sombre and taciturn. Sounds too much like John Bunyan, or John Milton, or names of that sort.'

'Well, I wouldn't be too sure about it until you see them. Better not make up your mind about the matter.'

'When shall I call for the five hundred dollars?'

'Oh, that you needn't trouble about. The better way is to get your dresses made, and tell the people to send the bills to our office.'

'Very well,' said the young woman. 'I shall be ready. Don't be frightened at the bills when they come in. If they come up to a thousand dollars, remember I told you I would let you off for five hundred dollars.'

The editor looked at her for a moment, and seemed to reflect that perhaps it was better not to give a young lady unlimited credit in New York. So he said:

'Wait a bit; I'll write you out the order, and you can take it downstairs.'

Miss Jennie took the paper when it was offered to her, and disappeared. When she presented the order in the business office, the cashier raised his eyebrows as he noticed the amount, and, with a low whistle, said to himself:

'Five hundred dollars! I wonder what game Jennie Brewster's up to now.'

CHAPTER II.

The last bell had rung. Those who were going ashore had taken their departure. Crowds of human beings clustered on the pier-head, and at the large doorways of the warehouse which stood open on the steamer wharf. As the big ship slowly backed out there was a fluttering of handkerchiefs from the mass on the pier, and an answering flutter from those who crowded along the bulwarks of the steamer. The tug slowly pulled the prow of the vessel round, and at last the engines of the steamship began their pulsating throbs—throbs that would vibrate night and day until the steamer reached an older civilization. The crowd on the pier became more and more indistinct to those on board, and many of the passengers went below, for the air was bitterly cold, and the boat was forcing its way down the bay among huge blocks of ice.

Two, at least, of the passengers had taken little interest in the departure. They were leaving no friends behind them, and were both setting their faces toward friends at home.

'Let us go down,' said Wentworth to Kenyon, 'and see that we get seats together at table before all are taken.'

'Very good,' replied his companion, and they descended to the roomy saloon, where two long tables were already laid with an ostentatious display of silver, glassware, and cutlery, which made many, who looked on this wilderness of white linen with something like dismay, hope that the voyage would be smooth, although, as it was a winter passage, there was every chance it would not be. The purser and two of his assistants sat at one of the shorter tables with a plan before them, marking off the names of passengers who wished to be together, or who wanted some particular place at any of the tables. The smaller side-tables were still uncovered because the number of passengers at that season of the year was comparatively few. As the places were assigned, one of the helpers to the purser wrote the names of the passengers on small cards, and the other put the cards on the tables.

One young woman, in a beautifully-fitting travelling gown, which was evidently of the newest cut and design, stood a little apart from the general group which surrounded the purser and his assistants. She eagerly scanned every face, and listened attentively to the names given. Sometimes a shade of disappointment crossed her brow, as if she expected some particular person to possess some particular name which that particular person did not bear. At last her eyes sparkled.

'My name is Wentworth,' said the young man whose turn it was.

'Ah! any favourite place, Mr. Wentworth?' asked the purser blandly, as if he had known Wentworth all his life.

'No, we don't care where we sit; but my friend Mr. Kenyon and myself would like places together.'

'Very good; you had better come to my table,' replied the purser. 'Numbers 23 and 24—Mr. Kenyon and Mr. Wentworth.'

The steward took the cards that were given him, and placed them to correspond with the numbers the purser had named. Then the young woman moved gracefully along, as if she were interested in the names upon the table. She looked at Wentworth's name for a moment, and saw in the place next to his the name of Mr. Brown. She gave a quick, apprehensive glance around the saloon, and observed the two young men who had arranged for their seats at table now walking leisurely toward the companion-way. She took the card with the name of Mr. Brown upon it, and slipped upon the table another on which were written the words 'Miss Jennie Brewster.' Mr. Brown's card she placed on the spot from which she had taken her own.

'I hope Mr. Brown is not particular which place he occupies,' said Jennie to herself; 'but at any rate I shall see that I am early for dinner, and I'm sure Mr. Brown, whoever he is, will not be so ungallant as to insist on having this place if he knows his card was here.'

Subsequent events proved her surmise regarding Mr. Brown's indifference to be perfectly well founded. That young man searched for his card, found it, and sat down on the chair opposite the young woman, who already occupied her chair, and was, in fact, the first one at table. Seeing there would be no unseemly dispute about places, she began to plan in her own mind how she would first attract the attention of Mr. Wentworth. While thinking how best to approach her victim, Jennie heard his voice.

'Here you are, Kenyon; here are our places.'

'Which is mine?' said the voice of Kenyon.

'It doesn't matter,' answered Wentworth, and then a thrill of fear went through the gentle heart of Miss Jennie Brewster. She had not thought of the young man not caring which seat he occupied, and she dreaded the possibility of finding herself next to Kenyon rather than Wentworth. Her first estimate of the characters of the two men seemed to be correct. She always thought of Kenyon as Bunyan, and she felt certain that Wentworth would be the easier man of the two to influence. The next moment her fears were allayed, for Kenyon, giving a rapid glance at the handsome young woman, deliberately chose the seat farthest from her, and Wentworth, with 'I beg your pardon,' slipped in and sat down on the chair beside her.

'Now,' thought Jennie, with a sigh of relief, 'our positions are fixed for the meals of the voyage.' She had made her plans for beginning an acquaintance with the young man, but they were rendered unnecessary by the polite Mr. Wentworth handing her the bill of fare.

'Oh, thank you,' said the girl, in a low voice, which was so musical that Wentworth glanced at her a second time and saw how sweet and pretty and innocent she was.

'I'm in luck,' said the unfortunate young man to himself. Then he remarked aloud: 'We have not many ladies with us this voyage.'

'No,' replied Miss Brewster; 'I suppose nobody crosses at this time of the year unless compelled to.'

'I can answer for two passengers that such is the case.'

'Do you mean yourself as one?'

'Yes, myself and my friend.'

'How pleasant it must be,' said Miss Brewster, 'to travel with a friend! Then one is not lonely. I, unfortunately, am travelling alone.'

'I fancy,' said the gallant Wentworth, 'that if you are lonely while on board ship, it will be entirely your own fault.'

Miss Brewster laughed a silvery little laugh.

'I don't know about that,' she said. 'I am going to that Mecca of all Americans—Paris. My father is to meet me there, and we are then going on to the Riviera together.'

'Ah, that will be very pleasant,' said Wentworth. 'The Riviera at this season is certainly a place to be desired.'

'So I have heard,' she replied.

'Have you not been across before?'

'No, this is my first trip. I suppose you have crossed many times?'

'Oh no,' answered the Englishman; 'this is only my second voyage, my first having been the one that took me to America.'

'Ah, then you are not an American,' returned Miss Brewster, with apparent surprise.

She imagined that a man is generally flattered when a mistake of this kind is made. No matter how proud he may be of his country, he is pleased to learn that there is no provincialism about him which, as the Americans say, 'gives him away.'

'I think,' said Wentworth, 'as a general thing, I am not taken for anything but what I am—an Englishman.'

'I have met so few Englishmen,' said the guileless young woman, 'that really I should not be expected to know.'

'I understand it is a common delusion among Americans that every Englishman drops his "h's," and is to be detected in that way.'

Jennie laughed again, and George Wentworth thought it one of the prettiest laughs he had ever heard.

Poor Kenyon was rather neglected by his friend during the dinner. He felt a little gloomy while the courses went on, and wished he had an evening paper. Meanwhile, Wentworth and the handsome girl beside him got on very well together. At the end of the dinner she seemed to have some difficulty in getting up from her chair, and Wentworth showed her how to turn it round, leaving her free to rise. She thanked him prettily.

'I am going on deck,' she said, turning to go; 'I am so anxious to get my first glimpse of the ocean at night from the deck of a steamer.'

'I hope you will let me accompany you,' returned young Wentworth. 'The decks are rather slippery, and even when the boat is not rolling it isn't quite safe for a lady unused to the motion of a ship to walk alone in the dark.'

'Oh, thank you very much,' replied Miss Brewster, with effusion. 'It is kind of you, I am sure; and if you promise not to let me rob you of the pleasure of your after-dinner cigar, I shall be most happy to have you accompany me. I will meet you at the top of the stairway in five minutes.'

'You are getting on,' said Kenyon, as the young woman disappeared.

'What's the use of being on board ship,' said Wentworth, 'If you don't take advantage of the opportunity for making shipboard acquaintances? There is an unconventionality about life on a steamer that is not without its charm, as perhaps you will find out before the voyage is over, John.'

'You are merely trying to ease your conscience because of your heartless desertion of me.'

George Wentworth had waited at the top of the companion-way a little more than five minutes when Miss Brewster appeared, wrapped in a cloak edged with fur, which lent an additional charm to her complexion, set off as it was by a jaunty steamer cap. They stepped out on the deck, and found it not at all so dark as they had expected. Little globes of electric light were placed at regular intervals on the walls of the deck building. Overhead was stretched a sort of canvas roof, against which the sleety rain pattered. One of the sailors, with a rubber mop, was pushing into the gutter by the side of the ship the moisture from the deck. All around the boat the night was as black as ink, except here and there where the white curl of a wave showed luminous for a moment in the darkness.

Miss Brewster insisted that Wentworth should light his cigar, which, after some persuasion, he did. Then he tucked her hand snugly under his arm, and she adjusted her step to suit his. They had the promenade all to themselves. The rainy winter night was not so inviting to most of the passengers as the comfortable rooms below. Kenyon, however, and one or two others came up, and sat on the steamer chairs that were tied to the brass rod which ran along the deckhouse wall. He saw the glow of Wentworth's cigar as the couple turned at the farther end of the walk, and when they passed him he heard a low murmur of conversation, and caught now and then a snatch of silvery laughter. It was not because Wentworth had deserted him that Kenyon felt so uncomfortable and depressed. He could not tell just what it was, but there had settled on his mind a strange, uneasy foreboding. After a time he went down into the saloon and tried to read, but could not, and so wandered along the seemingly endless narrow passage to his room (which was Wentworth's as well), and, in nautical phrase, 'turned in.' It was late when his companion came.

'Asleep, Kenyon?' asked the latter.

'No,' was the answer.

'By George! John, she is one of the most charming girls I ever met. Wonderfully clever, too; makes a man feel like a fool beside her. She has read nearly everything. Has opinions on all our authors, a great many of whom I've never heard of. I wish, for your sake, John, she had a sister on board.'

'Thanks, old man; awfully good of you, I'm sure,' said Kenyon. 'Don't you think it's about time to stop raving, get into your bunk, and turn out that confounded light?'

'All right, growler, I will.'

Meanwhile, in her own state-room, Miss Jennie Brewster was looking at her reflection in the glass. As she shook out her long hair until it rippled down her back, she smiled sweetly, and said to herself:

'Poor Mr. Wentworth! Only the first night out, and he told me his name was George.'

CHAPTER III.

The second day out was a pleasant surprise for all on board who had made up their minds to a disagreeable winter passage. The air was clear, the sky blue as if it were spring-time, instead of midwinter. They were in the Gulf Stream. The sun shone brightly and the temperature was mild. Nevertheless, it was an uncomfortable day for those who were poor sailors. Although there did not seem, to the casual observer, to be much of a sea running, the ship rolled atrociously. Those who had made heroic resolutions on the subject were sitting in silent misery in their deck-chairs, which had been lashed to firm stanchions. Few were walking the clean bright deck, because walking that morning was a gymnastic feat. Three or four who evidently wished to show they had crossed before, and knew all about it, managed to make their way along the deck. Those recumbent in the steamer-chairs watched with lazy interest the pedestrians who now and then stood still, leaning apparently far out of the perpendicular, as the deck inclined downward. Sometimes the pedestrian's feet slipped, and he shot swiftly down the incline. Such an incident was invariably welcomed by those who sat. Even the invalids smiled wanly.

Kenyon reclined in his deck-chair with his eyes fixed on the blue sky. His mind was at rest about the syndicate report now that it had been mailed to London. His thoughts wandered to his own affairs, and he wondered whether he would make money out of the option he had acquired at Ottawa. He was not an optimist man, and he doubted.

After their work for the London Syndicate was finished, the young men had done a little business on their own account. They visited together a mica-mine that was barely paying expenses, and which the proprietors were anxious to sell. The mine was owned by the Austrian Mining Company, whose agent, Von Brent, was interviewed by Kenyon in Ottawa. The young men obtained an option on this mine for three months from Von Brent. Kenyon's educated eye had told him that the white mineral they were placing on the dump at the mouth of the mine was even more valuable than the mica for which they were mining.

Kenyon was scrupulously honest—a quality somewhat at a discount in the mining business—and it seemed to him hardly the fair thing that he should take advantage of the ignorance of Von Brent regarding the mineral on the dump. Wentworth had some trouble in overcoming his friend's scruples. He claimed that knowledge always had to be paid for, in law, medicine, or mineralogy, and therefore that they were perfectly justified in profiting by their superior wisdom. So it came about that the young men took to England with them a three months' option on the mine.

Wentworth had been walking about all morning like a lost spirit apparently seeking what was not. 'It can't be,' he said to himself. No; the thought was too horrible, and he dismissed it from his mind, merely conjecturing that perhaps she was not an early riser, which was indeed the case. No one who works on a morning newspaper ever takes advantage of the lark's example.

'Well, Kenyon,' said Wentworth 'you look as if you were writing a poem, or doing something that required deep mental agony.'

'The writing of poems, my dear Wentworth, I leave to you. I am doing something infinitely more practical—something that you ought to be at. I am thinking what we are to do with our mica-mine when we get it over to London.'

'Oh, "sufficient for the day is the evil thereof,"' cried Wentworth jauntily; 'besides, half an hour's thinking by a solid-brained fellow like you is worth a whole voyage of my deepest meditation.'

'She hasn't appeared yet?' said Kenyon.

'No, dear boy; no, she has not. You see, I make no pretence with you as other less ingenuous men might. No, she has not appeared, and she has not breakfasted.'

'Perhaps——' began Kenyon.

'No, no!' cried Wentworth; 'I'll have no "perhaps." I thought of that, but I instantly dismissed the idea. She's too good a sailor.'

'It requires a very good sailor to stand this sort of thing. It looks so unnecessary, too. I wonder what the ship is rolling about?'

'I can't tell, but she seems to be rolling about half over. I say, Kenyon, old fellow, I feel horrible pangs of conscience about deserting you in this way, and so early in the voyage. I didn't do it last time, did I?'

'You were a model travelling companion on the last voyage,' returned Kenyon.

'I don't wish to make impertinent suggestions, my boy, but allow me to tell you that there are some other very nice girls on board.'

'You are not so bad as I feared, then,' replied Kenyon, 'or you wouldn't admit that. I thought you had eyes for no one but Miss—Miss—I really didn't catch her name.'

'I don't mind telling you confidentially, Kenyon, that her name is Jennie.'

'Dear me!' cried Kenyon, 'has it got so far as that? Doesn't it strike you, Wentworth, that you are somewhat in a hurry? It seems decidedly more American than English. Englishmen are apt to weigh matters a little more.'

'There is no necessity for weighing, my boy. I don't see any harm in making the acquaintance of a pretty girl when you have a long voyage before you.'

'Well, I wouldn't let it grow too serious, if I were you.'

'There isn't the slightest danger of seriousness about the affair. On shore the young lady wouldn't cast a second look at me. She is the daughter of a millionaire. Her father is in Paris, and they are going on to the Riviera in a few weeks.'

'All the more reason,' said Kenyon, 'that you shouldn't let this go too far. Be on your guard, my boy. I've heard it said that American girls have the delightful little practice of leading a man on until it comes to a certain point, and then arching their pretty eyebrows, looking astonished, and forgetting all about him afterwards. You had better wait until we make our fortunes on this mica-mine, and then, perhaps, your fair millionairess may listen to you.'

'John,' cried Wentworth, 'you are the most cold-blooded man I know of. I never noticed it so particularly before, but it seems to me that years and years of acquaintance with minerals of all kinds, hard and flinty, transform a man. Be careful that you don't become like the minerals you work among.'

'Well, I don't know anything that has less tendency to soften a man than long columns of figures. I think the figures you work at are quite as demoralizing as the minerals I have spent my life with.'

'Perhaps you are right, but a girl would have to be thrown into your arms before you would admit that such a thing as a charming young lady existed.'

'If I make all the money I hope to make out of the mica-mine, I expect the young ladies will not be thrown into my arms, but at my head. Money goes a long way toward reconciling a girl to marriage.'

'It certainly goes a long way toward reconciling her mother to the marriage. I don't believe,' said Wentworth slowly, 'that my—that Miss Brewster ever thinks about money.'

'She probably doesn't need to, but no doubt there is someone who does the thinking for her. If her father is a millionaire, and has, like many Americans, made his own money, you may depend upon it he will do the thinking for her; and if Miss Brewster should prove to be thoughtless in the matter, the old gentleman will very speedily bring you both to your senses. It would be different if you had a title.'

'I haven't any,' replied Wentworth, 'except the title George Wentworth, accountant, with an address in the City and rooms in the suburbs.'

'Precisely; if you were Lord George Wentworth, or even Sir George, or Baron Wentworth of something or other, you might have a chance; as it is, the title of accountant would not go far with an American millionaire, or his daughter either.'

'You are a cold, calculating wretch.'

'Nothing of the sort. I merely have my senses about me, and you haven't at this particular moment. You wouldn't think of trusting a book-keeper's figures without seeing his vouchers. Well, my boy, you haven't the vouchers— at least, not yet, so that is why I ask you to give your attention to what we are going to do with our mine; and if you take my advice you will not think seriously about American millionaires or their daughters.'

George Wentworth jumped to his feet, the ship gave a lurch at that particular moment, and he no sooner found his feet than he nearly lost them again; however, he was an expert at balancing himself as well as his accounts, and though for the moment his attention was occupied in keeping his equilibrium, he looked down on his companion, still placidly reclining in his chair, with a smile on his face.

'Kenyon,' he said, 'I am going to look for another girl.'

'Is one not enough for you?'

'No, I want two—one for myself, and one for you. No man can sympathize with another unless he is in the same position himself. John, I want sympathy, and I'm not getting it.'

'What you need more urgently,' said Kenyon calmly, 'is common-sense, and that I am trying to supply.'

'You are doing your duty in that direction; but a man doesn't live by common-sense alone. There comes a time when common-sense is a drug in the market. I don't say it has come to me yet, but I'm resolved to get you into a more sympathetic mood, so I am going to find a suitable young lady for you.'

'More probably you are going to look for your own,' answered Kenyon, as his friend walked off, and, disappearing round the corner, crossed to the other side of the ship.

Kenyon did not turn again to his figures when his companion left him. He mused over the curiously rapid turn of circumstances. He hoped Wentworth would not take it too seriously, for he felt that, somehow or other, Miss Brewster was just the sort of girl to throw him over after she had whiled away a tedious voyage. Of course he could not say this to his friend, who evidently admired Miss Brewster, but he had said as much as he could to put Wentworth on his guard.

'Now,' said Kenyon to himself, 'if she had been a girl like that, I wouldn't have minded.' The girl 'like that' was a young woman who for half an hour had been walking the deck alone with marvellous skill. She was not so handsome as the American girl, but she had a better complexion, and there was a colour in her cheek which seemed to suggest England. Her dress was not quite so smart nor so well-fitting as that of the American girl; but, nevertheless, she was warmly and sensibly clad, and a brown Tam o' Shanter covered her fair head. The tips of her hands were in the pockets of her short blue-cloth jacket; and she walked the deck with a firm, reliant tread that aroused the admiration of John Kenyon. 'If she were only a girl like that,' he repeated to himself, 'I wouldn't mind. There's something fresh and genuine about her. She makes me think of the breezy English downs.'

As she walked back and forward, one or two young men seemingly made an attempt to become acquainted with her, but it was evident to Kenyon that the young woman had made it plain to them, politely enough, that she preferred walking alone, and they raised their sea-caps and left her.

'She doesn't pick up the first man who comes,' he mused.

The ship was beginning to roll more and more, and yet the day was beautiful and the sea seemingly calm. Most of the promenaders had left the deck. Two or three of them had maintained their equilibrium with a gratifying success which engendered the pride that goeth before a fall, but the moment came at last when their feet slipped and they had found themselves thrown against the bulwark of the steamer. Then they had laughed a little in a crestfallen manner, picked themselves up, and promenaded the deck no more. Many of those who were lying in the steamer-chairs gave up the struggle and went down to their cabins. There was a momentary excitement as one chair broke from its fastenings and slid down with a crash against the bulwarks. The occupant was picked up in a hysterical condition and taken below. The deck steward tied the chair more firmly, so that the accident would not happen again. The young English girl was opposite John Kenyon when this disaster took place, and her attention being diverted by fear for the safety of the occupant of the sliding chair, her care for herself was withdrawn at the very moment when it was most needed. The succeeding lurch which the ship gave to the other side was the most tremendous of the day. The deck rose until the girl leaning outward could almost touch it with her hand, then, in spite of herself, she slipped with the rapidity of lightning against the chair John Kenyon occupied, and that tripping her up, flung her upon him with an unexpectedness that would have taken his breath away if the sudden landing of a plump young woman upon him had not accomplished the same thing. The fragile deck-chair gave way with a crash, and it would be hard to say which was the more discomfited by the sudden catastrophe, John Kenyon or the girl.

'I hope you are not hurt,' he managed to stammer.

'Don't think about me!' she cried. 'I have broken your chair, and—and——'

'The chair doesn't matter,' cried Kenyon. 'It was a flimsy structure at best. I am not hurt, if that is what you mean—and you mustn't mind it.'

Then there came to his recollection the sentence of George Wentworth: 'A girl will have to be thrown into your arms before you will admit that such a thing as a charming young woman exists.'

CHAPTER IV.

Edith Longworth could hardly be said to be a typical representative of the English girl. She had the English girl's education, but not her training. She had lost her mother in early life, which makes a great difference in a girl's bringing up, however wealthy her father may be; and Edith's father was wealthy, there was no doubt of that. If you asked any City man about the standing of John Longworth, you would learn that the 'house' was well thought of. People said he was lucky, but old John Longworth asserted that there was no such thing as luck in business—in which statement he was very likely incorrect. He had large investments in almost every quarter of the globe. When he went into any enterprise, he went into it thoroughly. Men talk about the inadvisability of putting all one's eggs into one basket, but John Longworth was a believer in doing that very thing—and in watching the basket. Not that he had all his eggs in one basket, or even in one kind of basket; but when John Longworth was satisfied with the particular variety of basket presented to him, he put a large number of eggs in it. When anything was offered for investment—whether it was a mine or a brewery or a railway—John Longworth took an expert's opinion upon it, and then the chances were that he would disregard the advice given. He was in the habit of going personally to see what had been offered to him. If the enterprise were big enough, he thought little of taking a voyage to the other end of the world for the sole purpose of looking the investment over. It was true that in many cases he knew nothing whatever of the business he went to examine, but that did not matter; he liked to have a personal inspection where a large amount of his money was to be placed. Investment seemed to be a sort of intuition with him. Often, when the experts' opinions were unanimously in favour of the project, and when everything appeared to be perfectly safe, Longworth would pay a personal visit to the business offered for sale, and come to a sudden conclusion not to have anything to do with it. He would give no reasons to his colleagues for his change of front; he simply refused to entertain the proposal any further, and withdrew. Several instances of this kind had occurred. Sometimes a large and profitable business, held out in the prospectus to be exceedingly desirable, had come to nothing, and when the company was wound up, people remembered what Longworth had said about it. So there came to be a certain superstitious feeling among those who knew him, that, if old Mr. Longworth was in a thing, the thing was safe, and if a company promoter managed to get his name on the prospectus, his project was almost certain to succeed.

* * * * *

When Edith Longworth was pronounced finished so far as education was concerned, she became more and more the companion of her father, and he often jokingly referred to her as his man of business. She went with him on his long journeys, and so had been several times to America, once to the Cape, and one long voyage, with Australia as the objective point, had taken her completely round the world. She inherited much of her father's shrewdness, and there is no doubt that, if Edith Longworth had been cast upon her own resources, she would have become an excellent woman of business. She knew exactly the extent of her father's investments, and she was his confidante in a way that few women are with their male relatives. The old man had a great faith in Edith's opinion, although he rarely acknowledged it. Having been together so much on such long trips, they naturally became, in a way, boon companions. Thus, Edith's education was very unlike that of the ordinary English girl, and this particular training caused her to develop into a different kind of woman than she might have been had her mother lived.

Perfect confidence existed between father and daughter, and only lately had there come a shadow upon their relations, about which neither ever spoke to the other since their first conversation on the subject.

Edith had said, with perhaps more than her usual outspokenness, that she had no thought whatever of marriage, and least of all had her thoughts turned toward the man her father seemed to have chosen. In answer to this, her father had said nothing, but Edith knew him too well to believe that he had changed his mind about the matter. The fact that he had invited her cousin to join them on this particular journey showed her that he evidently believed all that was necessary was to throw them more together than had been the case previously; and, although Edith was silent, she thought her father had not the same shrewdness in these matters that he showed in the purchasing of a growing business. Edith had been perfectly civil to the young man—as she would have been to anyone—but he saw that she preferred her own company to his; and so, much to the disgust of Mr. Longworth, he spent most of his time at cards in the smoking-room, whereas, according to the elder gentleman's opinion, he should have been promenading the deck with his cousin.

William Longworth, the cousin, was inclined to be a trifle put out, for he looked upon himself as quite an eligible person, one whom any girl in her senses would be glad to look forward to as a possible husband. He made no pretence of being madly in love with Edith, but he thought the marriage would be an admirable thing all round. She was a nice girl, he said to himself, and his uncle's money was well worth thinking about. In fact, he was becoming desirous that the marriage should take place; but, as there was no one upon whom he could look as a rival, he had the field to himself. He would therefore show Miss Edith that he was by no means entirely dependent for his happiness upon her company; and this he proceeded to do by spending his time in the smoking-room, and playing cards with his fellow-passengers. It was quite evident to anyone who saw Edith, that, if this suited him, it certainly suited her; so they rarely met on shipboard except at table, where Edith's place was between her father and her cousin. Miss Longworth and her cousin had had one brief conversation on the subject of marriage. He spoke of it rather jauntily, as being quite a good arrangement, but she said very shortly that she had no desire to change her name.

'You don't need to,' said Cousin William; 'my name is Longworth, and so is yours.'

'It is not a subject for a joke,' she answered.

'I am not joking, my dear Edith. I am merely telling you what everybody knows to be true. You surely don't deny that my name is Longworth?'

'I don't mean to deny or affirm anything in relation to the matter,' replied the young woman, 'and you will oblige me very much if you will never recur to this subject again.'

And so the young man betook himself once more to the smoking-room.

On this trip Edith had seen a good deal of American society. People over there had made it very pleasant for her, and, although the weather was somewhat trying, she had greatly enjoyed the sleigh-rides and the different festivities which winter brings to the citizen of Northern America. Her father and her cousin had gone to America to see numerous breweries that were situated in different parts of the country, and which it was proposed to combine into one large company. They had made a Western city their headquarters, and while Edith was enjoying herself with her newly-found friends, the two men had visited the breweries in different sections of the country—all, however, near the city where Edith was staying. The breweries seemed to be in a very prosperous condition, although the young man declared the beer they brewed was the vilest he had ever tasted, and he said he wouldn't like to have anything to do with the production of it, even if it did turn in money. His uncle had not tried the beer, but confined himself solely to the good old bottled English ale, which had increased in price, if not in excellence, by its transportation. But there was something about the combination that did not please him; and, from the few words he dropped on the subject, his nephew saw that Longworth was not going to be a member of the big Beer Syndicate. The intention had been to take a trip to Canada, and Edith had some hopes of seeing the city of Montreal in its winter dress; but that visit had been abandoned, as so much time had been consumed in the Western States. So they began their homeward voyage, with the elder Longworth sitting a good deal in his deck-chair, and young Longworth spending much of his time in the smoking-room, while Edith walked the deck alone. And this was the lady whom Fate threw into the arms of John Kenyon.

CHAPTER V.

Steamer friendships ripen quickly. It is true that, as a general thing, they perish with equal suddenness. The moment a man sets his foot on solid land the glamour of the sea seems to leave him, and the friend to whom he was ready to swear eternal fealty while treading the deck, is speedily forgotten on shore. Edith Longworth gave no thought to the subject of the innocent nature of steamer friendships when she reviewed in her own mind her pleasant walk along the deck with Kenyon. She had met many interesting people during her numerous voyages, but they had all proved to be steamer acquaintances, whose names she had now considerable difficulty in remembering. Perhaps she would not have given a second thought to Mr. Kenyon that night if it had not been for some ill-considered remarks her cousin saw fit to make at the dinner-table.

'Who was that fellow you were walking with today?' young Longworth asked.

Edith smiled upon him pleasantly, and answered:

'Mr. Kenyon you mean, I suppose?'

'Oh, you know his name, do you?' he answered gruffly.

'Certainly,' she replied; 'I would not walk with a gentleman whose name I did not know.'

'Really?' sneered her cousin. 'And pray were you introduced to him?'

'I do not think,' answered Edith quietly, 'any person has a right to ask me that question except my father. He has not asked it, and, as you have, I will merely answer that I was introduced to Mr. Kenyon.'

'I did not know you had any mutual acquaintance on board who could make you known to each other.'

'Well, the ceremony was a little informal. We were introduced by our mutual friend, old Father Neptune. Father Neptune, being, as you know, a little boisterous this morning, took the liberty of flinging me upon Mr. Kenyon. I weigh something more than a feather, and the result was—although Mr. Kenyon was good enough to say he was uninjured—that the chair on which he sat had not the same consideration for my feelings, and it went down with a crash. I thought Mr. Kenyon should take my chair in exchange for the one I had the misfortune to break, but Mr. Kenyon thought otherwise. He said he was a mining engineer, and that he could not claim to be a very good one if he found any difficulty in mending a deck-chair. It seems he succeeded in doing so, and that is the whole history of my introduction to, and my intercourse with, Mr. Kenyon, Mining Engineer.'

'Most interesting and romantic,' replied the young man; 'and do you think that your father approves of your picking up indiscriminate acquaintances in this way?'

Edith, flushing a little at this, said:

'I would not willingly do what my father disapproved of;' then in a lower voice she added: 'except, perhaps, one thing.'

Her father, who had caught snatches of the conversation, now leaned across towards his nephew, and said warningly:

'I think Edith is quite capable of judging for herself. This is my seventh voyage with her, and I have always found such to be the case. This happens to be your first, and so, were I you, I would not pursue the subject further.'

The young man was silent, and Edith gave her father a grateful glance. Thus it was that, while she might not have given a thought to Kenyon, the remarks which her cousin had made, brought to her mind, when she was alone, the two young men, and the contrast between them was not at all to the advantage of her cousin.

The scrubbing-brushes on the deck above him woke Kenyon early next morning. For a few moments after getting on deck he thought he had the ship to himself. One side of the deck was clean and wet; on the other side the men were slowly moving the scrubbing-brushes backward and forward, with a drowsy swish-swish. As he walked up the deck, he saw there was one passenger who had been earlier than himself.

Edith Longworth turned round as she heard his step, and her face brightened into a smile when she saw who it was.

Kenyon gravely raised his steamer cap and bade her 'Good-morning.'

'You are an early riser, Mr. Kenyon.'

'Not so early as you are, I see.'

'I think I am an exceptional passenger in that way,' replied the girl. 'I always enjoy the early morning at sea. I like to get as far forward on the steamer as possible, so that there is nothing between me and the boundless anywhere. Then it seems as if the world belongs to myself, with nobody else in it.'

'Isn't that a rather selfish view?' put in Kenyon.

'Oh, I don't think so. There is certainly nothing selfish in my enjoyment of it; but, you know, there are times when one wishes to be alone, and to forget everybody.'

'I hope I have not stumbled upon one of those times.'

'Oh, not at all, Mr. Kenyon,' replied his companion, laughing. 'There was nothing personal in the remark. If I wished to be alone, I would have no hesitation in walking off. I am not given to hinting; I speak plainly—some of my friends think a little too plainly. Have you ever been on the Pacific Ocean?'

'Never.'

'Ah, there the mornings are delicious. It is very beautiful here now, but in summer on the Pacific some of the mornings are so calm and peaceful and fresh, that it would seem as if the world had been newly made.'

'You have travelled a great deal, Miss Longworth. I envy you.'

'I often think I am a person to be envied, but there may come a shipwreck one day, and then I shall not be in so enviable a position.'

'I sincerely hope you may never have such an experience.'

'Have you ever been shipwrecked, Mr. Kenyon?'

'Oh no; my travelling experiences are very limited. But to read of a shipwreck is bad enough.'

'We have had a most delightful voyage so far. Quite like summer. One can scarcely believe that we left America in the depth of winter, with snow everywhere and the thermometer ever so far below zero. Have you mended your deck-chair yet, sufficiently well to trust yourself upon it again?'

'Oh!' said Kenyon, with a laugh, 'you really must not make fun of my amateur carpentering like that. As I told you, I am a mining engineer, and if I cannot mend a deck-chair, what would you expect me to do with a mine?'

'Have you had much to do with mines?' asked the young woman.

'I am just beginning,' replied Kenyon; 'this, in fact, is one of my first commissions. I have been sent with my friend Wentworth to examine certain mines on the Ottawa River.'

'The Ottawa River!' cried Edith. 'Are you one of those who were sent out by the London Syndicate?'

'Yes,' answered Kenyon with astonishment. 'What do you know about it?'

'Oh, I know everything about it. Everything, except what the mining expert's report is to be, and that information, I suppose, you have; so, between the two of us, we know a great deal about the fortunes of the London Syndicate.'

'Really! I am astonished to meet a young lady who knows anything about the matter. I understood it was rather a secret combination up to the present.'

'Ah! but, you see, I am one of the syndicate.'

'You!'

'Certainly,' answered Edith Longworth, laughing. 'At least, my father is, and that is the same thing, or almost the same thing. We intended to go to Canada ourselves, and I was very much disappointed at not going. I understand that the sleighing, and the snowshoeing, and the tobogganing are something wonderful.'

'I saw very little of the social side of life in the district, my whole time being employed at the mines; but even in the mining village where we stayed, they had a snowshoe club, and a very good toboggan slide—so good, in fact, that, having gone down once, I never ventured to risk my life on it again.'

'If my father knew you were on board, he would be anxious to meet you. Doubtless you know the London Syndicate will be a very large company.'

'Yes, I am aware of that.'

'And you know that a great deal is going to depend upon your report?'

'I suppose that is so, and I hope the syndicate will find my report at least an honest and thorough one.'

'Is the colleague who was with you also on board?'

'Yes, he is here.'

'He, then, was the accountant who was sent out?'

'Yes, and he is a man who does his business very thoroughly, and I think the syndicate will be satisfied with his work.'

'And do you not think they will be satisfied with yours also? I am sure you did your work conscientiously.'

Kenyon almost blushed as the young woman made this remark, but she looked intently at him, and he saw that her thoughts were not on him, but on the large interests he represented.

'Were you favourably impressed with the Ottawa as a mining region?' she asked.

'Very much so,' he answered, and, anxious to turn the conversation away from his own report, he said: 'I was so much impressed with it that I secured the option of a mine there for myself.'

'Oh! do you intend to buy one of the mines there?'

Kenyon laughed.

'No, I am no capitalist seeking investment for my money, but I saw that the mine contained possibilities of producing a great deal of money for those who possess it. It is very much more valuable, in my opinion, than the owners themselves suspect; so I secured an option upon it for three months, and hope when I reach England to form a company to take it up.'

'Well, I am sure,' said the young lady, 'if you are confident that the mine is a good one, you could see no one who would help you more in that way than my father. He has been looking at a brewery business he thought of investing in, but which he has concluded to have nothing to do with, so he will be anxious to find something reliable in its place. How much would be required for the purchase of the mine you mention?'

'I was thinking of asking fifty thousand pounds for it,' said Kenyon, flushing, as he thought of his own temerity in more than doubling the price of the mine.

Wentworth and he had estimated the probable value of the mine, and had concluded that even selling it at that price—which would give them thirty thousand pounds to divide between them—they were selling a mine that was really worth very much more, and would soon pay tremendous dividends on the fifty thousand pounds. He expected the young woman to be impressed by the amount, and was, therefore, very much surprised when she said:

'Fifty thousand pounds! Is that all? Then I am afraid my father would have nothing to do with it. He only deals with large businesses, and a company with a capitalization of fifty thousand pounds I am sure he would not look at.'

'You talk of fifty thousand pounds,' said Kenyon, 'as if it were a mere trifle. To me it seems an immense fortune. I only wish I had it, or half of it.'

'You are not rich, then?' said the girl, with apparent interest.

'No,' replied the young man. 'Far otherwise.'

At that moment the elder Mr. Longworth appeared in the door of the companion-way, and looked up and down the deck.

'Oh, here you are,' he said, as his daughter sprang from her chair.

'Father,' she cried, 'let me introduce to you Mr. Kenyon, who is the mining expert sent out by our syndicate to look at the Ottawa mines.'

'I am pleased to meet you,' said the elder gentleman.

The capitalist sat down beside the mining engineer, and began, somewhat to Kenyon's embarrassment, to talk of the London Syndicate.

CHAPTER VI.

A few mornings later Wentworth worked his way, with much balancing and grasping of stanchions, along the deck, for the ship rolled fearfully, but the person he sought was nowhere visible. He thought he would go into the smoking-room, but changed his mind at the door, and turned down the companion-way to the main saloon. The tables had been cleared of the breakfast belongings, but on one of the small tables a white cloth had been laid, and at this spot of purity in the general desert of red plush sat Miss Brewster, who was complacently ordering what she wanted from a steward, who did not seem at all pleased in serving one who had disregarded the breakfast-hour, to the disarrangement of all saloon rules. The chief steward stood by a door and looked disapprovingly at the tardy guest. It was almost time to lay the tables for lunch, and the young woman was as calmly ordering her breakfast as if she had been the first person at table.

She looked up brightly at Wentworth, and smiled as he approached her.

'I suppose,' she began, 'I'm dreadfully late, and the steward looks as if he would like to scold me. How awfully the ship is rolling! Is there a storm?'

'No. She seems to be doing this sort of thing for amusement. Wants to make it interesting for the unfortunate passengers who are not good sailors, I suppose. She's doing it, too. There's scarcely anyone on deck.'

'Dear me! I thought we were having a dreadful storm. Is it raining?'

'No. It's a beautiful sunshiny day; without much wind either, in spite of all this row.'

'I suppose you have had your breakfast long ago?'

'So long since that I am beginning to look forward with pleasant anticipation to lunch.'

'Oh dear! I had no idea I was so late as that. Perhaps you had better scold me. Somebody ought to do it, and the steward seems a little afraid.'

'You over-estimate my courage. I am a little afraid, too.'

'Then you do think I deserve it?'

'I didn't say that, nor do I think it. I confess, however, that up to this moment I felt just a trifle lonely.'

'Just a trifle! Well, that is flattery. How nicely you English do turn a compliment! Just a trifle!'

'I believe, as a race, we do not venture much into compliment making at all. We leave that for the polite foreigner. He would say what I tried to say a great deal better than I did, of course, but he would not mean half so much.'

'Oh, that's very nice, Mr. Wentworth. No foreigner could have put it nearly so well. Now, what about going on deck?'

'Anywhere, if you let me accompany you.'

'I shall be most delighted to have you. I won't say merely a trifle delighted.'

'Ah! Haven't you forgiven that remark yet?'

'There's nothing to forgive, and it is quite too delicious to forget. I shall never forget it.'

'I believe that you are very cruel at heart, Miss Brewster.'

The young woman gave him a curious side-look, but did not answer. She gathered the wraps she had taken from her cabin, and, handing them to him before he had thought of offering to take them, she led the way to the deck. He found their chairs side by side, and admired the intelligence of the deck-steward, who seemed to understand which chairs to place together. Miss Jennie sank gracefully into her own, and allowed him to adjust the wraps around her.

'There,' she said, 'that's very nicely done; as well as the deck-steward himself could do it, and I am sure it is impossible to pay you a more graceful compliment than that. So few men know how to arrange one comfortably in a steamer chair.'

'You speak as though you had vast experience in steamer life, and yet you told me this was your first voyage.'

'It is. But it doesn't take a woman more than a day to see that the average man attends to such little niceties very clumsily. Now just tuck in the corner out of sight. There! Thank you, ever so much. And would you be kind enough to—Yes, that's better. And this other wrap so. Oh, that is perfect. What a patient man you are, Mr. Wentworth!'

'Yes, Miss Brewster. You are a foreigner. I can see that now. Your professed compliment was hollow. You said I did it perfectly, and then immediately directed me how to do it.'

'Nothing of the kind. You did it well, and I think you ought not to grudge me the pleasure of adding my own little improvements.'

'Oh, if you put it in that way, I will not. Now, before I sit down, tell me what book I can get that will interest you. The library contains a very good assortment.'

'I don't think I care about reading. Sit down and talk. I suppose I am too indolent to-day. I thought, when I came on board, that I would do a lot of reading, but I believe the sea-air makes one lazy. I must confess I feel entirely indifferent to mental improvement.'

'You evidently do not think my conversation will be at all worth listening to.'

'How quick you are to pervert my meaning! Don't you see that I think your conversation better worth listening to than the most interesting or improving book you can choose from the library? Really, in trying to avoid giving you cause for making such a remark, I have apparently stumbled into a worse error. I was just going to say I would like your conversation much better than a book, when I thought you would take that as a reflection on your reading. If you take me up so sharply I will sit here and say nothing. Now then, talk!'

'What shall I say?'

'Oh, if I told you what to say I should be doing the talking. Tell me about yourself. What do you do in London?'

'I work hard. I am an accountant.'

'And what is an accountant? What does he do? Keep accounts?'

'Some of them do; I do not. I see, rather, that accounts which other people keep have been correctly kept.'

'Aren't they always correctly kept? I thought that was what book-keepers were hired for.'

'If books were always correctly kept there would be little for us to do; but it happens, unfortunately for some, but fortunately for us, that people occasionally do not keep their accounts accurately.'

'And can you always find that out if you examine the books?'

'Always.'

'Can't a man make up his accounts so that no one can tell there is anything wrong?'

'The belief that such a thing can be done has placed many a poor wretch in prison. It has been tried often enough.'

'I am sure they can do it in the States. I have read of it being done and continued for years. Men have made off with great sums of money by falsifying the books, and no one found it out until the one who did it died or ran away.'

'Nevertheless, if an expert accountant had been called in, he would have found out very soon that something was wrong, and just where the wrong was, and how much.'

'I didn't think such cleverness possible. Have you ever discovered anything like that?'

'I have.'

'What is done when such a thing is discovered?'

'That depends upon circumstances. Usually a policeman is called in.'

'Why, it's like being a detective. I wish you would tell me about some of the cases you have had. Don't make me ask so many questions. Talk.'

'I don't think my experiences would interest you in the least. There was one case with which I had something to do in London, two years ago, that——'

'Oh, London! I don't believe the book-keepers there are half so sharp as ours. If you had to deal with American accountants, you would not find out so easily what they had or had not done.'

'Well, Miss Brewster, I may say I have just had an experience of that kind with some of your very sharpest American book-keepers. I found that the books had been kept in the most ingenious way with the intent to deceive. The system had been going on for years.'

'How interesting! And did you call in a policeman?'

'No. This was one of the cases where a policeman was not necessary. The books were kept with the object of showing that the profits of the m—of the business—had been much greater than they really were. I may say that one of your American accountants had already looked over the books, and, whether through ignorance or carelessness, or from a worse motive, he reported them all right. They were not all right, and the fact that they were not, will mean the loss of a fortune to some people on your side of the water, and the saving of good money to others on my side.'

'Then I think your profession must be a very important one.'

'We think so, Miss Brewster. I would like to be paid a percentage on the money saved because of my report.'

'And won't you?'

'Unfortunately, no.'

'I think that is too bad. I suppose the discrepancy must have been small, or the American accountant would not have overlooked it?'

'I didn't say he overlooked it. Still, the size of a discrepancy does not make any difference. A small error is as easily found as a large one. This one was large. I suppose there is no harm in my saying that the books, taking them together, showed a profit of forty thousand pounds, when they should have shown a loss of nearly half that amount. I hope nobody overhears me.'

'No; we are quite alone, and you may be sure I will not breathe a word of what you have been telling me.'

'Don't breathe it to Kenyon, at least. He would think me insane if he knew what I have said.'

'Is Mr. Kenyon an accountant, too?'

'Oh no. He is a mineralogist. He can go into a mine, and tell with reasonable certainty whether it will pay the working or not. Of course, as he says himself, any man can see six feet into the earth as well as he can. But it is not every man that can gauge the value of a working mine so well as John Kenyon.'

'Then, while you were delving among the figures, your companion was delving among the minerals?'

'Precisely.'

'And did he make any such startling discovery as you did?'

'No; rather the other way. He finds the mines very good properties, and he thinks that if they were managed intelligently they would be good paying investments—that is, at a proper price, you know—not at what the owners ask for them at present. But you can have no possible interest in these dry details.'

'Indeed, you are mistaken. I think what you have told me intensely interesting.'

For once in her life Miss Jennie Brewster told the exact truth. The unfortunate man at her side was flattered.

'For what I have told you,' he said, 'we were offered twice what the London people pay us for coming out here. In fact, even more than that: we were asked to name our own price.'

'Really now! By the owners of the property, I suppose, if you wouldn't tell on them?'

'No. By one of your famous New York newspaper men. He even went so far as to steal the papers that Kenyon had in Ottawa. He was cleverly caught, though, before he could make any use of what he had stolen. In fact, unless his people in New York had the figures which were originally placed before the London Board, I doubt if my statistics would have been of much use to him even if he had been allowed to keep them. The full significance of my report will not show until the figures I have given are compared with those already in the hands of the London people, which were vouched for as correct by your clever American accountant.'

'You shouldn't run down an accountant just because he is American. Perhaps there will come a day, Mr. Wentworth, when you will admit that there are Americans who are more clever than either that accountant or that newspaper man. I don't think your specimens are typical.'

'I don't "run down," as you call it, the men because they are Americans. I "run down" the accountant because he was either ignorant or corrupt. I "run down" the newspaper man because he was a thief.'

Miss Brewster was silent for a few moments. She was impressing on her memory what he had said to her, and was anxious to get away, so that she could write out in her cabin exactly what had been told her. The sound of the lunch-gong gave her the excuse she needed, so, bidding her victim a pleasant and friendly farewell, she hurried from the deck to her state-room.

CHAPTER VII.

One morning, when Kenyon went to his state-room on hearing the breakfast-gong, he found the lazy occupant of the upper berth still in his bunk.

'Come, Wentworth,' he shouted, 'this won't do, you know. Get up! get up! breakfast, my boy! breakfast!—the most important meal in the day to a healthy man.'

Wentworth yawned and stretched his arms over his head.

'What's the row?' he asked.

'The row is, it's time to get up. The second gong has sounded.'

'Dear me! is it so late? I didn't hear it.' Wentworth sat up in his bunk, and looked ruefully over the precipice down the chasm to the floor. 'Have you been up long?' he asked.

'Long? I have been on deck an hour and a half,' answered Kenyon.

'Then, Miss What's-her-Name must have been there also.'

'Her name is Miss Longworth,' replied Kenyon, without looking at his comrade.

'That's her name, is it? and she was on deck?'

'She was.'

'I thought so,' said Wentworth; 'just look at the divine influence of woman! Miss Longworth rises early, therefore John Kenyon rises early. Miss Brewster rises late, therefore George Wentworth is not seen until breakfast-time. If the conditions were reversed, I suppose the getting-up time of the two men would be changed accordingly.'

'Not at all, George—not at all. I would rise early whether anybody else on board did or not. In fact, when I got on deck this morning, I expected to have it to myself.'

'I take it, though, that you were not grievously disappointed when you found you hadn't a monopoly?'

'Well, to tell the truth, I was not; Miss Longworth is a charmingly sensible girl.'

'Oh, they all are,' said Wentworth lightly. 'You had no sympathy for me the other day. Now you know how it is yourself, as they say across the water.'

'I don't know how it is myself. The fact is, we were talking business.'

'Really? Did you get so far?'

'Yes, we got so far, if that is any distance. I told her about the mica-mine.'

'Oh, you did! What did she say? Will she invest?'

'Well, when I told her we expected to form a company for fifty thousand pounds, she said it was such a small sum, she doubted if we could get anybody interested in it in London.'

Wentworth, who was now well advanced with his dressing, gave a long whistle.

'Fifty thousand pounds a small sum? Why, John, she must be very wealthy! Probably more so than the American millionairess.'

'Well, George, you see, the difference between the two young ladies is this: that while American heiresses are apt to boast of their immense wealth, English women say nothing about it.'

'If you mean Miss Brewster when you speak in that way, you are entirely mistaken. She has never alluded to her wealth at all, with the exception of saying that her father was a millionaire. So if the young woman you speak of has been talking of her wealth at all, she has done more than the American girl.'

'She said nothing to indicate she was wealthy. I merely conjectured it when I discovered she looked upon fifty thousand pounds as a triviality.'

'Well, the fault is easily remedied. We may raise the price of the mine to one hundred thousand pounds if we can get people to invest. Perhaps the young lady's father might care to go in for it at that figure.'

'Oh, by the way, Wentworth,' said Kenyon, 'I forgot to tell you, Miss Longworth's father is one of the London Syndicate.'

'By Jove! are you sure of that? How do you know? You weren't talking of our mission out there, were you?'

'Certainly not,' replied Kenyon, flushing. 'You don't think I would speak of that to a stranger, do you? nor of anything concerned with our reports.'

Wentworth proceeded with his dressing, a guilty feeling rising in his heart.

'I want to ask you a question about that.'

'About what?' said Wentworth shortly.

'About those mines. Miss Longworth's father being a member of the London Syndicate, suppose he asks what our views in relation to the matter are: would we be justified in telling him anything?'

'He won't ask me as I don't know him; he may ask you, and if he does, then you will have to decide the question for yourself.'

'Would you say anything about it if you were in my place?'

'Oh, I don't know. If we were certain it was all right—if you are sure he is a member of the syndicate, and he happens to ask you about it, I scarcely see how you can avoid telling him.'

'It would be embarrassing; so I hope he won't ask me. We should not speak of it until we give in our reports. He knows, however, that you are the accountant who has that part of the business in charge.'

'Oh, then you have been talking with him?'

'Just a moment or two, after his daughter introduced me.'

'What did you say his name was?'

'John Longworth, I believe. I am sure about the Longworth, but not about the John.'

'Oh, old John Longworth in the City! Certainly; I know all about him. I never saw him before, but I think we are quite safe in telling him anything he wants to know, if he asks.'

'Breakfast, gentlemen,' said the steward, putting his head in at the door.

After breakfast Edith Longworth and her cousin walked the deck together. Young Longworth, although in better humour than he had been the night before, was still rather short in his replies, and irritating in his questions.

'Aren't you tired of this eternal parade up and down?' he asked his cousin. 'It seems to me like a treadmill—as if a person had to work for his board and lodging.'

'Let us sit down then,' she replied; 'although I think a walk before lunch or dinner increases the attractiveness of those meals wonderfully.'

'I never feel the need of working up an appetite,' he answered pettishly.

'Well, as I said before, let us sit down;' and the girl, having found her chair, lifted the rug that lay upon it, and took her place.

The young man, after standing for a moment looking at her through his glistening monocle, finally sat down beside her.

'The beastly nuisance of living on board ship,' he said, 'is that you can't play billiards.'

'I am sure you play enough at cards to satisfy you during the few days we are at sea,' she answered.

'Oh, cards! I soon tire of them.'

'You tire very quickly of everything.'

'I certainly get tired of lounging about the deck, either walking or sitting.'

'Then, pray don't let me keep you.'

'You want me to go so you may walk with your newly-found friend, that miner fellow?'

'That miner fellow is talking with my father just now. Still, if you would like to know, I have no hesitation in telling you I would much prefer his company to yours if you continue in your present mood.'

'Yes, or in any mood.'

'I did not say that; but if it will comfort you to have me say it, I shall be glad to oblige you.'

'Perhaps, then, I should go and talk with your father, and let the miner fellow come here and talk with you.'

'Please do not call him the miner fellow. His name is Mr. Kenyon. It is not difficult to remember.'

'I know his name well enough. Shall I send him to you?'

'No. I want to talk with you in spite of your disagreeableness. And what is more, I want to talk with you about Mr. Kenyon. So I wish you to assume your very best behaviour. It may be for your benefit.'

The young man indulged in a sarcastic laugh.

'Oh, if you are going to do that, I have nothing more to say,' remarked Edith quietly, rising from her chair.

'I meant no harm. Sit down and go on with your talk.'

'Listen, then. Mr. Kenyon has the option of a mine in Canada, which he believes to be a good property. He intends to form a company when he reaches London. Now, why shouldn't you make friends with him, and, if you found the property is as good as he thinks it is, help him to form the company, and so make some money for both of you?'

'You are saying one word for me and two for Kenyon.'

'No, it would be as much for your benefit as for his, so it is a word for each of you.'

'You are very much interested in him.'

'My dear cousin, I am very much interested in the mine, and I am very much interested in you. Mr. Kenyon can speak of nothing but the mine, and I am sure my father would be pleased to see you take an interest in something of the sort. I mean, you know that if you would do something of your own accord—something that was not suggested to you by him—he would like it.'

'Well, it is suggested to me by you, and that's almost the same thing.'

'No, it is not the same thing at all. Father would indeed be glad if he saw you take up anything on your own account and make a success of it. Why can you not spend some of your time talking with Mr. Kenyon discussing arrangements, so that when you return to London you might be prepared to put the mine on the market and bring out the company?'

'If I thought you were talking to me for my own sake, I would do what you suggest; but I believe you are speaking only because you are interested in Kenyon.'

'Nonsense! How can you be so absurd? I have known Mr. Kenyon but for a few hours—a day or two at most.'

The young man pulled his moustache for a moment, adjusted his eyeglass, and then said:

'Very good. I will speak to Kenyon on the subject if you wish it, but I don't say that I can help him.'

'I don't ask you to help him. I ask you to help yourself. Here is Mr. Kenyon. Let me introduce you, and then you can talk over the project at your leisure.'

'I don't suppose an introduction is necessary,' growled the young man; but as Kenyon approached them, Edith Longworth said:

'We are a board of directors, Mr. Kenyon, on the great mica-mine. Will

241

you join the Board now, or after allotment?' Then, before he could reply, she said: 'Mr. Kenyon, this is my cousin, Mr. William Longworth.'

Longworth, without rising from his chair, shook hands in rather a surly fashion.

'I am going to speak to my father,' said the girl, 'and will leave you to talk over the mica-mine.'

When she had gone, young Longworth asked Kenyon:

'Where is the mine my cousin speaks of?'

'It is near the Ottawa River, in Canada,' was the answer.

'And what do you expect to sell it for?'

'Fifty thousand pounds.'

'Fifty thousand pounds! That will leave nothing to divide up among— by the way, how many are there in this thing—yourself alone?'

'No; my friend Wentworth shares with me.'

'Share and share alike?'

'Yes.'

'Of course, you think this mine is worth the money you ask for it— there is no swindle about it, is there?'

Kenyon drew himself up sharply as this remark was made. Then he answered coldly:

'If there was any swindle about it, I should have nothing to do with it.'

'Well, you see, I didn't know; mining swindles are not such rarities as you may imagine. If the mine is so valuable, why are the proprietors anxious to sell?'

'The owners are in Austria, and the mine in Canada, and so it is rather at arm's-length, as it were. They are mining for mica, but the mine is more valuable in other respects than it is as a mica property. They have placed a figure on the mine which is more than it has cost them so far.'

'You know its value in those other respects?'

'I do.'

'Does anyone know this except yourself?'

'I think not—no one but my friend Wentworth.'

'How did you come to learn its value?'

'By visiting the mine. Wentworth and I went together to see it.'

'Oh, is Wentworth also a mining expert?'

'No; he is an accountant in London.'

'Both of you were sent out by the London Syndicate, I understand, to look after their mines, or the mines they thought of purchasing, were you not?'

'We were.'

'And you spent your time in looking up other properties for yourselves, did you?'

Kenyon reddened at this question.

'My dear sir,' he said, 'if you are going to talk in this strain, you will have to excuse me. We were sent by the London Syndicate to do a certain thing. We did it, and did it thoroughly. After it was done the time was our own, as much as it is at the present moment. We were not hired by the day, but took a stated sum for doing a certain piece of work. I may go further and say that the time was our own at any period of our visit, so long as we fulfilled what the London Syndicate required of us.'

'Oh, I meant no offence,' said Longworth. 'You merely seemed to be posing as a sort of goody-goody young man when I spoke of mining swindles, so I only wished to startle you. How much have you to pay for the mine—

that is the mica-mine?'

Kenyon hesitated for a moment.

'I do not feel at liberty to mention the sum until I have consulted with my friend Wentworth.'

'Well, you see, if I am to help you in this matter, I shall need to know every particular.'

'Certainly. I shall have to consult Wentworth as to whether we require any help or not.'

'Oh, you will speedily find that you require all the help you can get in London. You will probably learn that a hundred such mines are for sale now, and the chances are you will find that this very mica-mine has been offered. What do you believe the mine is really worth?'

'I think it is worth anywhere from one hundred thousand pounds to two hundred thousand pounds, perhaps more.'

'Is it actually worth one hundred thousand pounds?'

'According to my estimate, it is.'

'Is it worth one hundred and fifty thousand pounds?'

'It is.'

'Is it worth two hundred thousand pounds?'

'I think so.'

'What percentage would it pay on two hundred thousand pounds?'

'It might pay ten per cent., perhaps more.'

'Why, in the name of all that is wonderful, don't you put the price at two hundred thousand pounds? If it will pay ten per cent and more on that amount of money, then that sum is what you ought to sell it for. Now we will investigate this matter, if you like, and if you wish to take me in with you, and put the price up to two hundred thousand pounds, I will see what can be done about it when we get to London. Of course, it will mean somebody going out to Canada again to report on the mine. Your report would naturally not be taken in such a case; you are too vitally interested.'

'Of course,' replied Kenyon, 'I shouldn't expect my report to have any weight.'

'Well, somebody would have to be sent out to report on the mine. Are you certain that it will stand thorough investigation?'

'I am convinced of it.'

'Would you be willing to make this proposition to the investors, that, if the expert did not support your statement, you would pay his expenses out there and back?'

'I would be willing to do that,' said Kenyon, 'if I had the money; but I haven't the money.'

'Then, how do you expect to float the mine on the London market? It cannot be done without money.'

'I thought I might be able to interest some capitalist.'

'I am much afraid, Mr. Kenyon, that you have vague ideas of how companies are formed. Perhaps your friend Wentworth, being an accountant, may know more about it.'

'Yes, I confess I am relying mainly on his assistance.'

'Well, will you agree to put the price of the mine at two hundred thousand pounds, and share what we make equally between the three of us?'

'It is a large price.'

'It is not a large price if the mine will pay good dividends upon it; if it will pay eight per cent. on that amount, it is the real price of the mine, while you say that you are certain it will pay ten per cent.'

'I say I think it will pay that percentage. One never can speak with entire certainty where a mine is concerned.'

'Are you willing to put the price of the mine at that figure? Otherwise, I will have nothing to do with it.'

'As I said, I shall have to consult my friend about it, but that can be done in a very short time, and I will answer you in the afternoon.'

'Good; there is no particular hurry. Have a talk over it with him, and while I do not promise anything, I think the scheme looks feasible, if the property is good. Remember, I know nothing at all about that, but if you agree to take me in, I shall have to know full particulars of what you are going to pay for the property, and what its peculiar value is.'

'Certainly. If we agree to take a partner, we will give that partner our full confidence.'

'Well, there is nothing more to say until you have had a consultation with your friend. Good-morning, Mr. Kenyon;' and with that Longworth arose and lounged off to the smoking-room.

Kenyon waited where he was for some time, hoping Wentworth would come along, but the young man did not appear. At last he went in search of him. He passed along the deck, but found no trace of his friend, and looked for a moment into the smoking-room, but Wentworth was not there. He went downstairs to the saloon, but his search below was equally fruitless. Coming up on deck again, he saw Miss Brewster sitting alone reading a paper-covered novel.

'Have you seen my friend Wentworth?' he asked.

She laid the book open-faced upon her lap, and looked quickly up at Kenyon before answering.

'I saw him not so very long ago, but I don't know where he is now. Perhaps you will find him in his state-room; in fact, I think it more than likely that he is there.'

With that, Miss Brewster resumed her book.

Kenyon descended to the state-room, opened the door, and saw his comrade sitting upon the plush-covered sofa, with his head in his hands. At the opening of the door, Wentworth started and looked for a moment at his friend, apparently not seeing him. His face was so gray and ghastly that Kenyon leaned against the door for support as he saw it.

'My God, George!' he cried, 'what is the matter with you? What has happened? Tell me!'

Wentworth gazed in front of him with glassy eyes for a moment, but did not answer. Then his head dropped again in his hands, and he groaned aloud.

CHAPTER VIII.

There was one man on board the Caloric to whom Wentworth had taken an extreme dislike. His name was Fleming, and he claimed to be a New York politician. As none of his friends or enemies asserted anything worse about him, it may be assumed that Fleming had designated his occupation correctly. If Wentworth were asked what he most disliked about the man, he would probably have said his offensive familiarity. Fleming seemed to think himself a genial good fellow, and he was immensely popular with a certain class in the smoking-room. He was lavishly free with his invitations to drink, and always had a case of good cigars in his pocket, which he bestowed with great liberality. He had the habit of slapping a man boisterously on the back, and saying, 'Well, old fellow, how are you? How's things?' He usually confided to his listeners that he was a self-made man: had landed at New York without a cent in his pocket, and look at him now!

Wentworth was icy towards this man; but frigidity had no effect whatever on the exuberant spirits of the New York politician.

'Well, old man!' cried Fleming to Wentworth, as he came up to the latter and linked arms affectionately. 'What lovely weather we are having for winter time!'

'It is good,' said Wentworth.

'Good? It's glorious! Who would have thought, when leaving New York in a snowstorm as we did, that we would run right into the heart of spring? I hope you are enjoying your voyage?'

'I am.'

'You ought to. By the way, why are you so awful stand-offish? Is it natural, or merely put on "for this occasion only"?'

'I do not know what you mean by "stand-offish."'

'You know very well what I mean. Why do you pretend to be so stiff and formal with a fellow?'

'I am never stiff and formal with anyone unless I do not desire his acquaintance.'

Fleming laughed loudly.

'I suppose that's a personal hint. Well, it seems to me, if this exclusiveness is genuine, that you would be more afraid of newspaper notoriety than of anything else.'

'Why do you say that?'

'Because I can't, for the life of me, see why you spend so much time with Dolly Dimple. I am sure I don't know why she is here; but I do know this: that you will be served up to the extent of two or three columns in the Sunday Argus as sure as you live.'

'I don't understand you.'

'You don't? Why, it's plain enough. You spend all your time with her.'

'I do not even know of whom you are speaking.'

'Oh, come now, that's too rich! Is it possible you don't know that Miss Jennie Brewster is the one who writes those Sunday articles over the signature of "Dolly Dimple"?'

A strange fear fell upon Wentworth as his companion mentioned the Argus. He remembered it as J.K. Rivers' paper; but when Fleming said Miss Brewster was a correspondent of the Argus, he was aghast.

'I—I—I don't think I quite catch your meaning,' he stammered.

'Well, my meaning's easy enough to see. Hasn't she ever told you? Then it shows she wants to do you up on toast. You're not an English politician, are you? You haven't any political secrets that Dolly wants to get at, have you? Why, she is the greatest girl there is in the whole United States for finding out just what a man doesn't want to have known. You know the Secretary of State'—and here Fleming went on to relate a wonderfully brilliant feat of

Dolly's; but the person to whom he was talking had neither eyes nor ears. He heard nothing and he saw nothing.

'Dear me!' said Fleming, drawing himself up and slapping the other on the back, 'you look perfectly dumfounded. I suppose I oughtn't to have given Dolly away like this; but she has pretended all along that she didn't know me, and so I've got even with her. You take my advice, and anything you don't want to see in print, don't tell Miss Brewster, that's all. Have a cigar?'

'No, thank you,' replied the other mechanically.

'Better come in and have a drink.'

'No, thank you.'

'Well, so long. I'll see you later.'

'It can't be true—it can't be true!' Wentworth repeated to himself in deep consternation, but still an inward misgiving warned him that, after all, it might be true. With his hands clasped behind him he walked up and down, trying to collect himself—trying to remember what he had told and what he had not. As he walked along, heeding nobody, a sweet voice from one of the chairs thrilled him, and he paused.

'Why, Mr. Wentworth, what is the matter with you this morning? You look as if you had seen a ghost.'

Wentworth glanced at the young woman seated in the chair, who was gazing up brightly at him.

'Well,' he said at last, 'I am not sure but I have seen a ghost. May I sit down beside you?'

'May you? Why, of course you may. I shall be delighted to have you. Is there anything wrong?'

'I don't know. Yes, I think there is.'

'Well, tell it to me; perhaps I can help you. A woman's wit, you know. What is the trouble?'

'May I ask you a few questions, Miss Brewster?'

'Certainly. A thousand of them, if you like, and I will answer them all if I can.'

'Thank you. Will you tell me, Miss Brewster, if you are connected with any newspaper?'

Miss Brewster laughed her merry, silvery little laugh.

'Who told you? Ah! I see how it is. It was that creature Fleming. I'll get even with him for this some day. I know what office he is after, and the next time he wants a good notice from the Argus he'll get it; see if he don't. I know some things about him that he would just as soon not see in print. Why, what a fool the man is! I suppose he told you out of revenge because I wouldn't speak to him the other evening. Never mind; I can afford to wait.'

'Then—then, Miss Brewster, it is true?'

'Certainly it is true; is there anything wrong about it? I hope you don't think it is disreputable to belong to a good newspaper?'

'To a good newspaper, no; to a bad newspaper, yes.'

'Oh, I don't think the Argus is a bad newspaper. It pays me well.'

'Then it is to the Argus that you belong?'

'Certainly.'

'May I ask, Miss Brewster, if there is anything I have spoken about to you that you intend to use in your paper?'

Again Miss Brewster laughed.

'I will be perfectly frank with you. I never tell a lie—it doesn't pay. Yes. The reason I am here is because you are here. I am here to find out what your report on those mines will be, also what the report of your friend will be. I have found out.'

'And do you intend to use the information you have thus obtained—if

I may say it—under false pretences?'

'My dear sir, you are forgetting yourself. You must remember that you are talking to a lady.'

'A lady!' cried Wentworth in his anguish.

'Yes, sir, a lady; and you must be careful how you talk to this lady. There was no false pretence about it, if you remember. What you told me was in conversation; I didn't ask you for it. I didn't even make the first advances towards your acquaintance.'

'But you must admit, Miss Brewster, that it is very unfair to get a man to engage in what he thinks is a private conversation, and then to publish what he has said.'

'My dear sir, if that were the case, how would we get anything for publication that people didn't want to be known? Why, I remember once, when the Secretary of State——'

'Yes,' interrupted Wentworth wearily; 'Fleming told me that story.'

'Oh, did he? Well, I'm sure I'm much obliged to him. Then I need not repeat it.'

'Do you mean to say that you intend to send to the Argus for publication what I have told you in confidence?'

'Certainly. As I said before, that is what I am here for. Besides, there was no "in confidence" about it.'

'And yet you pretend to be a truthful, honest, honourable woman?'

'I don't pretend it; I am.'

'How much truth, then, is there in your story that you are a millionaire's daughter about to visit your father in Paris, and accompany him from there to the Riviera?'

Miss Brewster laughed brightly.

'Oh, I don't call fibs, which a person has to tell in the way of business, untruths.'

'Then probably you do not think your estimable colleague, Mr. J.K. Rivers, behaved dishonourably in Ottawa?'

'Well, hardly. I think Rivers was not justified in what he did because he was unsuccessful, that is all. I'll bet a dollar if I had got hold of these papers they would have gone through to New York; but, then, J.K. Rivers is only a stupid man, and most men are stupid'—with a sly glance at Wentworth.

'I am willing to admit that, Miss Brewster, if you mean me. There never was a more stupid man than I have been.'

'My dear Mr. Wentworth, it will do you ever so much good if you come to a realization of that fact. The truth is, you take yourself much too seriously. Now, it won't hurt you a bit to have what I am going to send published in the Argus, and it will help me a great deal. Just you wait here for a few moments.'

With that she flung her book upon his lap, sprang up, and vanished down the companion-way. In a very short time she reappeared with some sheets of paper in her hand.

'Now you see how fair and honest I am going to be. I am going to read you what I have written. If there is anything in it that is not true, I will very gladly cut it out; and if there is anything more to be added, I shall be very glad to add it. Isn't that fair?'

Wentworth was so confounded with the woman's impudence that he could make no reply.

She began to read: '"By an unexampled stroke of enterprise the New York Argus is enabled this morning to lay before its readers a full and exclusive account of the report made by the two English specialists, Mr. George Wentworth and Mr. John Kenyon, who were sent over by the London Syndicate to examine into the accounts, and inquire into the true value of the mines of the Ottawa River."'

She looked up from the paper, and said, with an air of friendly confidence:

'I shouldn't send that if I thought the people at the New York end would know enough to write it themselves; but as the paper is edited by dull men, and not by a sharp woman, I have to make them pay twenty-five cents a word for puffing their own enterprise. Well, to go on: "When it is remembered that the action of the London Syndicate will depend entirely on the report of these two gentlemen—"'

'I wouldn't put it that way,' interrupted Wentworth in his despair. 'I would use the word "largely" for "entirely."'

'Oh, thank you,' said Miss Brewster cordially. She placed the manuscript on her knee, and, with her pencil, marked out the word 'entirely,' substituting 'largely.' The reading went on: '"When it is remembered that the action of the London Syndicate will depend largely on the report of these two gentlemen, the enterprise of the Argus in getting this exclusive information, which will be immediately cabled to London, may be imagined." That is the preliminary, you see; and, as I said, it wouldn't be necessary to cable it if women were at the head of affairs over there, which they are not. "Mr. John Kenyon, the mining expert, has visited all the mineral ranges along the Ottawa River, and his report is that the mines are very much what is claimed for them; but he thinks they are not worked properly, although, with judicious management and more careful mining, the properties can be made to pay good dividends. Mr. George Wentworth, who is one of the leading accountants of London—"'

'I wouldn't say that, either,' groaned George. 'Just strike out the words "one of the leading accountants of London."'

'Yes?' said Miss Brewster; 'and what shall I put in the place of them?'

'Put in place of them "the stupidest ass in London"!'

Miss Brewster laughed at that.

'No; I shall put in what I first wrote: "Mr. George Wentworth, one of the leading accountants of London, has gone through the books of the different mines. He has made some startling discoveries. The accounts have been kept in such a way as to completely delude investors, and this fact will have a powerful effect on the minds of the London Syndicate. The books of the different mines show a profit of about two hundred thousand dollars, whereas the actual facts of the case are that there has been an annual loss of something like one hundred thousand dollars—'"

'What's that? what's that?' cried Wentworth sharply.

'Dollars, you know. You said twenty thousand pounds. We put it in dollars, don't you see?'

'Oh,' said Wentworth, relapsing again.

'"One hundred thousand dollars"—where was I? Oh yes. "It is claimed that an American expert went over these books before Mr. Wentworth, and that he asserted they were all right. An explanation from this gentleman will now be in order."'

'There!' cried the young lady, 'that is the substance of the thing. Of course, I may amplify a little more before we get to Queenstown, so as to make them pay more money. People don't value a thing that doesn't cost them dearly. How do you like it? Is it correct?'

'Perfectly correct,' answered the miserable young man.

'Oh, I am so glad you like it! I do love to have things right.'

'I didn't say I liked it.'

'No, of course, you couldn't be expected to say that; but I am glad you think it is accurate. I will add a note to the effect that you think it is a good résumé of your report.'

'For Heaven's sake, don't drag me into the matter!' cried Wentworth.

'Well, I won't, if you don't want me to.'

There was silence for a few moments, during which the young woman seemed to be adding commas and full-stops to the MS. on her knee. Wentworth cleared his throat two or three times, but his lips were so dry that he could hardly speak. At last he said:

'Miss Brewster, how can I induce you not to send that from Queenstown to your paper?'

The young woman looked up at him with a pleasant bright smile.

'Induce me? Why, you couldn't do it—it couldn't be done. This will be one of the greatest triumphs I have ever achieved. Think of Rivers failing in it, and me accomplishing it!'

'Yes; I have thought of that,' replied the young man despondently. 'Now, perhaps you don't know that the full report was mailed from Ottawa to our house in London, and the moment we get to Queenstown I will telegraph my partners to put the report in the hands of the directors?'

'Oh, I know all about that,' replied Miss Brewster; 'Rivers told me. He read the letter that was enclosed with the documents he took from your friend. Now, have you made any calculations about this voyage?'

'Calculations? I don't know what you mean.'

'Well, I mean just this: We shall probably reach Queenstown on Saturday afternoon. This report, making allowance for the difference in the time, will appear in the Argus on Sunday morning. Your telegram will reach your house or your firm on Saturday night, when nothing can be done with it. Sunday nothing can be done. Monday morning, before your report will reach the directors, the substance of what has appeared in the Argus will be in the financial papers, cabled over to London on Sunday night. The first thing your directors will see of it will be in the London financial papers on Monday morning. That's what I mean, Mr. Wentworth, by calculating the voyage.'

Wentworth said no more. He staggered to his feet and made his way as best he could to the state-room, groping like a blind man. There he sat down with his head in his hands, and there his friend Kenyon found him.

CHAPTER IX.

'Tell me what has happened,' demanded John Kenyon.

Wentworth looked up at him.

'Everything has happened,' he answered.

'What do you mean, George? Are you ill? What is the matter with you?'

'I am worse than ill, John—a great deal worse than ill. I wish I were ill.'

'That wouldn't help things, whatever is wrong. Come, wake up. Tell me what the trouble is.'

'John, I am a fool—an ass—a gibbering idiot.'

'Admitting that, what then?'

'I trusted a woman—imbecile that I am; and now—now—I'm what you see me.'

'Has—has Miss Brewster anything to do with it?' asked Kenyon suspiciously.

'She has everything to do with it.'

'Has she—rejected you, George?'

'What! that girl? Oh, you're the idiot now. Do you think I would ask her?'

'I cannot be blamed for jumping at conclusions. You must remember "that girl," as you call her, has had most of your company during this voyage; and most of your good words when you were not with her. What is the matter? What has she to do with your trouble?'

Wentworth paced up and down the narrow limits of the state-room as if he were caged. He smote his hand against his thigh, while Kenyon looked at him in wonder.

'I don't know how I can tell you, John,' he said. 'I must, of course; but I don't know how I can.'

'Come on deck with me.'

'Never.'

'Come out, I say, into the fresh air. It is stuffy here, and, besides, there is more danger of being overheard in the state-room than on deck. Come along, old fellow.'

He caught his companion by the arm, and partly dragged him out of the room, closing the door behind him.

'Pull yourself together,' he said. 'A little fresh air will do you good.'

They made their way to the deck, and, linking arms, walked up and down. For a long time Wentworth said nothing, and Kenyon had the tact to hold his peace. Suddenly Wentworth noticed that they were pacing back and forth in front of Miss Brewster, so he drew his friend away to another part of the ship. After a few turns up and down, he said:

'You remember Rivers, of course.'

'Distinctly.'

'He was employed on that vile sheet, the New York Argus.'

'I suppose it is a vile sheet. I don't remember ever seeing it. Yes, I know he was connected with that paper. What then? What has Miss Brewster to do with Rivers?'

'She is one of the Argus staff, too.'

'George Wentworth, you don't mean to tell me that!'

'I do.'

'And is she here to find out about the mine?'

'Exactly. She was put on the job after Rivers had failed.'

'George!' said Kenyon, suddenly dropping his companion's arm and facing him. 'What have you told her?'

'There is the misery of it. I have told her everything.'

'My dear fellow, how could you be——'

'Oh, I know—I know! I know everything you would say. Everything you can say I have said to myself, and ten times more and ten times worse. There is nothing you can say of me more bitter than what I think about myself.'

'Did you tell her anything about my report?'

'I told her everything—everything! Do you understand? She is going to telegraph from Queenstown the full essence of the reports—of both our reports.'

'Heavens! this is fearful. Is there no way to prevent her sending it?'

'If you think you can prevent her, I wish you would try it.'

'How did you find it out? Did she tell you?'

'Oh, it doesn't matter how I found it out. I did find it out. A man told me who she was; then I asked her, and she was perfectly frank about it. She read me the report, even.'

'Read it to you?'

'Yes, read it to me, and punctuated it in my presence—put in some words that I suggested as being better than those she had used. Oh, it was the coolest piece of work you ever saw!'

'But there must be some way of preventing her getting that account to New York in time. You see, all we have to do is to wire your people to hand in our report to the directors, and then hers is forestalled. She has to telegraph from a British office, and it seems to me that we could stop her in some way.'

'As, for instance, how?'

'Oh, I don't know just how at the moment, but we ought to be able to do it. If it were a man, we could have him arrested as a dynamiter or something; but a woman, of course, is more difficult to deal with. George, I would appeal to her better nature if I were you.'

Wentworth laughed sneeringly.

'Better nature?' he said. 'She hasn't any; and that is not the worst of it. She has "calculated," as she calls it, all the possibilities in the affair; she "calculates" that we will reach Queenstown about Saturday night. If we do, she will get her report through in time to be published on Sunday in the New York Argus. If that is the case, then see where our telegram will be. We telegraph our people to send in the report. It reaches the office Saturday night, and is not read. The office closes at two o'clock; but even if they got it, and understood the urgency of the matter, they could not place the papers before the directors until Monday morning, and by Monday morning it will be in the London financial sheets.'

'George, that woman is a fiend.'

'No, she isn't, John. She is merely a clever American journalist, who thinks she has done a very good piece of work indeed, and who, through the stupidity of one man, has succeeded, that's all.'

'Have you made any appeal to her at all?'

'Oh, haven't I! Of course I have. What good did it do? She merely laughed at me. Don't you understand? That is what she is here for. Her whole voyage is for that one purpose; and it's not likely the woman is going to forego her triumph after having succeeded—more especially as somebody else in the same office has failed. That's what gives additional zest to what she has done. The fact that Rivers has failed and she has triumphed seems to be the great feather in her cap.'

'Then,' said Kenyon, 'I'm going to appeal to Miss Brewster myself.'

'Very well. I wish you joy of your job. But do what you can, John, there's a good fellow. Meanwhile, I want to be alone somewhere.'

Wentworth went down the stairway that led to the steerage department, and for a few moments sat among the steerage passengers. Then he climbed up another ladder, and got to the very front of the ship. Here he sat down on a coil of rope, and thought over the situation. Thinking, however, did him very little good. He realized that, even if he got hold of the paper Miss Brewster had, she could easily write another. She had the facts in her head, and all that she needed to do was to get to a telegraph office and there hand in her message.

Meanwhile, Kenyon took a few turns up and down the deck, thinking deeply on the same subject. He passed over to the side where Miss Brewster sat, but on coming opposite her had not the courage to take his place beside her. She was calmly reading her book. Three times he came opposite her, paused for a moment, and then continued his hopeless march. He saw that his courage was not going to be sufficient for the task, and yet he felt the task must be accomplished. He didn't know how to begin. He didn't know what inducement to offer the young woman for foregoing the fruits of her ingenuity. He felt that this was the weak point in his armour. The third time he paused in front of Miss Brewster; she looked up and motioned him to the chair beside her, saying:

'I do not know you very well, Mr. Kenyon, but I know who you are. Won't you sit down here for a moment?'

The bewildered man took the chair she indicated.

'Now, Mr. Kenyon, I know just what is troubling you. You have passed three or four times wishing to sit down beside me, and yet afraid to venture. Is that not true?'

'Quite true.'

'I knew it was. Now I know also what you have come for. Mr. Wentworth has told you what the trouble is. He has told you that he has given me all the particulars about the mines, hasn't he?'

'He has.'

'And he has gone off to his state-room to think over the matter, and has

261

left the affair in your hands, and you imagine you can come here to me and, perhaps, talk me out of sending that despatch to the Argus. Isn't that your motive?'

'That is about what I hope to be able to do,' said Kenyon, mopping his brow.

'Well, I thought I might just as well put you out of your misery at once. You take things very seriously, Mr. Kenyon—I can see that. Now, don't you?'

'I am afraid I do.'

'Why, of course you do. The publication of this, as I told Mr. Wentworth, will really not matter at all. It will not be any reflection on either of you, because your friends will be sure that, if you had known to whom you were talking, you would never have said anything about the mines.'

Kenyon smiled grimly at this piece of comfort.

'Now, I have been thinking about something since Mr. Wentworth went away. I am really very sorry for him. I am more sorry than I can tell.'

'Then,' said Kenyon eagerly, 'won't you——'

'No, I won't, so we needn't recur to that phase of the subject. That is what I am here for, and, no matter what you say, the despatch is going to be sent. Now, it is better to understand that at the first, and then it will create no trouble afterwards. Don't you think that is the best?'

'Probably,' answered the wretched man.

'Well, then, let us start there. I will say in the cablegram that the information comes from neither Mr. Kenyon nor Mr. Wentworth.'

'Yes, but that wouldn't be true.'

'Why, of course it wouldn't be true; but that doesn't matter, does it?'

'Well, on our side of the water,' said Kenyon, 'we think the truth does matter.'

Miss Brewster laughed heartily.

'Dear me!' she said, 'what little tact you have! How does it concern you whether it is true or not? If there is any falsehood, it is not you who tell it, so you are free from all blame. Indeed, you are free from all blame anyhow, in this affair; it is all your friend Wentworth's fault; but still, if it hadn't been Wentworth, it would have been you.'

Kenyon looked up at her incredulously.

'Oh yes, it would,' she said, nodding confidently at him. 'You must not flatter yourself, because Mr. Wentworth told me everything about it, that you wouldn't have done just the same, if I had had to find it out from you. All men are pretty much alike where women are concerned.'

'Can I say nothing to you, Miss Brewster, which will keep you from sending the message to America?'

'You cannot, Mr. Kenyon. I thought we had settled that at the beginning. I see there is no use talking to you. I will return to my book, which is very interesting. Good-morning, Mr. Kenyon.'

Kenyon felt the hopelessness of his project quite as much as Wentworth had done, and, thrusting his hands deep into his pockets, he wandered disconsolately up and down the deck.

As he went to the other side of the deck, he met Miss Longworth walking alone. She smiled a cordial welcome to him, so he turned and changed his step to suit hers.

'May I walk with you a few minutes?' he said.

'Of course you may,' was the reply, 'What is the matter? You are looking very unhappy.'

'My comrade and myself are in great trouble, and I thought I should like to talk with you about it.'

'I am sure if there is anything I can do to help you, I shall be most glad to do it.'

'Perhaps you may suggest something. You see, two men dealing with one woman are perfectly helpless.'

'Ah, who is the one woman—not I, is it?'

'No, not you, Miss Longworth. I wish it were, then we would have no trouble.'

'Oh, thank you!'

'You see, it is like this: When we were in Quebec—I think I told you about that—the New York Argus sent a man to find out what we had reported, or were going to report, to the London Syndicate.'

'Yes, you told me that.'

'Rivers was his name. Well, this same paper, finding that Rivers had failed after having stolen the documents, has tried a much more subtle scheme, which promises to be successful. They have put on board this ship a young woman who has gained a reputation for learning secrets not intended for the public. This young woman is Miss Brewster, who sits next Wentworth at the table. Fate seems to have played right into her hand and placed her beside him. They became acquainted, and, unfortunately, my friend has told her a great deal about the mines, which she professed an interest in. Or, rather, she pretended to have an interest in him, and so he spoke, being, of course, off his guard. There is no more careful fellow in the world than George Wentworth, but a man does not expect that a private conversation with a lady will ever appear in a newspaper.'

'Naturally not.'

'Very well, that is the state of things. In some manner Wentworth came to know that this young woman was the special correspondent of the New York Argus. He spoke to her about it, and she is perfectly frank in saying she is here solely for the purpose of finding out what the reports will be, and that the moment she gets to Queenstown she will cable what she has discovered to New York.'

'Dear me! that is very perplexing. What have you done?'

'We have done nothing so far, or rather, I should say, we have tried everything we could think of, and have accomplished nothing. Wentworth has appealed to her, and I made a clumsy attempt at an appeal also, but it was of no use. I feel my own helplessness in this matter, and Wentworth is completely broken down over it.'

'Poor fellow! I am sure of that. Let me think a moment.'

They walked up and down the deck in silence for a few minutes. Then Miss Longworth looked up at Kenyon, and said;

'Will you place this matter in my hands?'

'Certainly, if you will be so kind as to take any interest in it.'

'I take a great deal of interest. Of course, you know my father is deeply concerned in it also, so I am acting in a measure for him.'

'Have you any plan?'

'Yes; my plan is simply this: The young woman is working for money; now, if we can offer her more than her paper gives, she will very quickly accept, or I am much mistaken in the kind of woman she is.'

'Ah, yes,' said Kenyon; 'but we haven't the money, you see.'

'Never mind; the money will be quickly forthcoming. Don't trouble any more about it. I am sure that can be arranged.'

Kenyon thanked her, looking his gratitude rather than speaking it, for he was an unready man, and she bade him good-bye until she could think over her plan.

That evening there was a tap at the state-room door of Miss Jennie Brewster.

'Come in,' cried the occupant.

Miss Longworth entered, and the occupant of the room looked up, with a frown, from her writing.

'May I have a few moments' conversation with you?' asked the visitor gravely.

CHAPTER X.

Miss Jennie Brewster was very much annoyed at being interrupted, and she took no pains to conceal her feelings. She was writing an article entitled 'How People kill Time on Shipboard,' and she did not wish to be disturbed; besides, as she often said of herself, she was not 'a woman's woman,' and she neither liked, nor was liked by, her own sex.

'I desire a few moments' conversation with you, if I have your permission,' said Edith Longworth, as she closed the door behind her.

'Certainly,' answered Jennie Brewster. 'Will you sit down?'

'Thank you,' replied the other, as she took a seat on the sofa. 'I do not know just how to begin what I wish to say. Perhaps it will be better to commence by telling you that I know why you are on board this steamer.'

'Yes; and why am I on board the steamer, may I ask?'

'You are here, I understand, to get certain information from Mr. Wentworth. You have obtained it, and it is in reference to this that I have come to see you.'

'Indeed! and are you so friendly with Mr. Wentworth that you——'

'I scarcely know Mr. Wentworth at all.'

'Then, why do you come on a mission from him?'

'It is not a mission from him. It is not a mission from anyone. I was speaking to Mr. Kenyon, or, rather, Mr. Kenyon was speaking to me, about a subject which troubled him greatly. It is a subject in which my father is interested. My father is a member of the London Syndicate, and he naturally would not desire to have your intended cable message sent to New York.'

'Really; are you quite sure that you are not speaking less for your father than for your friend Kenyon?'

Anger burned in Miss Longworth's face, and flashed from her eyes as she answered:

'You must not speak to me in that way.'

'Excuse me, I shall speak to you in just the way I please. I did not ask for this conference; you did, and as you have taken it upon yourself to come into this room uninvited, you will have to put up with what you hear. Those who interfere with other people's business, as a general thing, do not have a nice time.'

'I quite appreciated all the possible disagreeableness of coming here, when I came.'

'I am glad of that, because if you hear anything you do not like, you will not be disappointed, and will have only yourself to thank for it.'

'I would like to talk about this matter in a spirit of friendliness if I can. I think nothing is to be attained by speaking in any other way.'

'Very well, then. What excuse have you to give me for coming into my state-room to talk about business which does not concern you?'

'Miss Brewster, it does concern me—it concerns my father, and that concerns me. I am, in a measure, my father's private secretary, and am intimately acquainted with all the business he has in hand. This particular business is his affair, and therefore mine. That is the reason I am here.'

'Are you sure?'

'Am I sure of what?'

'Are you sure that what you say is true?'

'I am not in the habit of speaking anything but the truth.'

'Perhaps you flatter yourself that is the case, but it does not deceive me. You merely come here because Mr. Kenyon is in a muddle about what I am going to do. Isn't that the reason?'

Miss Longworth saw that her task was going to be even harder than she had expected.

'Suppose we let all question of motive rest? I have come here—I have asked your permission to speak on this subject, and you have given me the permission. Having done so, it seems to me you should hear me out. You say that I should not be offended——'

'I didn't say so. I do not care a rap whether you are offended or not.'

'You at least said I might hear something that would not be pleasant. What I wanted to say is this: I have taken the risk of that, and, as you remark, whether I am offended or not does not matter. Now we will come to the point——'

'Just before you come to the point, please let me know if Mr. Kenyon told you he had spoken to me on this subject already.'

'Yes, he told me so.'

'Did he tell you that his friend Wentworth had also had a conversation with me about it?'

'Yes, he told me that also.'

'Very well, then, if those two men can do nothing to shake my purpose, how do you expect to do it?'

'That is what I am about to tell you. This is a commercial world, and I am a commercial man's daughter. I recognise the fact that you are going to cable this information for the money it brings. Is that not the case?'

'It is partly the case.'

'For what other consideration do you work, then?'

'For the consideration of being known as one of the best newspaper women in the city of New York. That is the other consideration.'

'I understood you were already known as the most noted newspaper woman in New York.'

This remark was much more diplomatic than Miss Longworth herself suspected.

Jennie Brewster looked rather pleased, then she said:

'Oh, I don't know about that; but I intend it shall be so before a year is past.'

'Very well, you have plenty of time to accomplish your object without using the information you have obtained on board this ship. Now, as I was saying, the New York Argus pays you a certain amount for doing this work. If you will promise not to send the report over to that paper, I will give you a cheque for double the sum the Argus will pay you, besides refunding all your expenses twice over.'

'In other words, you ask me to be bribed and refuse to perform my duty to the paper.'

'It isn't bribery. I merely pay you, or will pay you, double what you will receive from that paper. I presume your connection with it is purely commercial. You work for it because you receive a certain amount of money; if the editor found someone who would do the same work cheaper, he would at once employ that person, and your services would be no longer required. Is that not true?'

'Yes, it is true.'

'Very well, then, the question of duty hardly enters into such a compact. They have sent you on what would be to most people a very difficult mission. You have succeeded. You have, therefore, in your possession something to sell. The New York paper will pay you a certain sum in cash for it. I offer you, for the same article, double the price the New York Argus will pay you. Is not that a fair offer?'

Jennie Brewster had arisen. She clasped and unclasped her hands nervously. For a small space of time nothing was said, and Edith Longworth imagined she had gained her point. The woman standing looked down at the woman sitting.

'Do you know all the particulars about the attempt to get this information?' asked Miss Brewster.

'I know some of them. What particulars do you mean?'

'Do you know that a man from the Argus tried to get this information from Mr. Kenyon and Mr. Wentworth in Canada?'

'Yes; I know about that.'

'Do you know that he stole the reports, and that they were taken from him before he could use them?'

'Yes.'

'Do you know he offered Mr. Kenyon and Mr. Wentworth double the price the London Syndicate would have paid them, on condition they gave him a synopsis of the reports?'

'Yes, I know that also.'

'Do you know that, in doing what he asked, they would not have been keeping back for a single day the real report from the people who engaged them? You know all that, do you?'

'Yes; I know all that.'

'Very well, then. Now you ask me to do very much more than Rivers asked them, because you ask me to keep my paper completely in the dark about the information I have got. Isn't that so?'

'Yes, you can keep them in the dark until after the report has been given to the directors; then, of course, you can do what you please with the information.'

'Ah, but by that time it will be of no value. By that time it will have been published in the London financial papers. At that time anybody can get it. Isn't that the case?'

'I suppose so.'

'Now, I want to ask you one other question, Miss—Miss—I don't think you told me your name.'

'My name is Edith Longworth.'

'Very well, Miss Longworth. I want to ask you one more question. What do you think of the conduct of Mr. Kenyon and Mr. Wentworth in refusing to take double what they had been promised for making the report?'

'What do I think of them?' repeated the girl.

'Yes; what do you think of them? You hesitate. You realize that you are in a corner. You think Mr. Wentworth and Mr. Kenyon did very nobly in refusing Rivers' offer?'

'Of course I do.'

'So do I. I think they acted rightly, and did as honourable men should do. Now, when you think that, Miss Longworth, how dare you come and offer me double, or three times, or four times, the amount my paper gives to me for getting this information? Do you think that I am any less honourable than Kenyon or Wentworth? Your offer is an insult to me; nobody but a woman, and a woman of your class, would have made it. Kenyon wouldn't have made it. Wentworth wouldn't have made it. You come here to bribe me. You come here to do exactly what J. K. Rivers tried to do for the Argus in Canada. You think money will purchase anything—that is the thought of all your class. Now, I want you to understand that I am a woman of the people. I was born and brought up in poverty in New York. You were born and brought up amid luxury in London. I have suffered privation and hardships that you know nothing of, and, even if you read about them, you wouldn't understand. You, with the impudence of your class, think you can come to me and bribe me to betray my employer. I am here to do a certain thing, and I am going to do that certain thing in spite of all the money that all the Longworths ever possessed, or ever will possess. Do I make myself sufficiently plain?'

'Yes, Miss Brewster. I don't think anyone could misunderstand you.'

'Well, I am glad of that, because one can never tell how thickheaded some people may be.'

'Do you think there is any parallel between your case and Mr. Wentworth's?'

'Of course I do. We were each sent to do a certain piece of work. We each did our work. We have both been offered a bribe to cheat our employers of the fruits of our labour; only in my case it is very much worse than in Wentworth's, because his employers would not have suffered, while mine will.'

'This is all very plausible, Miss Brewster, but now allow me to tell you that what you have done is a most dishonourable thing, and that you are a disgrace to our common womanhood. You have managed, during a very short acquaintance, to win the confidence of a man—there is a kind of woman who knows how to do that: I thank Heaven I am not of that class; I prefer to belong to the class you have just now been reviling. Some men have an inherent respect for all women; Mr. Wentworth is apparently one of those, and, while he was on his guard with a man, he was not on his guard with a woman. You took advantage of that and you managed to secure certain information which you knew he would never have given you if he had thought it was to be published. You stole that information just as disreputably as that man stole the documents from Mr. Kenyon's pocket. You talk of your honour and your truth when you did such a contemptible thing! You prate of unbribeableness, when the only method possible is adopted of making you do what is right and just and honest! Your conduct makes me ashamed of being a woman. A thoroughly bad woman I can understand, but not a woman like you, who trade on the fact that you are a woman, and that you are pretty, and that you have a pleasing manner. You use those qualities as a thief or a counterfeiter would use the peculiar talents God had given him. How dare you pretend for a moment that your case is similar to Mr. Wentworth's? Mr. Wentworth is an honourable man, engaged in an honourable business; as for you and your business, I have no words to express my contempt for both. Picking pockets is reputable compared with such work.'

Edith Longworth was now standing up, her face flushed and her hands clenched. She spoke with a vehemence which she very much regretted when she thought of the circumstance afterwards; but her chagrin and disappointment at failure, where she had a moment before been sure of success, overcame her. Her opponent stood before her, angry and pale. At first Edith Longworth thought she was going to strike her, but if any such idea passed through the brain of the journalist, she thought better of it. For a few moments neither spoke, then Jennie Brewster said, in a voice of unnatural calmness:

'You are quite welcome to your opinion of me, Miss Longworth, and I presume I am entitled to my opinion of Kenyon and Wentworth. They are two fools, and you are a third in thinking you can control the actions of a woman where two young men have failed. Do you think for a moment I would grant to you, a woman of a class I hate, what I would not grant to a man like Wentworth? They say there is no fool like an old fool, but it should be said that there is no fool like a young woman who has had everything her own way in this world. You are——'

'I shall not stay and listen to your abuse. I wish to have nothing more to do with you.'

'Oh, yes! you will stay,' cried the other, placing her back against the door. 'You came here at your own pleasure; you will leave at mine. I will tell you more truth in five minutes than you ever heard in your life before. I will tell you, in the first place, that my business is quite as honourable as Kenyon's or Wentworth's. What does Kenyon do but try to get information about mines which other people are vitally interested in keeping from him? What does Wentworth do but ferret about among accounts like a detective trying to find out what other people are endeavouring to conceal? What is the whole mining business but one vast swindle, whose worst enemy is the press? No wonder anyone connected with mining fears publicity. If your father has made a million out of mines, he has made it simply by swindling unfortunate victims. I do my business my way, and your two friends do theirs in their way. Of the two, I consider my vocation much the more upright. Now that you have heard what I have to say, you may go, and let me tell you that I never wish to see you or speak with you again.'

'Thank you for your permission to go. I am sure I cordially echo your wish that we may never meet again. I may say, however, that I am sorry I spoke to you in the way I did. It is, of course, impossible for you to look on the matter from my point of view, just as it is impossible for me to look upon it from yours. Nevertheless, I wish you would forget what I said, and think over the matter a little more, and if you see your way to accepting my offer it will be always open to you. Should you forego the sending of that cablegram, I will willingly pay you three times what the New York Argus will give you for it. I do not offer that as a bribe; I merely offer it so that you will not suffer from doing what I believe to be a just action. It seems to me a great pity that two young men should have to endure a serious check to their own business advancement because one of them was foolish enough to confide in a woman in whom he believed.'

Edith Longworth was young, and therefore scarcely likely to be a mistress of diplomacy, but she might have known the last sentence she uttered spoiled the effect of all that had gone before.

'Really, Miss Longworth, I had some little admiration for you when you blazed out at me in the way you did; but now, when you coolly repeat your offer of a bribe, adding one-third to it, all my respect for you vanishes. You may go and tell those who sent you that nothing under heaven can prevent that cablegram being sent.'

In saying this, however, Miss Brewster somewhat exceeded her knowledge. Few of us can foretell what may or may not happen under heaven.

CHAPTER XI.

Edith Longworth went to her state-room and there had what women call 'a good cry' over her failure. Jennie Brewster continued her writing, every now and then pausing as she thought, with regret, of some sharp thing she might have said, which did not occur to her at the time of the interview. Kenyon spent his time in pacing up and down the deck, hoping for the reappearance of Miss Longworth—an expectation which, for a time at least, was the hope deferred which maketh the heart sick. Fleming, the New York politician, kept the smoking-room merry, listening to the stories he told. He varied the proceedings by frequently asking everybody to drink with him, an invitation that met with no general refusal. Old Mr. Longworth dozed most of his time in his steamer chair. Wentworth, who still bitterly accused himself of having been a fool, talked with no one, not even his friend Kenyon. All the time, the great steamship kept forging along through the reasonably calm water just as if nothing had happened or was going to happen. There had been one day of rain, and one night and part of a day of storm. Saturday morning broke, and it was expected that some time in the night Queenstown would be reached. Early on Saturday morning the clouds looked lowering, as they have a right to look near Ireland.

Wentworth, the cause of all the worry, gave Kenyon very little assistance in the matter that troubled his mind. He was in the habit, when the subject was referred to, of thrusting his hands into his hair, or plunging them down into his pockets, and breaking out into language which was as deplorable as it was expressive. The more Kenyon advised him to be calm, the less Wentworth followed that advice. As a general thing, he spent most of his time alone in a very gloomy state of mind. On one occasion when the genial Fleming slapped him on the shoulder, Wentworth, to his great astonishment, turned fiercely round and cried:

'If you do that again, sir, I'll knock you down.'

Fleming said afterwards that he was 'completely flabbergasted' by this—

whatever that may mean—and he added that the English in general were a queer race. It is true that he gathered himself together at the time and, having laughed a little over the remark, said to Wentworth:

'Come and have a drink; then you'll feel better.'

This invitation Wentworth did not even take the trouble to decline, but thrust his hands in his pockets once more, and turned his back on the popular New York politician.

Wentworth summed up the situation to John Kenyon when he said:

'There is no use in our talking or thinking any more about it. We can simply do nothing. I shall take the whole blame on my shoulders. I am resolved that you shall not suffer from my indiscretion. Now, don't talk to me any more about it. I want to forget the wretched business, if possible.'

So thus it came about quite naturally that John Kenyon, who was a good deal troubled about the matter, took as his confidante Edith Longworth, who also betrayed the greatest interest in the problem. Miss Longworth was left all the more alone because her cousin had taken permanently to the smoking-room. Someone had introduced him to the fascinating game of poker, and in the practice of this particular amusement Mr. William Longworth was now spending a good deal of his surplus cash, as well as his time.

Jennie Brewster was seldom seen on deck. She applied herself assiduously to the writing of those brilliant articles which appeared later in the Sunday edition of the New York Argus under the general title of 'Life at Sea,' and which have more recently been issued in book form. As everybody is already aware, her sketches of the genial New York politician, and also of the taciturn, glum Englishman, are considered the finest things in the little volume. They have been largely copied as typical examples of American humour.

When Jennie Brewster did appear on deck, she walked alone up and down the promenade, with a sort of half-defiant look in her eyes as she passed Kenyon and Edith Longworth, and she generally encountered them together.

On this particularly eventful Saturday morning, Kenyon and Edith had the deck to themselves. The conversation naturally turned to the subject which for the last few days had occupied the minds of both.

'Do you know,' said the girl, 'I have been thinking all along that she will come to me at the last for the money.'

'I am not at all sure about that,' answered Kenyon.

'I thought she would probably keep us on the tenterhooks just as long as possible, and then at the last moment come and say she would accept the offer.'

'If she does,' said Kenyon, 'I would not trust her. I would give her to understand that a cheque would be handed to her when we were certain the article had not been used.'

'Do you think that would be a safe way to act if she came and said she would take the money for not sending the cablegram? Don't you think it would be better to pay her and trust to her honour?'

Kenyon laughed.

'I do not think I would trust much to her honour.'

'Now, do you know, I have a different opinion of her. I feel sure that if she said she would do a thing, she would do it.'

'I have no such faith,' answered Kenyon. 'I think, on the contrary, that she is quite capable of asking you for the money and still sending her telegram.'

'Well, I doubt if she would do so. I think the girl really believes she is acting rightly, and imagines she has done a creditable action in a very smart way. If she were not what she calls "honest," she would not have shown so much temper as she did. Not but that I gave a deplorable exhibition of temper myself, for which there was really no excuse.'

'I am sure,' said Kenyon warmly, 'you did nothing of the kind. At all events, I am certain everything you did was perfectly right; and I know you were completely justified in anything you said.'

'I wish I could think so.'

'I want to ask you one question,' said Kenyon.

But what that question was will never be known. It was never asked; and when Edith Longworth inquired about it some time later, the question had entirely gone from Kenyon's mind. The steamship, which was ploughing along through the waters, suddenly gave a shiver, as if it were shaken by an earthquake; there were three tremendous bumps, such as a sledge might make by going suddenly over logs concealed in the snow. Both Kenyon and Miss Longworth sprang to their feet. There was a low roar of steam, and they saw a cloud rise amidships, apparently pouring out of every aperture through which it could escape. Then there was silence. The engines had stopped, and the vessel heeled distinctly over to the port side. When Edith Longworth began to realize the situation, she found herself very close to Kenyon, clasping his arm with both hands.

'What—what is it?' she cried in alarm.

'Something is wrong,' said Kenyon. 'Nothing serious, I hope. Will you wait here a moment while I go and see?'

'It is stupid of me,' she answered, releasing his arm; 'but I feel dreadfully frightened.'

'Perhaps you would rather not be left alone.'

'Oh no, it is all over now; but when the first of those terrible shocks came it seemed to me we had struck a rock.'

'There are no rocks here,' said Kenyon. 'The day is perfectly clear, and we are evidently not out of our course. Something has gone wrong with the machinery, I imagine. Just wait a moment, and I will find out.'

As Kenyon rushed towards the companion-way, he met a sailor hurrying in the other direction.

'What is the matter?' cried Kenyon.

The sailor gave no answer.

On entering the companion-way door, Kenyon found the place full of steam, and he ran against an officer.

'What is wrong? Is anything the matter?'

'How should I know?' was the answer, very curtly given. 'Please do not ask any questions. Everything will be attended to.'

This was scant encouragement. People began crowding up the companion-way, coughing and wheezing in the steam; and soon the deck, that but a moment before had been almost without an occupant, was crowded with excited human beings in all states of dress and undress.

'What is wrong?' was the question on every lip, to which, as yet, there was no answer. The officers who hurried to and fro were mute, or gave short and unsatisfactory replies to the inquiries which poured in upon them. People did not pause to reflect that even an officer could hardly be expected to know off-hand what the cause of the sudden stoppage of the engine might be. By-and-by the captain appeared, smiling and bland. He told them there was no danger. Something had gone amiss with the machinery, exactly what he could not, at the moment, tell; but there was no necessity for being panic-stricken, everything would be all right in a short time if they merely remained calm. These, and a lot of other nautical lies, which are always told on such occasions, served to calm the fears of the crowd; and by-and-by one after another went down to their state-rooms on finding the vessel was not going to sink immediately. They all appeared some time afterward in more suitable apparel. The steam which had filled the saloon soon disappeared, leaving the furniture dripping with warm moisture. Finally, the loud clang of the breakfast-gong sounded as if nothing had happened, and that did more, perhaps, than anything else to allay the fears of the passengers. If breakfast was about to be served, then, of course, things were not serious. Nevertheless, a great many people that morning had a very poor appetite for the breakfast served to them. The one blessing, as everybody said, was that the weather kept so fine and the sea so calm. To those few who knew anything about disasters at sea, the list of the ship to the port side was a most serious sign. The majority of the passengers, however, did not notice it. After breakfast people came up on deck. There was a wonderful avoidance of hurry, alike by officers and sailors. Orders were given calmly and quietly, and as calmly and quietly obeyed. Officers were still up on the bridge, although there were no commands to give to the man at the wheel and no screw turning. The helmsman stood at the wheel as if he expected at any time the order to turn it port or starboard. All this absence of rush had a very soothing effect on the passengers, many of whom wanted only a slight excuse to become hysterical. As the day wore on, however, a general feeling of security seemed to have come upon all on board. They one and all congratulated themselves on the fact that they had behaved in a most exemplary manner considering the somewhat alarming circumstances. Nevertheless, those who watched the captain saw that he swept the long line of the horizon through his glass every now and then with a good deal of anxiety, and they noticed on looking at the long level line where sea and sky met that not a sail was visible around the complete circle. Up from the engine-room came the clank of hammers, and the opinion was general that, whatever was amiss with the engine, it was capable of being repaired. One thing had become certain, there was nothing wrong with the shafts. The damage, whatever it was, had been to the engine alone. All of the passengers found themselves more or less affected by the peculiar sensation of the steamer being at rest—the awe-inspiring and helpless consciousness of complete silence—after the steady throb they had become so accustomed to all the way across. That night at dinner the captain took his place at the head of the table, urbane and courteous, as if nothing unusual had happened; and the people, who, notwithstanding their outward calmness, were in a state of anxious tension, noticed this with gratified feelings.

'What is the matter?' asked a passenger of the captain; 'and what is the extent of the accident?'

The captain looked down the long table.

'I am afraid,' said he, 'that if I went into technical details you would not understand them. There was a flaw in one of the rods connected with the engine. That rod broke, and in breaking it damaged other parts of the machinery. Doubtless you heard the three thuds which it gave before the engine was stopped. At present it is impossible to tell how long it will take to repair the damage. However, even if the accident were serious, we are right in the track of vessels, and there is no danger.'

This was reassuring; but those who lay awake that night heard the ominous sound of the pumps, and the swishing of water splashing down into the ocean.

CHAPTER XII.

Most of the passengers awoke next morning with a bewildering feeling of vague apprehension. The absence of all motion in the ship, the unusual and intense silence, had a depressing effect. The engines had not yet started; that at least was evident. Kenyon was one of the first on deck. He noticed that the pumps were still working at their full speed, and that the steamer had still the unexplained list to port. Happily, the weather continued good, so far as the quietness of the sea was concerned. A slight drizzle of rain had set in, and the horizon was not many miles from the ship. There would not be much chance of sighting another liner while such weather continued.

Before Kenyon had been many minutes on deck, Edith Longworth came up the companion-way. She approached him with a smile on her face.

'Well,' he said, 'you, at least, do not seem to be suffering any anxiety because of our situation.'

'Really,' she replied, 'I was not thinking of that at all, but about something else. Can you not guess what it is?'

'No,' he answered hesitatingly. 'What is it?'

'Have you forgotten that this is Sunday morning?'

'Is it? Of course it is. So far as I am concerned, time seemed to stop when the engines broke down. But I do not understand why Sunday morning means anything in particular.'

'Don't you? Well, for a person who has been thinking for the last two or three days very earnestly on one particular subject, I am astonished at you. Sunday morning and no land in sight! Reflect for a moment.'

Kenyon's face brightened.

'Ah,' he cried, 'I see what you mean now! Miss Brewster's cable message will not appear in this morning's New York Argus.'

'Of course it will not; and don't you see, also, that when we do arrive you will have an equal chance in the race. If we get in before next Sunday, your telegram to the London people will go as quickly as her cable despatch to New York; thus you will be saved the humiliation of seeing the substance of your report in the London papers before the directors see the report itself. It is not much, to be sure, but, still, it puts you on equal terms; while if we had got into Queenstown last night that would have been impossible.'

Kenyon laughed.

'Well,' he said, 'for such a result the cause is rather tremendous, isn't it? It is something like burning down the house to roast the pig!'

Shortly after ten o'clock the atmosphere cleared, and showed in the distance a steamer, westward bound. The vessel evidently belonged to one of the great ocean lines. The moment it was sighted there fluttered up to the masthead a number of signal-flags, and people crowded to the side of the ship to watch the effect on the outgoing vessel. Minute after minute passed, but there was no response from the other liner. People watched her with breathless anxiety, as though their fate depended on her noticing their signals. Of course, everybody thought she must see them, but still she steamed westward. A cloud of black smoke came out of her funnel, and then a long dark trail, like the tail of a comet, floated out behind; but no notice was taken of the fluttering flags at the masthead. For more than an hour the steamer was in sight. Then she gradually faded away into the west, and finally disappeared.

This incident had a depressing effect on the passengers of the disabled ship. Although every officer had maintained there was no danger, yet the floating away of that steamer seemed somehow to leave them alone; and people, after gazing toward the west until not a vestige of her remained in the horizon, went back to their deck-chairs, feeling more despondent than ever.

Fleming, however, maintained that if people had to drown, it was just as well to drown jolly as mournful, and so he invited everybody to take a drink at his expense—a generous offer, taken instant advantage of by all the smoking-room frequenters.

'My idea is this,' said Fleming, as he sipped the cocktail which was

283

brought to him, 'if anything happens, let it happen; if nothing happens, why, then let nothing happen. There is no use worrying about anything, especially something we cannot help. Here we are on the ocean in a disabled vessel—very good; we cannot do anything about it, and so long as the bar remains open, gentlemen, here's to you!'

And with this cheerful philosophy the New York politician swallowed the liquor he had paid for.

Still the swish of water from the pumps could be heard, but the metallic clanking of steel on steel no longer came up from the engine-room. This in itself was ominous to those who knew. It showed that the engineer had given up all hope of repairing the damage, whatever it was, and the real cause of the disaster was as much a mystery as ever. Shortly before lunch it became evident to people on board the ship that something was about to be done. The sailors undid the fastenings of one of the large boats, and swung it out on the davits until it hung over the sea.

Gradually rumour took form, and it became known that one of the officers and certain of the crew were about to make an attempt to reach the coast of Ireland and telegraph to Queenstown for tugs to bring the steamer in. The captain still asserted that there was no danger whatever, and it was only to prevent delay that this expedient was about to be tried.

'Do you know what they are going to do?' cried Edith Longworth, in a state of great excitement, to John Kenyon.

Kenyon had been walking the deck with Wentworth, who now had gone below.

'I have heard,' said Kenyon, 'that they intend trying to reach the coast.'

'Exactly. Now, why should you not send a telegram to your people in London, and have the reports forwarded at once? The chances are that Miss Brewster will never think of sending her cablegram with the officer who is going to make the trip; then you will be a clear day or two ahead of her, and everything will be all right. In fact, when she understands what has been done, she probably will not send her own message at all.'

'By George!' cried Kenyon, 'that is a good idea. I will see the mate at once, and find out whether he will take a telegram.'

He went accordingly, and spoke to the mate about sending a message with him. The officer said that any passenger who wished to send a telegraphic message would be at liberty to do so. He would take charge of the telegrams very gladly. Kenyon went down to his state-room and told Wentworth what was going to be done. For the first time in several days George Wentworth exhibited something like energy. He went to the steward and bought the stamps to put on the telegram, while John Kenyon wrote it.

The message was given to the officer, who put it into his inside pocket, and then Kenyon thought all was safe. But Edith Longworth was not so sure of that. Jennie Brewster sat in her deck-chair calmly reading her usual paper-covered novel. She apparently knew nothing of what was going on, and Edith Longworth, nervous with suppressed excitement, sat near her, watching her narrowly, while preparations for launching the boat were being completed. Suddenly, to Edith's horror, the deck-steward appeared, and in a loud voice cried:

'Ladies and gentlemen, anyone wishing to send telegrams to friends has a few minutes now to write them. The mate will take them ashore with him, and will send them from the first office that he reaches. No letters can be taken, only telegrams.'

Miss Brewster looked up languidly from her book during the first part of this recital. Then she sprang suddenly to her feet, and threw the book on the deck.

'Who is it will take the telegrams?' she asked the steward.

'The mate, miss. There he is standing yonder, miss.'

She made her way quickly to that official.

'Will you take a cable despatch to be sent to New York?'

'Yes, miss. Is it a very long one?' he asked.

'Yes, it is a very long one.'

'Well, miss,' was the answer, 'you haven't much time to write it. We leave now in a very few minutes.'

'It is all written out; I have only to add a few words to it.'

Miss Brewster at once flew to her state-room. The telegram about the mine was soon before her with the words counted, and the silver and gold that were to pay for it piled on the table. She resolved to run no risk of delay by having the message sent 'to collect.' Then she dashed off, as quickly as she could, a brief and very graphic account of the disaster which had overtaken the Caloric. If this account was slightly exaggerated, Miss Brewster had no time to tone it down. Picturesque and dramatic description was what she aimed at. Her pen flew over the paper with great rapidity, and she looked up every now and then, through her state-room window, to see dangling from the ropes the boat that was to make the attempt to reach the Irish coast. As she could thus see how the preparations for the departure were going forward, she lingered longer than she might otherwise have done, and added line after line to the despatch which told of the disaster. At last she saw the men take their places in the longboat. She hurriedly counted the words in the new despatch she had written, and quickly from her purse piled the gold that was necessary to pay for their transmission. Then she sealed the two despatches in an envelope, put the two piles of gold into one after rapidly counting them again, cast a quick look up at the still motionless boat, grasped the gold in one hand, the envelope in the other, and sprang to her feet; but, as she did so, she gave a shriek and took a step backwards.

Standing with her back to the door was Edith Longworth. When she had entered the state-room, Miss Brewster did not know, but her heart beat wildly as she saw the girl standing silently there, as if she had risen up through the floor.

'What are you doing here?' she demanded.

'I am here,' said Miss Longworth, 'because I wish to talk with you.'

'Stand aside; I have no time to talk to you just now. I told you I didn't want to see you again. Stand aside, I tell you.'

'I shall not stand aside.'

'What do you mean?'

'I mean that I shall not stand aside.'

'Then I will ring the bell and have you thrust out of here for your impudence.'

'You shall not ring the bell,' said Edith calmly, putting her hand over the white china plaque that held in its centre the black electric button.

'Do you mean to tell me that you intend to keep me from leaving my own state-room?'

'I mean to tell you exactly that.'

'Do you know that you can be imprisoned for attempting such a thing?'

'I don't care.'

'Stand aside, you vixen, or I will strike you!'

'Do it.'

For a moment the two girls stood there, the one flushed and excited, the other apparently calm, with her back against the door and her hand over the electric button. A glance through the window showed Miss Brewster that the mate had got into the boat, and that they were steadily lowering away.

'Let me pass, you—you wretch!'

'All in good time,' replied Edith Longworth, whose gaze was also upon the boat swinging in mid-air.

Jennie Brewster saw at once that, if it came to a hand-to-hand encounter, she would have no chance whatever against the English girl, who was in every way her physical superior. She had her envelope in one hand and the gold in the other. She thrust both of them into her pocket, which, after some fumbling, she found. Then she raised her voice in one of the shrillest screams which Edith Longworth had ever heard. As if in answer to that ear-piercing sound, there rose from the steamer a loud and ringing cheer. Both glanced up to see where the boat was, but it was not in sight. Several ropes were dangling down past the porthole. Miss Brewster sprang up on the sofa, and with her small hands turned round the screw which held the window closed.

Edith Longworth looked at her without making any attempt to prevent the unfastening of the window.

Jennie Brewster flung open the heavy brass circle which held the thick green glass, and again she screamed at the top of her voice, crying 'Help!' and 'Murder!'

The other did not move from her position. In the silence that followed, the steady splash of oars could be heard, and again a rousing cheer rang out from those who were left upon the motionless steamer. Edith Longworth raised herself on tiptoe and looked out of the open window. On the crest of a wave, five hundred yards away from the vessel, she saw the boat for a moment appear, showing the white glitter of her six dripping oars; then it vanished down the other side of the wave into the trough of the sea.

'Now, Miss Brewster', she said, 'you are at liberty to go.'

CHAPTER XIII.

After Edith Longworth left her, Jennie Brewster indulged in a brief spasm of hysterics. Her common-sense, however, speedily came to her rescue; and, as she became more calm, she began to wonder why she had not assaulted the girl who had dared to imprison her. She dimly remembered that she thought of a fierce onslaught at the time, and she also recollected that her fear of the boat leaving during the struggle had stayed her hand. But now that the boat had left she bitterly regretted her inaction, and grieved unavailingly over the fact that she had stopped to write the account of the disaster which befell the Caloric. Had she not done so, all might have been well, but her great ambition to be counted the best-newspaper woman in New York, and to show the editor that she was equal to any emergency that might arise, had undone her. While it would have been possible for her to send away one telegram, her desire to write the second had resulted in her sending none at all. Although she impugned her own conduct in language that one would not have expected to have heard from the lips of a millionaire's daughter, her anger against Edith Longworth became more intense, and a fierce desire for revenge took possession of the fair correspondent. She resolved that she would go up on deck and shame this woman before everybody. She would attract public attention to the affair by tearing Edith Longworth from her deck-chair, and in her present state of mind she had no doubt of her strength to do it. With the yearning for vengeance fierce and strong upon her, the newspaper woman put on her hat and departed for the deck. She passed up one side and down the other, but her intended victim was not visible. The rage of Miss Brewster increased when she did not find her prey where she expected. She had a fear that, when she calmed down, a different disposition would assert itself, and her revenge would be lost. In going to and fro along the deck she met Kenyon and Fleming walking together. Fleming had just that moment come up to Kenyon, who was quietly pacing the deck alone, and, slapping him on the shoulder, asked him to have a drink.

'It seems to me,' he said, 'that I never have had the pleasure of offering you a drink since we came on board this ship. I want to drink with everybody here, and especially now, when something has happened to make it worth while.'

'I am very much obliged to you,' said John Kenyon coldly, 'but I never drink with anybody.'

'What, never touch it at all? Not even beer?'

'Not even beer.'

'Well, I am astonished to hear that. I thought every Englishman drank beer.'

'There is at least one Englishman who does not.'

'All right, then; no harm done, and no offence given, I hope. I may say, however, that you miss a lot of fun in this world.'

'I suppose I miss a few headaches also.'

'Oh, not necessarily. I have one great recipe for not having a headache. You see, this is the philosophy of headaches.' And then, much to John's chagrin, he linked arms with him and changed his step to suit Kenyon's, talking all the time as if they were the most intimate friends in the world. 'I have a sure plan for avoiding a headache. You see, when you look into the matter, it is this way: The headache only comes when you are sober. Very well, then. It is as simple as A B C. Never get sober; that's my plan. I simply keep on, and never get sober, so I have no headaches. If people who drink would avoid the disagreeable necessity of ever getting sober, they would be all right. Don't you see what I mean?'

'And how about their brains in the meantime?'

'Oh, their brains are all right. Good liquor sharpens a man's brains wonderfully. Now, you try it some time. Let me have them mix a cocktail for you? I tell you, John, a cocktail is one of the finest drinks that ever was made, and this man at the bar—when I came on board, he thought he could make a cocktail, but he didn't know even the rudiments—I have taught him how to do it; and I tell you that secret will be worth a fortune to him, because if there is anything Americans like, it is to have their cocktails mixed correctly. There's no one man in all England can do it, and very few men on the Atlantic service. But I'm gradually educating them. Been across six times. They pretend to give you American drinks over in England, but you must know how disappointing they are.'

'I'm sure I don't see how I should know, for I never taste any of them.'

'Ah, true; I had forgotten that. Well, I took this bar-keeper here in hand, and he knows now how to make a reasonably good cocktail; and, as I say, that secret will be worth money to him from American passengers.'

John Kenyon was revolving in his mind the problem of how to get rid of this loquacious and generous individual, when he saw, bearing down upon them, the natty figure of Miss Jennie Brewster; and he wondered why such a look of bitter indignation was flashing from her eyes. He thought that she intended to address the American politician, but he was mistaken. She came directly at him, and said in an excited tone, with a ring of anger in it:

'Well, John Kenyon, what do you think of your work?'

'What work?' asked the bewildered man.

'You know very well what work I mean. A fine specimen of a man you are! Without the courage yourself to prevent my sending that telegram, you induced your dupe to come down to my state-room and brazenly keep me from sending it.'

The blank look of utter astonishment upon the face of honest John Kenyon would have convinced any woman in her senses that he knew nothing at all of what she was speaking. A dim impression of this, indeed, flashed across the young woman's heated brain. But before she could speak, Fleming said:

'Tut, tut, my dear girl! you are talking too loud altogether. Do you want to attract the attention of everybody on the deck? You mustn't make a scandal in this way on board ship.'

'Scandal!' she cried. 'We will soon see whether there will be a scandal or not. Attract the attention of those on deck! That is exactly what I am going to do, until I show up the villainy of this man you are talking to. He was the concocter of it, and he knows it. She never had brains enough to think of it. He was too much of a coward to carry it through himself, and so he set her to do his dastardly piece of work.'

'Well, well,' said Fleming, 'even if he has done all that, whatever it is, it will do no good to attract attention to it here on deck. See how everybody is listening to what you are saying. My dear girl, you are too angry to talk just now; the best thing you can do is to go down to your state-room.'

'Who asked you to interfere?' she cried, turning furiously upon him. 'I'll thank you to mind your own business, and let me attend to mine. I should have thought that you would have found out before this that I am capable of attending to my own affairs.'

'Certainly, certainly, my dear child,' answered the politician soothingly; 'I'm sorry I can't get you all to come and have a drink with me, and talk this matter over quietly. That's the correct way to do things, not to stand here scolding on the deck, with everybody listening. Now, if you will quietly discuss the matter with John here, I'm sure everything will be all right.'

'You don't know what you are talking about,' replied the young lady. 'Do you know that I had an important despatch to send to the Argus, and that this man's friend, doubtless at his instigation, came into my room and practically held me prisoner there until the boat had left, so that I could not send the despatch? Think of the cheek and villainy of that, and then speak to me of talking wildly!'

An expression of amazement upon Kenyon's face convinced the newspaper woman, more than all his protestations would have done, that he knew nothing whatever of the escapade.

'And who kept you from coming out?' asked Fleming.

'It is none of your business,' she replied tartly.

'If you will believe me,' said Kenyon at last, 'I had absolutely no knowledge of all this; so, you see, there is no use speaking to me about it. I won't pretend I am sorry, because I am not.'

This added fuel to the flames, and she was about to blaze out again, when Kenyon, turning on his heel, left her and Fleming standing facing each other. Then the young woman herself turned and quickly departed, leaving the bewildered politician entirely alone, so that there was nothing for him to do but to go into the smoking-room and ask somebody else to drink with him, which he promptly did.

Miss Brewster made her way to the captain's room and rapped at the door. On being told to enter, she found that officer seated at his table with some charts before him, and a haggard look upon his face, which might have warned her that this was not the proper time to air any personal grievances.

'Well?' he said briefly as she entered.

'I came to see you, captain,' she began, 'because an outrageous thing has been done on board this ship, and I desire reparation. What is more, I will have it!'

'What is the "outrageous thing"?' asked the captain.

'I had some despatches to send to New York, to the New York Argus, on whose staff I am.'

'Yes,' said the captain with interest; 'despatches relating to what has happened to the ship?'

'One of them did, the other did not.'

'Well, I hope,' said the captain, 'you have not given an exaggerated account of the condition we are in.'

'I have given no account at all, simply because I was prevented from sending the cablegrams.'

'Ah, indeed,' said the captain, a look of relief coming over his face, in spite of his efforts to conceal it; 'and pray what prevented you from sending your cablegrams? The mate would have taken any messages that were given to him.'

'I know that,' cried the young woman; 'but when I was in my room writing the last of the despatches, a person who is on board as a passenger here—Miss Longworth—came into my room and held me prisoner there until the boat had left the ship.'

The captain arched his eyebrows in surprise.

'My dear madam,' he said, 'you make a very serious charge. Miss Longworth has crossed several times with me, and I am bound to say that a better-behaved young lady I never had on board my ship.'

'Extremely well behaved she is!' cried the correspondent angrily, 'she stood against my door and prevented me from going out. I screamed for help, but my screams were drowned in the cheers of the passengers when the boat left.'

'Why did you not ring your bell?'

'I couldn't ring my bell because she prevented me. Besides, if I had reached the bell, it is not likely anybody would have answered it; everybody seemed to be bawling after the boat that was leaving.'

'You can hardly blame them for that. A great deal depends on the safety of that boat. In fact, if you come to think about it, you will see that whatever grievance you may have, it is, after all, a very trivial one compared with the burden that weighs on me just now, and I should much prefer not to have anything to do with disputes between the passengers until we are out of our present predicament.'

'The predicament has nothing whatever to do with it. I tell you a fact. I tell you that one of your passengers came and imprisoned me in my state-room. I come to you for redress. Now, there must be some law on shipboard that takes the place of ordinary law on land. I make this demand officially to you. If you decline to hear me, and refuse to redress my wrong, then I have public opinion, to which I can appeal through my paper, and perhaps there will also be a chance of obtaining justice through the law of the land to which

I am going.'

'My dear madam,' said the captain calmly, 'you must not use threats to me. I am not accustomed to be addressed in the tone you have taken upon yourself to use. Now tell me what it is you wish me to do?'

'It is for you to say what you will do. I am a passenger on board this ship, and am supposed to be under the protection of its captain. I therefore tell you I have been forcibly detained in my state-room, and I demand that the person who did this shall be punished.'

'You say that Miss Longworth is the person who did this?'

'Yes, I do.'

'Now, do you know you make a serious charge against that young lady—a charge that I find it remarkably difficult to believe? May I ask you what reason she had for doing what you say she has done?'

'That is a long story. I am quite prepared to show that she tried to bribe me not to send a despatch, and, finding herself unsuccessful, she forcibly detained me in my room until too late to send the telegram.'

The captain pondered over what had been said to him.

'Have you any proof of this charge?'

'Proof! What do you mean? Do you doubt my word?'

'I mean exactly what I say. Have you anybody to prove the exceedingly serious charge you bring?'

'Certainly not. I have no proof. If there had been a witness there, the thing would not have happened. If I could have summoned help, it would not have happened. How could I have any proof of such an outrage?'

'Well, do you not see that it is impossible for me to take action on your unsupported word? Do you not see that, if you take further steps in this extraordinary affair, Miss Longworth will ask you for proof of what you state? If she denies acting as you say she did, and you fail to prove your allegation, it seems to me that you will be in rather a difficult position. You would be liable to a suit for slander. Just think the matter over calmly for the rest of the day before you take any further action upon it, and I would strongly advise you not to mention this to anyone on board. Then to-morrow, if you are still in the same frame of mind, come to me.'

Thus dismissed, the young woman left the captain's room, and met Fleming just outside, who said:

'Look here, Miss Brewster, I want to have a word with you. You were very curt with me just now.'

'Mr. Fleming, I do not wish to speak to you.'

'Oh, that's all right—that's all right; but let me tell you this: you're a pretty smart young woman, and you have done me one or two very evil turns in your life. I have found out all about this affair, and it's one of the funniest things I ever heard of.'

'Very funny, isn't it?' snapped the young woman.

'Of course it's very funny; but when it appears in full in the opposition papers to the Argus, perhaps you won't see the humour of it—though everybody else in New York will, that's one consolation.'

'What do you mean?'

'I mean to say, Jennie Brewster, that unless you are a fool, you will drop this thing. Don't, for Heaven's sake, let anybody know you were treated by an English girl in the way you were. Take my advice: say no more about it.'

'And what business is it of yours?'

'It isn't mine at all; that is why I am meddling with it. Aren't you well enough acquainted with me to know that nothing in the world pleases me so much as to interfere in other people's business? I have found out all about the girl who kept you in, and a mighty plucky action it was too. I have seen that girl on the deck, and I like the cut of her jib. I like the way she walks. Her independence suits me. She is a girl who wouldn't give a man any trouble, now, I tell you, if he were lucky enough to win her. And I am not going to see that girl put to any trouble by you, understand that!'

'And how are you going to prevent it, may I ask?'

'May you ask? Why, of course you may. I will tell you how I am going to prevent it. Simply by restraining you from doing another thing in the matter.'

'If you think you can do that, you are very much mistaken. I am going to have that girl put in prison, if there is a law in the land.'

'Well, in the first place, we are not on land; and, in the second place, you are going to do nothing of the kind, because, if you do, I shall go to the London correspondents of the other New York papers and give the whole blessed snap away. I'll tell them how the smart and cute Miss Dolly Dimple, who has bamboozled so many persons in her life, was once caught in her own trap; and I shall inform them how it took place. And they'll be glad to get it, you bet! It will make quite interesting reading in the New York opposition papers some fine Sunday morning—about a column and a half, say. Won't there be some swearing in the Argus when that appears! It won't be your losing the despatch you were going to send, but it will be your utter idiocy in making the thing public, and letting the other papers on to it. Why, the best thing in the world for you to do, and the only thing, is to keep as quiet as possible about it. I am astonished at a girl of your sense, Dolly, making a public fuss like this, when you should be the very one trying to keep it secret.'

The newspaper correspondent pondered on these words.

'And if I keep quiet about it, will you do the same?'

'Certainly; but you must remember that if ever you attempt any of your tricks of interviewing on me again, out comes this whole thing. Don't forget that.'

'I won't,' said Miss Jennie Brewster.

And next morning, when the captain was anxiously awaiting her arrival in his room, she did not appear.

CHAPTER XIV.

After all, it must be admitted that George Wentworth was a man of somewhat changeable character. For the last two or three days he had been moping like one who meditated suicide; now when everyone else was anxiously wondering what was going to happen to the ship, he suddenly became the brightest individual on board. For a man to be moody and distraught while danger was impending was not at all surprising; but for a man, right in the midst of gloom, to blossom suddenly out into a general hilarity of manner, was something extraordinary. People thought it must be a case of brain trouble. They watched the young man with interest as he walked with a springy step up and down the deck. Every now and again a bright smile illuminated his face, and then he seemed to be ashamed that people should notice he was feeling so happy. When he was alone he had a habit of smiting his thigh and bursting out into a laugh that was long and low, rather than loud and boisterous. No one was more astonished at this change than Fleming, the politician. George met him on deck, and, to the great surprise of that worthy gentleman, smote him on the back and said:

'My dear sir, I am afraid the other day, when you spoke to me, I answered a little gruffly. I beg to apologize. Come and have a drink with me.'

'Oh, don't mention it,' said Fleming joyously; 'we all of us have our little down-turns now and then. Why, I have them myself, when liquor is bad or scarce! You mightn't believe it, but some days I feel away down in the mouth. It is true I have a recipe for getting up again, which I always use. And that reminds me: do you remember what the Governor of North Carolina said to the Governor of South Carolina?'

'I'm sure I don't know,' said Wentworth; 'you see, I'm not very well versed in United States politics.'

'Well, there wasn't much politics about his remark. He merely said, "It's a long time between drinks;" come in and have something with me. It seems to me you haven't tasted anything in my company since the voyage began.'

'I believe,' said Wentworth, 'that is a true statement. Let us amend it as soon as possible, only in this case let me pay for the drinks. I invited you to drink with me.'

'Not at all, not at all!' cried Fleming; 'not while I'm here. This is my treat, and it is funny to think that a man should spend a week with another man without knowing him. Really, you see, I haven't known you till now.'

And so the two worthy gentlemen disappeared into the smoking-room and rang the electric bell.

But it was in his own state-room that George Wentworth's jocularity came out at its best. He would grasp John Kenyon by the shoulder and shake that solemn man, over whose face a grim smile generally appeared when he noticed the exuberant jollity of his comrade.

'John,' Wentworth cried, 'why don't you laugh?'

'Well, it seems to me,' replied his comrade, 'that you are doing laughing enough for us both. It is necessary to have one member of the firm solid and substantial. I'm trying to keep the average about right. When you were in the dumps I had to be cheerful for two. Now that you feel so lively, I take a refuge in melancholy, to rest me after my hard efforts at cheerfulness.'

'Well, John, it seems to me too good to be true. What a plucky girl she was to do such a thing! How did she know but that the little vixen had a revolver with her, and might have shot her?'

'I suppose she didn't think about it at all.'

'Have you seen her since that dramatic incident?'

'Seen whom? Miss Brewster?'

'No, no; I mean Miss Longworth.'

'No, she hasn't appeared yet. I suppose she fears there will be a scene, and she is anxious to avoid it.'

'Very likely that is the case,' said Wentworth. 'Well, if you do see her, you can tell her there is no danger. Our genial friend, Fleming, has had a talk with that newspaper woman, so he tells me, and the way he describes it is exceedingly picturesque. He has threatened her with giving away the "snap," as he calls it, to the other New York papers, and it seems that the only thing on earth Miss Brewster is afraid of is the opposition press. So she has promised to say nothing more whatever about the incident.'

'Then, you have been talking with Fleming?'

'Certainly I have; a jovial good fellow he is, too. I have been doing something more than talking with him; I have been drinking with him.'

'And yet a day or two ago, I understand, you threatened to strike him.'

'A day or two ago, John! It was ages and ages ago. A day or two isn't in it. That was years and centuries since, as it appears to me. I was an old man then; now I have become young again, and all on account of the plucky action of that angel of a girl of yours.'

'Not of mine,' said Kenyon seriously; 'I wish she were.'

'Well, cheer up. Everything will come out right; you see, it always does. Nothing looked blacker than this matter about the telegram a few days ago, and see how beautifully it has turned out.'

Kenyon said nothing. He did not desire to discuss the matter even with his best friend. The two went up on deck together, and took a few turns along the promenade, during which promenade the eyes of Kenyon were directed to the occupants of the deckchairs, but he did not see the person whom he sought. Telling Wentworth he was going below for a moment, he left him to continue his walk alone, and on reaching the saloon Kenyon spoke to a stewardess.

'Do you know if Miss Longworth is in her stateroom?'

'Yes, sir, I think she is,' was the answer.

'Will you take this note to her?'

John sat down to wait for an answer. The answer did not come by the hand of the stewardess. Edith herself timorously glanced into the saloon, and, seeing Kenyon alone, ventured in. He sprang up to meet her.

'I was afraid,' he said, 'that you had been ill.'

'No, not quite, but almost,' she answered. 'Oh, Mr. Kenyon, I have done the most terrible thing! You could not imagine that I was so bold and wicked;' and tears gathered in the eyes of the girl.

Kenyon stretched out his hand to her, and she took it.

'I am afraid to stay here with you,' she said, 'for fear——'

'Oh, I know all about it,' said Kenyon.

'You cannot know about it; you surely do not know what I have done?'

'Yes, I know exactly what you've done; and we all very much admire your pluck.'

'It hasn't, surely, been the talk of the ship?'

'No, it has not; but Miss Brewster charged me with being an accomplice.'

'And you told her you were not, of course?'

'I couldn't tell her anything, for the simple reason that I hadn't the faintest idea what she was talking about; but that's how I came to know what had happened, and I am here to thank you, Miss Longworth, for your action. I really believe you have saved the sanity of my friend Wentworth. He is a different man since the incident we are speaking of occurred.'

'And have you seen Miss Brewster since?'

'Oh yes; as I was telling you, she met me on the deck. Dear me! how thoughtless of me! I had forgotten you were standing. Won't you sit down?'

'No, no; I have been in my room so long that I am glad to stand anywhere.'

'Then, won't you come up on deck with me?'

301

'Oh, I'm afraid,' she said. 'I am afraid of a public scene; and I am sure, by the last look I caught in that girl's eyes, she will stop at no scandal to have her revenge. I am sorry to say that I am too much of a coward to meet her. Of course, from her point of view I have done her eternal wrong. Perhaps it was wrong from anybody's point of view.'

'Miss Longworth,' said John Kenyon cordially, 'you need have no fear whatever of meeting her. She will say nothing.'

'How do you know that?'

'Oh, it is a long story. She went to the captain with her complaint, and received very little comfort there. I will tell you all about it on deck. Get a wrap and come with me.'

As Kenyon gave this peremptory order, he realized that he was taking a liberty he had no right to take, and his face flushed as he wondered if Edith would resent the familiarity of his tones; but she merely looked up at him with a bright smile, and said:

'I will do, sir, as you command.'

'No, no,' said Kenyon; 'it was not a command, although it sounded like one. It was a very humble request; at least, I intended it to be such.'

'Well, I will get my wrap.'

As she left for her state-room, a rousing cheer was heard from on deck. She stopped, and looked at Kenyon.

'What does that mean?' she asked.

'I do not know,' was the answer. 'Please get your things on and we will go up and see.'

When they reached the deck they saw everybody at the forward part of the ship. Just becoming visible in the eastern horizon were three trails of black smoke, apparently coming towards them.

The word was whispered from one to the other: 'It is the tug-boats. It is relief.'

Few people on board the steamer knew that their very existence depended entirely on the good weather. The incessant pumping showed everybody, who gave a thought to the matter, that the leak had been serious; but as the subsidence of the vessel was imperceptible to all save experts, no one but the officers really knew the grave danger they were in. Glad as the passengers were to see those three boats approach, the one who most rejoiced was the one who knew everything respecting the disaster and its effects—the captain.

Edith Longworth and John Kenyon paced the deck together, and did not form two of the crowd who could not tear themselves away from the front of the ship, watching the gradually approaching tug boats. Purposely, John Kenyon brought the girl who was with him past Miss Jennie Brewster, and although that person glared with a good deal of anger at Edith, who blushed to her temples with fear and confusion, yet nothing was said; and Kenyon knew that afterwards his companion would feel easier in her mind about meeting the woman with whom she had had such a stormy five minutes. The tug boats speedily took the big steamer in tow, and slowly the four of them made progress towards Queenstown, it having been resolved to land all the passengers there, and to tow the disabled vessel to Liverpool, if an examination of the hull showed such a course to be a safe one. The passengers bade each other good-bye after they left the tender, and many that were on board that ship never saw each other again. One at least, had few regrets and no good-byes to make, but a surprise was in store for her. Jennie Brewster found a cablegram from New York waiting for her. It said 'Cable nothing respecting mines. Letter follows.'

CHAPTER XV.

London again! Muddy, drizzly, foggy London, London, with its well filled omnibuses tearing along the streets, more dangerous than the chariots of Rome, London, with its bustling thoroughfares, with its traffic blocked at the corners by the raised white gloved hand of the policeman, London, with the four wheeled growler piled high with luggage, and the dashing hansom whirling along, missing the wheels of other vehicles by half an inch, while its occupant sits serenely smoking, or motioning his directions to his cabman with an umbrella; London, with its constantly moving procession of every sort of wheeled carriage, from the four-horsed coach to the coster barrow. London, London, London, London! the name seemed to ring in John Kenyon's ears as he walked briskly along the crowded pavement towards the City. The roar of its busy streets was the sweetest music in the world to him, as it is to every man who has once acquired the taste for London. Drink of the fountain of Trevi, and you will return to Rome. Drink of the roar and the bustle of London, and no other metropolis in the world, can ever satisfy the city-hunger in you again. London is London, and John Kenyon loved its very disadvantages as he strode along the streets.

He called at the office of George Wentworth, took that young man with him, and together they went to the place where the adjourned meeting of the London Syndicate was to be held. There were questions to be asked of the two young men, and the directors couldn't quite see why the reports had been so suddenly precipitated upon them, before the arrival of the experts they had sent out. So they had merely read the documents at the former meeting and adjourned until such time as the two young men could appear in person. Most of the directors were there, but, though Kenyon looked anxiously among them, he did not see the face of old Mr. Longworth. Questions were asked Kenyon about the position of the mines, about their output, and such other particulars as the directors wished to know. Then Wentworth underwent a similar examination. He pointed out the discrepancies which he had found in the accounts. He showed that there was an evident desire on the part of the owners of the different mines to make it appear that the properties paid better than they actually did, and he answered in a clear and satisfactory way all the questions asked him. The chairman thanked the young men for the evident care with which they had done their work, and the meeting then went into a private session to consider what action should be taken respecting the mines. When the two friends got out of the building, Kenyon said:

'Well, thank goodness that is over and done with. Now, George, what have you to suggest with reference to the mica-mine?'

'I think,' said Wentworth, 'we had better adjourn to my office and have a talk over the matter quietly there. Let us go into private session as the directors have done. I feel rich after having got my cheque, and the vote of thanks from the chairman; so I will spend a shilling on a hansom and get there with speed and comfort. Actually, since I have got back to London, I am spending all my surplus cash on hansoms. They are certainly the best and cheapest vehicles in the world. Think of what that pirate charged us for a ride from the hotel to the steamer in New York.'

'I don't like to think of it,' said Kenyon; 'it makes me shudder!'

'Do you know, John, I should not be inconsolable if I never saw the great city of New York again. London is good enough for me.'

'Oh, I don't know! New York is all right. I confess there are one or two of her citizens that I do not care much about.'

'Ah,' said Wentworth; then, after a few moments' reflection, he remarked suddenly, apropos of nothing: 'Do you know, John, I was very nearly in love with that girl?'

'I thought you were drifting in that direction.'

'Drifting! It wasn't drifting. It was a mad plunge down the rapids, and it is only lately I have begun to think what a close shave I had of it. The horror of those days, when I thought that despatch was going to New York, completely obliterated any other feeling in regard to her. If I had found she was a hopeless flirt, or something of that kind, who was trifling with me, I should have been very much shocked, of course, but I should have thought about my own feelings. Now, the curious thing is that I never began to think about them till I got to London.'

'Very well, Wentworth; I wouldn't think about them now, if I were you.'

'No, I don't intend to, particularly. The fact that I talk over them with you shows that the impression was not very deep.'

Wentworth drew a long breath that might have been mistaken for a sigh, if he had not just before explained how completely free he was from the thraldom in which Miss Brewster at one time held him.

'Still, she was a very pretty girl, John. You can't deny that.'

'I have no wish to deny it. I simply don't want to think about her at all.'

'No, and we don't need to, thank goodness. But she was very bright and clever. Of course you didn't know her as I did. I never before met anyone who—Well, that's all past and done with. I told her all about our mica-mine, and she gave me much sage advice.'

Kenyon smiled, but held his peace.

'Oh yes, I know what you are thinking of. I spoke of other mines as well; still, that was my folly, and not her fault exactly. She imagined she was doing right, and after all, you know, I think we sometimes don't make enough allowance for another's point of view.'

Kenyon laughed outright.

'It seems to me you are actually defending her. My remembrance is that you didn't make much allowance for her point of view when your own point was that coil of rope in the front of the ship—those days when you wouldn't speak even to me.'

'I admit it, John. No, I'm not defending her. I have succeeded in putting her entirely out of my mind—with an effort. How about your own case, John?'

'My own case! What do you mean?'

306

'You know very well what I mean.'

'I suppose I do forgive the little bit of affectation, will you? but a man gets somewhat nervous when such a question is sprung upon him. My own case is just where we left it at Queenstown.'

'Haven't you seen her since?'

'No.'

'Aren't you going to?'

'I really do not know what I am going to do.'

'John, that young woman has a decided personal interest in you.'

'I wish I were sure of that, or, rather, I wish I were sure of it and in a position to—But what is the use of talking? I haven't a penny to my name.'

'No; but if our mine goes through, you soon will have.'

'Yes, but what will it amount to? I never can forget the lofty disdain with which a certain person spoke of fifty thousand pounds. It sends a cold chill over me whenever I think of it. Fifty thousand pounds to her seemed so trivial; to me it was something that might be obtained after the struggle of a lifetime.'

'Well, I wouldn't let that discourage me too much if I were you; besides, you see—Oh! here we are. We'll talk about this some other time.'

Having paid the cabman, the two young men went upstairs into Wentworth's room, where they closed the door, and John drew up a seat by the side of his friend.

'Now, then,' said Wentworth, 'what have you done about the mine?'

'I have done absolutely nothing. I have been waiting for this conference with you.'

'Well, my boy, time is the great factor in anything of this sort.'

'Yes, I suppose it is.'

'You see, our option is running along; every day we lose is so much taken off our chances of success. Have you anything to propose?'

'I'll tell you what I thought of doing. You know young Longworth spoke to me a good deal about the mine at one time. His cousin introduced me to him, and she seemed to think he might take some interest in forming the company. I was to have a talk with you, because Longworth gave it as his opinion that the amount should be put at two hundred thousand pounds rather than at fifty thousand pounds.'

Wentworth gave a long whistle.

'Yes, it seems a very large amount; but he claims that if it would pay ten per cent. on that sum—if we could show that there was a reasonable chance of its paying so much—we could put it at two hundred thousand.'

'Well, that looks reasonable. What else did he say?'

'He did not say very much more about it, because I told him I should have to consult you.'

'And why didn't you? On board ship there was one of the best opportunities we could have had of having a talk with him. In fact, the whole matter might perhaps have been arranged there.'

'Oh, well, you know, I couldn't talk to you about it, because a certain circumstance arose, and you spent your time very much in the forward part of the steamer, sitting on a coil of rope and cursing the universe generally and yourself in particular'.

'Ah, yes, I remember, of course—yes. Very well, then, you have not seen young Longworth since, have you?'

'No, I have not.'

'Wouldn't the old gentleman go in for it?'

'His daughter seemed to think he would not, because the amount was too small.'

'Why couldn't he be got to go into it entirely by himself? If we put the price up to one hundred thousand pounds or two hundred thousand pounds, that ought to be large enough for him, if he were playing a lone hand.'

'Well, you see, I don't suppose they thought of going in for it at that, except as a matter of speculation. Of course, if they intended to buy some shares, it is not likely they would propose to raise the price from fifty thousand pounds to two hundred thousand pounds. Young Longworth spoke of dividing the profit. He claimed that whatever we made on fifty thousand pounds would be too small to be divided into three. I told him, of course, that you were my partner in this, and that is why he proposed the price should be made two hundred thousand pounds.'

'I suppose he seemed indifferent on the question whether it should pay a dividend on that amount of money or not?'

'He didn't mention that particularly—at least, he did not dwell upon it. He asked if it would pay a dividend on two hundred thousand, and I told him I thought it would pay ten per cent. if rightly managed; then he said of course that was its price, and we should be great fools to float it at fifty thousand pounds when it was really worth two hundred thousand.'

Wentworth pondered for a few minutes on this, tapping his pencil on the desk and knitting his brow.

'It seems an awful jump, from fifty thousand pounds to two hundred thousand pounds, doesn't it, John?'

'Yes, it does; it has a certain look of swindling about it. But what a glorious thing it would be if it could be done, and if it would pay the right percentage when we got the scheme working!'

'Of course I wouldn't be connected, nor you either, with anything that was bogus.'

'Certainly not. I wouldn't think for a moment of inflating it if I were not positive the property would stand it. I have been making, and have here in my pocket, an elaborate array of figures which will show approximately what the mine will yield, and I am quite convinced that it will pay at least ten per cent., and possible twelve or fifteen.'

'Well, nobody wants a better percentage on their money. Have you the figures with you?'

'Yes, here they are.'

'Very well, you had better leave them with me, and I will go over them as critically as if they were the figures of somebody I was deeply suspicious of, I hope they will hold water; but if they do not, I will point out to you where the discrepancies are.'

'But, you see, George, it is more a question of facts than of figures. I believe the whole mountain is made of the mineral which is so valuable, but I take only about an eighth of it as being possible to get out, which seems to me a very moderate estimate.'

'Yes, but how much demand is there for it? That is the real question. The thing may be valuable enough, but if there is only a limited demand—that is to say, if we have ten times the material that the world needs—the other nine parts are comparatively valueless.'

'That is true.'

'Do you know how many establishments there are in the world that use this mineral?'

'There are a great many in England, and also in the United States.'

'And how about the duty on it in the United States?'

'Ah, that I do not know.'

'Well, we must find that out. Just write down here what it is used for; then I shall try to get some information about the factories that require it, and also what quantities they need in a year. We shall have to get all these facts and figures to lay before the people who are going to invest, because, as I understand it, the great point we make is not on the mica, but on the other mineral.'

'Exactly.'

'Very well, then, you leave me what you know already about it, and I will try to supplement your information. In fact, we shall have to supplement it, before we can go before anybody with it. Now, I advise you to see the Longworths—both old and young Longworth—and you may find that talking with them in the City of London is very different from talking with them on the Caloric. By the way, I wonder why Longworth was not at the directors' meeting to-day.'

'I do not know. I noticed he was absent.'

'He very likely intends to have nothing more to do with the other mines, and so there may be a possibility of his investing in ours. Do you know his address?'

'Yes, I have it with me.'

'Then, if I were you, I would jump into a hansom and go there at once. Meanwhile, I will try to get your figures into shipshape order, and supplement them as far as it is possible to do so. This is going to be no easy matter, John. There are a great many properties now being offered to the public—the papers are full of them—and each of them appears to be the most money-making scheme in existence; so if we are going to float this mine without knowing any particular capitalist, we have our work cut out for us.'

'Then, you would be willing to put the price up to two hundred thousand pounds?'

'Yes, if you say the mine will stand it. That we can tell better after we have gone over the figures together. We ought to be sure of our facts first.'

'Very well. Good-bye; I will go and see Mr. Longworth.'

CHAPTER XVI.

John Kenyon did not take a cab. He walked so that he might have time to think. He wanted to arrange in his mind just what he would say to Mr. Longworth, so he pondered over the coming interview as he walked through the busy streets of the City.

He had not yet settled things satisfactorily to himself when he came to the door leading to Mr. Longworth's offices.

'After all,' he said to himself, as he paused there, 'Mr. Longworth has never said anything to me about the mica-mine; and, from what his daughter thought, it is not likely that he will care to interest himself in it. It was the young man who spoke about it.'

He felt that it was really the young man on whom he should call, but he was rather afraid of meeting him. The little he had seen of William Longworth on board the Caloric had not given him a very high opinion of that gentleman, and he wondered if it would not have been better to have told Wentworth that nothing was to be expected from the Longworths. However, he resolved not to shirk the interview, so passed up the steps and into the outer office. He found the establishment much larger than he had expected. At numerous desks there were numerous clerks writing away for dear life. He approached the inquiry counter, and a man came forward to hear what he had to say.

'Is Mr. Longworth in?'

'Yes, sir. Which Mr. Longworth do you want—the young gentleman or Mr. John Longworth?'

'I wish to see the senior member of the firm.'

'Ah! have you an appointment with him?'

'No, I have not; but perhaps if you will take this card to him, and if he is not busy, he may see me.'

'He is always very busy, sir.'

'Well, take the card to him; and if he doesn't happen to remember the name, tell him I met him on board the Caloric.'

'Very good, sir.' And with that the clerk disappeared, leaving Kenyon to ponder over in his mind the still unsettled question of what he should say to Mr. Longworth if he were ushered into his presence. As he stood there waiting, with the host of men busily and silently working around him, amid the general air of important affairs pervading the place, he made up his mind that Mr. Longworth would not see him, and so was rather surprised when the clerk came back without the card, and said, 'Will you please step this way, sir?'

Passing through a pair of swinging doors, his conductor tapped lightly at a closed one, and then opened it.

'Mr. Kenyon, sir,' he said respectfully, and then closed the door behind him, leaving John Kenyon standing in a large room somewhat handsomely furnished, with two desks near the window. From an inner room came the muffled click, click, click of a type-writer. Seated at one of the desks was young Longworth, who did not look round as Kenyon was announced. The elder gentleman, however, arose, and cordially held out his hand.

'How are you, Mr. Kenyon?' he said. 'I am very pleased to meet you again. The terror of our situation on board that ship does not seem to have left an indelible mark upon you. You are looking well.'

'Yes,' said John; 'I am very glad to be back in London again.'

'Ah, I imagine we all like to get back. By the way, it was a much more serious affair than we thought at the time on board the Caloric.'

'So I see by the papers.'

'How is your friend? He seemed to take it very badly.'

'Take what badly?' asked John in astonishment.

'Well, he appeared to me, at the time of the accident, to feel very

313

despondent about our situation.'

'Oh yes, I remember now. Yes, he did feel a little depressed at the time; but it was not on account of the accident. It was another matter altogether, which, happily, turned out all right.'

'I am glad of that. By the way, have you made your report to the directors yet?'

'Yes; we were at a meeting of the directors to-day.'

'Ah, I could not manage to be there. To tell the truth, I have made up my mind to do nothing with those Ottawa mines. You do not know what action the Board took in the matter, do you?'

'No, they merely received our report; in fact, they had had the report before, but there were some questions they desired to ask us, which we answered apparently to their satisfaction.'

'Who were there? Sir Ropes McKenna was in the chair, I suppose?'

'Yes, sir, he was there.'

'Ah, so I thought. Well, my opinion of him is that he is merely a guinea-pig—you know what that is? I have made up my mind to have nothing more to do with the venture, at any rate. And so they were pleased with your report, were they?'

'They appeared to be. They passed us a vote of thanks, and one or two of the gentlemen spoke in rather a complimentary manner of what we had done.'

'I am glad of that. By the way, William, you know Mr. Kenyon, do you not?'

The young man looked round with an abstracted air, and gazed past, rather than at, John Kenyon.

'Kenyon, Kenyon,' he said to himself, as if trying to recollect a name that he had once heard somewhere. 'I really don't——'

'Tut, tut!' said the old man, 'you remember Mr. Kenyon on board the Caloric?'

'Oh, ah, yes; certainly—oh, certainly. How do you do, Mr. Kenyon? I had forgotten for the moment. I thought I had met you in the City somewhere. Feeling first-rate after your trip, I hope.' And young Mr. Longworth fixed his one eyeglass in its place and flashed its glitter on Kenyon.

'I am very well, thanks.'

'That's right. Let me see, your business with the London Syndicate is concluded now, is it not?'

'Yes, it is done with.'

'Ah, and what are you doing? Have you anything else on hand?'

'Well, that is what I wish to see you about.'

'Really?'

'Yes; I—you remember, perhaps, we had some talk about a mica-mine near the Ottawa River?'

'On my soul, I don't. You see, the voyage rather—that was on board ship, I suppose?'

'Yes,' said John, crossing over to the young man's desk and taking a chair beside him. The old gentleman now turned to his own papers, and left the two young men to talk together.

'Do you mean to say you don't remember a talk we had on deck once about a mica-mine?'

Young Longworth looked at him with a puzzled expression, as if he could not quite make out what he was talking about.

'I remember,' he said, 'your telling me that you had been sent over by the London Syndicate to see after certain mines there; but I don't remember anything being said in reference to them.'

'It was not in reference to them at all; it was in reference to another mine, of which I have secured the option. You will, perhaps, recollect that your cousin introduced me to you. You seemed to think at the time that the price at which we were going to offer the mine was too low.'

'By Jove, yes! now I do recollect something about it, when you mention that. Let me see, how much was it? A million, was it not?'

'No, no' said Kenyon, mopping his brow. He did not at all like the turn the conversation had taken. 'Not a million, nor anything like that amount.'

'Ah, I am sorry for that. You see, my uncle and myself rarely touch anything that is not worth while; and anything under a million would be hardly worth bothering with, don't you know.'

'I don't think so; it seems to me that something below a million would be worth spending a little time on; at least, it would be worth my while.'

'That may be very true; but, you see, my uncle takes large interests only in large businesses.'

'If you remember, Mr. Longworth, your uncle was not mentioned in connection with this at all. Your cousin seemed to think you might take some interest in it yourself. You told me, when I said the price at which we wished to offer the mine was fifty thousand pounds, that the sum was altogether too small; at least, it left too little margin to divide amongst three.'

'Well, I think I was perfectly correct in that.'

'And you further said that, if we increased the capital to two hundred thousand pounds, you would take a share in it with us.'

'Did I say that?'

'Yes. It rested with my partner then. I said I would speak to him about it, and, if he were willing, I should be. Circumstances occurred which made it impossible for me to go into details with him on board the ship; but I have spoken to him to-day at his own office, and he is quite willing to offer the mine at two hundred thousand pounds, provided the figures which I have given him show that it will pay a handsome dividend on that sum.'

'Well, it seems to me that, if the mine is really worth two hundred thousand pounds, it is a pity to offer it at fifty thousand pounds. Doesn't it strike you that way?'

'Yes, it does; so I called to see you with reference to it. I wanted to say that Wentworth will go carefully over the figures I have given him, and see if there is any mistake about them. If there is not, and if we find that the mine will bear inflation to two hundred thousand pounds, we shall be very glad of your aid in the matter, and will divide everything equally with you. That is to say, each of us will take a third.'

'If I remember rightly, I asked you a question which you did not answer. I asked you how much you paid for the mine.'

Kenyon was astonished at this peculiar kind of memory, that could forget a whole conversation, and yet remember accurately one detail of it. However, he replied:

'Of course, at that time you had not said you would join us. I recognise that, if you are to be a partner, it is your right to know exactly what we pay for the mine. I may say that we have not paid for it, but have merely got an option on it at a certain price, and of course, if we can sell it for two hundred thousand pounds, we shall have a large amount to divide. Now, if you think you will go in with us, and do your best to make this project a success, I will tell you what our option is on the mica-mine.'

'Well, you see, I can hardly say that I will join you. It is really a very small matter. There ought not to be any difficulty in floating that mine on the London market, except that it is hardly worth one's while to take it up. Still, I should have to know exactly what you are to pay for the property before I went any further in the matter.'

'Very well, then, I tell you in confidence, and only because I expect you to become a partner with us, that the amount the mine is offered to us for is twenty thousand pounds.'

Young Longworth arched his eyeglass.

'It cannot be worth very much if that is all they ask for it.'

'The price they ask for it has really nothing at all to do with the value of the mine. They do not know the value of it. They are not working it, even now, so as to bring out all there is in it. They are mining for mica, and, as I told you, the mineral which they are throwing away is very much more valuable than all the mica they can get out of the mine. If it were worked rightly, the mica would pay all expenses, as well as a good dividend on fifty thousand pounds, while the other mineral would pay a large dividend on one hundred and fifty thousand pounds, or even two hundred thousand pounds.'

'I see. And you feel positive that there is enough of this mineral to hold out for some time?'

'Oh, I am positive of that. There is a whole mountain of it.'

'And do you get the mountain as well as the mine?'

'We get three hundred acres of it, and I think there would be no difficulty in buying the rest.'

'Well, that would seem to be a good speculation, and I am sure I hope you will succeed in forming your company. How much money are you prepared to spend in floating the mine?'

'I have practically nothing at all. My asset, as it were, is the option I have on the mine.'

'Then, how are you going to pay the preliminary fees, the advertising in the newspapers, the cost of counsel, and all that? These expenses will amount to something very heavy in the formation of a company. Of course you know that.'

'Well, you see, I think that perhaps we can get two or three men to go into this and form our company quietly, without having any of those heavy expenses which are necessary in the forming of some companies.'

'My dear sir, when you have been in this business a little longer, you will be very much wiser. That cannot be done—at least, I do not believe it can be done. I do not know of its having been done, and if you can do it, you are a very much cleverer man than I am. Companies are not formed for nothing in the City of London. You seem to have the vaguest possible notion about how this sort of thing is managed. I may tell you frankly I do not think I can go in with you; I have too much else on hand.'

Although Kenyon expected this, he nevertheless felt a grim sense of defeat as the young man calmly said these words. Then he blurted out:

'If you had no idea of going in with us, why have you asked me certain questions about the property which I would not have answered if I had not thought you were going to take an interest in it?'

'My dear sir,' said the other blandly, 'you were at perfect liberty to answer those questions or not, as you chose. You chose to answer them, and you have no one to blame but yourself if you are sorry you have answered them. It really doesn't matter at all to me, as I shall forget all you have said in a day or two at furthest.'

'Very well; I have nothing more to say except that what I have told you has been said in confidence.'

'Oh, of course. I shall mention it to nobody.'

'Then I wish you good-day.'

Turning to the elder gentleman, he said:

'Good-day, Mr. Longworth.'

The old man raised his eyes rather abstractedly from the paper he was reading, and then cordially shook hands with Kenyon.

'If I can do anything,' he said, 'to help you in any matter you have on hand, I shall be very pleased to do it. I hope to see you succeed. Good-day, Mr. Kenyon.'

'Good-day, Mr. Longworth.'

And with that the young man found himself again in the outer office, and shortly afterwards in the busy street, with a keen sense of frustration upon him. His first move in the direction of forming a company had been a disastrous failure; and thinking of this, he walked past the Mansion House and down Cheapside.

CHAPTER XVII.

John Kenyon walked along Cheapside feeling very much downhearted over his rebuff with Longworth. The pretended forgetfulness of the young man, of course, he took at its proper value. He, nevertheless, felt very sorry the interview had been so futile, and, instead of going back to Wentworth and telling him his experience, he thought it best to walk off a little of his disappointment first. He was somewhat startled when a man accosted him; and, glancing up, he saw standing there a tall footman, arrayed in a drab coat that came down to his heels.

'I beg your pardon, sir,' said the footman, 'but Miss Longworth would like to speak to you.'

'Miss Longworth!' cried Kenyon, in surprise; 'where is she?'

'She is here in her carriage, sir.'

The carriage had drawn up beside the pavement, and John Kenyon looked round in confusion to see that Miss Longworth was regarding him and the footman with an amused air. An elderly woman sat in the carriage opposite her, while a grave and dignified coachman, attired somewhat similarly to the footman, kept his place like a seated statue in front. John Kenyon took off his hat as he approached the young woman, whom he had not seen since the last day on the steamer.

'How are you, Mr. Kenyon?' said Edith Longworth brightly, holding out her hand to the young man by her carriage. 'Will you not step in? I want to talk with you, and I am afraid the police will not allow us to block such a crowded thoroughfare as Cheapside.'

As she said this, the nimble footman threw open the door of the carriage, while John, not knowing what to say, stepped inside and took his seat.

'Holborn,' said the young woman to the coachman; then, turning to Kenyon, she continued: 'Will you not tell me where you are going, so that I may know where to set you down?'

'To tell the truth,' said John, 'I do not think I was going anywhere. I am afraid I have not yet got over the delight of being back in London again, so I sometimes walk along the streets in rather a purposeless manner.'

'Well, you did not seem delighted when I first caught sight of you. I thought you looked very dejected, and that gave me courage enough to ask you to come and talk with me. I said to myself, "There is something wrong with the mica-mine," and, with a woman's I curiosity, I wanted to know all about it. Now tell me.'

'There is really very little to tell. We have hardly begun yet. Wentworth is to-day looking over the figures I gave him, and I have been making a beginning by seeing some people who I thought might be interested in the mine.'

'And were they?'

'No; they were not.'

'Then, that was the reason you were looking so distressed.'

'I suppose it was.'

'Well, now, Mr. Kenyon, if you get discouraged after an interview with the first person you think will be interested in the mine, what will you do when a dozen or more people refuse to have anything to do with it?'

'I'm sure I do not know. I am afraid I am not the right person to float a mine on the London market. I am really a student, you see, and flatter myself I am a man of science. I know what I am about when I am in a mine, miles away from civilization; but when I get among men, I feel somehow at a loss. I do not understand them. When a man tells me one thing to-day, and to-morrow calmly forgets all about it, I confess it—well, confuses me.'

'Then the man you have seen to-day has forgotten what he told you yesterday. Is that the case?'

'Yes; that is partly the case.'

'But, Mr. Kenyon, the success of your project is not going to depend upon what one man says, or two, or three, is it?'

'No; I don't suppose it is.'

'Then, if I were you, I would not feel discouraged because one man has forgotten. I wish I were acquainted with your one man, and I would make him ashamed of himself, I think.'

Kenyon flushed as she said this, but made no reply.

The coachman looked round as he came to Holborn, and Miss Longworth nodded to him; so he went on without stopping into Oxford Street.

'Now, I take a great interest in your mine, Mr. Kenyon, and hope to see you succeed with it. I wish I could help you, or, rather, I wish you would be frank with me, and tell me how I can help you. I know a good deal about City men and their ways, and I think I may be able to give you some good advice—at least, if you would have the condescension to consult me.'

Kenyon smiled.

'You are making game of me now, Miss Longworth. Of course, as you said on board ship, it is but a very small matter.'

'I never said any such thing. When did I say that?'

'You said that fifty thousand pounds was a small matter.'

'Did I? Well, I am like your man who has forgotten; I have forgotten that. I remember saying something about its being too small an amount for my father to deal with. Was not that what I said?'

'Yes, I think that was it. It conveyed the idea to my mind that you thought fifty thousand pounds a trifling sum indeed.'

Edith Longworth laughed.

'What a terrible memory you have! I do not wonder at your City man forgetting. Are you sure what you told him did not happen longer ago than yesterday?'

'Yes, it happened some time before.'

'Ah, I thought so; I am afraid it is your own terrible memory, and not his forgetfulness, that is to blame.'

'Oh, I am not blaming him at all. A man has every right to change his mind, if he wants to do so.'

'I thought only a woman had that privilege.'

'No; for my part I freely accord it to everybody, only sometimes it is a little depressing.'

'I can imagine that; in fact, I think no one could be a more undesirable acquaintance than a man who forgets to-day what he promised yesterday, especially if anything particular depends upon it. Now, why cannot you come to our house some evening and have a talk about the mine with my cousin or my father? My father could give you much valuable advice with reference to it, and I am anxious that my cousin should help to carry this project on to success. It is better to talk with them there than at their office, because they are both so busy during the day that I am afraid they might not be able to give the time necessary to its I discussion.'

John Kenyon shook his head.

'I am afraid,' he said, 'that would do no good. I do not think your cousin cares to have anything to do with the mine.'

'How can you say that? Did he not discuss the matter with you on board ship?'

'Yes; we had some conversation about it there, but I imagine that—I really do not think he would care to go any farther with it.'

'Ah, I see,' said Edith Longworth. 'My cousin is the man who "forgot to-day what he said yesterday."'

'What am I to say, Miss Longworth? I do not want to say "Yes," and I cannot truthfully say "No."'

'You need say nothing. I know exactly how it has been. So he does not want to have anything to do with it. What reason did he give?'

'You will not say anything to him about the matter? I should be very sorry if he thought that I talked to anyone else of my conference with him.'

'Oh, certainly not; I will say nothing to him at all.'

'He gave no particular reason; he simply seemed to have changed his mind. But I must say this: he did not appear to be very enthusiastic when I discussed it with him on board ship.'

'Well, you see, Mr. Kenyon, it rests with me now to maintain the honour of the Longworth family. Do you want to make all the profit there is to be made in the mica-mine—that is, yourself and your friend Mr. Wentworth?'

'How do you mean—"all the profit"?'

'Well, I mean—would you share the profit with anyone?'

'Certainly, if that person could help us to form the company.'

'Very well; it was on that basis you were going to take in my cousin as a partner, was it not?'

'Yes.'

'Then I should like to share in the profits of the mine if he does not take an interest in it. If you will let me pay the preliminary expenses of forming this company, and if you will then give me a share of what you make, I shall be glad to furnish the money you need at the outset.'

John Kenyon looked at Miss Longworth with a smile.

'You are very ingenious, Miss Longworth, but I can see, in spite of your way of putting it, that what you propose is merely a form of charity. Suppose we did not succeed in forming our company, how could we repay you the money?'

'You would not need to repay the money. I would take that risk. It is a sort of speculation. If you form the company, then I shall expect a very large reward for furnishing the funds. It is purely selfishness on my part. I believe I have a head for business. Women in this country do not get such chances of developing their business talents as they seem to have in America. In that country there are women who have made fortunes for themselves. I believe in your mine, and I am convinced you will succeed in forming your company. If you or Mr. Wentworth were capitalists, of course there would be no need of my assistance. If I were alone, I could not form a company. You and Mr. Wentworth can do what I cannot do. You can appear before the public and attend to all preliminaries. On the other hand, I believe I can do what neither of you can do; that is, I can supply a certain amount of money from time to time to pay the expenses of forming the company—because a company is not formed in London for nothing, I assure you. Perhaps you think you have simply to go and see a sufficient number of people and get your company formed. I fancy you will find it not so easy as all that. Besides this business interest I have in it, I have a very friendly interest in Mr. Wentworth.'

As she said this, she bent over towards John Kenyon, and spoke in a lower tone of voice:

'Please do not tell him so, because I think that he is a young man who has possibilities of being conceited.'

'I shall say nothing about it,' said Kenyon dolefully.

'Please do not. By the way, I wish you would give me Mr. Wentworth's address, so that I may communicate with him if a good idea occurs to me, or if I find out something of value in forming our company.'

Kenyon took out a card, wrote the address of Wentworth upon it, and handed it to her.

'Thank you,' she said 'You see, I deeply sympathized with Mr. Wentworth for what he had to pass through on the steamer.'

'He is very grateful for all you did for him on that occasion,' replied Kenyon.

'I am glad of that. People, as a general thing, are not grateful for what their friends do for them. I am glad, therefore, that Mr. Wentworth is an exception. Well, suppose you talk with him about what I have said, before you make up your own mind. I shall be quite content with whatever share of the profits you allow me.'

'Ah, that is not business, Miss Longworth.'

'No, it is not; but I am dealing with you—that is, with Mr. Wentworth—and I am sure both of you will do what is right. Perhaps it would be better not to tell him who is to furnish the money. Just say you have met a friend to-day who offers, for a reasonable share of the profits, to supply all the money necessary for the preliminary expenses. You will consult with him about it, will you not?'

'Yes, if it is your wish.'

'Certainly it is my wish; and I also wish you to do it so diplomatically that you will conceal my name from him more successfully than you concealed my cousin's name from me this afternoon.'

'I am afraid I am very awkward,' said John, blushing.

'No; you are very honest, that's all. You are not accomplished in the art of telling what is not true. Now, this is where we live; will you come in?'

'Thank you, no; I'm afraid not,' said John. 'I must really be going now.'

'Let the coachman take you to your station.'

'No, no, it is not worth the trouble; it is only a step from here.'

'It is no trouble. Which is your station—South Kensington?'

'Yes.'

'Very well. Drive to South Kensington Station, Parker,' she said to the coachman; and then, running up the steps, she waved her hand in good-bye, as the carriage turned.

And so John Kenyon, feeling abashed at his own poverty, was driven in this gorgeous equipage to the Underground Railway station, where he took the train for the City.

As he stepped from the carriage at South Kensington, young Mr. Longworth came out of the station on his way home, and was simply dumfounded to see Kenyon in the Longworths' carriage.

John passed him without noticing who he was, and just as the coachman was going to start again, Longworth said to him:

'Parker, have you been picking up fares in the street?'

'Oh no, sir,' replied the respectable Parker; 'the young gentleman as just left us came from the City with Miss Longworth.'

'Did he, indeed? Where did you pick him up, Parker?'

'We picked him up in Cheapside, sir.'

'Ah, indeed;' and with that, muttering some imprecations on the cheek of Kenyon, he stepped into the carriage and drove home.

CHAPTER XVIII.

George Wentworth was a very much better man than John Kenyon to undertake the commercial task they hoped to accomplish. Wentworth had mixed with men, and was not afraid of them. Although he had suffered keenly from the little episode on the steamer, and although at that trying time he appeared to but poor advantage so far as an exhibition of courage was concerned, the reason was largely because the blow had been dealt him by a woman, and not by a man. If one of Wentworth's fellow-men so far forgot himself as to make an insulting or cutting remark to him, Wentworth merely shrugged his shoulders and thought no more about it. On the other hand, notwithstanding his somewhat cold and calm exterior, John Kenyon was as sensitive as a child, and a rebuff such as he received from the Longworths was enough to depress him for a week. He had been a student all his life, and had not yet learnt the valuable lesson of knowing how to look at men's actions with an eye to proportion. Wentworth said to himself that nobody's opinion amounted to very much, but Kenyon knew too little of his fellows to have arrived at this comforting conclusion.

George Wentworth closed his door when he was alone, drew the mass of papers, which Kenyon had left, towards him on his desk, and proceeded systematically to find a flaw in them if possible. He said to himself: 'I must attack this thing without enthusiasm, and treat Kenyon as if he were a thief. I must find an error in the reasoning or something shaky about the facts.' He perused the papers earnestly, making pencil-marks on the margin here and there. At first he said to himself: 'It is quite evident that the mining of the mica will pay for the working of the mine. We can look upon the demand for mica as being in a certain sense settled. It has paid for the working of the mine so far, also a small dividend, and there is no reason to think it should not go on doing so. Now, the uncertain quantity is this other stuff, and the uncertain thing about this uncertain quantity is the demand for it in the markets of the world, also how much the carriage of it is going to cost.' Wentworth had a theory that all things were possible if you only knew a man who knew the man. There is always the man in everything—the man who is the authority on iron; the man who is the authority on mines; the man who is the authority on the currency, and the man who knows all about the printing trade. If you want any information on any particular subject, it was not necessary to know the man, but it was very essential to know a man who can put his finger on the man. Get a note of introduction from a man who knows the man, and there you are!

Wentworth touched his bell, and a boy answered his summons.

'Ask Mr. Close to step in here for a moment, will you, please?'

The boy disappeared, and shortly after an oldish man with a very deferential look, who was perpetually engaged in smoothing one hand over the other, came in, and, in a timid manner, closed the door softly behind him.

'Close,' said Wentworth, 'who is it that knows everything about the china trade?'

'About the china trade, sir?'

'Yes, about the china trade.'

'Wholesale or retail, sir?'

'I want to get at somebody who knows all about the manufacture of china.'

'Ah, the manufacture, sir,' said Close, in a tone that indicated this was another matter altogether; 'the manufacture, sir; yes, sir, I really do not know who could tell everything about the manufacture of china, sir, but I know of a man who could put you on the right track.'

'Very well; that is quite as good.'

'I would see Mr. Melville, if I were you, sir—Mr. Melville, of the great Scranton China Company.'

'And what is his address?'

'His address is——' And here the old man stooped over and wrote it on a card. 'That will find him, sir. If you can drop a note to Mr. Melville, sir, and say you want to learn who knows all about the production of china, he will be able to tell you just the man, sir. He is in the wholesale china trade himself, sir.'

'Would he be in at this hour, do you think?'

'Oh yes, sir, he is sure to be in his office now.'

'Very well, then; I think I will just run over and see him.'

'Very good, sir; anything more, sir?'

'Nothing more, Close, thank you.'

When the valuable Close had departed as softly and apologetically as he had entered, Wentworth picked up one of the specimens of spar which Kenyon had taken from the mine, and put it into his pocket. In two minutes more he was in a cab, dashing through the crowded streets towards Melville's office. By the side of the door of the china company's warehouse, inside the hall, were two parallel rows of names—one under the general heading of 'Out,' the other under the heading of 'In.' It appeared that Mr. Smith was out and Mr. Jones was in, but, what was more to the purpose, the name of Richard Melville happened to be in the column of those who were inside. After a few moments' delay, Wentworth was ushered into the office of this gentleman.

'Mr. Melville,' he said, 'I have been recommended to come to you for information regarding the china trade. The information I want, you will, perhaps, not be able to give me, but I believe you can tell me to whom I should apply for it.' Saying this, he took out of his pocket the specimen of mineral which he had brought with him. 'What I want to know is, how much of this material you use each year in the manufacture of china; what price you pay for it; and I should like to get at an estimate, if possible, of the quantity used in England every year.'

Melville picked up the specimen and turned it round and round, looking at it attentively.

'Well,' he said at last, 'I could tell you anything you wished about the wholesale china trade, but about the manufacture of it I am not so well informed. Where did you get this?'

'That,' said Wentworth, 'is from a mine in which I am interested.'

'Ah, where is the mine situated, may I ask?'

'It is in America,' said Wentworth vaguely.

'I see. Have you considered the question of carriage in proposing to put it on the English market? That, as you know, is an important question. The cost of taking a heavy article a long distance is a great factor in the question of its commercial value.'

'I recognise that,' said Wentworth; 'and it is to enable me to form some estimate of the value of this material that I ask for particulars of its price here.'

'I understand, but I am not able to answer your questions. If you have time to wait and see Mr. Brand, our manager of the works, who is also one of the owners, he could easily tell you everything about this mineral—whether used at all or not. He comes up to London once every fortnight, and to-day is his day. I am expecting him here at any time. You might wait, if you liked, and see him.'

'I do not think that will be necessary. I will write, if you will allow me, just what I want to know, and in two or three minutes he could jot down the information I require. Then I will call again to-morrow, if you don't mind.'

'Not in the least. I will submit the matter to him. You can leave me this piece of mineral, I suppose?'

'Certainly,' said Wentworth, writing on a sheet of paper the questions: 'First, What quantity of this mineral is used in your works in a year? second, What price per ton do you pay for it? third, Will you give me, if possible, an estimate of how much of this is used in England?'

'There,' he said, 'if you will give him this slip of paper, and show him the specimen of mineral, I shall be very much obliged.'

'By the way,' said Melville, 'is this mine in operation?'

'Yes, it is.'

'Is there anyone else beside yourself interested in it in this country?'

'Yes,' said Wentworth, with some hesitation; 'John Kenyon, a mining expert, is interested in it, and Mr. Longworth—young Mr. Longworth of the City.'

'Any relation to John Longworth?'

'His nephew.'

'Ah, well, anything that Longworth has an interest in is reasonably sure of being successful.'

'I am perhaps going too far in saying he has an interest in the mine, but in coming from America he seemed desirous of going in with us. My partner. John Kenyon, of whom I spoke just now, is with him at the present moment, I believe.'

'Very well. I will submit this specimen to Mr. Brand as you desire, and will let you know to-morrow what he says.'

With that Wentworth took his leave, and in going out through the hall he met the manager of the china works, although he didn't know at the time who he was. He was a very shrewd-faced individual, who walked with a brisk business step which showed he believed that time was money.

'Well, Melville,' he said when he entered, 'I am a little late to-day, am I not?'

'You are a little behind the usual time, but not much.'

'By the way——' began the manager, and then his eye wandered to the specimen on the desk before Melville. 'Hello!' he cried, 'where did you get this?'

'That was left here a moment ago by a gentleman whom I wanted to wait until you came, but he seemed to be in a hurry. He is going to call again to-morrow.'

'What is his name?'

'Wentworth. Here's his card.'

'Ah, of a firm of accountants, eh? How did he come to have this?'

'He wanted to get some information about it, and I told him I would show it to you. Here is the note he left.'

The manager turned the crystal over and over in his hand, put on his eyeglasses and peered into it, then picked up the piece of paper and looked at what Kenyon had written.

'Did he say where he had got this?'

'Yes; he says there is a mine of it in America.'

'In America, eh? Did he say how much of this stuff there was?

'No; he didn't tell me that. The mine is working, however.'

'It is very curious! I never heard of it.'

'I gathered from him,' said Mr. Melville, 'that he wishes to do something with the mine over here. He did not say much, but he told me his partner—I forget his name—was talking at the present moment with young Longworth about it.'

'Longworth—who's he?'

'He's a man who goes in for mines or other investments; that is, his uncle does—a very shrewd old fellow, too. He is always on the right side of the market, no matter how it turns.'

'Then, he would be a man certain to know the value of the property if he had it, wouldn't he?'

'I don't know anybody who knows the value of what he has better than Longworth.'

'Ah, that's a pity,' mused the manager.

'Why? Is it a mineral of any worth?'

'Worth! A quarry of this would be better for us than a gold-mine!'

'Well, it struck me, in talking with Mr. Wentworth, that he had no particular idea of its utility. He seemed to know nothing about it, and that's why he came here for information.'

Again the manager looked at the paper before him.

'I'm not so sure about that,' he said. 'He wants to know the quantity used in a year, how much of it is consumed in England, and the price we pay for it per ton. I should judge, from that, he has an inkling of its value, and wants merely to corroborate it. Yes, I feel certain that is his move. I fear nothing very much can be done with Mr. Wentworth.'

'What were you thinking of doing?'

'My dear Melville, if we could get hold of such a mine, supposing it has an unlimited quantity of this mineral in it, we could control the china markets of the world.'

'You don't mean it!'

'It's a fact, because of the purity of the mineral. The stuff that we use is heavily impregnated with iron; we have to get the iron out of it, and that costs money. Not that the stuff itself is uncommon at all, it is one of the most common substances in Nature; but anything so pure as this I have never seen. I wonder if it is a fair specimen of what they can get out of the mine? If it is, I would rather own that property than any gold-mine I know of.'

'Well, I will see Mr. Wentworth, if you like. He is going to call here about this time to-morrow, and I will find out if some arrangement cannot be made with him.'

'No, I wouldn't do that,' replied the manager, who preferred never to do things in a direct way. 'I think your best plan is to see Longworth. The chances are that a City man like him does not know the value of the property; and, if you don't mind, I will write a letter to Mr. Wentworth and give him my opinion on this mineral.'

'What shall I say to Longworth?'

'Say anything you like; you understand that kind of business better than I. Here are the facts of the case. If we can get a controlling interest in this mine, always supposing that it turns out mineral up to sample—I suspect that this is a picked specimen; of course we should have to send a man to America and see—if we could get hold of this property, it would be the greatest feat in business we have ever done, provided, of course, we get it at a cheap enough price.'

'What do you call a cheap enough price?'

'You find out what Longworth will sell the mine for.'

'But supposing Wentworth owns the mine, or as much of it as Longworth does?'

'I think, somehow, that if you know Longworth you can perhaps make better terms with him. Meanwhile I will send a letter to Wentworth. You have his address there?'

'Yes.'

'Very well.'

Taking his pen, he dashed off the following letter:

'DEAR SIR,

'I regret to say that the mineral you left at our office yesterday is of no value to us. We do not use mineral of this nature, and, so far as I know, it is not used anywhere in England.

'Yours truly,

'ADAM BRAND.'

CHAPTER XIX.

The chances are that, no matter under what circumstances young Longworth and Kenyon had first met, the former would have disliked the latter. Although strong friendships are formed between men who are dissimilar, it must not be forgotten that equally strong hatreds have arisen between people merely because they were of opposite natures. No two young men could have been more unlike each other; and as Longworth recalled the different meetings he had had with Kenyon, he admitted to himself that he had an extreme antipathy to the engineer. The evident friendship which his cousin felt for Kenyon added a bitterness to this dislike which was rapidly turning it into hate. However, he calmed down sufficiently, on going home in the carriage, to become convinced that it was better to say nothing about her meeting with Kenyon unless she introduced the subject. After all, the carriage was hers, not his, and he recognised that fact. He wondered how much Kenyon had told her of the interview at his uncle's office. He flattered himself, however, that he knew enough of women to be sure that she would very speedily refer to the subject, and then he hoped to learn just how much had been said. To his surprise, his cousin said nothing at all about the matter, neither that evening nor the next morning, and, consequently, he went to his office in a somewhat bewildered state of mind.

On arriving at his room in the City, he found Melville waiting for him.

Melville shook hands with young Longworth, and, taking a mineral specimen from his pocket, placed it on the young man's desk, saying;

'I suppose you know where that comes from?'

Longworth looked at it with an air of indecision which made Melville suspect he knew very little about it.

'I haven't the slightest idea, really.'

'No? I was told you were interested in the mine from which this was taken. Mr. Wentworth called on me yesterday, and gave your name as one of those who were concerned with the mine.'

'Ah, yes, I see; yes, yes, I have—some interest in the mine.'

'Well, it is about that I came to talk with you. Where is the mine situated?'

'It is near the Ottawa River, I believe, some distance above Montreal. I am not certain about its exact position, but it is somewhere in that neighbourhood.'

'I thought by the way Wentworth talked it was in the United States. He mentioned another person as being his partner in the affair; I forget his name.'

'John Kenyon, probably.'

'Kenyon! Yes, I think that was the name. Yes, I am sure it was. Now, may I ask what is your connection with that mine? Are you a partner of Wentworth's and Kenyon's? Are you the chief owner of the mine, or is the mine owned by them?'

'In the first place, Mr. Melville, I should like to know why you ask me these questions?'

Melville laughed.

'Well, I will tell you. We should like to know what chance there is of our getting a controlling interest in the mine. That is very frankly put, isn't it?'

'Yes, it is. But whom do you mean by "we"? Who else besides yourself?'

'By "we" I mean the china company to which I belong. This mineral is useful in making china. That I suppose you know.'

'Yes, I was aware of that,' answered Longworth, although he heard it now for the first time.

'Very well, then; I should like to know who is the owner of the mine.'

'The owner of the mine at present is some foreigner whose name and address I do not know. The two young men you speak of have an option on that mine for a certain length of time—how long I don't know. They have been urging me to go in with them to form a company for the floating of that mine for two hundred thousand pounds on the London market.'

'Two hundred thousand pounds!' said Melville. 'That seems to me rather a large amount.'

'Do you think so? Well, the objection I had to it was that it was too small.'

'Those two men must have an exaggerated idea of the value of this mineral if they think it will pay dividends on two hundred thousand pounds.'

'This mineral is not all there is in the mine. In fact, it is already paying a dividend on fifty thousand pounds or thereabouts, because of the mica in it. It is being mined for mica alone. To tell the truth, I did not know much about the other mineral.'

'And do you think the mine is worth two hundred thousand pounds?'

'Frankly, I do not.'

'Then why are you connected with it?'

'I am not connected with it—at least, not definitely connected with it. I have the matter under consideration. Of course, if there is anything approaching a swindle in it, I shall have nothing to do with it. It will depend largely on the figures that the two men show me whether I have anything to do with it or not.'

'I see; I understand your position.' Then, lowering his voice, Melville leaned over towards Longworth, and said: 'You are a man of business. Now, I want to ask you what would be the chance of our getting the mine at something like the original option priced which is, of course, very much less than two hundred thousand pounds? We do not want to have too many in it. In fact, if you could get it for us at a reasonable rate, and did not care to be troubled with the property yourself, we would take the whole ourselves.'

Young Longworth pondered a moment, and then said to Melville:

'Do you mean to freeze out the other two fellows, as they say in America?'

'I do not know about freezing out; but, of course, with the other two there is so much less profit to be divided. We should like to deal with just as few as if possible.'

'Exactly. I see what you mean. I think it can be done. Are you in any great hurry to secure the mine?'

'Not particularly. Why?'

'Well, if things are worked rightly, I don't know but what we could get it for the original option. That would mean, of course, to wait until this first option had run out.'

'Wouldn't there be a little danger in that? They may form their company in the meantime, and then we should lose everything. Our interest in the matter is as much to prevent anyone else getting hold of the mine as to get it ourselves.'

'I see. I will think it over. I believe it can be done without great risk; but, of course, we shall have to be reasonably quiet about the matter.'

'I see the necessity of that.'

'Very good. I will see you again after I have thought over the affair, and we can come to some arrangement.'

'I may say that our manager has written a note to Wentworth, saying that this mineral is of no particular use to us.'

'Exactly,' said young Longworth, with a look of intelligence.

'So, of course, in speaking with Wentworth about the mine, it is just as well not to mention us in any way.'

'I shall not.'

'Very well. I will leave the matter in your hands for the present.'

'Yes, do so. I will think over it this afternoon, and probably see Wentworth and Kenyon to-morrow. There is no immediate hurry, for I happen to know they have not done anything yet.'

With that Mr. Melville took his leave, and young Longworth paced up and down the room, evolving a plan that would at once bring him money and give him the satisfaction of making it lively for John Kenyon.

When he reached home, Longworth waited for his cousin to say something about Kenyon; but he soon saw that she did not intend to speak of him at all. So he said to her:

'Edith, do you remember Kenyon and Wentworth—who were on board our steamer?'

'I remember them very well.'

'Did you know they had a mining property for sale?'

'Yes.'

'I have been thinking about it—in fact, Kenyon called at my office a day or two ago, and at that time, not having given the subject much thought, I could not give him any encouragement; but I have been pondering over it since, and have almost decided to help them. What do you think about it?'

'Oh, I think it would be an excellent plan. I am sure the property is a good one, or Mr. Kenyon would have nothing to do with it. I shall write a note to them, if you think it advisable, inviting them here to talk with you about it.'

'That will not be necessary at all. I do not want people to come here to talk business. My office is the proper place.'

'Still, we met them in a friendly way on board the steamer, and I think it would be nice if they came here some evening and talked over the matter with you.'

'I don't believe in introducing business into a man's home. This would be a purely business conversation, and it may as well take place at my office, or at Wentworth's, if he has one, as I suppose he has.'

'Oh, certainly; his address is———'

'Oh, you know it, do you?'

Edith blushed as she realized what she had said; then she remarked:

'Is there any harm in my knowing the business address of Mr. Wentworth?'

'Oh, not at all—not at all. I merely wondered how you happened to know his address, when I didn't.'

'Well, it doesn't matter how I know it. I am glad you are going to join him, and I am sure you will be successful. Will you see them to-morrow?'

'I think so. I shall call on Wentworth and have a talk with him about it. Of course we may not be able to come to a workable arrangement. If not, it really does not matter very much. But if I can make satisfactory terms with them, I will help them to form their company.'

When Edith went to her own room she wrote a note. It was addressed to George Wentworth in the City, but above that address was the name John Kenyon. She said:

'DEAR MR. KENYON,

'I was certain at the time you spoke that my cousin was not so much at fault in forgetting his conversation as you thought. We had a talk to night about the mine, and when he calls upon you tomorrow, as he intends to do, I want you to know that I said nothing whatever to him of what you told me. He mentioned the subject first. I wanted you to know this because you might feel embarrassed when you met him by thinking I had sent him to you. That is not at all the case. He goes to you of his own accord, and I am sure you will find his assistance in forming a company very valuable. I am glad to think you will be partners.

'Yours very truly,

'EDITH LONGWORTH.'

She gave this letter to her maid to post, and young Longworth met the maid in the hall with the letter in her hand. He somehow suspected, after the foregoing conversation, to whom the letter was addressed.

'Where are you going with that?'

'To the post, sir.'

'I am going out; to save you the trouble I will take it.'

After passing the corner, he looked at the address on the envelope; then he swore to himself a little. If he had been a villain in a play he would have opened the letter; but he did not. He merely dropped it into the first pillar-box he came to, and in due time it reached John Kenyon.

CHAPTER XX.

Although Jennie Brewster arrived in London angry with the world in general, and with several of its inhabitants in particular, she soon began to revel in the delights of the great city. It was so old that it was new to her, and she visited Westminster Abbey and other of its ancient landmarks in rapid succession. The cheapness of the hansoms delighted her, and she spent most of her time dashing about in cabs. She put up at one of the big hotels, and ordered many new dresses at a place in Regent Street. She bought most of the newspapers, morning and evening, and declared she could not find an interesting article in any of them. From her point of view they were stupid and unenterprising, and she resolved to run down the editor of one of the big dailies when she got time, interview him, and discover how he reconciled it with his conscience to publish so dull a sheet every day.

She wrote to her editor in New York that London, though a slow town, was full of good material, and that nobody had touched it in the writing line since Dickens' time; therefore she proposed to write a series of articles on the Metropolis that would wake them up a bit. The editor cabled to her to go ahead, and she went.

Jennie engaged a chaperon, and took great satisfaction in this unwonted luxury. It had been intimated to her that Lady Willow was a sort of society St. Peter, who held keys that would open the gates of the social heaven, if she were sufficiently recompensed. Of all the ancient landmarks of England, none attracted Jennie so much as the aristocracy, and although she had written to New York for letters of introduction that would be useful in London, she was too impatient to await their arrival. Thus she came to secure the services of Lady Willow, the widow of Sir Debenham Willow, who had died abroad, insolvent, some years before, mourned by the creditors he left behind him.

Jennie was suspicious about the title, and demanded convincing proofs of its genuineness before she engaged Lady Willow. She was amazed that any real lady would, as it were, sell her social influence at so much a week;

but, as Lady Willow was equally astonished that an American girl earned her livelihood by writing for the papers, the surprise of the one found its counterpart in the wonder of the other.

Lady Willow thought all American girls were born daughters of millionaires, in accordance with some unexplained Western by-law of nature, and imagined that their sole object in desiring to enter London society was to purchase for themselves a more or less expensive scion of the aristocracy; she was therefore inclined to resent meeting a shrewd young woman apparently determined on getting the value for her money.

'It is not my custom to chaffer about terms,' said Lady Willow with much dignity.

'It is mine,' replied Jennie complacently; 'I always like to know what I am buying, and the price I am to pay for it.'

'You are dealing with me,' said the lady, rising indignantly, 'as if you were engaging a cook. I am sure we would not suit each other at all.'

'Please sit down, Lady Willow, and don't be offended. Let us talk it over in an amicable manner, even if we come to no arrangement. I think a cook an exceedingly important person, and I assure you I would treat one in the most deferential manner; while with you, on the other hand, I talk in an open and frank way, as between friend and friend. I take it that you and I are somewhat similarly situated. We are neither of us rich, and so we have each of us to earn the money we need in our own way. It would be dishonest if I pretended to you that I was wealthy, and then couldn't pay what you expected after you had done all you could for me—now, wouldn't it? Very well, if you have anyone else to chaperon who can afford to pay more than I can, you shouldn't bother about me at all, but secure a richer client.'

Lady Willow remembered that this was not the season when rich clients abounded; so she smothered her resentment, and sat down again.

'That's right,' said Jennie; 'we'll have a nice quiet talk, whatever comes of it. Now, if you like, I could write a lovely article about you in the Sunday Argus, and then all rich girls who come over here would go direct to you.'

'Oh dear! oh dear!' cried Lady Willow, evidently inexpressibly shocked at the idea, 'you would surely never do so cruel a thing as that? If my friends knew I chaperoned young ladies and took money for it, I would never be allowed to enter their doors again.'

'Ah, I didn't think of that. Of course it wouldn't do. What a curious thing it is that those who want to be written up in the papers generally never see their names in print; while those who don't want to have anything said about them are the people the reporters are always after.'

'Do you write for the papers, then?'

'For one of them.'

'How dreadful!' said Lady Willow, rising again, with an air of finality about her movement. It was evident that any dealings with this American girl were out of the question.

'Do sit down again, Lady Willow. We will take it that I am hopelessly ineligible, and so say no more about it; but I do want to have a talk with you.'

'But you will write something——'

'I shall not write a word about you or about anything you tell me. You see, your profession is as strange to me as mine is to you.'

'My profession? I have none.'

'Well, whatever you call it. I mean the way in which you make your money.'

Lady Willow sighed, and the tears came into her eyes.

'You little know, my child, to what straits one may come who is left unprovided for, and who has to do the best to keep up appearances.'

Jennie sprang up instantly and took the unresisting hand of the elder woman, smoothing it with her own caressingly.

'Why, of course I know,' she cried, with a little quaver in her voice; 'and there is nothing more terrible on earth than lack of money. If there was a single really civilized country in existence, it would make provision for its women. Every woman should be assured enough to live on, merely because she is a woman. If England had put aside as much for its women as it has spent in the last hundred years on foolish wars, or if America had made a fund of what its politicians have been allowed to steal, the women of both barbarous countries might have been provided with incomes that would at least keep them from the fear of want.'

Lady Willow seemed more alarmed than comforted by the vehemence of Miss Brewster. She said hesitatingly:

'I'm afraid you have some very strange ideas, my dear.'

'Perhaps; but I have one idea that isn't strange: it is that you are going to take charge of a lonesome, friendless girl for a few weeks at least—until the rich pork-packer's daughter from Chicago comes along, and she won't be here for a month or two yet. We won't say a word about terms; I'll pay you all that's left over from my hansom fares.'

'I shall be very happy to do what I can for you, my dear.'

Lady Willow had softened towards her fair client, and had now adopted a somewhat motherly tone with her, which Jennie evidently liked.

'I will try and be very little trouble to you, although I shall probably ask you ever so many questions. All I really want is merely to see the Zoo, hear the animals roar, and watch them being fed. I have no ambition to steal any of them.'

'Oh, that will be easily done,' said Lady Willow in surprise. 'We can get tickets from one of the Fellows of the Zoological Society which will admit us on Sunday, when there are but few people there.'

Jennie laughed merrily.

'I mean the social Zoo, Lady Willow; I have visited the other already. Please do not look so shocked at me, and don't be afraid; I really talk very nicely when I am in society, and I am sure you will not be in the least ashamed of me. You see, I haven't had a soul to speak with since I came to London, so

I think I ought to be allowed a little latitude at first.'

Lady Willow so far relaxed her dignity as to smile, although a little dubiously; and Jennie joyfully proclaimed that their compact was sealed and that she was sure they would be great friends.

'Now you must tell me what I am to do,' she continued. 'I suppose dresses are the most important preliminaries when one is meditating a siege on society. Well, I've ordered ever so many, so that's all right. What's the next thing?'

'Yes, dress is important; but I think the first thing to do is to choose pleasant rooms somewhere. You can't stay at this hotel, you know; besides, it must be very expensive.'

'Yes, it is rather; but it is so handy and central.'

'It is not central for society.'

'Oh, isn't it? I was thinking of Westminster Abbey and Trafalgar Square, and that sort of thing. Besides, there's always a nice hansom right at the door whenever one wants to go out.'

'Oh, but you mustn't ride in hansoms, you know!'

'Why? I thought the aristocracy—the very highest—rode in hansoms.'

'Some of them have private hansoms; but that's a very different thing.'

'And I heard somewhere that most of the hansoms in London are owned by the aristocracy. I am sure I rode in one belonging to the Marquis of Something—I forget his name. I don't suppose the Marquis himself drove it. Perhaps it was driven by his hired man; but the driver was such a nice young fellow, and he gave me a lot of information. He told me that the Marquis owned the hansom; for I asked him whose it was. I thought perhaps it belonged to the driver. I'll give up the hotel willingly, but I don't know about hansoms. I'm afraid to promise; for I feel sure I'll hail a hansom automatically the moment I go out alone. So we will postpone the hansom question until later. Now, where would you recommend me to stay while in London?'

'You could stop with me if you liked. I have not a large house; but there is room for one or two friends, and it is in a very good locality.'

'Oh, that will be delightful. I suppose the correct address on one's notepaper is everything, almost as good as a coat-of-arms—if they use coats-of-arms as letter-heads; and there is a difference between Drury and Park when they precede the word "Lane."'

The two ladies speedily came to an understanding that was satisfactory to each of them, and Lady Willow found, to the no small comforting of her dignity, that, although she came to the hotel in the attitude of one who, if it may be so expressed, sought a favour, the impetuous eagerness of the younger woman had so changed the situation that the elder lady now left with the gratifying self complacency of a generous person who has conferred a boon. Nor was her condescension without its reward, both material and intellectual, for not only did Jennie pay her way with some lavishness, but her immediate social success was flattering to Lady Willow as the introducer of a Transatlantic cousin so bright and vivacious.

So great an impression did Jennie make upon the more susceptible portion of the young men she met under Lady Willow's chaperonage, that even the rumour which got abroad, that she had no money, did not damp the devotion of all of them. Lord Frederick Bingham was quite as assiduous in his attentions as if she were the greatest heiress that ever crossed the ocean to exchange dubiously won gold for a title founded by some thief in the Middle Ages, thus bringing ancient and modern villainy into juxtaposition.

Lady Willow saw Lord Frederick's preference with pleasurable surprise. Although she did not altogether approve of the damsel in her care, she had become very fond of her; but she failed to see why Jennie was so much sought after, when other girls, almost as pretty and much more eligible, were neglected. She hinted delicately to the young woman one day that perhaps her visit to England would not be, after all, so futile.

'I don't think I understand you,' said Jennie.

'Well, my dear, with a little tact on your part, I'm not at all sure but Lord

Frederick Bingham might propose.'

Jennie, who was putting on her gloves, paused and looked at Lady Willow, with a merry twinkle in her eyes, and a demure smile hovering about the corners of her mouth.

'Do you imagine, then, that I have come over here to ensnare some poor unprotected nobleman—with a display of tact? Oh dear me! As if tact had anything to do with it! Never, never, never, Lady Willow! I wouldn't marry an Englishman if he were the last man left on earth.'

'Many Englishmen are very nice, my dear,' protested Lady Willow gently, with a deep sigh, for she thought of her own husband, who, having been all his life an irreclaimable reprobate, had commanded her utmost affection while he lived, and was the object of her tenderest regret now that he had taken his departure from a world that had never appreciated his talents; although its influence was, in the estimation of the widow, entirely to blame for those shortcomings which Sir Debenham had been unable to conceal.

'And yet,' continued Jennie inconsequently, as she buttoned her glove, 'I do adore a title; I wonder why that is? I suppose no woman is ever at heart a republican, and if the United States is to be wrecked, it is the women who will do the wrecking, and start a monarchy. I have no doubt the men would let us proclaim an empire now if they imagined it would please us.'

'I thought you were all sovereigns over there already,' said Lady Willow.

'Oh, we are, but that's just the trouble. There is too much competition in the queen business; there are too many of us, and so we exchange our sovereignty for the lesser titles of duchesses and countesses and all that.

"'It is no trivial thing, I ween,

To be a regular Royal Queen.

No half and half affair, I mean,

But a right down regular, regular regular regular Royal Queen."

I don't know that the words are right, but the sentiment is there. Oh dear me! I'm afraid I'm becoming quite English, you know.'

'I don't see many signs of it,' said Lady Willow, smiling in spite of herself as her voluble companion sang and danced about the room.

'Come, Lady Willow,' cried Jennie, 'get on your things; I am going to a City bank to cash a cheque, and I warn you that I will take a hansom. Lord Freddie agrees with me that a hansom is the jolliest kind of vehicle: please don't frown at me, Lady Willow—"jolliest" is Lord Freddie's word, not mine.'

'What I didn't like,' said Lady Willow, with as near an approach to severity as the kindly woman could assume, 'was your calling him Lord Freddie.'

'Oh, that's his phrase, too! He says everybody calls him Lord Freddie. But come along, and I'll call him Lord—Frederick—Bingham,' with a voice of awe and appropriate pauses between the words. 'He always seems so trivial compared with his name; he reminds me of a salesman at a remnant counter, and I don't wonder everybody calls him Lord Freddie. I'm afraid I'm a disappointed woman, Lady Willow. I suppose the men have retrograded since armour went out of fashion; they had to be big and strong then to carry so much hardware. Of course it makes a difference to a man whether his tailor cuts him a suit out of broadcloth or out of sheet iron. Yes, I begin to suspect that I've come to England several centuries too late.'

Lady Willow was too much shocked at these frivolous remarks to make any reply, so, attempting none, she went to her room to prepare for her trip to the City.

Leaving Lady Willow in the hansom, Jennie entered the bank and got the white notes, generally alluded to in fiction as 'crisp,' stuffing them with greater carelessness than their value warranted into her purse. She took from this receptacle of her wealth a bit of paper on which was written an address, and this she looked at for some moments before leaving the bank. On reaching the hansom, she handed up the slip of paper to the driver.

'Do you know where that is?' she asked.

'Yes, miss; it is just round the corner.'

'Well, drive to the opposite side of the street, and stop where I can see the door of No. 23.'

'Very good, miss.'

Arriving nearly opposite No. 23, the driver pulled up. Jennie looked across at the doorway where many hurrying men were entering and leaving. It was a large building evidently filled with offices; the girl drew a deep breath, but made no motion to leave the hansom.

'Have you business here, too?' asked Lady Willow, to whom the City was an unknown land, the rush and noise of which were unpleasantly bewildering.

'No,' said Jennie, with a doleful note in her voice, 'this is not business; it is pleasure. I want to sit here for a few minutes and think.'

'But, my dear child,' expostulated Lady Willow, 'you can't think in this babel; besides, the police will not allow the hansom to stand here unless one of us is shopping, or has business in an office.'

'Then, dear Lady Willow, do go shopping for ten minutes; I saw some lovely shops just down the street. Here are five pounds, and if you see anything that I ought to have, buy it for me. One must think now and then, you know. Our thoughts are like the letters we receive; we need to sort them out periodically, and discard those that we don't wish to keep. I want to rummage over my thoughts and see whether some of them are to be abandoned or not.'

When Lady Willow left her, Jennie sat with her chin in her hands and her elbows on her knees gazing across at No. 23. The faces of none who went in or came out were familiar to her. Frequently glances were cast at her by passers-by, but she paid no heed to the crowd, nor to the fleeting admiration her pretty face aroused in many a flinty stockbroking breast, if, indeed, she was conscious of the attention she received. She awoke from her reverie when Lady Willow stepped into the hansom.

'What, back already?' she cried.

'I have been away for a quarter of an hour,' said the elder woman reproachfully. 'Besides, the money is all spent, and here are the parcels.'

'Money doesn't go far in the City, does it?' said Jennie.

'Why, what's the matter with you, my dear?' asked the elder woman; 'your voice sounds as if you had been crying.'

'Nonsense! What an idea! This street reminds me so of Broadway that I have become quite homesick, that's all. I think I'll go back to New York.'

'Have you met somebody from over there?'

'No, no. I've seen no one I knew.'

'Did you expect to?'

'Perhaps.'

'I didn't know you had any friends in the City.'

'I haven't. He's an enemy.'

'Really? An enemy who was once a friend?'

'Yes. Why do you ask so many questions?'

Lady Willow took the girl's hand, and said soothingly:

'I am sorry there was a misunderstanding.'

'So am I,' agreed Jennie.

CHAPTER XXI.

When John Kenyon entered the office of his friend next morning, Wentworth said to him:

'Well, what luck with the Longworths?'

'No luck at all,' was the answer; 'the young man seemed to have forgotten all about our conversation on board the steamer, and the old gentleman takes no interest in the matter.'

Wentworth hemmed and tapped on the desk with the end of his lead pencil.

'I never counted much on that young fellow,' he said at last. 'What appeared to be his reason?'

'I don't know exactly. He didn't give any reason. He merely said that he would have nothing to do with it, after having got me to tell him what our option on the mine was.'

'Why did you tell him that?'

'Well, it seemed, after I had talked to him a little, that there was some hope of his going in with us. I told him point-blank that I didn't care to say at what figure we had the option unless he was going in with us. He said of course he couldn't consider the matter at all unless he knew to what he was committed; and so I told him.'

'And what excuse did he make for not joining us?'

'Oh, he merely said he thought he would have nothing to do with it.'

'Now, what do you imagine his object was in pumping you if he had no intention of taking an interest in the mine?'

'I'm sure I don't know. I do not understand that sort of man at all. In fact, I feel rather relieved he is going to have nothing to do with it. I distrust him.'

'That's all very well, John, you are prejudiced against him; but you know the name of Longworth would have a very great effect upon the minds of other City men. If we can get the Longworths into this, even for a small amount, I am certain that we shall have very little trouble in floating the company.'

'Well, all I can say is, my mission to the Longworths was a failure. Have you looked over the papers?'

'Oh yes, and that reminds me. The point on which the whole scheme turns is the availability of the mineral for the making of china, isn't it?'

'That is so.'

'Well, look at this letter; it came this morning.'

He tossed the letter over to Kenyon, who read it, and then asked:

'Who's Adam Brand? He doesn't know what he is talking about.'

'Ah, but the trouble is that he does. No man in England better, I should imagine. He is the manager and part owner of the big Scranton china works. I went to see Melville of that company yesterday. He could tell me nothing about the mineral, but kept the specimen I gave him, and told me he would show it to the manager when he came in. Brand is the manager of the works, and if anybody knows the value of the mineral, he ought to be the man.'

'Nevertheless,' said Kenyon, 'he is mistaken.'

'That is just the point of the whole matter—is he? The mineral is either valueless, as he says, or he is telling a deliberate lie for some particular purpose; and I can't see, for the life of me, why a stranger should not only tell a falsehood, but write it on paper. Now, John, what do you know about china manufacture?'

'I know very little indeed about it.'

'Very well, then, how can you put your knowledge against this man's, who is a practical manufacturer?'

Kenyon looked at Wentworth, who was evidently not feeling in the best of humours.

'Do you mean to say, George, that I do not know what I am talking about when I tell you that this mineral is valuable for a certain purpose?'

'Well, you have just admitted that you know nothing about the china trade.'

'Not "nothing," George—I know something about it; but what I do understand is the value of minerals. The reason I know anything at all about china manufacture is simply because I learned that this mineral is one of the most important components of china.'

'Then why did that man write such a letter?'

'I'm sure I don't know. As you saw the man, you can judge better than I whether he would tell a deliberate falsehood, or whether he was merely ignorant.'

'I didn't see Brand at all; I saw Melville. Melville was to submit this mineral to Brand, and let me know what he thought about it. Of course, everything depends upon the value of it in the china trade.'

'Of course.'

'Very well then, I took the only way that was open to me to find out what practical men say about it. If they say they will have nothing to do with it, then we might as well give up our mining scheme and send back our option to Mr. Von Brent.'

Kenyon read the letter again, and pondered deeply over it.

'You see, of course,' said George once more, 'everything hinges on that, don't you?'

'I certainly see that.'

'Then, what have you to say?'

'I have to say this—that I shall have to take a trip among the china works of Great Britain. I think it would be a good plan if you were to write to the different manufacturers in the United States and find out how much they use of it. There is no necessity for sending the mineral. They have to use that, and nothing else will do. Find out from them, if you can, how much of it they need, what price they will pay for pure material, and what they pay for the impure material they use now.'

'How do you know, John, that there are not a dozen mines with that material in them?'

'How do I know? Well, if you want to impugn my knowledge of mineralogy, I wish you would do so straight out. I either know my business or I do not. If you think I do not, then leave this matter entirely alone. I tell you that what I say about this mineral is true. What I say about its scarcity is true. There are no other mines with mineral so pure as this.'

'I am perfectly satisfied when you say that, but you must remember those who are going to put their money in this company will not be satisfied. They must have the facts and figures down before them, and they are not going to take either your word or mine as to the value of the mineral. Your proposal about seeing the different manufactories is good. I would act upon it at once, if I were you. We must have the opinions of practical men set forth clearly before we can make a move in the matter. Now, how much of this mineral have you got?'

'Only the few lumps I took with me in my portmanteau. The barrel full of it which we got at Burntpine has not arrived yet. I suppose it came by slow steamer and is probably on the ocean still.'

'Very good. Take what specimens you have, go to the North, and see those manufacturers. Get, in some way or another, whether from the principals or from the subordinates, the price they pay for it, and the cost of removing the adulteration from the stuff they employ now; because that is really the material we come into competition with. It is not with their first raw material, but with their material as cleared from the deleterious foreign substances, that we have to deal. Find out exactly what it costs to do this purifying, and then, when you get your facts and figures, I will arrange them for you in the best order. Meanwhile, as you suggest, I will learn what manufactories there are in the States. Nothing can be done except that until you come back, and, if I were you, I should leave at once.'

'I am quite ready. I don't want to lose any further time.'

So John Kenyon departed, and was soon on his way to the North, with a list of china manufactories in his note-book.

That afternoon Wentworth got the letters off by the American mail, and he felt that they were doing business as rapidly as could be expected. Next morning there was a letter for John Kenyon addressed to the care of Wentworth, and by a later mail there came a letter to Wentworth himself from John, who had reached his first district and had had an interview already with the manager of the works. He found the mineral was all he had expected, and they would be glad to take a certain quantity each year at a specified rate. This letter Wentworth filed away with a smile of satisfaction, and then he began again to wonder why Adam Brand, representing such a well-known manufactory, should have written a deliberate falsehood. Before he had time to fathom this mystery, the office-boy announced that a gentleman wished to see him, and handed Wentworth a card which bore the name of William Longworth. Wentworth arched his eyebrows as he looked at it.

'Ask the gentleman to step in, please,' he said; and the gentleman stepped in.

'How are you, Mr. Wentworth? I suppose you remember me, although I did not see much of you on board the steamer.'

'I remember you perfectly,' replied Wentworth. 'Won't you sit down?'

'Thank you. I did not know where to find Mr. Kenyon, and so, being aware that both of you were interested in this mica-mine, I called to see you with reference to it.'

'Indeed! I understood Mr. Kenyon to say that he had called upon you, and that you had decided to have nothing to do with it.'

357

'I hardly think he was justified in saying anything quite so definite. I got from him such particulars as he cared to give. He is not a very communicative man at the best, but he told me something about it, and I have been thinking over his proposal. I have now concluded to help you in this matter, if you care to have my aid. Perhaps, however, things have got to such a stage that you do not wish any assistance?'

'On the contrary, we have done very little. Mr. Kenyon is just now among the china manufactories in the North, finding out what demand there will be in England for this mineral.'

'Ah, I see. Have you had reports from him yet?'

'Nothing further than a letter this morning, which is very satisfactory.'

'There is no question, then, about the mineral being useful in the china trade?'

'No question whatever.'

'Well, I am glad of that. Now, Mr. Kenyon spoke to me on the steamer of going in share and share alike; that is, you taking a third, he taking a third, and I taking a third. We did not go very minutely into particulars, but I suppose we each share the expense in the same way—the preliminary expenses, I mean?'

'Yes,' said Wentworth; 'that would be the arrangement, I imagine.'

'Well, have you the authority to deal with me in the matter, or would it be better for me to wait until Kenyon comes back?'

'We can settle everything here and now.'

'Very good. Would you have any objection to my seeing the papers that relate to the mine? I should like to get the figures of the output as nearly as possible, and any other particulars you may have that would enable me to estimate the value of the property. Also I should like to see a copy of the option, or the original document by which you hold the mine.'

'Certainly; I shall be very pleased to give you all the information in my power.' Wentworth turned to his desk and wrote for a few moments, then blotted the paper he had been writing, and handed it to Longworth. 'You have no objection, before this is done, to signing this document, have you?'

Longworth adjusted his one eyeglass and looked at the paper, which read: 'I hereby agree to do my best to form a limited liability company for the purpose of taking over the Ottawa Mica-mine. I agree to pay my share of the expenses, and to accept one-third of the profits.'

'No, I don't object to sign this, though I think it should be a little more definite. I think it should state that the liability I incur is to be one-third of the whole preliminary expenses, the other two-thirds to be paid by Kenyon and yourself; and that, in return, I am to get one-third of the profits, the other two-thirds going to yourself and Kenyon. I think it should also state the amount of the capital of the new company; two hundred thousand pounds was suggested, if I remember rightly.'

'Very well,' answered Wentworth; 'I will rewrite that in accordance with your wishes.'

This he did, and Longworth, again adjusting his eyeglass, read it.

'Now,' he said, 'as we are so formal about the matter, perhaps it would be as well for you to give me a note which I can keep, setting forth these same particulars.'

'Undoubtedly,' said Wentworth, 'I shall do that. Probably it would be better for you to write the document to suit your own views, and I will sign it.'

'Oh no, not at all. Write whatever is embodied there, so that you will have one paper and I the other.'

This was done.

'Now then,' said Longworth, 'when does your option run out?'

Wentworth named the date.

'Who is the owner of the mine?'

'It is owned by the Austrian Mining Company, headquarters at Vienna, and the option is signed by a Mr. Von Brent, of Ottawa, who is manager of the mine and one of the owners.'

'You are perfectly certain that he has every right to sell the mine?'

'Yes; Mr. Kenyon's lawyer saw to that while he was in Ottawa.'

'And you are sure, also, that your option is a thoroughly legal instrument?'

'We are sure of that.'

'Has it been examined by a London solicitor?'

'It has been submitted to a Canadian lawyer. The bargain was made in Canada, and it will have to be carried out in Canada, under the laws of Canada.'

'Still, don't you think it would be just as well to get the opinion of an English lawyer on it?'

'I think that would be an unnecessary expense. However, if you wish to have that done, we will do it.'

'Yes; I think we shall need to have the opinion of a good lawyer upon it before we submit it to the stockholders.'

'Very well, I will have it done. Is there anyone whom you wish to give an opinion on it?'

'Oh, it is a matter of indifference to me; your own solicitor would do as well as anyone else. Perhaps, however, it will be better to have a legal adviser for the Mica Mining Company, Limited—we shall have to have one as we go on—and it might be as well to submit the document to whomever we are going to place in that position. It will not increase the legal expenses at all, or at least by only a very trifling amount. Have you anyone to suggest?'

'I have not thought about the matter,' said Wentworth.

'Suppose you let me look up a firm who will answer our purpose? My uncle is sure to know the right men, and that will be something towards my share of forming the company.'

'Very good,' said Wentworth; 'that will be satisfactory to me.'

'Now, there is a good deal to be done in the forming of a company, and it is going to take three men a good deal of time, besides some expense. What do you say to letting me look up offices?'

'Do you think it is necessary to have offices?'

'Oh, certainly. A great deal depends, in this sort of thing, on appearances. We shall need to get offices in a good locality.'

'To tell the truth, Mr. Longworth, Kenyon and I have not very much money, and we do not want to enter into any expense that is needless.'

'My dear sir, it is not needless. This business is one of those things into which, if you go boldly, you win; while if you go gingerly, on the economical plan, you lose everything. Of course, if there is to be a scarcity of cash, I shall have nothing to do with the scheme, because I know how these half-economically worked affairs turn out. I have seen too much of them. We are making a strike for sixty thousand pounds each. That is a sum worth risking something for, and, if you will believe me, you will not get it unless you venture something for it.'

'I suppose that is true.'

'Yes, it is very true. Of course I've had more experience in matters of this kind than either of you, and I know we shall have to get good offices, with a certain prosperous look about them. People are very much influenced by appearances. Now, if you like, I will see to getting the offices and to engaging a solicitor. Every step must be taken under legal advice, otherwise we may get into a very bad tangle and spend a great deal more money in the end.'

'Very well,' said Wentworth. 'Is there anything else you can suggest?'

'Not just at present; nothing need be done until Kenyon comes back, and then we can have a meeting to see what is the best way to proceed.'

Longworth then looked over the papers, took a note of some things mentioned in the option, and finally said:

'I wish you would get these papers copied for me, I suppose you have someone in the office who can do it?'

'Yes.'

'Then just have duplicates made of each of them. Good-morning, Mr. Wentworth.'

Wentworth mused for a few moments over the unexpected turn affairs had taken. He was very glad to get the assistance of Longworth; the name itself was a tower of strength in the City. Then, Kenyon's letter from the North was encouraging. Thinking of the letter brought the writer of it to his mind, so he took a telegraph-form from his desk, and wrote a message to the address given on the letter.

'Everything right. Longworth has joined us, and signed papers to assist in forming company.'

'There,' he said, as he sent the boy out with the message, 'that will cheer up old John when he gets it.'

CHAPTER XXII.

When John Kenyon returned from the North and entered the office of his friend Wentworth, he found that gentleman and young Longworth talking in the outer room.

'There's a letter for you on my desk,' said Wentworth, after shaking hands with him. 'I'll be there in a minute.'

Kenyon entered the room and found the letter. Then he did a very unbusinesslike thing. He pressed the writing to his lips and placed the letter in his pocket-book. This act deserves mention because it is an unusual thing in the City. As a general rule, City men do not press business communications to their lips, and the letter John had received was entirely a business communication, relating only to the mine, and to William Longworth's proposed connection with it. He wondered whether he should write an answer to it or not.

He sat down at Wentworth's desk, and came upon an obstacle at the very beginning. He did not know how to address the young woman. Whether to say 'My dear Miss Longworth,' or 'My dear madam,' or whether to use the adjective 'dear' at all, was a puzzle to him; and over this he was meditating when Wentworth came bustling in.

'Well,' said the latter, as John tore into small pieces a sheet of notepaper and threw the bits into the waste-basket, 'how have you got on? Your letters were very short indeed, but rather to the point. You seem to have succeeded.'

'Yes, I have succeeded very well. I have got all the figures and prices and everything else that it is necessary to have. I succeeded with everybody except Brand, who wrote that letter to you. I cannot make him out at all. He would give me no information, and he managed to prevent everyone else in his works from giving me any. He pooh-poohed the scheme—in fact, wouldn't listen to it. He said it was not usual for men to give away information regarding their business, and in that, of course, he was perfectly justified; but when I tried to argue with him as to whether this mineral was used in his manufactory or not, he would not listen. I asked him what he used in place of it, but he would not tell. All in all, he is a most extraordinary man, and I confess I do not understand him.'

'Oh, it doesn't matter about him in the least. I was speaking with Longworth just now about that curious letter of his, and he agrees with me that it makes no difference. He says, what is quite true, that in every business you find some man with whom it is difficult to deal.'

'Yes, that is so; but, still, he either uses this substance or he does not. I can understand a man who says, "We have no need for that, because we use another material." But that is one of the things Brand does not say.'

'Well, it is not worth while talking about him. By the way, you have all your figures and notes with you, I suppose?'

'Yes, I have everything.'

'Very well. Leave them with me, and I will get them into some sort of shape. Longworth says we shall have to have everything printed relating to this—your statements and all.'

'That will cost a great deal of money, will it not?'

'Oh, not very much. It is necessary, it seems. We must have printed matter to give to those who make application for information. It would be impossible to explain personally to everybody who inquires, and to show them these documents.'

'Yes, I suppose so.'

'Longworth was just now speaking to me about offices he has seen, and he is anxious to secure them at once. He is attending to that matter.'

'Do you think we need an office? Why could not the business be transacted here; or perhaps a room might be had on this floor that would do perfectly well; then we should be close together, and able to communicate when necessary.'

'Longworth seems to think differently. He says you must impress the public, and so he is going in for fine offices.'

'Yes, but who is to pay for them?'

'Why, we must, of course—you and Longworth and myself.'

'Have you the money?'

'I have a certain amount. I think we shall have enough to see it through, and if not, we can easily get it, and settle up when we finish the business.'

'Well, you know I have no money to spare.'

'Oh, I know that well enough. Perhaps Longworth will see us through, for, as he says, this sort of thing can be spoilt by niggardliness. He has known, and so have I, many a business go to pieces because of false economy.'

'But it seems to me all this is needless expense. We only want to get a few moneyed men interested in our project, and if they are sensible men, they will look to the probability of getting a good dividend, not at fine offices.'

'Very well, John; you get the men, and I shall be satisfied. I am sure I am as anxious to do this cheaply as you are. If you think you can go out and interest a dozen or twenty-four men in the City, and persuade them to go in for our mine, I will cry "Halt!" on our part until you do it. Will you try that?'

Kenyon pondered for a few minutes, and then said: 'I suppose that would be rather a difficult thing to do.'

'Yes, that is the way it strikes me. I do not know to whom I could go. Longworth is a good man, and we have gone to him. Now it seems to me, having got his assistance, the least we can do, unless we are prepared to produce the men ourselves forthwith, is to act as he wishes.'

'Yes, I quite appreciate that, and I also grasp the fact that too close economy is not the best thing; but, on the other hand, George, how are we to perform our part with Longworth? His ideas of economy and yours may be vastly different. What is a mere trifle to him would bankrupt us!'

'I know that. Well, he is coming here this afternoon at three. Suppose you manage to be in then, and talk with him. Meanwhile, I will go over the papers and get them into tabulated form.'

'Very well; I shall be here at three o'clock.'

It will hardly be credited that a business man like John Kenyon spent most of the time between that hour and three o'clock trying to compose a business letter in answer to the business communication he had received that morning. Yet such was the astonishing fact, and it showed, perhaps more than anything else, how utterly unfit Mr. John Kenyon was to join in a commercial undertaking in a city of hard-headed people. At last, however, the letter was posted, and Kenyon hurried away to be in time for his three-o'clock appointment. He found Wentworth and young Mr. Longworth together, the latter looking more like a young man from the West End than a typical City business man. His monocle was in his eye, and it shone on Kenyon as he entered. It was evident something was troubling Wentworth, and it was equally evident that the something, whatever it was, was not troubling young Longworth.

'You are late, John,' was Wentworth's greeting.

'A little,' he answered. 'I was detained.'

There was silence for a few moments, and Wentworth appeared to be waiting for Longworth to speak. At last Longworth said:

'I have succeeded in getting very nice offices indeed, and I was telling Mr. Wentworth about them. You see, it is not very easy to engage offices in a good part of the City by the week. They do not care to let them in that way, because, while a weekly tenant is occupying them, somebody else, who wants them for a longer time, might have to be sent away.'

'Yes,' said Kenyon in a non-committal manner.

'Well, I have got just the offices we need, and have now set the men at putting gilt lettering on the windows. I have taken the offices in the name of "The Canadian Mica Mining Company, Limited," which I shall have on the plate-glass windows in a very short time. Now, Mr. Wentworth here seems to think the offices rather expensive. I have told him before what my ideas are in the matter of expense. Perhaps, before anything more is said on the subject, we ought to go and look at the rooms.'

'How much are they a week?' asked Kenyon.

Young Mr. Longworth did not answer, because at that moment his monocle fell out of its place and had to be adjusted again; but Wentworth jerked out the two words, 'Thirty pounds.'

'A week?' cried John.

'Yes,' said Longworth, after having succeeded in replacing the round bit of glass—'yes; Mr. Wentworth seems to think that is rather high, but I defy him to get as fine offices in the City for anything less in price. It is merely ten pounds a week for each of us. However, before you can judge of their dearness or cheapness, you must see them. If you ask me, I think they are a bargain.'

'Very well,' said Kenyon. 'Have you the time, George?'

Wentworth, without answering, shoved the papers into his desk and closed it. The three young men went out together, and after a short walk came to large plate-glass windows, where a man on a ladder was chalking the words 'The Canadian Mica Mining Company, Limited,' in a semicircle.

'You see,' said Longworth, 'this is one of the very best situations in the City. As I said before, I doubt if you could get anything like it for the price.'

They could not deny the excellence of the position, or that the plate-glass looked very imposing and the gilt letters exceedingly fine; but the cost of this running on perhaps for two or three months seemed to appal them.

'Come inside,' said young Longworth suavely; 'I am sure you will be pleased with the rooms we have. You see,' he said, entering and nodding to the carpenters who were at work there, 'this will be the front office, where the public is received. Here you have room for an accountant or two and your secretary. The back-room, which you see is also well lighted, is just the spot for our people to meet. We will get in a large long table here, and a number of chairs, and there we are—capital directors' room.'

'Does the thirty pounds a week include the furnishing of the place?' asked Kenyon.

'Oh, bless you, no! You surely couldn't expect that? We shall have to put in the furniture, of course.'

'And do you intend to put in desks and counter and everything of that sort here?'

'Of course. Beside that, we will get in a large safe. There is nothing like a ponderous safe, with the name of the company in gilt letters on it, for impressing the general public.'

'And how much is the furnishing of this place to cost?'

'Really, I don't know that. The men I have engaged will do it very reasonably. They have done work for me before. You don't get it done any cheaper by haggling about the price beforehand—I've found that out.'

'I do not see how we are to pay our share of all this,' said Kenyon.

'Nothing easier, my boy; I've arranged all that. I will pay them my third in cash when it is finished, and, they have agreed to wait three months for the remainder. By that time you will have sixty thousand pounds each, and a little bill like this will be nothing to you.'

Kenyon looked grave.

'It's a little like counting your chickens,' he said.

'Ah, they'll hatch all right,' laughed Longworth. And then his eyeglass dropped out.

CHAPTER XXIII.

It is never wise to despise an enemy, no matter how humble he may be. The mouse liberated the enmeshed lion. Jennie Brewster should have been thankful that circumstances, working in her favour, had rendered her account of the discoveries she made about the mines unnecessary. She was saved the bitterness of acknowledged defeat by the cable despatch that awaited her at Queenstown, telling her not to forward her information. The letter she received from the editor of the Argus later explained the cable message. The Argus had obtained from a different source what purported to be an account of the reports on the mines, and this had been published. If Jennie's contribution corroborated this article, it was unnecessary; if it contradicted what had been already published, then, of course, it was equally unavailable, for the Argus was a paper that never stultified itself by acknowledging an error. So the editor sent his correspondent a short cable message to save the expense of a long and costly despatch that would have been useless when it reached the Argus office.

Instead, however, of being grateful to the stars that fought so well for her, Jennie became bitterly resentful against Fleming, and hardly less so against Miss Longworth. If it had not been for the meddling politician's interference, Wentworth would never have discovered who she was, and the whole train of humiliating events that followed would not have taken place. She would have parted with Wentworth on a friendly basis, at least. She was forced, reluctantly, to admit to herself that she liked Wentworth better than any young man she had ever before met; and now that there was little chance of seeing him again, her regret had become more and more poignant as time went on. He had told her all his hopes about the mica-mine before their unfortunate disaster, and had taken her into his confidence in a way, she felt sure, he had never done with any other woman. She saw the earnest look in his honest eyes whenever she closed her own, and this look haunted her day and night, alternating with the remembrance of that gaze of incredulous reproach with which he regarded her when he discovered her mission, which was even harder to bear than the recollection of his confidence and esteem.

And the sting of the situation lay in the fact that it had all been so useless and unnecessary. She had wounded her friend and humiliated herself all for nothing! The rapid changes that had taken place in the newspaper office since she left, had rendered her sacrifices futile, and while she had buoyed herself up on shipboard by holding that she was merely doing her duty to her employers, even that consolation had been made naught by the editor's letter.

Thus it ever is in that kaleidoscopic, gigantic and fascinating lottery, the modern press. The sensation for which an editor to-day would sell his soul, is to-morrow worthless. The greatest fool in the office will sometimes stumble stupidly upon the most important news of the day, while the cleverest reporter may be baffled in his constant fight against time, for the paper goes to press at a certain hour, and after that, effort is useless. The conductor of a great paper is like the driver of a Roman chariot; he needs a cool head and a strong arm, with a clear eye that peers into the future, and that pays little heed to the victims of the whirling scythe-blades at the hub. He may overturn a Government or be himself thrown, by an unexpected jolt, under the wheels. The fiery steeds never stop, and when one drops the reins, another grasps them, to be in turn lost and forgotten in the mad race, wherein never a glance is cast to the rear. The best brains in the country are called into requisition, squeezed, and flung aside. With a lavish but indiscriminating hand are thrown broadcast fame and dishonour, riches and disaster. Unbribable in the ordinary sense of the word, the press will, for the accumulation of the smallest coins of the realm, exaggerate a cholera scare and paralyze the business of a nation; then it will turn on a corrupt Government and rend it, although millions might be made by taking another course. It is the terror of scoundrels and the despair of honest men.

Jennie Brewster, in the midst of her unavailing regrets, clenched her little fist when she thought of Fleming. It is both customary and consoling to place the blame on other shoulders than our own. Human nature is such an erring quantity, that usually we can find a scapegoat among our fellow-beings, who can be made responsible for any misdeeds or failings which are so much a part of ourselves that they escape recognition. If Fleming had only attended his own business, as a man should, Wentworth would never have known that Jennie wrote for the Argus, and Jennie might have had a friend in London who would have added that spice of interest to her visit which usually accompanies the friendship of an agreeable young man for a girl so pretty and fascinating.

Fleming put up at the hotel that Jennie had at first selected, and now and then she met him in the extensive halls of the great building; but she invariably passed him with the dignity of an offended queen, although the unfortunate man always took off his hat, and once or twice paused as if about to speak with her.

On the last day of her stay at the hotel, she met Fleming oftener than ever before; but it did not occur to her that the unhappy politician was lying in wait for her, never being able to muster up enough courage to address her when his opportunity came. At last a note was brought up to the room she occupied, from Fleming, in which he said that he would like to have a few moments' conversation with her, and would wait for a reply.

'Tell him there is no reply,' said the girl to the messenger.

It is sometimes well to know the point of view, even of an enemy, but Jenny was too angry with him to think of that. However, a politician, to be successful, must not be easily rebuffed, and as a rule he is not.

Fleming, when he got the curt reply to his note, threw away his cigar, put on his hat, took the lift, passed through the long corridor, and knocked at Jennie's door.

The girl's amazement at seeing her enemy there was so great that the obvious act of shutting the door in his face did not occur to her until it was too late, and Fleming had carelessly placed his large foot in the way of its closing.

'How dare you come here, when I refused to see you?' she cried, with her eyes ablaze.

'Oh, I understood the messenger to say I might come,' replied the untruthful politician. 'You see, it's not a personal matter, but the very biggest sensation that ever went under the ocean on a cable, and I thought—Well, you know, I felt I had done you—quite unintentionally—a mean trick on board the Caloric and this was kind of to make up for it, don't you know.

'You can never repair what you have done.'

'Oh yes, I can, Jennie.'

'I shall be obliged to you if you remember that my name is Miss Brewster,' said the girl, drawing herself up; but Fleming noticed, with relief, that since he had mentioned the sensation she had made no motion to close the door, while the eagerness of the newspaper woman was gradually replacing the anger with which she had at first regarded him.

'All right, Miss Brewster. I meant no disrespect, you know; and, honestly, I would rather give you a big item than anybody else.'

'Oh, you're very honest—I know that.'

'Well, I am, you know, Jen—I mean Miss Brewster; although I tell you it don't pay in politics any more than in the newspaper business.'

'If you only came to speak like that of the newspapers, I don't care to listen to you.'

'Wait a minute. I don't blame you for being angry——'

'Thank you.'

'But, all the same, if you let this item get away, you'll be sorry. I'm giving you the straight tip. I could get more gold than you ever saw for giving this snap away, yet here you're treating me as if I were——'

'A New York politician. Why do you come to me with this valuable piece of information? Just because you have a great regard for me, I suppose?'

'That's right. That's it exactly.'

'I thought so. Very well. There is a parlour on this floor where we can talk without being interrupted. Come with me.'

Jennie closed the door and walked down the passage, followed by Fleming, who smiled with satisfaction at his own tact and shrewdness, as, indeed, he had every right to do.

In the deserted sitting-room was a writing-table, and Jennie sat down beside it, motioning Fleming to a chair opposite her.

'Now,' she said, drawing some paper towards her, and taking up a pen, 'what is this important bit of news?'

'Well, before we begin,' replied Fleming, 'I would like to tell you why I interfered on shipboard and let that Englishman know who you were.'

'Never mind that. Better let it rest.' There was a flash of anger in the girl's eye, but, in spite of it, Fleming continued. He was a persistent man.

'But it has some bearing on what I'm going to tell you. When I saw you on board the Caloric, my heart went down into my boots. I thought the game was up, and that you were after me. I was bound to find out whether the Argus knew anything of my trip or not, and whether it had put you on my track. Only five men in New York knew of my journey across, and as a good deal depended on secrecy, I had to find out in some way whether you were there for the purpose of—well, you know. So I spoke to the Englishman, and raised a hornets' nest about my ears; but I soon saw you had no suspicion of what I was engaged in, otherwise I would have had to telegraph to certain persons then in London, and scatter them.'

'Dear me! And what villainy were you concocting? Counterfeiting?'

'No; politics. Just as bad, I suppose you think. Now, do you know where Crupper is?'

'The Boss of New York? I heard before I left that he was at Carlsbad for his health.'

'He was there,' said Fleming mysteriously; 'but now——'

The politician solemnly pointed downwards with his forefinger.

'What! Dead?' cried Jennie, the ominous motion of Fleming's finger naturally suggesting what all good people believed to be the arch-thief's ultimate destination.

'No,' said Fleming, laughing; 'he's in this hotel.'

'Oh!'

'Yes, and Senator Smollet, leader of the Conscientious Party, is here too, although you don't meet them in the halls as often as you do me. These good men supposed to be political opponents, are lying low and saying nothing.'

'I see. And they've had a conference.'

'Exactly. Now, it's like this.' Fleming pulled a sheet of paper towards him, and drew on it an oval. 'That's New York. We'll call it a pumpkin-pie, if you like, the material of which it is composed being typical of the heads of its conscientious citizens. Or a pigeon-pie, perhaps, for the New Yorker is made to be plucked. Well, look here.' Fleming drew from a point in the centre several radiating lines. 'That's what Crupper and Smollet are doing in London. They're dividing the pie between the two parties.'

'That's very interesting, but how are they going to deliver the pieces?'

'Simple as shelling peas. You see, our great pull is the conscientious citizen—the voter who wants to vote right, and for a good man. If it weren't for the good men as candidates and the good men as voters, New York politics would be a pretty uncertain game. You see, the so-called respectable element in both parties is our only hope. Each believes in his party, thinks his crowd is better than the other fellow's, so all you have to do is to nominate an honest man to represent each party, and then that divides what they call the reputable vote, and we real politicians get our man in between the two. That's all there is in New York politics. Well, Senator Smollet threatened not to put up a good man on the conscientious ticket, and that would have turned the whole unbribable vote of both parties against us, so we had to make a deal with him, and throw in the next Presidential election. Crupper's no hog; he knows when he's had plenty, and New York's good enough for him. He don't care who gets the Presidency.'

'And this conference has been held?'

'That's right. It took place in this hotel.'

'The bargain was made, I suppose?'

'It was. The pie was divided.'

'And you didn't get a slice?'

'Oh, I beg your pardon, I did!'

'Then, why do you come to me and tell me all this—if it's true?'

Honest indignation shone in Fleming's face.

'If it's true? Of course it's true. Why do I come to you? Because I want to be friendly with you, that's why.'

Jennie, nibbling the end of her pen, looked thoughtfully across at him for a few moments, then slowly shook her head.

'If you get me to believe that, Mr. Fleming, I'll not cable a word. No, I must have an adequate motive, for I won't cable anything I don't believe to be absolutely true.'

'I assure you, Jennie——'

'Wait a moment. You say you are promised your share in the new deal, but it is not as big a slice as what you have now. It stands to reason that, if Crupper is to divide with Smollet's rascals, each of Crupper's rascals must content himself with a smaller piece. The greater the number of thieves, the smaller each portion of booty. You didn't see that when you left New York, and therefore you were afraid of publicity. You see it now, and you want a sensational article published, so that Senator Smollet will be forced to deny it, or further arouse the suspicions of the honest men in his party. In either case publicity will nullify the results of the deal, and you will hold the share you have. As you didn't know any of the regular London representatives of the New York papers, you couldn't trust them not to tell on you, and so you came to me. Now that I see a good substantial selfish motive for your action, I am ready to believe you.'

An expression of dismay at first overspread the countenance of the politician, but this gave way to a look of undisguised admiration as the girl went on.

'By Jove, Jennie!' he cried, bringing his fist down on the table when she had finished; 'you're wasted in the newspaper business; you ought to be a politician! Say, girl, if you marry me, I'll be President of the United States yet.'

'Oh no, you wouldn't,' said Jennie, quite unabashed by his handsome, if excited, proposal. 'No corrupt New York politician will ever be President of the United States. You have the great honest bulk of the people to deal with there, and I'm Democrat enough to believe in them when it comes to big issues, however much you may befog them in small; you can't fool all people for all time, Mr. Fleming, as a man who was not in little politics once said. Every now and then the awakened people will get up and smash you.'

Fleming laughed boisterously.

'That's just it,' he said. 'It's every now and then. If they did it every year I would have to quit politics. But will you send the particulars of this meeting to the Argus without giving me away?'

'Yes, I recognise its importance. Now, I want you to give me every detail—the number of the room they met in, the exact hour, and all that. What I like to get in a report of a secret meeting is absolute accuracy in small matters, so that those who were there will know it is not guesswork. That always takes the backbone out of future denials. I'll mention your name——'

'Bless my soul, don't do that!'

'I must say you were present.'

'Why?'

'Why? Dear me! you can't be so stupid as not to see that, if your name is left out, suspicion will at once point to you as the divulger?'

'Yes I suppose that is so.'

'And this man is a ruler in one of the greatest cities in the world! Go on, Mr. Fleming; who else was there besides Crupper, Smollet, and yourself?'

The account—two columns and a half—was a bombshell in political New York the morning it appeared in the Argus. Senator Smollet cabled from Paris that there wasn't a word of truth in it, that he wasn't in London on the date mentioned, and had never seen Crupper there or elsewhere. Crupper cabled from Carlsbad that he was ill, and had not been out of bed for a month. He would sue the Argus for libel, which, by the way, he never did. The reporters flocked to meet Fleming when his steamer came in, but of course he knew nothing about it; he had been across the ocean solely on private business that had no connection with politics. He knew nothing of Crupper's whereabouts, but he knew one thing, which was that Crupper was too honest and honourable a man to traffic with the enemy.

Notwithstanding all these denials, the report bore the marks of truth on its face, and everybody believed it, although many pretended not to. The division of the spoils aroused the greatest consternation and indignation among Crupper's own following, and a deputation went over to see the old man.

Meanwhile, the Argus, with much dignity of diction, explained that it stood for the best interests of the people, and in the people's cause was fearless. It defied all and sundry to bring libel suits if they wanted to; it was prepared to battle for the people's rights. And its circulation went up and up, its many web presses being taxed to their utmost in supplying the demand. Thus are the truly good rewarded.

A great newspaper is as lavishly generous as a despotic monarch, to those who serve it well, and the cheque which Jennie cashed when Lady Willow accompanied her to the City lined her purse with banknotes to a fulness that receptacle had never known before.

After a few weeks with Lady Willow, Jennie seemed to tire of the frivolities of society, and even of the sedate company of the good lady with whom she lived. She announced that she was going to Paris for a week or two, but, owing to uncertainty of address, her letters were not to be forwarded. She merely took a hand-bag, leaving the rest of her luggage with Lady Willow, who was thus sustained by the hope that her paying guest would soon return.

Jennie took a hansom to Charing Cross, but instead of departing on the Paris express, she hailed a four-wheeler, and, giving a West End address to the driver, entered the closed vehicle.

CHAPTER XXIV.

On the big plate-glass windows of the new rooms there soon appeared, in gilt letters with black edges, the words, 'Canadian Mica Mining Company, Limited: London Offices.' But the workmen who were finishing the interior were not so quick as the painters and gilders. The new offices took a long time to prepare, and both Kenyon and Wentworth chafed at the delay, because Longworth said nothing could be done until the rooms were occupied.

'It is like this, Longworth,' said Wentworth to him: 'every moment is of value. Time is running on, and we have not for ever in which to form this company.'

'And you must remember,' replied young Mr. Longworth, gazing reproachfully at him through his glittering monocle, 'that I am equally interested in this project with you. It is just as much to my interest to save time as it is to yours. You must not worry about the matter, Mr. Wentworth; everything is all right. The men are doing a good job for us, and it will not be long before their work is completed. As I have told you time and again, a great deal depends on the appearance we present to the public. We have nearly the best offices in the City. The workmen have certainly taken longer than I expected they would, but, you see, they have a great deal of work on hand. When we get this started it will not take long. I, in the meanwhile, have not been idle. At least half a dozen moneyed men are ready to go in with us on this project. The moment the offices are finished we will have a meeting of the proposed shareholders. If they subscribe sufficiently large amounts—and I think they will—all the rest is a mere matter of detail which our solicitors will attend to. But if you imagine that you and Mr. Kenyon can manage everything better than I am doing, you are perfectly at liberty to go ahead. I am sure I have no desire to monopolize all the work. What have you done, for instance? What has Mr. Kenyon done?'

'Kenyon, as I think you know, has got all the facts in reference to the demand for the mineral, and I have arranged them. We have had everything printed as you suggested, and the papers are ready. They were delivered at my office to-day.'

'Very well,' answered young Longworth; 'we are getting on. That is so much done which will not have to be done over again. Perhaps it will be as well to send me some of the printed matter, so that I can give it to the men I was speaking of. Meanwhile, don't worry about the offices; they will be ready in good time.'

Wentworth and Kenyon visited the new offices time and again, but still the work seemed to drag. At last Wentworth said very sharply to the foreman:

'Unless this is finished by next Monday, we will have nothing to do with it.'

The foreman seemed astonished.

'I understood from Mr. Longworth,' he said, 'from whom we take our instructions, that there was no particular hurry about this job.'

'Well, there is a particular hurry. We must be in here by the first of next week, and if you have not finished by that time, we shall have to come in with it unfinished.'

'In that case,' said the foreman, 'I will do the best I can. I think we can finish it this week.'

And finished it was accordingly.

When Kenyon entered his new offices, he found them rather oppressive for so modest a man as himself. Wentworth laughed at his doleful expression as he viewed the general grandeur of his surroundings.

'What bothers me,' said John, 'is knowing that all this has to be paid for.'

'Ah, yes,' answered Wentworth; 'but by the time the debts become due I hope we shall have plenty of money.'

'I must confess I do not understand Longworth in this matter. He seems to be doing nothing; at least, he has nothing to show for what he has done, and he does not appear to realize that time is an object with us; in fact, that our company-forming has really become a race against time.'

'Well, we shall see very shortly what he is going to do. I have sent a messenger for him to meet us here—he ought to be here now—and we must certainly push things. There is no time to lose.'

'Has he said anything to you—he talks more freely with you than he does to me—about what the next move is to be?'

'No; he has said nothing.'

'Well, don't you see the situation in which we stand? We are practically doing nothing—leaving everything in his hands. Now, if he should tell us some fine day that he can have nothing more to do with our project (and I believe he is quite capable of it), here we are with our time nearly spent, deeply in debt, and nothing done.'

'My dear John, what a brain you have for conjuring up awful possibilities! Trust me, Longworth won't act in the way you suggest. It would be dishonourable, and he is, so far as I know, an honourable man of business. I think you take a certain prejudice against a person, and then can see nothing good in anything he does. Longworth told me the other day that he had five or six people who are ready to go into this business with us, and if such is the case he has certainly done his share.'

'Yes, I admit that. Did he give you their names?'

'No, he did not.'

'The thing that troubles me is our own helplessness. We seem, in some way or other, to have been shoved into the background.'

'So far from that being the case,' said Wentworth, 'Longworth told me that, if anything suggested itself to us, we were to go ahead with it. He asked what you had done and what I had done, and I told him. He seemed quite anxious that we should do everything we could, as he is doing.'

'Well, but, don't you see, the situation is this: if we make a move at all, we may do something of which he does not approve. Haven't you noticed that whenever I suggest anything, or whenever you suggest anything, for that matter, he always has something counter to it? And I don't like the solicitors he has engaged for this business. They are what is known as "shady"; you know that as well as I do.'

'Bless me, John! then suggest something yourself if you have such dark suspicions of Longworth. I'm sure I'm willing to do anything you want done. Suggest something.'

Before John could make the required suggestion, the messenger Wentworth had sent to young Longworth returned.

'His uncle says, sir,' began the messenger, 'that Master William has gone to the North, and will not be back for a week.'

'A week!' cried both the young men together.

'Yes, sir, a week was what he said. He left a note to be given to either of you if you called. Here is the note, sir.'

Wentworth took the envelope handed to him and tore it open. The contents ran thus:

'I have been suddenly called away to the North, and may be gone for a week or ten days. I am sorry to be away at this particular juncture, but as it is not likely that the men will have the offices finished before I come back, no great harm will be done. Meanwhile I shall see several gentlemen I have in my mind's eye, men that seldom come to London, who will be of great service to us. If you think of anything to forward the mica-mine, pray go on with it. You can send any letters for me to my uncle, and I shall get them. As there is no hurry in the matter of time, however, I should strongly advise that nothing be done until my return, when we can all go at the business with a will.

'Yours truly,

'WILLIAM LONGWORTH.'

When Wentworth had finished reading this letter, the two young men looked at each other.

'What do you make of that?' said Kenyon.

'I'm sure I do not know. In the first place, he is gone for a week.'

'Yes; that one thing is certain.'

'Well now, John, one of two things has to be done. We have either to trust this Longworth, or we have to go on alone without him. Which is it to be?'

'I am sure I don't know,' answered Kenyon.

'But, my dear fellow, we have come to a point when we must decide. You are, evidently, suspicious of Longworth. What you say really amounts to this: that he, for some reason of his own, which I confess I cannot see or understand, desires to delay forming this company until it is too late.'

'I didn't say that.'

'You say what practically amounts to that. Either he is honest or he is not. Now, we have to decide to-day, and here, whether we are going to ignore him and go on with the forming of the company, or work with him. Unless you can give some good reason for doing otherwise, I propose to work with him. I think it will be very much worse if he leaves us now than if he had never gone into it. People will ask why he left.'

'Probably he wouldn't leave, even if you wanted him to do so. He has your signature to an agreement, and you have his.'

'Certainly.'

'I do not see how we can help ourselves.'

'Then I think these suspicions should be dropped, because you cannot work with a man whom you suspect of being a rascal.'

'I quite admit of the justice of that, so I shall say nothing more. Meanwhile, do you propose to wait until he comes back?'

'I shall write him to-night and ask him what he intends to do. I shall tell him, as I have told him before, that time is pressing, and we want to know what is being done.'

'Very well,' said John; 'I will wait till you get the answer to your letter. In the meantime, I do not see that there is anything to do but occupy this gorgeous office as well as I can, and wait to see what turns up.'

'That is my own idea. I think, myself, it is rather unfair to suspect a man of being a villain when he has really done nothing to show that he is one.'

To this John made no answer.

The next day Kenyon occupied the new offices, and set himself to the task of getting accustomed to them. The first day a few people dropped in, made inquiries about the mine, took some printed matter, and generally managed to ask several questions to which Kenyon was unable to reply. On the second day a number of newspaper men called—advertising canvassers, most of them, who left cards or circulars with Kenyon, showing that unless a commercial venture was advertised in their particular papers it was certain not to be a success. One very swell individual, with a cast of countenance that betokened a frugal, money-making, and shrewd race, asked Kenyon for a private interview. He said he belonged to the Financial Field, the great newspaper of London, which was read by every investor both in the City and in the country. All he wanted was some particulars of the mine.

Had the company been formed yet?

No, it had not.

When did they intend to go to the public?

That Kenyon could not say.

What was the peculiarity about the mine which constituted its recommendation to investors?

Kenyon said the full particulars would be found in the printed sheet he handed him, and with profuse thanks the newspaper man put it in his pocket.

How had the mine paid in previous years?

It had paid a small dividend.

On what amount?

That Kenyon was not prepared to answer.

How long had it been in operation?

For several years.

Had it ever been placed on the London market before?

Not so far as Kenyon was aware.

Who was at present interested in the mine?

That Mr. Kenyon did not care to answer, and he further stated, so far as giving out advertisements was concerned, he was not yet prepared to do any advertising. The visitor, who had taken down these notes, said his object was not to get an advertisement, but to obtain information about the mine. People could advertise in his paper or not, as they chose. The journal was such a well-known medium for reaching investors that everyone who knew his business advertised in it as a matter of course, and so they kept no canvassers, and made no applications for advertisements.

'The chances are,' said the newspaper man, as he took his leave, 'that our editor will write an editorial on this mine, and, in order that there may be no inaccuracy, I shall bring it to you to read, and shall be very much obliged if you will correct any mistakes.'

'I shall be glad to do so,' returned Kenyon, as the representative of the Financial Field took his leave.

The newspaper men were rather hard to please, and to get rid of; but John had a visitor on the afternoon of the second day who almost caused his wits to desert him. He looked up from his desk as the door opened, and was astonished to see the smiling face of Edith Longworth, while behind her came the old lady who had been an occupant of the carriage when John had taken his drive to the west.

'You did not expect to see me here among the investors who have been calling upon you, Mr. Kenyon, did you?'

Kenyon held out his hand, and said:

'I am very pleased indeed to see you, whether you come as an investor or not.'

'And so this is your new office?' she cried, looking round. 'How you have blossomed out, haven't you? These offices are as fine as any in the City.'

'Yes,' said John; 'they are too fine to suit me.'

'Oh, I don't see why you should not have handsome offices as well as anyone else. You have been in my father's place of business, of course. But it is not so grand as these rooms.'

'I think that helps to show the absurdity of ours. Your father's house is an old-standing one, and this gives us an air of new riches which, I must confess, I don't like, especially as we have not the riches.'

'Then, why did you agree to have such offices? I suppose you had something to say about them?'

'Very little, I must own. They were engaged while I was in the North, and after they had been engaged, of course I did not like to say anything against them.'

'Well, and how is the mine getting on? You have not applied to me yet to fulfil my offer, which I think was a very fair one.'

'I have not needed to do so,' said Kenyon.

'Ah, then, subscriptions are coming in, are they? Where is the list?'

'We have no list yet. We are waiting for your cousin, who is in the North.'

'In the North!' said Edith, with her eyes open wide. 'He is not in the North; he is in Paris, and we expect him home to-night.'

'Oh, indeed!' said John, who made no further comment.

'Now, where's your subscription-list? Oh, you told me you have none yet. Very well; this sheet of paper will do.' And the young woman drew some lines across the paper, heading it, 'The Canadian Mica-mine.' Then underneath she wrote the name Edith Longworth, and after it—'For ten thousand pounds.' 'There! I am the first subscriber to the new company; if you get the others as easily, you will be very fortunate.'

And, before John could thank her, she laughingly turned to her companion, and said:

'We must go.'

CHAPTER XXV.

When Wentworth dropped in to see if anything had happened, Kenyon told him that young Longworth was not in the North at all, but in Paris. Wentworth pondered over this piece of information for a moment, and said:

'I have written him, but have received no answer. I have just been to see the solicitors, and have told them that time was pressing; that we must do something. They quite agreed it was desirable some action should be taken at once, but, of course, as they said, they merely waited our instructions. They are willing to do anything we ask them to do. However, they advised waiting until Longworth got back, and then they proposed we should have a meeting at the offices here. They said, moreover, that, if Longworth had five or six men who would go at work with a will, the whole affair would be finished in a week at most. They did not appear to be at all alarmed at the shortening time, but said everything depended upon the men Longworth was going to bring with him. If they were the right men, there would be no trouble. So, all in all, they advised me not to worry about it, but to communicate with Longworth, if I could, and get him to come as soon as possible. I had to admit myself that this was the only thing to do, so I called round to see if you had heard anything from him.'

'I have heard nothing about him,' said Kenyon, 'except that he has lied, and has gone to Paris instead of going North.'

'Well,' mused Wentworth, 'I don't know that that is a very important point. He may have business in Paris, and he may have thought it was no affair of ours where he went, in which he was partly right and partly wrong. He thought, no doubt, that if he said he was going North, to see some men who could not be seen without his going there, it would relieve our minds, and make us imagine we were going on all right.'

'That is just what I object to, Wentworth. His whole demeanour seems to show that he wants us to think things are all right when they are not all right.'

'Well, John, as I said before, you've got to do one thing or the other. You have to trust Longworth or to go on without him. Now, for Heaven's sake make up your mind which it is to be, and don't grumble.'

'I am not grumbling. A man that is really honest will not say what is false, even about a small thing.'

'Oh, you are too particular. Wait till you have been in the City ten years longer, and you won't mind a little thing like that.'

'Little things like that, as you call them, are indicative of general character.'

'Sometimes yes, and sometimes no. You mustn't take things too seriously. I do not see that anything can be done until Longworth chooses to exhibit himself. If you can suggest anything better, as I said before, tell me what it is, and I am ready to do my part.'

'I confess I don't see what we can do. We might wait a day or two longer yet, and then, if we hear nothing more from Longworth, dismiss those solicitors he has chosen, and take the gentlemen who act for you.'

'The people Longworth has engaged do not bear a very good reputation; still, I must admit they talk in a very straightforward manner. As you say, it is perhaps better to let matters rest for a day or two.'

And so the days passed. Wentworth wrote again to Longworth at his office, and said they would wait for two days, and if he did not put in an appearance, before that time, they would go on forming the company as if he did not exist.

To this no answer came, and Kenyon and Wentworth again held consultation in the sumptuous offices which had been chosen for them.

'No news yet, I suppose?' said Kenyon.

'None whatever,' was the answer.

'Very well; I have made up my mind what to do——'

But before John Kenyon could say what he had resolved to do, the door opened, and there entered unto them Mr. William Longworth, with his silk hat as glossy as a mirror, a general trim and prosperous appearance about him, a flower in his buttonhole and his eyeglass in its place.

'Good-morning, gentlemen,' he said. 'I thought I should find you here, and so I did not call at your office, Wentworth. Ah,' he cried, looking round, 'this is the proper caper! These offices look even better than I thought they would. I just got back this morning,' he added, turning to his partners.

'Indeed,' said Wentworth, 'we are very glad to see you. How did you enjoy your trip to Paris?'

The young man did not appear in the least abashed by this remark. He merely elevated his eyebrows, shrugged his shoulders, and said:

'Ah, well, as both of you are doubtless aware, Paris is not what it used to be. Still, I had a very good time there.'

'I'm glad of that,' said Wentworth; 'and did you see the gentlemen you expected to meet?'

'I must confess I did not. I did not think it was necessary. I have five or six men interested already, practically pledged to furnish all the capital.' And, saying this, he walked round the desk at which they stood, and sat down, throwing the right leg across the left and clasping his knee in his hands.

'Well, what has been done during my absence? The mine floated yet?'

'No,' said Wentworth; 'the mine is not yet floated. Now, Mr. Longworth, the time has come for plain speaking. You have gone off to Paris without a word of warning to us at a very critical time, and you have not answered any of the letters I sent to you.'

'Well, my dear boy, the reason was that I expected every day to get back here, and each day was detained a little longer.'

'Very good; the point I want to impress upon you is this—time is getting short. If we are going to form this company, we have to set about it at once.'

'My dear fellow,' said Longworth, in an expostulating tone of voice, 'that is exactly what I told myself. The time is getting short, as you say. Of course, as I said when I joined you, I cannot give my whole time to this. We are equal partners, and the fact that I had to leave for a few days should not interrupt the business we have on hand. What did you expect to do if I had not been a partner at all?'

'If you were not a partner,' replied Wentworth with some heat, 'we should have gone on and formed our company, or failed; but the very fact that you are a partner is just what now retards us. We do not feel justified in doing anything until it has your approval, or until we know that it does not run counter with something you have already done.'

'Well, gentlemen, if you feel like that about it, I am quite willing to withdraw. I am ready to give up the paper I hold from you, and receive back the paper you hold from me. Of course we cannot work together if there are to be any recriminations. I have done my best; I have done everything that I promised to do—even more than that; but if you think for a moment you can get on better without me, I am ready at any time to retire.'

'It is easy to say that, Mr. Longworth, now that the time of the option has only a month further to run. You must remember that a great deal of time has been lost, and not through our fault.'

'Ah! do you mean it has been lost through my fault?'

'I mean that if we had been alone something would have been done, whereas we are now in the same position as when we started. We are in a worse position than we were at the beginning, because we have not only spent our money, but are deeply in debt into the bargain.'

'Well, Mr. Wentworth, I did not propose to withdraw until you, as a matter of fact, almost suggested it. I am quite willing and anxious to help, but if I do stay with you it must be understood that we have no such recriminations as these. You must do your best, and I must do my best.'

'Very well, then,' said Wentworth; 'your leaving us at this time is entirely out of the question. Now, will you give me the names of those gentlemen who have offered to go in with us?'

'Certainly.'

And Longworth pulled out a note-book from his inside pocket, while Wentworth took up a pen from the desk and pulled a sheet of paper towards him.

'First, Mr. Melville.'

'Is that the Melville I saw in relation to this mineral?'

'I am sure I do not know. He is at the head of the Scranton China Company.'

'Has he spoken of going in with us?'

'Yes, he seems to think the scheme is a good one. Why do you ask?'

'Well, merely because I took a specimen of the mineral to him and his manager wrote to me that it was of no value. It seems rather remarkable that he should go in for the mine if his manager believes it to be worthless.'

'Oh, he goes in entirely in his own private capacity. He is not at all affected by what the manager says. The manager has nothing to do with Melville's private affairs.'

'Still, it seems very strange, because, when Kenyon saw the manager in the North, he claimed they did not use this material, and said it would be of no benefit whatever to him.'

'That is very singular,' mused Longworth. 'Well, all I can say is, Melville has intimated that he should like to have a share in this mine, so, I take it, he and the manager do not agree as to the value of the mineral. You can set down Mr. Melville's name with perfect confidence. I know him very well, and I know that he's a thorough man of business. Besides, it will be a great advantage to have a man connected with the china trade in with us.'

There was no denying this point, so Wentworth said nothing more. Longworth named five other persons, none of whom Wentworth knew. Then he closed his note-book and put it in his pocket.

'The question now is: Have these gentlemen stated how much they will subscribe?' asked Wentworth.

'No, they have not. Of course, everything will depend on how they are impressed with what we can tell them. The great thing is to get men who are willing even to listen to you. The rest depends on the inducements you offer.'

'Do you expect to get any more men interested?'

'I don't think any more are needed. The best thing to do now is to get those we have together and summon our solicitors here. Then our friend Kenyon, who is a fluent speaker, can lay the case before them.'

Kenyon, who had not spoken at all during the interview, did not even look up, and apparently did not hear the satirical allusion to his eloquence.

'Very well; when would be a good time to call this meeting?'

'As soon as possible, I think,' said Longworth. 'What do you say to Monday, at three o'clock? Men come from lunch about that hour, and are in a good humour. If you send out a letter saying a meeting will be held here in the directors' room at three o'clock, prompt, on Monday, I will see the men and get them to come. Of course they are generally busy, and may have other appointments; still, we must do something, and nothing can be done until we get them together.'

'Right; the invitations to the meeting shall be sent out at once.'

Longworth rose, went to the desk and picked up a paper.

'What is this?' he said.

Kenyon looked up suddenly.

'That,' he said, flushing slightly, 'is our first subscription.'

'Who wrote the name of Miss Edith Longworth here?'

'The young lady herself.'

'Has she been here?'

'She called, and desired to be the first subscriber.'

'Nonsense!' cried Longworth, with a frown; 'we don't want any women in this business;' and, saying that, he tore the paper in two.

Kenyon clenched his fist and was about to say something, when Wentworth's hand came down on his shoulder.

'I don't think I would refuse ten thousands pounds,' said Wentworth, 'from anybody who offered it, woman or man. Perhaps we had better see whether your men will subscribe as much before we throw away a subscription already received.'

'But she hasn't the ten thousand pounds.'

'I fancy,' said Wentworth, 'that whatever Miss Longworth puts her name to, she is ready to stand by;' and with that he placed the two pieces of paper in a drawer. 'Now, I think that is all,' he added; 'we will call the meeting for Monday, and see what comes of it.'

CHAPTER XXVI.

William Longworth had an eye for beauty. One of his eyes was generally covered by a round disc of glass, save when the disc fell out of its place and dangled in front of his waistcoat. Whether the monocle assisted his sight or not, it is certain that William knew a pretty girl when he saw her. One of the housemaids in the Longworth household left suddenly, without just cause or provocation, as the advertisements say, and in her place a girl was engaged who was so pretty that, when William Longworth caught sight of her, his monocle dropped from its usual position, and he stared at her with his two natural eyes, unassisted by science. He tried to speak to her on one or two occasions when he met her alone; but he could get no answer from the girl, who was very shy and demure, and knew her place, as people say. All this only enhanced her value in young Longworth's estimation, and he thought highly of his cousin's taste in choosing this young person to dust the furniture.

William had a room in the house which was partly sitting-room and partly study, and there he kept many of his papers. He was supposed to ponder over matters of business in this room, and it gave him a good excuse for arriving late at the office in the morning. He had been sitting up into the small hours, he would tell his uncle; although he would sometimes vary the excuse by saying that it was quieter at home than in the City, and that he had spent the early part of the morning in reading documents.

The first time William got an answer from the new housemaid was when he expressed his anxiety about the care of this room. He said that servants generally were very careless, and he hoped she would attend to things, and see that his papers were kept nicely in order. This, without glancing up at him, the girl promised to do, and William thereafter found his apartment kept with a scrupulous neatness which would have delighted the most particular of men.

One morning when he was sitting by his table, enjoying an after-breakfast cigarette, the door opened softly, and the new housemaid entered. Seeing him there, she seemed confused, and was about to retire, when William, throwing his cigarette away, sprang to his feet.

'No, don't go,' he said; 'I was just about to ring.'

The girl paused with her hand on the door.

'Yes,' he continued, 'I was just going to ring, but you have saved me the trouble; but, by the way, what is your name?'

'Susy, if you please, sir,' replied the girl modestly.

'Ah well, Susy, just shut the door for a moment.'

The girl did so, but evidently with some reluctance.

'Well, Susy,' said William jauntily, 'I suppose that I'm not the first one who has told you that you are very pretty.'

'Oh, sir!' said Susy, blushing and looking down on the carpet.

'Yes, Susy, and you take such good care of this room that I want to thank you for it,' continued William.

Here he fumbled in his pocket for a moment, and drew out half a sovereign.

'Here, my girl, is something for your trouble. Keep this for yourself.'

'Oh, I couldn't think of taking money, sir,' said the girl, drawing back. 'I couldn't indeed, sir!'

'Nonsense!' said William; 'isn't it enough?'

'Oh, it's more than enough. Miss Longworth pays me well for what I do, sir, and it's only my duty to keep things tidy.'

'Yes, Susy, that is very true; but very few of us do our duty, you know, in this world.'

'But we ought to, sir,' said the girl, in a tone of quiet reproof that made the young man smile.

'Perhaps,' said he; 'but then, you see, we are not all pretty and good, like you. I'm sorry you won't take the money. I hope you are not offended at me for offering it;' and William adjusted his eye-glass, looking his sweetest at the young person standing before him.

'Oh no, sir,' she said, 'I'm not at all offended, and I thank you very much, very much indeed, sir, and I would like to ask you a question, if you wouldn't think me too bold.'

'Bold?' cried William. 'Why, I think you are the shyest little woman I have ever seen. I'll be very pleased to answer any question you may ask me. What is it?'

'You see, sir, I've got a little money of my own.'

'Well, I declare, Susy, this is very interesting. I'd no idea you were an heiress.'

'Oh, not an heiress, sir—far from it. It's only a little matter of four or five hundred pounds, sir,' said Susy, dropping him an awkward little curtsy, which he thought most charming. 'The money is in the bank, and earns no interest, and I thought I would like to invest it where it would bring in something.'

'Certainly, Susy, and a most laudable desire on your part. Was it about that you wished to question me?'

'Yes, if you please, sir. I saw this paper on your desk, and I thought I would ask you if it would be safe for me to put my money in these mines, sir. Seeing the paper here, I supposed you had something to do with it.'

William whistled a long incredulous note, and said:

'So you have been reading my papers, have you, miss?'

'Oh no, sir,' said the girl, looking up at him with startled eyes. 'I only saw the name Canadian Mica-mine on this, and the paper said it would pay ten per cent., and I thought if you had anything to do with it that my money would be quite safe.'

'Oh, that goes without saying,' said William; 'but if I were you, my dear,

I should not put my money in the mica-mine.'

'Oh, then, you haven't anything to do with the mine, sir?'

'Yes, Susy, I have. You know, fools build houses, and wise men live in them.'

'So I have heard,' said Susy thoughtfully.

'Well, two fools are building the house that we will call the Canadian Mica-mine, and I am the wise man, don't you see, Susy?' said the young man, with a sweet smile.

'I'm afraid I don't quite understand, sir.'

'I don't suppose, Susy,' replied the young man, with a laugh, 'that there are many who do; but I think in a month's time I shall own this mica-mine, and then, my dear, if you still want to own a share or two, I shall be very pleased to give you a few without your spending any money at all.'

'Oh, would you, sir?' cried Susy in glad surprise; 'and who owns the mine now?'

'Oh, two fellows; you wouldn't know their names if I told them to you.'

'And are they going to sell it to you, sir?'

William laughed heartily, and said:

'Oh no! they themselves will be sold.'

'But how can that be if they don't own the mine? You see, I'm only a very stupid girl, and don't understand business. That's why I asked you about my money.'

'I don't suppose you know what an option is, do you, Susy?'

'No, sir, I don't; I never heard of it before.'

'Well, these two young men have what is called an option on the mine, which is to say that they are to pay a certain sum of money at a certain time and the mine is theirs; but if they don't pay the certain sum at the certain time, the mine isn't theirs.'

'And won't they pay the money, sir?'

'No, Susy, they will not, because, don't you know, they haven't got it. Then these two fools will be sold, for they think they are going to get the money, and they are not.'

'And you have the money to buy the mine when the option runs out, sir.'

'By Jove!' said William in surprise, 'you have a prodigious head for business, Susy; I never saw anyone pick it up so fast. You will have to take lessons from me, and go on the market and speculate yourself.'

'Oh, I should like to do that, sir—I should indeed.'

'Well,' said William kindly, 'whenever you have time, come to me, and I will give you lessons.'

The young man approached her, holding out his hand, but the girl slipped away from him and opened the door.

'I think,' he said in a whisper, 'that you might give me a kiss after all this valuable information.'

'Oh, Mr. William!' cried Susy, horrified.

He stepped forward and tried to catch her, but the girl was too nimble for him, and sprang out into the passage.

'Surely,' protested William, 'this is getting information under false pretences; I expected my fee, you know.'

'And you shall have it,' said the girl, laughing softly, 'when I get ten per cent. on my money.'

'Egad!' said William to himself as he entered his room again, 'I will see that you get it. She's as clever an outside broker.'

When young Longworth had left for his office, Susy swept and dusted out his room again, and then went downstairs.

'Where's the mistress?' she asked a fellow-servant.

'In the library,' was the answer, and to the library Susy went, entering the room without knocking, much to the amazement of Edith Longworth, who sat near the window with a book in her lap. But further surprise was in store for the lady of the house. The housemaid closed the door, and then, selecting a comfortable chair, threw herself down into it, exclaiming:

'Oh dear me! I'm so tired.'

'Susy,' said Miss Longworth, 'what is the meaning of this?'

'It means, mum,' said Susy, 'that I'm going to chuck it.'

'Going to what?' asked Miss Longworth, amazed.

'Going to chuck it. Didn't you understand? Going to give up my situation. I'm tired of it.'

'Very well,' said the young woman, rising, 'you may give notice in the proper way. You have no right to come into this room in this impudent manner. Be so good as to go to your own room.'

'My!' said Susy, 'you can do the dignified! I must practise and see if I can accomplish an attitude like that. If you were a little prettier, Miss Longworth, I should call that striking;' and the girl threw back her head and laughed.

Something in the laugh aroused Miss Longworth's recollection, and a chill of fear came over her; but, looking at the girl again, she saw she was mistaken. Susy jumped up, still laughing, and drew a pin from the little cap she wore, flinging it on the chair; then she pulled off her wig, and stood before Edith Longworth her natural self.

'Miss Brewster!' gasped the astonished Edith. 'What are you doing in my house in that disguise?'

'Oh,' said Jennie, 'I'm an amateur housemaid. How do you think I have acted the part? Now sit down, Miss Dignity, and I will tell you something about your own family. I thought you were a set of rogues, and now I can prove it.'

'Will you leave my house this instant?' cried Edith, in anger. 'I shall not listen to you.'

'Oh yes, you will,' said Jennie, 'for I shall follow your own example, and not let you out until you do hear what I have to tell you.'

Saying which the amateur housemaid skipped nimbly to the door, and placed her back against it.

CHAPTER XXVII.

Jennie Brewster stood with her back to the door, a sweet smile on her face.

'This is my day for acting, Miss Longworth. I think I did the rôle of housemaid so well that it deceived several members of this family. I am now giving an imitation of yourself in your thrilling drama, "All at Sea." Don't you think I do it most admirably?'

'Yes,' said Edith, sitting down again. 'I wonder you did not adopt the stage as a profession.'

'I have often thought of doing so, but journalism is more exciting.'

'Perhaps. Still, it has its disappointments. When I gave my thrilling drama, as you call it, on shipboard, I had my stage accessories arranged to better advantage than you have now.'

'Do you mean the putting off of the boat?'

'No; I mean that the electric button was under my hand—it was impossible for you to ring for help. Now, while you hold the door, you cannot stop me from ringing, for the bell-rope is here beside me.'

'Yes, that is a disadvantage, I admit. Do you intend to ring, then, and have me turned out?'

'I don't think that will be necessary. I imagine you will go quietly.'

'You are a pretty clever girl, Miss Longworth. I wish I liked you, but I don't, so we won't waste valuable time deploring that fact. Have you no curiosity to hear what I was going to tell you?'

'Not the slightest; but there is one thing I should like to know.'

'Oh, is there? Well, that's human, at any rate. What do you wish to know?'

'You came here well recommended. How did you know I wanted a housemaid, and were your testimonials——'

Edith paused for a word, which Jennie promptly supplied.

'Forged? Oh dear no! There is no necessity for doing anything criminal in this country, if you have the money. I didn't forge them—I bought them. Didn't you write to any of the good ladies who stood sponsor for me?'

'Yes, and received most flattering accounts of you.'

'Certainly. That was part of the contract. Oh, you can do anything with money in London; it is a most delightful town. Then, as for knowing there was a vacancy, that also was money. I bribed the other housemaid to leave.'

'I see. And what object had you in all this?'

Jennie Brewster laughed—the same silvery laugh that had charmed William Longworth an hour or two before, a laugh that sometimes haunted Wentworth's memory in the City. She left her sentinel-like position at the door and threw herself into a chair.

'Miss Longworth,' she said, 'you are not consistent. You first pretend that you have no curiosity to hear what I have to say, then you ask me exactly what I was going to tell you. Of course, you are dying to know why I am here; you wouldn't be a woman if you weren't. Now, I've changed my mind, and I don't intend to tell you. I will say, though, that my object in coming here was, first, to find out for myself how servants are treated in this country. You see, my sympathies are all with the women who work, and not with women— well, like yourself, for instance.'

'Yes, I think you said that once before. And how do we treat our servants?'

'So far as my experience goes, very well indeed.'

'It is most gratifying to hear you say this. I was afraid we might not have met with your approval. And now, where shall I send your month's money, Miss Brewster?'

Jennie Brewster leaned back in her chair, her eyes all but closed; an angry light shooting from them reminded Edith of her glance of hatred on board the steamship. A rich warm colour overspread her fair face, and her lips closed tightly. There was a moment's silence, and then Jennie's indignation passed away as quickly as it came. She laughed, with just a touch of restraint in her tone.

'You can say an insulting thing more calmly and sweetly than anyone I ever met before; I envy you that. When I say anything low down and mean, I say it in anger, and my voice has a certain amount of acridity in it. I can't purr like a cat and scratch at the same time—I wish I could.'

'Is it an insult to offer you the money you have earned?'

'Yes, it is, and you knew it was when you spoke. You don't understand me a little bit.'

'Is it necessary that I should?'

'I don't suppose you think it is,' said Jennie meditatively, resting her elbow on her knee and her chin on her palm. 'That is where our point of view differs. I like to know everything. It interests me to learn what people think and talk about, and somehow it doesn't seem to matter to me who the people are, for I was even more interested in your butler's political opinions than I was in Lord Frederick Bingham's. They are both Conservatives, but Lord Freddie seems shaky in his views, for you can argue him down in five minutes, but the butler is as steadfast as a rock. I do admire that butler. I hope you will break the news of my departure gently to him, for he proposed to me, and he has not yet had his answer.'

'There is still time,' said Edith, smiling in spite of herself. 'Shall I ring for him?'

'Please do not. I want to avoid a painful scene, because he is so sure of himself, and never dreams of a refusal. It is such a pity, too, for the butler is my ideal of what a member of the aristocracy should be. His dignity is positively awe-inspiring; while Lord Freddie is such a simple, good-natured, everyday young fellow, that if I imported him to the States I am sure no one would believe he was a real lord. With the butler it would be so different,' added Jennie, with a deep sigh.

'It is too bad that you cannot exchange the declaration of the butler for one from Lord Frederick.'

'Too bad!' cried Jennie, looking with wide-open eyes at the girl before her; 'why, bless you! I had a proposal from Lord Freddie two weeks before I ever saw the butler. I see you don't believe a word I say. Well, you ask Lord Freddie. I'll introduce you, and tell him you don't believe he asked me to be Lady Freddie, if that's the title. He'll look sheepish, but he won't deny it. You see, when I found I was going to stay in England for a time, I wrote to the editor of the Argus to get me a bunch of letters of introduction and send them over, as I wanted particularly to study the aristocracy. So he sent them, and, I assure you, I found it much more difficult to get into your servants' hall than I did into the halls of the nobility—besides, it costs less to mix with the Upper Ten.'

Edith sat in silence, looking with amazed interest at the girl, who talked so rapidly that there was sometimes difficulty in following what she said.

'No, Lord Freddie is not half so condescending as the butler, neither is his language so well chosen; but then, I suppose, the butler's had more practice, for Freddie is very young. I am exceedingly disappointed with the aristocracy. They are not nearly so haughty as I had imagined them to be. But what astonishes me in this country is the way you women spoil the men. You are much too good to them. You pet them and fawn on them, and naturally they get conceited. It is such a pity, too; for they are nice fellows, most of them. It is the same everywhere I've been—servants' hall included. Why, when you meet a young couple, of what you are pleased to call the "lower classes," walking in the Park, the man hangs down his head as he slouches along, but the girl looks defiantly at you, as much as to say, "I've got him. Bless him! What have you to say about it?" while the man seems to be ashamed of himself, and evidently feels that he's been had. Now, a man should be made to understand that you're doing him a great favour when you give him a civil word. That's the proper state of mind to keep a man in, and then you can do what you like with him. I generally make him propose, so as to get it over before any real harm's done, and to give an artistic finish to the episode. After that we can be excellent friends, and have a jolly time. That's the way I did with Lord Freddie. Now, here am I, chattering away as if I were paid for talking instead of writing. Why do you look at me so? Don't you believe what I tell you?'

'Yes, I believe all you say. What I can't understand is, why a bright girl like you should enter a house and,—well, do what you have done here, for instance.'

'Why shouldn't I? I am after accurate information. I get it in my own way. Your writers here tell how the poor live, and that sort of thing. They enter the houses of the poor quite unblushingly, and print their impressions of the poverty-stricken homes. Now, why should the rich man be exempt from a similar investigation?'

'In either case it is the work of a spy.'

'Yes; but a spy is not a dishonourable person—at least, he need not be. I saw a monument in Westminster Abbey to a man who was hanged as a spy. A spy must be brave; he must have nerve, caution, and resource. He sometimes does more for his country than a whole regiment. Oh, there are worse persons than spies in this world.'

'I suppose there are, still——'

'Yes, I know. It is easy for persons with plenty of money to moralize on the shortcomings of others. I'll tell you a secret. I'm writing a book, and if it's a success, then good-bye to journalism. I don't like the spy business myself any too well; I'm afraid England is contaminating me, and if I stayed here a few years I might degenerate so far as to think your newspapers interesting. By the way, have you seen Mr. Wentworth lately?'

Edith hesitated a moment, and at last answered:

'Yes, I saw him a day or two ago.'

'Was he looking well? I think I ought to write him a note of apology for all the anxiety I caused him on board ship. You may not believe it, but I have actually had some twinges of conscience over that episode. I suppose that's why I partially forgave you for stopping the cablegram.'

Edith Longworth was astonished at herself for giving the young woman information about Wentworth, but she gave it, and the amateur housemaid departed in peace, saying, by way of farewell:

'I'm not going to write up your household, after all.'

CHAPTER XXVIII.

One day when Kenyon entered the office, the clerk said to him:

'That young gentleman has been here twice to see you. He said it was very important, sir.'

'What young gentleman?'

'The gentleman—here is his card—who belongs to the Financial Field, sir.'

'Did he leave any message?'

'Yes, sir; he said he would call again at three o'clock.'

'Very good,' said Kenyon; and he began composing his address to the proposed subscribers.

At three o'clock the smooth, oily person from the Financial Field put in an appearance.

'Ah, Mr. Kenyon,' he said, 'I am glad to meet you. I called in twice, but had not the good fortune to find you in. Can I see you in private for a moment?'

'Yes,' answered Kenyon. 'Come into the directors' room;' and into the directors room they went, Kenyon closing the door behind them.

'Now,' said the representative of the Financial Field, 'I have brought you a proof of the editorial we propose using, which I am desired by the proprietor to show you, so that it may be free, if possible, from any error. We are very anxious to have things correct in the Financial Field;' and with this he handed to John a long slip of paper with a column of printed matter upon it.

The article was headed, 'The Canadian Mica Mining Company, Limited.' It went on to show what the mine had been, what it had done, and what chances there were for investors getting a good return for their money by buying the shares. John read it through carefully.

'That is a very handsome article,' he said; 'and it is without an error, so far as I can see.'

'I am glad you think so,' replied the young gentleman, folding up the proof and putting it in his inside pocket. 'Now, as I said before, although I am not the advertising canvasser of the Financial Field, I thought I would see you with reference to an advertisement for the paper.'

'Well, you know, we have not had a meeting of the proposed stockholders yet, and therefore are not in a position to give any advertisements regarding the mine. I have no doubt advertisements will be given, and, of course, your paper will be remembered among the rest.'

'Ah,' said the young man, 'that is hardly satisfactory to us. We have a vacant half-page for Monday, the very best position in the paper, which the proprietor thought you would like to secure.'

'As I said a moment ago, we are not in a position to secure it. It is premature to talk of advertising at the present state of affairs.'

'I think, you know, it will be to your interest to take the half-page. The price is three hundred pounds, and besides that amount we should like to have some shares in the company.'

'Do you mean three hundred pounds for one insertion of the advertisement?'

'Yes.'

'Doesn't that strike you as being a trifle exorbitant? Your paper has a comparatively limited circulation, and they do not ask us such a price even in the large dailies.'

'Ah, my dear sir, the large dailies are quite different. They have a tremendous circulation, it is true, but it is not the kind of circulation we have. No other paper circulates so largely among investors as the Financial Field. It is read by exactly the class of people you desire to reach, and I may say that, except through the Financial Field, you cannot get at some of the best men in the City.'

'Well, admitting all that, as I have said once or twice, we are not yet in a position to give an advertisement.'

'Then, I am very sorry to say that we cannot, on Monday, publish the article I have shown you.'

'Very well; I cannot help it. You are not compelled to print it unless you wish. I am not sure, either, that publishing the article on Monday would do us any good. It would be premature, as I say. We are not yet ready to court publicity until we have had our first meeting of proposed stockholders.'

'When is your first meeting of stockholders?'

'On Monday, at three o'clock.'

'Very well, we could put that announcement in another column, and I am sure you would find the attendance at your meeting would be very largely and substantially increased.'

'Possibly; but I decline to do anything till after the meeting.'

'I think you would find it pay you extremely well to take that half-page.'

'I am not questioning the fact at all. I am merely saying what I have said to everyone else, that we are not ready to consider advertising.'

'I am sorry we cannot come to an arrangement, Mr. Kenyon—very sorry indeed;' and, saying this, he took another proof-sheet out of his pocket, which he handed to Kenyon. 'If we cannot come to an understanding, the manager has determined to print this, instead of the article I showed you. Would you kindly glance over it, because we should like to have it as correct as possible.'

Kenyon opened his eyes, and unfolded the paper. The heading was the same, but he had read only a sentence or two when he found that the mica-mine was one of the greatest swindles ever attempted on poor old innocent financial London!

'Do you mean to say,' cried John, looking up at him, with his anger kindling, 'that if I do not bribe you to the extent of three hundred pounds, besides giving you an unknown quantity of stock, you will publish this libel?'

'I do not say it is a libel,' said the young man smoothly; 'that would be a matter for the courts to decide. You might sue us for libel, if you thought we had treated you badly. I may say that has been tried several times, but with indifferent success.'

'But do you mean to tell me that you intend to publish this article if I do not pay you the three hundred pounds?'

'Yes; putting it crudely, that is exactly what I do mean.'

Kenyon rose in his wrath and flung open the door.

'I must ask you to leave this place, and leave it at once. If you ever put in an appearance here again while I am in the office, I will call a policeman and have you turned out!'

'My dear sir,' expostulated the other suavely, 'it is merely a matter of business. If you find it impossible to deal with us, there is no harm done. If our paper has no influence, we cannot possibly injure you. That, of course, is entirely for you to judge. If, any time between now and Sunday night, you conclude to act otherwise, a wire to our office will hold things over until we have had an opportunity of coming to an arrangement with you. If not, this article will be published on Monday morning. I wish you a very good afternoon, sir.'

John said nothing, but watched his visitor out on the pavement, and then returned to the making of his report.

On Monday morning, as he came in by train, his eye caught a flaming poster on one of the bill-boards at the station. It was headed Financial Field, and the next line, in heavy black letters, was, 'The Mica Mining Swindle,' Kenyon called a newsboy to him and bought a copy of the paper. There, in leaded type, was the article before him. It seemed, somehow, much more important on the printed page than it had looked in the proof.

As he read it, he noticed an air of truthful sincerity about the editorial that had escaped him during the brief glance he had given it on Friday. It went on to say that the Austrian Mining Company had sunk a good deal of money in the mine, and that it had never paid a penny of dividends; that they merely kept on at a constant loss to themselves in the hope of being able to swindle some confiding investors—but that even their designs were as nothing compared to the barefaced rascality contemplated by John Kenyon. He caught his breath as he saw his own name in print. It was a shock for which he was not prepared, as he had not noticed it in the proof. Then he read on. It seemed that this man, Kenyon, had secured the mine at something like ten thousand pounds, and was trying to palm it off on the unfortunate British public at the enormous increase of two hundred thousand pounds; but this nefarious attempt would doubtless be frustrated so long as there were papers of the integrity of the Financial Field, to take the risk and expense of making such an exposure as was here set forth.

The article possessed a singular fascination for Kenyon. He read and re-read it in a dazed way, as if the statement referred to some other person, and he could not help feeling sorry for that person.

He still had the paper in his hand as he walked up the street, and he felt numbed and dazed as if someone had struck him a blow. He was nearly run over in crossing one of the thoroughfares, and heard an outburst of profanity directed at him from a cab-driver and a man on a bus; but he heeded them not, walking through the crowd as if under a spell.

He passed the door of his own gorgeous office, and walked some distance up the street before he realized what he had done. Then he turned back again, and, just at the doorstep, paused with a pang at his heart.

'I wonder if Edith Longworth will read that article,' he said to himself.

CHAPTER XXIX.

When John Kenyon entered his office, he thought the clerk looked at him askance. He imagined that innocent employee had been reading the article in the Financial Field; but the truth is, John was hardly in a frame of mind to form a correct opinion on what other people were doing. Everybody he met in the street, it seemed to him, was discussing the article in the Financial Field.

He asked if anybody had been in that morning, and was told there had been no callers. Then he passed into the directors' room, closed the door behind him, sat down on a chair, and leaned his head on his hands with his elbows on the table. In this position Wentworth found him some time later, and when John looked up his face was haggard and aged.

'Ah, I see you have read it.'

'Yes.'

'Do you think Longworth is at the bottom of that article?'

John shook his head.

'Oh no,' he said; 'he had nothing whatever to do with it.'

'How do you know?'

Kenyon related exactly what had passed between the oily young man of the Financial Field and himself in that very room. While this recital was going on, Wentworth walked up and down, expressing his opinion now and then, in remarks that were short and pithy, but hardly fit for publication. When the story was told he turned to Kenyon.

'Well,' he said, 'there is nothing for it but to sue the paper for libel.'

'What good will that do?'

'What good will it do? Do you mean to say that you intend to sit here under such an imputation as they have cast upon you, and do nothing? What good will it do? It will do all the good in the world.'

'We cannot form our company and sue the paper at the same time. All our energies will have to be directed towards the matter we have in hand.'

'But, my dear John, don't you see the effect of that article? How can we form our company if such a lie remains unchallenged? Nobody will look at our proposals. Everyone will say, "What have you done about the article that appeared in the Financial Field?" If we say we have done nothing, then, of course, the natural inference is that we are a pair of swindlers, and that our scheme is a fraud.'

'I have always thought,' said John, 'that the capitalization is too high.'

'Really, I believe you think that article is not so unfair, after all. John, I'm astonished at you!'

'But if we do commence a libel suit, it cannot be finished before our option has expired. If we tell people that we have begun a suit against the Financial Field for libel, they will merely say they prefer to wait and hear what the result of the case is. By that time our chances of forming a company will be gone.'

'There is a certain amount of truth in that; nevertheless, I do not see how we are to go on with our company unless suit for libel is at least begun.'

Before John could reply there was a knock at the door, and the clerk entered with a letter in his hand which had just come in. Kenyon tore it open, read it, and then tossed it across the table to Wentworth. Wentworth saw the name of their firm of solicitors at the top of the letter-paper. Then he read:

'DEAR SIR,

'You have doubtless seen the article in the Financial Field of this morning, referring to the Canadian Mica Mining Company. We should be pleased to know what action you intend to take in the matter. We may say that, in justice to our reputation, we can no longer represent your company unless a suit is brought against the paper which contains the article.

'Yours truly,

'W. HAWK.'

Wentworth laughed with a certain bitterness.

'Well,' he said, 'if it has come to such a pass that Hawk fears for his reputation, the sooner we begin a libel suit against the paper the better!'

'Perhaps,' said John, with a look of agony on his face, 'you will tell me where the money is to come from. The moment we get into the Law Courts money will simply flow like water, and doubtless the Financial Field has plenty of it. It will add to their reputation, and they will make a boast that they are fighting the battle of the investor in London. Everything is grist that comes to their mill. Meanwhile, we shall be paying out money, or we shall be at a tremendous disadvantage, and the result of it all will probably be a disagreement of the jury and practical ruin for us. You see, I have no witnesses.'

'Yes, but what about the mine? How can we go on without vindicating ourselves?'

Before anything further could be said, young Mr. Longworth came in, looking as cool, calm, and unruffled as if there were no such things in the world as financial newspapers.

'Discussing it, I see,' were his first words.

'Yes,' said Wentworth; 'I am very glad you have come. We have a little difference of opinion in the matter of that article. Kenyon here is averse to suing that paper for libel; I am in favour of prosecuting it. Now, what do you say?'

'My dear fellow,' replied Longworth, 'I am delighted to be able to agree with Mr. Kenyon for once. Sue them! Why, of course not. That is just what they want.'

'But,' said Wentworth, 'if we do not, who is going to look at our mine?'

'Exactly the same number of people as would look at it before the article appeared.'

'Don't you think it will have any effect?'

'Not the slightest.'

'But look at this letter from your own lawyers on the subject.' Wentworth handed Longworth the letter from Hawk. Longworth adjusted his glass and read it carefully through.

'By Jove!' he said with a laugh, 'I call that good; I call that distinctly good. I had no idea old Hawk was such a humorist! His reputation indeed; well, that beats me! All that Hawk wants is another suit on his hands. I wish you would let me keep this letter. I will have some fun with my friend Hawk over it.'

'You are welcome to the letter, so far as I am concerned,' said Wentworth; 'but do you mean to say, Mr. Longworth, that we have to sit here calmly under this imputation and do nothing?'

'I mean to say nothing of the kind; but I don't propose to play into their hands by suing them—at least, I should not if it were my case instead of Kenyon's.'

'What would you do?'

'I would let them sue me if they wanted to. Of course, their canvasser called to see you, didn't he, Kenyon?'

'Yes, he did.'

'He told you that he had a certain amount of space to sell for a certain sum in cash?'

'Yes.'

'And, if you did not buy that space, this certain article would appear; whereas, if you did, an article of quite a different complexion would be printed?'

'You seem to know all about it,' said Kenyon suspiciously.

'Of course I do, my dear boy! Everybody knows all about it. That's the way those papers make their money. I think myself, as a general rule, it is cheaper to buy them off. I believe my uncle always does that when he has anything special on hand, and doesn't want to be bothered with outside issues. But we haven't done so in this instance, and this is the result. It can be easily remedied yet, mind you, if you like. All that you have to do is to pay his price, and there will be an equally lengthy article saying that, from outside information received with regard to the Canadian Mining Company, he regrets very much that the former article was an entire mistake, and that there is no more secure investment in England than this particular mine. But now, when he has come out with his editorial, I think it isn't worth while to have any further dealings with him. Anything he can say now will not matter. He has done all the harm he can. But I would at once put the boot on the other foot. I would write down all the circumstances just as they happened— give the name of the young man who called upon you, tell exactly the price he demanded for his silence, and I will have that printed in an opposition paper to-morrow. Then it will be our friend the Financial Field's turn to squirm! He will say it is all a lie, of course, but nobody will believe him, and we can tell him, from the opposition paper, that if it is a lie he is perfectly at liberty to sue us for libel. Let him begin the suit if he wants to do so. Let him defend his reputation. Sue him for libel! I know a game worth two of that. Could you get out the statement before the meeting this afternoon?'

Kenyon, who had been looking, for the first time in his life, gratefully at Longworth, said he could.

'Very well; just set it down in your own words as plainly as possible, and give date, hour, and full particulars. Sign your name to it, and I will take it when I come to the meeting this afternoon. It would not be a bad plan to read it to those who are here. There is nothing like fighting the devil with fire. Fight a paper with another paper. Nothing new, I suppose?'

'No,' said Kenyon; 'nothing new except what we are discussing.'

'Well, don't let that trouble you. Do as I say, and we will begin an interesting controversy. People like a fight, and it will attract attention to the mine. Good-bye. I shall see you this afternoon.'

He left both Kenyon and Wentworth in a much happier frame of mind than that in which he had found them.

'I say, Kenyon,' said Wentworth, 'that fellow is a trump. His advice has cleared the air wonderfully. I believe his plan is the best, after all, and, as you say, we have no money for an expensive lawsuit. I shall leave you now to get on with your work, and will return at three o'clock.'

At that hour John had his statement finished. The first man to arrive was Longworth, who read the article with approval, merely suggesting a change here and there, which was duly made. Then he put the communication into an envelope, and sent it to the editor of the opposition paper. Wentworth came in next, then Melville, then Mr. King. After this they all adjourned to the directors' room, and in a few minutes the others were present.

'Now,' said Longworth, 'as we are all here, I do not see any necessity for delay. You have probably read the article that appeared in this morning's Financial Field. Mr. Kenyon has written a statement in relation to that, which gives the full particulars of the inside of a very disreputable piece of business. It was merely an attempt at blackmailing which failed. I intended to have had the statement read to you, but we thought it best to get it off as quickly as possible, and it will appear to-morrow in the Financial Eagle, where, I hope, you will all read it. Now, Mr. Kenyon, perhaps you will tell us something about the mine.'

Kenyon, like many men of worth and not of words, was a very poor speaker. He seemed confused, and was often a little obscure in his remarks, but he was listened to with great attention by those present. He was helped here and there by a judicious question from young Longworth, and when he sat down the impression was not so bad as might have been expected. After a moment's silence, it was Mr. King who spoke.

'As I take it,' he said, 'all we wish to know is this: Is the mine what it is represented to be? Is the mineral the best for the use Mr. Kenyon has indicated? Is there a sufficient quantity of that mineral in the mountain he speaks of to make it worth while to organize this company? It seems to me that this can only be answered by some practical man going out there and seeing the mine for himself. Mr. Melville is, I understand, a practical man. If he has the time to spare, I would propose that he should go to America, see this mine, and report.'

Another person asked when the option on the mine ran out. This was answered by Longworth, who said that the person who went over and reported on the mine could cable the word 'Right' or 'Wrong'; then there would be time to act in London in getting up the list of subscribers.

'I suppose,' said another, 'that in case of delay there would be no trouble in renewing the option for a month or two?'

To this Kenyon replied that he did not know. The owners might put a higher price on the property, or the mine might be producing more mica than it had been heretofore, and they perhaps might not be inclined to sell. He thought that things should be arranged so that there would be no necessity of asking for an extension of the option, and to this they all agreed.

Melville then said he had no objection to taking a trip to Canada. It was merely a question of the amount of the mineral in sight, and he thought he could determine that as well as anybody else. And so the matter was about to be settled, when Longworth rose, and said that he was perfectly willing to go to Canada himself, in company with Mr. Melville; that he would pay all his own expenses, and give them the benefit of his opinion as well. This was received with applause, and the meeting terminated. Longworth shook hands with Kenyon and Wentworth.

'We will sail by the first steamer,' he said, 'and, as I may not see you again, you might write me a letter of introduction to Mr. Von Brent, and tell him that I am acting for you in this affair. That will make matters smooth in getting an extension of the option, if it should be necessary.'

CHAPTER XXX.

Kenyon was on his way to lunch next day, when he met Wentworth at the door.

'Going to feed?' asked the latter.

'Yes.'

'Very well; I'll go with you. I couldn't stay last night to have a talk with you over the meeting; but what did you think of it?'

'Well, considering the article which appeared in the morning, and considering also the exhibition I made of myself in attempting to explain the merits of the mine, I think things went off rather smoothly.'

'So do I. It doesn't strike you that they went off a little too smoothly, does it?'

'What do you mean?'

'I don't know exactly what I mean. I merely wanted to get your own opinion about it. You see, I have attended a great many gatherings of this sort, and it struck me there was a certain cut-and-driedness about the meeting. I can't say whether it impressed me favourably or unfavourably, but I noticed it.'

'I still don't understand what you mean.'

'Well, as a general thing in such meetings, when a man gets up and proposes a certain action there is some opposition, or somebody has a suggestion to make, or something better to propose—or thinks he has—and so there is a good deal of talk. Now, when King got up and proposed calmly that Melville should go to America, it appeared to me rather an extraordinary thing to do, unless he had consulted Melville beforehand.'

'Perhaps he had done so.'

'Yes, perhaps. What do you think of it all?'

Kenyon mused for a moment before he replied:

'As I said before, I thought things went off very smoothly. Whom do you suspect—young Longworth?'

'I do not know whom I suspect. I am merely getting anxious about the shortness of the time. I think, myself, you ought to go to America. There is nothing to be done here. You should go, see Von Brent, and get a renewal of the option. Don't you see that when they get over there, allowing them a few days in New York, and a day or two to get out to the mine, we shall have little more than a week, after the cable despatch comes, in which to do anything, should they happen to report unfavourably.'

'Yes, I see that. Still, it is only a question of facts on which they have to report, and you know, as well as I do, that no truthful men can report unfavourably on what we have certified. We have understated the case in every instance.'

'I know that. I am perfectly well aware of that. Everything is all right if—if—Longworth is dealing honestly with us. If he is not, then everything is all wrong, and I should feel a great deal easier if we had in our possession another three months' option of the mine. We are now at the fag-end of this option, and, it seems to me, as protection to ourselves, we ought either to write to Von Brent—By the way, have you ever written to him?'

'I wrote one letter telling him how we were getting on, but have received no answer; perhaps he is not in Ottawa at present.'

'Well, I think you ought to go to the mine with Longworth and Melville. It is the conjunction of those two men that makes me suspicious. I can't tell what I distrust. I can give nothing definite; but I have a vague uneasiness when I think that the man who tried to mislead us regarding the value of the mineral is going with the man who has led us into all this expense. Longworth refused to go into the scheme in the first place, pretended he had forgotten all about it in the second place, and then suddenly developed an interest.'

John knitted his brows and said nothing.

'I don't want to worry you about it, but I am anxious to have your candid opinion. What had we better do?'

'It seems to me,' said John, after a pause, 'that we can do nothing. It is a very perplexing situation. I think, however, we should turn it over in our minds for a few days, and then I can get to America in plenty of time, if necessary.'

'Very well, suppose we give them ten days to get to the mine and reply. If no reply comes by the eleventh day then you will still have eighteen or nineteen days before the option expires. Put it at twelve days. I propose, if you hear nothing by then, you go over.'

'Right,' said John; 'we may take that as settled.'

'By the way, you got an invitation to-day, did you not?'

'Yes.'

'Are you going?'

'I do not know. I should like to go and yet, you know, I am entirely unused to fashionable assemblages. I should not know what to say or do while I was there.'

'As I understand, it is not to be a fashionable party, but merely a little friendly gathering which Miss Longworth gives because her cousin is about to sail for Canada. I don't want to flatter you, John, at all, but I imagine Miss Longworth would be rather disappointed if you did not put in an appearance. Besides, as we are partners with Longworth in this, and as he is going away on account of the mine. I think it would be a little ungracious of us not to go.'

'Very well, I will go. Shall I call for you, or will you come for me?'

'I will call for you and we will go there together in a cab. Be ready about eight o'clock.'

The mansion of the Longworths was brilliantly lighted, and John felt rather faint-hearted as he stood on the steps before going in. The chances are he would not have had the courage to allow himself to be announced if his friend Wentworth had not been with him. George, however, had no such qualms, being more experienced in this kind of thing than his comrade. So they entered together, and were warmly greeted by the young hostess.

'It is so kind of you to come,' she said, 'on such short notice. I was afraid you might have had some prior engagement, and would have found it impossible to be with us.'

'You must not think that of me,' said Wentworth. 'I was certain to come; but I must confess my friend Kenyon here was rather difficult to manage. He seems to frown on social festivities, and actually had the coolness to propose that we should both plead more important business.'

Edith looked reproachfully at Kenyon, who flushed to the temples, as was his custom, and said:

'Now, Wentworth, that is unfair. You must not mind what he says, Miss Longworth; he likes to bring confusion on me, and he knows how to do it. I certainly said nothing about a prior engagement.'

'Well, now you are here, I hope you will enjoy yourselves. It is quite an informal little gathering, with nothing to abash even Mr. Kenyon.'

They found young Longworth there in company with Melville, who was to be his companion on the voyage. He shook hands, but without exhibiting the pleasure at meeting them which his cousin had shown.

'My cousin,' said the young man, 'seems resolved to make the going of the prodigal nephew an occasion for killing the fatted calf. I'm sure I don't know why, unless it is that she is glad to be rid of me for a month.'

Edith laughed at this, and left the men together. Wentworth speedily contrived to make himself agreeable to the young ladies who were present; but John, it must be admitted, felt awkward and out of place. He was not enjoying himself. He caught himself now and then following Edith Longworth with his eyes, and when he realized he was doing this, would abruptly look at the floor. In her handsome evening dress she appeared supremely lovely, and this John Kenyon admitted to himself with a sigh, for her very loveliness seemed to place her further and further away from him. Somebody played something on the piano, and this was, in a way, a respite for John. He felt that nobody was looking at him. Then a young man gave a recitation, which was very well received, and Kenyon began to forget his uneasiness. A German gentleman with long hair sat down at the piano with a good deal of importance in his demeanour. There was much arranging of music, and finally, when the leaves were settled to his satisfaction, there was a tremendous crash of chords, the beginning of what was evidently going to be a troublesome time for the piano. In the midst of this hurricane of sound John Kenyon became aware that Edith Longworth had sat down beside him.

'I have got everyone comfortably settled with everyone else,' she said in a whisper to him, 'and you seem to be the only one who is, as it were, out in the cold, so, you see, I have done you the honour to come and talk to you.'

'It is indeed an honour,' said John earnestly.

'Oh, really,' said the young woman, laughing very softly, 'you must not take things so seriously. I didn't mean quite what I said, you know—that was only, as the children say, "pretended"; but you take one's light remarks as if they were most weighty sentences. Now, you must look as if you were entertaining me charmingly, whereas I have sat down beside you to have a very few minutes' talk on business; I know it's very bad form to talk business at an evening party, but, you see, I have no other chance to speak with you. I understand you have had a meeting of shareholders, and yet you never sent me an invitation. I told you that I wished to help you in forming a company; but that is the way you business men always treat a woman.'

'Really, Miss Longworth,' began Kenyon; but she speedily interrupted him.

'I am not going to let you make any explanation. I have come over here to enjoy scolding you, and I am not to be cheated out of my pleasure.'

'I think,' said John, 'if you knew how much I have suffered during this last day or two, you would be very lenient with me. Did you read that article upon me in the Financial Field?'

'No, I did not, but I read your reply to it this morning, and I think it was excellent.'

'Ah, that was hardly fair. A person should read both sides of the question before passing judgment.'

'It is a woman's idea of fairness,' said Edith, 'to read what pertains to her friend, and to form her judgment without hearing the other side. But you must not think I am going to forego scolding you because of my sympathy with you. Don't you remember you promised to let me know how your company was progressing from time to time, and here I have never had a word from you; now tell me how you have been getting on.'

'I hardly know, but I think we are doing very well indeed. You know, of course, that your cousin is going to America to report upon the mine. As I have stated nothing but what is perfectly true about the property, there can be no question as to what that report will be, so it seems to me everything is going on nicely.'

'Why do not you go to America?'

'Ah, well, I am an interested party, and those who are thinking of going in with us have my report already. It is necessary to corroborate that. When it is corroborated, I expect we shall have no trouble in forming the company.'

'And was William chosen by those men to go to Canada?'

'He was not exactly chosen; he volunteered. Mr. Melville here was the one who was chosen.'

'And why Mr. Melville more than you, for instance?'

'Well, as I said, I am out of the question because I am an interested party. Melville is a man connected with china works, and as such, in a measure, an expert.'

'Is Mr. Melville a friend of yours?'

'No, he is not. I never saw him until he came to the meeting.'

'Do you know,' she said, lowering her voice and bending towards him, 'that I do not like Mr. Melville's face?' Kenyon glanced at Melville, who was at the other side of the room, and Edith went on: 'You must not look at people when I mention them in that way, or they will know we are talking about them. I do not like his face. He is too handsome a man, and I don't like handsome men.'

'Don't you, really,' said John; 'then, you ought to——'

Edith laughed softly, a low, musical laugh that was not heard above the piano din, and was intended for John alone, and to his ears it was the sweetest music he had ever heard.

'I know what you were going to say,' she said; 'you were going to say that in that case I ought to like you. Well, I do; that is why I am taking such an interest in your mine, and in your friend Mr. Wentworth. And so my cousin volunteered to go to Canada. Now, I think you ought to go yourself.'

'Why?' said Kenyon, startled that she should have touched the point that had been discussed between Wentworth and himself.

'I can only give you a woman's reason—"because I do." It seems to me you ought to be there to know what they report at the time they do report. Perhaps they won't understand the mine without your explanation, and then you see an adverse report might come back in perfect good faith. I think you ought to go to America, Mr. Kenyon.'

'That is just what George Wentworth says.'

'Does he? I always thought he was a very sensible young man, and now I am sure of it. Well, I must not stay here gossiping with you on business. I see the professor is going to finish, and so I shall have to look after my other guests. If I don't see you again this evening, or have no opportunity of speaking with you, think over what I have said.'

And then, with the most charming hypocrisy, the young woman thanked the professor for the music to which she had not listened in the least.

'Well, how did you enjoy yourself?' said Wentworth when they had got outside again.

It was a clear, starlight night, and they had resolved to walk home together.

'I enjoyed myself very well indeed,' answered Kenyon; 'much better than I expected. It was a little awkward at first, but I got over that.'

'I noticed you did—with help.'

'Yes, "with help."'

'If you are inclined to rave, John, now that we are under the stars, remember I am a close confidant, and a sympathetic listener. I should like to hear you rave, just to learn how an exasperatingly sensible man acts under the circumstances.'

'I shall not rave about anything, George, but I will tell you something. I am going to Canada.'

'Ah, did she speak about that?'

'She did.'

'And of course her advice at once decides the matter, after my most cogent arguments have failed?'

'Don't be offended, George, but—it does.'

CHAPTER XXXI.

'What name, please?'

'Tell Mr. Wentworth a lady wishes to see him.'

The boy departed rather dubiously, for he knew this message was decidedly irregular in a business office. People should give their names.

'A lady to see you, sir,' he said to Wentworth; and, then, just as the boy had expected, his employer wanted to know the lady's name.

Ladies are not frequent visitors at the office of an accountant in the City, so Wentworth touched his collar and tie to make sure they were in their correct position, and, wondering who the lady was, asked the boy to show her in.

'How do you do, Mr. Wentworth?' she said brightly, advancing towards his table and holding out her hand.

Wentworth caught his breath, and took her extended hand somewhat limply, then he pulled himself together; saying:

'This is an unexpected pleasure, Miss Brewster.'

Jennie blushed very prettily, and laughed a laugh that Wentworth thought was like a little ripple of music from a mellow flute.

'It may be unexpected,' she said, 'but you don't look a bit like a man suffering from an overdose of pure joy. You didn't expect to see me, did you?'

'I did not; but now that you are here, may I ask in what way I can serve you?'

'Well, in the first place, you may ask me to take a chair, and in the second place you may sit down yourself; for I've come to have a long talk with you.'

The prospect did not seem to be so alluring to Wentworth as one might have expected, when the announcement was made by a girl so pretty, and dressed in such exquisite taste; but the young man promptly offered her a chair, and then sat down, with the table between them. She placed her parasol and a few things she had been carrying on the table, arranging them with some care; then, having given him time to recover from his surprise, she flashed a look at him that sent a thrill to the finger-tips of the young man. Yet a danger understood is a danger half overcome; and Wentworth, unconsciously drawing a deep breath, nerved himself against any recurrence of a feeling he had been trying with but indifferent success to forget, saying grimly, but only half convincingly, to himself:

'You are not going to fool me a second time, my girl, lovely as you are.'

A glimmer of a smile hovered about the red lips of the girl, a smile hardly perceptible, but giving an effect to her clear complexion as if a sunbeam had crept into the room, and its reflection had lit up her face.

'I have come to apologize, Mr. Wentworth,' she said at last. 'I find it a very difficult thing to do, and, as I don't quite know how to begin, I plunge right into it.'

'You don't need to apologize to me for anything, Miss Brewster,' replied Wentworth, rather stiffly.

'Oh yes, I do. Don't make it harder than it is by being too frigidly polite about it, but say you accept the apology, and that you're sorry—no, I don't mean that—I should say that you're sure I'm sorry, and that you know I won't do it again.'

Wentworth laughed, and Miss Brewster joined him.

'There,' she said, 'that's ever so much better. I suppose you've been thinking hard things of me ever since we last met.'

'I've tried to,' replied Wentworth.

'Now, that's what I call honest; besides, I like the implied compliment. I think it's very neat indeed. I'm really very, very sorry that I—that things happened as they did. I wouldn't have blamed you if you had used exceedingly strong language about it at the time.'

'I must confess that I did.'

'Ah!' said Jennie, with a sigh, 'you men have so many comforts denied to us women. But I came here for another purpose; if I had merely wanted to apologize, I think I would have written. I want some information which you can give me, if you like.'

The young woman rested her elbows on the table, with her chin in her hands, gazing across at him earnestly and innocently. Poor George felt that it would be almost impossible to refuse anything to those large beseeching eyes.

'I want you to tell me about your mine.'

All the geniality that had gradually come into Wentworth's face and manner vanished instantly.

'So this is the old business over again,' he said.

'How can you say that!' cried Jennie reproachfully. 'I am asking for my own satisfaction entirely, and not for my paper. Besides, I tell you frankly what I want to know, and don't try to get it by indirect means—by false pretences, as you once said.'

'How can you expect me to give you information that does not belong to me alone? I have no right to speak of a business which concerns others without their permission.'

'Ah, then, there are at least two more concerned in the mine,' said Jennie gleefully. 'Kenyon is one, I know; who is the other?'

'Miss Brewster, I will tell you nothing.'

'But you have told me something already. Please go on and talk, Mr. Wentworth—about anything you like—and I shall soon find out all I want to know about the mine.'

She paused, but Wentworth remained silent, which, indeed, the bewildered young man realized was the only safe thing to do.

'They speak of the talkativeness of women,' Miss Brewster went on, as if soliloquizing, 'but it is nothing to that of the men. Once set a man talking, and you learn everything he knows—besides ever so much more that he doesn't.'

Miss Brewster had abandoned her very taking attitude, with its suggestion of confidential relations, and had removed her elbows from the table, sitting now back in her chair, gazing dreamily at the dingy window which let the light in from the dingy court. She seemed to have forgotten that Wentworth was there, and said, more to herself than to him:

'I wonder if Kenyon would tell me about the mine.'

'You might ask him.'

'No; it wouldn't do any good,' she continued, gently shaking her head. 'He's one of your silent men, and there are so few of them in this world. Perhaps I had better go to William Longworth himself; he's not suspicious of me.'

As she said this, she threw a quick glance at Wentworth, and the unfortunate young man's face at once told her that she had hit the mark. She bent her head over the table, and laughed with such evident enjoyment that Wentworth, in spite of his helpless anger, smiled grimly.

Jennie raised her head, but the sight of his perplexed countenance was too much for her, and it was some time before her merriment allowed her to speak. At last she said:

'Wouldn't you like to take me by the shoulders and put me out of the room, Mr. Wentworth?'

'I'd like to take you by the shoulders and shake you.'

'Ah! that would be taking a liberty, and could not be permitted. We must leave punishment to the law, you know, although I do think a man should be allowed to turn an objectionable visitor into the street.'

'Miss Brewster,' cried the young man earnestly, leaning over the table towards her, 'why don't you abandon your horrible inquisitorial profession, and put your undoubted talents to some other use?'

'What, for instance?'

'Oh, anything.'

Jennie rested her fair cheek against her open palm again, and looked at the dingy window. There was a long silence between them—Wentworth absorbed in watching her clear-cut profile and her white throat, his breath quickening as he feasted his eyes on her beauty.

'I have always got angry,' she said at last, in a low voice with the quiver of a suppressed sigh in it, 'when other people have said that to me—I wonder why it is I merely feel hurt and sad when you say it? It is so easy to say, "Oh, anything"—so easy, so easy. You are a man, with the strength and determination of a man, yet you have met with disappointments and obstacles that have required all your courage to overcome. Every man has, and with most men it is a fight until the head is gray, and the brain weary with the ceaseless struggle. The world is utterly merciless; it will trample you down relentlessly if it can, and if your vigilance relaxes for a moment, it will steal your crust and leave you to starve. Every time I think of this incessant sullen contest, with no quarter given or taken, I shudder, and pray that I may die before I am at the mercy of the pitiless world. When I came to London, I saw, for the first time in my life, that hopeless, melancholy promenade of the sandwich-men; human wreckage drifting along the edge of the street, as if cast there by the rushing tide sweeping past them. They—they seemed to me like a tottering procession of the dead; and on their backs was the announcement of a play that was making all London roar with laughter. The awful comedy and tragedy of it! Well, I simply couldn't stand it. I had to run up a side-street and cry like the little fool I was, right in broad daylight.'

Jennie paused and tried to laugh, but the effort ended in a sound suspiciously like a sob. She dashed her hand with quick impatience across her eyes, from which Wentworth had never taken his own, seeing them become dim, as if the light from the window proved too strong for them, and finally fill as she ceased to speak. Searching ineffectually about her dress for a handkerchief, which lay on the table beside her parasol unnoticed by either, Jennie went on with some difficulty:

'Well, these poor forlorn creatures were once men—men who have gone down—and if the world is so hard on a man with all his strength and resourcefulness, think—think what it is for a woman thrown into this inhuman turmoil—a woman without friends—without money—flung among these relentless wolves—to live if she can—or—to die—if she can.'

The girl's voice broke, and she buried her face in her arms, which rested on the table.

Wentworth sprang to his feet and came round to where she sat.

'Jennie,' he said, putting his hand on her shoulder. The girl, without looking up, shook off the hand that touched her.

'Go back to your place,' she cried, in a smothered voice. 'Leave me alone.'

'Jennie,' persisted Wentworth.

The young woman rose from her chair and faced him, stepping back a pace.

'Don't you hear what I say? Go back and sit down. I came here to talk business, not to make a fool of myself. It's all your fault, and I hate you for it—you and your silly questions.'

But the young man stood where he was, in spite of the dangerous sparkle that shone in his visitor's wet eyes. A frown gathered on his brow.

'Jennie,' he said slowly, 'are you playing with me again?'

The swift anger that blazed up in her face, reddening her cheeks, dried the tears.

'How dare you say such a thing to me!' she cried hotly. 'Do you flatter yourself that, because I came here to talk business, I have also some personal interest in you? Surely even your self-conceit doesn't run so far as that!'

Wentworth stood silent, and Miss Brewster picked up her parasol, scattering, in her haste, the other articles on the floor. If she expected Wentworth to put them on the table again, she was disappointed, for, although his eyes were upon her, his thoughts were far away upon the Atlantic Ocean.

'I shall not stay here to be insulted,' she cried resentfully, bringing Wentworth's thoughts back with a rush to London again. 'It is intolerable that you should use such an expression to me. Playing with you indeed!'

'I had no intention of insulting you, Miss Brewster.'

'What is it but an insult to use such a phrase? It implies that I either care for you, or——'

'And do you?'

'Do I what?'

'Do you care for me?'

Jennie shook out the lace fringes of her parasol; and smoothed them with some precision. Her eyes were bent on what she was doing; consequently, they did not meet those of her questioner.

'I care for you as a friend, of course,' she said at last, still giving much attention to the parasol. 'If I had not looked on you as a friend, I would not have come here to consult with you, would I?'

'No, I suppose not. Well, I am sorry I used the words that displeased you, and now, if you will permit it, we will go on with the consultation.'

'It wasn't a pretty thing to say.'

'I'm afraid I'm not good at saying pretty things.'

'You used to be.'

The parasol being arranged to her liking, she glanced up at him.

'Still, you said you were sorry, and that's all a man can say—or a woman either, for that's what I said myself when I came in. Now, if you will pick up those things from the floor—thanks—we will talk about the mine.'

Wentworth seated himself again, and said;

'Well, what is it you wish to know about the mine?'

'Nothing at all.'

'But you said you wanted information.'

'What a funny reason to give! And how a man misses all the fine points of a conversation! No; just because I asked for information, you might have known that was not what I really wanted.'

'I'm afraid I'm very stupid. I hate to ask boldly what you did want, but I would like to know.'

'I wanted a vote of confidence. I told you I was sorry because of a certain episode. I wished to see if you trusted me, and I found you didn't. There!'

'I think that was hardly a fair test. You see, the facts did not belong to me alone.'

Miss Brewster sighed, and slowly shook her head.

'That wouldn't have made the least difference if you had really trusted me.'

'Oh, I say! You couldn't expect a man to——'

'Yes I could.'

'What, merely a friend?'

Miss Brewster nodded.

'Well, all I can say,' remarked Wentworth, with a laugh, 'is that friendship has made greater strides in the States than it has in this country.'

Before Jennie could reply, the useful boy knocked at the door and brought in a tea-tray, which he placed before his master; then silently departed, closing the door noiselessly.

'May I offer you a cup of tea?'

'Please. What a curious custom this drinking of tea is in business offices! I think I shall write an article on "A Nation of Tea-tipplers." If I were an enemy of England, instead of being its greatest friend, I would descend with my army on this country between the hours of four and five in the afternoon, and so take the population unawares while it was drinking tea. What would you do if the enemy came down on you during such a sacred national ceremony?'

'I would offer her a cup of tea,' replied Wentworth, suiting the action to the phrase.

'Mr. Wentworth,' said the girl archly, 'you're improving. That remark was distinctly good. Still, you must remember that I come as a friend, not as an enemy. Did you ever read the "Babes in the Wood"? It is a most instructive, but pathetic, work of fiction. You remember the wicked uncle, surely? Well, you and Mr. Kenyon remind me of the "Babes," poor innocent little things! and London—this part of it—is the dark and pathless forest. I am the bird hovering about you, waiting to cover you with leaves. The leaves, to do any good, ought to be cheques fluttering down on you, but, alas! I haven't any. If negotiable cheques only grew on trees, life would not be so difficult.'

Miss Brewster sipped her tea pensively, and Wentworth listened contentedly to the musical murmur of her voice. Such an entrancing effect had it on him that he paid less heed to what she said than a man ought when a lady is speaking. The tea-drinking had added a touch of domesticity to the tête-a-tête which rather went to the head of the young man. He clinched and unclinched his hand out of sight under the table, and felt the moisture on his palm. He hoped he would be able to retain control over himself, but the difficulty of his task almost overcame him when she now and then appealed to him with glance or gesture, and he felt as if he must cry out, 'My girl, my girl, don't do that, if you expect me to stay where I am.'

'I see you are not paying the slightest attention to what I am saying,' she said, pushing the cup from her. She rested her arms on the table, leaning slightly forward, and turning her face full upon him: 'I can tell by your eyes that you are thinking of something else.'

'I assure you,' said George, drawing a deep breath, 'I am listening with intense interest.'

'Well, that's right, for what I am going to say is important. Now, to wake you up, I will first tell you all about your mine; you will understand thereafter that I did not need to ask anyone for information regarding it.'

Here, to Wentworth's astonishment, she gave a rapid and accurate sketch of the negotiations and arrangements between the three partners, and the present position of affairs.

'How do you know all this?' he asked.

'Never mind that; and you mustn't ask how I know what I am now going to tell you, but you must believe it implicitly, and act upon it promptly. Longworth is fooling both you and Kenyon. He is marking time, so that your option will run out; then he will pay cash for the mine at the original price, and you and Kenyon will be left to pay two-thirds of the debt incurred. Where is Kenyon?'

'He has gone to America.'

'That's good. Cable him to get the option renewed. You can then try to form the company yourselves in London. If he can't obtain a renewal, you have very little time to get the cash together, and if you are not able to do that, then you lose everything. This is what I came to tell you, although I have been a long time about it. Now I must go.'

She rose, gathered her belongings from the table, and stood with the parasol pressed against her. Wentworth came around to where she was standing, his face paler than usual, probably because of the news he had heard. One hand was grasped tightly around one wrist in front of him. He felt that he should thank her for what she had done, but his lips were dry, and, somehow, the proper words were not at his command.

She, holding her fragile lace-fringed parasol against her with one arm, was adjusting her long neatly fitting glove, which she had removed before tea. A button, one of many, was difficult to fasten, and as she endeavoured to put

437

it in its place, her sleeve fell away, showing a round white arm above the glove.

'You see,' she said, a little breathlessly, her eyes upon her glove, 'it is a very serious situation, and time is of immense importance.'

'I realize that.'

'It would be such a pity to lose everything now, when you have had so much trouble and worry.'

'It would.'

'And I think that whatever is done should be done quickly. You should act at once and with energy.'

'I am convinced that is so.'

'Of course it is. You are of too trusting a nature; you should be more suspicious, then you wouldn't be tricked as you have been.'

'No. The trouble is I have been too sceptical, but that is past. I won't be again.'

'What are you talking about?' she said, looking quickly up at him. 'Don't you know you'll lose the mine if——'

'Hang the mine!' he cried, flinging his wrist free, and clasping her to him before she could step back or move from her place. 'There is something more important than mines or money.'

The parasol broke with a sharp snap, and the girl murmured 'Oh!' but the murmur was faint.

'Never mind the parasol,' he said, pulling it from between them and tossing it aside; 'I'll get you another.'

'Reckless man!' she gasped; 'you little know how much it cost, and I think, you know, I ought to have been consulted—in an—in an—affair of this kind—George.'

'There was no time. I acted upon your own advice—promptly. You are not angry, Jennie, my dear girl, are you?'

'I suppose I'm not, though I think I ought to be; especially as I know only too well that I held my heart in my hand the whole time, almost offering it to you. I hope you won't treat it as you have treated the sunshade.'

He kissed her for answer.

'You see,' she said, putting his necktie straight, 'I liked you from the very first, far more than I knew at the time. If you—I'm not trying to justify myself, you know—but if you had, well, just coaxed me a little yourself, I would never have sent that cable message. You seemed to give up everything, and you sent Kenyon to me, and that made me angry. I expected you to come back to me, but you never came.'

'I was a stupid fool. I always am when I get a fair chance.'

'Oh no, you're not, but you do need someone to take care of you.'

She suddenly held him at arm's length from her.

'You don't imagine for a moment, George Wentworth, that I came here to-day for—for this.'

'Certainly not!' cried the honest young man, with much indignant fervour, drawing her again towards him.

'Then it's all right. I couldn't bear to have you think such a thing, especially—well, I'll tell you why some day. But I do wish you had a title. Do they ever ennoble accountants in this country, George?'

'No; they knight only rich fools.'

'Oh, I'm so glad of that; for you'll get rich on the mine, and I'll be Lady Wentworth yet.'

Then she drew his head down until her laughing lips touched his.

CHAPTER XXXII.

Although the steamship that took Kenyon to America was one of the speediest in the Atlantic service, yet the voyage was inexpressibly dreary to him. He spent most of his time walking up and down the deck, thinking about the other voyage of a few weeks before. The one consolation of his present trip was its quickness.

When he arrived at his hotel in New York, he asked if there was any message there for him, and the clerk handed him an envelope, which he tore open. It was a cable despatch from Wentworth, with the words:

'Longworth at Windsor. Proceed to Ottawa immediately. Get option renewed. Longworth duping us.'

John knitted his brows and wondered where Windsor was. The clerk, seeing his perplexity, asked if he could be of any assistance.

'I have received this cablegram, but don't quite understand it. Where is Windsor?'

'Oh, that means the Windsor Hotel. Just up the street.'

Kenyon registered, told the clerk to assign him a room, and send his baggage up to it when it came. Then he walked out from the hotel and sought the Windsor.

He found that colossal hostelry, and was just inquiring of the clerk whether a Mr. Longworth was staying there, when that gentleman appeared at the desk, took some letters and his key.

Kenyon tapped him on the shoulder.

Young Longworth turned round with more alacrity than he usually displayed, and gave a long whistle of surprise when he saw who it was.

'In the name of all the gods,' he cried, 'what are you doing here?' Then, before Kenyon could reply, he said: 'Come up to my room.'

They went to the elevator, rose a few stories, and passed down an apparently endless hall, carpeted with some noiseless stuff that gave no echo of the footfall. Longworth put the key into his door and opened it. They entered a large and pleasant room.

'Well,' he said, 'this is a surprise. What is the reason of your being here? Anything wrong in London?'

'Nothing wrong, so far as I am aware. We received no cablegram from you, and thought there might be some hitch in the business; therefore I came.'

'Ah, I see. I cabled over to your address, and said I was staying at the Windsor for a few days. I sent a cablegram almost as long as a letter, but it didn't appear to do any good.'

'No, I did not receive it.'

'And what did you expect was wrong over here?'

'That I did not know. I knew you had time to get to Ottawa and see the mine in twelve days from London. Not hearing from you in that time, and knowing the option was running out, both Wentworth and I became anxious, and so I came over.'

'Exactly. Well, I'm afraid you've had your trip for nothing.'

'What do you mean? Is not the mine all I said it was?'

'Oh, the mine is all right; all I meant was, there was really no necessity for your coming.'

'But, you know, the option ends in a very short time.'

'Well, the option, like the mine, is all right. I think you might quite safely have left it in my hands.'

It must be admitted that John Kenyon began to feel he had acted with unreasonable rashness in taking his long voyage.

'Is Mr. Melville here with you?'

'Melville has returned home. He had not time to stay longer. All he wanted was to satisfy himself about the mine. He was satisfied, and he has gone home. If you were in London now, you would be able to see him.'

'Did you meet Mr. Von Brent?'

'Yes, he took us to the mine.'

'And did you say anything about the option to him?'

'Well, we had some conversation about it. There will be no trouble about the option. What Von Brent wants is to sell his mine, that is all.' There was a few moments' silence, then Longworth said: 'When are you going back?'

'I do not know. I think I ought to see Von Brent. I am not at all easy about leaving matters as they are. I think I ought to get a renewal of the option. It is not wise to risk things as we are doing. Von Brent might at any time get an offer for his mine, just as we are forming our company, and, of course, if the option had not been renewed, he would sell to the first man who put down the money. As you say, all he wants is to sell his mine.'

Longworth was busy opening his letters, and apparently paying very little attention to what Kenyon said. At last, however, he spoke:

'If I were you—if you care to take my advice—I would go straight back to England. You will do no good here. I merely say this to save you any further trouble, time, and expense.'

'Don't you think it would be as well to get a renewal of the option?'

'Oh, certainly; but, as I told you before, it was not at all necessary for you to come over. I may say, furthermore, that Von Brent will not renew the option without a handsome sum down, to be forfeited if the company is not formed. Have you the money to pay him?'

'No, I have not.'

'Very well, then, why waste time and money going to Ottawa?' Young Mr. Longworth arched his eye-brows and gazed at John through his eyeglass. 'I will let you have my third of the money, if that will do any good.'

'How much money does Von Brent want?'

'How should I know? To tell you the truth, Mr. Kenyon—and truth never hurts, or oughtn't to—I don't at all like this visit to America. You and Mr. Wentworth have been good enough to be suspicious about me from the very first. You have not taken any pains to conceal it, either of you. Your appearance in America at this particular juncture is nothing more nor less than an insult to me. I intend to receive it as such.'

'I have no intention of insulting you,' said Kenyon, 'if you are dealing fairly with me.'

'There it is again. That remark is an insult. Everything you say is a reflection upon me. I wish to have nothing more to say to you. I give you my advice that it is better for you, and cheaper, to go back to London. You need not act on it unless you like. I have nothing further to say to you and so this interview may be considered closed.'

'And how about the mine?'

'I imagine the mine will take care of itself.'

'Do you think this is courteous treatment of a business partner?'

'My dear sir, I do not take my lessons in courtesy from you. Whether you are pleased or displeased with my treatment of you is a matter of supreme indifference to me. I am tired of living in an atmosphere of suspicion, and I have done with it—that is all. You think some game is being played on you—both you and Mr. Wentworth think that—and yet you haven't the "cuteness," as they call it here, or sharpness, to find it out. Now, a man who has suspicions he cannot prove to be well founded should keep those suspicions to himself until he can prove them. That is my advice to you. I wish you a good-day.'

John Kenyon walked back to his hotel with more misgivings than ever. He wrote a letter to Wentworth detailing the conversation, telling him Melville had sailed for home, and advising him to see that gentleman when he arrived. He stayed in New York that night, and took the morning train to Montreal. In due time he arrived at Ottawa, and called on Von Brent. He found that gentleman in his chambers, looking as if he had never left the room since the option was signed. Von Brent at first did not recognise his visitor, but after gazing a moment at him he sprang from his chair and held out his hand.

'I really did not know you,' he said; 'you have changed a great deal since I saw you last. You look haggard, and not at all well. What is the matter with you?'

'I do not think anything is the matter. I am in very good health, thank you; I have had a few business worries, that is all.'

'Ah, yes,' said Von Brent; 'I am very sorry indeed you failed to form your company.'

'Failed!' echoed Kenyon.

'Yes; you haven't succeeded, have you?'

'Well, I don't know about that; we are in a fair way to succeed. You met Longworth and Melville, who came out to see the mine? I saw Longworth in New York, and he told me you had taken them out there.'

'Are they interested with you in the mine?'

'Certainly; they are helping me to form the company.'

Von Brent seemed amazed.

'I did not understand that at all. In fact, I understood the exact opposite. I thought you had attempted to form a company, and failed. They showed me an attack in one of the financial papers upon you, and said that killed your chances of forming a company in London. They were here, apparently, on their own business.'

'And what was their business?'

'To buy the mine.'

'Have they bought it?'

'Practically, yes. Of course, while your option holds good I cannot sell it, but that, as you know, expires in a very few days.'

Kenyon, finding his worst suspicions confirmed, seemed speechless with amazement, and in his agony mopped from his brow the drops collected there.

'You appear to be astonished at this,' said Von Brent.

'I am very much astonished.'

'Well, you cannot blame me. I have acted perfectly square in the matter. I had no idea Longworth, and the gentleman who was with him, had any connection with you whatever. Their attention had been drawn to the mine, they said, by that article. They had investigated it and appeared to be satisfied there was something in it—in the mine, I mean, not in the article. They said they had attended a meeting which you had called, but it was quite evident you were not going to be able to form the company. So they came here and made me a cash offer for the mine. They have deposited twenty thousand pounds at the bank here, and on the day your option closes they will give me a cheque for the amount.'

'It serves me right,' said Kenyon. 'I have been cheated and duped. I had grave suspicions of it all along, but I did not act upon them. I have been too timorous and cowardly. This man Longworth has made a pretence of helping me to form a company. Everything he has done has been to delay me. He came out here, apparently, in the interests of the company I was forming, and now he has got the option for himself.'

'Yes, he has,' said Von Brent. 'I may say I am very sorry indeed for the turn affairs have taken. Of course, as I have told you, I had no idea how the land lay. You see, you had placed no deposit with me, and I had to look after my own interests. However, the option is open for a few days more, and I will not turn the mine over to them till the last minute of the time has expired. Isn't there any chance of your getting the money before then?'

'Not the slightest.'

'Well, you see, in that case I cannot help myself. I am bound by a legal document to turn the mine over to them on receipt of the twenty thousand pounds the moment your option is ended. Everything is done legally, and I am perfectly helpless in the matter.'

'Yes, I see that,' said John. 'Good-bye.'

He went to the telegraph-office and sent a cablegram.

Wentworth received the message in London the next morning. It read:

'We are cheated. Longworth has the option on the mine in his own name.'

CHAPTER XXXIII.

When George Wentworth received this message, he read it several times over before its full meaning dawned upon him. Then he paced up and down his room, and gave way to his feelings. His best friends, who had been privileged to hear George's vocabulary when he was rather angry, admitted that the young man had a fluency of expression which was very more terse than proper. When the real significance of the despatch became apparent to him, George outdid himself in this particular line. Then he realized that, however consolatory such language is to a very angry man, it does little good in any practical way. He paced silently up and down the room, wondering what he could do, and the more he wondered the less light he saw through the fog. He put on his hat and went into the other room.

'Henry,' he said to his partner, 'do you know anybody who would lend me twenty thousand pounds?'

Henry laughed. The idea of anybody lending that sum of money, except on the very best security, was in itself extremely comic.

'Do you want it to-day?' he said.

'Yes, I want it to-day.'

'Well, I don't know any better plan than to go out into the street and ask every man you meet if he has that sum about him. You are certain to encounter men who have very much more than twenty thousand pounds, and perhaps one of them, struck by your very sane appearance at the moment, might hand over the sum to you. I think, however, George, that you would be more successful if you met the capitalist in a secluded lane some dark night, and had a good reliable club in your hand.'

'You are right,' said George. 'Of course, there is just as much possibility of my reaching the moon as getting that sum of money on short notice.'

'Yes, or on long notice either, I imagine. I know plenty of men who have the money, but I wouldn't undertake to ask them for it, and I don't believe you would. Still there is nothing like trying. He who tries may succeed, but no one can succeed who doesn't try. Why not go to old Longworth? He could let you have the money in a moment if he wanted to do so. He knows you. What's your security? What are you going to do with it—that eternal mine of yours?'

'Yes, that "eternal mine"; I want it to be mine. That is why I need the twenty thousand pounds.'

'Well, George, I don't see much hope for you. You never spoke to old Longworth about it, did you? He wasn't one of the men you intended to get into this company?'

'No, he was not. I wish he had been. He would have treated us better than his rascally nephew has done.'

'Ah, that immaculate young man has been playing you tricks, has he?'

'He has played me one trick, which is enough.'

'Well, why don't you go and see the old man, and lay the case before him? He treats that nephew as if he were his son. Now, a man will do a great deal for his son, and perhaps old Longworth might do something for his nephew.'

'Yes; but I should have to explain to him that his nephew is a scoundrel.'

'Very well; that is just the kind of explanation to bring the twenty thousand pounds. If his nephew really is a scoundrel, and you can prove it, you could not want a better lever than that on the old man's money-bags.'

'By Jove!' said Wentworth, 'I believe I shall try it. I want to let him know, anyhow, what sort of man his nephew is. I'll go and see him.'

'I would,' said the other, turning to his work.

And so George Wentworth, putting the cablegram in his pocket, went to see old Mr. Longworth in a frame of mind in which no man should see his fellow-man. He did not wait to be announced, but walked, to the astonishment of the clerk, straight through into Mr. Longworth's room. He found the old man seated at his desk.

'Good-day, Mr. Wentworth,' said the financier cordially.

'Good-day,' replied George curtly. 'I have come to read a cable despatch to you, or to let you read it.'

He threw the paper down before the old gentleman, who adjusted his spectacles and read it. Then he looked up inquiringly at Wentworth.

'You don't understand it, do you?' said the latter.

'I confess I do not. The Longworth in this telegram does not refer to me, does it?'

'No, it does not refer to you, but it refers to one of your house. Your nephew, William Longworth, is a scoundrel!'

'Ah!' said the old man, placing the despatch on the desk again, and removing his glasses, 'have you come to tell me that?'

'Yes, I have. Did you know it before?'

'No, I did not,' answered the old gentleman, his colour rising; 'and I do not know it now. I know you say so, and I think very likely you will be glad to take back what you have said. I will at least give you the opportunity.'

'So far from taking it back, Mr. Longworth, I shall prove it. Your nephew formed a partnership with my friend Kenyon and myself to float on the London market a certain Canadian mine.'

'My dear sir,' broke in the old gentleman, 'I have no desire to hear of my nephew's private speculations; I have nothing to do with them. I have nothing to do with your mine. The matter is of no interest whatever to me, and I must decline to hear anything about it. You are, also, if you will excuse my saying so, not in a fit state of temper to talk to any gentleman. If you like to come back here when you are calmer, I shall be very pleased to listen to what you have to say.'

'I shall never be calmer on this subject. I have told you that your nephew is a scoundrel. You are pleased to deny the accusation.'

'I do not deny it; I merely said I did not know it was the case, and I do not believe it, that is all.'

'Very well; the moment I begin to show you proof that things are as I say———'

'My dear sir,' cried the elder man, with some heat, 'you are not showing proof. You are merely making assertions, and assertions about a man who is absent—who is not here to defend himself. If you have anything to say against William Longworth, come and say it when he is here, and he shall answer for himself. It is cowardly of you, and ungenerous to me, to make a number of accusations which I am in no wise able to refute.'

'Will you listen to what I have to say?'

'No; I will not.'

'Then, by God, you shall!' and with that Wentworth strode to the door and turned the key, while the old man rose from his seat and faced him.

'Do you mean to threaten me, sir, in my own office?'

'I mean to say, Mr. Longworth, that I have made a statement which I am going to prove to you. I mean that you shall listen to me, and listen to me now!'

'And I say, if you have anything to charge against my nephew, come and say it when he is here.'

'When he is here, Mr. Longworth, it will be too late to say it; at present you can repair the injury he has done. When he returns to England you cannot do so, no matter how much you might wish to make the attempt.'

The old man stood irresolute for a moment, then he sat down in his chair again.

'Very well,' he said, with a sigh; 'I am not so combative as I once was. Go on with your story.'

'My story is very short,' said Wentworth; 'it simply amounts to this: You know your nephew formed a partnership with us in relation to the Canadian mine?'

'I know nothing about it, I tell you,' answered Mr. Longworth.

'Very well, you know it now.'

'I know you say so.'

'Do you doubt my word?'

'I shall tell you more definitely when I hear what you have to say. Go on.'

'Well, your nephew, pretending to aid us in forming this company, did everything to retard our progress. He engaged offices that took a long time to fit up, and which we had at last to take in hand ourselves. Then he left for a week, leaving us no address, and refusing to answer the letters I sent to his office for him. On one pretext or another, the forming of the company was delayed; until at length, when the option by which Mr. Kenyon held the mine had less than a month to run, your nephew went to America in company with Mr. Melville, ostensibly to see and report upon the property. After waiting a certain length of time and hearing nothing from him (he had promised to cable us), Kenyon went to America to get a renewal of the option. This cablegram explains his success. He finds, on going there, that your nephew has secured the option of the mine in his own name, and, as Kenyon says, we are cheated. Now have you any doubt whether your nephew is a scoundrel or not?'

Mr. Longworth mused for a few moments on what the young man had told him.

'If what you say is exactly true, there is no doubt William has been guilty of a piece of very sharp practice.'

'Sharp practice!' cried the other. 'You might as well call robbery sharp practice!'

'My dear sir, I have listened to you; now I ask you to listen to me. If, as

451

I say, what you have stated is true, my nephew has done something which I think an honourable man would not do; but as to that I cannot judge until I hear his side of the story. It may put a different complexion on the matter, and I have no doubt it will; but even granting your version is true in every particular, what have I to do with it? I am not responsible for my nephew's actions. He has entered into a business connection, it seems, with two young men, and has outwitted them. That is probably what the world would say about it. Perhaps, as you say, he has been guilty of something worse, and has cheated his partners. But even admitting everything to be true, I do not see how I am responsible in any way.'

'Legally, you are not; morally, I think you are.'

'Why?'

'If he were your son——'

'But he is not my son; he is my nephew.'

'If your son had committed a theft, would you not do everything in your power to counteract the evil he had done?'

'I might, and I might not. Some fathers pay their sons' debts, others do not. I cannot say what action I should take in a purely imaginary case.'

'Very well; all I have to say is, our option runs out in two or three days. Twenty thousand pounds will secure the mine for us. I want that twenty thousand pounds before the option ceases.'

'And do you expect me to pay you twenty thousand pounds for this?'

'Yes, I do.'

Old Mr. Longworth leaned back in his office chair, and looked at the young man in amazement.

'To think that you, a man of the City, should come to me, another man of the City, with such an absurd idea in your head, is simply grotesque.'

'Then the name of the Longworths is nothing to you—the good name,

I mean?'

'The good name of the Longworths, my dear sir, is everything to me; but I fancy it will be able to take care of itself without any assistance from you.'

There was silence for a few moments. Then Wentworth said, in a voice of suppressed anguish:

'I thought, Mr. Longworth, one of your family was a scoundrel; I now wish to say I believe the epithet covers uncle as well as nephew. You have had a chance to repair the mischief a member of your family has done. You have answered me with contempt. You have not shown the slightest indication of wishing to make amends.'

He unlocked the door.

'Come, now,' said old Mr. Longworth, rising, 'that will do, that will do, Mr. Wentworth.' Then he pressed an electric bell, and, when the clerk appeared, he said: 'Show this gentleman the door, please, and if ever he calls here again, do not admit him.'

And so George Wentworth, clenching his hands with rage, was shown to the door. He had the rest of the day to ponder on the fact that an angry man seldom accomplishes his purpose.

CHAPTER XXXIV.

The stormy interview with Wentworth disturbed the usual serenity of Mr. Longworth's temper. He went home earlier than was customary with him that night, and the more he thought over the attack, the more unjustifiable it seemed. He wondered what his nephew had really done, and tried to remember what Wentworth had charged against him. He could not recollect, the angrier portions of the interview having, as it were, blotted the charges from his mind. There remained, however, a very bitter resentment against Wentworth. Mr. Longworth searched his conscience to see if he could be in the least to blame, but he found nothing in the recollections of his dealings with the young men to justify him in feeling at all responsible for the disaster that had overtaken them. He read his favourite evening paper with less than his usual interest, for every now and then the episode in his office would occur to him. Finally he said sharply:

'Edith!'

'Yes, father,' answered his daughter.

'You remember a person named Wentworth, whom you had here the evening William went away?'

'Yes, father.'

'Very well. Never invite him to this house again.'

'What has he been doing?' asked the young woman in rather a tremulous voice.

'I desire you also never to ask anyone connected with him—that man Kenyon, for instance,' continued her father, ignoring her question.

'I thought,' she answered, 'that Mr. Kenyon was not in this country at present.'

'He is not, but he will be back again, I suppose. At any rate, I wish to have nothing more to do with those people. You understand that?'

'Yes, father.'

Mr. Longworth went on with his reading. Edith saw her father was greatly disturbed, and eagerly desired to know the reason, but knew enough of human nature to understand that in a short time he would relieve her anxiety. He again appeared to be trying to fix his attention on the paper. At length he threw it down, and turned towards her.

'That man, Wentworth,' he said bitterly, 'behaved to-day in a most unjustifiable manner to me in my own office. It seems that William and he and Kenyon embarked in some mine project. I knew nothing of their doings, and was not even consulted with regard to them. Now it appears William has gone to America and done something Wentworth considers wrong. Wentworth came to me and demanded twenty thousand pounds—the most preposterous thing ever heard of—said I owed it to clear the good name of Longworth. As if the good name were dependent on him, or anyone like him! I turned him out of the office.'

Edith did not answer for a few moments, while her father gave expression to his indignation by various ejaculations that need not be here recorded.

'Did he say,' she spoke at length, 'in what way William had done wrong?'

'I do not remember now just what he said. I know I told him to come again when my nephew was present, and then make his charges against him if he wanted to do so. Not that I admitted I had anything to do with the matter at all, but I simply refused to listen to charges against an absent man. I paid no attention to them.'

'That certainly was reasonable,' replied Edith. 'What did he say to it?'

'Oh, he abused me, and abused William, and went on at a dreadful rate, until I was obliged to order him out of the office.'

'But what did he say about meeting William when he returned, and making the charges against him then?'

'What did he say? I don't remember. Oh yes! he said it would be too late then; that they had only a few days to do what business they have to do, and that is why he made the demand for twenty thousand pounds. It was to repair the harm, whatever the harm was, William had done. I look on it simply as some blackmailing scheme of his, and I am astonished that a man belonging to so good a house as he does should try that game with me. I shall speak to the elder partner about it to-morrow, and if he does not make the young man apologize in the most abject manner he will be the loser by it, I can tell him that.'

'I would think no more about it, father, if I were you. Do not let it trouble you in the least.'

'Oh, it doesn't trouble me, but young men nowadays seem to think they can say anything to their elders.'

'I mean,' she continued, 'that I would not go to his partner for a day or two. Wait and see what happens. I have no doubt, when he considers the matter, he will be thoroughly ashamed of himself.'

'Well, I hope so.'

'Then give him the chance of being ashamed of himself, and take no further steps in the meantime.'

Edith shortly afterwards went to her own room; there, clasping her hands behind her, she walked up and down thinking, with a very troubled heart, of what she had heard. Her view of the occurrence was very different from that taken by her father. She felt certain something dishonourable had been done by her cousin. For a long time she had mistrusted his supposed friendship for the two young men, and now she pictured to herself John Kenyon in the wilds of Canada, helpless and despondent because of the great wrong that had been done him. It was far into the night when she retired, and it was early next morning when she arose. Her father was bright and cheerful at breakfast, and had evidently forgotten all about the unpleasant incident of the day before. A good night's sleep had erased it from his memory. Edith was glad of this, and she did not mention the subject. After he had gone to the City, his daughter prepared to follow him. She did not take her carriage, but hailed a hansom, and gave the driver the number of Wentworth's offices. That young man was evidently somewhat surprised to see her. He had been trying to write to Kenyon an account of his interview with old Mr. Longworth; but after he had finished, he thought John Kenyon would not approve of his zeal, so had just torn the letter up.

'Take this chair,' he said, wheeling an armchair into position. 'It is the only comfortable one we have in the room.'

'Comfort does not matter,' said Miss Longworth. 'I came to see you about the mica-mine. What has my cousin done?'

'How do you know he has done anything?'

'That does not matter. I know. Tell me as quickly as you can what he has done.'

'It is not a very pleasant story to tell,' he said, 'to a young lady about one of her relatives.'

'Never mind that. Tell me.'

'Very well, he has done this: He has pretended he was our friend, and professed to aid us in forming this company. He has delayed us by every means in his power until the option has nearly expired. Then he has gone to Canada and secured for himself, and a man named Melville, the option of the mine when John Kenyon's time is up—that is to say, at twelve o'clock to-morrow, when Kenyon's option expires, your cousin will pay the money and own the mine; after which, of course, Kenyon and myself will be out of it. I don't mind the loss at all—I would gladly give Kenyon my share—but for John it is a terrible blow. He had counted on the money to pay debts which he considers he owes to his father for his education. He calls them debts of honour, though they are not debts of honour in the ordinary sense of the words. Therefore, it seemed to me a terrible thing that—' Here he paused and did not go on. He saw there were tears in the eyes of the girl to whom he was talking. 'It is brutal,' he said, 'to tell you all this. You are not to blame for it and neither is your father, although I spoke to him in a heated manner yesterday.'

'When did you say the option expires?'

'At twelve o'clock to-morrow.'

'How much money is required to buy the mine?'

'Twenty thousand pounds.'

'Can money be sent to Canada by cable?'

'Yes, I think so.'

'Aren't you quite sure?'

'No, I am not. It can be sent by telegraph in this country, and in America.'

'How long will it take you to find out?'

'Only a few moments.'

'Very well. Where is Mr. Kenyon now?'

'Kenyon is in Ottawa. I had a cablegram from him yesterday.'

'Then, will you write a cablegram that can be sent away at once, asking him to wait at the telegraph-office until he receives a further message from you?'

'Yes, I can do that; but what good will it do?'

'Never mind that; perhaps it will do no good. I am going to try to make it worth doing. Meanwhile remember, if I succeed, John Kenyon must never know the particulars of this transaction.'

'He never will—if you say so.'

'I say so. Now, there is six hours' difference of time between this country and Canada, is there not?'

'About that, I think.'

'Very well; lose no time in getting the cable-message sent to him, and tell him to answer, so that we shall be sure he is at the other end of the wire. Then find out about the cabling of the money. I shall be back here, I think, as soon as you are.'

With that she left the office, and, getting into her cab, was driven to her father's place of business.

'Well, my girl,' said the old man, pushing his spectacles up on his brow, and gazing at her, 'what is it now—some new extravagance?'

'Yes, father, some new extravagance.'

His daughter was evidently excited, and her breath came quickly. She closed the door, and took a chair opposite her father.

'Father,' she said, 'I have been your business man, as you call me, for a long time.'

'Yes, you have. Are you going to strike for an increase of salary?'

'Father,' she said earnestly, not heeding the jocularity of his tone, 'this is very serious. I want you to give me some money for myself—to speculate with.'

'I will do that very gladly. How much do you want?'

The old man turned his chair round and pulled out his cheque-book.

'I want thirty thousand pounds,' she answered.

Mr. Longworth wheeled quickly round in his chair and looked at her in astonishment.

'Thirty thousand what?'

'Thirty thousand pounds, father; and I want it now.'

'My dear girl,' he expostulated, 'have you any idea how much thirty thousand pounds is? Do you know that thirty thousand pounds is a fortune?'

'Yes, I know that.'

'Do you know that there is not one in twenty of the richest merchants in London who could at a moment's notice produce thirty thousand pounds in ready money?'

'Yes, I suppose that is true. Have you not the ready money?'

'Yes, I have the money. I can draw a cheque for that amount, and it will be honoured at once; but I cannot give you so much money without knowing what you are going to do with it.'

'And suppose, father, you do not approve of what I am going to do with it?'

'All the more reason, my dear, that I should know.'

'Then, father, I suppose you mean that whatever services I have rendered you, whatever comfort I have given you, what I have been to you all my life, is not worth thirty thousand pounds?'

'You shouldn't talk like that, my daughter. Everything I have is yours, or will be, when I die. It is for you I work; it is for you I accumulate money. You will have everything I own the moment I have to lay down my work.'

'Father!' cried the girl, standing up before him, 'I do not want your money when you die. I do not want you to die, as you know; but I do want thirty thousand pounds to-day, and now. I want it more than I ever wanted anything else before in my life, or ever shall again. Will you give it to me?'

'No, I will not, unless you tell me what you are going to do with it.'

'Then, father, you can leave your money to your nephew when you die; I shall never touch a penny of it. I now bid you good-bye. I will go out from this room and earn my own living.'

With that the young woman turned to go, but her father, with a sprightliness one would not have expected from his years, sprang to the door and looked at her with alarm.

'Edith, my child, you never talked to me like this before in your life. What is wrong with you?'

'Nothing, father, except that I want a cheque for thirty thousand pounds, and want it now.'

'And do you mean to say that you will leave me if I do not give it to you?'

'Have you ever broken your word, father?'

'Never, my child, that I know of.'

'Then remember I am your daughter. I have said, if I do not get that money now, I shall never enter our house again.'

'But thirty thousand pounds is a tremendous amount. Remember, I have given my word, too, that I would not give you the money unless you told me what it was for.'

'Very well, father, I will tell what it is for when you ask me. I would advise you, though, not to ask me; and I would advise you to give me the money. It will all be returned to you if you want it.'

'Oh, I don't care about the money at all, Edith. I merely, of course, don't want to see it wasted.'

'And, father, have you no trust in my judgment?'

'Well, you know I haven't much faith in any woman's wisdom, in the matter of investing money.'

'Trust me this time, father. I shall never ask you for any more.'

The old man went slowly to his desk, wrote out a cheque, and handed it to his daughter. It was for thirty thousand pounds.

CHAPTER XXXV.

Edith Longworth, with that precious bit of paper in her pocket, once more got into her hansom and drove to Wentworth's office. Again she took the only easy-chair in the room. Her face was very serious, and Wentworth, the moment he saw it, said to himself. 'She has failed.'

'Have you telegraphed to Mr. Kenyon?' she asked.

'Yes.'

'Are you sure you made it clear to him what was wanted? Cablegrams are apt to be rather brief.'

'I told him to keep in communication with us. Here is a copy of the cablegram.'

Miss Longworth read it approvingly, but said:

'You have not put in the word "answer."'

'No; but I put it in the despatch I sent. I remember that now.'

'Have you had a reply yet?'

'Oh no; you see, it takes a long time to get there, because there are so many changes from the end of the cable to the office where Kenyon is. And then, again, you see, they may have to look for him. He may not be expecting a message; in fact, he is sure not to be expecting any. From his own cablegram to me, it is quite evident he has given up all hope.'

'Show me that cablegram, please.'

Wentworth hesitated.

'It is hardly couched in language you will enjoy reading,' he said.

'That doesn't matter. Show it to me. I must see all the documents in the case.'

He handed her the paper, which she read in silence, and gave it back to him without a word.

'I knew you wouldn't like it,' he said.

'I have not said I do not like it. It is not a bit too strong under the circumstances. In fact, I do not see how he could have put it in other words. It is very concise and to the point.'

'Yes; there is no doubt about that, especially the first three words, "We are cheated!" Those are the words that make me think Kenyon has given up all hope; so there may be some trouble in finding him.'

'Did you learn whether money could be sent by cable or not?'

'Oh yes; there is no difficulty about that. The money is deposited in a bank here, and will be credited to Kenyon in the bank at Ottawa.'

'Very well, then,' said Miss Longworth, handing him the piece of paper, 'there is the money.'

Wentworth gave a long whistle as he looked at it. 'Excuse my rudeness,' he said; 'I don't see a bit of paper like this every day. You mean, then, to buy the mine?'

'Yes, I mean to buy the mine.'

'Very well; but there is ten thousand pounds more here than is necessary.'

'Yes. I mean not only to buy the mine, but to work it; and so some working capital will be necessary. How much do you suppose.'

'About that I have no idea,' said Wentworth. 'I should think five thousand pounds would be ample.'

'Then, we shall leave five thousand pounds in the bank here for contingencies, and cable twenty-five thousand pounds to Mr. Kenyon. I shall expect him to get me a good man to manage the mine. I am sure he will be glad to do that.'

'Most certainly he will. John Kenyon, now that the mine has not fallen into the hands of those who tried to cheat him, will be glad to do anything for the new owner of it. He won't mind, in the least, losing his money if he knows that you have the mine.'

'Ah, but that is the one thing he must not know. As to losing the money, neither you nor Mr. Kenyon are to lose a penny. If the mine is all you think it is, then it will be an exceedingly profitable investment; and I intend that we shall each take our third, just as if you had contributed one-third of the money, and Mr. Kenyon another.'

'But, my dear Miss Longworth, that is absurd. We could never accept any such terms.'

'Oh yes, you can. I spoke to John Kenyon himself about being a partner in this mine. I am afraid he thought very little of the offer at the time. I don't intend him to know anything at all about my ownership now. He has discovered the mine—you and he together. If it is valueless, then you and he will be two of the sufferers; if it is all you think it is, then you will be the gainers. The labourer is worthy of his hire, and I am sure both you and Mr. Kenyon have laboured hard enough in this venture. Should he guess I bought it, the chances are that he will be stupidly and stubbornly conscientious, and decline to share the fruits of his labours.'

'And do you think, Miss Longworth, I am not conscientious enough to refuse?'

'Oh, yes; you are conscientious, but you are sensible. Mr. Kenyon isn't.'

'I think you are mistaken about that. He is one of the most sensible men in the world—morbidly sensible, perhaps.'

'Well, I think, if Mr. Kenyon knew I owned the mine, he would not take a penny as his share. So I trust you will never let him know I am the person who gave the money to buy the mine.'

'But is he never to know it, Miss Longworth?'

'Perhaps not. If he is to learn, I am the person to tell him.'

'I quite agree with you there, and I shall respect your confidence.'

'Now, what time,' said the young woman, looking at her watch, 'ought we to get an answer from Mr. Kenyon?'

'Ah, that, as I said before, no one can tell.'

'I suppose, then, the best plan is to send the money at once, or put it in the way of being sent, to some bank in Ottawa.'

'Yes, that is the best thing to do; although, of course, if John Kenyon is not there——'

'If he is not there what shall we do?'

'I do not exactly know. I could cable to Mr. Von Brent. Von Brent is the owner of the mine, and the man who gave John the option. I do not know how far he is committed to the others. If he is as honest as I take him to be, he will accept the money, providing it is sent in before twelve o'clock, and then we shall have the mine. Of that I know nothing whatever, because I have no particulars except John's cable-message.'

'Then, I can do no more just now?'

'Yes, you can. You will have to write a cheque for the twenty-five thousand pounds. You see, this cheque is crossed, and will go into your banking account. An other cheque will have to be drawn to get the money out.'

'Ah, I see. I have not my cheque-book here, but perhaps you can send this cheque to the bank, and I will return. There will be time enough, I suppose, before the closing hour of the bank?'

'Yes, there will be plenty of time. Of course, the sooner we get the money away the better.'

'I shall return shortly after lunch. Perhaps you will then have heard from Mr. Kenyon. If anything comes sooner, will you send me a telegram? Here is my address.'

'I will do that,' said Wentworth, as he bade her good-bye.

As soon as lunch was over, Miss Longworth, with her cheque-book, again visited Wentworth's office. When she entered he shook his head.

'No news yet,' he said.

'This is terrible,' she answered; 'suppose he has left Ottawa and started for home?'

'I do not think he would do that. Still, I imagine he would think there was no reason for staying in Ottawa. Nevertheless, I know Kenyon well enough to believe that he will wait there till the last minute of the option has expired, in the hope that something may happen. He knows, of course, that I shall be doing everything I can in London, and he may have a faint expectation that I shall be able to accomplish something.'

'It would be useless to cable again?'

'Quite. If that message does not reach him, none will.'

As he was speaking, a boy entered the room with a telegram in his hand. Its contents were short and to the point:

'Cablegram received.

'KENYON.'

'Well, that's all right,' said Wentworth; 'now I shall cable that we have the money, and advise him to identify himself at the bank, so that there can be no formalities about the drawing of it, to detain him.'

Saying this, Wentworth pulled the telegraph-forms towards him, and, after considerable labour, managed to concoct a satisfactory despatch.

'Don't spare money on it,' urged his visitor; 'be sure and make it plain to him.'

'I think that will do, don't you?'

'Yes,' she answered, after reading the despatch; 'that will do.'

'Now,' she said, 'here is the cheque. Shall I wait here while you do all that is necessary to cable the money, or had I better go, and return again to see if everything is all right?'

'If you don't mind, just sit where you are. You may lock this door, if you like, and you will not be disturbed.'

It was an hour before Wentworth returned, but his face was radiant.

'We have done everything we can,' he said, 'the money is at his order there, if the cablegram gets over before twelve o'clock to-morrow, as of course it will.'

'Very well, then, good-bye,' said the girl with a smile, holding out her hand.

CHAPTER XXXVI.

If any man more miserable and dejected than John Kenyon existed in the broad dominion of Canada, he was indeed a person to be pitied. After having sent his cablegram to Wentworth, he returned to his very cheerless hotel. Next morning when he awoke he knew that Wentworth would have received the message, but that the chances were ten thousand to one that he could not get the money in time, even if he could get it at all. Still, he resolved to stay in Ottawa, much as he detested the place, until the hour the option expired. Then, he thought, he would look round among the mines, and see if he could not get something to do in the management of one of them. This would enable him to make some money, wherewith to pay the debts which he and Wentworth would have incurred as a result of their disastrous speculation. He felt so depressed that he did what most other Englishmen would have done in his place—took a long walk. He stood on the bridge over the Ottawa River and gazed for a while at the Chaudière Falls, watching the mist rising from the chasm into which the waters plunged. Then he walked along the other side of the river, among big saw-mills and huge interminable piles of lumber, with their grateful piny smell. By-and-by he found himself in the country, and then the forest closed in upon the bad road on which he walked. Nevertheless, he kept on and on, without heeding where he was going. Here and there he saw clearings in the woods, and a log shanty, or perhaps a barn. The result of all this was that, being a healthy man, he soon developed an enormous appetite, which forced itself upon his attention in spite of his depression. He noticed the evening was closing around him, and so was glad to come to a farmhouse that looked better than the ordinary shanties he had left behind. Here he asked for food, and soon sat down to a plentiful meal, the coarseness of which was more than compensated for by the excellence of his appetite. After dinner he began to realize how tired he was, and felt astonished to hear from his host how far he was from Ottawa.

'You can't get there to-night,' said the farmer; 'it is no use your trying. You stay with us, and I'll take you in to-morrow. I'm going there in the afternoon.'

And so Kenyon remained all night, and slept the dreamless sleep of health and exhaustion.

It was somewhat late in the afternoon when he reached the city of Ottawa. Going towards his hotel, he was astonished to hear his name shouted after him. Turning round, he saw a man, whom he did not recognise, running after him.

'Your name is Kenyon, isn't it?' asked the man, somewhat out of breath.

'Yes, that is my name.'

'I guess you don't remember me. I am the telegraph operator. We have had a despatch waiting for you for some time, a cablegram from London. We have searched all over the town for you, but couldn't find you.'

'Ah,' said Kenyon, 'is it important?'

'Well, that I don't know. You had better come with me to the office and get it. Of course, they don't generally cable unimportant things. I remember it said something about you keeping yourself in readiness for something.'

They walked together to the telegraph-office. The boy was still searching for Kenyon with the original despatch, but the operator turned up the file and read the copy to him.

'You see, it wants an answer,' he said; 'that's why I thought it was important to get you. You will have plenty of time for an answer to-night.'

John took a lead pencil and wrote the cable despatch which Wentworth received. He paid his money, and said:

'I will go to my hotel; it is the —— House. I will wait there, and if anything comes for me, send it over as soon as possible.'

'All right,' said the operator, 'that is the best plan; then we will know exactly where to find you. Of course, there is no use in your waiting here, because we can get you in five minutes. Perhaps I had better telephone to the hotel for you if anything comes.'

'Very well,' said Kenyon; 'I will leave it all in your hands.'

Whether it was the effect of having been in the country or not, John felt that the cablegram he had received was a good omen. He meditated over the tremendous ill-fortune he had suffered in the whole business from beginning to end, and thought of old Mr. Longworth's favourite phrase, 'There's no such thing as luck.'

Then came a rap at his door, and the bell-boy said:

'There is a gentleman here wishes to speak to you.'

'Ask him to come up,' was the answer; and two minutes later Von Brent entered.

'Any news?' he asked.

John, who was in a state of mind which made him suspicious of everything and everybody, answered:

'No, nothing new.'

'Ah, I am sorry for that. I had some hopes that perhaps you might be able to raise the money before twelve o'clock to-morrow. Of course you know the option ends at noon to-morrow?'

'Yes, I know that.'

'Did you know that Longworth was in Ottawa?'

'No,' said Kenyon; 'I have been out of town myself.'

'Yes, he came last night. He has the money in the bank, as I told you. Now, I will not accept it until the very latest moment. Of course, legally, I cannot accept it before that time, and, just as legally, I cannot refuse his money when he tenders it. I am very sorry all this has happened—more sorry than I can tell you. I hope you will not think that I am to blame in the matter?'

'No, you are not in the slightest to blame. There is nobody in fault except myself. I feel that I have been culpably negligent, and altogether too trustful.'

'I wish to goodness I knew where you could get the money; but, of course, if I knew that, I would have had it myself long ago.'

'I am very much obliged to you,' said Kenyon; 'but the only thing you can do for me is to see that your clock is not ahead of time to-morrow. I may, perhaps, be up at the office before twelve o'clock—that is where I shall find you, I suppose?'

'Yes; I shall be there all the forenoon. I shall not leave until twelve.'

'Very good; I am much obliged to you, Mr. Von Brent, for your sympathy. I assure you, I haven't many friends, and it—well, I'm obliged to you, that's all. An Englishman, you know, is not very profuse in the matter of thanks, but I mean it.'

'I'm sure you do,' said Von Brent, 'and I'm only sorry that my assistance cannot be something substantial. Well, good-bye, hoping to see you to-morrow.'

After he had departed, Kenyon's impatience increased as the hours went on. He left the hotel, and went direct to the telegraph-office; but nothing had come for him.

'I'm afraid,' said the operator, 'that there won't be anything more to-night. If it should come late, shall I send it to your hotel?'

'Certainly; no matter at what hour it comes, I wish you would let me have it as soon as possible. It is very important.'

Leaving the office, he went up the street and, passing the principal hotel in the place, saw young Longworth standing under the portico of the hotel as dapper and correct in costume as ever, his single eyeglass the admiration of all Ottawa, for there was not another like it in the city.

'How do you do, Kenyon?' said that young man.

'My dear sir,' replied Kenyon, 'the last time you spoke to me you said you desired to have nothing more to say to me. I cordially reciprocated that sentiment, and I want to have nothing to say to you.'

'My dear fellow,' cried Longworth jauntily, 'there is no harm done. Of course, in New York I was a little out of sorts. Everybody is in New York—beastly hole! I don't think it is worse than Ottawa, but the air is purer here. By the way, perhaps you and I can make a little arrangement. I am going to buy that mine to-morrow, as doubtless you know. Now, I should like to see it in the hands of a good and competent man. If a couple of hundred pounds a year would be any temptation to you, I think we can afford to let you develop the mine.'

'Thank you!' said Kenyon.

'I knew you would be grateful; just think over the matter, will you? and don't come to any rash decision. We can probably give a little more than that; but until we see how the mine is turning out, it is not likely we shall spend a great deal of money on it.'

'Of course,' said John, 'the proper answer to your remark would be to knock you down; but, besides being a law-abiding citizen, I have no desire to get into gaol to-night for doing it, because there is one chance in a thousand, Mr. Longworth, that I may have some business to do with that mine myself before twelve o'clock to-morrow.'

'Ah, it is my turn to be grateful now!' said Longworth. 'In a rough-and-tumble fight I am afraid you would master me easier than you would do in a contest of diplomacy.'

'Do you call it diplomacy? You refer, I suppose, to your action in relation to the mine. I call it robbery.'

'Oh, do you? Well, that is the kind of conversation which leads to breaches of the peace; and as I also am a law-abiding subject, I will not continue the discussion any further. I bid you a very good evening, Mr. Kenyon.'

The young man turned on his heel and went into the hotel. John walked to his own much more modest inn, and retired for the night. He did not sleep well. All night long, phantom telegraph-messengers were rapping at the door, and he started up every now and then to receive cablegrams which faded away as he awoke. Shortly after breakfast he went to the telegraph-office, but found that nothing had arrived for him.

'I am afraid,' said the operator, 'that nothing will come on before noon.'

'Before noon!' echoed John. 'Why?'

'The wires are down in some places in the East, and messages are delayed a good deal. Perhaps you noticed the lack of Eastern news in the morning papers? Very little news came from the East last night.' Seeing John's look of anxious interest, the operator continued: 'Does the despatch you expect pertain to money matters?'

'Yes, it does.'

'Do they know you at the bank?'

'No, I don't think they do.'

'Then, if I were you, I would go up to the bank and be identified, so that, if it is a matter of minutes, no unnecessary time may be lost. You had better tell them you expect a money-order by cable, and, although such orders are paid without any identification at the bank, yet they take every precaution to see that it does not get into the hands of the wrong man.'

'Thank you,' said Kenyon. 'I am much obliged to you for your suggestion. I will act upon it.'

And as soon as the bank opened, John Kenyon presented himself to the cashier.

'I am expecting a large amount of money from England to-day. It is very important that, when it arrives, there shall be no delay in having it placed at my disposal. I want to know if there are any formalities to be gone through.'

'Where is the money coming from?' said the clerk.

'It is coming from England.'

'Is there anyone in Ottawa who can identify you?'

'Yes; I know the telegraph operator here.'

'Ah!' said the cashier somewhat doubtfully. 'Anybody else?'

'Mr. Von Brent knows me very well.'

'That will do. Suppose you get Mr. Von Brent to come here and identify you as the man who bears the name of Kenyon. Then the moment your cablegram comes the money will be at your disposal.'

Kenyon hurried to Von Brent's rooms and found him alone.

'Will you come down to the bank and identify me as Kenyon?'

'Certainly. Has the money arrived?'

'No, it has not; but I expect it, and want to provide for every contingency. I do not wish to have any delay in my identification when it does come.'

'If it comes by cable,' said Von Brent, 'there will be no need of identification. The bank is not responsible, you know. They take the money entirely at the sender's risk. They might pay it to the telegraph operator who receives the message! I believe they would not be held liable. However, it is better to see that nothing is left undone.'

Going over to the bank, Von Brent said to the cashier: 'This is John Kenyon.'

'Very good,' replied the cashier. 'Have you been at the telegraph-office lately, Mr. Kenyon?'

'No, I have not—at least, not for half an hour or so.'

'Well, I would go there as soon as possible, if I were you.'

'That means,' said Von Brent, as soon as they had reached the door, 'that they have had their notice about the money. I believe it is already in the bank for you. I will go back to my rooms and not leave them till you come.'

John hurried to the telegraph-office.

'Anything for me yet?' he said.

'Nothing as yet, Mr. Kenyon; I think, however,' he added with a smile, 'that it will be all right. I hope so.'

The moments ticked along with their usual rapidity, yet it seemed to Kenyon the clock was going fearfully fast. Eleven o'clock came and found him still pacing up and down the office of the telegraph. The operator offered him the hospitality of the private room, but this he declined. Every time the machine clicked, John's ears were on the alert, trying to catch a meaning from the instrument.

Ten minutes after eleven!

Twenty minutes after eleven, and still no despatch! The cold perspiration stood on John's brow, and he groaned aloud.

'I suppose it's very important,' said the operator.

'Very important.'

'Well, now, I shouldn't say so, but I know the money is in the bank for you. Perhaps if you went up there and demanded it, they would give it to you.'

It was twenty-five minutes past the hour when John hurried towards the bank.

'I have every belief,' he said to the cashier, 'that the money is here for me now. Is it possible for me to get it?'

'Have you your cablegram?'

'No, I have not.'

'Well, you know, we cannot pay the money until we see your cablegram. If time is of importance, you should not leave the telegraph-office, and the moment you get your message, come here; then there will be no delay whatever. Do you wish to draw all the money at once?'

'I don't know how much there is, but I must have twenty thousand pounds.'

'Very well, to save time you had better make out a cheque for twenty thousand pounds; that will be——'

And here he gave the number of dollars at the rate of the day on the pound. 'Just make out a cheque for that amount, and I will certify it. A certified cheque is as good as gold. The moment you get your message I will hand you the certified cheque.'

John wrote out the order and gave it to the cashier, glancing at the clock as he did so. It was now twenty-five minutes to twelve. He rushed to the telegraph-office with all the speed of which he was capable, but met only a blank look again from the chief operator.

'It has not come yet,' he said, shaking his head.

Gradually despair began to descend on the waiting man. It was worse to miss everything now, than never to have had the hope of success. It was like hanging a man who had once been reprieved. He resumed his nervous pace up and down that chamber of torture. A quarter to twelve. He heard chimes ring somewhere. If the message did not come before they rang again, it would be for ever too late.

Fourteen   minutes—thirteen   minutes—twelve   minutes—eleven minutes—ten minutes to twelve, and yet, no—

'Here you are!' shouted the operator in great glee, 'she's a-coming—it's all right—"John Kenyon, Ottawa."' Then he wrote as rapidly as the machine ticked out the message. 'There it is; now rush!'

John needed no telling to rush. People had begun to notice him as the man who was doing nothing but running between the bank and the telegraph-office.

It was seven minutes to twelve when he got to the bank.

'Is that despatch right?' he said, shoving it through the arched aperture.

The clerk looked at it with provoking composure, and then compared it with some papers.

'For God's sake, hurry!' pleaded John.

'You have plenty of time,' said the cashier coolly, looking up at the clock and going on with his examination. 'Yes,' he added, 'that is right. Here is your certified cheque.'

John clasped it, and bolted out of the bank as a burglar might have done. It was five minutes to twelve when he got to the steps that led to the rooms of Mr. Von Brent. Now all his excitement seemed to have deserted him. He was as cool and calm as if he had five days, instead of so many minutes, in which to make the payment. He mounted the steps quietly, walked along the passage, and knocked at the door of Von Brent's room.

'Come in!' was the shout that greeted him.

He opened the door, glancing at the clock behind Von Brent's head as he did so.

It stood at three minutes to twelve.

Young Mr. Longworth was sitting there, with just a touch of pallor on his countenance, and there seemed to be an ominous glitter in his eyeglass. He said nothing, and John Kenyon completely ignored his presence.

'There is still some life left in my option, I believe?' he said to Von Brent, after nodding good-day to him.

'Very little, but perhaps it will serve. You have two minutes and a half,' said Von Brent.

'Are the papers ready?' inquired John.

'All ready, everything except putting in the names.'

'Very well, here is the money.'

Von Brent looked at the certified cheque. 'That is perfectly right,' he said, 'the mine is yours.'

Then he rose and stretched his hand across the table to Kenyon, who grasped it cordially.

Young Mr. Longworth also rose, and said languidly 'As this seems to be a meeting of long-lost brothers, I shall not intrude. Good-day, Mr. Von Brent.'

Then, adjusting his eyeglass in a leisurely manner, he walked out of the room.

CHAPTER XXXVII.

When Edith Longworth entered the office of George Wentworth, that young gentleman somewhat surprised her. He sprang from his chair the moment she entered the room, rushed out of the door, and shouted at the top of his voice to the boy, who answered him, whereupon Wentworth returned to the room, apparently in his right mind.

'I beg your pardon, Miss Longworth,' he said, laughing; 'the fact was, I had just sent my boy with a telegram for you, and now, you see, I have saved sixpence.'

'Then you have heard from Canada?' said the young lady.

'Yes; a short message, but to the point.' He handed her the cablegram, and she read:

'Mine purchased; shall take charge temporarily.'

'Then, the money got there in time,' she said, handing him back the telegraphic message.

'Oh yes,' said George, with the easy confidence of a man who doesn't at all know what he is talking about. 'We had plenty of time; I knew it would get there all right.'

'I am glad of that; I was afraid perhaps we might have sent it too late. One can never tell what delays or formalities there may be.'

'Evidently there was no trouble. And now, Miss Longworth, what are your commands? Am I to be your agent here, in Great Britain?'

'Have you written to Mr. Kenyon?'

'Yes, I wrote to him just after I sent the cable message.'

'Of course you didn't——'

'No, I didn't say a word that would lead him to suspect who was the mistress of the mine. In my zeal I even went so far as to give you a name. You are hereafter to be known in the correspondence as Mr. Smith, the owner of the mine.'

Miss Longworth laughed.

'And—oh, by the way,' cried Wentworth, 'here is a barrel belonging to you.'

'A barrel!' she said, and, looking in the direction to which he pointed, she saw in the corner of the room a barrel with the head taken away. 'If it is my property,' continued the young woman, 'who has taken the liberty of opening it?'

'Oh, I did that as your agent. That barrel contains the mineral from the mine, which we hope will prove so valuable. It started from Canada over three months ago, and only arrived here the other day. It seems that the idiot who sent it addressed it by way of New York, and it was held by some Jack-in-office belonging to the United States Customs. We have had more diplomatic correspondence and trouble about that barrel than you can imagine, and now it comes a day behind the fair, when it is really of no use to anyone.'

Miss Longworth rose and went to the barrel. She picked out some of the beautiful white specimens that were in it.

'Is this the mineral?' she asked.

Wentworth laughed.

'Imagine a person buying a mine at an exorbitant price, and not knowing what it produces. Yes, that is the mineral.'

'This is not mica, of course?'

'No, it is not mica. That is the stuff used for the making of china.'

'It looks as if it would take a good polish. Will it, do you know?'

'I do not know. I could easily find out for you.'

'I wish you would, and get a piece of it polished, which I will use as a paper-weight.'

'What are your orders for the rest of the barrel?'

'What did you intend doing with it?' said the young woman.

'Well, I was thinking the best plan would be to send some of it to each of the pottery works in this country, and get their orders for more of the stuff, if they want to use it.'

'I think that an extremely good idea. I understand from the cablegram that Mr. Kenyon says he will take charge of the mine temporarily.'

'Yes; I imagine he left Ottawa at once, as soon as he had concluded his bargain. Of course, we shall not know for certain until he writes.'

'Very well, then, it appears to me the best thing you could do over here would be to secure what orders can be obtained in England for the mineral. Then, I suppose, you could write to Mr. Kenyon, and ask him to engage a proper person to work the mine.'

'Yes, I will do that.'

'When he comes over here, you and he can have a consultation as to the best thing to do next. I expect nothing very definite can be arranged until he comes. You may make whatever excuse you can for the absence of the mythical Mr. Smith, and say that you act for him. Then you may tell Mr. Kenyon, in whatever manner you choose, that Mr. Smith intends both you and Mr. Kenyon to share conjointly with him. I think you will have no trouble in making John—that is, in making Mr. Kenyon—believe there is such a person as Mr. Smith, if you put it strongly enough to him. Make him understand that Mr. Smith would never have heard of the mine unless Mr. Kenyon and you had discovered it, and that he is very glad indeed to have such a good opportunity of investing his money; so that, naturally, he wishes those who have been instrumental in helping him to this investment to share in its profits. I imagine you can make all this clear enough, so that your friend will suspect nothing. Don't you think so?'

'Well, with any other man than John Kenyon I should have my doubts, because, as a fabricator, I don't think I have a very high reputation; but with John I have no fears whatever. He will believe everything I say. It is almost a pity to delude so trustful a man, but it's so very much to his own advantage that I shall have no hesitation in doing it.'

'Then, you will write to him about getting a fit and proper person to manage the mine?'

'Yes. I don't think there will be any necessity for doing so, but I will make sure. I imagine John will not leave there until he sees everything to his satisfaction. He will be very anxious indeed for the mine to prove the great success he has always believed it to be, even though, at present, he does not know he is to have any pecuniary interest in its prosperity.'

'Very well then, I shall bid you good-bye. I may not be here again, but whenever you hear from Mr. Kenyon, I shall be very glad if you will let me know.'

'Certainly; I will send you all the documents in the case, as you once remarked. You always like to see the original papers, don't you?'

'Yes, I suppose I do.' Miss Longworth lingered a moment at the door, then, looking straight at Wentworth, she said to him, 'You remember you spoke rather bitterly to my father the other day?'

'Yes,' said Wentworth, colouring; 'I remember it.'

'You are a young man; he is old. Besides that, I think you were entirely in the wrong. He had nothing whatever to do with his nephew's action.'

'Oh, I know that,' said Wentworth. 'I would have apologized to him long ago, only—well, you know, he told me I shouldn't be allowed in the office again, and I don't suppose I should.'

'A letter from you would be allowed in the office,' replied the young lady, looking at the floor.

'Of course it would,' said George; 'I will write to him instantly and apologize.'

'It is very good of you,' said, Edith, holding out her hand to him; the next moment she was gone.

George Wentworth turned to his desk and wrote a letter of apology. Then he mused to himself upon the strange and incomprehensible nature of women. 'She makes me apologize to him, and quite right too; but if it hadn't been for the row with her father, she never would have heard about the transaction, and therefore couldn't have bought the mine, which she was anxious to do for Kenyon's sake—lucky beggar John is, after all!'

CHAPTER XXXVIII.

When the business of transferring the mine to its new owner was completed, John Kenyon went to the telegraph-office, and sent a short cable-message to Wentworth. Then he turned his steps to the hotel, an utterly exhausted man. The excitement and tension of the day had been too much for him, and he felt that, if he did not get out of the city of Ottawa and into the country, where there were fewer people and more air, he was going to be ill. He resolved to leave for the mine as soon as possible. There he would get affairs in as good order as might be, and keep things going until he heard from the owner. When he reached his hotel, he wrote a letter to Wentworth, detailing briefly the circumstances under which he had secured the mine, and dealing with other more personal matters. Having posted this, he began to pack his portmanteau, preparatory to leaving early next morning. While thus occupied, the bell-boy came into his room, and said:

'There is a gentleman wants to see you.'

He imagined at once that it was Von Brent, who wished to see him with regard to some formality relating to the transfer, and he was, therefore, very much astonished—in fact, for the moment speechless—when Mr. William Longworth entered and calmly gazed round the rather shabby room with his critical eyeglass.

'Ah,' he said, 'these are your diggings, are they? This is what they call a dollar hotel, I suppose, over here. Well, some people may like it, but, I confess, I don't care much about it, myself. Their three or four dollars a day hotels are bad enough for me. By the way, you look rather surprised to see me; being strangers together in a strange country, I expected a warmer greeting. You said last night, in front of the Russell House, that it would please you very much to give me a warm greeting; perhaps you would like to do so to-night.'

'Have you come up here to provoke a quarrel with me?' asked Kenyon.

'Oh, bless you, no! Quarrel! Nothing of the sort. What should I want to quarrel about?'

'Perhaps you will be good enough to tell me why you come here, then?'

'A very reasonable request. Very reasonable indeed, and perfectly natural, but still quite unnecessary. It is not likely that a man would climb up here into your rooms, and then not be prepared to tell you why he came. I came, in the first place, to congratulate you on the beautiful and dramatic way in which you secured the mine at the last moment, or apparently at the last moment. I suppose you had the money all the time?'

'No, I had not.'

'Then you came in to Von Brent just as soon as you received it?'

'Well, now, I don't see that it is the business of anyone else but myself. Still, if you want to know, I may say that I came to Mr. Von Brent's room at the moment I received the money.'

'Really! Then it was sent over by cable, I presume?'

'Your presumption is entirely correct.'

'My dear Kenyon,' said the young man, seating himself without being asked, and gazing at John in a benevolent kind of way, 'you really show some temper over this little affair of yours. Now, here is the whole thing in a nutshell——'

'My dear sir, I don't wish to hear the whole thing, in a nutshell. I know all about it—all I wish to know.'

'Ah, precisely; of course you do; certainly; but, nevertheless, let me have my say. Here is the whole thing. I tried to—well, to cheat you. I thought I could make a little money by doing so, and my scheme failed. Now, if anybody should be in a bad temper, it is I, not you. Don't you see that? You are not acting your part well at all. I'm astonished at you!'

'Mr. Longworth, I wish to have nothing whatever to say to you. If you have anything to ask, I wish you would ask it as quickly as possible, and then leave me alone.'

'The chief fault I find with you, Kenyon,' said Longworth, throwing one leg over the other, and clasping his hands round his knee—'the chief fault I have to find is your painful lack of a sense of humour. Now, you remember last night I offered you the managership of the mine. I thought, certainly, that by this time to-day I should be owner of it, or, at least, one of the owners. Now, you don't appear to appreciate the funniness of the situation. Here you are the owner of the mine, and I am out in the cold—"left," as they say here in America. I am the man who is left——'

'If that is all you have to talk about,' said Kenyon gravely, 'I must ask you to allow me to go on with my packing. I am going to the mine to-morrow.'

'Certainly, my dear fellow; go at once and never mind me. Can I be of any assistance to you? It requires a special genius, you know, to pack a portmanteau properly. But what I wanted to say was this: Why didn't you turn round, when you had got the mine, and offer me the managership of it? Then you would have had your revenge. The more I think of that episode in Von Brent's office, the more I think you utterly failed to realize the dramatic possibilities of the situation.'

Kenyon was silent.

'Now, all this time you are wondering why I came here. Doubtless you wish to know what I want.'

'I have not the slightest interest in the matter,' said Kenyon.

'That is ungracious, but, nevertheless, I will continue. It is better, I see, to be honest with you, if a man wants to get anything from you. Now, I want to get a bit of information from you. I want to know where you got the money with which you bought the mine?'

'I got it from the bank.'

'Ah, yes, but I want to know who sent it over to you?'

'It was sent to me by George Wentworth.'

'Quite so; but now I want to know who gave Wentworth the money?'

'You will have a chance of finding that out when you go to England, by asking him.'

'Then you won't tell me?'

'I can't tell you.'

'You mean by that, of course, that you won't.'

'I always mean, Mr. Longworth, exactly what I say. I mean that I can't tell you. I don't know myself.'

'Really?'

'Yes, really. You seem to have some difficulty in believing that anybody can speak the truth.'

'Well, it isn't a common vice, speaking the truth. You must forgive a little surprise.' He nursed his knee for a moment, and looked meditatively up at the ceiling. 'Now, would you like to know who furnished that money?'

'I have no curiosity in the matter whatever.'

'Have you not? You are a singular man. It seems to me that a person into whose lap twenty thousand pounds drops from the skies would have some little curiosity to know from whom the money came.'

'I haven't the slightest.'

'Nevertheless, I will tell you who gave the money to Wentworth. It was my dear friend Melville. I didn't tell you in New York, of course, that Melville and I had a little quarrel about this matter, and he went home decidedly huffy. I had no idea he would take this method of revenge; but I see it quite clearly now. He knew I had secured the option of the mine. There was a little trouble as to what our respective shares were to be, and I thought, as I had secured the option, I had the right to dictate terms. He thought differently. He was going to Von Brent to explain the whole matter; but I pointed out that such a course would do no good, the option being legally made out in my name, so that the moment your claim expired mine began. When this dawned upon him, he took the steamer and went to England. Now, I can see his hand in this artistic finish to the affair. It was a pretty sharp trick of Melville's, and I give him credit for it. He is a very much shrewder and cleverer man than I thought he was.'

'It seems to me, Mr. Longworth, that your inordinate conceit makes you always underestimate your friends, or your enemies either, for that matter.'

'There is something in that, Kenyon; I think you are more than half right, but I thought, perhaps, I could make it advantageous to you to do me a favour in this matter. I thought you might have no objection to writing a little document to the effect that the money did not come in time, and consequently, I had secured the mine. Then, if you would sign that, I would take it over to Melville and make terms with him. Of course, if he knows that he has the mine there will not be much chance of coming to any arrangement with him.'

'You can make no arrangements with me, Mr. Longworth, that involve sacrifice of the truth.'

'Ah, well, I suspected as much; but I thought it was worth trying. However, my dear sir, I may make terms with Melville yet, and then, I imagine, you won't have much to do with the mine.'

'I shall not have anything to do with it if you and Melville have a share in it; and if, as you suspect, Melville has the mine, I consider you are in a bad way. My opinion is that, when one rascal gets advantage over another rascal, the other rascal will be, as you say, "left."'

Longworth mused over this for a moment, and said:

'Yes, I fear you are right—in fact, I am certain of it. Well, that is all I wanted to know. I will bid you good-bye. I shan't see you again in Ottawa, as I shall sail very shortly for England. Have you any messages you would like given to your friends over there?'

'None, thank you.'

'Well, ta-ta!' And John was left to his packing. That necessary operation concluded, Kenyon sat down and thought over what young Longworth had told him. His triumph, after all, had been short-lived. The choice between the two scoundrels was so small that he felt he didn't care which of them owned the mine. Meditating on this disagreeable subject, he suddenly remembered a request he had asked Wentworth to place before the new owner of the mine. He wanted no favour from Melville, so he wrote a second letter, contradicting the request made in the first, and, after posting it, returned to his hotel, and went to bed, probably the most tired man in the city of Ottawa.

CHAPTER XXXIX.

This chapter consists largely of letters. As a general rule, letters are of little concern to anyone except the writers and the receivers, but they are inserted here in the hope that the reader is already well enough acquainted with the correspondents to feel some interest in what they have written.

It was nearly a fortnight after the receipt of the cablegram from Kenyon that George Wentworth found, one morning, on his desk two letters, each bearing a Canadian postage-stamp. One was somewhat bulky and one was thin, but they were both from the same writer. He tore open the thin one first, without looking at the date stamped upon it. He was a little bewildered by its contents, which ran as follows:

'MY DEAR GEORGE,

'I have just heard that Melville is the man who has bought the mine. The circumstances of the case leave no doubt in my mind that such is the fact; therefore, please disregard the request I made as to employment in the letter I posted to you a short time ago. I feel a certain sense of disappointment in the fact that Melville is the owner of the mine. It seems I have only kept one rascal from buying it in order to put it in the hands of another rascal.

'Your friend,

'JOHN KENYON.'

'Melville the owner!' cried Wentworth to himself. 'What could have put that into John's head? This letter is evidently the one posted a few hours before, so it will contain whatever request he has to make;' and, without delay, George Wentworth tore open the envelope of the second letter, which was obviously the one written first.

It contained a number of documents relating to the transfer of the mine. The letter from John himself went on to give particulars of the buying of the property. Then it continued:

'I wish you would do me a favour, George. Will you kindly ask the owner of the mine if he will give me charge of it? I am, of course, anxious to make it turn out as well as possible, and I believe I can more than earn my salary, whatever it is. You know I am not grasping in the matter of money, but get me as large a salary as you think I deserve. I desire to make money for reasons that are not entirely selfish, as you know. To tell you the truth, George, I am tired of cities and of people. I want to live here in the woods, where there is not so much deceit and treachery as there seems to be in the big towns. When I reached London last time, I felt like a boy getting home. My feelings have undergone a complete change, and I think, if it were not for you and a certain young lady, I should never care to see the big city again. What is the use of my affecting mystery, and writing the words "a certain young lady"? Of course, you know whom I mean—Miss Edith Longworth. You know, also, that I am, and have long been, in love with her. If I had succeeded in making the money I thought I should by selling the mine, I might have had some hopes of making more, and of ultimately being in a position to ask her to be my wife; but that and very many other hopes have disappeared with my recent London experiences. I want to get into the forest and recover some of my lost tone, and my lost faith in human nature. If you can arrange matters with the owner of the mine, so that I may stay here for a year or two, you will do me a great favour.'

George Wentworth read over the latter part of this letter two or three times. Then he rose, paced the floor, and pondered.

'It isn't a thing upon which I can ask anyone's advice,' he muttered to himself. 'The trouble with Kenyon is, he is entirely too modest; a little useful self-esteem would be just the thing for him.' At last he stopped suddenly in his walk. 'By Jove!' he said to himself, slapping his thigh, 'I shall do it, let the consequences be what they may.'

Then he sat down at his desk and wrote a letter.

'DEAR Miss LONGWORTH' (it began),

'You told me when you were here last that you wanted all the documents pertaining to the mine, in every instance. A document has come this morning that is rather important. John Kenyon, as you will learn by reading the letter, desires the managership of the mine. I need not say that I think he is the best man in the world for the position, and that everything will be safe in his hands. I therefore enclose you his letter. I had some thought of cutting out a part of it, but knowing your desire to have all the documents in the case, I take the liberty of sending this one exactly as it reached me, and if anyone is to blame, I am the person.

'I remain, your agent,

'GEORGE WENTWORTH.'

He sent this letter out at once, so that he would not have a chance to change his mind.

'It will reach her this afternoon, and doubtless she will call and see me.'

It is, perhaps, hardly necessary to say she did not call, and she did not see him for many days afterwards; but next morning, when he came to his office, he found a letter from her. It ran:

'DEAR MR. WENTWORTH,

'The sending of Mr. Kenyon's letter to me is a somewhat dangerous precedent, which you must on no account follow by sending any letters you may receive from any other person to Mr. Kenyon. However, as you were probably aware when you sent the letter, no blame will rest on your shoulders, or on those of anyone else, in this instance. Still, be very careful in future, because letter-sending, unabridged, is sometimes a risky thing to do. You are to remember that I always want all the documents in the case, and I want them with nothing eliminated. I am very much obliged to you for forwarding the letter.

'As to the managership of the mine, of course I thought Mr. Kenyon would desire to come back to London. If he is content to stay abroad, and really wants to stay there, I wish you would tell him that Mr. Smith is exceedingly pleased to know he is willing to take charge of the mine. It would not look businesslike on the part of Mr. Smith to say that Mr. Kenyon is to name his own salary, but, unfortunately, Mr. Smith is very ignorant as to what a proper salary should be, so will you kindly settle that question? You know the usual salary for such an occupation. Please write down that figure, and add two hundred a year to it. Tell Mr. Kenyon the amount named is the salary Mr. Smith assigns to him.

'Pray be very careful in the wording of the letters, so that Mr. Kenyon will not have any idea who Mr. Smith is.

'Yours truly,

'EDITH LONGWORTH.

When Wentworth received this letter, being a man, he did not know whether Miss Longworth was pleased or not. However, he speedily wrote to John, telling him that he was appointed manager of the mine, and that Mr. Smith was very much pleased to have him in that capacity. He named the salary, but said if it was not enough, no doubt Mr. Smith was so anxious for his services that the amount would be increased.

John, when he got the letter, was more than satisfied.

At the time Wentworth was reading his letters, John had received those which had been sent when the mine was bought. He was relieved to find that Melville was not, after all, the owner; and he went to work with a will, intending to put in two or three years of his life, with hard labour, in developing the resources of the property. The first fortnight, before he received any letters, he did nothing but make himself acquainted with the way work was being carried on there. He found many things to improve. The machinery had been allowed to run down, and the men worked in the listless way men do when they are under no particular supervision. The manager of the mine was very anxious about his position. John told him the property had changed hands but, until he had further news from England, he could not tell just what would be done. When the letters came, John took hold with a will, and there was soon a decided improvement in the way affairs were going. He allowed the old manager to remain as a sort of sub-manager; but that individual soon found that the easy times of the Austrian Mining Company were for ever gone.

Kenyon had to take one or two long trips in Canada and the United States, to arrange for the disposal of the products of the mine; but, as a general rule, his time was spent entirely in the log village near the river.

When a year had passed, he was able to write a very jubilant letter to Wentworth.

'You see,' he said, 'after all, the mine was worth the two hundred thousand pounds we asked for it. It pays, even the first year, ten per cent. on that amount. This will give back all the mine has cost, and I think, George, the honest thing for us to do would be to let the whole proceeds go to Mr. Smith this year, who advanced the money at a critical time. This will recoup him for his outlay, because the working capital has not been touched. The mica has more than paid the working of the mine, and all the rest is clear profit. Therefore, if you are willing, we will let our third go this year, and then we can take our large dividend next year with a clear conscience. I enclose the balance-sheet.'

To this letter there came an answer in due time from Wentworth, who said that he had placed John's proposal before Mr. Smith; but it seemed the gentleman was so pleased with the profitable investment he had made that he would hear of no other division of the profits but that of share and share alike. He appeared to be very much touched by the offer John had made, and respected him for making it, but the proposed rescinding on his part and Wentworth's was a thing not to be thought of. This being the case, John sent a letter and a very large cheque to his father. The moment of posting that letter was, doubtless, one of the happiest of his life, and this ends the formidable array of letters which appears in this chapter.

CHAPTER XL.

Wentworth had written to Kenyon that Mr. Smith absolutely refused to take more than one-third of the profits of the mine. It was true that the offer had been declined, but Wentworth never knew how much tempted the Mistress of the Mine had been when he made it. Her one great desire was to pay back the thirty thousand pounds to her father, and she wanted to do it as speedily as possible. At the end of the second year her profits from the mine, including the return of the five thousand pounds which had been sent to Ottawa as working capital, was still about five thousand pounds under the thirty thousand pounds. She looked forward eagerly to the time when she would be able to pay the thirty thousand pounds to her father. Old Mr. Longworth had never spoken a word to his daughter about the money. She had expected he would ask her what she had done with it, but he had never mentioned the subject. Her conscience troubled her very frequently about the method she had taken to obtain that large amount. She saw that her father had changed in his manner towards her since that day. He had given her the money, but he had given it, as one might say, almost under compulsion, and there was no doubt that, generous as he was, he did not like being coerced into parting with his money. Edith Longworth had paid more for the mine than the amount of cash she had deposited in Ottawa. She had paid for it by being cut off from her father's confidence. Now he never asked her advice about any of his business ventures, and, for the first time in many years, he had taken a long sea-voyage without inviting her to accompany him. All this made the girl more and more anxious to obtain the money to pay back her indebtedness, and, if Wentworth had made the same offer at the end of the second year which he had made at the close of the first, she would have accepted it. The offer, however, was not made, and Miss Longworth said nothing, but took her share of the profits and put them into the bank.

The plan of placing all one's eggs into the same basket is a good one—until something happens to the basket! It is said that lightning never strikes twice in the same place, and, as the small boy remarked, 'it never needed to.'

In Mr. Longworth's affairs lightning struck in three places, and in each of those strokes it hit a large basket. A new law had been passed in one part of the world that vitally affected great interests he held there. In another part of the world, at the same time, there occurred a revolution, and every business in that country stopped for the time being. In still another part of the world there had been a commercial crisis; and, in sympathy with all these financial disasters, the money market in London was exceedingly stringent.

Everybody wanted to sell, and nobody wished to buy. This unfortunate combination of circumstances hit old Mr. Longworth hard. It was not that he did not believe all his investments were secure, could he only weather the gale, but there was an immediate need of ready money which it seemed absolutely impossible to obtain. Day by day his daughter saw him ageing perceptibly. She knew worry was the cause of this, and she knew the events that were happening in different parts of the world must seriously embarrass her father. She longed to speak to him about his business, but one attempt she made in this direction had been very rudely rebuffed, and she was not a woman to tempt a second repulse of that kind. So she kept silent, and saw with grief the havoc business troubles were making with her father's health.

'The old man,' said young Longworth, 'seems to be in a corner.'

'I do not want you ever again to allude to my father as "the old man"— remember that!' cried the girl indignantly.

Young Longworth shrugged his shoulders, and said:

'I don't think you can insist on my calling him a young man much longer. If he isn't an old man, I should like to know who is?'

'That doesn't matter,' said Edith. 'You must not use such a phrase again in my hearing. What do you mean by saying he is in a corner?'

'Well,' returned the young man, 'I don't know much about his business. He does not take me into his confidence at all. In fact, the older he grows, the closer he gets, and the chances are he will make some very bad speculation before long, if he has not done so already. That is the way with old men, begging your pardon for using the phrase. It is not levelled against your father in this instance, but at old men as a class, especially men who have been successful. They seem to resent anybody giving them advice.'

One day Edith received a telegram, asking her to come to the office in the City without delay. She was panic-stricken when she read the message, feeling sure her father had been stricken down in his office, and was probably dying—perhaps dead. She had feared some such result for a long time, because of the intense anxiety to which he had been subjected, and he was not a man who could be counselled to take care of himself on the plea that he was getting old. He resented any intimation that he was not as good a business man as he had ever been, and so it was extremely difficult to get him to listen to reason, if anyone had the courage to talk reason to him.

Edith, without a moment's delay, sprang lightly into a hansom, and went to the District Railway without waiting for her carriage. From the Mansion House Station another cab took her quickly to her father's office.

She was immensely relieved, as she passed through, to see the clerks working as if nothing particular had happened. On entering her father's room, she found him pacing up and down the apartment, while her cousin sat, apparently absorbed in his own affairs, at his desk. Her father was evidently greatly excited.

'Edith,' he cried the moment she entered, 'where is that money I gave you two years ago?'

'It is invested,' she answered, turning slightly pale.

Her father laughed—a hoarse, dry laugh.

'Just as I thought,' he sneered—'put in such shape that a person cannot touch a penny of it, I suppose. In what is it invested? I must have that money.'

'How soon do you need it, father?

'I want it just now, at this moment; if I don't have that money I am a ruined man.'

'This moment. I suppose, means any time to-day, before the bank closes?'

Her father looked at her for a moment, then said:

'Yes that is what it means.'

'I will try and get you the money before that time.'

'My dear girl,' he said bitterly, 'you don't know what you are talking about. If you have that money invested, even if your investment is worth three times now what it was then, you could not get a penny on it. Don't you know the state of the London money market? Don't you know how close money is? I thought perhaps you might have some portion of it yet, not sunk in your silly investment, whatever it is. I have never asked you what it was. You told me you would tell me, but you never have done so. I looked on that money as lost. I look on it still as lost. If you can get me a remnant of it, it will help me now more than the whole amount, or double the amount, would have done at the time I gave it to you. What have you done with the money? What is it invested in?'

'It is invested in a mine.'

'A mine. Of all things in the world in which to sink money, a mine is the worst. Just what a woman or a fool would do! How do you expect to raise money on a mine in the present state of the market? What, in the name of wonder, made you put it into a mine? Whose mine did you buy?'

'I do not know whose it was, father, but I was willing to tell you all I knew at the time you asked me and if you ask me now what mine I bought, I will tell you.'

'Certainly I ask you. What mine did you buy?'

'I bought the mine for which John Kenyon was agent.'

The moment these words were said, her cousin sprang to his feet and glared at her like a man demented.

'You bought that mine—you? Then Wentworth lied to me. He said a Mr. Smith had given him the money.'

'I am the Mr. Smith, William.'

498

'You are the Mr. Smith! You are the one who has cheated me out of that mine!'

'My dear cousin, the less we say about cheating, the better. I am talking to my father just now, and I do not wish to be interrupted. Will you be so kind as to leave the room until my interview with him is over?'

'So you bought the mica-mine, did you! Pretending to be friendly with me, and knowing all the time that you were doing your best to cheat——'

'Come, come!' interrupted the old gentleman; 'William, none of this. If anyone is to talk roughly to Edith, it will be me, not you. Come, sir, leave the room, as she has asked you to do. Now, my daughter,' he continued, in a much milder tone of voice, after young Longworth had left the office, 'have you any ready money? It is no use saying the mine is worth a hundred thousand pounds, or a million, just now, if you haven't the ready money. Edith, my child,' he cried, 'sit down with me a moment, and I will explain the whole situation to you. It seems to me that ever since I stopped consulting you things have gone wrong. Perhaps, even if you have the money, it is better not to risk it just now; but one pound will do what two pounds will not do a year hence, or perhaps six months from now, when this panic is over.'

Edith sat down beside her father and heard from him exactly how things stood. Then she said:

'All you really need is about fifteen thousand pounds?'

'Yes, that would do; I'm sure that would carry me over. Can you get it for me, my child?'

'Yes, and more. I will try to get you the whole amount. Wait for me here twenty minutes or half an hour.'

George Wentworth was very much surprised when he saw Edith Longworth enter his office. It had been many months since she was there before, and he cordially held out his hand to the girl.

'Mr. Wentworth,' she began at once, 'have you any of the money the mica mine has brought you?'

'Yes. I invested the first year's proceeds, but, since I got the last amount, things have been so shaky in the City that it is still at the bank.'

'Will you lend me—can you lend me five thousand pounds of it?'

'Of, course I can, and will; and very glad I am to get the chance of doing so.'

'Then, please write me out a cheque for it at once, and whatever papers you want as security, make them out, and I will see that you are secured.'

'Look here, Miss Longworth,' said the young man, placing his hands on his hips and gazing at her, 'do you mean to insult me? Do you not know that the reason I am able to write out a cheque for five thousand pounds, that will be honoured, is entirely because you trusted your money to me and Kenyon without security? Do you think I want security? Take back the word, Miss Longworth.'

'I will—I will,' she said; 'but I am in a great hurry. Please write me out the cheque, for I must have it before the bank closes.'

The cheque was promptly written out and handed to her.

'I am afraid,' she said, 'I am not very polite to-day, and rather abrupt; but I will make up for it some other time.'

And so, bidding the young man good-bye, she drove to the bank, deposited the cheque, drew her own for thirty thousand pounds, and carried it to her father.

'There,' she said, 'is thirty thousand pounds, and I still own the mine, or, at least, part of it. All the money is made from the cheque you gave me, or, rather, two-thirds of it, because one-third was never touched. Now, it seems to me, father, that, if I am a good enough business woman to more than double my money in two years, I am a good enough business woman to be consulted by my father whenever he needs a confidant. My dear father, I want to take some of the burden off your shoulders.'

There were tears in her father's eyes as he put his arm round her waist and whispered to her:

'There is no one in all London like you, my dear—no one, no one. I'll have no more secrets from you, my own brave girl.'

CHAPTER XLI.

Kenyon's luck, as he said to himself, had turned. The second year was even more prosperous than the first, and the third as successful as the second. He had a steady market for his mineral, and, besides, he had the great advantage of knowing the rogues to avoid. Some new swindles he had encountered during his first year's experience had taught him lessons that he profited by in the second and third. He liked his home in the wilderness, and he liked the rough people amongst whom he found himself.

Notwithstanding his renunciation of London, however, there would now and then come upon him a yearning for the big city, and he promised himself a trip there at the end of the third year. Wentworth had been threatening month after month to come out and see him, but something had always interfered.

Taking it all in all, John liked it better in the winter than in the summer, in spite of the extreme cold. The cold was steady and could be depended upon; moreover, it was healthful and invigorating. In summer, John never quite became accustomed to the ravages of the black fly, the mosquito, and other insect pests of that region. His first interview with the black fly left his face in such a condition that he was glad he lived in a wilderness.

At the beginning of the second winter John treated himself to a luxury. He bought a natty little French Canadian horse that was very quick and accustomed to the ice of the river, which formed the highway by which he reached Burntpine from the mine in the cold season. To supplement the horse, he also got a comfortable little cutter, and with this turn-out he made his frequent journeys between the mine and Burntpine with comfort and speed, wrapped snugly in buffalo robes.

If London often reverted to his mind, there was another subject that obtruded itself even more frequently. His increased prosperity had something to do with this. He saw that, if he was to have a third of the receipts of the mine, he was not to remain a poor man for very long, and this fact gave him a certain courage which had been lacking before. He wondered if she remembered him. Wentworth had said very little about her when he wrote, for his letters were largely devoted to enthusiastic eulogies of Jennie Brewster, and Kenyon, in spite of the confession he had made when his case seemed hopeless, was loath to write and ask his friend anything about Edith.

One day, on a clear sharp frosty winter morning, Kenyon had his little pony harnessed for his weekly journey to Burntpine. After the rougher part of the road between the mine and the river had been left behind, and the pony got down to her work on the ice, with the two white banks of snow on either side of the smooth track, John gave himself up to thinking about the subject which now so often engrossed his mind. Wrapped closely in his furs, with the cutter skimming along the ice, these thoughts found a pleasant accompaniment in the silvery tinkle of the bells which jingled around his horse's neck. As a general thing, he met no one on the icy road from the mine to the village. Sometimes there was a procession of sleighs bearing supplies for his own mine and those beyond, and when this procession was seen, Kenyon had to look out for some place by the side of the track where he could pull up his horse and cutter and allow the teams to pass. The snow on each side of the cutting was so deep that these bays were shovelled out here and there to permit teams to get past each other. He had gone halfway to the village, when he saw ahead of him a pair of horses which he at once recognised as those belonging to the hotel-keeper. He drew up in the first bay and awaited the approach of the sleigh. He saw that it contained visitors for himself, because the driver, on recognising him, had turned round and spoken to the occupants of the vehicle. As it came along, the man drew up and nodded to Kenyon, who, although ordinarily the most polite of men, did not return the salutation. He was stricken dumb with astonishment on seeing who was in the sleigh. One woman was so bundled up that not even her nose appeared out in the cold, but the smiling rosy face of the other needed no introduction to John Kenyon.

'Well, Mr. Kenyon,' cried a laughing voice, 'you did not expect to see me this morning, did you?'

'I confess I did not,' said John, 'and yet—.' Here he paused; he was going to say, 'and yet I was thinking of you,' but he checked himself.

Miss Longworth, who had a talent for reading the unspoken thoughts of John Kenyon, probably did not need to be told the end of the sentence.

'Are you going to the village?' she asked.

'I was going. I am not going now.'

'That's right. I was just about to invite you to turn round with us. You see, we are on our way to look at the mine, and, I suppose, we shall have to obtain the consent of the manager before we can do so.'

Miss Longworth's companion had emerged for a moment from her wraps and looked at John, but instantly retired among the furs again with a shiver. She was not so young as her companion, and she considered this the most frightful climate she had ever encountered.

'Now,' said John, 'although your sleigh is very comfortable, I think this cutter of mine is even more so. It is intended for two; won't you step out of the sleigh into the cutter? Then, if the driver will move on, I can turn, and we will follow the sleigh.'

'I shall be delighted to do so,' said the young woman, shaking herself free from the buffalo robe, and stepping lightly from the sleigh into the cutter, pausing, however, for a moment, before she did so, to put her own wraps over her companion. John tucked her in beside himself, and, as the sleigh jingled on, he slowly turned his pony round into the road again.

'I have got a pretty fast pony,' he said, 'but I think we will let them drive on ahead. It irritates this little horse to see anything in front of it.'

'Then we can make up speed,' said Edith, 'and catch them before they get to the mine. Is it far from here?'

'No, not very far; at least, it doesn't take long to get there with a smart horse.'

'I have enjoyed this experience ever so much,' she said; 'you see, my father had to come to Montreal on business, so I came with him, as usual, and, being there, I thought I would run up here and see the mine. I wanted,' she continued, looking at the other side of the cutter and trailing her well-gloved fingers in the snow—'I wanted to know personally whether my manager was conducting my property in the way it ought to be conducted, notwithstanding the very satisfactory balance-sheets he sends.'

'Your property!' exclaimed John, in amazement.

'Certainly. You didn't know that, did you?' she replied, looking for a moment at him, and then away from him. 'I call myself the Mistress of the Mine.'

'Then you are—you are———'

'Mr. Smith,' said the girl coming to his rescue.

There was a moment's pause, and the next words John said were not at all what she expected.

'Take your hand out of the snow,' he commanded, 'and put it in under the buffalo robe; you have no idea how cold it is here, and your hand will be frozen in a moment.'

'Really,' said the girl, 'an employee must not talk to his employer in that tone! My hand is my own, is it not?'

'I hope it is,' said John, 'because I want to ask you for it.'

For answer Miss Edith Longworth placed her hand in his.

Actions speak louder than words. The sleigh was far in advance, and there were no witnesses on the white topped hills.

'Were you astonished?' she said, 'when I told you that I owned the mine?'

'Very much so indeed. Were you astonished when I told you I wished to own the owner of the mine?'

'Not in the slightest.'

'Why?'

'Because your treacherous friend Wentworth sent me your letter applying for a situation. You got the situation, didn't you, John?'

THE END

THE SWORD MAKER

I. AN OFFER TO OPEN THE RIVER

Considering the state of the imperial city of Frankfort, one would not expect to find such a gathering as was assembled in the Kaiser cellar of the Rheingold drinking tavern. Outside in the streets all was turbulence and disorder; a frenzy on the part of the populace taxing to the utmost the efforts of the city authorities to keep it within bounds, and prevent the development of a riot that might result in the partial destruction at least of this once prosperous city. And indeed, the inhabitants of Frankfort could plead some excuse for their boisterousness. Temporarily, at any rate, all business was at a standstill. The skillful mechanics of the town had long been out of work, and now to the ranks of the unemployed were added, from time to time, clerks and such-like clerical people, expert accountants, persuasive salesmen, and small shopkeepers, for no one now possessed the money to buy more than the bare necessities of life. Yet the warehouses of Frankfort were full to overflowing, with every kind of store that might have supplied the needs of the people, and to the unlearned man it seemed unjust that he and his family should starve while granaries were packed with the agricultural produce of the South, and huge warehouses were glutted with enough cloth from Frankfort and the surrounding districts to clothe ten times the number of tatterdemalions who clamored through the streets.

The wrath of the people was concentrated against one man, and he the highest in the land; to blame, of course, in a secondary degree, but not the one primarily at fault for this deplorable state of things. The Emperor, always indolent from the time he came to the throne, had grown old and crabbed and fat, caring for nothing but his flagon of wine that stood continually at his elbow. Laxity of rule in the beginning allowed his nobles to get the upper hand, and now it would require a civil war to bring them into subjection again. They, sitting snug in their strongholds, with plenty of wine in their cellars and corn in their bins, cared nothing for the troubles of the city. Indeed, those who inhabited either bank of the Rhine, watching from their elevated castles the main avenue of traffic between Frankfort and Cologne, her chief market, had throughout that long reign severely taxed the merchants conveying goods downstream. During the last five years, their exactions became so piratical that finally they killed the goose that laid the golden eggs, so now the Rhine was without a boat, and Frankfort without a buyer.

For too long Frankfort had looked to the Emperor, whose business it was to keep order in his domain, and when at last the merchants, combining to help themselves, made an effort towards freedom, it was too late. The result of their combination was a flotilla of nearly a hundred boats, which, gathering at Frankfort and Mayence, proceeded together down the river, convoyed by a fleet containing armed men, and thus they thought to win through to Cologne, and so dispose of their goods. But the robber Barons combined also, hung chains across the river at the Lorely rocks, its narrowest part, and realizing that this fleet could defeat any single one of them, they for once acted in concert, falling upon the boats when their running against the chains threw them into confusion.

The nobles and their brigands were seasoned fighters all, while the armed men secured by the merchants were mere hirelings, who fled in panic; and those not cut to pieces by their savage adversaries became themselves marauders on a small scale, scattered throughout the land, for there was little use of tramping back to the capital, where already a large portion of the population suffered the direst straits.

Not a single bale of goods reached Cologne, for the robbers divided everything amongst themselves, with some pretty quarrels, and then they sank the boats in the deepest part of the river as a warning, lest the merchants of Frankfort and Mayence should imagine the Rhine belonged to them. Meantime, all petitions to the Emperor being in vain, the merchants gave up the fight. They were a commercial, not a warlike people. They discharged their servants and underlings, and starvation slowly settled down upon the distressed city.

After the maritime disaster on the Rhine, some of the merchants made a futile attempt to amend matters, for which their leaders paid dearly. They appealed to the seven Electors, finding their petitions to the Emperor were in vain, asking these seven noblemen, including the three warlike Archbishops of Cologne, Treves, and Mayence, to depose the Emperor, which they had power to do, and elect his son in his stead. But they overlooked the fact that a majority of the Electors themselves, and probably the Archbishops also, benefited directly or indirectly by the piracies on the Rhine. The answer to this request was the prompt hanging of three leading merchants, the imprisonment of a score of others, and a warning to the rest that the shoemaker should stick to his last, leaving high politics to those born to rule. This misguided effort caused the three Archbishops to arrest Prince Roland, the Emperor's only son, and incarcerate him in Ehrenfels, a strong castle on the Rhine belonging to the Archbishop of Mayence, who was thus made custodian of the young man, and responsible to his brother prelates of Cologne and Treves for the safe-keeping of the Prince. The Archbishops, as has been said, were too well satisfied with the weak administration then established at Frankfort to wish a change, so the lad was removed from the capital, that the citizens of Frankfort might be under no temptation to place him at their head, and endeavor to overturn the existing order of things.

This being the state of affairs in Frankfort, with every one gloomy, and a majority starving, it was little wonder that the main cellar of the Rheingold tavern should be empty, although when times were good it was difficult to find a seat there after the sun went down. But in the smaller Kaiser cellar, along each side of the single long table, sat young men numbering a score, who ate black bread and drank Rhine wine, to the roaring of song and the telling of story. They formed a close coterie, admitting no stranger to their circle if one dissenting voice was raised against his acceptance, yet in spite of this exclusiveness there was not a drop of noble blood in the company. They belonged, however, to the aristocracy of craftsmen; metal-workers for the most part, ingenious artificers in iron, beaters of copper, fashioners of gold and silver. Glorious blacksmiths, they called themselves; but now, like every one else, with nothing to do. In spite of their city up-bringing all were stalwart, well-set-up young men; and, indeed, the swinging of hammers is good exercise for the muscles of the arm, and in those turbulent days a youth who could not take care of himself with his stick or his fists was like to fare ill if he ventured forth after nightfall.

This, indeed, had been the chief reason for the forming of their guild, and if one of their number was set upon, the secret call of the organization shouted aloud brought instant help were any of the members within hearing. Belonging neither to the military nor the aristocracy, they were not allowed to wear swords, and to obtain this privilege was one of the objects of their organization. Indeed, each member of the guild secretly possessed a weapon of the best, although he risked his neck if ever he carried it abroad with him. Among their number were three of the most expert sword makers in all Germany.

These three sword makers had been instrumental in introducing to their order the man who was now its leader. This youth came to one of them with ideas concerning the proper construction of a sword, and the balancing of it, so that it hung easily in the hand as though part of the fore-arm. Usually, the expert has small patience with the theories of an amateur; but this young fellow, whose ambition it was to invent a sword, possessed such intimate knowledge of the weapon as it was used, not only in Germany, but also in France and Italy, that the sword maker introduced him to fellow-craftsmen at other shops, and they taught him how to construct a sword. These instructors, learning that although, as Roland laughingly said, he was not allowed to wear a sword, he could wield it with a precision little short of marvelous, the guild gave permission for this stranger to be a guest at one of their weekly meetings at the Kaiser cellar, where he exhibited his wonderful skill.

Not one of them, nor, indeed, all of them together, stood any chance when confronting him. They clamored to be taught, offering good money for the lessons, believing that if they acquired but a tithe of his excellence with the blade they might venture to wear it at night, and let their skill save them from capture. But the young fellow refused their money, and somewhat haughtily declined the rôle of fencing-master, whereupon they unanimously elected him a member of the coterie, waiving for this one occasion the rule which forbade the choice of any but a metal-worker. When the stranger accepted the election, he was informed that it was the duty of each member to come to the aid of his brethren when required, and they therefore requested him to teach them swordsmanship. Roland, laughing, seeing how he had been trapped, as it were, with his own consent, acceded to the universal wish, and before a year had passed his twenty comrades were probably the leading swordsmen in the city of Frankfort.

Shortly after the disaster to the merchants' fleet at the Lorely, Roland disappeared without a word of farewell to those who had come to think so much of him. He had been extremely reticent regarding his profession, if he had one, and no one knew where he lodged. It was feared that the authorities had arrested him with the sword in his possession, for he grew more reckless than any of the others in carrying the weapon. One night, however, he reappeared, and took his seat at the head of the table as if nothing had happened. Evidently he had traveled far and on foot, for his clothes were dusty and the worse for wear. He refused to give any account of himself, but admitted that he was hungry, thirsty, and in need of money.

His hunger and thirst were speedily satisfied, but the money scarcity was not so easily remedied. All the score were out of employment, with the exception of the three sword makers, whose trade the uncertainty of the times augmented rather than diminished. To cheer up Roland, who was a young fellow of unquenchable geniality, they elected him to the empty honor of being their leader, Kurzbold's term of office having ended.

The guild met every night now, instead of once a week, and it may be shrewdly suspected that the collation of black bread and sausage formed the sole meal of the day for many of them. Nevertheless, their hilarity was undiminished, and the rafters rang with song and laugh, and echoed also maledictions upon a supine Government, and on the rapacious Rhine lords. But the bestowal of even black bread and the least expensive of wine could not continue indefinitely. They owed a bill to the landlord upon which that worthy, patient as he had proved himself, always hoping for better times, wished for at least something on account. All his other customers had deserted him, and if they drank at all, chose some place where the wine was thin and cheap. The landlord held out bravely for three months after Roland was elected president, then, bemoaning his fate, informed the guild that he would be compelled to close the Rheingold tavern.

"Give me a week!" cried Roland, rising in his place at the head of the table, "and I will make an effort to get enough gold to settle the bill at least, with perhaps something over for each of our pockets."

This promise brought forth applause and a rattle of flagons on the table, so palpably empty that the ever-hopeful landlord proceeded forthwith to fill them.

"There is one proviso," said Roland, as they drank his health in the wine his offer produced. "To get this money I must do something in return. I have a plan in mind which it would be premature to disclose. If it succeeds, none of us will ever need to bend back over a workman's bench again, or hammer metal except for our own pleasure. But acting alone I am powerless, so I must receive your promise that you will stand by any pledge I make on your behalf, and follow me into whatever danger I choose to lead you."

There was a great uproar at this, and a boisterous consent.

"This day week, then," said Roland, as he strapped sword to side, threw cloak over shoulders, so that it completely concealed the forbidden weapon, waved a hand to his cheering comrades, and went out into the night.

Once ascended the cellar steps, the young man stood in the narrow street as though hesitating what to do. Faintly there came to him the sound of singing from the cellar he had quitted, and he smiled slightly as he listened to the rousing chorus he knew so well. From the direction of the Palace a more sinister echo floated on the night air; the unmistakable howl of anger, pain, and terror; the noise that a pursued and stricken mob makes when driven by soldiers. The populace had evidently been engaged in its futile and dangerous task of demonstrating, and proclaiming its hunger, and the authorities were scattering it; keeping it ever on the move.

It was still early; not yet ten o'clock, and a full moon shone over the city, unlighted otherwise. Drawing his cloak closer about him, Roland walked rapidly in an opposite direction to that from which the tumult of the rabble came, until he arrived at the wide Fahrgasse, a street running north and south, its southern end terminating at the old bridge. Along this thoroughfare lived the wealthiest merchants of Frankfort.

Roland turned, and proceeded slowly towards the river, critically examining the tall, picturesque buildings on either hand, cogitating the question which of them would best answer his purpose. They all seemed uninviting enough, for their windows were dark, most of them tightly shuttered; and, indeed, the thoroughfare looked like a street of the dead, the deserted appearance enhanced, rather than relieved, by the white moonlight lying on its cobble-stones.

Nearing the bridge, he discovered one stout door ajar, and behind it shone the yellow glow of a lamp. He paused, and examined critically the façade of the house, which, with its quiet, dignified architectural beauty, seemed the abode of wealth. Although the shutters were closed, his intent inspection showed him thin shafts of light from the chinks, and he surmised that an assemblage of some sort was in progress, probably a secret convention, the members of which entered unannounced, and left the door ajar ready for the next comer.

For a moment he thought of venturing in, but remembering his mission required the convincing of one man rather than the persuasion of a group, he forbore, but noted in his mind the position and designation of the house, resolving to select this building as the theater of his first effort, and return to it next morning. It would serve his purpose as well as another.

Roland's attention was then suddenly directed to his own position, standing in the bright moonlight, for there swung round from the river road, into the Fahrgasse, a small and silent company, who marched as one man. The moon was shining almost directly up the street, but the houses to the west stood in its radiance, while those in the east were still in shadow. Roland pressed himself back against the darkened wall to his left, near the partially opened door; between it and the river. The silent procession advanced to the door ajar, and there paused, forming their ranks into two lines, thus making a passage for a tall, fine-looking, bearded man, who walked to the threshold, then turned and raised his bonnet in salute.

"My friends," he said, "this is kind of you, and although I have been silent, I ask you to believe that deeply I appreciate your welcome escort. And now, enter with me, and we will drink a stoup of wine together, to the somber toast, 'God save our stricken city!'"

"No, no, Herr Goebel. To-night is sacred. We have seen you safely to your waiting family, and at that reunion there should be no intruders. But to-morrow night, if you will have us, we will drink to the city, and to your own good health, Herr Goebel."

This sentiment was applauded by all, and the merchant, seeing that they would not accept his present invitation, bowed in acquiescence, and bade them good-by. When the door closed the delegation separated into units, and each went his own way. Roland, stepping out of the shadow, accosted the rearmost man.

"Pardon me, mein Herr," he said, "but may I ask what ceremony is this in which you have been taking part?"

The person accosted looked with some alarm at his questioner, but the moonlight revealed a face singularly gentle and winning; a face that in spite of its youth inspired instinctive confidence. The tone, too, was very persuasive, and seemed devoid even of the offense of curiosity.

"'Tis no ceremony," said the delegate, "but merely the return home of our friend, Herr Goebel."

"Has he, then, been on a journey?"

"Sir, you are very young, and probably unacquainted with Frankfort."

"I have lived here all my life," said Roland. "I am a native of Frankfort."

"In that case," replied the other, "you show yourself amazingly ignorant of its concerns; otherwise you would know that Herr Goebel is one of the leading merchants of the city, a man honorable, enlightened, and energetic—an example to us all, and one esteemed alike by noble or peasant. We honor ourselves in honoring him."

"Herr Goebel should be proud of such commendation, mein Herr, coming I judge, from one to whom the words you use might also be applied."

The merchant bowed gravely at this compliment, but made no remark upon it.

"Pardon my further curiosity," continued the young man, "but from whence does Herr Goebel return?"

"He comes from prison," said the other. "He made the mistake of thinking that our young Prince would prove a better ruler than his father, our Emperor, and but that the Archbishops feared a riot if they went to extremes, Herr Goebel ran great danger of losing his life rather than his liberty."

"What you say, mein Herr, interests me very much, and I thank you for your courtesy. My excuse for questioning you is this. I am moved by a desire to enter the employ of such a man as Herr Goebel, and I purpose calling upon him to-morrow, if you think he would be good enough to receive me."

"He will doubtless receive you," replied the other, "but I am quite certain your mission will fail. At the present moment none of us are engaging clerks, however competent. Ignorant though you are of civic affairs, you must be aware that all business is at a standstill in Frankfort. Although Herr Goebel has said nothing about it, I learn from an unquestionable source that he himself is keeping from starvation all his former employees, so I am sure he would not take on, for a stranger, any further obligation."

"Sir, I am well acquainted with the position of affairs, and it is to suggest a remedy that I desire speech with Herr Goebel. I do not possess the privilege of acquaintance with any merchant in this city, so one object of my accosting you was to learn, if possible, how I might secure some note of introduction to the merchant that would ensure his receiving me, and obtain for me a hearing when once I had been admitted to his house."

If Roland expected the stranger to volunteer such a note, he quite underestimated the caution of a Frankfort merchant.

"As I said before, you will meet with no difficulty so far as entrance to the house is concerned. May I take it that you yourself understand the art of writing?"

"Oh yes," replied Roland.

"Then indite your own letter of introduction. Say that you have evolved a plan for the redemption of Frankfort, and Herr Goebel will receive you without demur. He will listen patiently, and give a definite decision regarding the feasibility of your project. And now, good sir, my way lies to the left. I wish you success, and bid you good-night."

The stranger left Roland standing at the intersection of two streets, one of which led to the Saalhof. They had been approaching the Romerberg, or market-place, the center of Frankfort, when the merchant so suddenly ended the conversation and turned aside. Roland remembered that no Jew was allowed to set foot in the Romerberg, and now surmised the nationality of his late companion. The youth proceeded alone through the Romerberg, and down directly to the river, reaching the spot where the huge Saalhof faced its flood. Roland saw that triple guards surrounded the Emperor's Palace. The mob had been cleared away, but no one was allowed to linger in its precincts, and the youth was gruffly ordered to take himself elsewhere, which he promptly did, walking up the Saalgasse, and past the Cathedral, until he came once more into the Fahrgasse, down which he proceeded, pausing for another glance at Goebel's house, until he came to the bridge, where he stood with arms resting on the parapet, thoughtfully shaping in his mind what he would say to Herr Goebel in the morning.

Along the opposite side of the river lay a compact mass of barges; ugly, somber, black in the moonlight, silent witnesses to the ruin of Frankfort. The young man gazed at this melancholy accumulation of useless floating stock, and breathed the deeper when he reflected that whoever could set these boats in motion again would prove himself, temporarily at least, the savior of the city.

When the bells began to toll eleven, Roland roused himself, walked across the bridge to Sachsenhausen, and so to his squalid lodging, consoling himself with the remembrance that the great King Charlemagne had made this his own place of residence. Here, before retiring to bed, he wrote the letter which he was to send in next day to Herr Goebel, composing it with some care, so that it aroused curiosity without satisfying it.

It was half-past ten next morning when Roland presented himself at the door of the leading merchant in the Fahrgasse, and sent in to that worthy his judiciously worded epistle. He was kept waiting in the hall longer than he expected, but at last the venerable porter appeared, and said Herr Goebel would be pleased to receive him. He was conducted up the stair to the first floor, and into a front room which seemed to be partly library and partly business office. Here seated at a stout table, he recognized the grave burgher whose home-coming he had witnessed the night before.

The keen eyes of the merchant seemed to penetrate to his inmost thought, and it struck Roland that there came into them an expression of disappointment, for he probably did not expect so youthful a visitor.

"Will you be seated, mein Herr," said his host; and Roland, with an inclination of the head, accepted the invitation. "My time is very completely occupied to-day," continued the elder man, "for although there is little business afoot in Frankfort, my own affairs have been rather neglected of late, and I am endeavoring to overtake the arrears."

"I know that," said Roland. "I stood by your doorcheek last night when you returned home."

"Did you so? May I ask why?"

"There was no particular reason. It happened that I walked down the Fahrgasse, endeavoring to make up my mind upon whom I should call to-day."

"And why have I received the preference?"

"Perhaps, sir, it would be more accurate to say your house received the preference, if it is such. I was struck by its appearance of solidity and wealth, and, differing from all others in the door being ajar, I lingered before it last night with some inclination to enter. Then the procession which accompanied you came along. I heard your address to your friends, and wondered what the formality was about. After the door was closed I accosted one of those who escorted you, and learned your name, business, and reputation."

"You must be a stranger in Frankfort when you needed to make such inquiry."

"Those are almost the same words that my acquaintance of last night used, and he seemed astonished when I replied that I was born in Frankfort, and had lived here all my life."

"Ah, I suppose no man is so well known as he thinks he is, but I venture to assert that you are not engaged in business here."

"Sir, you are in the right. I fear I have hitherto led a somewhat useless existence."

"On money earned by some one else, perhaps."

"Again you hit the nail on the head, Herr Goebel. I lodge on the other side of the river, and coming to and fro each day, the sight of all those useless barges depresses me, and I have formulated a plan for putting them in motion again."

"I fear, sir, that wiser heads than yours have been meditating upon that project without avail."

"I should have been more gratified, Herr Goebel, if you had said 'older heads.'"

The suspicion of a smile hovered for a brief instant round the shrewd, firm lips of the merchant.

"Young sir, your gentle reproof is deserved. I know nothing of your wisdom, and so should have referred to the age, and not to the equipment of your head. It occurs to me, as I study you more closely, that I have met you before. Your face seems familiar."

"'Tis but a chance resemblance, I suspect. Until very recently I have been absorbed in my studies, and rarely left my father's house."

"I am doubtless mistaken. But to return to our theme. As you are ignorant of my name and standing in this city, you are probably unaware of the efforts already made to remove the deadlock on the Rhine."

"In that, Herr Goebel, you are at fault. I know an expedition of folly was promoted at enormous expense, and that the empty barges, numbering something like fivescore, now rest in the deepest part of the Rhine."

"Why do you call it an expedition of folly?"

"Surely the result shows it to be such."

"A plan may meet with disaster, even where every precaution has been taken. We did the best we could, and if the men we had paid for the protection of the flotilla had not, with base cowardice, deserted their posts, these barges would have reached Cologne."

"Never! The defenders you chose were riff-raff, picked up in the gutters of Frankfort, and you actually supposed such cattle, undisciplined and untrained, would stand up against the fearless fighters of the Barons, swashbucklers, hardened to the use of sword and pike. What else was to be expected? The goods were not theirs, but yours. They had received their pay, and so speedily took themselves out of danger."

"You forget, sir, or you do not know, that several hundred of them were cut to pieces."

"I know that, also, but the knowledge does not in the least nullify my contention. I am merely endeavoring to show you that the heads you spoke of a moment ago were only older, but not necessarily wiser than mine. It would be impossible for me to devise an expedition so preposterous."

"What should we have done?"

"For one thing, you should have gone yourselves, and defended your own bales."

The merchant showed visible signs of a slowly rising anger, and had the young man's head contained the wisdom he appeared to claim for it, he would have known that his remarks were entirely lacking in tact, and that he was making no progress, but rather the reverse. "You speak like a heedless, untutored youth. How could we defend our bales, when no merchant is allowed to wear a sword?"

Roland rose and put his hands to the throat of his cloak.

"I am not allowed to wear a sword;" and saying this, he dramatically flung wide his cloak, displaying the prohibited weapon hanging from his belt. The merchant sat back in his chair, visibly impressed.

"You seem to repose great confidence in me," he said. "What if I were to inform the authorities?"

The youth smiled.

"You forget, Herr Goebel, that I learned much about you from your friend last night. I feel quite safe in your house."

He flung his cloak once more over the weapon, and sat down again.

"What is your occupation, sir?" asked the merchant.

"I am a teacher of swordsmanship. I practice the art of a fencing-master."

"Your clients are aristocrats, then?"

"Not so. The class with which I am now engaged contains twenty skilled artisans of about my own age."

"If they do not belong to the aristocracy, your instruction must be surreptitious, because it is against the law."

"It is both surreptitious and against the law, but in spite of these disadvantages, my twenty pupils are the best swordsmen in Frankfort, and I would willingly pit them against any twenty nobles with whom I am acquainted."

"So!" cried the merchant. "You are acquainted with twenty nobles, are you?"

"Well, you see," explained the young man, flushing slightly, "these metal-workers whom I drill, being out of employment, cannot afford to pay for their lessons, and naturally, as you indicated, a fencing-master must look to the nobles for his bread. I used the word acquaintance hastily. I am acquainted with the nobles in the same way that a clerk in the woolen trade might say he was acquainted with a score of merchants, to none of whom he had ever spoken."

"I see. Am I to take it that your project for opening the Rhine depends for its success on those twenty metal-workers, who quite lawlessly know how to handle their swords?"

"Yes."

"Tell me what your plan is."

"I do not care to disclose my plan, even to you."

"I thought you came here hoping I should further your project, and perhaps finance it. Am I wrong in such a surmise?"

"Sir, you are not. The very first proviso is that you pay to me across this table a thousand thalers in gold."

The smile came again to the lips of the merchant.

"Anything else?" he asked.

"Yes. You will select one of your largest barges, and fill it with whatever class of goods you deal in."

"Don't you know what class of goods I deal in?"

"No! I do not."

Goebel's smile broadened. That a youth so ignorant of everything pertaining to the commerce of Frankfort, should come in thus boldly and demand a thousand thalers in gold from a man whose occupation he did not know, seemed to the merchant one of the greatest pieces of impudence he had encountered in his long experience of men.

"After all, my merchandise," he said, "matters little one way or another when I am engaged with such a customer as you. What next?"

"You will next place a price upon the shipload; a price such as you would accept if the boat reached Cologne intact. I agree to pay you that money, together with the thousand thalers, when I return to Frankfort."

"And when will that be, young sir?"

"You are better able to estimate the length of time than I. I do not know, for instance, how long it takes a barge to voyage from Frankfort to Cologne."

"Given fair weather, which we may expect in July, and premising that there are no interruptions, let us say a week."

"Would a man journeying on horseback from Cologne to Frankfort reach here sooner than the boat?"

"The barge having to make headway against a strong current, I should say the horseman would accomplish the trip in a third of the time."

"Very well. To allow for all contingencies, I promise to pay the money one month from the day we leave the wharf at Frankfort."

"That would be eminently satisfactory."

"I forgot to mention that I expect you, knowing more about navigation than I, to supply a trustworthy captain and an efficient crew for the manning of the barge. I should like men who understand the currents of the river, and who, if questioned by the Barons, would not be likely to tell more than they were asked."

"I can easily provide such a set of sailors."

"Very well, Herr Goebel. Those are my requirements. Will you agree to supply them?"

"With great pleasure, my young and enthusiastic friend, provided that you comply with one of the most common of our commercial rules."

"And what is that, mein Herr?"

"Before you depart you will leave with me ample security that if I never see you again, the value of the goods, plus the thousand thalers, will be repaid to me when the month is past."

"Ah," said the young man, "you impose an impossible condition."

"Give me a bond, then, signed by three responsible merchants."

"Sir, as I am acquainted with no merchant in this city except yourself, how could I hope to obtain the signature of even one responsible man?"

"How, then, do you expect to obtain my consent to a project which I know cannot succeed, while I bear all the risk?"

"Pardon me, Herr Goebel. I and my comrades risk our lives. You risk merely your money and your goods."

"You intend, then, to fight your way down the Rhine?"

"Surely. How else?"

"Supported by only twenty followers?"

"Yes."

"And you hope to succeed where a thousand of our men failed?"

"Yes; they were hirelings, as I told you. With my twenty I could put them all to flight. Aside from this, I should like to point out to you that the merchants of Frankfort formed their combination at public meetings, called together by the burgomaster. There was no secrecy about their deliberations. Every robber Baron along the Rhine knew what you were going to attempt, and was prepared for your coming. I intend that your barge shall leave Frankfort at midnight. My company will proceed across country, and join her at some agreed spot, probably below Bingen."

"I see. Well, my young friend, you have placed before me a very interesting proposal, but I am a business man, and not an adventurer. Unless you can furnish me with security, I decline to advance a single thaler, not to mention a thousand."

The young man rose to his feet, and the merchant, with a sigh, seemed glad that the conference was ended.

"Herr Goebel, you deeply disappoint me."

"I am sorry for that, and regret the forfeiting of your good opinion, but despite that disadvantage I must persist in my obstinacy."

"I do not wonder that this fair city lies desolate if her prosperity depends upon her merchants, and if you are chief among them; yet I cannot forget that you risked life and liberty on my behalf, though now you will not venture a miserable thousand thalers on my word of honor."

"On your behalf? What do you mean?"

"I mean, Herr Goebel, that I am Prince Roland, only son of the Emperor, and that you placed your neck in jeopardy to elevate me to the throne."

II. THE BARGAIN IS STRUCK

Every epoch seems to have possessed a two-word phrase that contained, as it were, the condensed wisdom of the age, and was universally believed by the people. For instance, the aphorism "Know thyself" rose to popularity when cultured minds turned towards science. In the period to which this recital belongs the adage "Blood tells" enjoyed universal acceptance. It was, in fact, that erroneous statement "The King can do no wrong" done up into tabloid form. From it, too, sprang that double-worded maxim of the days of chivalry, "Noblesse oblige."

In our own time, the two-worded phrase is "Money talks," and if diligent inquirers probe deeply into the matter, they will find that the aspirations of the people always correspond with reasonable accuracy to the meaning of the phrase then in use. Nothing could be more excellent, for instance, than the proverb "Money talks" as representing two commercial countries like America and England. In that short sentence is packed the essence of many other wise and drastic sayings, as, for instance, "The devil take the hindmost;" for, of course, if money talks, then the man without it must remain silent, and his place is at the tail of the procession, where the devil prowls about like a Cossack at the rear of Napoleon's army.

Confronting each other in that ancient house on the Fahrgasse, we witness, then, the personification of the two phrases, ancient and modern: blood represented by the standing lad, and money by the seated merchant.

"I am Prince Roland, only son of the Emperor," the young man had said, and he saw at once by the expression on the face of his host that, could he be convinced of the truth of the assertion, the thousand thalers that the Prince had demanded would be his on the instant.

For a full minute Roland thought he had succeeded, but as the surprise died out of the merchant's countenance, there replaced it that mask of caution which had had so much to do with the building of his fortune. During their conference Herr Goebel cudgeled his brain, trying to remember where he had seen this young man before, but memory had roamed among clerks, salesmen, and industrious people of that sort where, somehow, this young fellow did not fit in. When Roland suddenly sprung on him the incredible statement that he was a member of the Imperial family, the merchant's recollection then turned towards pageants he had seen, in one of which this young stranger might very well have borne a part. Blood was beginning to tell.

But now experience came to the merchant's aid. Only in romances did princes of the blood royal wander about like troubadours. Even a member of the lesser nobility did not call unheralded at the house of a merchant. The aristocracy always wanted money, it is true, "but what they thought they might require, they went and took," as witness the piratical Barons of the Rhine, whose exactions brought misery on the great city of Frankfort.

Then all at once came the clinching remembrance that when the Electors were appealed to on behalf of the young Prince, the three Archbishops had promptly seized his Royal Highness, and, in spite of the pleadings of the Empress (the Emperor was drunk and indifferent) placed him in the custody of the Archbishop nearest to Frankfort, the warrior prelate of Mayence, who imprisoned him in the strong fortress of Ehrenfels, from which, well guarded and isolated as it was upon a crag over-hanging the Rhine, no man could escape.

"Will you kindly be seated again, sir," requested the merchant, and if he had spoken a short time before, he would have put the phrase "your Royal Highness" in the place of the word "sir."

Roland, after a moment's hesitation, sat down. He saw that his coup had failed, because he was unable to back it up by proofs. His dramatic action had been like a brilliant cavalry charge, for a moment successful, but coming to naught because there was no solid infantry to turn the temporary confusion of the enemy into complete rout. Realizing that the battle must be fought over again, the Prince sat back with a sigh of disappointment, a shade of discontent on his handsome face.

"I find myself in rather a quandary," proceeded the merchant. "If indeed you are the Emperor's son, it is not for such as I to cross-examine you."

"Ask me any questions you like, sir. I shall answer them promptly enough."

"If I beg you to supply proof of the statement you make, you would be likely to reply that as you dared not enter your father's Palace, you are unable to furnish me with corroboration."

"Sir, you put the case in better language than I could employ. In more halting terms that is what I should have said."

"When were you last in the Palace?"

"About the same time, sir, that you took up your residence in prison."

"Ah, yes; that naturally would be your answer. Now, my young friend, you have shown me that you know nothing of mercantile practice; therefore it may perhaps interest you if I explain some of our methods."

"Herr Goebel, you may save your breath. Such a recital must not only fail to interest me, but will bore me extremely. I care nothing for your mercantile procedure, and, to be quite plain with you, I despise your trade, and find some difficulty in repressing my contempt for those who practice it."

"If an emissary of mine," returned Goebel, unperturbed, "approached a client or customer for the purpose of obtaining a favor, and used as little tact as you do, I should dismiss him."

"I'm not asking any favors from you."

"You wish me to hand over to you a thousand thalers, otherwise why came you here?"

"I desire to bestow upon you the greatest of boons, namely to open up the Rhine, and bring back prosperity to Frankfort, which you brainless, cowardly merchants have allowed to slip through your fingers, blaming now the Barons, now the Emperor, now the Electors; censuring everybody, in fact, except the real culprits ... yourselves. You speak of the money as a favor, but it is merely an advance for a few weeks, and will be returned to you; yet because I desire to confer this inestimable gift upon you and your city, you expect me to cringe to you, and flatter you, as if I were a member of your own sycophantic league. I refuse to do anything of the kind, and yet, by God, I'll have the money!"

The merchant, for the first time during their conference, laughed heartily. The young man's face was aflame with anger, yet the truculent words he used did more to convince Herr Goebel that he belonged to the aristocracy than if he had spoken with the most exemplary humility. Goebel felt convinced he was not the Prince, but some young noble, who, intimate with the Royal Family, and knowing the Emperor's son to be out of the way, thought it safe to assume his name, the better to carry forward his purpose, whatever that purpose might actually be. That it was to open the Rhine he did not for a moment credit, and that he would ever see his cash again, if once he parted with it, he could not believe.

"At the risk of tiring you, I shall nevertheless proceed with what I was about to say. We merchants, for our own protection, contribute to a fund which might be entitled one for secret service. This fund enables us to procure private information that may be of value in our business. Among other things we need to know are accurate details pertaining to the intentions and doings of our rulers, for whatever our own short-comings may be, the actions of those above us affect business one way or the other. May I read you a short report that came in while I was serving my term of imprisonment?"

"Oh, read what you like," said Roland indifferently, throwing back his head, and partially closing his eyes, with an air of ennui.

The merchant drew towards him a file of papers, and going through them carefully, selected a document, and drew it forth, then, clearing his throat, he read aloud—

"'At an hour after midnight, on St. Stanislas' Day, three nobles, one representing the Archbishop of Mayence, the second the Archbishop of Treves, and the third the Archbishop of Cologne, armed with authority from these three Electors and Princes of the Church, entered the Saalhof from the side facing the river, and arrested in his bed the young Prince Roland. They assured the Empress, who protested, that the Prince would be well cared for, and that, as an insurrection was feared in Frankfort, it was considered safer that the person whom they intended to elevate to the throne on the event of the Emperor's death, should be out of harm's way, being placed under the direct care of the Archbishop of Mayence. They informed the Empress that the Archbishops would not remove the Prince from the Palace in opposition to the wishes of either the Emperor or herself, but if this permission was not given, a meeting of the Electors would at once be called, and some one else selected to succeed the present ruler.

"'This consideration exerted a great influence upon the Empress, who counseled her son to acquiesce. The young man was led to a boat then in waiting by the river steps of the Palace, and so conveyed down the Main to the Rhine, which was reached just after daybreak. Without landing, and keeping as much as possible to the middle of the river, the party proceeded down the Rhine, past Bingen, to the foot of the crag on which stands the castle of Ehrenfels. The Prince was taken up to the Castle, where he now remains.

"'The Archbishops from their revenues allot to him seven hundred thalers a month, in addition to his maintenance. It is impossible for him to escape from this stronghold unaided, and as the Emperor takes no interest in the matter, and the Empress has given her consent, he is like to be an inmate of Ehrenfels during the pleasure of the Archbishops, who doubtless will not elect him to the throne in succession unless he proves compliant to their wishes. The Prince being a young man of no particular force of character'" (the merchant paused in his reading, and looked across at his vis-à-vis with a smile, but the latter appeared to be asleep), "'he will probably succumb to the Archbishops, therefore merchants are advised to base no hopes upon an improvement in affairs, even though the son should succeed the father. Despite the precautions taken, the arrest and imprisonment of the Prince, and even the place of his detention, became rather generally known in Frankfort, but the news is in the form of rumor only, and excites little interest throughout the city.'

"There, Sir Roland, what do you say to that?"

"Oh, nothing much," replied Roland. "The account might have stated that in the boat were five rowers, who worked lustily until we reached the Rhine, when, the wind being favorable, a sail was hoisted, and with the current assisting the wind, we made excellent time to Ehrenfels. I observe, further, that your secret service keeps you very well informed, and therefore withdraw a tithe of the harsh things I said regarding the stupidity of the merchants."

"Many thanks for the concession," said Goebel, replacing the document with its fellows. "Now, as a plain and practical man, what strikes me is this: you need only return to Ehrenfels for two months, and as there is little use for money in that fortress, your maintenance being guaranteed, and seven hundred thalers allowed, you can come away with four hundred thalers more than the sum you demand from me, and thus put your project into force without being under obligations to any despised merchant."

"True, Herr Goebel, but can you predict what will happen in Frankfort before two months are past? You learn from that document that the shrewd Archbishops anticipate an insurrection, and doubtless they command the force at hand ready to crush it, but during this conflict, which you seem to regard so lightly, does it ever occur to you that the merchants' palaces along the Fahrgasse may be sacked and burnt?"

"That, of course, is possible," commented the merchant.

"Nay, it is absolutely certain. Civil war means ruin, to innocent and guilty alike."

"You are in the right. Now, will you tell me how you escaped from Ehrenfels?"

"Yes; if you agree to my terms without further haggling."

"I shall agree to your terms if I believe your story."

"It seems impossible, sir, to pin you down to any definite bargain. Is this the way you conduct your business?"

"Yes; unless I am well assured of the good faith of my customer. I offered you ordinary business terms when I asked for security, or for the signature of three responsible merchants to your bond. It is because I am a merchant, and not a speculator, that I haggle, as you term it."

"Very well, then, I will tell you how I got away, but I begin my recital rather hopelessly, for you always leave yourself a loophole of escape. If you believe my story, you say! Yes: could I weave a romance about tearing my sheets into ropes; of lowering myself in the dark from the battlements to the ground; of an alarm given; of torches flashing; of diving into the Rhine, and swimming under the water until I nearly strangled; of floating down over the rapids, with arrows whizzing round me in the night; of climbing dripping to the farther shore, far from sight of Ehrenfels, then, doubtless, you would believe. But my escape was prosaically commonplace, depending on the cupidity of one man. The material for it was placed in my hands by the Archbishops themselves. Your account states that the Castle is well guarded. So it is, but when the Archbishop needs an augmentation of his force, he withdraws his men from Ehrenfels to Mayence, as my prison is the nearest of his possessions to his capital city, and thus at times it happens that the Castle is bereft of all save the custodian and his family. His eldest son happens to be of my own age, and not unlike me in appearance. None of the guards saw me, except the custodian, and you must remember he was a very complacent jailer, for the reason that he knew well every rising sun might bring with it tidings that I was his Emperor, so he cultivated my acquaintance, to learn in his own thrifty, peasant way what manner of ruler I might become, and I, having no one else to talk to, made much of his company.

"Frequently he impressed upon me that his task of jailer was most irksome to him, but poverty compelling, what could he do? He swore he would accomplish whatever was in his power to mitigate my captivity, and this indeed did; so at last when the Castle was empty I made him a proposal. Now remember, Sir Merchant, that what I tell you is in confidence, and should you break faith with me, I will have you hanged if I become Emperor, or slit your throat with my own sword if I don't."

"Go on. I shall tell no one."

"I said to my jailer: 'There are not half a dozen people in this world who know me by sight, and among that half-dozen no Elector is included. Outside the Palace at Frankfort I am acquainted with a sword maker or two, and about a score of good fellows who are friends of theirs, but to them I am merely a fencing-master. Now, seven hundred thalers a month pass through your honest hands to mine, and will continue to do so. Your son seems to be even more silent than yourself, and he is a young fellow whom I suspect knows the difference between a thaler and a button on his own coat. If you do what I wish, there will be some slight risk, but think of the reward immediate and in future! At once you come into an income of seven hundred thalers a month. If I am elected Emperor, I shall ennoble you, and present you with the best post in the land. If you don't do what I wish, I shall cause your head cut off as the first act of my first day of power.'"

"You did not threaten to slit his throat with your own sword, failing your elevation?" asked the merchant, with a smile.

"No. He was quite safe from my vengeance unless I came to the throne."

"In that case I should say the custodian need not fear the future. But please go on with your account."

"I proposed that his son and I should exchange costumes; in short, the young man was to take my place, occupying the suite of rooms assigned to me in the Castle. I told his father there was not the slightest fear of discovery, for if the Archbishop of Mayence sent some one to see that the Prince was safe, or even came himself, all the young man need do was to follow my example and keep silent, for I had said nothing from the time I was roused in my room in the Saalhof until I was lodged in Ehrenfels. I promised, if set at liberty, to keep within touch of Frankfort, where, at the first rumor of any crisis, I could return instantly to Ehrenfels.

"The custodian is a slow-minded man, although not so laggard in coming to an agreement as yourself. He took a week to turn the matter over in his mind, and then made the plunge. He is now jailer to his own son, and that young peasant lives in a style he never dreamed of before. The Archbishops are satisfied, because they believe I cannot escape from the stronghold— like yourself, holding but a poor opinion of my abilities; and their devout

Lordships know that outside the fortress no person, not even my mother, wishes me forth. I took in my wallet five hundred thalers, and fared like the peasant I seemed to be, down the Rhine, now on one side, now on the other, until I came to the ancient town of Castra Bonnensia of the Romans, which name the inhabitants now shorten to Bonn. There I found the Archbishop in residence, and not at Cologne, as I had supposed. The town being thronged with soldiers and inquisitive people of Cologne's court, I returned up the Rhine again, remembering I had gone rather far afield, and although you may not believe it, I called upon my old friend the custodian of Ehrenfels, and enjoyed an excellent meal with him, consuming some of the seductive wine that is grown on the same side of the river about a league above Ehrenfels."

"I dare say," said the merchant, "that I can give the reason for this apparently reckless visit of yours to Ehrenfels. You were in want of money, the five hundred thalers being spent."

"Sir, you are exactly in the right, and I got it, too, without nearly so much talk as I have been compelled to waste on the present occasion."

"What was your object in going down the river instead of turning to Frankfort?"

"I had become interested in my prison, and had studied methods by which it could be successfully attacked. I knew that my father allowed the Barons of the Rhine to override him, and I wondered if his wisdom was greater than I thought. Probably, said I to myself, he knew their castles to be impregnable, but, with the curiosity of youth, I desired to form an opinion of my own. I therefore lodged as a wayfarer at every castle to I could gain admittance, making friends with some underling, and getting a bed on occasion in the stables, although often I lodged within the castle itself. Thus I came to the belief, which I bring to you, that assisted by twenty fearless men I can capture any castle on the Rhine with the exception of three. And now, Herr Goebel, I have said all I intend to say. Do you discredit my story?"

The merchant gazed across at him quizzically for some time without making any reply, then he said:

"Do you think I believe you?"

"Frankly, I do not."

"If I am unable to give you the gold, I can at least furnish some good advice. Set up as a poet, good Master Roland, and weave for our delectation stories of the Rhine. I think your imagination, if cultivated, would give you a very high place among the romancers of our time."

With a patience that Herr Goebel had not expected, Roland replied:

"It grieves me to return empty-handed to my twenty friends, who last night bade me a very confident adieu."

"Yes, they will be disappointed, and I shrewdly suspect that my thousand thalers would not go towards the prosecuting of the expedition you have outlined, but rather in feasting and in wine."

"Again, sir, you are right. It is unfortunate that I am so often compelled to corroborate your statements, when all the acumen with which you credit my mind is turned towards the task of proving you a purse-proud fool, puffed up in your own conceit, and as short-sighted as an owl in the summer sunlight. However, let us stick to our text. If what I said had been true, although of course you know it isn't, you have nevertheless enough common sense to be aware that I would certainly show a pardonable reluctance about visiting my father's Palace. It is thronged with spies of the Archbishop, and although, as I have said, I am not very well known, there is a chance that one or another might recognize me, and then, almost instantly, a man on a swift horse would be on his way to Mayence. If I knew that I had been discovered, I should make at once for Ehrenfels, arriving there before an investigation was held. But my twenty comrades would wait for me in vain. Nevertheless, I shall venture into the Saalhof this very afternoon, and bring to you a letter written by my mother certifying that I am her son. Would that convince you?"

"Yes; were I sure the signature was genuine."

"Ah, there you go again! Always a loophole!"

The young man spoke in accents of such genuine despair that his host was touched despite his incredulity.

"Look you here," he said, bending across the table. "There is, of course, one chance in ten thousand that you are what you say. I have never seen the signature of the Empress, and such a missive could easily be forged by a scholar, which I take you to be. If, then, you wish to convince me, I'll put before you a test which will be greatly to your advantage, and which I will accept without the loophole."

"In Heaven's name, let's hear what it is."

"There is something that you cannot forge: the Great Seal of the Realm, attached to all documents signed by the Emperor."

"I have had no dealings with my father for years," cried the young man. "I have not even seen him these many months past. I can obtain the signature of my mother to anything I like to write, but not that of my father."

"Patience, patience," said the merchant, holding up his hand. "'Tis well known that the Empress can bend the Emperor to her will when she chooses to exert it. You see, in spite of all, I am quite taking it for granted that you are the Prince, otherwise 'twere useless to waste time in this talk. You display all the confidence of youth in speaking of the exploits you propose, and, indeed, it is cheering for a middle-aged person like myself to meet one so confident of anything in these pessimistic days. But have you considered what will happen if something goes wrong during one of your raids?"

"Nothing can go wrong. I feel no fear on that score."

"I thought as much. Very well, I will tell you what could go wrong. Some Baron may entrap you and your score, and forthwith hang you all from his battlements. Now, it is but common sense to prevent such a termination, if it be possible. Therefore seek out the Empress. Tell her that you and your twenty companions are about to embark on an enterprise greatly beneficial to the land. Say that you go incognito, and that, even should you fail, 'twill bring no discredit to your Royal House. But point out the danger of which I forewarn you. Ask her to get the signature of the Emperor attached to a safe-conduct, together with the device of the Great Seal; then if the Baron who captures you cannot read, he will still know the potency of the picture, and as there is no loophole to my acceptance of this proof, I will, for your convenience, and for my own protection, write the safe-conduct on as sound a bit of parchment as ever was signed in a palace."

Saying this, Herr Goebel rose, and went to his desk in a corner of the room, where he indited the memorial he had outlined, and, after sprinkling it with sand, presented it to Roland, who read:

"These presents warn him to whom they are presented that Roland the bearer is my son, and that what he has done has been done with my sanction, therefore he and his twenty comrades are to be held scathless, pending an appeal to me in my capital city of Frankfort.

"Whomsoever disobeys this instrument forfeits his own life, and that of his family and followers, while his possessions will be confiscated by the State."

Roland frowned.

"Doesn't it please you?" asked Goebel, his suspicions returning.

"Well, it seems to me rather a plebeian action, to attack a man's castle, and then, if captured, crawl behind a drastic threat like this."

The merchant shrugged his shoulders.

"That's a sentimental objection, but of course you need not use the document unless you wish, though I think if you see twenty-one looped ropes dangling in the air your hesitation will vanish. Oh, not on your own account," cried Goebel, as a sign of dissent from his visitor, "but because of those twenty fine young fellows who doubtless wait to drink wine with you."

"That is true," said Roland, with a sigh, folding up the stiff parchment, opening his cloak, and thrusting it under his belt, standing up as he did this.

"Bring me that parchment, bearing the Emperor's signature and the Great Seal, and you will find the golden coins awaiting you."

"Very well. At what time this evening would it please you to admit me?"

"Friends of mine are coming to-night, but they are not likely to stop long; merely a few handshakes, and a few cups of wine. I shall be ready for you when the Cathedral clock strikes ten."

With this the long conference ended, and the aged servitor in the hall showed Roland into the Fahrgasse.

As the young man proceeded down the Weckmarkt into the Saalgasse, he muttered to himself:

"The penurious old scoundrel! God keep me in future from dealing with such! To the very last he suspects me of being a forger, and has written this with his own hand, doubtless filling it with secret marks. Still, perhaps it is as well to possess such a safeguard. This is my loophole out of the coming enterprise, I fear we are all cowards, noble and merchant alike."

He walked slowly past the city front of the Palace, cogitating some means of entering without revealing his identity, but soon found that even this casual scrutiny made him an object of suspicion. He could not risk being accosted, for, if taken to the guard-room and questioned—searched, perhaps, and the sword found on him—a complication would arise adding materially to the difficulties already in his way. Quickening his pace, he passed through the Fahrthor, and so to the river-bank, where he saw that the side of the Saalhof fronting the Main was guarded merely by one or two sentries, for the mob could not gather on the surface of the waters, as it gathered on the cobble-stones of the Saalgasse and the Fahrthor.

Retracing his steps, the Prince walked rapidly until he came to the bridge, advancing to the iron Cross which commemorates the fowl sacrifice to the devil, as the first living creature venturing upon that ancient structure. Here he leaned against the parapet, gazed at the river façade of the Palace, and studied his problem. There were three sets of steps from the terrace to the water, a broad flight in the center for use upon state occasions, and a narrow flight at either end; the western staircase being that in ordinary use, and the eastern steps trodden by the servants carrying buckets of water from the river to the kitchen.

"The nearer steps," he said to himself, "offer the most feasible opportunity. I'll try them."

He counted his money, for here was probably a case for bribery. He found twenty-four gold pieces, and some loose silver. Returning the coins to his pouch, he walked to the land, and proceeded up the river until he reached a wharf where small skiffs were to let. One of these he engaged, and refusing the services of a waterman, stepped in, and drifted down the stream. He detached sword and scabbard from his belt, removed the cloak and wrapped the weapon in it, placing the folded garment out of sight under the covering at the prow. With his paddle he kept the boat close to the right bank, discovering an excellent place of concealment under the arch supporting the steps, through which the water flowed. He waited by the steps for a few moments until a scullion in long gabardine came down and dipped his bucket in the swift current.

"Here, my fine fellow," accosted Roland, "do you wish to earn a pair of gold pieces?" and he showed the yellow coins in the palm of his hand.

The menial's eyes glistened, and he cast a rapid glance over his shoulder.

"Yes," he replied breathlessly.

"Then leave your bucket where it is, and step into this wherry."

The underling, again with a cautious look around, did as he was ordered.

"Now throw off that outer garment, and give it to me."

Roland put it on over his own clothes, and flung his bonnet beside the cloak and sword, for the servant was bareheaded.

"Get under that archway, and keep out of sight until you hear me whistle."

Taking the bucket, Roland mounted the steps, and strode out of the brilliant sunlight into the comparative gloom of the corridor that led to the kitchen. He had been two hours with the merchant, and it was now the time of midday eating. Every one was hurrying to and fro, with no time to heed anything that did not pertain to the business in hand, so placing the bucket in a darkened embrasure, the intruder flung off the gabardine beside it, and searching, found a back stair which he ascended.

Once in the upper regions, he knew his way about, and proceeded directly to his mother's room, being sure at this hour to find her within. On his unannounced entrance the Empress gave utterance to an exclamation that indicated dismay rather than pleasure, but she hurried forward to meet and embrace him.

"Oh, Roland!" she cried, "what do you here? How came you to the Palace?"

"By way of the river. My boat is under the arch of the servants' stairway, and I have not a moment to lose."

"How did you escape from Ehrenfels, and why have you come here? Surely you know the Palace will be the first place searched for you?"

"There will be no search, mother. Take my word for it that no one is aware of my absence from Ehrenfels but the custodian, and for the best of reasons he dare not say a word. Do not be alarmed, I beg of you. I am free by his permission, and shall return to the Castle before he needs me. Indeed, mother, so far from jeopardizing my own safety, I am here to preserve it."

He drew from under his belt Herr Goebel's parchment, and handed it to her.

"In case it should occur to the good Archbishop, or any other noble, to hang me, I thought it best to get such a declaration signed by the Emperor, and decorated with the Great Seal of the Empire. Then, if any attempt is made on my life, as well as on my liberty, I may produce this Imperial decree, and bring my case to Frankfort."

"Surely, surely," exclaimed the agitated lady, her hands trembling as she held the document and tried to read it; "I can obtain your father's signature, but the Great Seal must be attached by the Chamberlain."

"Very good, mother. The Chamberlain will do as his Majesty orders. The seal is even more important than the signature, if it comes to that, and I am sure the Chamberlain will make no objection when the instrument is for the protection of your son's life. It is not necessary to say that I am here, or have anything to do with the matter. But lose not a moment, and give orders that no one shall enter this room."

The empress hastened away with the parchment, while the young man walked impatiently up and down the room. It seemed hours before she returned, but at last she came back with the document duly executed. Roland thrust it under his belt again, and reassuring his mother, who was now weeping on his shoulder, he tried to tear himself away. The Empress detained him until, with fumbling hands, she unlocked a drawer in a cabinet, and took from it a bag that gave forth a chink of metal as she pressed it on her son.

"I must not take it," he said. "I am quite well provided. The generous Archbishops allow me seven hundred thalers a month, which is paid with exemplary regularity."

"There are only five hundred thalers here," replied the Empress. "I wish there were more, but you must accept it, for I should feel easier in my mind to know that you possess even that much. Do they misuse you at Ehrenfels, my son?"

"Oh, no, no, no! I live like a burgomaster. You need feel no fear on my account, mother. Ehrenfels is a delightful spot, with old Bingen just across the water. I like it much better than I did Frankfort, with its howling mobs, and shall be very glad to get quit again of the city."

Then, with a hurried farewell, he left the weeping woman, and descending the back stair, secured the abandoned gabardine, put it on, and so came to the water's edge, entering into possession of his boat again. Returning the craft to its owner, he resumed sword and cloak once more, and found his way to a tavern, where he ordered a satisfactory meal.

In the evening he arrived at the Rheingold, and meeting the landlord in the large, empty, public cellar, asked that worthy if his friends had assembled yet, and was told they were all within the Kaiser cellar.

"Good!" he cried. "I said I would be gone a week, but here I am within a day. If that's not justifying a man's word, I should like to know what is. And now, landlord, set forth the best meal you can provide, with a double quantity of wine."

"For yourself, sir?"

"For all, landlord. What else? The lads have had no supper, I'll warrant."

"A little black bread has gone the rounds."

"All the more reason that we should have a huge pasty, steaming hot, or two or three of them if necessary. And your best wine, landlord. That from the Rheingau."

But the landlord demurred.

"A meal for yourself, sir, as leader, I could venture upon, but feeding a score of hungry men is a different matter. Remember, sir, I have not seen the color of their silver for many a long day, and, since these evil times have set in, I am a poor man."

"Sordid silver? Out upon silver! unless it is some silvery fish from the river, fresh and firm; and that's a good idea. We will begin with fish while you prepare the meat. 'Tis gold I deal with to-night, and most of it is for your pouch. Run your hand in here and enjoy the thrill," and Roland held open the mouth of the bag which contained his treasure.

"Ah!" cried the inn-keeper, his face aglow. "No such meal is spread to-night in Frankfort as will be set before you."

There was a great shout as Roland entered the Kaiser cellar, and a hurrah of welcome.

"Ha, renegade!" cried one. "Have you shirked your task so soon?"

"Coward, coward, poltroon!" was the cry. "I see by his face he has failed. Never mind them, Roland. Your chair at the head of the table always awaits you. There is a piece of black bread left, and though the wine is thin, it quenches thirst."

Roland flung off his cloak, hung it and the sword on a peg, and took his seat at the head of the table. Pushing away the flagons that stood near him, he drew the leathern bag from his belt, and poured the shining yellow coins on the table, at the sight of which there arose such a yell that the stout beams above them seemed to quake.

"Apologize!" demanded Roland, when the clamor quieted down. "The man who refuses to apologize, and that abjectly, must take down his sword from the peg and settle with me!"

A shout of apology was the response.

"We grovel at your feet, High Mightiness!" cried the man who had called him poltroon.

"I have taken the liberty of ordering a fish and meat supper, with a double quantity of Rudesheimer wine. Again I offer to fight any man who resents this encroachment on my part."

"I could spit you with a hand tied behind my back," cried one, "but I am of a forgiving nature, and will wait instead for the spitted fowl."

"Most of this money," continued Roland quietly, "goes, I suspect, to the landlord, as a slight recognition of past kindness, but I am promised a further supply this evening, which will be divided equally among ourselves. I ask you, therefore, to be sparing of the wine." Here he was compelled to pause for some moments, and listen to groans, hoots, howls, and the rapping of empty flagons on the stout table.

The commotion was interrupted by the entrance of the landlord, who brought with him the promised Rhine wine; for, hearing the noise, he supposed it represented impatience of the company at the delay, a mistake which no one thought it worth while to rectify. He promised that the fish would follow in a very few minutes, and went out to see that his word was kept.

"Why should we be sparing of the wine?" asked a capable drinker, who had drained his flagon before asking the question. "With all that money on the table it seems to me a scandalous proviso."

"'Tis not a command at all," replied Roland, "but merely a suggestion.

I spoke in the interests of fair-play. An appointment was made by me for ten o'clock this evening, and I wish to keep it and remain uninfluenced by wine."

"What's her name, Roland?" inquired the wine-bibber.

"I was about to divulge that secret when you interrupted me. The name is Herr Goebel."

"What! the cloth merchant on the Fahrgasse?"

"Is it cloth he deals in? I didn't know the particulars of his occupation beyond the facts that he is a merchant, and lives in the Fahrgasse. This morning I enjoyed the privilege of presenting to Herr Goebel a mutually beneficial plan which would give us all something to do."

"Oh, is Goebel to be our employer? I'm a sword forger, and work for no puny cloth merchant," said Kurzbold.

"This appointment," continued Roland, unheeding, "is set for ten o'clock, and I expect to return here before half-past, therefore—"

"Therefore we're not to drink all the wine."

"Exactly."

Their leader sat down as the landlord, followed by an assistant, entered, carrying the paraphernalia for the substantial repast, and proceeded to set the table.

When the hilarious meal was finished, the company sat for another half-hour over its wine, then Roland rose, buckled on his sword, and flung his cloak over his shoulders.

"Roland, I hope you have not sold your soul for this gold?"

"No; but I have pledged your bodies, and my own as well. Greusel, will you act as secretary and treasurer? Scrutinize the landlord's bill with a generous eye, and pay him the amount we owe. If anything is left, we will divide it equally," and with that he waved his hand to them, departing amidst a round of cheers, for the active youths were tired of idleness.

Punctuality is the politeness of kings, and as the bells of Frankfort were ringing ten o'clock, Roland knocked at the door of the merchant's house in the Fahrgasse. It was promptly opened by the ancient porter, who, after securing it again, conducted the young man up the solid stairway to the office-room on the first floor.

Ushered in, the Prince found the merchant seated in his usual chair, as if he had never moved from the spot where Roland had left him at noon that day. Half a dozen candles shed their soft radiance over the table, and on one corner of it, close by Herr Goebel's right elbow, the visitor saw a well-filled doeskin bag which he fancied might contain the thousand thalers.

"Good even to you, Herr Goebel," said the young man, doffing his bonnet. "I hope I have not trodden too closely on the heels of my appointment, thus withdrawing you prematurely from the festivities, which I trust you enjoyed all the more that you breathed the air of liberty again."

"The occasion, sir, was solemn rather than festive, for although I was glad to see my old friends again, and I believe they were glad to see me, the condition of the city is such, and growing rapidly worse, that merchants cannot rejoice when they are gathered together."

"Ah, well, Herr Goebel, we will soon mend all that. How long will it require to load your boat and choose your crew?"

"Everything can be ready by the evening of the day after to-morrow."

"You will select one of your largest barges. Remember, it must house twenty-one men besides the crew and the goods."

"Yes; I shall see that complete arrangements are made for your comfort."

"Thank you. But do not provide too much luxury. It might arouse suspicion from the Barons who search the boat."

"But the Barons will see you and your men in the boat."

"I think not. At least, we don't intend to be seen. I will call upon you again to-morrow at ten o'clock. Will you kindly order your captain to be here to meet me? I wish you to give him instructions in my presence that he is to do whatever I ask of him. We will join the boat on the Rhine between Ehrenfels and Assmannshausen. Instruct him to wait for us midway between the two places, on the right bank. And now the money, if you please."

"The money is here," said the merchant, sitting up a little more stiffly in his chair as he patted the well-stuffed bag. "The money is here if you have brought the instrument that authorizes you to take it."

"I have brought it with me, mein herr."

"Then show it to me," demanded the merchant, adjusting his horn glasses with the air of one who will not allow himself to be hoodwinked.

"With the greatest pleasure," returned the young man, standing before him. He unfastened his cloak, and allowed it to fall at his feet, then whisked out his sword, and presented the point of it to the merchant's throat.

Goebel, who had been fumbling with his glasses, suddenly became aware of his danger, and shrank back so far as his chair allowed, but the point of the sword followed him.

"What do you mean by that?" he gasped.

"I mean to show you that in this game iron is superior to gold. Your card is on the table, represented by that bag. Mine is still in my hand, and unplayed, but it takes the trick, I think. I hope you see the uselessness of resistance. You cannot even cry out, for at the first attempt a thrust of this blade cuts the very roots of utterance. It will be quite easy for me to escape, because I shall go quietly out with the bag under my cloak, telling the porter that you do not wish to be disturbed."

"It is the Prince of Thieves you are, then," said Herr Goebel.

"So it would appear. With your right hand pass that bag of gold across the table, and beg of me to accept it."

The merchant promptly did what he was told to do.

The young man put his sword back in its place, laughing joyously, but there was no answering smile on the face of Herr Goebel. As he had said, the condition of things in Frankfort, especially in that room, failed to make for merriment. Roland, without being invited, drew up a chair, and sat down at the opposite side of the table.

"Please do not attempt to dash for the door," he warned, "because I can quite easily intercept you, as I am nearer to it than you are, and more active. Call philosophy to your aid, and take whatever happens calmly. I assure you, 'tis the best way, and the only way."

He untied the cord, and poured the bulk of the gold out upon the table. The merchant watched him with amazement. For all the robber knew, the door might be opened at any moment, but he went on with numbering the coins as nonchalantly as if seated in the treasury of the Corn Exchange. When he had counted half the sum the bag contained, he poured the loose money by handfuls into the wallet that had held his mother's contribution, and pushed towards the merchant the bag, in which remained five hundred thalers.

"You are to know," he said with a smile, abandoning his bent-forward posture, "that when I visited my mother this afternoon, she quite unexpectedly gave me five hundred thalers, so I shall accept from you only half the sum I demanded this morning."

"Your mother!" cried the merchant. "Who is your mother?"

"The Empress, as I told you. Oh, at last I understand your uneasiness. You wished to see that document! Why didn't you ask for it? I asked for the money plainly enough. Well, here it is. Examine Seal and sign-manual."

The merchant minutely scrutinized the Great Seal and the signature above it.

"I don't know what to think," stammered Herr Goebel at last, gazing across the table with bewildered face.

"Think of your good fortune. A moment ago you imagined a thousand thalers were lost. Now it is but five hundred thalers invested, and you are a partner with the Royal House of the Empire."

III. DISSENSION IN THE IRONWORKERS' GUILD

Up to the time of his midnight awakening, Prince Roland had led a care-free, uneventful life. Although he received the general education supposed to be suitable for a youth of his station, he interested himself keenly in only two studies, but as one of these challenged the other, as it were, the result was entirely to the good. He was a very quiet boy, much under the influence of his mother, seeing little or nothing of his easy-going, inebriated father. It was his mother who turned her son's attention towards the literature of his country, and he became an omnivorous reader of the old monkish manuscripts with which the Palace was well supplied. Especially had his mind been attracted by the stories and legends of the Rhine. The mixture of history, fiction, and superstition which he found in these vellum pages, so daintily limned, and so artistically embellished with initial letters in gold and crimson and blue, fascinated him, and filled him with that desire to see those grim strongholds on the mountain-sides by the river, which later on resulted in his journey from Ehrenfels to Bonn, when his ingenuity, and the cupidity of his custodian, freed him from the very slight thraldom in which he was held by the Archbishop of Mayence.

If his attention had been entirely absorbed by the reading of these tomes, he might have become a mere dreamy bookworm, his intellect saturated with the sentimental and romantic mysticism permeating Germany even unto this day, and, as he cared nothing for the sports of boyhood, body might have suffered as brain developed.

But, luckily, he had been placed under the instruction of Rinaldo, the greatest master of the sword that the world had up to that period produced. Rinaldo was an Italian from Milan, whom gold tempted across the Alps for the purpose of instructing the Emperor's son in Frankfort. He was a man of grace and politeness, and young Roland took to him from the first, exhibiting such aptitude in the art of fencing that the Italian was not only proud of one who did such credit to his tuition, but came to love the youth as if he were his own son.

For the sword-making of Germany the Italian expressed the utmost contempt. The coarse weapons produced by the ironworkers of Frankfort needed strength rather than skill in their manipulation. Between the Italian method and the German was all the contrast that exists between the catching of salmon with a delicate line and a gossamer fly, or clubbing the fish to death as did the boatmen at that fishery called the Waag down the Rhine by St. Goar.

Roland listened intently and without defense to the diatribe against his country's weapons and the clumsy method of using them, but although he said nothing, he formed opinions of his own, believing there was some merit in strength which the Italian ignored; so, studying the subject, he himself invented a sword which, while lacking the stoutness of the German weapon, retained some of its stability, and was almost as easily handled as the Italian rapier, without the disadvantage of its extreme frailty.

Thus it came about that young Roland stole away from the Palace and made the acquaintance of the sword makers. The practice of fencing exercises every muscle in the body, and Roland's constant bouts with Rinaldo did more than make him a master of the weapon, with equal facility in his right arm or his left; it produced an athlete of the first quality; agile and strong, developing his physical powers universally, and not in any one direction.

Meanwhile Roland remained deplorably ignorant regarding affairs of State, this being a subject of which his mother knew nothing. The Emperor, who should have been his son's natural teacher, gave his whole attention to the wine-flagon, letting affairs drift towards disaster, allowing the power that deserted his trembling fingers to be grasped by stronger but unauthorized hands. Roland's surreptitious excursions into the city to confer with the sword makers taught him little of politics, for his conversations with these mechanics were devoted entirely to metal-working. He was hustled now and again by the turbulent mob, in going to and fro, but he did not know why it clamored, and, indeed, took little interest in the matter, conscious only that he came more and more to hate the city and loathe its inhabitants. When he could have his own way, he said to himself, he would retire to some country castle which his father owned, and there devote himself to such employment as fell in with his wishes.

But he was to receive a sharp lesson that no man, however highly placed, is independent of his fellows. He was unaware of the commotion that arose round his own name, and of the grim hanging of the leaders who chose him as their supreme head. When, bewildered and sleepy, he was aroused at midnight, and saw three armed men standing by his bedside, he received a shock that did more to awaken him than the grip of alien hands on his shoulders. During that night ride in the boat he said nothing but thought much. He had heard his mother plead for him without for a moment delaying his departure. She, evidently, was powerless. There was then in the land a force superior to that of the Throne. Something that had been said quieted his mother's fears, for at last she allowed him to go without further protest, but weeping a little, and embracing him much. There was no roughness or rudeness on the part of those who conveyed him down the river Main, and finally along the Rhine to Ehrenfels, but rather the utmost courtesy and deference, yet Roland remained silent throughout the long journey, agitated by this new, invisible, irresistible sovereignty animated with the will and power to do what it liked with him.

At the Castle of Ehrenfels he found awaiting him no rigorous imprisonment. He was treated as a welcome guest of an invisible host. It was his conversations with the garrulous custodian, who was a shrewd observer of the passing show, that gradually awakened the young Prince to some familiarity with the affairs of the country. He learned now in what a deplorable state the capital stood, through the ever-increasing exactions of the robber Barons along the Rhine. He asked his instructor why the merchants did not send their goods by some other route, which was a very natural query, but was told there existed no other route. A great forest extended for the most part between Frankfort and Cologne, and through the wilderness were no roads, for even those constructed by the Romans had been allowed to fall into decay; overgrown with trees, Nature thus destroying the neglected handiwork of man; the forest reclaiming its own.

"Indeed," continued the custodian, "for the last ten years things have been going to the devil, for the lack of a strong hand in the capital. A strong hand is needed by nobles and outlaws alike. We want a new Frederick

Barbarossa; the hangman's rope and the torch judiciously applied might be the saving of the country."

Ehrenfels, belonging to the Archbishop, was not a nest of piracy, and so its guardian could talk in this manner if he chose, but had he uttered these sentiments farther down the Rhine, he would himself have experienced the utility of the hangman's rope. Roland, knowing by this time who had taken him into custody, said:

"Why do not the three Archbishops put a stop to it? They possess the power."

The old jailer shrugged his shoulders.

"My chief, the great prelate of Mayence, would do it speedily enough if he stood alone, but the Archbishops of Treves have ever been robbers themselves, and Cologne is little better, therefore they neutralize one another. No two of them will allow the other to act, fearing he may gain in power, and thus upset the balance of responsibility, which I assure your Highness is very nicely adjusted. Each of the three claim allegiance from this Baron or the other, and although the Archbishops themselves may not lay toll directly on the Rhine, their ardent partisans do, which produces a deadlock."

Thus Roland received an education not to be had in palaces, and, saying little beyond asking an occasional question, he thought much, and came to certain conclusions. He arrived at an ambition to open the lordly Rhine and spent his time gathering knowledge and forming plans.

Twelve hours after receiving the five hundred thalers from the merchant, he again presented himself at the now familiar door in the Fahrgasse. In the room on the first floor he found with Herr Goebel a thick-set, heavily-bearded, weather-beaten man, who stood bonnet in hand while the merchant gave him final instructions.

"Good-morning, Sir Roland," cried Herr Goebel cheerfully. He exhibited no resentment for his treatment of the night before, and apparently daylight brought with it renewed confidence that the young man might succeed in his mission. There was now no hesitation in the merchant's manner; alert and decided, all mistrust seemed to have vanished. "This is Captain Blumenfels, whom I put in charge of the barge, and who has gathered together a crew on which he can depend although, of course, you must not expect them to fight."

"No," said Roland, "I shall attend to that portion of the enterprise."

"Now, Captain Blumenfels," continued Herr Goebel, "this young man is commander. You are to obey him in every particular, just as you would obey me."

The captain bowed without speaking.

"I shall not detain you any longer, captain, as you will be anxious to see the bales disposed of to your liking on the barge."

The captain thereupon took himself off, and Roland came to the conclusion that he liked this rough-and-ready mariner with so little to say for himself; a silent man of action, evidently.

Herr Goebel turned his attention to Roland.

"I have ordered bales of cloth to the value of a trifle more than four thousand thalers to be placed in the barge," he said. "The bales are numbered, and I have given the captain an inventory showing the price of each. I suppose you despise our vulgar traffic, and, indeed, I had no thought of asking so highly placed a person as yourself to sell my goods, therefore Blumenfels will superintend the marketing when you reach Cologne—that is, if you ever get so far."

"Your pardon, Herr Goebel, but I have my own plans regarding the disposal of your goods. I intend to be quit of them long before I see Cologne. Indeed, should I prosper, I hope your boat will set its nose southward for the return journey some distance this side of Coblentz."

The merchant gazed up at him in astonishment.

"Your design is impossible. There is no sale for cloth nearer than Coblentz. Your remarks prove you unacquainted with the river."

"I have walked every foot of both sides of the river between Ehrenfels and Bonn. There are many wealthy castles on this side of Coblentz."

"True, my good sir, true; but how became they wealthy? Simply by robbing the merchants. Are you not aware that each of these castles is inhabited by a titled brigand? You surely do not expect to sell my cloth to the Barons?"

"Why not? Remember how long it is since a cloth-barge went down the Rhine. Think for a moment of the arduous life which these Barons lead, hunting the boar, the bear, and the deer, tearing recklessly through thicket and over forest-covered ground. Why, our noble friends must be in rags by this time, or clad in the skins of the beasts they kill! They will be delighted to see and handle a piece of well-woven cloth once more."

For a full minute the merchant gaped aghast at this senseless talk so seriously put forward; then a smile came to his lips.

"Prince Roland, I begin to understand you. Your words are on a par with the practical joke you played upon me so successfully last night. Of course, you know as well as I that the Barons will buy nothing. They will take such goods as they want if you but give them opportunity. What you say is merely your way of intimating it is none of my affair how the goods are disposed of, so long as you hand over to me four thousand thalers."

"Four thousand five hundred, if you please."

"I shall be quite content with the four thousand, regarding the extra five hundred as paid for services rendered. Now, can I do anything further to aid you?"

"Yes. I wish you to send a man on horseback to Lorch, there to await the barge. Choose a man as silent as your captain; one whom you trust implicitly, for I hope to send back with him four thousand five hundred thalers, and also some additional gold, which I beg of you to keep safely for me until I return."

"Prince Roland, there can be no gold for me at Lorch."

"Dispatch a trustworthy man in case I receive the money. You will be anxious to know how we prosper, and I can at least forward a budget of news."

"But should there be gold, he cannot return safely with it to Frankfort."

"Oh, yes, if he keeps to the eastern bank of the Rhine. There is no castle between Lorch and Frankfort except Ehrenfels, and that, being the property of the Archbishop, may be passed safely."

"Very well. The man shall await you at Lorch. Inquire for Herr Kruger at Mergler's Inn."

That night, in the Kaiser cellar, another excellent supper was spread before the members of the metal-workers' league. It was quite as hilarious as the banquet of the night before; perhaps more so, because now, for the first time in months, the athletic young men were well fed, with money in their pouches. Each was clad in a new suit of clothes. Nothing like uniformity in costume had been attempted, there being but one day in which to replenish the wardrobes, which involved the acquiring of garments already made. However no trouble was experienced about this, for each branch of the metal-workers had its own recognized outfit, which was kept on hand in all sizes by various dealers catering to the wants of artisans, from apprentices to masters of their trade. The costumes were admirably adapted to the use for which they were intended. There was nothing superfluous in their make-up, and, being loosely cut, they allowed ample play to stalwart limbs. For dealing with metal the wearers required a cloth tightly woven, of a texture as nearly as possible resembling leather, and better accouterment for a rough-and-tumble, freebooter's excursion could not have been found, short of coats of mail, or, failing that, of leather itself.

Roland appeared in the trousers and doublet of a sword maker, and his comrades cheered loudly when he threw off his cloak and displayed for the first time that he was actually one of themselves. Hitherto something in the fashioning of his wearing apparel had in a manner differentiated him from the rest of the company, but now nothing in his dress indicated that he was leader of the coterie, and this pleased the independent metal-workers.

The previous night, after the landlord's bill was generously liquidated, each man had received upwards of thirty thalers. Roland then related to them his adventure with the merchant, and the result of his sword-play in the vicinity of Herr Goebel's throat. Two accomplishments he possessed endeared Roland to his comrades: first, the ability to sing a good song; and second, his talent for telling an interesting story, whether it was a personal adventure, a legend of the Rhine, or some tale of the gnomes which, as every one knows, haunt the gloomy forests in the mountain regions. His account of the evening spent with Herr Goebel aroused much laughter and applause, which greatly augmented when the material advantages of the interview were distributed among the guild.

This evening he purposed making a still more important disclosure; thus when the meal was finished, and the landlord, after replenishing the flagons, had retired, the new sword maker rose in his place at the head of the table.

"I crave your strict attention for a few minutes. Although I refused to confide my plans to Herr Goebel, I consider it my duty to inform you minutely of what is before us, and if I speak with some solemnity, it is because I realize we may never again meet around this table. We depart from Frankfort to-morrow upon a hazardous expedition, and some of us may not return."

"Oh, I say, Roland," protested Conrad Kurzbold, "don't mar a jovial evening with a note of tragedy. It's bad art, you know."

Kurzbold was one of the three actual sword makers, and had been president of the guild until he gave place to Roland. He was the oldest of the company; an ambitious man, a glib talker, with great influence among his fellows, and a natural leader of them. What he said generally represented the opinion of the gathering.

"For once, Kurzbold, I must ask you to excuse me," persisted Roland. "It is necessary that on this, the last, opportunity I should place before you exactly what I intend to do. I am very anxious not to minimize the danger. I wish no man to follow me blindfold, thus I speak early in the evening, that you may not be influenced by the enthusiasm of wine in coming to a decision. I desire each man here to estimate the risk, and choose, before we separate to-night, whether or not he will accompany the expedition.

"Here is the compact made with Herr Goebel: I promised that, with the help of my comrades, I would endeavor to open the Rhine to mercantile traffic. On the strength of such promise he gave me the money."

At this announcement rose a wild round of applause, and with the thunder of flagons on the table, and the shouting of each member, no single voice could make itself heard above the tumult. These lads had no conception of the perils they were to face, and Roland alone remained imperturbable, becoming more and more serious as the uproar went on. When at last quiet was restored, he continued, with a gravity in striking contrast to the hilarity of his audience:

"Herr Goebel is filling his largest barge with bales of cloth, and he has engaged an efficient crew, and a capable captain who will assume charge of the navigation. The barge will proceed to-morrow night down the Main, leaving Frankfort as unostentatiously as possible, while we march across the country to Assmannshausen, and there join this craft. It is essential that no hint of our intention shall spread abroad in gossipy Frankfort, therefore, depending on Captain Blumenfels to get his boat clear of the city without observation, and before the moon rises, I ask you to leave to-morrow separately by different gates, meeting me at Hochst, something more than two leagues down the river. I dare say you all know the Elector's palace, whose beautiful tower is a landmark for the country round."

"I protest against such a rendezvous," objected Kurzbold. "Make it the tavern of the Nassauer Hof, Roland. We shall all be thirsty after a walk of two leagues."

"Not at that time in the morning, I hope," said Roland, "for I shall await you in the shadow of the tower at nine o'clock. Let every man drink his fill to-night, for I intend to lead a sober company from Hochst to-morrow."

"Oh, you're optimistic, Roland," cried John Gensbein. "Give us till twelve o'clock to cool our heads."

"Drink all you wish this evening," repeated Roland, "but to-morrow we begin our work, with a long day's march ahead of us, so nine is none too early for a start from Hochst."

"Sufficient to the day is the wine thereof," said Conrad Kurzbold, rising to his feet. "Wine, blessed liquor as it is, possesses nevertheless one defect, which blot on its escutcheon is that it cannot carry over till next day, except in so far as a headache is concerned, and a certain dryness of the mouth. It is futile to bid us lay in a supply to-night that will be of any use to-morrow morning. For my part, I give you warning, Roland, that I shall make directly for the Nassauer Hof, or for the Schone Aussicht, where they keep most excellent vintages."

To this declaration Roland made no reply, but continued his explanatory remarks.

"We shall join the barge, as I have said, above Assmannshausen, probably at night, and then cross directly over the river. The first castle with which I intend to deal is that celebrated robber's roost, Rheinstein, standing two hundred and sixty feet above the water. Disembarking about a league up the river from Rheinstein, before daybreak we will all lie concealed in the forest within sight of the Castle gates. When the sun is well risen, Captain Blumenfels will navigate his boat down the river, and as it approaches Rheinstein we shall probably enjoy the privilege of seeing the gates open wide, as the company from the Castle descend precipitously to the water. While they rifle the barge we shall rifle the Castle, overpowering whoever we may find there, and taking in return for the cloth they steal such gold or silver as the treasury affords. We will then imprison all within the Castle, so that a premature alarm may not be given. If we are hurried, we may lock them in cellars, or place them in dungeons, then leave the Castle with our booty, but I do not purpose descending to the river until we have traversed a league or more of the mountain forest, where we may remain concealed until the barge appears, and so take ship again.

"The next castle is Falkenberg, the third Sonneck, both on the same side of the river as Rheinstein, and within a short distance from the stronghold, but the plan with each being the same as that already outlined, it is not necessary for me to repeat it."

"An excellent arrangement!" cried several; but John Gensbein spoke up in criticism.

"Is there to be no fighting?" he asked. "I expected you to say that after we had secured the gold we would fall on the robbers to the rear, and smite them hip and thigh."

"There is likely to be all the fighting you can wish for," replied Roland, "for at some point our scheme may go awry. It is not my intention to attack, but I expect you to fight like heroes in our own defense."

"I agree with Herr Roland," put in Conrad Kurzbold, rising to his feet. "If we purpose to win our way down to Cologne, it is unnecessary to search for trouble, because we shall find enough of it awaiting us at one point or another. But Roland stopped his account at what seems to me the most interesting juncture. What is the destination of the gold we loot from the castles?"

"The first call upon our accumulation will be the payment of four thousand five hundred thalers to Herr Goebel."

"Oh, damn the merchant!" cried Conrad. "We are risking our lives, and I don't see why he should reach out his claws. He will profit enough through our exertions if we open the Rhine."

"True; but that was the bargain I made with him. We risk our lives, as you say, but he risks his goods, besides providing barge, captain, and crew. He also furnished us with the five hundred thalers now in our pockets. We must deal honestly with the man who has supported us in the beginning."

"Oh, very well," growled Kurzbold, "have it your own way; but in my opinion the merchants should combine and raise a fund with which to reward us for our exertions if we succeed. Still, I shall not press my contention in the face of an overwhelming sentiment against me. However, I should like to speak to our leader on one matter which it seemed ungracious to mention last night. The merchant offered him a thousand thalers in gold, and he, with a generosity which I must point out to him was exercised at our expense, returned half that money to Herr Goebel. I confess that all I received has been spent; my hand is lonesome when it enters my pouch. I should be glad of that portion which might have been mine (and when I speak for myself, I speak for all) were it not for the misplaced prodigality of our leader who, possessing the money, was so thoughtless of our fellowship that he actually handed over five hundred thalers to a man who had not the slightest claim upon it."

"Herr Kurzbold," said Roland, with some severity, "many penniless nights passed over our heads in this room. If you know so much better than I how to procure money, why did you not do so? I should not venture to criticise a man who, without any effort on my part, placed thirty thalers at my disposal."

There was a great clamor at this, every one except Kurzbold, who stood stubbornly in his place, and Gensbein, who sat next to him, becoming vociferous in defense of their leader.

"It is uncomrade-like," cried Ebearhard above the din, "to spend the money and then growl."

"I speak in the interests of us all," shouted Kurzbold. "In the interests of our leader, no less than ourselves," but the others howled him down.

Roland, holding up his right hand, seemed to request silence and obtained it.

"I am rather glad," he said, "that this discussion has arisen, because there is still time to amend our programme. Herr Goebel's barge will not be loaded until to-morrow night, so the order may even yet be countermanded. The five hundred thalers which belonged to me I say nothing about, but the five hundred advanced by Herr Goebel must be returned to him unless we are in perfect unanimity."

At this suggestion Kurzbold sat down with some suddenness.

"I told you, when I left this room, promising to find the money within a week, that one condition was the backing of my fellows. You empowered me to pledge the efforts of our club as though it contained but one man. If that promise is not to be kept in spirit as well as in letter, I shall retire from the position I now hold, and you may elect in my stead Conrad Kurzbold, John Gensbein, or any one else that pleases you. But first I must be in a position to give back intact Herr Goebel's money; then, as I have divulged to you my plans, Conrad Kurzbold may approach him, and make better terms than I was able to arrange."

There were cries of "Nonsense! Nonsense!" "Don't take a little opposition in that spirit, Roland." "We are all free-speaking comrades, you know." "You are our leader, and must remain so."

Kurzbold rose to his feet for the third time.

"Literally and figuratively, my friend Roland has me on the hip, for my hip-pocket contains no money, and it is impossible for me to refund. I imagine, if the truth were told, we are all more or less in the same condition, for we have had equipment to buy, and what-not."

"Also Hochheimer," said one, at which there was a laugh, as Kurzbold was noted for his love of good wine. Up to this point Roland had carried the assemblage with him, but now he made an injudicious remark that instantly changed the spirit of the room.

"I am astonished," he said, "that any objection should be made to the fair treatment of Herr Goebel, for you are all of the merchant class, and should therefore hold by one of your own order."

He could proceed no farther. Standing there, pale and determined, he was simply stormed down. His ignorance of affairs, of which on several occasions the merchant himself had complained, led him quite unconsciously to touch the pride of his hearers. It was John Gensbein who angrily gave expression to the sentiment of the meeting.

"To what class do you belong, I should like to know? Do you claim affinity with the merchant class? If you do, you are no leader of ours. I inform you, sir, that we are skilled artisans, with the craft to turn out creditable work, while the merchants are merely the vendors of our products. Which, therefore, takes the higher place in a community, and which deserves it better: he who with artistic instinct unites the efforts of brain and hand to produce wares that are at once beautiful and useful, or he who merely chaffers over his counter to get as much lucre as he can for the creations that come from our benches?"

To Roland's aristocratic mind, every man who lacked noble blood in his veins stood on the same level, and it astonished him that any mere plebeian should claim precedence over another. He himself felt immeasurably superior to those present, sensible of a fathomless gulf between him and them, which he, in his condescension, might cross as suited his whim, but over which none might follow him back again; and this, he was well aware, they would be the first to admit did they but know his actual rank.

For a moment he was tempted to acknowledge his identity, and crush them by throwing the crown at their heads, but some hitherto undiscovered stubbornness in his nature asserted itself, arousing a determination to stand or fall by whatever strength of character he might possess.

"I withdraw that remark," he said, as soon as he could obtain a hearing. "I not only withdraw it, but I apologize to you for my folly in making it. It was merely thoughtlessness on my part, and, resting on your generosity, I should like you to consider the words unsaid."

Once more eighteen of the twenty swung round to his side. Roland now turned his attention to Conrad Kurzbold, ignoring John Gensbein, who had sat down flushed after his declamation, bewildered by the mutability of the many as Coriolanus had been before him.

"Herr Kurzbold," began Roland sternly, "have you any further criticism to offer?"

"No; but I stand by what I have already said."

"Well, I thank you for your honest expression of that determination, and I announce that you cannot accompany this expedition."

Again Roland instantaneously lost the confidence of his auditors, and they were not slow in making him of the fact.

"This is simply tyranny," said Ebearhard. "If a man may not open his mouth without running danger of expulsion, then all comradeship is at an end, and I take it that good comradeship is the pivot on which this organization turns. I do not remember that we ever placed it in the power of our president merely by his own word to cast out one of us from the fellowship. I may add, Roland, that you seem to harbor strange ideas concerning rank and power. I have been a member of this guild much longer than you, and perhaps understand better its purpose. Our leader is not elected to govern a band of serfs. Indeed, and I say it subject to correction from my friends, the very opposite is the case. Our leader is our servant, and must conduct himself as we order. It is not for him to lay down the law to us, but whatever laws exist for our governance, and I thank Heaven there are few of them, must be settled in conclave by a majority of the league."

"Right! Right!" was the unanimous cry, and when Ebearhard sat down all were seated except Roland, who stood at the end of the table with pale face and compressed lips.

"We are," he said, "about to set out against the Barons of the Rhine, entrenched in their strong castles. Hitherto these men have been completely successful, defying alike the Government and the people. It was my hope that we might reverse this condition of things. Now, Brother Ebearhard, name me a single Baron along the whole length of the Rhine who would permit one of his men-at-arms to bandy words with him on any subject whatever."

"I should hope," replied Ebearhard, "that we do not model our conduct after that of a robber."

"The robbers, I beg to point out to you, Ebearhard, are successful. It is success we are after, also a portion of that gold of which Herr Kurzbold has pathetically proclaimed his need."

"Do you consider us your men-at-arms, then, in the same sense that a Rhine Baron would employ the term?"

"Certainly."

"You claim the liberty of expelling any one you choose?"

"Yes; I claim the liberty to hang any of you if I find it necessary."

"Oh, the devil!" cried Ebearhard, sitting down as if this went beyond him. He gazed up and down the table as much as to say, "I leave this in your hands, gentlemen."

The meeting gave immediate expression of its agreement with Ebearhard.

"Gentlemen," said Roland, "I insist that Conrad Kurzbold apologizes to me for the expressions he has used, and promises not again to offend in like manner."

"I'll do nothing of the sort," asserted Kurzbold, with equal firmness.

"In that case," exclaimed Roland, "I shall retire, and I ask you to put me in a position to repay Herr Goebel the money I extracted from him. I resign the very thankless office of so-called leadership."

At this several wallets came out upon the table, but their contents clinked rather weakly. The majority of the guild sat silent and sobered by the crisis that had so unexpectedly come upon them. Joseph Greusel, seeing that no one else made a move, uprose, and spoke slowly. He was a man who never had much to say for himself; a listener rather than a talker, in whom Roland reposed great confidence, believing him to be one who would not flinch if trial came, and he had determined to make Greusel his lieutenant if the expedition was not wrecked before it set out.

"My friends," said Greusel gloomily, "we have arrived at a deadlock, and I should not venture to speak but that I see no one else ready to make a suggestion. I cannot claim to be non-partisan in the matter. This crisis has been unnecessarily brought about by what I state firmly is a most ungenerous attack on the part of Conrad Kurzbold."

There were murmurs of dissent, but Greusel proceeded stolidly, taking no notice.

"It is not disputed that Kurzbold accepted the money from Roland last night, spent it to-day, and now comes penniless amongst us, quite unable to refund the amount when his unjust remarks produce their natural effect. He is like a man who makes a wager knowing he hasn't the money to pay should he lose. If Roland retires from this guild, I retire also, ashamed to keep company with men who uphold a trick worthy of a ruined gambler."

"My dear Joseph," cried Ebearhard, springing up with a laugh, "you were misnamed in your infancy. You should have been called Herod, practically justifying a slaughter of us innocents."

"I stand by Benjamin," growled Gruesel, "the youngest and most capable of our circle; the one who produced the money while all the rest of us talked."

"You never talked till now, Joseph," said Ebearhard, still trying to ease the situation with a laugh, "and what you say is not only deplorably severe, but uttered, as I will show you, upon entirely mistaken grounds. We did not, and do not, support Conrad Kurzbold in what he said at first. Now you rate us as if we were no better than thieves. Dishonest gamblers, you call us, and Lord knows what else, and then you threaten withdrawal. I submit that your diatribe is quite undeserved. We all condemn Kurzbold for censuring Roland's generosity to the merchant, unanimously upholding Roland in that action, and have said so plainly enough. What we object to is this: Roland arrogates to himself power which he does not possess, of peremptorily expelling any member whose remarks displease him. Surely you cannot support him in that any more than we."

"Let us take one thing at a time," resumed Greusel, "not forgetting from whom came the original provocation. I must know where we stand. I therefore move a vote of censure on Conrad Kurzbold for his unmerited attack upon our president anent his dealings with Herr Goebel."

"I second that with great pleasure," said Ebearhard.

"Now, as we cannot ask our leader to put that motion, I shall take the liberty of submitting it myself," continued Greusel. "All in favor of the vote of censure which you have heard, make it manifest by standing up."

Every one arose except Roland, Gensbein, and Kurzbold.

"There, we have removed that obstacle to a clear understanding of the case, and before I formally deliver this vote of censure to Herr Kurzbold, I request him to reconsider his position, and of his own motion to make such delivery unnecessary.

"If it is the case that Roland assumes authority to expel whom he pleases from this guild, I shall not support him."

"It is the case! It is the case!" shouted several.

"Pardon me, comrades; I have the floor," continued Greusel. "I am not attempting oratory, but trying to disentangle a skein in which we have involved ourselves. I wish to receive neither applause nor hissing until I have finished the business. You say it is the case. I say it is not. Roland gave Herr Kurzbold the alternative either of apologizing or of paying over the money, so that it might be returned to the merchant. As I understand the matter, our president does not insist on Kurzbold leaving the guild, but merely announces his own withdrawal from it. You have allowed Kurzbold to put you in the position of being compelled to choose between himself and Roland. If you are logical men you cannot pass a vote of censure on Kurzbold, and then choose him instead of Roland. I therefore move a vote of confidence in our chief, the man who has produced the money, a thousand thalers in all, half of which was his own, and has divided it equally amongst us, when the landlord's bill was paid, withholding not a single thaler, nor arrogating—I think that was your word, friend Ebearhard—to himself a stiver more of the money than each of the others received. While Kurzbold has prated of comradeship, Roland has given us an excellent example of it, and I think he deserves our warmest thanks and our cordial support. I therefore submit to you the following motion: This meeting tenders to the president its warmest thanks for his recent efforts on behalf of the guild, and begs to assure him of its most strenuous assistance in carrying out the project he has put before it to-night."

"Joseph," said Ebearhard, rising, with his usual laugh, "you are a very clever man, although you usually persist in hiding your light under a bushel. I desire to associate myself with the expressions you have used, and therefore second your motion."

"I now put the resolution which you have all heard," said Greusel, "and I ask those in favor of it to stand."

Every one stood up promptly enough except the two recalcitrants, and of those two John Gensbein showed signs of hesitation and uneasiness. He half rose, sat down again; then, apparently at the urging of the man next him, stood up, a picture of irresolution. Kurzbold, finding himself now alone, laughed, and got upon his feet, thus making the vote unanimous. As the company seated itself, Greusel turned to the president.

"Sir, it is said that all's well that ends well. It gives me pleasure to tender you the unanimous vote of thanks and confidence of the iron-workers' guild, and before calling upon you to make any reply, if such should be your intention, I will ask Conrad Kurzbold to say a few words, which I am sure we shall all be delighted to hear."

Kurzbold rose bravely enough, in spite of the fact that Joseph Greusel's diplomacy had made a complete separation between him and all the others.

"I should like to say," he began, with an air of casual indifference, "that my first mention of the money was wholly in jest. Our friend Roland took my remarks seriously, which, of course, I should not have resented, and there is little use in recapitulating what followed. As, however, my utterances gave offense which was not intended by me, I have no hesitation in apologizing for them, and withdrawing the ill-advised sentences. No one here feels a greater appreciation of what our president has done than I, and I hope he will accept my apology in the same spirit in which it is tendered."

"Now, Master of the Guild," said Greusel, and Roland took the floor once more.

"I have nothing to say but 'Thank you.' The antagonists whom we hope to meet are men brave, determined, and ruthless. If any one in this company holds rancor against me, I ask him to turn it towards the Barons, and punish me after the expedition is accomplished. Let us tolerate no disagreements in face of the foe."

The young man took his cloak and sword from the peg on which they hung, passed down along the table, and thrust across his hand to Kurzbold, who shook it warmly. Arriving at the door, Roland turned round.

569

"I wish to see Captain Blumenfels, and give him final instructions regarding our rendezvous on the Rhine, so good-night. I hope to meet you all under the shadow of the Elector's tower in Hochst to-morrow morning at nine," and with that the president departed, being too inexperienced to know that soft words do not always turn away wrath, and that mutiny is seldom quelled with a handshake.

IV. THE DISTURBING JOURNEY OF FATHER AMBROSE

The setting summer sun shone full on the western side of Sayn Castle, sending the shadow of that tenth-century edifice far along the greensward of the upper valley. Upon a balcony, perched like a swallow's nest against the eastern end of Sayn Castle, a lovely girl of eighteen leaned, meditating, with arms resting on the balustrade, the harshness of whose stone surface was nullified by the soft texture of a gaudily-covered robe flung over it. This ample cloth, brought from the East by a Crusading ancestor of the girl, made a gay patch of scarlet and gold against the somber side of the Castle.

The youthful Countess Hildegunde von Sayn watched the slow oncoming of a monk, evidently tired, who toiled along the hillside deep in the shadow of the Castle, as if its cool shade was grateful to him. Belonging, as he did, to the very practical Order of the Benedictines, whose belief was in work sanctioned by prayer, the Reverend Father did not deny himself this temporary refuge from the hot rays of the sun, which had poured down upon him all day.

Looking up as he approached the stronghold, and seeing the girl, little dreaming of the frivolous mission she would propose, he waved his hand to her, and she responded gracefully with a similar gesture.

Indeed, however strongly the monk might disapprove, there was much to be said in favor of the resolution to which the young lady had come. She was well educated, probably the richest heiress in Germany, and carefully as the pious Sisters of Nonnenwerth Convent may have concealed the fact from her, she was extremely beautiful, and knew it, and although the valley of the Saynbach was a very haven of peace and prosperity, the girl became just a trifle lonely, and yearned to know something of life and the Court in Frankfort, to which her high rank certainly entitled her.

It is true that very disquieting rumors had reached her concerning the condition of things in the capital city; nevertheless she determined to learn from an authoritative source whether or not it was safe to take up a temporary residence in Frankfort, and for this purpose the reluctant Father Ambrose would journey southward.

Father Ambrose was more than sixty years old, and if he had belonged to the world, instead of to religion, would have been entitled to the name Henry von Sayn. His presence in the Benedictine Order was proof of the fact that money will not accomplish everything. His famous, or perhaps we should say infamous, ancestor, Count Henry III. of Sayn, who died in 1246, was a robber and a murderer, justly esteemed the terror of the Rhine. Concealed as it was in the Sayn valley, half a league from the great river, the situation of his stronghold favored his depredations. He filled his warehousing rooms with merchandise from barges going down the river, and with gold seized from unhappy merchants on their way up. He thought no more of cutting a throat than of cutting a purse, and it was only when he became amazingly wealthy that the increase of years brought trouble to a conscience which all men thought had ceased to exist. Thereupon, for the welfare of his soul, he built the Abbey of Sayn, and provided for the monks therein. Yet, when he came to die, he entertained fearsome, but admittedly well-founded doubts regarding his future state, so he proceeded to sanctify a treasure no longer of any use to him, by bequeathing it to the Church, driving, however, a bargain by which he received assurance that his body should rest quietly in the tomb he had prepared for himself within the Abbey walls.

He was buried with impressive ceremony, and the monks he had endowed did everything to carry out their share of the pact. The tomb was staunchly built with stones so heavy that no ordinary ghost could have emerged therefrom, but to be doubly sure a gigantic log was placed on top of it, strongly clamped down with concealed bands of iron, and, so that this log might not reveal its purpose, the monks cunningly carved it into some semblance of Henry himself, until it seemed a recumbent statue of the late villainous Count.

But despite such thoughtfulness their plan failed, for when next they visited the tomb the statue lay prone, face downwards, as if some irresistible, unseen power had flung it to the stone flags of the floor. Replacing the statue, and watching by the tomb, was found to be of little use. The watchers invariably fell asleep, and the great wooden figure, which during their last waking moments lay gazing towards the roof, was now on its face on the monastery floor, peering down in the opposite direction, and this somehow was regarded by the brethren as a fact of ominous significance.

The new Count von Sayn, heir to the title and estate of the late Henry III. was a gloomy, pious man, very different indeed from his turbulent predecessor. Naturally he was much perturbed by the conduct of the wooden statue. At first he affected disbelief in the phenomena despite the assurances of the monks, and later on the simple brethren deeply regretted they had made any mention of the manifestations. The new Count himself took up the task of watching, and paced all night before the tomb of the third Henry. He was not a man to fall asleep while engaged on such a somber mission, and the outcome of his vigil was so amazing that in the morning he gathered the brethren together in the great hall of the Abbey, that he might relate to them his experience.

The wooden statue had turned over, and fallen to the floor, as was its habit, but on this occasion it groaned as it fell. This mournful sound struck terror into the heart of the lonely watcher, who now, he confessed, regretted he had not accepted the offer of the monks to share his midnight surveillance. The courage of the House of Sayn is, however, a well-known quality, and, notwithstanding his piety, the new holder of the title was possessed of it, for although admitting a momentary impulse towards flight, and the calling for assistance which the monks would readily have given, he stood his ground, and in trembling voice asked what he could do to forward the contentment of his deceased relative.

The statue replied, still face downward on the stone floor, that never could the late wicked Count rest in peace unless the heir to his titles and lands should take upon himself the sins Henry had committed during his life, while a younger member of the family should become a monk of the Benedictine Order, and daily intercede for the welfare of his soul.

"With extreme reluctance," continued the devout nobleman, "I gave my assent to this unwelcome proposal, providing only that it should receive the sanction of the Abbot and brethren of the Monastery of Sayn, hoping by a life of continuous rectitude to annul, in some measure at least, the evil works of Henry III.; and that holy sanction I now request, trusting if given it may remove any doubts regarding the righteousness of my promise."

Here the Count bowed low to the enthroned Abbot and, with less reverence, to the assembled brethren. The Abbot rose to his feet, and in a few well-chosen words complimented the nobleman on the sacrifice he made, predicting that it would redound greatly to his spiritual welfare. Speaking for himself, he had no hesitation in giving the required sanction, but as the Count made it a proviso that the brethren should concur, he now requested their acquiescence.

This was accorded in silent unanimity, whereupon Count von Sayn, deeply sighing as one accepting a burden almost too heavy to bear, spoke with a tremor of grief in his voice.

"It is not for me," he said, "to question your wisdom, nor shrink from my allotted task. After all, I am but human, and up to this decisive moment had hoped, alas! in vain, that some one more worthy than I might be chosen in my place. The most grievous part of the undertaking, so far as I am concerned, was outlined in the last words spoken by the wooden statue. The evil deeds my ancestor has committed will in time be obliterated by the prayers of the younger member of my family who becomes a monk, but the accumulated gold carries with it a continual curse, which can be wiped off each coin only by that coin benefiting the merchants who have been robbed. The contamination of this metal, therefore, I must bear, for it adds to the agony of my ancestor that, little realizing what he was doing, he bequeathed this poisonous dross to the Abbey he founded. I am required to lend it in Frankfort, upon undoubted security and suitable usury, that it may stimulate and fertilize the commerce of the land, much as the contents of a compost heap, disagreeable in the senses, and defiling to him who handles it, when spread upon the fields results in the production of flower, fruit, and food, giving fragrance, delight, and sustenance to the human frame."

The count, bowing for the third time to the conclave, passed from its presence with mournful step and sorrowful countenance; whereupon the brethren, seeing themselves thus denuded of wealth they had hoped to enjoy, gave utterance to a groan doubtless much greater in volume than that emitted by the carven statue, which wooden figure may be seen to-day in the museum of the modern Castle of Sayn by any one who cares to spend the fifty pfennigs charged for admission.

All that has been related happened generations before the time when the Countess Hildegunde reigned as head of the House of Sayn, but Father Ambrose formed a link with the past in that he was the present scion of Sayn who, as a Benedictine, daily offered prayer for the repose of the wicked Henry III. The gold which Henry's immediate successor so craftily deflected from the monks seemed to be blessed rather than cursed, for under the care of that subtle manager it multiplied greatly in Frankfort, and scandal-mongers asserted that besides receiving the usury exacted, the pietistic Count tapped the treasure-casks of upward-sailing Rhine merchants quite as successfully, if more quietly, than the profane Henry had done. Thus the House of Sayn was one of the richest in Germany.

The aged monk and the youthful Countess were distant relatives, but he regarded her as a daughter, and her affection was given to him as to a father, in other than the spiritual sense.

In his youth Ambrose the Benedictine, because of his eloquence in discourse, and also on account of his aristocratic rank, officiated at the court in Frankfort. Later, he became spiritual and temporal adviser to that great prelate, the Archbishop of Cologne, and the Archbishop, being guardian of the Countess von Sayn, sent Father Ambrose to the castle of his ancestor to look after the affairs of Sayn, both religious and material. Under his gentle rule the great wealth of his House increased, although he, the cause of prosperity, had no share in the riches he produced, for, as has been written of the Benedictines:

"It was as teachers of ... scientific agriculture, as drainers of fens and morasses, as clearers of forests, as makers of roads, as tillers of the reclaimed soil, as architects of durable and even stately buildings, as exhibiting a visible type of orderly government, as establishing the superiority of peace over war as the normal condition of life, as students in the library which the rule set up in every monastery, as the masters in schools open not merely to their own postulants but to the children of secular families also, that they won their high place in history as benefactors of mankind."

"Oh, Father Ambrose," cried the girl, when at last he entered her presence, "I watched your approach from afar off. You walked with halting step, and shoulders increasingly bowed. You are wearing yourself out in my service, and that I cannot permit. You return this evening a tired man."

"Not physically tired," replied the monk, with a smile. "My head is bowed with meditation and prayer, rather than with fatigue. Indeed, it is others who do the harassing manual labor, while I simply direct and instruct. Sometimes I think I am an encumberer in the vineyard, lazily using brain instead of hand."

"Nonsense!" cried the girl, "the vineyard would be but a barren plantation without you; and speaking of it reminds me that I have poured out, with my own hand, a tankard of the choicest, oldest wine in our cellars, which I allow no one but yourself to taste. Sit down, I beg of you, and drink."

The wise old man smiled, wondering what innocent trap was being set for him. He raised the tankard to his lips, but merely indulged in one sip of the delectable beverage. Then he seated himself, and looked at the girl, still smiling. She went on speaking rapidly, a delicate flush warming her fair cheeks.

"Father, you are the most patient and indefatigable of agriculturists, sparing neither yourself nor others, but there is danger that you grow bucolic through overlong absence from the great affairs of this world."

"What can be greater, my child, than increasing the productiveness of the land; than training men to supply all their needs from the fruitful earth?"

"True, true," admitted the girl, her eyes sparkling with eagerness, "but to persist overlong even in well-doing becomes ultimately tedious. If the laborer is worthy of his hire, so, too, is the master. You should take a change, and as I know your fondness for travel, I have planned a journey for you."

The old man permitted himself another sip of the wine.

"Where?" he asked.

"Oh, an easy journey; no farther than the royal city of Frankfort, there to wander among the scenes of your youth, and become interested for a time in the activities of your fellow-men. You have so long consorted with those inferior to you in intellect and learning that a meeting with your equals—though I doubt if there are any such even in Frankfort—must prove as refreshing to your mind as that old wine would to your body, did you but obey me and drink it."

Father Ambrose slowly shook his head.

"From what I hear of Frankfort," he said, "it is anything but an inspiring town. In my day it was indeed a place of cheer, learning, and prosperity, but now it is a city of desolation."

"The rumors we hear, Father, may be exaggerated; and even if the city itself be doleful, which I doubt, there is sure to be light and gayety in the precincts of the Court and in the homes of the nobility."

"What have I to do with Court or palaces? My duty lies here."

"It may be," cried the girl archly, "that some part of your duty lies there. If Frankfort is indeed in bad case, your sage advice might be of the greatest benefit. Prosperity seems to follow your footsteps, and, besides, you were once a chaplain in the Court, and surely you have not lost all interest in your former charge?"

Again that quiet, engaging smile lit up the monk's emaciated features, and then he asked a question with that honest directness which sometimes embarrassed those he addressed:

"Daughter Hildegunde, what is it you want?"

"Well," said the girl, sitting very upright in her chair, "I confess to loneliness. The sameness of life in this castle oppresses me, and in its continuous dullness I grow old before my time. I wish to enjoy a month or two in Frankfort, and, as doubtless you have guessed, I send you forth as my ambassador to spy out the land."

"In such case, daughter, you should present your petition to that Prince of the Church, the Archbishop of Cologne, who is your guardian."

"No, no, no, no!" cried the girl emphatically; "you are putting the grapes into the barrel instead of into the vat. Before I trouble the worthy Archbishop with my request, I must learn whether it is practicable or not. If the city is indeed in a state of turbulence, of course I shall not think of going thither. It is this I wish to discover, but if you are afraid." She shrugged her shoulders and spread out her hands.

And now the old monk came as near to laughing as he ever did.

"Clever, Hildegunde, but unnecessary. You cannot spur me to action by slighting the well-known valor of our race. I will go where and when you command me, and report to you faithfully what I see and hear. Should the time seem favorable for you to visit Frankfort, and if your guardian consents, I shall raise not even one objection."

"Oh, dear Father, I do not lay this as a command upon you."

"No; a request is quite sufficient. To-morrow morning I shall set out."

"Along the Rhine?" queried the girl, so eagerly that the old man's eyes twinkled at the celerity with which she accepted his proposition.

"I think it safer," he said, "to journey inland over the hills. The robbers on the Rhine have been so long bereft of the natural prey that one or other of them may forget I am Father Ambrose, a poor monk, remembering me only as Henry of the rich House of Sayn, and therefore hold me for ransom. I would not willingly be a cause of strife, so I shall go by way of Limburg on the Lahn, and there visit my old friend the Bishop, and enjoy once more a sight of the ancient Cathedral on the cliff by the river."

When the young Countess awoke next morning, and reviewed in her mind the chief event of the preceding day, remembering the reluctance of

Father Ambrose to undertake the quest she had outlined without the consent of his overlord the Archbishop, a feeling of compunction swept over her. She berated her own selfishness, resolving to send her petition to her guardian, the Archbishop, and abide by his decision.

When breakfast was finished, she asked her lady-in-waiting to request the presence of Father Ambrose, but instead of the monk came disturbing news.

"The seneschal says that Father Ambrose left the Castle at daybreak this morning, taking with him frugal rations for a three days' journey."

"In which direction did he go?" asked the lady of Sayn.

"He went on horseback up the valley, after making inquiries about the route to Limburg on the Lahn."

"Ah!" said the Countess. "He spoke yesterday of taking such a journey, but I did not think he would leave so early."

This was the beginning of great anxiety for the young lady of the Castle. She knew at once that pursuit was useless, for daybreak comes early in summer, and already the good Father had been five hours on his way—a way that he was certain to lose many times before he reached the capital city. An ordinary messenger might have been overtaken, but the meditative Father would go whither his horse carried him, and when he awoke from his thoughts and his prayers, would make inquiries, and so proceed. A day or two later came a message that he had achieved the hospitality of Limburg's bishop, but after that arrived no further word.

Nearly two weeks had elapsed when, from the opposite direction, Hildegunde received a communication which added to her already painful apprehension. It was a letter from her guardian in Cologne, giving warning that within a week he would call at her Castle of Sayn.

"Matters of great import to you and me," concluded the Archbishop, "are toward. You will be called upon to meet formally my two colleagues of Mayence and Treves, at the latter's strong Castle of Stolzenfels, above Coblentz.

From the moment we enter that palace-fortress, I shall, temporarily, at least, cease to be your guardian, and become merely one of your three overlords. But however frowningly I may sit in the throne of an Elector, believe me I shall always be your friend. Tell Father Ambrose I wish to consult with him the moment I arrive at your castle, and that he must not absent himself therefrom on any pretext until he has seen me."

Here was trouble indeed, with Father Ambrose as completely disappeared as if the dragons of the Taunus had swallowed him. Never before on his journeys had he failed to communicate with her, even when his travels were taken on account of the Archbishop, and not, as in this case, on her own. She experienced the darkest forebodings from this incredible silence. Imagine, then, her relief, when exactly two weeks from the day he had left Schloss Sayn, she saw him coming down the valley. As when she last beheld him, he traveled on foot, leading his horse, that had gone lame.

Throwing etiquette to the wind, she flew down the stairway, and ran to meet her thrice-welcome friend.

She realized with grief that he was haggard, and the smile he called up to greet her was wan and pitiful.

"Oh, Father, Father!" she cried, "what has happened to you? I have been nearly distraught with doubt and fear, hearing nothing of you since your message from Limburg."

"I was made a prisoner," said the old man quietly, "and allowed to communicate with no one outside my cell. 'Tis a long and sad story, and, worse than all one that bodes ill for the Empire. I should have arrived earlier in the day, but my poor, patient beast has fallen lame."

"Yes!" said the girl indignantly, "and you spare him instead of yourself!"

The monk laid his left hand affectionately on her shoulder.

"You would have done the same, my dear," he said, and she looked up at him with a sweet smile. They were kin, and if she censured any quality in him, the comment carried something of self-reproach.

A servitor took away the lame horse; another waited on Father Ambrose in his small room, which was simple as that of a monastery cell, and as meagerly furnished. After a slight refection, Father Ambrose received peremptory command to rest for three full hours, the lady of the Castle saying it was impossible for her to receive him until that time had elapsed. The order was welcome to the tired monk, although he knew how impatient Hildegunde must be to unpack his budget of news, and he fell asleep even as he gave instructions that he should be awakened at nine.

Descending at that time, the supper hour of the Castle, he found a dainty meal awaiting him, flanked by a flagon of that rare wine which he sipped so sparingly.

"I lodged with my brethren in their small and quiet monastery on the opposite side of the Main from Frankfort, in that suburb of the workingmen which is called Sachsenhausen. Even if my eyes had not seen the desolation of the city, with the summer grass growing in many of its streets, the description given of its condition by my brethren would have been saddening enough to hear. All authority seems at an end. The nobles have fled to their country estates, for defense in the city is impossible should once a universal riot break out, and thinking men look for an insurrection when continued hunger has worn down the patience of the people. Up to the present sporadic outbreaks have been cruelly suppressed, starving men falling mutilated before the sword-cuts of the soldiers; but now disaffection has penetrated the ranks of the Army itself, through short rations and deferred pay, and when the people learn that the military are more like to join them than oppose, destruction will fall upon Frankfort. The Emperor sits alone in drunken stupor, and it is said cannot last much longer, he who has lasted too long already; while the Empress is as much a recluse as a nun in a convent."

"But the young Prince?" interrupted the Countess. "What of him? Is there no hope if he comes to the throne?"

"Ah!" cried the monk, with a long-drawn sigh, dolefully shaking his head.

"But, Father Ambrose, you knew him as a lad, almost as a young man. I have heard you speak highly of his promise."

"He denied me; denied his own identity; threatened my life with his sword, and finally flung me into the most loathsome dungeon in all Frankfort!"

The girl uttered an ejaculation of dismay. If so harsh an estimate of the heir-presumptive came from so mild and gentle a critic as Father Ambrose, then surely was this young man lower in the grade of humanity than even his bestial father.

"And yet," said the girl to herself, "what else was to be expected? Go on," she murmured; "tell me from the beginning."

"One evening, crossing the old bridge from Frankfort to Sachsenhausen, I saw approach me a swaggering figure that seemed familiar, and as he drew nearer I recognized Prince Roland, son of the Emperor, despite the fact that he held his cloak over the lower part of his face, as if, in the gathering dusk, to avoid recognition.

"'Your Highness!' I cried in surprise. On the instant his sword was out, and as the cloak fell from his face, displaying lips which took on a sinister firmness, I saw that I was not mistaken in so accosting him. He threw a quick glance from side to side, but the bridge, like the silent streets, was deserted. We stood alone, beside the iron Cross, and there under the Figure of Christ he denied me, with the sharp point of his sword against my breast.

"'Why do you dare address me by such a title?'

"'You are Prince Roland, son of the Emperor.'

"The sword-point pressed more sharply.

"'You lie!' he cried, 'and if you reiterate that falsehood, you will pay the penalty instantly with your life, despite your monkish cowl. I am nobody. I have no father.'

"'May I ask, then, sir, who you are?'

"'You may ask, but there is no reason for me to answer. Nevertheless, to satisfy your impertinent curiosity, I inform you that I am an ironworker, a maker of swords, and if you desire a taste of my handiwork, you have but to persist in your questioning. I lodge in the laboring quarter of Sachsenhausen, and am now on my way into Frankfort, which surely I have the right to enter free from any inquiry unauthorized by the law.'

"'In that case I beg your pardon,' said I. 'The likeness is very striking. I had once the honor to be chaplain at Court, where frequently I saw the young Prince in company with that noble lady, noble in every sense of the word, his mother, the Empress.'

"I watched the young man narrowly as I said this, and despite his self-control, he winced perceptibly, and I thought I saw a gleam of recognition in his eyes. He thrust the sword back into its scabbard, and said with a light laugh:

"''Tis I that should beg your pardon for my haste and roughness. I assure you I honor the cloth you wear, and would not willingly offer it violence. We are all liable to make mistakes at times. I freely forgive yours and trust you will extend a like leniency to mine.'

"With that he doffed his hat, and left me standing there."

"Surely," said the Countess, deeply interested in the recital, "so far as speech was concerned he made amends?"

"Yes, my daughter; such speech never came from the lips of an ironworker."

"You are convinced he was the Prince?"

"Never for one instant did I doubt it."

"Be that as it may, Father Ambrose, why should not the young man walk the streets of his own capital city, and even explore the laborers' quarter of Sachsenhausen, if he finds it interesting to do so? Is it not his right to wear a sword, and go where he lists; and is it such a very heinous thing that, being accosted by a stranger, he should refuse to make the admission demanded? You took him, as one might say, unaware."

The monk bowed his head, but did not waste time in offering any defense of his action.

"I followed him," he went on, "through the narrow and tortuous streets of Frankfort, an easy adventure, because darkness had set in, but even in daylight my course would have been safe enough, for never once did he look over his shoulder, or betray any of that suspicion characteristic of our laboring classes."

"I think that tells in his favor," persisted the girl.

"He came to the steps of the Rheingold, a disreputable drinking cellar, and disappeared from my sight down its steps. A great shout greeted him, and the rattle of tankards on a table, as he joined what was evidently his coterie. Standing outside, I heard song and ribaldry within. The heir-presumptive to the throne of the Empire was too obviously a drunken brawler; a friend and comrade of the lowest scum in Frankfort.

"After a short time he emerged alone, and once more I followed him. He went with the directness of a purposeful man to the Fahrgasse, the street of the rich merchants, knocked at a door, and was admitted. Along the first-floor front were three lighted windows, and I saw his form pass the first two of these, but from my station in the street could not witness what was going on within. Looking about me, I found to my right a narrow alley, occupied by an outside stairway. This I mounted, and from its topmost step I beheld the interior of the large room on the opposite side of the way.

"It appeared to me that Prince Roland had been expected, for the elderly man seated at the table, his calm face toward me, showed no surprise at the Prince's entrance. His Highness sat with his back towards me, and for a time it seemed that nothing was going forward but an amiable conversation. Suddenly the Prince rose, threw off his cloak, whisked out his sword, and presented its point at the throat of the merchant.

"It was clear, from the expression of dismay on the merchant's face, that this move on the part of his guest was entirely unexpected, but its object was speedily manifested. The old man, with trembling hand, pushed across the table to his assailant a well-filled bag, which the Prince at once untied.

Pouring out a heap of yellow gold, he began with great deliberation to count the money, which, when you consider his precarious situation, showed the young man to be old in crime. Some portion of the gold he returned to the merchant; the rest he dropped into an empty bag, which he tied to his belt.

"I did not wait to see anything more, but came down to the foot of the stairs, that I might learn if Roland took his money to his dissolute comrades. He came out, and once more I followed him, and once more he led me to the Rheingold cellar. On this occasion, however, I took step by step with him until we entered the large wineroom at the foot of the stairs, he less than an arm's length in front of me, still under the illusion that he was alone. Prince though he was, I determined to expostulate with him, and if possible persuade a restitution of the gold.

"'Your Highness!' I began, touching him lightly on the shoulder.

"Instantly he turned upon me with a savage oath, grasped me by the throat, and forced me backward against the cellar wall.

"'You spying sneak!' he cried. 'In spite of my warning you have been hounding my footsteps!'

"The moment I attempted to reply, he throttled me so as to choke every effort at utterance. There now approached us, with alarm in his wine-colored face, a gross, corpulent man, whom the Prince addressed as proprietor of the place, which doubtless he was.

"'Landlord,' said Roland very quietly, 'this unfortunate monk is weak in the head, and although he means no harm with his meddling, he may well cause disaster to my comrades and myself. Earlier in the evening he accosted on the bridge, but I spared him, hoping never to see his monkish costume again. You may judge the state of his mind when I tell you he accuses me of being the Emperor's son, and Heaven only knows what he would estimate to be the quality of my comrades were he to see them.'

"Two or three times I attempted to speak, but the closing of his fingers upon my throat prevented me, and even when they were slightly relaxed I was scarcely able to breathe."

The Countess listened with the closest attention, fixing upon the narrator her splendid eyes, and in them, despite their feminine beauty and softness, seemed to smoulder a deep fire of resentment at the treatment accorded her kinsman, a luminant of danger transmitted to her down the ages from ancestors equally ready to fight for the Sepulcher in Palestine or for the gold on the borders of the Rhine. In the pause, during which the monk wiped from his wrinkled brow the moisture brought there by remembrance of the indignity he had undergone, kindliness in the eyes of the Countess overcame their menace, and she said gently:

"I am quite confident, Father, that such a ruffian could not be Prince Roland. He was indeed the rude mechanic he proclaimed himself. No man of noble blood would have acted thus."

"Listen, my child, listen," resumed Father Ambrose. "Turning to the landlord, the Prince asked:

"'Is there a safe and vacant room in your establishment where I could bestow this meddlesome priest for a few days?'

"'There is a wine vault underneath this drinking cellar,' responded the landlord.

"'Does anyone enter that vault except yourself?'

"'No one,'

"'Will you undertake charge of the priest, seeing that he communicates with none outside?'

"'Of a surety, Captain,'

"'Good. I will pay you well, and that in advance.'"

"This ruffian was never the Prince," interrupted the Countess firmly.

"I beg you to listen, Hildegunde, and my next sentence will convince you. The Prince continued:

"'Not only prevent his communication with others, but do not listen

586

to him yourself. He will endeavor to persuade you that his name is Father Ambrose, and that he is a monk in good standing with the Benedictine Order. If he finds you care little for that, he may indeed pretend he is of noble origin himself; that he is Henry von Sayn, and thus endeavor to work on whatever sympathy you may feel for the aristocrats. But I assure you he is no more a Sayn than I am Prince Roland.'

"'Indeed, Captain,' replied the host, 'I have as little liking for an aristocrat as for a monk, so you may depend that I will keep him safe enough until you order his release.'

"Now, my dear Hildegunde, you see there was no mistake on my part. This young man asserted he knew nothing of me, and indeed, I believed he had forgotten the time of my chaplaincy at the Court, often as he listened to my discourses, yet all the time he knew me, and now, with an effrontery that seems incredible, he showed no hesitation in proving me right when I accosted him as son of the Emperor. I must in justice, however, admit that he instructed the landlord when he paid him, to treat me with gentleness, and to see that I had plenty to eat and drink. When three days had expired, I was to be allowed my liberty.

"'He can do no harm then,' concluded the Prince, in his talk with the landlord, 'for by that time I shall have succeeded or failed.'

"I was led down a narrow, broken stairway by the proprietor, and thrust into a dark and damp cellar, partially filled with casks of wine, and there I remained until set at liberty a few days ago.

"I returned at once to the Benedictine Monastery where I had lodged, expecting to find my brethren filled with anxiety concerning me, but such was not the case. Any one man is little missed in this world, and my comrades supposed that I was invited to the Court, and had forgotten them as I saw they had forgotten me, so I said nothing of my adventure, but mounted my waiting horse and journeyed back to the Castle of Sayn."

For a long time there was silence between the two, then the younger spoke.

"Do you intend to take any action regarding your unauthorized imprisonment?"

"Oh, no," replied the forgiving monk.

"Is it certain that this dissolute young man will be chosen Emperor?"

"There is a likelihood, but not a certainty."

"Would not the election of such a person to the highest position in the State prove even a greater misfortune to the land than the continuance of the present regime, for this young man adds to his father's vice of drunkenness the evil qualities, of dishonesty, cruelty, ribaldry, and a lack of respect for the privileges both of Church and nobility?"

"Such indeed is my opinion, daughter."

"Then is it not your duty at once to acquaint the three Archbishops with what you have already told me, so that the disaster of his election may be avoided?"

"It is a matter to which I gave deep thought during my journey thither, and I also invoked the aid of Heaven in guiding me to a just conclusion."

"And that conclusion, Father?"

"Is to say nothing whatever about my experiences in Frankfort."

"Why?"

"Because it is not given to a humble man like myself, occupying a position of no authority, to fathom what may be in the minds of those great Princes of the Church, the Archbishops. In effect they rule the country, and it is possible that they prefer to place on the throne a drunken nonentity who will offer no impediment to their ambitions, rather than to elect a moral young man who might in time prove too strong for them."

"I am sure no such motive would actuate the Archbishop of Cologne."

"His Lordship of Cologne, my child, dare not break with their Lordships of Treves and Mayence, so you may be sure that if these two wish to elect

Prince Roland Emperor, nothing I could say to the Archbishop of Cologne would prevent that choice."

"Oh, I had forgotten, in the excitement of listening to your adventures, but talking of the Archbishop reminds me his Highness of Cologne will visit us to-morrow, and he especially wishes to see you. You may imagine my anxiety when I received his message a few days ago, knowing nothing of your whereabouts."

"Wishes to see me?" ejaculated Father Ambrose, wrinkling a perplexed brow. "I wonder what for. Can he have any knowledge of my visit to Frankfort?"

"How could he?"

"The Archbishops possess sources of enlightenment that we wot not of. If he charges me with being absent from my post, I must admit the fact."

"Of course. Let me confess to him as soon as he arrives; your journey was entirely due to my persistence. I alone am to blame."

The old man slowly shook his head.

"I am at least equally culpable," he said. "I shall answer truthfully any question asked me, but I hope I am not in the wrong if I volunteer no information."

The girl rose.

"You could do no wrong, Father, even if you tried; and now good-night. Sleep soundly and fear nothing. On the rare occasions when the good Archbishop was angry with me, I have always managed to placate him, and I shall not fail in this instance."

Father Ambrose bade her good-night, and left the room with the languid air of one thoroughly tired. As the young Countess stood there watching his retreat and disappearance, her dainty little fist clenched, and her eyebrows came together, bringing to her handsome face the determined expression which marked the countenances of some of her Crusader ancestors whose portraits decorated the walls.

"If ever I get that ruffian Prince Roland into my power," she said to herself, "I will make him regret his treatment of so tolerant and forbearing a man as Father Ambrose."

V. THE COUNTESS VON SAYN AND THE ARCHBISHOP OF COLOGNE

It was high noon when that great Prince of the Church, the Archbishop of Cologne, arrived at Castle Sayn, with a very inconsiderable following, which seemed to indicate that he traveled on no affair of State, for on such occasions he led a small army. The lovely young Countess awaited him at the top of the Castle steps, and he greeted her with the courtesy of a polished man of the world, rather than with the more austere consideration of a great Churchman. Indeed, it seemed to the quick apprehension of the girl that as he raised her fair hand to his lips his obeisance was lower, more deferential, than their differing stations in life justified.

He shook hands with Father Ambrose in the manner of old friend accosting old friend, and nothing in his salutation indicated displeasure of any sort in the background.

Perhaps, then, that sense of uneasiness felt by both the aged Father Ambrose and the youthful Countess Hildegunde in the Archbishop's presence came from their consciousness of conspiracy, resulting in the ill-fated journey to Frankfort. Nevertheless, all that afternoon the two were oppressed by the shadow of some impending danger, and the good spirits of the Archbishop seemed to them assumed for the occasion, and indeed in this they were not far wrong. His Lordship of Cologne was keenly apprehensive regarding an important conference set down for the next day, and the exuberance of an essentially serious man in such a crisis is prone to be overdone.

Father Ambrose, who, in the midst of luxury and plenty, lived with the abstemiousness of an anchorite, and always partook of his scant refreshment alone in his cell, was invited by the Archbishop to a seat at the table in the dining-hall.

"So long as you cast no look of reproach upon me for my enjoyment of Sayn's most excellent cuisine, and my appreciation of its unequaled cellar, I shall not comment on your dinner of parched peas and your unexhilarating tankard of water. Besides, I wish to consult with Ambrose the librarian of Sayn, touching the archives of this house, rather than with Ambrose the superintendent of farms, or Father Ambrose the monk."

During the midday meal the Archbishop led, and at times monopolized, the conversation.

"While you were under the tutelage of the good Sisters at Nonnenwerth Convent, Hildegunde, the Abbess frequently spoke of your proficiency in historical studies. Did you ever turn your attention to the annals of your own House?"

"No, Guardian. From what I heard casually of my ancestors a record of their doings would be scarcely the sort of reading recommended to a young girl."

"Ah, very true, very true," agreed the Archbishop. "Some of the Counts of Sayn led turbulent lives, and except with a battle-ax it was difficult to persuade them not to meddle with the goods and chattels of their neighbors. A strenuous line they proved in those olden days; but many noble women have adorned the Castle of Sayn whose lives shine out like an inspiration against the dark background of medieval tumult. Did you ever hear of your forebear, the gracious Countess Matilda von Sayn, who lived some hundreds of years ago? Indeed, the letters I have been reading, written in her quaint handwriting, are dated about the middle of the thirteenth century. I cannot learn whether she was older or younger than the Archbishop of Cologne of that period, and thus I wish to enlist the interest of Father Ambrose in searching the archives of Sayn for anything pertaining to her. The Countess sent many epistles to the Archbishop which he carefully preserved, while documents of much more importance to the Archbishopric were allowed to go astray.

"Her letters breathe a deep devotion to the Church, and a warm kindliness to its chief ornament of that day, the then Archbishop of Cologne. She was evidently his most cherished adviser, and in points of difficulty her counsel exhibits all the clarity of a man's brain, to which is added a tenderness and a sense of justice entirely womanly. I could not help fancying that this great prelate's success in his Archbishopric was largely due to the disinterested advice of this noble woman. It is clearly to be seen that the Countess was the benignant power behind the throne, and she watched his continued advancement with a love resembling that lavished on a favorite son. Her writings now and then betray an affection of a quality so motherly that I came to believe she was much older than the great Churchman, but then there is the fact that she long outlived him, so it is possible she may have been the younger."

"Why, my Lord, are you about to weave us a romance?"

The Archbishop smiled, and for a moment placed his hand upon hers, which rested on the table beside him.

"A romance, perhaps, between myself and the Countess of long ago, for as I read these letters I used much of their contents for my own guidance, and found her precepts as wise to-day as they were in 1250, and to me ... to me," the Archbishop sighed, "she seems to live again. Yes, I confess my ardent regard for her, and if you call that romance, it is surely of a very innocent nature."

"But the other Archbishop? Your predecessor, the friend of Matilda; what of him?"

"There, Hildegunde, I have much less evidence to go upon, for his letters, if they exist, are concealed somewhere in the archives of Sayn Castle."

"To-morrow," cried the girl, "I shall robe myself in the oldest garments I possess, and will rummage those dusty archives until I find the letters of him who was Archbishop in 1250."

"I have bestowed that task upon one less impulsive. Father Ambrose is the searcher, and he and I will put our wise old heads together in consultation over them before entrusting them to the perusal of that impetuous young noblewoman, the present Countess von Sayn."

The impetuous person referred to brought down her hand with a peremptory impact upon the table, and exclaimed emphatically:

"My Lord Archbishop, I shall read those letters to-morrow."

Once more the Archbishop placed his hand on hers, this time, however, clasping it firmly in his own. There was no smile on his face as he said gravely:

"My lady, to-morrow you will face three living Archbishops, more difficult, perhaps, to deal with than one who is dust."

"Three!" she cried, startled, a gleam of apprehension troubling her fine eyes. "My Lords of Mayence, Treves, and yourself? Are they coming here?"

"The conclave of the Archbishops will be held at Castle Stolzenfels, the Rhine residence of my brother of Treves."

"Why is this Court convened?"

"That will be explained to you, Hildegunde, by his Highness of Mayence. I did not intend to speak to you about this until later, so I will merely say that there is nothing to fear. I, being your guardian, am sent to escort you to Stolzenfels, and as we ride there together I wish to place before you some suggestions which you may find useful when the meeting takes place."

"I shall faithfully follow any advice you give me, my Lord."

"I am sure of it, Hildegunde, and you will remember that I speak as guardian, not as Councilor of State. My observations will be requests and not commands. You see, we have reversed the positions of my predecessor and the Countess Matilda. It was always she who tendered advice, which he invariably accepted. Now I must take the rôle of advice-giver; thus you and I transpose the parts of the former Archbishop of Cologne, and the former Countess of Sayn, who, I am sorry to note, have been completely banished from your thoughts by my premature announcement regarding the three living Archbishops."

"Oh, not at all, not at all! I am still thinking of those two. Have you told me all you know about them?"

"Far from it. Although I was handicapped in my reconstitution of their friendship by lack of the Archbishop's letters, he had nevertheless made a note here and there upon the communications he received from the Countess. Throughout the letters certain paragraphs are marked with a cross, as if for reperusal, these paragraphs being invariably most delicately and charmingly written. But now I come to the last very important document, the only one of which a copy has been kept, written in the Archbishop's own hand.

"In the year 1250, the Countess von Sayn had ceded to him the Rhine town of Linz. Linz seems to have been a rebellious and troublesome fief, which the Sayns held by force of arms. When it came into the possession of the Archbishop, the foolish inhabitants, remembering that Cologne was a long distance down the river compared with the up-river journey to Sayn, broke out into open revolt. The Archbishop sent up his army, and most effectually crushed this outbreak, severely punishing the rebels. He returned from this subdued town to his own city of Cologne, and whether from the exposure of the brief campaign, or some other cause, he was taken ill and shortly after died.

"The new Archbishop was installed, and nearly two years passed, so far as I can learn, before the Countess Matilda made claim that the town of Linz should come again within her jurisdiction, saying that this restitution had been promised by the late Archbishop. His successor, however, disputed this claim. He possessed, he said, the deed of gift making over the town of Linz to his predecessor, and this document was definite enough. If then, it was the intention of the late Archbishop to return Linz to the House of Sayn, the Countess doubtless held some document to that effect, and in this case he would like to know its purport.

"The Countess replied that an understanding had existed between the late Archbishop and herself regarding the subjugation of the town of Linz and its return to her after the rebellion was quelled. But for the untimely death of the late Archbishop she did not doubt that his part of the contract would have been kept long since. Nevertheless, she did possess a document, in the late Archbishop's own hand, setting out the terms of their agreement, and of this manuscript she sent a copy.

"The crafty Archbishop, without casting doubt on the authenticity of the copy, said that of course it would be illegal for him to act upon it. He must have the original document. Matilda replied, very shrewdly, that on her part she could not allow the original document to quit her custody, as upon it rested her rights to the town of Linz. She would, however, exhibit this document to any ecclesiastical committee her correspondent might appoint, and the members of the committee so chosen should be men well acquainted with the late Archbishop's writing and signature. In reply the Archbishop regretted that he could not accept her suggestion. The people of Cologne, believing that their overlord had rightfully acquired Linz, cheerfully consented to make good their title by battle, thus having, as it were, bought the town with their blood, and indeed, a deplorable sacrifice of life, it would become a dangerous venture to give up the town unless indisputable documentary evidence might be exhibited to them showing that such a bargain was made by the deceased prelate.

"But before proceeding farther in this matter, he asked the Countess if she were prepared to swear that the copy forwarded to him was a full and faithful rendition of the original. Did it contain every word the late Archbishop had written in that letter?

"To this the Countess made no reply, and allowed to lapse any title she might have to the town of Linz."

"I think," cried the girl indignantly, "that my ancestress was in the right, refusing further communication with this ignoble Churchman who dared to impugn her good faith."

The Archbishop smiled at her vehemence.

"I shall make no attempt to defend my astute predecessor. A money-lender's soul tenanted his austere body, but what would you say if his implication of the Countess Matilda's good faith was justified?"

"You mean that the copy which she sent of the Archbishop's letter was fraudulent? I cannot believe it."

"Not fraudulent. So far as it went her copy was word perfect. She neglected to add, however, a final sentence, and rather than make it public forfeited her rightful claim to great possessions. Of the Archbishop's communications to her there remains in our archives a copy of this last epistle written in his own hand. I cannot imagine why he added the final clauses to what was in essence an important business communication. The premonition he admits may have set his thoughts upon things not of this world, but undoubtedly he believed that he would live long enough to conquer the rebels of Linz, and restore to the Countess her property. This is what he wrote, and she refused to publish:

"'Matilda, I feel that my days are numbered, and that their number is scant. To all the world my life seems to have been successful beyond the wishes of mortal man, but to me it is a dismal failure, in that I die bachelor Archbishop of Cologne, and you are the spinster Countess von Sayn.'"

VI. TO BE KEPT SECRET FROM THE COUNTESS

There are few favored spots occupied by blue water and greensward over which a greater splendor is cast by the rising sun on a midsummer morning than that portion of the Rhine near Coblentz, and as our little procession emerged from the valley of the Saynbach every member of it was struck with the beauty of the flat country across the Rhine, ripening toward a yellow harvest, flooded by the golden glory of the rising sun.

Their route led to the left by the foot of the eastern hills, and not yet along the margin of the great river. Gradually, however, as they journeyed in a southerly direction, the highlands deflected them westward until at last there was but scant room for the road between rock and water. Always they were in the shade, a comforting feature of a midsummer journey, an advantage, however, soon to be lost when they crossed the Rhine by the ferry to Coblentz. The distance from Sayn Castle to Schloss Stolzenfels was a little less than four leagues, so their early start permitted a leisurely journey.

The Archbishop and the Countess rode side by side. Following them at some distance came Father Ambrose, deep in his meditations, and paying little attention to the horse he rode, which indeed, faithful animal, knew more about the way than did his rider. Still farther to the rear rode half a dozen mounted lancemen, two and two, the scant escort of one who commanded many thousands of armed men.

"How lovely and how peaceful is the scene," said the Countess. "How beautiful are the fields of waving grain; their color of dawn softened by the deep green of interspersed vineyards, and the water without a ripple, like a slumbering lake rather than a strong river. It seems as though anger, contention, and struggle could not exist in a realm so heavenly."

"'Seems' is the word to use," commented the Archbishop gravely, "but the unbroken placidity of the river you so much admire is a peace of defeat. I had much rather see its flood disturbed by moving barges and the turmoil of commerce. It is a peace that means starvation and death to our capital city, and, indeed, in a lesser degree, to my own town of Cologne, and to Coblentz, whose gates we are approaching."

"But surely," persisted the girl, "the outlook is improving, when you and I travel unmolested with a mere handful of men to guard us. Time was when a great and wealthy Archbishop might not stir abroad with less than a thousand men in his train."

The Archbishop smiled.

"I suppose matters mend," he said, "as we progress in civilized usage. The number of my escort, however, is not limited by my own modesty, but stipulated by the Court of Archbishops. Mayence travels down the Rhine and Treves down the Moselle, each with a similar following at his heels."

"You are pessimistic this lovely morning, my Lord, and will not even admit that the world is beautiful."

"It all depends on the point of view, Hildegunde. I regard it from a position toward the end of life, and you from the charming station of youth: the far-apart outlook of an old man and a young girl."

"Nonsense, Guardian, you are anything but old. Nevertheless I am much disappointed with your attitude this morning. I fully expected to be complimented by you."

"Doesn't my whole attitude breathe of compliment?"

"Ah, but I expected a particular compliment to-day!"

"What have I overlooked?"

"You overlooked the fact that yesterday you aroused my most intense curiosity regarding the journey we are now taking together, and the conference which is to follow. Despite deep anxiety to learn what is before me I have not asked you a single question, nor even hinted at the subject until this moment. Now, I think I should be rewarded for my reticence."

"Ah, Countess, you are an exception among women, and I merely withheld the well-earned praise until such time as I could broach the subject occupying my mind ever since we left the Castle. With the awkwardness of a man I did not know how to begin until you so kindly indicated the way."

"Perhaps, after all, I make a false claim, because I have guessed your secret, and therefore my deep solicitude is assumed."

"Guessed it?" queried the Archbishop, a shade of anxiety crossing his face.

"Yes. Your story of the former Archbishop and the Countess Matilda gave me a clue. You have discovered a document proving my right to the town of Linz on the Rhine."

The Archbishop bowed his head, but said nothing.

"Your sense of justice urges you to make amends, but such a long time has elapsed that my claim is doubtless outlawed, and you do not quite know how restoration may be effected. You have, I take it, consulted with one or other of your colleagues, Mayence or Treves, or perhaps with both. They have made objection to your proposed generosity, and put forward the argument that you are but temporary trustee of the Cologne Archbishopric; that you must guard the rights of your successor; and this truism could not help but appeal to that quality of equity which distinguishes you, so a conference of the prelates has been called, and a majority of that Court will decide whether or not the town of Linz shall be tendered to me. Perhaps a suggestion will be made that I allow things to remain as they are, in which case I shall at once refuse to accept the town of Linz. Now, Guardian, how near have I come to solving the mystery?"

They rode along in silence together, the Archbishop pondering on the problem of her further enlightenment. At last he said:

"Cologne is ruled by its Archbishop, wisely or the reverse as the case may be. The Archbishop, much as he reveres the opinion of his distinguished colleagues, would never put them to the inconvenience of giving a decision on any matter not concerning them. Linz's fate was settled when the handwriting of my predecessor, prelate of 1250 A.D., convinced me that this Rhine town belonged to the House of Sayn. Restitution has already been accomplished in due legal form, and when next the Countess Hildegunde rides through Linz, she rides through her own town."

"I shall never, never accept it, Guardian."

"It is yours now, Countess. If you do not wish to hold the town, use it as a gift to the fortunate man you marry. And now, Hildegunde, this long-postponed advice I wish to press upon your attention, must be given, for we are nearing the ferry to Coblentz, and between that town and Stolzenfels we may have company. Of the three Archbishops you will meet to-day, there is only one of whom you need take account."

"Oh, I know that," cried the girl, "his Lordship of Cologne!"

The Archbishop smiled, but went on seriously:

"Where two or three men are gathered together, one is sure to be leader. In our case the chief of the trio supposed to be equal is his Highness of Mayence. Treves and I pretend not to be under his thumb, but we are: that is to say, Treves holds I am under his thumb, and I hold Treves is under his thumb, and so when one or the other of us join the Archbishop of Mayence, there is a majority of the Court, and the third member is helpless."

"But why don't you and Treves join together?"

"Because each thinks the other a coward, and doubtless both are right. The point of the matter is that Mayence is the iron man of the combination; therefore I beg you beware of him, and I also entreat you to agree with the proposal he will make. It will be of tremendous advantage to you."

"In that case, my Lord, how could I refuse?"

"I hope, my child, you will not, but if you should make objection, do so with all the tact at your disposal. In fact, refrain wholly from objection if you can, and plead for time to consider, so that you and I may consult together, thus affording me opportunity of bringing arguments to bear that may influence your decision."

"My dear Guardian, you alarm me by the awesome way in which you speak. What fateful choice hangs over my head?"

"I have no wish to frighten you, my daughter, and, indeed, I anticipate little chance of disagreement at the conference. I merely desire that you shall understand something of Mayence. He is a man whom opposition may drive to extremity, and being accustomed to crush those who disagree with him, rather than conquer by more diplomatic methods, I am anxious you should not be led into any semblance of dissent from his wishes. By agreement between Mayence, Treves, and myself, I am not allowed to enlighten you regarding the question at issue. I perhaps strain that agreement a little when I endeavor to put you on your guard. If, at any point in the discussion, you wish a few moments to reflect, glance across the table at me, and I shall immediately intervene with some interruption which must be debated by the three members of the Court. Of course, I shall do everything in my power to protect you should our grim friend Mayence lose his temper, as may happen if you thwart him."

"Why am I likely to thwart him?"

"Why indeed? I see no reason. I am merely an old person perhaps over-cautious. Hence this warding off of a crisis which I hope will never arise."

"Guardian, I have one question to ask, and that will settle the matter here on the border of the Rhine, before we reach Stolzenfels. Do you thoroughly approve, with your heart, mind, and conscience, of the proposition to be made to me?"

"I do," replied the Archbishop, in a tone of conviction that none could gainsay. "Heart and soul, agree."

"Then, Guardian, your crisis that never came vanishes. I shall tell his Lordship of Mayence, in my sweetest voice and most ingratiating manner, that I will do whatever he requests."

Here the conversation ceased, for the solitude now gave way to a scene of activity, as they came to the landing alongside which lay the floating bridge, a huge barge, capable of carrying their whole company at one voyage. Several hundred persons, on horseback or on foot, gathered along the river-bank, raised a cheer as the Archbishop appeared. The Countess thought they waited to greet him, but they were merely travelers or market people who found their journey interrupted at this point. An emissary of the Archbishop had commanded the ferry-boat to remain at its eastern landing until his Lordship came aboard. When the distinguished party embarked, the crew instantly cast off their moorings, and the tethered barge, impelled by the swift current, gently swung across to the opposite shore.

A great concourse of people greeted their arrival at Coblentz, and if vociferous shouts and hurrahs are signs of popularity, the Archbishop had reason to congratulate himself upon his reception. The prelate bowed and smiled, but did not pause at Coblentz, and, to the evident disappointment of the multitude, continued his way up the Rhine. When the little cavalcade drew away from the mob, the Countess spoke:

"I had no thought," she said, "that Coblentz contained so many inhabitants."

"Neither does it," replied the Archbishop.

"Then is this simply an influx of people from the country, and is the conclave of the Archbishops of such importance that it draws so many sightseers?"

"The Court held by the Archbishops on this occasion is very important. I suspect, however, that those are no sightseers, for the general public is quite unaware that we meet to-day. They who cheered so lustily just now are, I think, men of Treves."

"Do you mean soldiers?"

"Aye. Soldiers in the dress of ordinary townsmen, but I dare say they all know where to find their weapons should a war-cry arise."

"Do you imply that the Archbishop of Treves has broken his compact? I understood that your escort was limited to the few men following you."

His Lordship laughed.

"The Archbishop of Treves," he said, "is not a great strategist, yet I surmise he is ready in case of trouble to seize the city of Coblentz."

"What trouble could arise?"

"The present moment is somewhat critical, for the Emperor lies dying in Frankfort. We three Electors hope to avoid all commotion by having our plans prepared and acting upon them promptly. But the hours between the death of an Emperor and the appointment of his successor are fateful with uncertainty. I suppose the good Sisters at Nonnenwerth taught you about the Election of an Emperor?"

"Indeed, Guardian, I am sorry to confess that if they did I have forgotten all about it."

"There are seven Electors; four high nobles of the Empire and three Archbishops, Lords Temporal and Lords Spiritual. The present Count Palatine of the Rhine is, like my friend Treves, completely under the dominion of the Archbishop of Mayence, so the three Lords Spiritual, with the aid of the Count Palatine, form a majority of the Electoral Court."

"I understand. And now I surmise that you assemble at Stolzenfels to choose our future Emperor."

"No; he has already been chosen, but his name will not be announced to any person save one before the Emperor dies."

"Doubtless that one is the Count Palatine."

"No, Countess, he remains ignorant; and I give you warning, Madam, I am not to be cross-questioned by indirection. You should be merciful: I am but clay in your hands, yet there is certain information I am forbidden to impart, so I will merely say that if the Archbishop happens to be in good-humor this afternoon, he is very likely to tell you who will be the future Emperor."

The girl gave an exclamation of surprise.

"To tell me? Why should he do so?"

"I said I was not to be cross-examined any further. I tremble now with apprehension lest I have let slip something I should not, therefore we will change the subject to one of paramount importance; namely, our midday meal. I intended to stop at Coblentz for that repast, but the Archbishop of Treves, whose guests we are, was good enough to accept a menu I suggested, therefore we will sit at table with him."

"You suggested a menu?"

"Yes; I hope you will approve of it. There is some excellent Rhine salmon, with a sauce most popular in Treves, a sauce that has been celebrated for centuries. Next some tender venison from the forest behind Stolzenfels, which is noted for its deer. There are, beside, cakes and various breads, also vegetables, and all are to be washed down by delicate Oberweseler wine. How does my speis-card please you, Countess?"

"I am committing it to memory, Guardian, so that I shall know what to prepare for you when next you visit my Castle of Sayn."

"Oh, this repast is not in my honor, but in yours. I feared you might object to the simplicity of it. It is upon record that this meal was much enjoyed by a young lady some centuries ago, at this very Castle of Stolzenfels, shortly after it was completed. Indeed, I think it likely she was the noble castle's first guest. Stolzenfels was built by Arnold von Isenberg, the greatest Archbishop that ever ruled over Treves, if I may except Archbishop Baldwin, the fighter. Isenberg determined to have a stronghold on the Rhine midway between Mayence and Cologne, and he made it a palace as well as a fortress, taking his time about it—in all seventeen years. He began its erection in 1242, and so was building at the time your ancestress Matilda ceded Linz to the Archbishop of Cologne, therefore I imagine Cologne probably wished to have a stronghold within striking distance of Treves' new castle.

"One of the first to visit Stolzenfels was a charming young English girl named Isabella, who was no other than the youngest daughter of John, King of England. Doubtless she came here with an imposing suite of attendants, and I surmise that the great prelate's castle saw impressive pageants and festivities, for the chronicler, after setting down the menu whose excellence I hope to test to-day, adds:

"'They ate well, and drank better, and the Royal maiden danced a great deal.'

"Her brother then occupied the English throne. He was Henry III., and of course much attention was paid over here to his dancing sister."

"Why, Guardian, what you say gives a new interest to old Stolzenfels. I have never been within the Castle, but now I shall view it with delight, wondering through which of the rooms the English Princess danced. Why did Isabella come from England all the way to the Rhine?"

"She came to meet the three Archbishops."

"Really? For what purpose?"

"'That they might in ecclesiastical form, and upon the highest ecclesiastical authority, announce her betrothal."

"Announce in Stolzenfels the betrothal of an English Princess, the daughter of one king and sister of another! Did she, then, marry a German?"

"Yes; she married the Emperor, Frederick II.; Frederick of Hohenstaufen."

Slowly the girl turned her head, and looked steadfastly at the Archbishop, who was gazing earnestly up the road as if to catch a glimpse of the Castle which had been the scene of the events he related. Her face became pale, and a questioning wonder rose in her eyes. What did the Archbishop really mean by this latest historical recital? True, he was a man who had given much study to ancient lore; rather fond of exhibiting his proficiency therein when he secured patient listeners. Could there be any secret meaning in his story of the English Princess who danced? Was there any hidden analogy between the journey of the English Isabella, and the short trip taken that day by Hildegunde of Sayn? She was about to speak when the Archbishop made a slight signal with his right hand, and a horseman who had followed them all the way from Coblentz now spurred up alongside of his Lordship, who said sharply to the newcomer:

"How many of Treves' men are in Coblentz?"

"Eight hundred and fifty, my Lord."

"Enough to capture the town?"

"Coblentz is already in their possession, my Lord."

"They seem to be unarmed."

"Their weapons are stored under guard in the Church of St. Castor, and can be in the hands of the soldiers within a few minutes after a signal is rung by the St. Castor's bells."

"Are there any troops in Coblentz from Mayence?"

"No, my Lord."

"How many of my men have been placed behind the Castle of Stolzenfels?"

"Three thousand are concealed in the forest near the hilltop."

"How many men has my Lord of Mayence within call?"

"Apparently only the scant half-dozen that reached Stolzenfels with him yesterday."

"Are you sure of that?"

"Scouts have been sent all through the forest to the south, and have brought us no word of an advancing company. Other scouts have gone up the river as far as Bingen, but everything is quiet, and it would have been impossible for his Lordship to march a considerable number of men from any quarter towards Stolzenfels without one or other of our hundred spies learning of the movement."

"Then doubtless Mayence depends on his henchman Treves."

"It would seem so, my Lord."

"Thank you; that will do."

The rider saluted, turned his horse towards the north, and galloped away, and a few moments later the little procession came within sight of Stolzenfels, standing grandly on its conical hill beside the Rhine, against a background of green formed by the mountainous forests to the rear.

This conversation, which she could not help but hear, had driven entirely from the mind of Hildegunde the pretty story of the English Princess.

"Why, Guardian!" she said, "we seem to be in the midst of impending civil war."

The Archbishop smiled.

"We are in the midst of an assured peace," he replied.

"What! with Coblentz practically seized, and three thousand of your men lurking in the woods above us?"

"Yes. I told you that Treves was no strategist. I suppose he and Mayence imagine that by seizing the town of Coblentz they cut off my retreat to Cologne. They know it would be useless in a crisis for me to journey up the river, as I should then be getting farther and farther from my base of supplies both in men and provisions, therefore the Archbishop of Mayence has neglected to garrison that quarter."

"But, Guardian, you are surely entrapped, with Coblentz thus held?"

"Not so, my child, while I command three thousand men to their eight hundred."

"But that means a battle!"

"A battle that will never take place, Hildegunde, because I shall seize something much more valuable than any town, namely, the persons of the two Archbishops. With their Lordships of Treves and Mayence in my custody, cut off from communication with their own troops, I have slight fear of a leaderless army. The very magnitude of the force at my command is an assurance of peace."

They now arrived at the branching hill-road leading up to the gates of Stolzenfels just above them, and conversation ceased, but the Countess was fated to remember before the afternoon grew old the final words Cologne spoke so confidently.

VII. MUTINY IN THE WILDERNESS

It was a lovely morning in July when Prince Roland walked into the shadow of the handsome tower which to-day is all that survives of the Elector's palace at Hochst, on the river Main. He found Greusel there awaiting him, but none of the others. When the two had greeted one another, the Prince said:

"Joseph, I determined several days ago to appoint you my lieutenant on this expedition."

"If you take my advice, Roland, you will do nothing of the kind."

"Why?"

"Because it may be looked upon as favoritism, and so promote jealously in the ranks, which is a thing to avoid."

"Whom would you suggest for the place?"

"Conrad Kurzbold."

"What! and run the risk of divided authority? I am determined to be commander, you know."

"Kurzbold, even if made lieutenant, would be as much under your orders as the rest of us. He is an energetic man, and you may thus direct his energy along the right path. From being a critic, he will become one of the criticised, giving him something to think about. Then your appointment of him would show that you bear no ill-feeling for what he said last night."

"You appear to think, Greusel, that it is the duty of a commander to curry favor with his following."

"No; but I regard tact as a useful quality. You see, you are not in the position of a general with an army. The members of the guild can depose you whenever they like and elect a successor, or they may desert you in a body, and you have no redress. Your methods should not be drastic, but rather those of a man who seeks election to some high office."

"I fear I am not constituted for such a rôle, Greusel."

"If you are to succeed in the task you have undertaken, Roland, you must adapt yourself to your situation as it actually is, and not as you would wish to have it. I stood by you yesterday evening, and succeeded in influencing the others to do the same, yet there is no denying that you spoke to those men in a most overbearing manner. Why, you could not have been more downright had you been an officer of the Emperor himself. What passed through my mind as I listened was, 'Where did this youth get his swagger?' You ordered Kurzbold out of the ranks, you know."

"Then why favor my action?"

"Because I was reluctant to see a promising marauding adventure wrecked at the very outset for lack of a few soothing words."

Roland laughed heartily. The morning was inspiring, and he was in good fettle.

"Your words to Kurzbold were anything but soothing."

"Oh, I was compelled to crush him. He was the cause of the disturbance, and therefore I had no mercy so far as the affair impinged upon him. But the others, with the exception of Gensbein perhaps, are good, honest, sweet-tempered fellows, whom I did not wish to see misled. I think you must put out of your mind all thought of punishment, no matter what the offense against your authority may be."

"Then how would you deal with insubordination when it arises?"

"I should trust to the good sense of the remaining members of your company to make it uncomfortable for the offender."

"But suppose they don't?"

Greusel shrugged his shoulders.

"In that case you are helpless, I fear. At any rate, talking of hanging, or the infliction of any other punishment, is quite futile so long as you do not possess the power to carry out your sentence. To return to my simile of the general: a general can order any private in his army to be hanged, and the man is taken out and hanged accordingly, but if one of the guild is to be executed, he must be condemned by an overwhelming vote of his fellows, because even if a bare majority sentenced one belonging to the minority it would mean civil war among us. Suppose, for example, it was proposed to hang you, and eleven voted for the execution and nine against it. Do you think we nine would submit to the verdict of the eleven? Not so. I am myself the most peaceful of men, but the moment it came to that point, I should run my sword through the proposer of the execution before he had time to draw his weapon. In other words, I'd murder him to lessen the odds, and then we'd fight it out like men."

"Why didn't you say all this last night, Greusel?"

"Last night my whole attention was concentrated on inducing Kurzbold to forget that you had threatened the company with a hangman's rope. Had he remembered that, I could never have carried the vote of confidence. But you surely saw that the other men were most anxious to support you if your case was placed fairly before them, a matter which, for some reason, you thought it beneath your dignity to attempt."

"My dear Joseph, your wholesale censure this morning does much to nullify the vote I received last night."

"My dear Roland, I am not censuring you at all; I am merely endeavoring to place facts before you so that you will recognize them."

"Quite so, but what I complain of is that these facts were not exhibited in time for me to shoulder or shirk the responsibility. I do not believe that military operations can be successfully carried on by a little family party, the head of which must coddle the others in the group, and beg pardon before he says 'Devil take you!' I would not have accepted the leadership last night had I known the conditions."

"Well, it is not yet too late to recede. The barge does not leave Frankfort until this evening, and it is but two leagues back to that city. Within half an hour at the farthest, every man of us will be assembled here. Now is the time to have it out with them, because to-morrow morning the opportunity to withdraw will be gone."

"It is too late even now, Greusel. If last night the guild could not make up the money we owe to Goebel, what hope is there that a single coin remains in their pockets this morning? Do I understand, then, that you refuse to act as my lieutenant?"

"No; but I warn you it will be a step in the wrong direction. You are quite sure of me; and as merely a man-at-arms, as you called us last night, I shall be in a better position to speak in your favor than if I were indebted to you for promotion from the ranks."

"I see. Therefore you counsel me to nominate Kurzbold?"

"I do."

"Why not Gensbein, who was nearly as mutinous as Kurzbold?"

"Well, Gensbein, if you prefer him."

"He showed a well-balanced mind last night, being part of the time on one side and part on the other."

"My dear commander, we were all against you last night, when you spoke of hanging, and even when you only went as far as expulsion."

"Yes, I suppose you were, and the circumstances being such as you state, doubtless you were justified. I am to command, then, a regiment that may obey or not, according to the whim of the moment; a cheering prospect, and one I had not anticipated. When I received the promise of twenty men that they would carry out faithfully whatever I undertook on their behalf, I expected them to stand by it."

"I think you are unjust, Roland. No one has refused, and probably no one will. If any one disobeys a command, then you can act as seems best to you, but I wish you fully to realize the weakness of your status should it come to drastic punishment."

"Quite so, quite so," said Roland curtly. He clasped his hands behind his back, and without further words paced up and down along the bank of the river, head bowed in thought.

Ebearhard was the next arrival, and he greeted Greusel cordially, then one after another various members of the company came upon the scene. To the new-comers Roland made no salutation, but continued his meditating walk.

At last the bell in the tower pealed forth nine slow, sonorous strokes, and Roland raised his head, ceasing his perambulations. Greusel looked anxiously at him as he came forward to the group, but his countenance gave no indication whether or not he had determined to abandon the expedition.

"Are we all here?" asked Roland.

"No," was the reply; "Kurzbold, Eiselbert, Rasselstein, and Gensbein have not arrived yet."

"Then we will wait for them a few moments longer," said the commander, with no trace of resentment at their unpunctuality, and from this Greusel assumed that he not only intended to go on, but had taken to heart the warning given him. Ebearhard and a comrade walked up the road rapidly toward Frankfort, hoping for some sign of the laggards, and Roland resumed his stroll beside the river. At last Ebearhard and his companion returned, and the former approached Roland.

"I see nothing of those four," he said. "What do you propose to do?"

Roland smiled.

"I think sixteen good men, all of a mind, will accomplish quite as much as twenty who are divided in purpose. I propose, therefore, to go on, unless you consider the missing four necessary, in which case we can do nothing but wait."

"I am in favor of going forward," said Ebearhard; then turning to the rest, who had gathered themselves around their captain, he appealed to them. All approved of immediate action.

"Do you intend to follow the river road, Captain?" asked Ebearhard.

"Yes, for two or three leagues, but after that we strike across the country."

"Very well. We can proceed leisurely along the road, and our friends may overtake us if they have any desire to do so."

"Right!" said Roland. "Then let us set out."

The seventeen walked without any company formation through the village, then, approaching a wayside tavern, they were hailed by a loud shout from the drinkers in front of it. Kurzbold was the spokesman for the party of four, which he, with his comrades, made up.

"Come here and drink success to glory," he shouted. "Where have you lads been all the morning?"

"The rendezvous," said Roland sternly, "was at the Elector's tower."

"My rendezvous wasn't. I have been here for more than an hour," said Kurzbold. "I told you last night that when I arrived at Hochst I should be thirsty, and would try to mitigate the disadvantage at a tavern."

"Yes," said Ebearhard, with a laugh, "we can all see you have succeeded in removing the disadvantage."

"Oh, you mean I'm drunk, do you? I'll fight any man who says I'm drunk. It was a tremendous thirst caused by the dryness of my throat from last night, and the dust on the Frankfort road this morning. It takes a great deal of wine to overcome two thirsts. Come along, lads, and drink to the success of the journey. No hard feeling. Landlord, set out the wine here for seventeen people, and don't forget us four in addition."

The whole company strolled in under the trees that fronted the tavern, except Roland, who stood aloof.

"Here's a salute to you, Captain," cried Kurzbold. "I drink wine with you."

"Not till we return from a successful expedition," said Roland.

"Oh, nonsense!" hiccoughed Kurzbold. "Don't think that your office places you so high above us that it is infra dig. to drink with your comrades."

To this diatribe Roland made no reply, and the sixteen, seeing the attitude of their leader, hesitated to raise flagon to lip. The diplomatic Ebearhard seized a measure of wine and approached Roland.

"Drink with us, Commander," he said aloud; and then in a whisper, "Greusel and I think you should."

"Thank you, comrade," said Roland, taking the flagon from him. "And now, brethren, I give you a toast."

"Good, good, good!" cried Kurzbold, with drunken hilarity. "Here's to the success of the expedition. That's the toast, I make no doubt, eh, Captain?"

"The sentiment is included in the toast I shall offer you. Drink to the health of Joseph Greusel, whom I have this morning appointed my lieutenant. If we all conduct ourselves as honorably and capably as he, our project is bound to prosper."

Greusel, who was seated at a table, allowed his head to sink into his hands. Here was his advice scouted, and a direct challenge flung in the face of the company. He believed now that, after all, Roland had resolved to return to Frankfort, money or no money. If he intended to proceed to the Rhine, then even worse might happen, for it was plain he was bent on rule or ruin. Instantly the challenge was accepted. Kurzbold stood up, swaying uncertainly, compelled to maintain his upright position by grasping the top of the table at which he had been seated.

"Stop there, stop there!" he cried. "No man drinks to that toast just yet. Patience, patience! all things in their order. If we claim the power to elect our captain, by the cock-crowned Cross of the old bridge we have a right to name the lieutenant! This is a question for the companionship to decide, and a usurpation on the part of Roland."

"Sit down, you fool!" shouted Ebearhard savagely. "You're drunk. The Captain couldn't have made a better selection. What say you, comrades?"

A universal shout of "Aye!" greeted the question, and even Kurzbold's three comrades joined in it.

"And now, gentlemen, no more talk. Here's to the health of the new lieutenant, Joseph Greusel."

The toast was drunk enthusiastically, all standing, with the exception of Kurzbold, who came down in his seat with a thud.

"All right!" he cried, waving his hand. "All right; all right! That's what I said. Greusel's good man, and now he's elected by the companionship, he's all right. I drink to him. Drink to anybody, I will!"

In groping round for the flagon, he upset it, and then roared loudly for the landlord to supply him again.

"Now, comrades," said Roland sharply, "fall in! We've a long march ahead of us. Come, Greusel, we must lead the van, for I wish to instruct you in your duties."

It was rather a straggling procession that set out from Hochst.

"Perhaps," began Roland, as he strode along beside Greusel, "I should make some excuse for not following the advice you so strenuously urged upon me this morning regarding the appointment of a lieutenant. The truth is I wished to teach you a lesson, and could not resist the temptation of proving that a crisis firmly and promptly met disappears, whereas if you compromise with it there is a danger of being overwhelmed."

"I admit. Commander, that you were successful just now, and the reason is that most of our brigade are sane and sober this morning. But wait until to-night, when the wine passes round several times, and if you try conclusions with them then you are likely to fail."

"But the wine won't pass round to-night."

"How can you prevent it?"

"Wait, and you will see," said Roland, with a laugh.

By this time they arrived at a fork in the road, one section going southwest and the other straight west. The left branch was infinitely the better thoroughfare, for the most part following the Main until it reached the Rhine. Roland, however, chose the right-hand road.

"I thought you were going along by the river," said his lieutenant.

"I have changed my mind," replied Roland, without further explanation.

At first Kurzbold determined to set the pace. He would show the company he was not drunk, and tax them to follow him, but, his stout legs proving unable to carry out this excellent resolution, he gradually fell to the rear. As the sun rose higher, and grew hotter, the pace began to tell on him, and he accepted without protest the support of two comrades who had been drinking with him at Hochst. He retrograded into a condition of pessimistic dejection as the enthusiasm of the wine evaporated. A little later he wished to lie down by the roadside and allow a cruel and unappreciative world to pass on its own way, but his comrades encouraged him to further efforts, and in some manner they succeeded in dragging him along at the tail of the procession.

As they approached the village of Zeilsheim, Roland requested his lieutenant to inform the marchers that there would be no halt until mittagessen.

Zeilsheim is rather more than a league from Hochst, and Kurzbold allowed himself to wake up sufficiently to maintain that the distance earned another drink, but his supporters dragged him on with difficulty past those houses which displayed a bush over the door. At the larger town of Hofheim, five leagues from Frankfort, the same command was passed down the ranks, and at this there was some grumbling, for the day had become very hot, and the way was exceedingly trying, up hill and down dale.

Well set up as these city lads were, walking had never been their accustomed exercise. The interesting Taunus mountains, which to-day constitute an exercise ground full of delights to the pedestrian, forming, as they do, practically a suburb of Frankfort, were at that time an unexplored wilderness, whose forests were infested by roving brigands, where no man ventured except at the risk of an untimely grave. The mediæval townsman rarely trusted himself very far outside the city gates, and our enterprising marauders, whom to outward view seemed stalwart enough to stand great fatigue, proved so soft under the hot sun along the shadeless road that by the time they reached Breckenheim, barely six leagues from Frankfort, there was a mopping of brows and a general feeling that the limit of endurance had been reached.

At Breckenheim Roland called a halt for midday refreshment, and he was compelled to wait nearly half an hour until the last straggler of his woebegone crew limped from the road on to the greensward in front of the Weinstaube which had been selected for a feeding-place. Black bread and a coarse kind of country cheese were the only provisions obtainable, but of these eatables there was an ample supply, and, better than all to the jaded wayfarers, wine in abundance, of good quality, too, for Breckenheim stands little more than a league to the north of the celebrated Hochheim.

The wanderers came in by ones and twos, and sank down upon the benches before the tavern, or sprawled at full length on the short grass, where Kurzbold and his three friends dropped promptly off into sleep. A more dejected and amenable gang even Roland could not have wished to command. Every ounce of fight, or even discussion, was gone from them. They cared not where they were, or what any one said to them. Their sole desire was to be let alone, and they took not the slightest interest even in the preparing of their frugal meal. A mug of wine served to each mitigated the general depression, although Kurzbold showed how far gone he was by swearing dismally when roused even to drink the wine. He said he was resolved to lead a temperate life in future, but nevertheless managed to dispose of his allowance in one long, parched draught.

Greusel approached his chief.

"There will be some difficulty," he said, "when this meal has to be paid for. I find that the men are all practically penniless."

"Tell them they need anticipate no trouble about that," replied Roland. "I have settled the bill, and will see that they do not starve or die of thirst before we reach the Rhine."

"It is proposed," continued Greusel, "that each man should give all the money he possesses into a general fund to be dealt with by a committee the men will appoint. What do you say to this?"

"There is nothing to say. I notice that the proposal was not made until the proposers' pouches were empty."

"They know that some of us have money," Greusel went on, "myself, for instance, and they wish us to share as good comrades should—at least, that is their phrase."

"An admirable phrase, yet I don't agree with it. How much money have you, Greusel?"

"The thirty thalers are practically intact, and Ebearhard has about the same."

"Well, fifty thalers lie safe in my pouch, but not a coin goes into the treasury of any committee the men may appoint. If they choose a committee, let them finance it themselves."

"There will be some dissatisfaction at that decision, Commander."

"I dare say. Still, as you know, I am always ready to do anything conducive to good feeling, so you may inform them that you and Ebearhard and myself, that is, three of us, will contribute to the committee's funds an amount equal to that subscribed by the other eighteen. Such lavishness on our part ought to satisfy them."

"It won't, Commander, because there's not a single kreuzer among the eighteen."

"So be it. That's as far as I am willing to go. Appeal to their reasoning powers, Greusel. If each of the eighteen contributes one thaler, we three will contribute six thalers apiece. Ask them whether they do not think we are generous when we do six times more than any one of them towards providing capital for a committee."

"'Tis not willingness they lack, Commander, but ability."

"They are not logical, Joseph. They prate of comradeship, and when it comes to an exercise of power they demand equality. How, then, can they, with any sense of fairness, prove ungrateful to us when we offer to bear six times the burden they are asked to shoulder?"

The lieutenant said no more, but departed to announce the decision to the men, and either the commander's reasoning overcame all opposition, or else the company was too tired to engage in a controversy.

When the black bread and cheese were served, with a further supply of wine, all sat up and ate heartily. The banquet ended, Greusel made an announcement to the men. There would now be an hour's rest, he said, before taking to the road again. The meal and the wine had been paid for by the commander, so no one need worry on that account, but if any man wished more wine he must pay the shot himself. However, before the afternoon's march was begun flagons of wine would be served at the commander's expense. This information was received in silence, and the men stretched themselves out on the grass to make the most of their hour of rest. Roland strolled off alone to view the village. The lieutenant and Ebearhard sat together at a table, conversing in low tones.

"Well," said Ebearhard, "what do you think of it all?"

"I don't know what to think," replied Greusel. "If the Barons of the Rhine could see us, and knew that we intended to attack them, I imagine there would be a great roar of laughter."

Ebearhard emulated the Barons, and laughed. He was a cheerful person.

"I don't doubt it," he said; "and talking of prospects, what's your opinion of the Commander?"

"I am quite adrift on that score also. This morning I endeavored to give him some good advice. I asked him not to appoint me lieutenant, but to choose Kurzbold or Gensbein from among the malcontents, for I thought if responsibility were placed on their shoulders we should be favored with less criticism."

"A very good idea it seems to me," remarked Ebearhard.

"Well, you saw how promptly he ignored it, yet after all there may be more wisdom in that head of his than I suspected. Look you how he has made a buffer of me. He gives no commands to the men himself, but merely orders me to pass along the word for this or that. He appears determined to have his own way, and yet not to bring about a personal conflict between himself and his following."

"Do you suppose that to be cowardice on his part?"

"No; he is not a coward. He doubtless intends that I shall stand the brunt of any ill-temper on the part of the men. Should disobedience arise, it will be my orders that are disobeyed, not his. If the matter is of no importance one way or the other, I take it he will say nothing, but I surmise that when it comes to the vital point, he will brush me aside as though I were a feather, and himself confront the men regardless of consequences. This morning I thought they would win in such a case, but, by the iron Cross, I am not so confident now. Remember how he sprung my appointment on the crowd, counting, I am sure, on your help. He said to me, when we were alone by the tower, that you were the most fair-minded man among the lot, and he evidently played on that, giving them not a moment to think, and you backed him up. He carried his point, and since then has not said a word to them, all orders going through me, but I know he intended, as he told you, to take the river road, instead of which he has led us over this hilly district until every man is ready to drop. He is himself very sparing of wine, and is in fit condition. I understand he has tramped both banks of the Rhine, from Ehrenfels to Bonn, so this walk is nothing to him. At the end of it he was off for a stroll, and here are these men lying above the sod like the dead underneath it."

"I cannot make him out," mused Ebearhard. "What has been his training? He appears to be well educated, and yet in some common matters is ignorant as a child, as, for instance, not knowing the difference in status between a skilled artisan and a chaffering merchant! What can have been his up-bringing? He is obviously not of the merchant class, yet he persuades the chief of our merchants, and the most conservative, to engage in this wild goose chase, and actually venture money and goods in supporting him. This expedition will cost Herr Goebel at least five thousand thalers, all because of the blandishments of a youth who walked in from the street, unintroduced. Then he is not an artisan of any sort, for when he joined us his hands were quite useless, except upon the sword-hilt."

"He said he was a fencing-master," explained Greusel.

"I know he did, and yet when he was offered a fee to instruct us he wouldn't look at it. The first duty of a fencing-master, like the rest of us, is to make money. Roland quite evidently scorns it, and at the last instructs us for nothing. Fencing-masters don't promote freebooting expeditions, and, besides, a fencing-master is always urbane and polite, cringing to every one. I have watched Roland closely at times, trying to study him, and in doing so have caught momentary glimpses of such contempt for us, that, by the good Lord above us, it made me shrivel up. You know, Greusel, that youth has more of the qualities usually attributed to a noble than those which go to the make-up of any tradesman."

"He is a puzzle to me," admitted Greusel, "and if this excursion does not break up at the outset, I am not sure that it will be a success."

Noticing a look of alarm in Ebearhard's eyes, Greusel cast a glance over his shoulder, and saw Roland standing behind him. The young man said quietly:

"It hasn't broken up at the outset, for we are already more than five leagues from Frankfort. Our foray must be a success while I have two such wise advisers as I find sitting here."

Neither of the men replied. Both were wondering how much their leader had overheard. He took his place on the bench beside Ebearhard, and said to him:

"I wish you to act as my second lieutenant. If anything happens to me,

Greusel takes my place and you take his. This, by the way, is an appointment, rather than an election. It is not to be put before the guild. You simply act as second lieutenant, and that is all there is about it."

"Very good, Commander," said Ebearhard.

"Greusel, how much money have you?"

"Thirty thalers."

"Economical man! Will you lend me the sum until we reach Assmannshausen?"

"Certainly." Greusel pulled forth his wallet, poured out the gold, and Roland took charge of it.

"And you, Ebearhard? How are you off for funds?"

"I possess twenty-five thalers."

"May I borrow from you as well?"

"Oh, yes."

"I was thinking," continued the young man, as he put away the gold, "that this committee idea of the men has merits of its own; therefore I have formed myself into a committee, appointed, not elected, and will make the disbursements. How much money does our company possess?"

"Not a stiver, so far as I can learn."

"Ah, in that case there is little use in my attempting a collection. Now, as I was saying, Greusel, if anything happens to me, you carry on the enterprise along the lines I have laid down. The first thing, of course, is to reach Assmannshausen."

"Nothing can happen to you before we arrive there," hazarded Greusel.

"I'm not so sure. The sun is very powerful to-day, and should it beat me down, let me lie where I fall, and allow nothing to interrupt the march. Once at Assmannshausen, you two must keep a sharp lookout up the river. When you see the barge, gather your men and lead them up to it. It is to await us about half a league above Assmannshausen."

The three conversed until the hour was consumed, then Roland, throwing his cloak over his arm, rose, and said to his lieutenant:

"Just rouse the men, if you please; and you, Ebearhard, tell the landlord to give each a flagon of wine. We take the road to Wiesbaden. I shall walk slowly on ahead, so that you and the company may overtake me."

With this the young leader sauntered indifferently away, leaving to his subordinates the ungracious task of setting tired men to their work again. Greusel looked glum, but Ebearhard laughed.

Some distance to the east of Wiesbaden the leader deflected his company from the road, and thus they passed Wiesbaden to the left, arriving at the village of Sonnenberg. The straggling company made a halt for a short time, while provisions were purchased, every man carrying his own share, which was scantly sufficient for supper and breakfast, and a quantity of wine was acquired to gratify each throat with about a liter and a half; plenty for a reasonable thirst, but not enough for a carouse.

The company grumbled at being compelled to quit Sonnenberg. They had hoped to spend the night at Wiesbaden, and vociferously proclaimed themselves satisfied with the amount of country already traversed. Their leader said nothing, but left Greusel and Ebearhard to deal with them. He paid for the provisions and the wine, and then, with his cloak loosely over his arm, struck out for the west, as if the declining sun were his goal. The rest followed him slowly, in deep depression of spirits. They were in a wild country, unknown to any of them. The hills had become higher and steeper, and there was not even a beaten path to follow; but Roland, who apparently knew his way, trudged steadily on in advance even of his lieutenants. A bank of dark clouds had risen in the east, the heat of the day being followed by a thunderstorm that growled menacingly above the Taunus mountains, evidently accompanying a torrent of rain, although none fell in the line of march.

The sun had set when the leader brought his company down into the valley of the Walluf, about two and a half leagues from Sonnenberg. Here the men found themselves in a wilderness through which ran a brawling stream. Roland announced to them that this would be their camping place for the night. At once there was an uproar of dissent. How were they to camp out without tents? A heavy rain was impending. Listen to the thunder, and taking warning from the swollen torrent.

"Wrap your cloaks around you," said Roland, "and sleep under the trees. I have often done it myself, and will repeat the experience to-night. If you are not yet tired enough to ensure sound slumber, I shall be delighted to lead you on for another few leagues."

The men held a low-voiced, sullen consultation, gathered in a circle. They speedily decided upon returning to Sonnenberg, which it was the unanimous opinion of the company they should never have left. Townsmen all, who had not in their lives spent a night without a roof over their heads, such accommodation as their leader proposed they should endure seemed like being cast away on a desert island. The mystery of the forest affrighted them. For all they could tell the woods were full of wild animals, and they knew that somewhere near lurked outlaws no less savage. The eighteen, ignoring Greusel and Ebearhard, who stood on one side, watching their deliberations with anxious faces, moved in a body upon their leader, who sat on the bank of the torrent, his feet dangling down towards the foaming water.

"We have resolved to return to Sonnenberg," said the leader of the conclave.

"An excellent resolution," agreed Roland cheerfully. "It is a pleasant village, and I have passed through it several times. By the way, Wiesbaden, which is much larger, possesses the advantage to tired men of being half a league nearer."

The spokesman seemed taken aback by Roland's nonchalant attitude.

"We do not know the road to Wiesbaden, and, indeed, are in some doubt whether or no we can find our way to Sonnenberg with darkness coming on."

"Then if I were you, I shouldn't attempt it. Why not eat your supper, and drink your wine in this sheltering grove?"

"By that time it will be as dark as Erebus," protested the spokesman.

"Then remain here, as I suggested, for the night."

"No; we are determined to reach Sonnenberg. A storm impends."

"In that case, gentlemen, don't let me detain you. The gloom thickens as you spend your time in talk."

"Oh, that's all very well, but when we reach Sonnenberg we shall need money."

"So you will."

"And we intend to secure it."

"Quite right."

"We demand from you three thalers for each man."

"Oh, you want the money from me?"

"Yes, we do."

"That would absorb all the funds I possess."

"No matter. We mean to have it."

"You propose to take it from me by force?"

"Yes."

"Ah, well, such being the case, perhaps it would be better for me to yield willingly?"

"I think so."

"I quite agree with you. There are eighteen of you, all armed with swords, while I control but one blade."

Saying this he unfastened his cloak, which he had put on in the gathering chill of the evening, and untying from his belt a well-filled wallet, held it up to their gaze.

"As this bag undisputedly belongs to me, I have a right to dispose of it as I choose. I therefore give it to the brook, whose outcry is as insistent as yours, and much more musical."

"Stop, Roland, stop!" shouted Ebearhard, but the warning came too late. The young man flung the bag into the torrent, where it disappeared in a smother of foam. He rose to his feet and drew his sword.

"If you wish a fight now, it will be for the love of it, no filthy lucre being at stake."

"By Plutus, you are an accursed fool!" cried the spokesman, making no further show of aggression now that nothing but steel was to be gained by a contest.

"A fool; yes!" said Roland. "And therefore the better qualified to lead all such. Now go to Sonnenberg, or go to Hades!"

The men did neither. They sat down under the trees, ate their supper, and drank their wine.

"Will you dine with me?" said Roland, approaching his two gloomy lieutenants, who stood silent at some distance from the circle formed by the others.

"Yes," said Greusel sullenly, "but I would have dined with greater pleasure had you not proven the spokesman's words true."

"You mean about my being a fool? Oh, you yourself practically called me that this morning. Come, let us sit down farther along the stream, where they cannot overhear what we say."

This being done, Roland continued cheerfully:

"I may explain to you that a week ago I had only a wallet of my own, but before leaving on this journey I called upon my mother, and she presented me with another bag. I foresaw during mittagessen that a demand would be made upon us for money, therefore I borrowed all that you two possessed. Walking on ahead, I prepared for what I knew must come, filling the empty wallet with very small stones picked up along the road. That wallet went into the stream. It is surprising how prone human nature is to jump at conclusions. Why should any of you think that I am simpleton enough to throw away good money? Dear, dear, what a world this is, to be sure!"

Half an hour later all were lying down enveloped in their cloaks, sleeping soundly because of their fatigue, despite being out of doors. Next morning there was consternation in the camp, real or pretended. Roland was nowhere to be found, nor did further search reveal his whereabouts.

VIII. THE MISSING LEADER AND THE MISSING GOLD

Probably because of the new responsibility resting upon him, Joseph Greusel was the first to awaken next morning. He let his long cloak fall from his shoulders as he sat up, and gazed about him with astonishment. It seemed as if some powerful wizard of the hills had spirited him away during the night. He had gone to sleep in a place of terror. The thunder rolled threateningly among the peaks of Taunus, and the reflection of the lightning flash, almost incessant in its recurrence, had lit up the grove with an unholy yellow glare. The never-ceasing roar of the foaming torrent, which in the darkness gleamed with ghostly pallor, had somehow got on his nerves. Under the momentary illumination of the lightning, the waves appeared to leap up at him like a pack of hungry wolves, flecked with froth, and the noise strove to emulate the distant thunder. The grove itself was ominous in its gloom, and sinister shapes seemed to be moving about among the trees.

How different was the aspect now! The sun was still beneath the eastern horizon. The cloudless sky gave promise of another warm day, and the air, of crystalline clearness, was inspiring to breathe. To Greusel's mind, tinged with religious feeling, the situation in which he found himself seemed like a section of the Garden of Eden. The stream, which the night before had been to his superstitious mind a thing of terror, was this morning a placid, smiling, rippling brook that a man might without effort leap across.

He rubbed his eyes in amazement, thinking the mists of sleep must be responsible for this magic transformation, until he remembered the distant thunderstorm of the night before among the eastern mountains, and surmised that a heavy rainfall had deluged these speedily drained peaks and valleys.

"What a blessed thing," he said to himself fervently, "is the ever-recurring morning. How it clears away the errors and the passions of darkness! It is as if God desired to give man repeated opportunities of reform, and of encouragement. How sane everything seems now, as compared with the turbulence of the sulphurous night."

As he rose he became aware of an unaccustomed weight by his side, and putting down his hand was astonished to encounter a bag evidently filled with coin. It had been tied by its deerskin thong to his belt, just as was his own empty wallet. He sat down again, drew it round to the front of him, and unfastened it. Pouring out the gold, he found that the wallet contained a hundred and fifteen thalers, mostly in gold, with the addition of a few silver coins. At once it occurred to him that these were Roland's sixty thalers, his own thirty, and Ebearhard's twenty-five. For some reason, probably fearing the men would suspect the ruse practiced on them the night before, Roland had made him treasurer of the company. But why should he have done it surreptitiously?

Readjusting the leathern sack, he again rose to his feet, but now cast his cloak about him, thus concealing the purse. Ebearhard lay sound asleep near him. Farther away the eighteen remaining members of the company were huddled closely together, as if they had gone to rest in a room too small for them, although the whole country was theirs from which to choose sleeping quarters.

Remembering how the brook had decreased in size, and was now running clear and pellucid, he feared that the bag of stones Roland had so dramatically flung into it might be plainly visible. He determined to rouse his commander, and seek the bag for some distance downstream; for he knew that when the men awakened, all night-fear would have departed from them, and seeing the shrinkage of the brook they might themselves institute a search.

On looking round for Roland he saw no sign of him, but this caused little disquietude, for he supposed that the leader had risen still earlier than himself, wishing to stroll through the forest, or up and down the rivulet.

Greusel, with the purpose of finding the bag, and in the hope, also, of encountering his chief, walked down the valley by the margin of the waterway. Peering constantly into the limpid waters, he discovered no trace of what he sought. Down and down the valley, which was wooded all the way, he walked, and sometimes he was compelled to forsake his liquid guide, and clamber through thickets to reach its border again.

At last he arrived at a little waterfall, and here occurred a break in the woods, causing him to stand entranced by the view which presented itself. Down the declivity the forest lasted for some distance, then it gave place to ever-descending vineyards, with here and there a house showing among the vines. At the foot of this hill ran a broad blue ribbon, which he knew to be the Rhine, although he had never seen it before. Over it floated a silvery gauze of rapidly disappearing mist. The western shore appeared to be flat, and farther along the horizon was formed by hills, not so lofty as that on which he stood, but beautiful against the blue sky, made to seem nearer than they were by the first rays of the rising sun, which tipped the summits with crimson.

Greusel drew a long breath of deep satisfaction. He had never before realized that the world was so enchanting and so peaceful. It seemed impossible that men privileged to live in such a land could find no better occupation than cutting one another's throats.

The gentle plash of the waterfall at his right hand accentuated the stillness. From his height he glanced down into the broad, pellucid pool, into whose depths the water fell, and there, perfectly visible, lay the bag of bogus treasure. Cautiously he worked his way down to the gravelly border of the little lake, flung off his clothes, and plunged head-first into this Diana's pool. It was a delicious experience, and he swam round and round the circular basin, clambered up on the gravel and allowed the stream to fall over his glistening shoulders, reveling in Nature's shower-bath. Satisfied at length, he indulged in another rainbow plunge, grasped the bag, and rose again to the surface. Coming ashore, he unloosened the swollen thongs, poured out the stones along the strand, then, after a moment's thought, he wrung the water out of the bag itself, and tied it to his belt, for there was no predicting where the men would wander when once they awoke, and if he threw it away among the bushes, it might be found, breeding first wonder how it came there, and then suspicion of the trick.

Greusel walked back to camp by the other bank of the stream. Although the early rays of the sun percolated through the upper branches of the trees above them, the eighteen prone men slept as if they were but seven. He sprang over the brook, touched the recumbent Ebearhard with his foot, and so awoke him. This excellent man yawned, and stretched out his arms above his head.

"You're an early bird, Greusel," he said. "Have you got the worm?"

"Yes, I have," replied the latter. "I found it in the basin of a waterfall nearly a league from here," and with that he drew aside his cloak, showing the still wet but empty bag.

For a few moments Ebearhard did not understand. He rose and shook himself, glancing about him.

"Great Jove!" he cried, "this surely isn't the stream by which we lay down last night? Do you mean to tell me that thread of water struck terror into my heart only a few hours ago? I never slept out of doors before in all my life, and could not have imagined it would produce such an effect. I see what you mean now. You have found the bag which Roland threw into the foaming torrent."

"Yes; I was as much astonished at the transformation as you when I awoke, and then it occurred to me that when our friends saw the reduction of the rivulet, they would forthwith begin a treasure-hunt, so I determined to obliterate the evidence."

"Was the bag really full of stones?"

"Oh, yes."

"Well, that is a lesson to me. I believe after all that Roland is helplessly truthful, but last night I thought he befooled us. I was certain it was the bag of coin he had thrown away, and becoming ashamed of himself, had lied to us."

"How could you imagine that? He showed us both the bag of money."

"He produced a bag full of something, but I, being the doubting Thomas of the group, was not convinced it contained money."

"Ah, that reminds me, Ebearhard; here is the bag we saw last night. I discovered it attached to my belt this morning."

"He attached it to the wrong belt, then, for you believed him. He should have tied it to mine. What reason does he give for presenting it to you?"

"Ah, now you touch a point of anxiety in my own mind. I have seen nothing of Roland this morning. I surmised that he had arisen before me, and expected to meet him somewhere down the stream, but have not done so."

"He may have gone farther afield. As you found the bag, he of course, missed it, and probably continued his search."

"I doubt that, because I came upon a point of view reaching to the Rhine and the hills beyond. I could trace the stream for a considerable distance, and watched it for a long time, but there appeared to be nothing alive in the forest."

"You don't suppose he has gone back to Frankfort, do you?"

"I am at loss what to think."

"If he has abandoned this gang of malcontents, I should be the last to blame him. The way these pigs acted yesterday was disgraceful, ending up their day with rank mutiny and threats of violence. By the iron Cross, Greusel, he has forsaken this misbegotten lot, and it serves them perfectly right, prating about comradeship and carrying themselves like cut-throats. This is Roland's method of returning our money, for I suppose that bag contains your thirty thalers and my twenty-five."

"Yes, and his own sixty as well. Poor disappointed devil, generous to the last. It was he who obtained all the money at the beginning, then these drunken swine spend it on wine, and prove so generous and brave that eighteen of them muster courage enough to face one man, and he the man who had bestowed the gold upon them."

"Greusel, the whole situation fills me with disgust. I propose we leave the lot sleeping there, go to Wiesbaden for breakfast, and then trudge back to Frankfort. It would serve the brutes right."

"No," said Greusel quietly; "I shall carry out Roland's instructions."

"I thought you hadn't seen him this morning?"

"Not a trace of him. You heard his orders at Breckenheim."

"I don't remember. What were they?"

"That if anything happened to him, I was to drive the herd to Assmannshausen. I quite agree with you, Ebearhard, that he is justified in deserting this menagerie, but, on the other hand, you and I have stood faithfully by him, and it doesn't seem to me right that he should leave us without a word. I don't believe he has done so, and I expect any moment to see him return."

"You're wrong, Greusel. He's gone. That purse is sufficient explanation, and as you recall to my mind his instructions, I believe something of this must have suggested itself to him even that early in the day. He has divested himself of every particle of money in his possession, turning it over to you, but instead of returning to Frankfort he has made his way over the hills to Assmannshausen, and will await us there."

"What would be the object of that?"

"One reason may be that he will learn whether or not you have enough control over these people to bring them to the Rhine. He will satisfy himself that your discipline is such as to improve their manners. It may be in his mind to resign, and make you leader, if you prove yourself able to control them."

"Suppose I fail in that?"

"Well, then—this is all fancy, remember—I imagine he may look round Assmannshausen to find another company who will at least obey him."

"What you say sounds very reasonable. Still, I do not see why he should have left two friends like us without a word."

"A word, my dear Greusel, would have led to another, and another, and another. One of the first questions asked him would be 'But what are Ebearhard and I to do?' That's exactly what he doesn't wish to answer. He desires to know what you will do of your own accord. He is likely rather hopeless about this mob, but is giving you an opportunity, and then another chance. Why, his design is clear as that rivulet there, and as easily seen through.

You will either bring those men across the hills, or you won't. If you and I are compelled to clamber over to Assmannshausen alone, Roland will probably be more pleased to see us than if we brought this rogues' contingent straggling at our heels. He will appoint you chief officer of his new company, and me the second. If you doubt my conclusions, I'll wager twenty-five thalers against your thirty that I am in the right."

"I never gamble, Ebearhard, especially when certain to lose. You are a shrewder man than I, by a long bowshot."

In a work of fiction it would of course be concealed till the proper time came that all of these men were completely wrong in their prognostications regarding the fate of Roland, but this being history it may be stated that the young man had not the least desire to test Greusel's ability, nor would his lieutenants find him awaiting them when they reached Assmannshausen.

"Hello! Rouse up there! What have we for breakfast? Has all the wine been drunk? I hope not. My mouth's like a brick furnace!"

It was the brave Kurzbold who spoke, as he playfully kicked, not too gently, those of his comrades who lay nearest him. He was answered by groans and imprecations, as one by one the sleeping beauties aroused themselves, and wondered where the deuce they were.

"Who has stolen the river?" cried Gensbein.

"Oh, stealing the river doesn't matter," said a third. "It's only running water. Who drank all the wine? That's a more serious question."

"Well, whoever's taken away the river, I can swear without searching my pouch has made no theft from me, for I spent my last stiver yesterday."

"Don't boast," growled Kurzbold. "You're not alone in your poverty. We're all in the same case. Curse that fool of a Roland for throwing away good money just when it's most needed."

"Good money is always most needed," exclaimed the philosophic Gensbein.

He rose and shook himself, then looked down at the beautiful but unimportant rivulet.

"I say, lads, were we as drunk as all that last night? Was there an impassable torrent here or not?"

"How could we be drunk, you fool, on little more than a liter of wine each," cried Kurzbold.

"Please be more civil in your talk," returned his friend. "You were drunk all day. The liter and a half was a mere nightcap. If you are certain there was a torrent, then I must have been in the same condition as yourself."

The spokesman of the previous night, who had been chided for not springing on Roland before he succeeded in doing away with the treasure, here uttered a shout.

"This water," he said, "is clear as air. You can see every pebble at the bottom. Get to work, you sleepyheads, and search down the stream. We'll recover that bag yet, and then it's back to Sonnenberg for breakfast. Whoever finds it, finds it for the guild; a fair and equal division amongst us. That is, amongst the eighteen of us. I propose that Roland, Greusel, and Ebearhard do not share. They were all in the plot to rob us."

"Agreed!" cried the others, and the treasure-hunt impetuously began.

Greusel and Ebearhard watched them disappear through the forest down the stream.

"Greusel," said Ebearhard, "what a deplorable passion is the frantic quest for money in these days, especially money that we have not earned. Our excited treasure-hunters do not realize that at such a moment in the early morning the only subject worth consideration is breakfast. Being unsparing and prodigal last night, it would take a small miracle of the fishes to suffice them to-day. There is barely enough for two hungry men, and as we are rid of these chaps for half an hour at least, I propose we sit down to our first meal."

Greusel made no comment upon this remark, but the advice commended itself to him, for he followed it.

Some time after they had finished breakfast, the unsuccessful company returned by twos and threes. Apparently they had not wandered so far as the waterfall, for no one said anything of the amazing view of the Rhine. Indeed, it was plain that they considered themselves involved in a boundless wilderness, and were too perplexed to suggest a way out. After a storm of malediction over the breakfastless state of things, and a good deal of quarreling among themselves anent who had been most greedy the night before, they now turned their attention to the silent men who were watching them.

"Where's Roland?" they demanded.

"I don't know," replied Greusel.

"Didn't he tell you where he was going?"

"We have not seen him this morning," explained Ebearhard gently. "He seems to have disappeared in the night. Perhaps he fell into the stream. Perhaps, on the other hand, he has deliberately deserted us. He gave us no hint of his intentions last night, and we are as ignorant as yourselves regarding his whereabouts."

"This is outrageous!" cried Kurzbold. "It is the duty of a leader to provide for his following."

"Yes; if the following follows."

"We have followed," said Kurzbold indignantly, "and have been led into this desert, not in the least knowing where in Heaven's name we are. And now to be left like this, breakfastless, thirsty—" Here Kurzbold's language failed him, and he drew the back of his hand across parched lips.

"When you remember, gentlemen," continued Ebearhard, in accents of honey, "that your last dealings with your leader took place with eighteen swords drawn; when you recollect that you expressed your determination to rob him, and when you call to mind that you brave eighteen threatened him with personal violence if he resisted this brigandage on your part, I cannot understand why you should be surprised at his withdrawal from your fellowship."

"Oh, you always were a glib talker, but the question now is what are we to do?"

"Yes, and that is a question for you to decide," said Ebearhard. "When you mutinied last night, you practically deposed Roland from the leadership. To my mind, he had no further obligations towards you, so, having roughly taken the power into your own hands, it is for you to deal with it as you think best. I should never so far forget myself as to venture even a suggestion."

"As I hinted to you," said Kurzbold, "you are talking too much. You are merely one of ourselves, although you have kept yourself separate from us. Greusel has been appointed lieutenant by our unanimous vote, and if his chief proves a poltroon, he is the man to act. Therefore, Joseph Greusel, I ask on behalf of the company what you intend to do?"

"Before I can answer that question," replied Greusel, "I must know whether or not you will act as you did yesterday?"

"What do you mean by that?" Several, speaking together, put the question.

"I wish to know whether you will follow cheerfully and without demur where I lead? I refuse to act as guide if I run the risk of finding eighteen sword-points at my throat when I have done my best."

"Oh, you talk like a fool," commented Kurzbold. "We followed Roland faithfully enough until he brought us into this impasse. You make entirely too much of last night's episode. None of us intended to hurt him, as you are very well aware, and besides, we don't want a leader who is frightened, and runs away at the first sign of danger."

"Make up your minds what you propose to do," said Greusel stubbornly, "and give me your decision; then you will receive mine."

Greusel saw that although Kurzbold talked like the bully he was, the others were rather subdued, and no voice but his was raised in defense of their previous conduct.

"There is one thing you must tell us before we can come to a decision," went on Kurzbold. "How much money have you and Ebearhard?"

"At midday yesterday I had thirty thalers, and Ebearhard had twenty-five. While you were all sleeping on the grass, after our meal at Breckenheim, Roland asked us for the money."

"You surely were not such idiots as to give it to him?"

"He was our commander, and we both considered it right to do what he asked of us."

"He said," put in Ebearhard, "that your suggestion about a finance committee was a good one, and that he had determined to be that committee. He asked us if any of you had money, but I told him I thought it was all spent, which probably accounts for his restricting the application to us two."

"Then we are here in an unknown wilderness, twenty men, hungry, and without a florin amongst us," wailed Kurzbold, and the comments of those behind him were painful to hear.

"I am glad that at last you thoroughly appreciate our situation, and I hope that in addition you realize it has been brought about not through any fault of Roland's, who gave in to your whims and childishness until you came to the point of murder and robbery. Therefore blame yourselves and not him. You now know as much of our position as I do, so make up your minds about the next step, and inform me what conclusion you come to."

"You're a mighty courageous leader," cried Kurzbold scornfully, and with this the hungry ones retired some distance into the grove, from whence echoes of an angry debate came to the two men who sat by the margin of the stream. After a time they strode forward again. Once more Kurzbold was the spokesman.

"We have determined to return to Frankfort."

"Very good."

"I suppose you remember enough of the way to lead us at least as far as Wiesbaden. Beyond that point we can look to ourselves."

"I should be delighted," said Greusel, "to be your guide, but unfortunately

I am traveling in the other direction with Ebearhard."

"Why, in the name of starvation?" roared Kurzbold. "You know no more of the country ahead of us than we do. By going back we can get something to eat, and a drink, at one of the farmhouses we passed this side of Sonnenberg."

"How?" inquired Greusel.

"Why, if they ask for payment we will give them iron instead of silver. No man need starve with a sword by his side."

"Granted that this is feasible, and that the farmers yield instead of raising the country-side against you, when you reach Frankfort what are you going to do? Eat and drink with the landlord of the Rheingold until he becomes bankrupt? You must remember that it was Roland who liquidated our last debt there, without asking or receiving a word of thanks, and he did that not a moment too soon, for the landlord was at the end of his resources and would have closed his tavern within another week."

Kurzbold stormed at this harping on the subject of Roland and his generosity, but those with him were hungry, and they now remembered, too late, that what Greusel said was strictly true. If Roland had put in an appearance then, he would have found a most docile company to lead. They were actually murmuring against Kurzbold, and blaming him and his clan for the disaster that had overtaken them.

"Why will you not come back with us?" pleaded the penitents, with surprising mildness.

"Because the future in Frankfort strikes me as hopeless. Not one amongst us has the brains of Roland, whom we have thrown out. Besides, it is nine and a half long leagues to Frankfort, and only three and a half leagues to Assmannshausen. I expect to find Roland there, and although I know nothing of his intentions, I imagine he has gone to enlist a company of a score or thereabouts that will obey his commands. There is some hope by going forward to Assmannshausen; there is absolutely none in retreating to Frankfort. Then, as I said, Assmannshausen is little more than three leagues away; a fact worth consideration by hungry men. On the Rhine we are in the rich wine country, where there is plenty to eat and drink, probably for the asking, whereas if we turn our faces towards the east we are marching upon starvation."

The buzz of comment aroused by this speech proved to the two men that Kurzbold stood once more alone. Greusel, without seeming to care which way the cat jumped, had induced that unreasoning animal to leap as he liked. His air of supreme indifference aroused Ebearhard's admiration, especially when he remembered that under his cloak there rested a hundred and fifteen thalers in gold and silver.

"But you know nothing of the way," protested Kurzbold. "None of us are acquainted with the country to the west."

"We don't need to be acquainted with it," said Greusel. "We steer westward by glancing at the sun now and then, and cannot go astray, because we must come to the Rhine; then it's either up or down the river, as the case may be, to reach Assmannshausen."

"To the Rhine! To the Rhine!" was now the universal cry.

"Before we begin our journey," said Greusel, as if he accepted the leadership with reluctance, "I must have your promise that you will obey me without question. I am not so patient a man as Roland, but on my part I guarantee you an excellent meal and good wine as soon as we reach Assmannshausen."

"How can you promise that," growled Kurzbold, "when you have given away your money?"

"Because, as I told you, I expect to meet Roland there."

"But he threw away his bag."

"Yes; I told him it was a foolish thing to do, and perhaps that is why he left without saying a word, even to me. He is an ingenious man. Assmannshausen is familiar to him, and I dare say he would not have discarded his money without knowing where to get more."

"To the Rhine! To the Rhine! To the Rhine!" cried the impatient host, gathering up their cloaks, and tightening their belts, as the savage does when he is hungry.

"To the Rhine, then," said Greusel, springing across the little stream in company with Ebearhard.

"You did that very well, Greusel," complimented the latter.

"I would rather have gone alone with you," replied the new leader, "for I have condemned myself to wear this heavy cloak, which is all very well to sleep in, but burdensome under a hot sun."

"The sun won't be so oppressive," predicted his friend, "while we keep to the forest."

"That is very true, but remember we are somewhere in the Rheingau, and that we must come out into the vineyards by and by."

"Don't grumble, Greusel, but hold up your head as a great diplomatist. Roland himself could not have managed these chaps so well, you flaunting hypocrite, the only capitalist amongst us, yet talking as if you were a monk sworn to eternal poverty."

Greusel changed the subject.

"Do you notice," he said, "that we are following some sort of path, which we must have trodden last evening, without seeing it in the dusk."

"I imagine," said Ebearhard, "that Roland knew very well where he was going. He strode along ahead of us as if sure of his ground. I don't doubt but this will lead us to Assmannshausen."

Which, it may be remarked, it did not. The path was little more than a trail, which a sharp-eyed man might follow, and it led up-hill and down dale direct to the Archbishop's Castle of Ehrenfels.

The forest lasted for a distance that the men in front estimated to be about two leagues, then they emerged into open country, and saw the welcome vines growing. Climbing out of the valley, they observed to the right, near the top of a hill, a small hamlet, which had the effect of instantaneously raising the spirits of the woebegone company.

"Hooray for breakfast!" they shouted, and had it not been for their own fatigue, and the steepness of the hill, they would have broken into a run.

"Halt!" cried Greusel sternly, standing before and above them. At once they obeyed the word of command, which caused Ebearhard to smile.

"You will climb to the top of this hill," said Greusel, "and there rest under command of my lieutenant, Ebearhard. As we now emerge into civilization, I warn you that if we are to obtain breakfast it must be by persuasion, and not by force. Therefore, while you wait on the hilltop, I shall go alone into the houses on the right, and see what can be done towards providing a meal for eighteen men. Ebearhard and I will fast until we reach Assmannshausen. On the other hand, you should be prepared for disappointment; loaves of bread are not to be picked up on the point of a sword. If I return and order you to march on unfed, you must do so as cheerfully as you can."

This ultimatum called forth not a word of opposition, and Ebearhard led the van while Greusel deflected up the hill to his right, the sooner to reach the village.

He learned that the name of the place was Anton-Kap; that the route he had been following would take him to Ehrenfels, and that he must adopt a reasonably rough mountain-road to the right in order to reach Assmannshausen.

By somewhat straining the resources of the place, which proved to possess no inn, he collected bread enough for the eighteen, and there was no dearth of wine, although it proved a coarse drink that reflected little credit on the reputation of the Rheingau. He paid for this meal in advance, saying that they were all in a hurry to reach Assmannshausen, and wished to leave as soon as the frugal breakfast was consumed.

Mounting a small elevation to the west of the village, he signaled to the patient men to come on, which they lost no time in doing. The bread was eaten and the wine drunk without a word being said by any one. And now they took their way down the hill again, crossed the little Geisenheim stream, and up once more, traversing a high table-land giving them a view of the Rhine, finally descending through another valley, which led them into Assmannshausen, celebrated for its red wine, a color they had not yet met with.

Assmannshausen proved to be a city as compared with the hamlets they had passed, yet was small enough to make a thorough search of the place a matter that consumed neither much effort nor time. Greusel led his men to a Weinstaube a short distance out of the village, and, to their delight, succeeded in establishing a credit for them to the extent of one liter of wine each, with a substantial meal of meat, eggs, and what-not. Greusel and Ebearhard left them there in the height of great enjoyment, all the more delightful after the hunger and fatigue they had encountered, for the three and a half leagues had proved almost without a single stretch of level land. The two officers inquired for Roland, without success, at the various houses of entertainment which Assmannshausen boasted, then canvassed every home in the village, but no one had seen anything of the man they described.

Coming out to the river front, deeply discouraged, the two gazed across the empty water, from which all enlivening traffic had departed. It was now evident to both that Roland had not entered Assmannshausen, for in so small and gossipy a hamlet no stranger could even have passed through without being observed.

"Well, Joseph," asked Ebearhard, "what do you intend to do?"

"There is nothing to do but to wait until our money is gone. It is absolutely certain that Roland is not here. Can it be possible that after all he returned?"

"How could he have done so? We know him to have been without money; therefore why to Frankfort, even if such a trip were possible for a penniless man?"

"I am sorry now," said Greusel despondently, "that I did not follow a suggestion that occurred to me, which was to take the men direct down the valley where we encamped, to the banks of the Rhine, and there make inquiries."

"You think he went that way?"

"I did, until you persuaded me out of it."

"Again I ask what could be his object?"

"It seems to me that this mutiny made a greater impression on his mind than I had supposed. After all, he is not one of us, and never has been. You yourself pointed that out when we were talking of him at Breckenheim. If you caught glances of contempt for us while we were all one jolly family in the Kaiser cellar, what must be his loathing for the guild after such a day as yesterday?"

"That's true. You must travel with a man before you learn his real character."

"Meaning Roland?"

"Meaning this crew, guzzling up at the tavern. Meaning you, meaning me; yes, and meaning Roland also. I never knew until yesterday and to-day what a capable fellow you were, and when I remember that I nominated Kurzbold for our leader before Roland appeared on the scene, I am amazed at my lack of judgment of men. As for Roland himself, my opinion of him has fallen. Nothing could have persuaded me that he would desert us all without a word of explanation, no matter what happened. My predictions regarding his conduct are evidently wrong. What do you think has actually occurred?"

"It's my opinion that the more he thought over the mutiny, the angrier he became; a cold, stubborn anger, not vocal at all, as Kurzbold's would be. I think that after fastening the money to my belt he went down the valley to the Rhine. He knows the country, you must remember. He would then either wait there until the barge appeared, or more likely would proceed up along the margin of the river, and hail the boat when it came in sight. The captain would recognize him, and turn in, and we know the captain is under his command. At this moment they are doubtless poling slowly up the Rhine to the Main again, and will thus reach Frankfort. Herr Goebel has confidence in

Roland, otherwise he would never have risked so much on his bare word. He will confess to his financier that he has been mistaken in us, and doubtless tell him all that happened, and the merchant will appreciate that, even though he has lost his five hundred thalers, Roland would not permit him to lose his goods as well."

"Do you suppose Roland will enlist another company?"

"It is very likely, for Herr Goebel trusts him, and, goodness knows, there are enough unemployed men in Frankfort for Roland to select a better score than we have proved to be."

It was quite certain that Roland was not in Assmannshausen, yet Greusel was a prophet as false as Ebearhard.

IX. A SOLEMN PROPOSAL OF MARRIAGE

When Roland wrapped his cloak about him, and lay down on the sward at some distance from the spot where his officers already slept, he found that he could not follow their example. Although, he had remained outwardly calm when the attack was made upon him, his mind was greatly perturbed over the outlook. He reviewed his own conduct, wondering whether it would be possible for him so to amend it that he could acquire the respect and maintain the obedience of his men. If he could not accomplish this, then was his plan foredoomed to failure. His cogitations drove away sleep, and he called to mind the last occasion on which he made this same spot his bedroom. Then he had slumbered dreamlessly the night through. He was on the direct trail between Ehrenfels Castle and the town of Wiesbaden, the route over which supplies had been carried to the Castle time and again when the periodical barges from Mayence failed to arrive. It had been pointed out to him by the custodian of the Castle when the young man first became irked by the confined limits of the Schloss, and frequently since that time he had made his way through the forest to Wiesbaden and back.

Never before had he seen the little Walluf so boisterous, pretending that it was important, and he quite rightly surmised that the cause was a sudden downpour in the mountains farther east. The distant mutterings of thunder having long since ceased, he recognized that the volume of the stream was constantly lessening. As the brook gradually subsided to its customary level, the forest became more and more silent. The greater his endeavor to sleep, the less dormant Roland felt, and all his senses seemed unduly quickened by this ineffectual beckoning to somnolence. He judged by the position of the stars, as he lay on his back, that it was past midnight, when suddenly he became aware of a noise to the west of him, on the other side of the brook. Sitting up, and listening intently, he suspected, from the rustle of the underbrush, that some one was following the trail, and would presently come upon his sleeping men.

He rose stealthily, unsheathed his sword, leaped across the rivulet, and proceeded with caution up the acclivity, keeping on the trail as best he could in the darkness. He was determined to learn the business of the wayfarer, without disturbing his men, so crept rapidly up the hill. Presently he saw the glimmer of a light, and conjectured that some one was coming impetuously down, guided by a lanthorn swinging in his hand. Roland stood on guard with sword extended straight in front of him, and the oncomer's breast was almost at the point of it when he hauled himself up with a sudden cry of dismay, as the lanthorn revealed an armed man holding the path.

"I have no money," were the first words of the stranger.

"Little matter for that," replied Roland. "'Tis information I wish, not gear. Why are you speeding through the forest at night, for no sane man traverses this path in the darkness?"

"I could not wait for daylight," said the stranger, breathing heavily. "I carry a message of the greatest importance. Do not delay me, I beg of you. I travel on affairs of State; Imperial matters, and it is necessary I should reach Frankfort in time, or heads may fall."

"So serious as that?" asked Roland, lowering the point of his sword, for he saw the messenger was unarmed. "Whom do you seek?"

"That I dare not tell you. The message concerns those of the highest, and I am pledged to secrecy. Be assured, sir, that I speak the truth."

"Your voice sounds honest. Hold up the lanthorn at arm's length, that I may learn if your face corresponds with it. Ha, that is most satisfactory! And now, my hurrying youth, will you reveal your mission, or shall I be compelled to run my sword through your body?"

"You would not learn it even then," gasped the young man, shrinking still farther up the hill.

Roland laughed.

"That is true enough," he said, "therefore shall I not impale you, but will instead relate to you the secret you carry. You are making not for Frankfort—"

"I assure you, sir, by the sacred Word, that I am, and grieve my oath does not allow me to do your bidding, even though you would kill me, which is easily done, since I am unarmed."

"You pass through Frankfort, I doubt not, but your goal is a certain small room in the neighboring suburb of Sachsenhausen, and he whom you seek is a youth of about your own age, named Roland. You travel on the behest of your father, who was much agonized in mind when you left him, and he, I take it, is custodian of Ehrenfels Castle."

"In God's name!" cried the youth, aghast, "how did you guess all that?"

Again Roland laughed quietly.

"Why, Heinrich," he said, "your agitation causes you to forget old friends. Hold up your lanthorn again, and learn whether or not you recognize me, as I recognized you."

"Heaven be praised! Prince Roland!"

"Yes; your journey is at an end, my good Heinrich, thank the fortune that kept me awake this night. Do you know why you are sent on this long and breathless journey?"

"Yes, Highness. There has come to the Castle from the Archbishop of Mayence a lengthy document for you to sign, and you are informed that the day after to-morrow their Lordships of Mayence, Treves, and Cologne, meet together at the Castle to hold some conversation with you."

"By my sword, then, Heinrich, had you found me in Sachsenhausen we had never attained Ehrenfels in time."

"I think I could have accomplished it," replied the young man. "I should have reached Wiesbaden before daybreak, and there bought the fastest horse that could be found. My father told me to time myself, and if by securing another horse at Frankfort for you I could not make the return journey speedily enough, I was to engage a boat with twenty rowers, if necessary, and convey you to Ehrenfels before the Archbishops arrived."

"Then, Heinrich, you must have deluded me when you said you had no money."

"No, Highness, I have none, but I carry an order for plenty upon a merchant in Wiesbaden, who would also supply me with a horse."

"Heinrich, there are many stars burning above us to-night, and I have been watching them, but your star must be blazing the brightest of all. Sit you down and rest until I return. Make no noise, for there are twenty others asleep by the stream. My cloak is at the bottom of the hill, and I must fetch it. I shall be with you shortly, so keep your candle alight, that I may not miss you."

With that Roland returned rapidly down the slope, untying his bag of money as he descended. Cautiously he fastened it to the belt of Greusel, then, snatching his cloak from the ground, he sprang once more across the stream, and climbed to the waiting Heinrich.

It was broad daylight before they saw the towers of Ehrenfels, and they found little difficulty in rousing Heinrich's father, for he had slept as badly that night as Roland himself.

The caretaker flung his arms around the young prisoner.

"Oh, thank God, thank God!" was all he could cry, and "Thank God!" again he repeated. "Never before have I felt my head so insecure upon my shoulders. Had you not been here when they came, Highness, their Lordships would have listened to no explanation."

"Really you were in little danger with such a clever son. The Archbishops would never have suspected that he was not I, for none of the three has ever seen me. I am quite sure Heinrich would have effected my signature excellently, and answered to their satisfaction all questions they might ask. So long as he complied with their wishes, there would be no inquiries set afoot, for none would suspect the change. Indeed, custodian, you have missed the opportunity of your life in not suppressing me, thus allowing your son to be elected Emperor."

"Your Highness forgets that my poor boy cannot write his own name, much less yours. Besides, it would be a matter of high treason to forge your signature, so again I thank God you are here. Indeed, your Highness, I am in great trouble about my son."

"Oh, the danger is not so serious as you think."

"'Tis not the danger, Highness. That it is his duty to face, but he takes advantage of his position as prisoner. He knows I dare refuse him nothing, and he calls for wine, wine, wine, spending his days in revelry and his nights in stupor."

"You astonish me. Why not cudgel the nonsense out of him? Your arm is strong enough."

"I dare not lay stick on him, and I beg you to breathe nothing of what I have told you, for he holds us both in his grasp, and he knows it. If I called for help to put him in a real dungeon, he would blurt out the whole secret."

"In that case you must even make terms with him. 'Twill be for but a very short time, and after that we will reform him. He was frightened enough of my sword in the forest, and I shall make him dance to its point once this crisis is over."

"I shall do the best I can, Highness. But you must have been on your way to Ehrenfels. Had you heard aught of what is afoot?"

"Nothing. 'Twas mere chance that Heinrich and I met in the forest, and he was within a jot of impinging himself upon my sword in his hurry. I stood in the darkness, while he himself held a light for the better convenience of any chance marauder who wished to undo him."

"Unarmed, and without money," said the custodian, "I thought he was safer than otherwise. But you are surely hungry, Highness. Advance then within, and I will see to your needs."

So presently the errant Prince consumed an excellent, if early breakfast, and, without troubling to undress, flung himself upon a couch, sleeping dreamlessly through the time that Greusel and Ebearhard were conjuring up motives for him, of which he was entirely innocent.

When Roland woke in the afternoon, he had quite forgotten that a score of men who, nominally, at least, acknowledged him master, were wondering what had become of him. He called the custodian, and asked for a sight of the parchments that his Lordship of Mayence had sent across the river for his perusal. He found the documents to be a very carefully written series of demands disguised under the form of requests.

The pledges which were asked of the young Prince were beautifully engrossed on three parchments, each one a duplicate of the other two. If Roland accepted them, they were to be signed next day, in presence of the three Archbishops. Two certainties were impressed upon him when he had read the scroll: first, the Archbishops were determined to rule; and second, if he did not promise to obey they would elect some other than himself Emperor on the death or deposition of his father. The young man resolved to be acquiescent and allow the future to settle the question whether he or the Archbishops should be the head of the Empire. A strange exultation filled him at the prospect, and all thought of other things vanished from his mind.

Leaving the parchments on the table in the knights' hall, where he had examined them, he mounted to the battlements to enjoy the fresh breeze that, no matter how warm the day, blows round the towers of Ehrenfels. Here a stone promenade, hung high above the Rhine, gave a wonderful view up and down the river and along the opposite shore. From this elevated, paved plateau he could see down the river the strongholds of Rheinstein and Falkenberg, and up the river almost as far as Mayence. He judged by the altitude of the sun that it was about four o'clock in the afternoon. The sight of Rheinstein should have suggested to him his deserted company, for that was the first castle he intended to attack, but the prospect opened up to him by the communication of the Archbishops had driven everything else from his mind.

Presently the cautious custodian joined him in his eyrie, and Roland knew instinctively why he had come. The old man was wondering whether or not he would make difficulties about signing the parchments. He feared the heedless impetuosity and conceit of youth; the natural dislike on the part of a proud young prince to be restricted and bound down by his elders, and the jailer could not conceal his gratification when the prisoner informed him that of course he would comply with the desires of the three prelates.

"You see," he continued, with a smile, "I must attach my signature to those instruments in order to make good my promises to you."

He was interrupted by a cry of astonishment from his aged comrade.

"Will wonders never cease!" cried the old man. "Those merchants in Frankfort must be irredeemable fools. Look you there, Highness! Do you see that barge coming down the river, heavily laden, as I am a sinner, for she lies low in the water. It is one of the largest of the Frankfort boats, and those hopeful simpletons doubtless imagine they can make their way through to Cologne with enough goods left to pay for the journey. 'Tis madness! Why, the knights of Rheinstein and Falkenberg alone will loot them before they are out of our sight. If they think to avoid those rovers by hugging our shore, their mistake will be apparent before they have gone far."

Roland gazed at the approaching craft, and instantly remembered that he was responsible for its appearance on the Rhine. He recognized Herr Goebel's great barge, with its thick mast in the prow, on which no sail was hoisted because the wind blew upstream. On recollecting his deserted men, he wondered whether or not Greusel had brought them across the hills to Assmannshausen. Had they yet discovered that Joseph carried the bag of gold? He laughed aloud as he thought of the scrimmage that would ensue when this knowledge came to them. But little as he cared for the eighteen, he experienced a pang of regret as he estimated the predicament in which both Greusel and Ebearhard had stood on learning he had left them without a word. Still, even now he could not see how any explanation on his part was possible without revealing his identity, and that he was determined not to do.

Turning round, he said abruptly to the custodian:

"Were the seven hundred thalers paid to you each month?"

"Of a surety," was the reply.

"That will be two thousand one hundred thalers altogether. Did you spend the money?"

"I have not touched a single coin. That amount is yours, and yours alone, Prince Roland. If I have been of service I am quite content to wait for my reward, or should I not be here, I know you will remember my family."

"May the Lord forget me if I don't. Still, the twenty-one hundred thalers are all yours, remember, but I beg of you to lend me a thousand, for I possess not a single gold piece in my bag. Indeed, if it comes to that, I do not possess even a bag. I had two yesterday, but one I gave away and the other I threw away."

The old man hurried down, and presently returned with the bag of money that Roland had asked of him. Before this happened, however, Roland, watching the barge, saw it round to, and tie up at the shore some distance above Assmannshausen. He took the gold, and passed down the stone stair to the courtyard.

"I shall return," he said, "before the sun sets," and without more ado, this extraordinary captive left his prison, and descended the hill in the direction of the barge.

After greeting Captain Blumenfels, he learned that the boat had been delayed by running on a sandbank in the Main during the night, but they had got it off at daybreak, and here they were. As, standing on the shore, Roland talked with the captain on the barge, he saw approaching from Assmannshausen two men whom he recognized. Telling the captain he might not be ready for several days, he walked along the shore to meet his astonished friends, who, as was usual with them, jumped at an erroneous conclusion, and supposed that he arrived on the barge which they had seen rounding to for the purpose of taking up her berth by the river-bank.

Greusel and Ebearhard stood still until he came up to them.

"Good afternoon, gentlemen. Are you here alone, or have you brought the mob with you?"

"Your capable lieutenant, sir," said Ebearhard, before his slower companion could begin to frame a sentence, "allowed the men to think they were having their own way, but in reality diverted them into his, so they are now enjoying a credit of one liter each at the tavern of the Golden Anker."

"That," said Roland, "is but as a drop of water in a parched desert. Have they discovered you hold the money, Greusel?"

"No, not yet; but I fear they will begin to suspect by and by. I suppose you went down the valley of the brook to the Rhine, and overhauled the barge there?"

"I suppose so," said Roland. "What else did you think I could do?"

"I was sure you had done that, but I feared you would turn the barge back to Frankfort."

"I never thought of such a thing. Indeed, the captain told me he met difficulty enough navigating the shallow Main, and I think he prefers the deeper Rhine. Of course, you know why I left you."

The men looked at each other without reply, and Roland laughed.

"I see you have been harboring dark suspicions, but the case is very simple. The pious monks tell us that the Scriptures say if a man asks us to go one league with him, we should go two. My good friends of the guild last night made a most reasonable request, namely, that I should bestow upon them three thalers each, and surely, to quote the monks again, the laborer is worthy of his hire."

"Oh, that is the way you look upon it, then," said Greusel.

"From a scriptural point of view, yes; and I am going to better the teachings of my young days by giving each of the men ten times the amount he desired. Thirty thalers each are waiting in this bag for them."

"By my sword!" cried Ebearhard, "if that isn't setting a premium on mutiny it comes perilously close."

"Not so, Ebearhard; not so. You and Greusel did not mutiny, therefore to each of you I give a hundred and thirty thalers, which is the thirty thalers the mutineers receive, and a hundred thalers extra, as a reward of virtue because you did not join them. After all, there is much to be said for the men's point of view. I had led them ruthlessly under a burning July sun, along a rough and shadeless road, then dragged them away from the ample wine-vaults of

Sonnenberg; next guided them on through brambles, over streams, into bogs and out again; and lastly, when they were dog-tired, hungry and ill-tempered, I carelessly pointed to a section of the landscape, and said, 'There, my dear chaps, is your bedroom'; lads who had never before slept without blankets and a roof. No wonder they mutinied; but even then, by the love of God for His creatures, they did not actually attack me when I stood up with drawn sword in my hand."

"Of course you have that at least to be thankful for," said Ebearhard. "Eighteen to one was foul odds."

"I be thankful! Surely you are dreaming, Ebearhard. Why should I be thankful, except that I escaped the remorse for at least killing a dozen of them!"

Ebearhard laughed heartily.

"Oh, if so sure of yourself as all that, you need no sympathy from me."

"You thought I would be outmatched? By the Three Kings! do you imagine me such a fool as to teach you artisans the higher qualities of the sword? There would have been a woeful surprise for the eighteen had they ventured another step farther. However, that's all past and done with, and we'll say no more about it. Let us sit down here on the sward, and indulge in the more agreeable recreation of counting money."

He spread his cloak on the grass, and poured out the gold upon it.

"I am keeping two hundred thalers for myself, as leader of the expedition, and covetous. Here are your hundred and thirty thalers, Greusel, and yours, Ebearhard. You will find remaining five hundred and forty, which, if divided with reasonable accuracy, should afford thirty thalers to each of our precious eighteen."

"Aren't you coming with us to Assmannshausen, that you may give this money to the men yourself?" asked Greusel.

"No; that pleasure falls to my lieutenants, first and second. One may divide the money while the other delivers the moral lecture against mutiny, illustrated by the amount that good behavior gains. Say nothing to the men about the barge being here, merely telling them to prepare for action. Now that you are in funds, engage a large room, exclusively for yourselves, at the Golden Anker. Thus you will be the better able to keep the men from talking with strangers, and so prevent any news of our intentions drifting across the river to Rheinstein or Falkenberg. You might put it to them, should they object to the special room, that you are reconstituting, as it were, the Kaiser cellar of Frankfort in the village of Assmannshausen. Go forward, therefore, with your usual meetings of the guild, as it was before I lowered its tone by becoming a member. Knowing the lads as I do, I suggest that you make your bargain with them before you deliver the money. No promise; no thirty thalers. And now, good-by. I shall be exceedingly busy for some days arranging for a further supply of money, so do not seek me out no matter what happens."

With this Roland shook hands, and returned to Ehrenfels Castle.

The three sumptuous barges of the Archbishops hove in sight at midday, two coming up the river and one floating down. They maneuvered to the landing so that all reached it at the same time, and thus the three Archbishops were enabled to set foot simultaneously on the firm ground, as was right and proper, no one of them obtaining precedence over the other two. On entering the Castle of Ehrenfels in state, they proceeded to the large hall of the knights, and seated themselves in three equal chairs that were set along the solid table. Here a repast was spread before them, accompanied by the finest wine the Rheingau produced, and although the grand prelates ate lustily, they were most sparing in their drink, for when they acted in concert none dared risk putting himself at a disadvantage with the others. They would make up for their abstinence when each rested in the security of his own castle.

The board being cleared, Roland was summoned, and bowing deeply to each of the three he took his place, modestly standing on the opposite side of the table. The Archbishop of Mayence, as the oldest of the trio, occupied the middle chair; Treves, the next in age, at his right hand, and Cologne at his left. A keen observer might have noticed that the deferential, yet dignified, bearing of the young Prince made a favorable impression upon these rulers who, when they acted together, formed a power that only nominally was second in the realm.

It was Mayence who broke the silence.

"Prince Roland, some months ago turbulence in the State rendered it advisable that you, as a probable nominee to the throne, should be withdrawn from the capital to the greater safety which this house affords. I hope it has never been suggested to you that this unavoidable detention merited the harsh name of imprisonment?"

"Never, your Lordships," said Roland, with perfect truth.

The three slightly inclined their heads, and Mayence continued:

"I trust that in the carrying out of our behests you have been put to no inconvenience during your residence in my Castle of Ehrenfels, but if you find cause for complaint I shall see to it that the transgressor is sharply punished."

"My Lord, had such been the case I should at once have communicated with your Lordship at Mayence. The fact that you have received no such protest from me answers your question, but I should like to add emphasis to this reply by saying I have met with the greatest courtesy and kindness within these walls."

"I speak for my brothers and myself when I assert we are all gratified to hear the expression that has fallen from your lips. There was sent for your perusal a document in triplicate. Have you found time to read it?"

"Yes, my Lord, and I beg to state at once that I will sign it with the greater pleasure since in any case, if called to the high position you propose, I should have consulted your Lordships on every matter that I deemed important enough to be worthy of your attention, and in no instance could I think of setting up my own opinion against the united wisdom of your Lordships."

For a few minutes there ensued a whispered conversation among the three, then Mayence spoke again:

"Once more I voice the sentiments of my colleagues, Prince Roland, when I assure you that the words you have just spoken give us the utmost satisfaction. In the whole world to-day there is no prouder honor than that which it is in the Electors' power to bestow upon you, and it is a blessed augury for the welfare of our country when the energy and aspiration of youth in this high place associates itself with the experience of age."

Here he made a signal, and the aged custodian, who had been standing with his back against the door, well out of earshot, for the conversation was carried on in the most subdued and gentle tones, hurried forward, and Mayence requested him to produce the documents entrusted to his care. These were spread out before the young man, who signed each of them amidst a deep silence, broken only by the scratching of the quill.

Up to this point Roland had been merely a Prince of the Empire; now, to all practical purposes, he was heir-apparent to the throne. This distinction was delicately indicated by Mayence, who asked the attendant to bring forward a chair, and then requested the young man to seat himself. Roland had supposed the ceremonies at an end, but it was soon evident that something further remained, for the three venerable heads were again in juxtaposition, and apparently there was some whispered difference as to the manner of procedure. Then Cologne, as the youngest of the three, was prevailed upon to act as spokesman, and with a smile he regarded the young man before he began.

"I reside farther than my two colleagues from your fair, if turbulent, city of Frankfort, and perhaps that is one reason why I know little of the town and its ways from personal observation. You are a young man who, I may say, has greatly commended himself to us all, and so in whatever questions I may put, you will not, I hope, imagine that there is anything underneath them which does not appear on the surface."

Roland drew a long breath, and some of the color left his face.

"What in the name of Heaven is coming now," he said to himself, "that calls for so ominous a prelude? It must be something more than usually serious. May the good Lord give me courage to face it!"

But outwardly he merely inclined his head.

"We have all been young ourselves, and I trust none of us forget the temptations, and perhaps the dangers, that surround youth, especially when highly placed. I am told that Frankfort is a gay city, and doubtless you have mixed, to some extent at least, in its society." Here the Archbishop paused, and, as he evidently expected a reply, Roland spoke:

"I regret to say, my Lord, that my opportunities for social intercourse have hitherto been somewhat limited. Greatly absorbed in study, there has been little time for me to acquire companions, much less friends."

"What your Highness says, so far from being a drawback, as you seem to imagine, is all to the good. It leaves the future clear of complications that might otherwise cause you embarrassment." Here the Archbishop smiled again, and Roland found himself liking the august prelate. "It was not, however, of men that I desired to speak, but of women."

"Oh, is that all?" cried the impetuous youth. "I feared, my Lord, that you were about to treat of some serious subject. So far as women are concerned, I am unacquainted with any, excepting only my mother."

At this the three prelates smiled in differing degrees; even the stern lips of Mayence relaxing at the young man's confident assumption that consideration of women was not a matter of importance.

"Your Highness clears the ground admirably for me," continued Cologne, "and takes a great weight from my mind, because I am entrusted by my brethren with a proposal which I have found some difficulty in setting forth. It is this. The choice of an Empress is one of the most momentous questions that an Emperor is called upon to decide. In all except the highest rank personal preference has much to do with the selection of a wife, but in the case of a king do you agree with me that State considerations must be kept in view?"

"Undoubtedly, my Lord."

"This is a matter to which we three Electors have given the weightiest consideration, finally agreeing on one whom we believe to possess the necessary qualifications; a lady highly born, deeply religious, enormously wealthy, and exceedingly beautiful. She is related to the most noble in the land. I refer to Hildegunde Lauretta Priscilla Agnes, Countess of Sayn. If there is any reason why your preference should not coincide with ours, I beg you quite frankly to state it."

"There is no reason at all, your Lordships," cried Roland, with a deep sigh of relief on learning that his fears were so unfounded. "I shall be most happy and honored to wed the lady at any time your Lordships and she may select."

"Then," said the Archbishop of Mayence, rising to his feet and speaking with great solemnity, "you are chosen as the future Emperor of our land."

X. A CALAMITOUS CONFERENCE

The prelate and his ward were met at the doors of Stolzenfels by the Archbishop of Treves in person, and the welcome they received left nothing to be desired in point of cordiality. There were many servants, male and female, about the Castle, but no show of armed men.

The Countess was conducted to a room whose outlook fascinated her. It occupied one entire floor of a square tower, with windows facing the four points of the compass, and from this height she could view the Rhine up to the stern old Castle of Marksburg, and down past Coblentz to her own realm of Sayn, where it bordered the river, although the stronghold from which she ruled this domain was hidden by the hills ending in Ehrenbreitstein.

When she descended on being called to mittagessen, she was introduced to a sister of the Archbishop of Treves, a grave, elderly woman, and to the Archbishop's niece, a lady about ten years older than Hildegunde. Neither of these grand dames had much to say, and the conversation at the meal rested chiefly with the two Archbishops. Indeed, had the Countess but known it, her presence there was a great disappointment to the two noblewomen, for the close relationship of the younger to the Archbishop of Treves rendered it impossible that she should be offered the honor about to be bestowed upon the younger and more beautiful Countess von Sayn.

The Archbishop of Mayence, although a resident of the Castle, partook of refreshment in the smallest room of the suite reserved for him, where he was waited upon by his own servants and catered for by his own cook.

When the great Rhine salmon, smoking hot, was placed upon the table, Cologne was generous in his praise of it, and related again, for the information of his host and household, the story of the English Princess who had partaken of a similar fish, doubtless in this same room. Despite the historical bill of fare, and the mildly exhilarating qualities of the excellent Oberweseler wine, whose delicate reddish color the sentimental Archbishop compared to the blush on a bride's cheeks, the social aspect of the midday refection was overshadowed by an almost indefinable sense of impending danger. In the pseudogenial conversation of the two Archbishops there was something forced: the attitude of the elderly hostess was one of unrelieved gloom. After a few conventional greetings to her young guest, she spoke no more during the meal. Her daughter, who sat beside the Countess on the opposite side of the table from his Lordship of Cologne, merely answered "Yes" or "No" to the comments of the lady of Sayn praising the romantic situation of the Castle, its unique qualities of architecture, and the splendid outlook from its battlements, eulogies which began enthusiastically enough, but finally faded away into silence, chilled by a reception so unfriendly.

Thus cast back upon her own thoughts, the girl grew more and more uneasy as the peculiar features of the occasion became clearer in her own mind. Here was her revered, beloved friend forcing hilarity which she knew he could not feel, breaking bread and drinking wine with a colleague while three thousand of his armed men peered down on the roof that sheltered him, ready at a signal to pounce upon Stolzenfels like birds of prey, capturing, and if necessary, slaying. She remembered the hearty cheers that welcomed them on their arrival at Coblentz, yet every man who thus boisterously greeted them, waving his bonnet in the air, was doubtless an enemy. The very secrecy, the unknown nature of the danger, depressed her more and more as she thought of it; the fierce soldiers hidden in the forest, ready to leap up, burn and kill at an unknown sign from a Prince of religion; the deadly weapons concealed in a Church of Christ: all this grim reality of a Faith she held dear had never been hinted at by the gentle nuns among whom she lived so happily for the greater part of her life.

At last her somber hostess rose, and Hildegunde, with a sigh of relief, followed her example. The Archbishop of Cologne gallantly held back the curtain at the doorway, and bowed low when the three ladies passed through. The silent hostess conducted her guest to a parlor on the same floor as the dining-room; a parlor from which opened another door connecting it with a small knights' hall; the kleine Rittersaal in which the Court of the Archbishops was to be held.

The Archbishop's sister did not enter the parlor, but here took formal farewell of Countess von Sayn, who turned to the sole occupant of the room, her kinsman and counselor, Father Ambrose.

"Were you not asked to dine with us?" she inquired.

"Yes; but I thought it better to refuse. First, in case the three Archbishops might have something confidential to say to you; and second, because at best I am poor company at a banquet."

"Indeed, you need not have been so thoughtful: first, as you say, there were not three Archbishops present, but only two, and neither said anything to me that all the world might not hear; second, the rest of the company, the sister and the niece of Treves, were so doleful that you would have proved a hilarious companion compared with them. Did my guardian make any statement to you yesterday afternoon that revealed the object of this coming Court?"

"None whatever. Our conversation related entirely to your estate and my management of it. We spoke of crops, of cultivation, and of vineyards."

"You have no knowledge, then, of the reason why we are summoned hither?"

"On that subject, Hildegunde, I am as ignorant as you."

"I don't think I am wholly in the dark," murmured the Countess, "although I know nothing definite."

"You surmise, in spite of your guardian's disclaimer, that the discussion will pertain to your recovery of the town of Linz?"

"Perhaps; but not likely. Did you say anything of your journey to Frankfort?"

"Not a word. I understood from you that no mention should be made of my visit unless his Lordship asked questions proving he was aware of it, in which case I was to tell the truth."

"You were quite right, Father. Did my guardian ask you to accompany us to Stolzenfels?"

"Assuredly, or I should not have ventured."

"What reason did he give, and what instructions did he lay upon you?"

"He thought you should have by your side some one akin to you. His instructions were that in no circumstances was I to offer any remark upon the proceedings. Indeed, I am not allowed to speak unless in answer to a question directly put to me, and then in the fewest possible words."

Hildegunde ceased her cross-examination, and seated herself by a window which gave a view of the steep mountain-side behind the Castle, where, sheltered by the thick, dark forest, she knew that her guardian's men lay in ambush. She shuddered slightly, wondering what was the meaning of these preparations, and in the deep silence became aware of the accelerated beating of her heart. She felt but little reassured by the presence of her kinsman, whose lips moved without a murmur, and whose grave eyes seemed fixed on futurity, meditating the mystery of the next world, and completely oblivious to the realities of the earth he inhabited.

She turned her troubled gaze once more to the green forest, and after a long lapse of time the dual reveries were broken by the entrance of an official gorgeously appareled. This functionary bowed low, and said with great solemnity:

"Madam, the Court of my Lords the Archbishops awaits your presence."

The kleine Rittersaal occupied a fine position on the river-side front of Stolzenfels, its windows giving a view of the Rhine, with the strong Castle of Lahneck over-hanging the mouth of the Lahn, and the more ornamental Schloss Martinsburg at the upper end of Oberlahnstein. The latter edifice, built by a former Elector of Mayence, was rarely occupied by the present Archbishop, but, as he sat in the central chair of the Court, he had the advantage of being able to look across the river at his own house should it please him to do so.

The three Archbishops were standing behind the long table when the

Countess entered, thus acknowledging that she who came into their presence, young and beautiful, was a very great lady by right of descent and rank. She acknowledged their courtesy by a graceful inclination of the head, and the three Princes of the Church responded each with a bow, that of Mayence scarcely perceptible, that of Treves deferential and courtly, that of Cologne with a friendly smile of encouragement.

In the center of the hall opposite the long table had been placed an immense chair, taken from the grand Rittersaal, ornamented with gilded carving, and covered in richly-colored Genoa velvet. It looked like a throne, which indeed it was, used only on occasions when Royalty visited the Castle. To this sumptuous seat the scarcely less gorgeous functionary conducted the girl, and when she had taken her place, the three Archbishops seated themselves. The glorified menial then bent himself until his forehead nearly touched the floor, and silently departed. Father Ambrose, his coarse, ill-cut clothes of somber color in striking contrast to the richness of costume worn by the others, stood humbly beside the chair that supported his kinswoman.

The Countess gave a quick glance at the Archbishop of Mayence, then lowered her eyes. Cologne she had known all her life; Treves she had met that day, and rather liked, although feeling she could not esteem him as she did her guardian, but a thrill of fear followed her swift look at the man in the center.

"A face of great strength," she said to herself, "but his thin, straight lips, tightly compressed, seemed cruel, as well as determined." With a flash of comprehension she understood now her guardian's warning not to thwart him. It was easy to credit the acknowledged fact that this man dominated the other two. Nevertheless, when he spoke his voice was surprisingly mild.

"Madam," he said, "we are met here in an hour of grave anxiety. The Emperor, who has been ill for some time, is now upon his death-bed, and the physicians who attend him inform me that at any moment we may be called upon to elect his successor. That successor has already been chosen; chosen, I may add, in an informal manner, but his selection is not likely to be canceled, unless by some act of his own which would cause us to reconsider our decision.

Our adoption was made very recently in my castle of Ehrenfels, and we are come together again in the Castle of my brother Treves, not in our sacred office as Archbishops, but in our secular capacity as Electors of the Empire, to determine a matter which we consider of almost equal importance. It is our privilege to bestow upon you the highest honor that may be conferred on any woman in the realm; the position of Empress.

"When you have signified your acceptance of this great elevation, I must put to you several questions concerning your future duties to the State, and these are embodied in a document which you will be asked to sign."

The Countess did not raise her eyes. While the Archbishop was speaking the color flamed up in her cheeks, but faded away again, and her guardian, who watched her very intently across the table, saw her face become so pale that he feared she was about to faint. However, she rallied, and at last looked up, not at her dark-browed questioner, but at the Archbishop of Cologne.

"May I not know," she said, in a voice scarcely audible, "who is my future husband?"

"Surely, surely," replied her guardian soothingly, "but the Elector of Mayence is our spokesman here, and you must address your question to his Lordship."

She now turned her frightened eyes upon Mayence, whose brow had become slightly ruffled at this interruption, and whose lips were more firmly closed. He sat there imperturbable, refusing the beseechment of her eyes, and thus forced her to repeat her question, though to him it took another form.

"My Lord, who is to be the next Emperor?"

"Countess von Sayn, I fear that in modifying my opening address to accord with the comprehension of a girl but recently emerged from convent life, I have led you into an error. The Court of Electors is not convened for the purpose of securing your consent, but with the duty of imposing upon you a command. It is not for you to ask questions, but to answer them."

"You mean that I am to marry this unknown man, whether I will or

667

no?"

"That is my meaning."

The girl sat back in her chair, and the moisture that had gathered in her eyes disappeared as if licked up by the little flame that burned in their depths.

"Very well," she said. "Ask your questions, and I will answer them."

"Before I put any question, I must have your consent to my first proposition."

"That is quite unnecessary, my Lord. When you hear my answer to your questions, you will very speedily withdraw your first proposition."

The Elector of Treves, who had been shifting uneasily in his chair, now leaned forward, and spoke in an ingratiating manner.

"Countess, you are a neighbor of mine, although you live on the opposite side of the river, and I am honored in receiving you as my guest. As guest and neighbor, I appeal to you on our behalf: be assured that we wish nothing but your very greatest good and happiness." The spark in her eyes died down, and they beamed kindly on the courtier Elector. "You see before you three old bachelors, quite unversed in the ways of women. If anything that has been said offends you, pray overlook our default, for I assure you, on behalf of my colleagues and myself, that any one of us would bitterly regret uttering a single word to cause you disquietude."

"My disquietude, my Lord, is caused by the refusal to utter the single name I have asked for. Am I a peasant girl to be handed over to the hind that makes the highest offer?"

"Not so. No such thought entered our minds. The name is, of course, a secret at the present moment, and I quite appreciate the reluctance of my Lord of Mayence to mention it, but I think in this instance an exception may safely be made, and I now appeal to his Lordship to enlighten the Countess."

Mayence answered indifferently:

"I do not agree with you, but we are here three Electors of equal power, and two can always outvote one."

The Elector of Cologne smiled slightly; he had seen this comedy enacted before, and never objected to it. The carrying of some unimportant point in opposition to their chief always gave Treves a certain sense of independence.

"My Lord of Cologne," said the latter, bending forward and addressing the man at the other end of the table "do you not agree with me?"

"Certainly," replied Cologne, with some curtness.

"In that case," continued Treves, "I take it upon myself to announce to you, Madam, that the young man chosen for our future ruler is Prince Roland, only son of the dying Emperor."

The hands of the Countess nervously clutched the soft velvet on the arms of her chair.

"I thank you," she said, addressing Treves, and speaking as calmly as though she were Mayence himself. "May I ask you if this marriage was proposed to the young man?"

Treves looked up nervously at the stern face of Mayence, who nodded to him, as much as to say:

"You are doing well; go on."

"Yes," replied Treves.

"Was my name concealed from him?"

"No."

"Had he ever heard of me before?"

"Surely," replied the diplomatic Treves, "for the fame of the Countess von Sayn has traveled farther than her modesty will admit."

"Did he agree?"

"Instantly; joyfully, it seemed to me."

"In any case, he has never seen me," continued the Countess. "Did he make any inquiry, whether I was tall or short, old or young, rich or poor, beautiful or ugly?"

"He seemed very well satisfied with our choice."

Treves had his elbows on the table, leaning forward with open palms supporting his chin. He had spoken throughout in the most ingratiating manner, his tones soft and honeyed. He was so evidently pleased with his own diplomacy that even the eye of the stern Mayence twinkled maliciously when the girl turned impulsively toward the other end of the table, and cried:

"Guardian, tell me the truth! I know this young man accepted me as if I were a sack of grain, his whole mind intent on one thing only: to secure for himself the position of Emperor. Is it not so?"

"It is not so, Countess," said Cologne solemnly.

"Prince Roland, it is true, made no stipulation regarding you."

"I was sure of it. Any Gretchen in Germany would have done just as well. I was merely part of the bargain he was compelled to make with you, and now I announce to the Court that no power on earth will induce me to marry Prince Roland. I claim the right of my womanhood to wed only the man whom I love, and who loves me!"

Mayence gave utterance to an exclamation that might be coarsely described as a snort of contempt. The Elector of Treves was leaning back in his chair discomfited by her abrupt desertion of him. The Elector of Cologne now leaned forward, dismayed at the turn affairs had taken, deep anxiety visible on his brow.

"Countess von Sayn," he began, and thus his ward realized how deeply she had offended, "in all my life I never met any young man who impressed me so favorably as Prince Roland of Germany. If I possessed a daughter whom I dearly loved, I could wish her no better fortune than to marry so honest a youth as he. The very point you make against him should have told most strongly in his favor with a young girl. My reading of his character is that so far as concerns the love you spoke of, he knows as little of it as yourself, and thus he agreed to our proposal with a seeming indifference which you entirely misjudge. If you, then, have any belief in my goodwill towards you, in my deep anxiety for your welfare and happiness, I implore you to agree to the suggestion my Lord of Mayence has made. You speak of love knowing nothing concerning it. I call to your remembrance the fact that one noble lady of your race may have foregone the happiness that love perhaps brings, in her desire for the advancement of one whom she loved so truly that she chose for her guide the more subdued but steadier star of duty. The case is presented to you, my dear, in different form, and I feel assured that duty and love will shine together."

As the venerable Archbishop spoke with such deep earnestness, in a voice she loved so well, the girl buried her face in her hands, and he could see the tears trickle between her fingers. A silence followed her guardian's appeal, disturbed only by the agitated breathing of Hildegunde.

The cold voice of the Elector of Mayence broke the stillness, like a breath from a glazier:

"Do you consent, Madam?"

"Yes," gasped the girl, her shoulders quivering with emotion, but she did not look up.

"I fear that the object of this convocation was like to be forgotten in the gush of sentiment issuing from both sides of me. This is a business meeting, and not a love-feast. Will you do me the courtesy, Madam, of raising your head and answering my question?"

The girl dashed the tears from her eyes, and sat up straight, grasping with nervous hands the arms of the throne, as if to steady herself against the coming ordeal.

"I scarcely heard what you said. Do you consent to marry Prince Roland of Germany?"

"I have consented," she replied firmly.

"Will you use your influence with him that he may carry out the behests of the three Archbishops?"

"Yes, if the behests are for the good of the country."

"I cannot accept any qualifications, therefore I repeat my question. Will you use your influence with him that he may carry out the behests of the three Archbishops?"

"I can have no influence with such a man."

"Answer my question, Madam."

"Say yes, Hildegunde," pleaded Cologne.

She turned to him swimming eyes.

"Oh, Guardian, Guardian!" she cried, "I have done everything I can, and all for you; all for you. I cannot stand any more. This is torture to me. Let me go home, and another day when I am calmer I will answer your questions!"

The perturbed Archbishop sat back again with a deep sigh. The ignorance of women with which his colleague of Treves had credited all three was being amazingly dispelled. He could not understand why this girl should show such emotion at the thought of marrying the heir to the throne, when assured the young man was all that any reasonable woman could desire.

"Madam, I pray you give your attention to me," said the unimpassioned voice of Mayence. "I have listened to your conversation with my colleagues, and the patience I exhibited will, I hope, be credited to me. This matter of business"—he emphasized the word—"must be settled to-day, and to clear away all misapprehension, I desire to say that your guardian has really no influence on this matter. It was settled before you came into the room. You are merely allowed a choice of two outcomes: first, marriage with Prince Roland; second, imprisonment in Pfalz Castle, situated in the middle of the Rhine."

"What is that?" demanded the Countess.

"I am tired of repeating my statements."

"You would imprison me—me, a Countess of Sayn?"

Again the tears evaporated, and in their place came the smoldering fire bequeathed to her by the Crusaders, and, if the truth must be known, by Rhine robbers as well.

"Yes, Madam. A predecessor of mine once hanged one of your ancestors."

"It is not true," cried the girl, in blazing wrath. "'Twas the Emperor Rudolph who hanged him; the same Emperor that chastised an Archbishop of Mayence, and brought him, cringing, to his knees, begging for pardon, which the Emperor contemptuously flung to him. You dare not imprison me!"

"Refuse to marry Prince Roland, and learn," said the Archbishop very quietly.

The girl sprang to her feet, a-quiver with anger.

"I do refuse! Prince Roland has hoodwinked the three of you! He is a libertine and a brawler, consorting with the lowest in the cellars of Frankfort; a liar and a thief, and not a brave thief at that, but a cutthroat who holds his sword to the breast of an unarmed merchant while he filches from him his gold. Added to that, a drunkard as his father is; and, above all, a hypocrite, as his father is not, yet clever enough, with all his vices, to cozen three men whose vile rule has ruined Frankfort, and left the broad Rhine empty of its life-giving commerce;" she waved her hand toward the vacant river.

The Archbishop of Cologne was the first to rise, horror-stricken.

"The girl is mad!" he murmured.

Treves rose also, but Mayence sat still, a sour smile on his lips, yet a twinkle of admiration in his eyes.

"No, my poor Guardian, I am not mad," she cried, regarding him with a smile, her wrath subsiding as quickly as it had risen. "What I say is true, and it may be that our meeting, turbulent as it has been, will prevent you from making a great mistake. He whom you would put on the throne is not the man you think."

"My dear ward!" cried Cologne, "how can you make such accusations against him? What should a girl living in seclusion as you live, know of what is passing in Frankfort."

"It seems strange, Guardian, but it is true, nevertheless. Sit down again, I beg of you, and you, my Lord of Treves. Even my Lord of Mayence will, I think, comprehend my abhorrence when such a proposal was made to me, and I hope, my Lord, you will forgive my outburst of anger just now."

She heard the trembling Treves mutter:

"Mayence never forgives."

"Now, Father Ambrose, come forward."

"Why?" asked Ambrose, waking from his reverie.

"Tell them your experiences in Frankfort."

"I am not allowed to speak," objected the monk.

"Speak, speak!" cried Cologne. "What, sir, have you had to do with this girl's misleading?"

"I thought," he said wistfully to his kinswoman, "that I was not to mention my visit to Frankfort unless my Lord the Archbishop brought up the subject."

"Have you not been listening to these proceedings?" cried the girl impatiently. "The subject is brought up before three Archbishops, instead of before one. Tell their Lordships what you know of Prince Roland."

Father Ambrose, with a deep sigh, began his recital, to which Treves and Cologne listened with ever-increasing amazement, while the sullen Mayence sat back in his chair, face imperturbable, but the thin lips closing firmer and firmer as the narrative went on.

When the monologue ended, his Reverence of Cologne was the first to speak:

"In the name of Heaven, why did you not tell me all this yesterday?"

Father Ambrose looked helplessly at his kinswoman, but made no reply.

"I forbade him, my Lord," said the girl proudly, and for the first time addressing him by a formal title, as if from now on he was to be reckoned with her enemies. "I alone am responsible for the journey to Frankfort and its consequences, whatever they may be. You invoked the name of Heaven just now, my Lord, and I would have you know that I am convinced Heaven itself intervened on my behalf to expose the real character of Prince Roland, who has successfully deluded three men like yourselves, supposed to be astute!"

The Archbishop turned upon her sorrowful eyes, troubled yet kindly.

"My dear Countess," he said, "I have not ventured to censure you; nevertheless I am, or have been, your guardian, and should, I think, have been consulted before you committed yourself to an action that threatens disaster to our plans."

The girl replied, still with the hauteur so lately assumed:

"I do not dispute my wardship, and have more than once thanked you for your care of me, but at this crisis of my life—a crisis transforming me instantly from a girl to a woman—you fail me, seeing me here at bay. I wished to spend a month or two at the capital city, but before troubling you with such a request I determined to learn whether or not the state of Frankfort was as disturbed as rumor alleged. Finding matters there to be hopeless, the project of a visit was at once abandoned, and knowing nothing of the honor about to be conferred on Prince Roland, I thought it best to keep what had been discovered regarding his character a secret between the Reverend Father and myself. I dare say an attempt will be made to cast doubt on the Reverend Father's story, and perhaps my three judges may convince themselves of its falseness, but they cannot convince me, and I tell you finally and formally that no power on earth will induce me to marry a marauder and a thief!"

This announcement effectually silenced the one friend she possessed among the three. Mayence slowly turned his head, and looked upon the colleague at his right, as much as to say, "Do you wish to add your quota to this inconsequential talk?"

Treves, at this silent appeal, leaned forward, and spoke to the perturbed monk, who knew that, in some way he did not quite understand, affairs were drifting towards a catastrophe.

"Father Ambrose," began the Elector of Treves, "would you kindly tell us the exact date when this encounter on the bridge took place?"

"Saint Cyrille's Day," replied Father Ambrose.

"And during the night of that day you were incarcerated in the cellar among the wine-casks?"

"Yes, my Lord."

"Would it surprise you to know, Father Ambrose, that during Saint Cyrille's Day, and for many days previous to that date, Prince Roland was a close prisoner in his Lordship of Mayence's strong Castle of Ehrenfels, and that it was quite impossible for you to have met him in Frankfort, or anywhere else?"

"Nevertheless, I did meet him," persisted Father Ambrose, with the quiet obstinacy of a mild man.

Treves smiled.

"Where did you lodge in Frankfort, Father?"

"At the Benedictine Monastery in Sachsenhausen."

"Do the good brethren supply their guests with a potent wine? Frankfort is, and always has been, the chief market of that exhilarating but illusion-creating beverage."

The cheeks of the Countess flushed crimson at this insinuation on her kinsman's sobriety. The old monk's hand rested on the arm of her throne, and she placed her own hand upon his as if to encourage him to resent the implied slander. After all, they were two Sayns hard pressed by these ruthless potentates. But Ambrose answered mildly:

"It may be that the monastery contains wine, my Lord, and doubtless the wine is good, but during my visit I did not taste it."

Cross-examination at an end, the Lord of Mayence spoke scarcely above a whisper, a trace of weariness in his manner.

"My Lords," he said, "we have wandered from the subject. The romance by Father Ambrose is but indifferently interesting, and nothing at all to the point. Even a child may understand what has happened, for it is merely a case of mistaken identity, and my sympathy goes out entirely towards the unknown; a man who knew his own mind, and being naturally indignant at an interference both persistent and uncalled for, quite rightly immured the meddler among the casks, probably shrewd enough to see that this practicer of temperance would not interfere with their integrity.

"Madam, stand up!"

The Countess seemed inclined to disobey this curt order, but a beseeching look from her now thoroughly frightened guardian changed her intention, and she rose to her feet.

"Madam, the greatest honor which it is in the power of this Empire to bestow upon a woman has been proffered to you, and rejected with unnecessary heat. I beg therefore, to inform you, that in the judgment of this Court you are considered unworthy of the exalted position which, before knowing your true character, it was intended you should fill. The various calumnies you have poured upon the innocent head of Prince Roland amount in effect to high treason."

"Pardon, my Lord!" cried the Archbishop of Cologne, "your contention will hold neither in law nor in fact. High treason is an offense that can be committed only against the realm as a whole, or against its ruler in person. Prince Roland is not yet Emperor of Germany, and however much we may regret the language used in his disparagement, it has arisen through a misunderstanding quite patent to us all. A good but dreamy man made a mistake, which, however deplorable, has been put forward with a sincerity that none of us can question; indeed, it was the intention of Father Ambrose to keep his supposed knowledge a secret, and you both saw with what evident reluctance he spoke when commanded to do so by my colleague of Treves. Whatever justice there may be in disciplining Father Ambrose, there is none at all for exaggerated censure upon my lady, the Countess of Sayn, and before pronouncing a further censure I beg your Lordship to take into consideration the circumstances of the case, by which a young girl, without any previous warning or preparation, is called upon suddenly to make the most momentous decision of her life. I say it is to her ladyship's credit that she refused the highest station in the land in the interests of what she supposes to be, however erroneously, the cause of honesty, sobriety, and, I may add, of Christianity; qualities for which we three men should stand."

"My Lord," objected Treves, "we meet here as temporal Princes, and not as Archbishops of the Church."

"I know that, my brother of Treves, and my appeal is to the temporal law. Prince Roland, despite his high lineage, is merely a citizen of the Empire, and a subject of his Majesty, the Emperor. It is therefore impossible that the crime of treason can be committed against him."

During this protest and discussion the Elector of Mayence had leaned back again in his usual attitude of tired indifference; his keen eyes almost closed. When he spoke he made no reference to what either of his two confrères had said.

"Madam," he began, without raising his voice, "it is the sentence of this Court that you shall be imprisoned during its pleasure in the Castle of Pfalzgrafenstein, which stands on a rock in the middle of the Rhine. Under the guardianship of the Pfalzgraf von Stahleck, who will be responsible for your safe keeping, I hope you will listen to the devout counsel of his excellent wife to such effect that when next you are privileged to meet a Court so highly constituted as this you may be better instructed regarding the language with which it should be addressed. You are permitted to take with you two waiting-women, chosen by yourself from your own household, but all communication with the outside world is forbidden. You said something to the effect that this Court dared not pronounce such sentence against you, but if you possessed that wisdom you so conspicuously lack, you might have surmised that a power which ventured to imprison the future Emperor of this land would not hesitate to place in durance a mere Countess von Sayn."

The Countess bowed her head slightly, and without protest sat down again. The Elector of Cologne arose.

"My Lord, I raised a point of law which has been ignored."

"This is the proper time to raise it," replied Mayence, "and you shall be instantly satisfied. This Court is competent to give its decision upon any point of law. If my Lord of Treves agrees with me, your objection is disallowed."

"I agree," said the Elector of Treves.

"My Lord of Cologne," said Mayence, turning towards the person addressed, "the decision of the Court is against you."

Hildegunde was already learning a lesson. Although dazed by the verdict, she could not but admire the quiet, conversational tone adopted by the three men before her, as compared with her own late vehemence.

"The decision of the Court is not unexpected," said Cologne, "and I regret that I am compelled to appeal."

"To whom will you appeal?" inquired Mayence mildly, "The Emperor, as you know, is quite unfit for the transaction of public business, and even if such were not the case, would hesitate to overturn a decision given by a majority of this Court."

"I appeal," replied Cologne, "to a power that even Emperors must obey; the power of physical force."

"You mean," said Mayence sadly, "to the three thousand men concealed in the forest behind this house in which you are an honored guest?"

The Elector of Cologne was so taken aback by this almost whispered remark that he was momentarily struck speechless. A sudden pallor swept the usual ruddiness from his face. The Lord of Mayence gently inclined his head as if awaiting an answer, and when it did not come, went on impassively:

"I may inform you, my Lord, that my army occupies the capital city of Frankfort, able and ready to quell any disturbance that may be caused by the announcement of the Emperor's death, but there are still plenty of seasoned troops ready to uphold the decisions of this Court. When your spies scoured the country in the forests, and along the river almost to the gates of my city of Mayence, they appeared to labor under the illusion that I could move my soldiers only overland. Naturally, they met no sign of such an incursion, because I had requisitioned a hundred barges which I found empty in the river Main by Frankfort. These were floated down the Main to Mayence, and there received their quota of a hundred men each. The night being dark they came down the Rhine, it seems, quite unobserved, and are now concealed in the mouth of the river Lahn directly opposite this Castle.

"When my flag is hoisted on the staff of the main tower this flotilla will be at the landing below us within half an hour. You doubtless have made similar arrangements for bringing your three thousand down upon Stolzenfels, but the gates of this Castle are now closed. Indeed, Stolzenfels was put in condition to withstand a siege very shortly after you and your ward entered it, and it is garrisoned by two hundred fighting men, kindly provided at my suggestion by my brother of Treves. I doubt if its capture is possible, even though you gave the signal, which we will not allow. Of course, your plan of capturing Treves and myself was a good one could it be carried out, for a man in jeopardy will always compromise, and as I estimate you are in that position I should be glad to know what arrangement you propose."

The Archbishop of Cologne did not reply, but stood with bent head and frowning brow. It was the Countess von Sayn who, rising, spoke:

"My Lord Archbishop of Mayence," she said, "I could never forgive myself if through action of mine a fatal struggle took place between my countrymen. I have no desire to enact the part of Helen of Troy. I am therefore ready and willing to be imprisoned, or to marry Prince Roland of Frankfort, whichever alternative you command, so long as no disadvantage comes to my friend, his Lordship of Cologne."

"Madam," said Mayence suavely, "there are not now two alternatives, as you suppose."

"In such case, your Highness, I betake myself instantly to Pfalz Castle, and I ask that my guardian be allowed to escort me on the journey."

680

"Madam, your determination is approved, and your request granted, but, as the business for which the three Electors were convened is not yet accomplished, I request you to withdraw until such time as an agreement has been arrived at. Father Ambrose is permitted to accompany you."

The gallant Elector of Treves sprang at once to his feet, pleading for the privilege of conducting the Countess to the apartments of his sister and her daughter. As the door to the ante-room opened the Elector of Cologne, whose eyes followed his departing ward, did not fail to observe that the lobby was thronged with armed men, and he realized now, if he had not done so from Mayence's observation, how completely he was trapped. Even had a hundred thousand of his soldiers stood in readiness on the hills, it was impossible for him to give the signal bringing them to his rescue.

A few minutes later the Elector of Treves returned, and took his place at Mayence's right hand. The latter spoke as though the conference had been unanimous and amiable.

"Now that we three are alone together, I think we shall discuss our problems under a feeling of less apprehension if the small army in the forest is bade God-speed on its way to Cologne. Such being the case," he went on, turning to Cologne, "would you kindly write an order to that effect to your commander. Inform him that we three Electors wish to review your troops from the northern balcony, and bid them file past from the hills to the river road. They are to cross the Moselle by the old bridge, and so return to your city. You will perhaps pledge faith that no signal will be made to your officers as they pass us. I make this appeal with the greater confidence since you are well aware three thousand men would but destroy themselves in any attempt to capture this Castle, with an army of ten thousand on their flank to annihilate them. Do you agree?"

"I agree," replied Cologne.

He wrote out the order required, and handed it to Mayence, who scrutinized the document with some care before passing it on to Treves. Mayence addressed Cologne in his blandest tones:

"Would you kindly instruct our colleague how to get that message safely into the hands of your commander."

"If he will have it sent to the head of my small escort, ordering him to take it directly up the hill behind this Castle until he comes to my sentinels, whom he knows personally, they will allow him to pass through, and deliver my written command to the officer in charge."

This being done, and Treves once more returned, Mayence said:

"I am sure we all realize that the Countess von Sayn, however admirable in other respects, possesses an independent mind and a determined will rendering her quite unsuited for the station we intended her to occupy. I think her guardian must be convinced now, even though he had little suspicion of it before, that this lady would not easily be influenced by any considerations we might place before her. The regrettable incidents of this conference have probably instilled into her mind a certain prejudice against us."

Here, for the first time, the Elector of Cologne laughed.

"It is highly probable, my Lord," he said, "and, indeed, your moderate way of putting the case is unanswerable. Her ladyship as an Empress under our influence is out of the question. I therefore make a proposal with some confidence, quite certain it will please you both. I venture to nominate for the position of Empress that very demure and silent lady who is niece of my brother the Elector of Treves."

Treves strangled a gasp in its birth, but could not suppress the light of ambition that suddenly leaped into his eyes. The elevation of his widowed sister's child to the Imperial throne was an advantage so tremendous, and came about so unexpectedly, that for the moment his slow brain was numbed by the glorious prospect. It seemed incredible that Cologne had actually put forward such a proposition.

The eyes of Mayence veiled themselves almost to shutting point, but in no other manner did emotion show. Like a flash his alert mind saw the full purport of the bombshell Cologne had so carelessly tossed between himself and his henchman. Cologne, having lost everything, had now proved clever enough to set by the ears those who overruled him by their united vote. If this girl were made Empress she would be entirely under the influence of her uncle, of whose household she had been a pliant member ever since childhood. Yet what was Mayence to do? Should he object to the nomination, he would at once obliterate the unswerving loyalty of Treves, and if this happened, Treves and Cologne, joining, would outvote him, and his objection would prove futile. He would enrage Treves without carrying his own point, and he knew that he held his position only because of the dog-like fidelity of the weaker man. Slow anger rose in his heart as he pictured the conditions of the future. Whatever influence he sought to exert upon the Emperor by the indirect assistance of the Empress, must be got at through the complacency of Treves, who would gradually come to appreciate his own increased importance.

All this passed through the mind of Mayence, and his decision had been arrived at before Treves recovered his composure.

"It gives me great pleasure," said the Elector of Mayence, firmly suppressing the malignancy of his glance towards the man seated on his left,— "it gives me very great pleasure indeed to second so admirable a nomination, the more so that I am thus permitted to offer my congratulations to an esteemed colleague and a valued friend. My Lord of Treves, I trust that you will make this nomination unanimous, for, to my delight, his Lordship of Cologne anticipated, by a few moments the proposal I was about to submit to you."

"My Lord," stammered Treves, finding his voice with difficulty, "I—I— of course will agree to whatever the Court decides. I—I thank you, my Lord, and you too, my brother of Cologne."

"Then," cried Mayence, almost joyfully, "the task for which we are convened is accomplished, and I declare this Court adjourned."

He rose from his chair. The overjoyed Prince at his right took no thought of the fact that their chairman had not called upon the lady that she might receive the decision of the conclave and answer the questions to be put to her, but Cologne perceived the omission, and knew that from that moment Mayence would set his subtility at work to nullify the nomination. Even though his bombshell had not exploded, and the two other Electors were apparently greater friends than ever, Cologne had achieved his immediate object, and was satisfied.

Through the open windows came the sound of the steady tramping of disciplined men, and the metallic clash of armor and arms in transit.

"Ah, now," cried Mayence, "we will enjoy the advantage of reviewing the brave troops of Cologne. Lead the way, my Lord of Treves. You know the Castle better than we do."

The proud Treves, treading on air, guided his guests to the northern balcony.

XI. GOLD GALORE THAT TAKES TO ITSELF WINGS

In the thick darkness Roland paced up and down the east bank of the Rhine at a spot nearly midway between Assmannshausen and Ehrenfels. The night was intensely silent, its stillness merely accentuated by the gentle ripple of the water current against the barge's blunt nose, which pointed upstream. Standing motionless as a statue, the massive figure of Captain Blumenfels appeared in deeper blackness against the inky hills on the other side of the Rhine. Long sweeps lay parallel to the bulwarks of the barge, and stalwart men were at their posts, waiting the word of command to handle these exaggerated oars, in defiance of wind and tide. On this occasion, however, the tide only would be against them, for the strong southern breeze was wholly favorable. Their voyage that night would be short, but strenuous; merely crossing the river, and tying up against the opposite bank; but the Rhine swirled powerfully round the rock of Ehrenfels above them, and the men at the sweeps must pull vigorously if they were not to be carried down into premature danger.

Roland, who when they left Frankfort was in point of time the youngest member of the guild, now seemed, if one could distinguish him through the gloom of the night, to have become years older, and there was an added dignity in his bearing, for, although now but a potential freebooter, he had received assurance that he would be eventually elected Emperor.

He had sent word that morning to Greusel at the Golden Anker, bidding him get together his men, and lead them up to the barge not later than an hour before the moon rose, for Roland was anxious to reach the other side of the Rhine unseen from either shore. He cautioned Greusel to make his march a silent one, and this order Joseph at first found some difficulty in carrying out, but in any case he need have entertained no fear. The strong red wine of Assmannshausen is a potent liquid, and the inhabitants of the town were accustomed to song and laughter on the one street of the place at all hours of the night.

When they arrived, the men were quiet enough, and speedily stowed themselves away in their quarters at the stern of the barge, whereupon Roland, the last to spring aboard, waved his hand at the captain to cast off. The nose of the boat was shoved away from land, and then the powerful sweeps dipped into the water. Slowly but surely she made her way across the river; silent and invisible from either bank. The current, however, swept them down opposite the twinkling lights of Assmannshausen, after which, in the more tranquil waters of the western shore, they rowed steadily upstream for about half a league, and then, with ropes tied round trees growing at the water's edge, laid up for the remainder of the night.

Roland now counseled his company to enjoy what sleep was possible, as they would be roused at the first glint of daybreak; so, with great good-nature, each man wrapped himself up in his cloak and lay down on the cabin floor.

When the eastern sky became gray, the slumberers were awakened, and a ration of bread and wine served to each. The captain already had received his instructions, and the men discarding their cloaks, followed their leader into the still gloomy forest. Here, with as little noise as might be, they climbed the steep wooded hill, and arriving at something almost like a path, a hundred yards up from the river, they turned to the right, and so marched, no man speaking above a whisper.

The forest became lighter and lighter, and at last Roland, holding up his hand to sign caution, turned to the left from the path, and farther up into the unbroken forest. They had traversed perhaps a league when another silent order brought them to a standstill, and peering through the trees to the east, the men caught glimpses of the grand, gray battlements of that famous stronghold, Rheinstein, seeing at the corner nearest them a square tower, next a machicolated curtain of wall, and a larger square tower almost as high as the first hanging over the precipice that descended to the Rhine. Inside this impregnable enclosure rose the great bulk of the Castle itself, and near at hand the massive square keep, with an octagonal turret on the southeast corner, the top of which was the highest point of the stronghold, although a round tower rising directly over the Rhine was not much lower.

Roland, advancing through the trees, but motioning his men to remain where they were, peered across to the battlements and down at the entrance gate.

Baron von Hohenfels sat so secure in his elevated robber's nest, which he deemed invincible—and, indeed, the cliff on which it stood, nearly a hundred yards high, made it so if approached from the Rhine—that he kept only one man on watch, and this sentinel was stationed on the elevated platform of the round tower. Roland saw him yawn wearily as he leaned against his tall lance, and was glad to learn that even one man kept guard, for at first he feared that all within the Castle were asleep, the round tower, until Roland had shifted his position to the north, being blotted out by the nearer square donjon keep. Now satisfied, he signaled his men to sit down, which they did. He himself took up a position behind a tree, where, unseen, he could watch the man with the lance.

So indolent was the sentry that Roland began to fear the barge would pass by unnoticed. Not for months had any sailing craft appeared on the river, and doubtless the warden regarded his office as both useless and wearisome. Brighter and brighter became the eastern sky, and at last a tinge of red appeared above the hills across the silent Rhine. Suddenly the guardian straightened up, then, shading his eyes with his right hand, he leaned over the battlements, peering to the south. A moment later the stillness was rent by a lusty shout, and the man disappeared as if he had fallen through a trap-door. Presently the notes of a bugle echoed within the walls, followed by clashes of armor and the buzzing sound of men, as though a wasp's nest had been disturbed. Half a dozen came into sight on top of the various towers and battlements, glanced at the river, and vanished as hastily as the sentinel had done.

At last the gates came ponderously open, and the first three men to emerge were on horseback, one of them hastily getting into an outer garment, but the well-trained horses, who knew their business quite as thoroughly as their riders, for they were accustomed to plunge into the river if any barge disobeyed the order commanding it to halt, turned from the gate, and dashed down the steep road that descended through the forest. The men-at-arms poured forth with sword or pike, and in turn went out of sight. They appeared to be leaderless, dashing forward in no particular formation, yet, like the horses, they knew their business. All this turmoil was not without its effect on Roland's following, who edged forward on hands and knees to discover what was going on, everyone breathless with excitement; but they saw their leader cool and motionless, counting on his fingers the number of men who passed out, for he knew exactly how many fighters the Castle contained.

"Not yet, not yet!" he whispered.

Finally three lordly individuals strode out; officers their more resplendent clothing indicated them to be, and the trio followed the others.

"Ha!" cried Roland, "old Baron Hugo drank too deeply last night to be so early astir."

He was speaking aloud now.

"Take warning from that, my lads, and never allow wine to interfere with business. Follow me, but cautiously, one after the other in single file, and look to your footing. 'Tis perilous steep between here and the gate;" and, indeed, so they found it, but all reached the level forecourt in safety, and so through the open portal.

"Close and bar those gates," was the next command, instantly obeyed.

Down the stone steps of the Castle, puffing and grunting, came a gigantic, obese individual, his face bloated with excess, his eyes bleary with the lees of too much wine. He was struggling into his doublet, assisted by a terrified old valet, and was swearing most deplorably. Seeing the crowd at the gate, and half-blindly mistaking them for his own men, he roared:

"What do you there, you hounds? To the river, every man of you, and curse your leprous, indolent souls! Why in the fiend's name—" But here he came to an abrupt stop on the lowest step, the sting of a sword's point at his throat, and now, out of breath, his purple face became mottled.

"Good morning to you, Baron Hugo von Hohenfels. These men whom you address so coarsely obey no orders but mine."

"And who, imp of Satan, are you?" sputtered the old man.

"By profession a hangman. From our fastnesses in the hills, seeing a barge float down the river, we thought it likely you would leave the Castle undefended, and so came in to execute the Prince of Robbers."

The Baron was quaking like a huge jelly. It was evident that, although noted for his cruelty, he was at heart a coward.

"You—you—you—" he stammered, "are outlaws! You are outlaws from the Hunsruck."

"How clever of you, Baron, to recognize us at once. Now you know what to expect. Greusel, unwind the rope I gave you last night. I will show you its purpose."

Greusel did as he was requested without comment, but Ebearhard approached closely to his chief, and whispered:

"Why resort to violence? We have no quarrel with this elephant. 'Tis his gold we want, and to hang him is a waste of time."

"Hush, Ebearhard," commanded Roland sternly. "The greater includes the less. I know this man, and am taking the quickest way to his treasure-house."

Ebearhard fell back, but by this time the useful Greusel had made a loop of the rope, and threw it like a cravat around the Baron's neck.

"No, no, no!" cried the frightened nobleman. "'Tis not my life you seek. That is of no use to such as you; and, besides, I have never harmed the outlaws."

"That is a lie," said Roland. "You sent an expedition against us just a year ago."

"'Twas not I," protested Hohenfels, "but the pirate of Falkenberg. Still, no matter. I'll buy my life from you. I am a wealthy man."

"How much?" asked Roland, hesitating.

"More than all of you can carry away."

"In gold?"

"Of a surety in gold."

"Where are the keys of your treasury?"

"In my chamber. I will bring them to you," and the Baron turned to mount the steps again.

"Not so," cried Roland. "Stand where you are, and send your man for them. If they are not here before I count twoscore, you hang, and nothing will save you."

The Baron told the trembling valet where to find the keys.

"Greusel, you and Ebearhard accompany him, and at the first sign of treachery, or any attempt to give an alarm, run him through with your swords. Does your man know where the treasury is?" he continued to the Baron.

"Oh, yes, yes!"

"How is your gold bestowed?"

"In leathern bags."

"Good. Greusel, take sixteen of the men, and bring down into the courtyard all the gold you can carry. Then we will estimate whether or not it is sufficient to buy the Baron's life, for I hold him in high esteem. He is a valuable man. See to it that there is no delay, Greusel, and never lose sight of this valet. Bring him back, laden with gold."

They all disappeared within the Castle, led by the old servitor.

"Sit you down, Baron," said Roland genially. "You seem agitated, for which there is no cause should there prove to be gold enough to outweigh you."

The ponderous noble seated himself with a weary sigh.

"And pray to the good Lord above us," went on Roland, "that your men may not return before this transaction is completed, for if they do, my first duty will be to strangle you. Even gold will not save you in that case. But still, you have another chance for your life, should such an untoward event take place. Shout to them through the closed gates that they must return to the edge of the river until you join them; then, if they obey, you are spared. Remember, I beg of you, the uselessness of an outcry, for we are in possession of Rheinstein, and you know that the Castle is unassailable from without."

The Baron groaned.

"Do not be hasty with your cord," he said dejectedly. "I will follow your command."

The robbers, however, did not return, but the treasure-searchers did, piling the bags in the courtyard, and again Hohenfels groaned dismally at the sight. Roland indicated certain sacks with the point of his sword, ordering them to be opened. Each was full of gold.

"Now, my lads," he cried, "oblige the Baron by burdening yourselves with this weight of metal, then we shall make for the Hunsruck. Open the gates. Lead the men to the point where we halted, Greusel, and there await me."

The rich company departed, and Roland beguiled the time and the weariness of the Baron by a light and interesting conversation to which there was neither reply nor interruption. At last, having allowed time for his band to reach their former halting-place, he took the rope from the Baron's neck, tied the old robber's hands behind him, then bound his feet, cutting the rope in lengths with his sword. He served the trembling valet in the same way, shutting him up within the Castle, and locking the door with the largest key in the bunch, which bunch he threw down beside his lordship.

"Baron von Hohenfels," he said, "I have kept my word with you, and now bid farewell. I leave you out-of-doors, because you seem rather scant of breath, for which complaint fresh air is beneficial. Adieu, my lord Baron."

The Baron said nothing as Roland, with a sweep of his bonnet, took leave of him, climbed the steep path and joined his waiting men. He led them along the hillside, through the forest for some distance, then descended to the water's edge. The river was blank, so they all sat down under the trees out of sight, leaving one man on watch. Here Roland spent a very anxious half-hour, mitigated by the knowledge that the men of Rheinstein were little versed in woodcraft, and so might not be able to trace the fugitives. It was likely they would make a dash in quite the opposite direction, towards the Hunsruck, because Hohenfels believed they were outlaws from that district, and did not in any way associate them with the plundered barge.

But if the robbers of Rheinstein took a fancy to sink the barge, an act only too frequently committed, then were Roland and his company in a quandary, without food, or means of crossing the river. However, he was sure that Captain Blumenfels would follow his instructions, which were to offer no resistance, but rather to assist the looters in their exactions.

"Within a league," said Roland to his men, "stand three pirate castles: Rheinstein, which we have just left; Falkenberg, but a short distance below, and then Sonneck. If nothing happens to the barge, I expect to finish with all three before nightfall; for, the strongholds being so close together, we must work rapidly, and not allow news of our doings to leap in advance of us."

"But suppose," said Kurzbold, "that Hohenfels' men hold the barge at the landing for their own use?"

"We will wait here for another half-hour," replied Roland, "and then, if we see nothing of the boat, proceed along the water's edge until we learn what has become of her. I do not think the thieves will interfere with the barge, as they have not been angered either by disobedience of their orders to land, or resistance after the barge is by the shore. Besides, I count on the fact that the officers, at least, will be anxious to let the barge proceed, hoping other laden boats may follow, and, indeed, I think for this reason they will be much more moderate in their looting than we have been."

Before he had finished speaking, the man on watch by the water announced the barge in sight, floating down with the current. At this they all emerged from the forest. Captain Blumenfels, carefully scanning the shore, saw them at once, and turned the boat's head towards the spot where they stood.

The bags of gold were bolted away in the stout lockers extending on each side of the cabin. While this was being done, Roland gave minute instructions to the captain regarding the next item in the programme, and once more entered the forest with his men.

The task before them was more difficult than the spoiling of Rheinstein, because the huge bulk of Falkenberg stood on a summit of treeless rock; the Castle itself, a gigantic, oblong gray mass, with a slender square campanile some distance from it, rising high above its battlements on the slope that went down towards the Rhine, forming thus an excellent watch-tower. But although the conical hill of rock was bare of the large trees that surrounded Rheinstein, there were plenty of bowlders and shrubbery behind which cover could be sought. On this occasion the marauding guild could not secure a position on a level with the battlements of the Castle, as had been the case behind Rheinstein, and, furthermore, they were compelled to make their dash for the gate up-hill.

But these disadvantages were counterbalanced by the fact that Falkenberg was situated much higher than Rheinstein, and was farther away from the river, so that when the garrison descended to the water's edge it could not return as speedily as was the case with Hohenfels' men. Rheinstein stood directly over the water, and only two hundred and sixty feet above it, while, comparatively speaking, Falkenberg was back in the country. Still all these castles had been so long unmolested, and considered themselves so secure, that adequate watching had fallen into abeyance, and at Falkenberg guard was kept by one lone man on the tall campanile. The attacking party saw no one on the battlements of the Castle, so worked their way round the hill until the man on the tower was hidden from them by the bulk of the Castle itself, and thus they crawled like lizards from bush to bush, from stone to stone, and from rock-ledge to rock-ledge, taking their time, and not deserting one position of obscurity until another was decided upon. The fact that the watchman was upon the Rhine side of the Castle greatly favored a stealthy approach from any landward point.

At last the alarm was given; the gate opened, and, as it proved, every man in the Castle went headlong down the hill. The amateur cracksmen therefore had everything their own way, and while this at first seemed an advantage, they speedily found it the reverse, for although they wandered from room to room, the treasure could not be discovered. The interior of Falkenberg was unknown to Roland, this being one of the strongholds where he had been compelled to sleep in an outhouse. At last they found the door to the treasure-chamber, for Roland suggested it was probably in a similar position to that at Rheinstein, and those who had accompanied Hohenfels' valet made search according to this hint, and were rewarded by coming upon a door so stoutly locked that all their efforts to force it open were fruitless.

Deeply disappointed, with a number of the men grumbling savagely, they were compelled to withdraw empty handed, warned by approaching shouts that the garrison was returning, so the men crawled away as they had come, and made for the river, where on this occasion the boat already awaited them.

The lord of Falkenberg proved as moderate in his exactions as the men of Rheinstein. Many bales had been cut open, and the thieves, with the knowledge of cloth-weavers, selected in every case only the best goods, but of these had taken merely enough for one costume each.

Although the company had made so early a beginning, it was past noon by the time they reached the barge on the second occasion. A substantial meal was served, for every man was ravenously hungry, besides being disgusted to learn that there were ups and downs even in the trade of thievery.

Early in the afternoon they made for the delicate Castle of Sonneck, whose slender turrets stood out beautifully against the blue sky. Here excellent cover was found within sight of the doorway, for Sonneck stood alone on its rock without the protection of a wall.

In this case the experience of Rheinstein was repeated, with the exception that it was not the master of the Castle they encountered, but a frightened warder, who, with a sharp sword to influence him, produced keys and opened the treasury. Not nearly so large a haul of gold was made as in the first instance, yet enough was obtained to constitute a most lucrative day's work, and with this they sought the barge in high spirits.

They waited in the shadow of the hills until dusk, then quietly made their way across the river behind the shelter of the two islands, and so came to rest alongside the bank, just above the busy town of Lorch, scarcely two leagues down the river from the berth they had occupied the night before. After the barge was tied up, Roland walked on deck with the captain, listening to his account of events from the level of the river surface. It proved that, all in all, Roland could suggest no amendment of the day's proceedings. So far as Blumenfels was concerned, everything had gone without a hitch.

As they promenaded thus, one of the men came forward, and said, rather cavalierly:

"Commander, your comrades wish to see you in the cabin."

Roland made no reply, but continued his conversation with the captain until he learned from that somewhat reticent individual all he wished to know. Then he walked leisurely aft, and descended into the cabin, where he found the eighteen seated on the lockers, as if the conclave were a deliberate body like the Electors, who had come to some momentous decision.

"We have unanimously passed a resolution," said Kurzbold, "that the money shall be divided equally amongst us each evening. You do not object, I suppose?"

"No; I don't object to your passing a resolution."

"Very good. We do not wish to waste time just now in the division, because we are going to Lorch, intending to celebrate our success with a banquet. Would Greusel, Ebearhard, and yourself care to join us?"

"I cannot speak for the other two," returned Roland quietly; "but personally I shall be unable to attend, as there are some plans for the future which need thinking over."

"In that case we shall not expect you," went on Kurzbold, who seemed in no way grieved at the loss of his commander's company.

"Perhaps," suggested John Gensbein, "our chief will drop in upon us later in the evening. We learned at Assmannshausen that the Krone is a very excellent tavern, so we shall sup there."

"How did you know we were to stop at Lorch?" asked Roland, wondering if in any way they had heard he was to meet Goebel's emissary in this village.

"We were not sure," replied Gensbein, "but we made inquiries concerning all the villages and castles down the Rhine, and have taken notes."

"Ah, in that case you are well qualified as a guide. I may find occasion to use the knowledge thus acquired."

"We are all equally involved in this expedition," said Kurzbold impatiently, "and you must not imagine yourself the only person to be considered. But we lose time. What we wish at the present moment is that you will unlock one of these chests, and divide amongst us a bag of gold. The rest is to be partitioned when we return this evening; and after that, Herr Roland, we shall not need to trouble you by asking for more money."

"Are the thirty thalers I gave you the other day all spent, Herr Kurzbold?"

"No matter for that," replied this insubordinate ex-president. "The money in the lockers is ours, and we demand a portion of it now, with the remainder after the banquet."

Without another word, Roland took the bunch of keys from his belt, opened one of the lockers, lifted out a bag of gold, untied the thongs, and poured out the coins on the lid of the chest, which he locked again.

"There is the money," he said to Kurzbold. "I shall send Greusel and Ebearhard to share in its distribution, and thus you can invite them to your banquet. My own portion you may leave on the lid of the locker."

With that he departed up on deck again, and said to his officers:

"Kurzbold, on behalf of the men, has demanded a bag of gold. You will go to the cabin and receive your share. They will also invite you to a banquet at the Krone. Accept that invitation, and if possible engage a private room, as you did at Assmannshausen, to prevent the men talking with any of the inhabitants. Keep them roystering there until all the village has gone to bed;

then convoy them back to the barge as quietly as you can. A resolution has been passed that the money is to be divided amongst our warriors on their return, but I imagine that they will be in no condition to act as accountants when I have the pleasure of beholding them again, so if anything is said about the apportionment, suggest a postponement of the ceremony until morning. I need not add that I expect you both to drink sparingly, for this is advice I intend to follow myself."

Roland paced the deck deep in thought until his difficult contingent departed towards the twinkling lights of the village, then he went to the cabin, poured his share of the gold into his pouch, and followed the company at a distance into Lorch. He avoided the Krone, and after inquiring his way, stopped at the much smaller hostelry, Mergler's Inn. Here he gave his name, and asking if any one waited for him, was conducted upstairs to a room where he found Herr Kruger just about to sit down to his supper. A stout lad nearing twenty years of age stood in the middle of the room, and from his appearance Roland did not need the elder man's word for it that this was his son.

"I took the precaution of bringing him with me," said Kruger, "as I thought two horsemen were better than one in the business I had undertaken."

"You were quite right," returned Roland, "and I congratulate you upon so stalwart a traveling companion. With your permission I shall order a meal, and sup with you, thus we may save time by talking while we eat, because you will need to depart as speedily as possible."

"You mean in the darkness? To-night?"

"Yes; as soon as you can get away. There are urgent reasons why you should be on the road without delay. How came you here?"

"On horseback; first down the Main, then along the Rhine."

"Very well. In the darkness you will return by the way you came, but only as far as the Castle of Ehrenfels, three leagues from here. There you are to rouse up the custodian, and in safety spend the remainder of the night. To-morrow morning he will furnish you a guide to conduct you through the forest to Wiesbaden, and from thence you know your way to Frankfort, which you should reach not later than evening."

At this point the landlord, who had been summoned, came in.

"I will dine with my friends here," said Roland. "I suppose I need not ask if you possess some of the good red wine of Lorch, which they tell me equals that of Assmannshausen?"

"Of the very best, mein Herr, the product of my own vineyard, and I can therefore guarantee it sound. As for equaling that of Assmannshausen, we have always considered it superior, and, indeed, many other good judges agree with us."

"Then bring me a stoup of it, and you will be enabled to add my opinion to that of the others."

When the landlord produced the wine, Roland raised it to his lips, and absorbed a hearty draught.

"This is indeed most excellent, landlord, and does credit alike to your vines and your inn. I wish to send two large casks of so fine a wine to a merchant of my acquaintance in Frankfort, and my friend, Herr Kruger, has promised to convey it thither. If you can spare me two casks of such excellent vintage, they will make an evenly balanced burden for the horse."

"Surely, mein Herr."

"Choose two of those long casks, landlord, with bung-holes of the largest at the sides. Do you possess such a thing as a pack-saddle?"

"Oh, yes."

"And you, my young friend," he said, turning to Kruger's son, "rode here on a saddle?"

"No," interjected his father; "I ride a saddle, but my son was forced to content himself with a length of Herr Goebel's coarse cloth, folded four times, and strapped to the horse's back."

"Then the cloth may still be used as a cushion for the pack-saddle, and you, my lad, will be compelled to walk, to which I dare venture you are well accustomed."

The lad grinned, but made no objection.

"Now, landlord, while we eat, fill your casks with wine, then place the pack-saddle on the back of this young man's horse, and the casks thereon, for I dare say you have men expert in such a matter."

"There are no better the length of the Rhine," said the landlord proudly.

"Lay the casks so that the bung-holes are upward, and do not drive the bungs more tightly in place than is necessary, for they are to be extracted before Frankfort is reached, that another friend of mine may profit by the wine. When this is done, bring me word, and let me know how much I owe you."

The landlord gone, the three men fell to their meal.

"There is more gold," said Roland, "than I expected, and it is impossible even for two of you to carry it in bags attached to your belts. Besides, if you are molested, such bestowal of it would prove most unsafe. A burden of wine, however, is too common either to attract notice or arouse cupidity. I propose, then, when we leave here, to bring you to the barge belonging to Herr Goebel, and taking out the bungs, we will pour the gold into the barrels, letting the wine that is displaced overflow to the ground. Then we will stoutly drive in the bungs, and should the guards question you at the gates of Frankfort, you may let them taste the wine if they insist, and I dare say it will contain no flavor of the metal."

"A most excellent suggestion," said Herr Kruger with enthusiasm. "An admirable plan; for I confess I looked forward with some anxiety to this journey, laden down with bags of gold under my cloak."

"Yes. You are simply an honest drinker, tired of the white wine of Frankfort, and providing yourself with the stronger fluid that Lorch produces. I am sure you will deliver the money safely to Herr Goebel, somewhat in drink, it is true, but, like the rest of us, none the worse for that when the fumes are gone."

The repast finished, and all accounts liquidated, the trio left the inn, and, leading the two horses, reached the barge without observation. Here the bungs were removed from the casks, and the three men, assisted by the captain, quietly and speedily opened bag after bag, pouring the coins down into the wine; surely a unique adulteration, astonishing even to so heady a fluid as the vintage of Lorch. From the whole amount Roland deducted two thousand thalers, which he divided equally between two empty bags.

"This thousand thalers," said he to Kruger, "is to be shared by your son and yourself, in addition to whatever you may receive from Herr Goebel. The other you will hand to the custodian of Ehrenfels Castle, saying it came from his friend Roland, and is recompense for the money he lent the other day. That will be an effective letter of introduction to him. Say that I ask him to send his son with you as guide through the forest to Wiesbaden; and so good-night and good luck to you."

It was long after midnight when the guild came roystering up the bank of the Rhine to the barge. The moon had risen, and gave them sufficient light to steer a reasonably straight course without danger of falling into the water. Ebearhard was with them, but Greusel walked rapidly ahead, so that he might say a few words to his chief before the others arrived.

"I succeeded in preventing their talking with any stranger, but they have taken aboard enough wine to make them very difficult and rather quarrelsome if thwarted. When I proposed that they should leave the counting until to-morrow morning they first became suspicious, and then resented the imputation that they were not in fit condition for such a task. I recommend, therefore, that you allow them to divide the money to-night. It will allay their fear that some trick is to be played upon them, and if you hint at intoxication, they are likely to get out of hand. As it does not matter when the money is distributed, I counsel you to humor them to-night, and postpone reasoning until to-morrow."

"I'll think about it," said Roland.

"They have bought several casks of wine, and are taking turns in carrying them. Will you allow this wine to come aboard, even if you determine to throw it into the water to-morrow?"

"Oh, yes," said Roland, with a shrug of the shoulders. "Coax them into the cabin as quietly as possible, and keep them there if you can, for should they get on deck, we shall lose some of them in the river."

Greusel turned back to meet the bellowing mob, while Roland roused the captain and his men.

"Get ready," he said to Blumenfels, "and the moment I raise my hand, shove off. Make for this side of the larger island, and come to rest there for the remainder of the night. Command your rowers to put their whole force into the sweeps."

This was done accordingly, and well done, as was the captain's custom. The late moon threw a ghostly light over the scene, and the barren island proved deserted and forbidding, as the crew tied up the barge alongside. Most of the lights in Lorch had gone out, and the town lay in the silence of pallid moonbeams like a city of the dead. Roland stood on deck with Greusel and Ebearhard by his side, the latter relating the difficulties of the evening. There had been singing in the cabin during the passage across, then came a lull in the roar from below, followed by a shout that betokened danger. An instant later the crowd came boiling up the short stair to the deck, Kurzbold in command, all swords drawn, and glistening in the moonlight.

"You scoundrel!" he cried to Roland, "those lockers are full of empty bags."

"I know that," replied Roland, quietly. "The money is in safe keeping, and will be honestly divided at the conclusion of this expedition."

"You thief! You robber!" shouted Kurzbold, flourishing his weapon.

"Quite accurate," replied Roland, unperturbed. "I was once called a Prince of Thieves when I did not deserve the title. Now I have earned it."

"You have earned the penalty of thieving, and we propose to throw you into the Rhine."

"Not, I trust, before you learn where the money is deposited."

Drunk as they were, this consideration staggered them, but Kurzbold was mad with rage and wine.

"Come on, you poltroons!" he shouted. "There are only three of them."

"Draw your swords, gentlemen," whispered Roland, flashing his own blade in the moonlight.

Greusel and Ebearhard obeyed his command.

XII. THE LAUGHING RED MARGRAVE OF FURSTENBERG

Ebearhard laughed, and took two steps forward. Whenever affairs became serious, one could always depend on a laugh from Ebearhard.

"Excuse me, Commander," he said, "but you placed Greusel and me in charge of this pious and sober party; therefore I, being the least of your officers, must stand the first brunt of our failure to keep these lambs peaceable for the night. Greusel, stand behind me, and in front of the Commander. I, being reasonably sober, believe I can cut down six of the innocents before they finish with me. You will attend to the next six, leaving exactly half a dozen for Roland to eliminate in his own fashion. Now, Herr Conrad Kurzbold, come on."

"We have no quarrel with you," said Kurzbold. "Stand aside."

"But I force a quarrel upon you, undisciplined pig. Defend yourself, for, by the Three Kings, I am going to tap your walking wine-barrel!"

Kurzbold, however, retreating with more haste than caution, one or two behind him were sent sprawling, and the half-dozen which were Roland's portion tumbled over one another down the steep ladder into the cabin.

Ebearhard laughed again when the last man disappeared.

"I think," he said to Roland, "that you will meet no further trouble from our friends. They evidently broke open the lockers, alarmed because Greusel and I asked for a postponement of the counting, probably intending to make the division without our assistance."

"Have you hidden the money?" asked Greusel.

"Not exactly," replied Roland; "but, in case anything should happen to me, I will tell you what I have done with it."

When he finished his recital, he added:

"I will give each of you a letter to Herr Goebel, identifying you. He is entitled to four thousand five hundred thalers of the money. The balance you will divide among those of us who survive."

Roland slept on deck, wrapped in his cloak. His two lieutenants took turn in keeping watch, but nothing except snores came up from the cabin. The mutineers were not examples of early rising next morning. The sun gave promise of another warm day, and Roland walked up and down the deck, anxiety printed on his brow. He had made up his mind to knock at the door of the Laughing Baron, a giant in stature, reported to be the most ingenious, most cruel, and bravest of all the robber noblemen of the Rhine, whose Castle was notoriously the hardest nut to crack along the banks of that famous river. For several reasons it would not be wise to linger much longer in the neighborhood of Lorch. The three castles they had entered the day before were still visible on the western bank. News of the raid would undoubtedly travel to Furstenberg, also within sight down the river, and thus the hilarious Margrave would be put on his guard, overjoyed at the opportunity of trapping the moral marauders. Furstenberg was also a fief of Cologne, and any molestation of it would involve the meddler, if identified, in complications with the Church and the Archbishop.

It was necessary, therefore, to move with caution, and to retreat, if possible, unobserved. These difficulties alone were enough to give pause to the most intrepid, but Roland was further handicapped by his own following. How could he hope to accomplish any subtle movement requiring silence, prompt obedience, and great alertness, supported by men whose brains were muddled with drink, and whose conduct was saturated with conspiracy against him? They had wine enough on board to continue their orgy, and he was quite unable to prevent their carouse. With a deep sigh he realized that he would be compelled to forego Furstenberg, and thus leave behind him a virgin citadel, which he knew was bad tactics from a military point of view.

During his meditations his men were coming up from the fuming cabin into the fresh air and the sunlight. They appeared by twos and threes, yawning and rubbing their eyes, but no one ventured to interrupt the leader as, with bent head, he paced back and forth on the deck. The men, indeed, seemed exceedingly subdued. They passed with almost overdone nonchalance from the boat to the island, and sauntered towards its lower end, from which, in the clear morning air, the grim fortress of Furstenberg could be plainly discerned diagonally across the river. It was Ebearhard who broke in upon Roland's reverie.

"Our friends appear very quiet this morning, but I observe they have all happened to coincide upon the northern part of the island as a rendezvous for their before-breakfast walk. I surmise they are holding a formal meeting of the guild, but neither Greusel nor I have been invited, so I suppose that after last night's display we two are no longer considered their brethren. This meekness on their part seems to me more dangerous than last night's flurry. I think they will demand from you a knowledge of what has been done with the gold. Have you decided upon your answer?"

"Yes; it is their right to know, so I shall tell them the truth. By this time Kruger is on his way somewhere between Ehrenfels and Wiesbaden. He will reach Frankfort to-night, and cannot be overtaken."

"Is there not danger that they will desert in a body, return to Frankfort, and demand from Herr Goebel their share of the spoil?"

"No matter for that," returned Roland. "Goebel will not part with a florin except under security of such letters as I purpose giving you and Greusel, and even then only when you have proven to him that I am dead."

"That is all very well," demurred Ebearhard, "but don't you see what a dangerous power you put into the hands of the rebels? Goebel is merely a merchant, and, though rich, politically powerless. He has already come into conflict with the authorities, and spent a term in prison. Do not forget that the Archbishops have refused to take action against these robber Barons. Our men, if there happen to be one of brains among them, can easily terrify Goebel into parting with the treasure by threatening to confess their own and his complicity in the raids. Consider what an excellent case they can put forward, stating quite truly that they joined this expedition in ignorance of its purport, but on the very first day, learning what was afoot, they deserted their criminal leader, and are now endeavoring to make restitution. Goebel is helpless. If he says that they first demanded the gold from him, they as strenuously deny it, and their denial must be believed, because they come of their own free-will to the authorities. The merchant, already tainted with treason, having suffered imprisonment, and narrowly escaped hanging, proves on investigation to be up to the neck in this affair. There is no difficulty in learning that his barge went down the river, manned by a crew of his own choosing. Of course, it need never come to this, because Goebel, being a shrewd man, could at once see in what jeopardy he stood, and convinced from the men's own story that they were part, at least, of your contingent, would deliver up the treasure to them. Don't you see he must do so to save his own neck?"

Roland pondered deeply on what had been said to him, but for the moment made no reply. Greusel, who joined them during the conversation, remaining silent until Ebearhard had finished, now spoke:

"I quite agree with all that has been said."

"What, then, would you advise me to do?" asked Roland.

"I have been talking with one or two of the men," said Greusel. "(They won't speak to Ebearhard because he drew his sword on them.) I find they believe you took advantage of their absence to bury the gold in what you suppose to be a safe place. They are sure you are acquainted with no one in Lorch to whom you could safely entrust it, and of course do not suspect an emissary from Frankfort. I should advise you to say that arrangements have been made for every man to get his share so long as nothing untoward happens to you. This will preserve your life should they go so far as to threaten it, and compel them to stay on with us. After all, we are merely artisans, and not fighting men. I am convinced that if ever we are really attacked, we shall make a very poor showing, even though we carry swords. Remember how the men tumbled over one another in their haste to get out of reach when Ebearhard flourished his blade."

"I think Greusel's suggestion is an excellent one," put in Ebearhard.

"Very well," said Roland, "I shall adopt it, although I had made up my mind fully to enlighten them."

"There is one more matter that I should like to speak to you about,"

arranging that if nothing happens to me, this money shall be properly divided in my presence."

"Do you deny, sir, that the money belongs to us?"

"Part of it undoubtedly does, but I, as leader of the expedition, am morally, if not legally, responsible to you all for its safe keeping. Our barge has stopped three times so far, and Captain Blumenfels tells me that he has had no real violence to complain of, but as we progress farther down the river, we are bound to encounter some Baron who is not so punctilious; for instance, the Margrave von Katznellenbogenstahleck, whose stronghold you doubtless saw from the latest meeting-place of the guild. Such a man as the Margrave is certain to do what you yourselves did without hesitation last night, that is, break open the lockers, and if gold were there you may depend it would not long remain in our possession after the discovery."

"You miss, or rather, evade the point, Commander. Is the gold ours, or is it yours?"

"I have admitted that part of it is yours."

"Then by what right do you assert the power to deal with it, lacking our consent? If you will pardon me for saying so, you, the youngest of our company, treat the rest of us as though we were children."

"If I possessed a child that acted at once so obstreperously and in so cowardly a manner as you did last night, I should cut a stick from the forest here, and thrash him with such severity that he would never forget it. As I have not done this to you, I deny that I treat you like children. The truth is that, although the youngest, I am your commander. We are engaged in acts of war, therefore military law prevails, and not the code of Justinian. It is my duty to protect your treasure and my own, and ensure that each man shall receive his share. After the division you may do what you please with the money, for you will then be under the common law, and I should not presume even to advise concerning its disposal."

"You refuse to tell us, then, what you have done with the gold?"

"I do. Now proceed with your suggestion."

"I fear I put the case too mildly when I called it a suggestion, considering the unsatisfactory nature of your reply to my question, therefore I withdraw the word 'suggestion,' and substitute the word 'command.'"

Kurzbold paused, to give his ultimatum the greater force. Behind him rose a murmur of approval.

"Words do not matter in the least. I deal with deeds. Out, then, with your command!" cried Roland, for the first time exhibiting impatience.

"The command unanimously adopted is this: the Castle of Furstenberg must be left alone. We know more of that Castle than you do, especially about its owner and his garrison. We have been gathering information as we journeyed, and have not remained sulking in the barge."

"Well, that is encouraging news to hear," said Roland. "I thought you were engaged in sampling wine."

"You hear the command. Will you obey?"

"I will not," said Roland decisively.

Ebearhard took a step forward to the side of his chief, and glanced at him reproachfully. Greusel remained where he was, but neither man spoke.

"You intend to attack Furstenberg?"

"Yes."

"When?"

"This afternoon."

Kurzbold turned to his following:

"Brethren," he said, "you have heard this conversation, and it needs no comment from me."

Apparently the discussion was to receive no comment from the others either. They stood there glum and disconcerted, as if the trend of affairs had taken an unexpected turn.

710

"I think," said one, "we had better retire and consult again."

This was unanimously agreed to, and once more they disembarked upon the island, and moved forward to their Witenagemot. Still Greusel and Ebearhard said nothing, but watched the men disappear through the trees. Roland looked at one after another with a smile.

"I see," he said, "that you disapprove of my conduct."

Greusel remained silent, but Ebearhard laughed and spoke.

"You came deliberately to the conclusion that it was unwise to attack Furstenberg. Now, because of Kurzbold's lack of courtesy, you deflect from your own mature judgment, and hastily jump into a course opposite to that which you marked out for yourself after sober, unbiased thought."

"My dear Ebearhard, the duty of a commander is to give, and not to receive, commands."

"Quite so. Command and suggestion are merely words, as you yourself pointed out, saying that they did not matter."

"In that, Ebearhard, I was wrong. Words do matter, although Kurzbold wasn't clever enough to correct me. For example, I hold no man in higher esteem than yourself, yet you might use words that would cause me instantly to draw my sword upon you, and fight until one or other of us succumbed."

Ebearhard laughed.

"You put it very flatteringly, Roland. Truth is, you'd fight till I succumbed, my swordsmanship being no match for yours. I shall say the words, however, that will cause you to draw your sword, and they are: Commander, I will stand by you whatever you do."

"And I," said Greusel curtly.

Roland shook hands in turn with the two men.

"Right," he cried. "If we are fated to go down, we will fall with banners flying."

After a time the captain returned with his supplies, but still the majority of the guild remained engaged in deliberation. Evidently discussion was not proceeding with that unanimity which Kurzbold always insisted was the case.

At noon Roland requested the captain to send some of his men with a meal for those in prolonged session, and also to carry them a cask which had been half-emptied either that morning or the night before.

"They will enjoy a picnic under the trees by the margin of the river," said Roland, as he and his two backers sat down in the empty cabin to their own repast.

"Do you think they are purposely delaying, so that you cannot cross over this afternoon?"

"'Tis very likely," said Roland. "I'll wait here until the sun sets, and then when they realize that I am about to leave them on an uninhabited island, without anything to eat, I think you will see them scramble aboard."

"But suppose they don't," suggested Greusel. "There are at least three of them able to swim across this narrow branch of the Rhine, and engage a boatman to take them off, should their signaling be unobserved."

"Again no matter. My plan for the undoing of the castles does not depend on force, but on craft. We three cannot carry away as much gold as can twenty-one, but our shares will be the same, and then we are not likely to find again so full a treasury as that at Rheinstein. My belief that these chaps would fight was dispelled by their conduct last night. Think of eighteen armed men flying before one sword!"

"Ah, you are scarce just in your estimate, Commander. They were under the influence of wine."

"True; but a brave man will fight, drunk or sober."

Although the sun sank out of sight, the men did not return. There had been more wine in the cask than Roland supposed, for the cheery songs of the guild echoed through the sylvan solitude. Roland told the captain to set his men at work and row round the top of the island into the main stream of the Rhine. The revelers had evidently appointed watchmen, for they speedily came running through the woods, and followed the movements of the boat from the shore, keeping pace with it. When the craft reached the opposite side of the island, the rowers drew in to the beach.

"Are you coming aboard?" asked Roland pleasantly.

"Will you agree to pass Furstenberg during the night?" demanded Kurzbold.

"No."

"Do you expect to succeed, as you did with the other castles?"

"Certainly; otherwise I shouldn't make the attempt."

"I was wrong," said Kurzbold mildly, "in substituting the word 'command' for 'suggestion,' which I first employed. There are many grave reasons for deferring an attempt on Furstenberg. In the heat of argument these reasons were not presented to you. Will you consent to listen to them if we go on board?"

"Yes; if you, on your part, will unanimously promise to abide by my decision."

"Do you think," said Kurzbold, "that your prejudice against me, which perhaps you agree does exist—"

"It exists," confessed Roland.

"Very well. Will you allow that prejudice to prevent you from rendering a decision in the men's favor?"

"No. If they present reasons that convince Greusel and Ebearhard against the attack on Furstenberg, I shall do what these two men advise, even although I myself believe in a contrary course. Thus you see, Herr Kurzbold, that my admitted dislike of you shall not come into play at all."

"That is quite satisfactory," said Kurzbold. "Will you tie up against the farther shore until your decision is rendered?"

"With pleasure," replied Roland; and accordingly the raiders tumbled impetuously on board the barge, whereupon the sailors bent to their long oars, and quickly reached the western bank, at a picturesque spot out of sight of any castle, where the trees came down the mountain-side to the water's edge. Here the sailors, springing ashore, tied their stout ropes to the tree-trunks, and the great barge lay broadside on to the land, with her nose pointing down the stream.

"You see," said Roland to his lieutenants, "without giving way in the least I allow you two the decision, and so I take it Furstenberg or ourselves will escape disaster on this occasion."

"Aside from all other considerations," replied the cautious Greusel, "I think it good diplomacy on this occasion to agree with the men, since they have stated their case so deferentially. They are improving, Commander."

"It really looks like it," he agreed. "You and Ebearhard had better go aft, and counsel them to begin the conference at once, for if we are to attack we must do so before darkness sets in. I'll remain here as usual at the prow."

Some of the men were strolling about the deck, but the majority remained in the cabin, down whose steps the lieutenants descended. Roland's impatience increased with the waning of the light.

Suddenly a cry that was instantly smothered rose from the cabin, then a shout:

"Treachery! Look out for yourself!"

Roland attempted to stride forward, but four men fell on him, pinioning his arms to his side, preventing the drawing of his weapon. Kurzbold, with half a dozen others, mounted on deck.

"Disarm him!" he commanded, and one of the men drew Roland's sword from its sheath, flinging it along the deck to Kurzbold's feet. The others now came up, bringing the two lieutenants, both gagged, with their arms tied behind them. Roland ceased his struggles, which he knew to be fruitless.

"We wish an amicable settlement of this matter," said Kurzbold, addressing the lieutenants, "and regret being compelled to use measures that may appear harsh. I do this only to prevent unnecessary bloodshed. Earlier in the day," he continued, turning to Roland, "when we found all appeals to you were vain, we unanimously deposed you from the leadership, which is our right, and also our duty."

"Not under martial law," said Roland.

"I beg to point out that there was no talk of martial law before we left Frankfort. It was not till later that we learned we had appointed an unreasoning tyrant over us. We have deposed him, and I am elected in his place, with John Gensbein as my lieutenant. We will keep you three here until complete darkness sets in, then put you ashore unarmed. Bacharach, on this side of the Rhine, is to be our next resting-place, and doubtless so clever a man as you, Roland, may say that we choose Bacharach because it is named for Bacchus, the god of drunkards. Nevertheless, to show our good intentions towards you, we will remain there all day to-morrow. You can easily reach Bacharach along the hilltops before daybreak. We have written a charter of comradeship which all have signed except yourselves. If at Bacharach you give us your word to act faithfully under my leadership, we will reinstate you in the guild, and return your swords. By way of recompense for this leniency, we ask you to direct the captain to obey my commands as he has done yours."

"Captain Blumenfels," said Roland to the honest sailor, who stood looking on in amaze at this turn of affairs, "you are to wait here until it is completely dark. See that no lights are burning to give warning to those in Furstenberg; and, by the way," added Roland, turning to his former company, "I advise you not to drink anything until you are well past the Castle. If you sing the songs of the guild within earshot of Furstenberg, you are like to sing on the other side of your mouths before morning. Don't forget that Margrave Hermann von Katznellenbogenstahleck is the chief hangman of Germany." Then once more to the captain:

"As the Castle of Furstenberg stands high above the river, and well back from it, you will be out of sight if you keep near this shore. However, you can easily judge your distance, because the towers are visible even in the darkness against the sky. No man on the ramparts of the Castle can discern you down here on the black surface of the water, so long as you do not carry a light."

"Roland, my deposed friend," said Kurzbold, "I fear you bear resentment, for you are giving the captain orders instead of telling him to obey mine."

"Kurzbold, you are mistaken. I resign command with great pleasure, and, indeed, Greusel and Ebearhard will testify that I had already determined to pass Furstenberg unseen. As my former lieutenants are disarmed, surely the company, with eighteen swords, is not so frightened as to keep them gagged and bound. 'Tis no wonder you wish to avoid the Laughing Baron, if that is all the courage you possess."

Stung by these taunts, Kurzbold gruffly ordered his men to release their prisoners, but when the gags were removed, and before the cords were cut, he addressed the lieutenants:

"Do you give me your words not to make any further resistance, if I permit you to remain unbound?"

"I give you my word on nothing, you mutinous dog!" cried Greusel; "and if I did, how could you expect me to keep it after such an example of treachery from you who pledged your faith, and then broke it? I shall obey my Commander, and none other."

"I am your Commander," asserted Kurzbold.

"You are not," proclaimed Greusel.

Ebearhard laughed.

"No need to question me," he said. "I stand by my colleagues."

"Gag them again," ordered Kurzbold.

"No, no!" cried Roland. "We are quite helpless. Give your words, gentlemen."

Gloomily Greusel obeyed, and merrily Ebearhard. Darkness was now gathering, and when it fell completely the three men were put off into the forest.

"You have not yet," said Kurzbold to Roland, "ordered the captain to obey me. I do not object to that, but it will be the worse for him and his men if they refuse to accept my instructions."

"Do you know this district, Captain Blumenfels?" asked Roland.

"Yes, mein Herr."

"Is there a path along the top that will lead us behind Furstenberg on to Bacharach?"

"Yes, mein Herr, but it is a very rough track."

"Is it too far for you to guide us there, and return before the moon rises?"

"Oh no, mein Herr, I can conduct you to the trail in half an hour if you consent to climb lustily."

"Very good. Herr Kurzbold, if you are not impatient to be off, and will permit the captain to direct us on our way, I will tell him to obey you."

"How long before you can return, captain?" asked Kurzbold.

"I can be back well within the hour, mein Herr."

"You will obey me if the late Commander orders you to do so?"

"Yes, mein Herr."

"Captain," said Roland, "I inform you in the hearing of these men that Herr Kurzbold occupies my place, and is to be obeyed by you until I resume command."

Kurzbold laughed.

"You mean until you are re-elected to membership in the guild, for we do not propose to make you commander again. Now, captain, to the hill, and see that your return is not delayed."

The four men disappeared into the dark forest.

"Captain," said Roland, when they reached the track, "I have taken you up here not that I needed your guidance, for I know this land as well as you do. You will obey Kurzbold, of course, but if he tells you to make for Lorch, allow your boat to drift, and do not get beyond the middle of the river until opposite Furstenberg. There is a buoyed chain—"

"I know it well," interrupted the captain. "I have many times avoided it, but twice became entangled with it, in spite of all my efforts, and was robbed by the Laughing Baron."

"Very well; I intend you to be entrapped by that chain to-night. Offer no resistance, and you will be safe enough. Do not attempt to help these lads should they be set upon, and it will be hard luck if I am not in command again before midnight. Keep close to this shore, but if they order you into the middle of the river, or across it, dally, my good Blumenfels, dally, until you are stopped by the chain for the third time."

When the captain returned to his barge, he found Kurzbold pacing the deck in a masterly manner, impatient to be off. For once the combatants, with an effort, were refraining from drink.

"We will open a cask," said Kurzbold, "as soon as we have passed the Schloss."

He ordered the captain to follow the shore as closely as was safe, and take care that they did not come within sight of Furstenberg's tall, round tower. All sat or reclined on the dark deck, saying no word as the barge slid silently down the swift Rhine. Suddenly the speed of the boat was checked so abruptly that one or two of the standing men were flung off their feet. From up on the hillside there tolled out the deep note of a bell. The barge swung round broadside on the current, and lay there with the water rushing like hissing serpents along its side, the bell pealing out a loud alarm that seemed to keep time with the shuddering of the helpless boat.

"What's wrong, captain?" cried Kurzbold, getting on his feet again and running aft.

"I fear, sir, 'tis an anchored chain."

"Can't you cut it?"

"That is impossible, mein Herr."

"Then get out your sweeps, and turn back. Where are we, do you think?"

"Under the battlements of Furstenberg Castle."

"Damnation! Put some speed into your men, and let us get away from here."

The captain ordered his crew to hurry, but all their efforts could not release the boat from the chain, against which it ground up and down with a tearing noise, and even the un-nautical swordsmen saw that the current was impelling it diagonally toward the shore, and all the while the deep bell tolled on.

"What in the fiend's name is the meaning of that bell?" demanded Kurzbold.

"It is the Castle bell, mein Herr," replied the captain.

Before Kurzbold could say anything more the air quivered with shout after shout of laughter. Torches began to glisten among the trees, and there was a clatter of horses' hoofs on the echoing rock. A more magnificent sight was never before presented to the startled eyes of so unappreciative a crowd. Along the zigzag road, and among the trees, spluttered the torches, each with a trail of sparks like the tail of a comet. The bearers were rushing headlong down the slope, for woe to the man who did not arrive at the water's edge sooner than his master.

The torchlight gleamed on flashing swords and glittering points of spears, but chief sight of all was the Margrave Hermann von Katznellenbogenstahleck, a giant in stature, mounted on a magnificent stallion, as black as the night, and of a size that corresponded with its prodigious rider. The Margrave's long beard and flowing hair were red; scarlet, one may say, but perhaps that was the fiery reflection from the torches. Servants, scullions, stablemen carried the lights; the men-at-arms had no encumbrance but their weapons, and the business-like way in which they lined up along the shore was a study in discipline, and a terror to any one unused to war. Above all the din and clash of arms rang the hearty, stentorian laughter of the Red Margrave actually echoing back in gusts of fiendish merriment from the hills on the other side of the Rhine.

Now the boat's nose came dully against the ledge of rock, to whose surface the swaying chain rose dripping from the water, sparkling like a jointed snake under the torchlight.

"God save us all!" cried the Margrave, "what rare show have we here? By my sainted patron, the Archbishop, merchants under arms! Whoever saw the like? Ha! stout Captain Blumenfels, do I recognize you? Once more my chain has caught you. This makes the third time, does it not, Blumenfels?"

"Yes, your Majesty."

"You may as well call me 'your Holiness' as 'your Majesty.' I'm contented with my title, the 'Laughing Baron,' Haw-haw-haw-haw! And so your merchants have taken to arms again? The lesson at the Lorely taught them nothing! Are there any ropes aboard, captain?"

"Plenty, my lord."

"Then fling a coil ashore. Now, my tigers," he roared to his men-at-arms, "hale me to land those damned shopkeepers."

With a clash of armor and weapons the brigands threw themselves on the boat, and in less time than is taken to tell it, every man of the guild was disarmed and flung ashore. Here another command of the Red Margrave gave them the outlaw's knot, as he termed it, a most painful tying-up of the body and the limbs until each victim was rigid as a red of iron. They were flung face downwards in a row, and beaten black and blue with cudgels, despite their screams of agony and appeals for mercy.

"Now turn them over on their backs," commanded the Margrave, and it was done. The glare of the pitiless torches fell upon contorted faces. The Baron turned his horse athwart the line of helpless men, and spurred that animal over it from end to end, but the intelligent horse, more merciful than its rider, stepped with great daintiness, despite its unusual size, and never trod on one of the prostrate bodies. During what followed, the Red Baron, shaking with laughter, marched his horse up and down over the stricken men.

"Now, unload the boat, but do not injure any of the sailors! I hope to see them often again. You cannot tell how we have missed you, captain. What are you loaded with this time? Sound Frankfort cloth?"

"Yes, your Majesty—I mean, my lord."

"No, you mean my Holiness, for I expect to be an Archbishop yet, if all goes well," and his laughter echoed across the Rhine. "Uplift your hatches, Blumenfels, and tell your men to help fling the goods ashore."

Delicately paced the fearful horse over the prone men, snorting, perhaps in sympathy, from his red nostrils, his jet-black coat a-quiver with the excitement of the scene. The captain obeyed the Margrave with promptness and celerity. The hatches were lifted, and his sailors, two and two, flung on the ledge of rock the merchant's bales. The men-at-arms, who proved to be men-of-all-work, had piled their weapons in a heap, and were carrying the bales a few yards inland. Through it all the Baron roared with laughter, and rode his horse along its living pavement, turning now at this end and now at the other.

"Do not be impatient," he cried down to them, "'twill not take long to strip the boat of every bale, then I shall hang you on these trees, and send back your bodies in the barge, as a lesson to Frankfort. You must return, captain," he cried, "for you cannot sell dead bodies to my liege of Cologne."

As he spoke a ruddy flush spread over the Rhine, as if some one had flashed a red lantern upon the waters. The glow died out upon the instant.

"What!" thundered the Margrave, "is that the reflection of my beard, or are Beelzebub and his fiends coming up from below for a portion of the Frankfort cloth? I will share with good brother Satan, but with no one else. Boil me if I ever saw a sight like that before! What was it, captain?"

"I saw nothing unusual, my lord."

"There, there!" exclaimed the Margrave, and as he spoke it seemed that a crimson film had fallen on the river, growing brighter and brighter.

"Oh, my lord," cried the captain, "the Castle is on fire!"

"Saints protect us!" shouted the Red Margrave, crossing himself, and turning to the west, where now both hearing and sight indicated that a furnace was roaring. The whole western sky was aglow, and although the flames could not be seen for the intervening cliff, every one knew there was no other dwelling that could cause such an illumination.

Spurring his horse, and calling his men to come on, the nobleman dashed up the steep acclivity, and when the last man had departed, Roland, followed by his two lieutenants, stepped from the forest to the right down upon the rocky plateau.

XIII. "A SENTENCE; COME, PREPARE!"

"Captain," said Roland quietly, "bring your crew ashore, and fling these bales on board again as quickly as you can."

An instant later the sailors were at work, undoing their former efforts.

"In mercy's name, Roland," wailed one of the stricken, "get a sword and cut our bonds."

"All in good time," replied Roland. "The bales are more valuable to me than you are, and we have two barrels of gold at the foot of the cliff to bring in, if they haven't sunk in the Rhine. Greusel, do you and Ebearhard take two of the crew, launch the small boat, and rescue the barrels if you can find them."

"Mercy on us, Roland! Mercy!" moaned his former comrades.

"I have already wasted too much mercy upon you," he said. "If I rescue you now, I shall be compelled to hang you in the morning as breakers of law, so I may as well leave you where you are, and allow the Red Margrave to save me the trouble. The loss of his castle will not make him more compassionate, especially if he learns you were the cause of it. You will then experience some refined tortures, I imagine; for, like myself, he may think hanging too good for you. I should never have fired his castle had it not been for your rebellion."

The men on the ground groaned but made no further appeal. Some of them were far-seeing enough to realize that an important change had come over the young man they thought so well known to them, who stood there with an air of indifference, throwing out a suggestion now and then for the more effective handling of the bales; suggestions carrying an impalpable force of authority that caused them to be very promptly obeyed. They did not know that this person whom they had regarded as one of themselves, the youngest at that, treating him accordingly, had but a day or two before received a tremendous assurance, which would have turned the head of almost any individual in the realm, old or young; the assurance that he was to be supreme ruler over millions of creatures like themselves; a ruler whose lightest word might carry their extinction with it.

Yet such is the strange littleness of human nature that, although this potent knowledge had been gradually exercising its effect on Roland's character, it was not the rebellion of the eighteen or their mutinous words that now made him hard as granite towards them. It was the trivial fact that four of them had dared to manhandle him; had made a personal assault upon him; had pinioned his helpless arms, and flung his sword, that insignia of honor, to the feet of Kurzbold, leader of the revolt.

The Lord's Anointed, he was coming to consider himself, although not yet had the sacred ointment been placed upon his head. A temporal Emperor and a vice-regent of Heaven upon earth, his hand was destined to hold the invisible hilt of the Almighty's sword of vengeance. The words "I will repay" were to reach their fulfillment through his action. Notwithstanding his youth, or perhaps because of it, he was animated by deep religious feeling, and this, rather than ambition, explained the celerity with which he agreed to the proposals of the Archbishops.

The personage the prisoners saw standing on the rock-ledge of Furstenberg was vastly different from the young man who, a comrade of comrades, had departed from Frankfort in their company. They beheld him plainly enough, for there was now no need of torches along the foreshore; the night was crimson in its brilliancy, and down the hill came a continuous roar, like that of the Rhine Fall seventy leagues away.

Into this red glare the small boat and its four occupants entered, and Roland saw with a smile that two well-filled casks formed its freight. The bales were now aboard the barge again, and the Commander ordered the crew to help the quartette in the small boat with the lifting of the heavy barrels. Greusel and Ebearhard clambered over the side, and came thus to the ledge where Roland stood, as the crew rolled the barrels down into the cabin.

"Lieutenants," said the Commander, "select two stout battle-axes from that heap. Follow the chain up the hill until you reach that point where it is attached to the thick rope. Cut the rope with your axes, and draw down the chain with you, thus clearing a passage for the barge."

The two men chose battle-axes, then turned to their leader.

"Should we not get our men aboard," they said, "before the barge is free?"

"These rebels are prisoners of the Red Margrave. They belong to him, and not to me. Where they are, there they remain."

The lieutenants, with one impulse, advanced to their Commander, who frowned as they did so. A cry of despair went up from the pinioned men, but Kurzbold shouted:

"Cut him down, Ebearhard, and then release us. In the name of the guild I call on you to act! He is unarmed; cut him down! 'Tis foul murder to desert us thus."

The cutting down could easily have been accomplished, for Roland stood at their mercy, weaponless since the émeute on the barge. Notwithstanding the seriousness of the occasion, the optimistic Ebearhard laughed, although every one else was grave enough.

"Thank you, Kurzbold, for your suggestion. We have come forward, not to use force, but to try persuasion. Roland, you cannot desert to death the men whom you conducted out of Frankfort."

"Why can I not?"

"I should have said a moment ago that you will not, but now I say you cannot. Kurzbold has just shown what an irreclaimable beast he is, and on that account, because birth, or training, or something has made you one of different caliber, you cannot thus desert him to the reprisal of that red fiend up the hill."

"If I save him now, 'twill be but to hang him an hour later. I am no hangman, while the Margrave is. I prefer that he should attend to my executions."

Again Ebearhard laughed.

"'Tis no use, Roland, pretending abandonment, for you will not abandon. I thoroughly favor choking the life out of Kurzbold, and one or two of the others, and will myself volunteer for the office of headsman, carrying, as I do, the ax, but let everything be done decently and in order, that a dignified execution may follow on a fair trial."

"Commander," shouted the captain from the deck of the barge, "make haste, I beg of you. The rope connecting with the Castle has been burnt, and the chain is dragging free. The current is swift, and this barge heavy. We shall be away within the minute."

"Get your crew ashore on the instant," cried Roland, "and fling me these despicable burdens aboard. A man at the head, another at the heels, and toss each into the barge. Is there time, captain, to take this heap of cutlery with us as trophies of the fray?"

"Yes," replied the captain, "if we are quick about it."

The howling human packages were hurled from ledge to barge; the strong, unerring sailors, accustomed to the task, heaved no man into the water. Others as speedily fell upon the heap of weapons, and threw them, clattering, on the deck. All then leaped aboard, and Roland, motioning his lieutenants to precede him, was the last to climb over the prow.

The chain came down over the stones with a clattering run, and fell with a great splash into the river. The barge, now clear, swung with the current stern foremost; the sailors got to their oars, and gradually drew their craft away from the shore. A little farther from the landing, those on deck, looking upstream, enjoyed an uninterrupted view of the magnificent conflagration. The huge stone Castle seemed to glow white hot. The roof had fallen in, and a seething furnace reddened the midnight sky. Like a flaming torch the great tower roared to the heavens. The whole hilltop resembled the crater of an active volcano. Timber floors and wooden partitions, long seasoned, proved excellent material for the incendiaries, and even the stones were crumbling away, falling into the gulf of fire, sending up a dazzling eruption of sparks, as section after section tumbled into this earthly Hades.

The long barge floated placidly down a river resembling molten gold.

The boat was in disarray, covered with bales of cloth not yet lowered into the hold, cluttered here and there with swords, battle-axes, and spears. In the various positions where they had been flung lay the helpless men, some on their faces, some on their backs. The deck was as light as if the red setting sun were casting his rays upon it. Roland seated himself on a bale, and said to the captain:

"Turn all these men face upward," and the captain did so.

"Ebearhard, you said execution should take place after a fair trial. There is no necessity to call witnesses, or to go through any court of law formalities. You two are perfectly cognizant of everything that has taken place, and no testimony will either strengthen or weaken that knowledge. As a preliminary, take Kurzbold, the new president, and Gensbein, his lieutenant, from among that group, and set them apart. Two members of the crew will carry out this order," which was carried out accordingly.

Roland rose, walked along the prostrate row, and selected, apparently at haphazard, four others, then said to the members of his crew:

"Place these four men beside their leader. Left to myself," he continued to his lieutenants, "I should hang the six. However, I shall take no hand in the matter. I appoint you, Joseph Greusel, and you, Gottlieb Ebearhard, as judges, with power of life and death. If your verdict on any or all of the accused is death, I shall use neither the ax nor the cord, but propose flinging them into the river, and if God wills them to reach the shore alive, their binding will be no hindrance to escape."

Kurzbold and his lieutenant broke out into alternate curses and appeals, protesting that Greusel and Ebearhard had not been expelled from the guild, and calling upon them by their solemn oath of brotherhood to release them now that they possessed the power. To these appeals the newly-appointed judges made no reply, and for once Ebearhard did not laugh.

The other four directed their supplications to Roland himself. They had been misled, they cried, and deeply regretted it. Already they suffered punishment of a severity almost beyond power of human endurance, and they feared their bones were broken with the cudgeling, since which assault their bonds grievously tortured them. All swore amendment, and their grim commander still remaining silent, they asked him in what respect they were more guilty than the dozen others whom seemingly he intended to spare. At last Roland replied.

"You four," he said sternly, "dared to lay hands upon me, and for that I demand from the judges a sentence of death."

Even his two lieutenants gazed at him in amazement, that he should make so much of an action which they themselves had endured and nothing said of it. Surely the laying-on of hands, even in rudeness, was not a capital crime, yet they saw to their astonishment that Roland was in deadly earnest.

The leader turned a calm face toward their scrutiny, but there was a frown upon his brow.

"Work while ye have the light," he said. "Judges, consider your decision, and deliver your verdict."

Greusel and Ebearhard turned their backs on every one, walked slowly aft, and down into the cabin. Roland resumed his seat on the bale of cloth, elbows on his knees, and face in his hands. All appeals had ceased, and deep silence reigned, every man aboard the boat in a state of painful tension. The fire in the distant castle lowered and lowered, and darkness was returning to the deck of the barge. At last the judges emerged from the cabin, and came slowly forward.

It was Greusel who spoke.

"We wish to know if only these six are on trial?"

"Only these six," replied Roland.

"Our verdict is death," said Greusel. "Kurzbold and Gensbein are to be thrown into the Rhine bound as they lie, but the other four receive one chance for life, in that the cords shall be cut, leaving their limbs free."

This seeming mercy brought no consolation to the quartette, for each plaintively proclaimed that he could not swim.

"I thank you for your judgment," said Roland, "which I am sure you must have formed with great reluctance. Having proven yourself such excellent judges, I doubt not you will now act with equal wisdom as advisers. A phrase of yours, Ebearhard, persists in my mind, despite all efforts to dislodge it. You uttered on the ledge of rock yonder something to the effect that we left Frankfort as comrades together. That is very true, and unless you override my resolution, I have come to the conclusion that if any of us are fated to die, the penalty shall be dealt by some other hand than mine. The twelve who lie here are scarcely less guilty than the six now under sentence, and I propose, therefore, to put ashore on the east bank Kurzbold and Gensbein, one a rogue, the other a fool. The sixteen who remain have so definitely proven themselves to be simpletons that I trust they will not resent my calling them such. If however, they abandon all claim to the comradeship that has been so much prated about, swearing by the Three Kings of Cologne faithfully to follow me, and obey my every word without cavil or argument, I will pardon them, but the first man who rebels will show that my clemency has been misplaced, and I can assure them that it shall not be exercised again. Captain, your sailors are familiar with knotted ropes. Bid them release all these men except the six condemned."

The boatmen, with great celerity, freed the prostrate captives from their bonds, but some of the mutineers had been so cruelly used in the cudgeling that it was necessary to assist them to their feet. The early summer daybreak was at hand, its approach heralded by the perceptible diluting of the darkness that surrounded them, and a ghastly, pallid grayness began to overspread the surface of the broad river. Down the stream to the west the towers of Bacharach could be faintly distinguished, looking like a dream city, the lower gloom of which was picked out here and there by points of light, each betokening an early riser.

It was a deeply dejected, silent group that stood in this weird half-light, awaiting the development of Roland's mind regarding them; he, the youngest of their company, quiet, unemotional, whose dominion no one now thought of disputing.

"Captain," he continued, "steer for the eastern shore. I know that Bacharach is the greatest wine mart on the Rhine, and well sustains the reputation of the drunken god for whom it is named, but we will nevertheless avoid it. There is a long island opposite the town, but a little farther down. I dare say you know it well. Place that island between us and Bacharach, and tie up to the mainland, out of view from the stronghold of Bacchus. He is a misleading god, with whom we shall hold no further commerce.

"Now, Joseph Greusel, and Gottlieb Ebearhard, do you two administer the oath of the Three Kings to these twelve men; but before doing so, give each one his choice, permitting him to say whether he will follow Kurzbold on the land or obey me on the water."

Here Kurzbold broke out again in trembling anger:

"Your pretended fairness is a sham, and your bogus option a piece of your own sneaking dishonesty. What chance have we townsmen, put ashore, penniless, in an unknown wilderness, far from any human habitation, knowing nothing of the way back to Frankfort? Your fraudulent clemency rescues us from drowning merely to doom us to starvation."

The daylight had so increased that all might see the gentle smile coming to Roland's lips, and the twinkle in his eye as he looked at the wrathful Kurzbold.

"A most intelligent leader of men are you, Herr Conrad. I suppose this dozen will stampede to join your leadership. They must indeed be proud of you when they learn the truth. I shall present to each of you, out of my own store of gold that came from the castle you so bravely attacked last night, one half the amount that is your due. This will be more money than any of you ever possessed before; each portion, indeed, excelling the total that you eighteen accumulated during your whole lives. I could easily bestow your share without perceptible diminution of the fund we three, unaided, extracted from the coffers of the Red Margrave. The reason I do not pay in full is this. When you reach Frankfort, I must be assured that you will keep your foolish tongues silent. If any man speaks of our labors, I shall hear of it on my return, and will fine that man his remaining half-share.

"It distresses me to expose your ignorance, Kurzbold, but I put you ashore amply provided with money, barely two-thirds of a league from Lorch, where you spent so jovial an evening, and where a man with gold in his pouch need fear neither hunger nor thirst. Lorch may be attained by a leisurely walker in less than half an hour; indeed, it is barely two leagues from this spot to Assmannshausen, and surely you know the road from that storehouse of red wine to the capital city of Frankfort, having once traversed it. A child of six, Kurzbold, might be safely put ashore where you shall set foot on land. Therefore, lieutenants, let each man know he will receive a bag of coin, and may land unmolested to accompany the brave and intelligent Kurzbold."

As he finished this declamation, that caused even some of the beaten warriors to laugh at their leader, the barge came gently alongside the strand, well out of sight of Bacharach. Each of the dozen swore the terrible, unbreakable oath of the Three Kings to be an obedient henchman to Roland.

"You may," said Roland, "depart to the cabin, where a flagon of wine will be served to every man, and also an early breakfast. After that you are permitted to lie down and relax your swollen limbs, meditating on the extract from Holy Writ which relates the fate of the blind when led by the blind."

When the dozen limped away, the chief turned to his prisoners.

"Against you four I bear resentment that I thought could not be appeased except by your expulsion, but reflection shows me that you acted under instruction from the foolish leader you selected, and therefore the principal, not the agent, is most to blame. I give you the same choice I have accorded to the rest. Unloose them, captain; and while this is being done, Greusel, get two empty bags from the locker, open one of the casks, and place in each bag an amount which you estimate to be one half the share which is Kurzbold's due."

The four men standing up took the oath, and thanked Roland for his mercy, hurrying away at a sign from him to their bread and wine.

"Send hither," cried Roland after them, "two of the men who have already refreshed themselves, each with a loaf of bread and a full flagon of wine. And now, captain, release Kurzbold and Gensbein."

When these two stood up and stretched themselves, the bearers of bread and wine presented them with this refreshment, and after they had partaken of it, Greusel gave them each a bag of gold, which they tied to their belts without a word, while Greusel and Ebearhard waited to escort them to land.

"We want our swords," said Kurzbold sullenly.

Ebearhard looked at his chief, but he shook his head.

"They have disgraced their swords," he said, "which now by right belong to the Margrave Hermann von Katznellenbogenstahleck. Put them ashore, lieutenant."

It was broad daylight, and the men had all come up from the cabin, standing in a silent group at the stern. Kurzbold, on the bank, foaming at the mouth with fury, shook his fist at them, roaring:

"Cowards! Pigs! Dolts! Asses! Poltroons!"

The men made no reply, but Ebearhard's hearty laugh rang through the forest.

"You have given us your titles, Kurzbold," he cried. "Send us your address whenever you get one!"

"Captain," said Roland, "cast off. Cross to this side of that island, and tie up there for the day. Set a man on watch, relieving the sentinel every two hours. We have spent an exciting night, and will sleep till evening."

"Your honor, may I first stow away these bales, and dispose of the battle-axes, spears, and broadswords, so to clear the deck?"

"You may do that, captain, at sunset. As for the bales, they make a very comfortable couch upon which I intend to rest."

XIV. THE PRISONER OF EHRENFELS

There is inspiration in the sight of armed men marching steadily together; men well disciplined, keeping step to the measured clank of their armor. Like a great serpent the soldiers of Cologne issued from the forest, coming down two and two, for the path was narrow. They would march four abreast when they reached the river road, and the evolutions which accomplished this doubling of the columns, without changing step or causing confusion, called forth praise from the two southern Archbishops.

A beautiful tableau of amity and brotherly love was presented to the troops as they looked up at the three Archbishops standing together on the balcony in relief against the gray walls of the Castle. The officers, who were on horseback, raised their swords sky-pointing from their helmets, for they recognized their overlord and his two notable confrères. With the motion of one man the three Archbishops acknowledged the salute. The troops cheered and cheered as the anaconda made its sinuous way down the mountainside, and company after company came abreast the Castle. The Archbishops stood there until the last man disappeared down the river road on his way to Coblentz.

"May I ask you," said Mayence, addressing Treves, "to conduct me to the flat roof of your Castle? Will you accompany us?" he inquired of Cologne.

Cologne and Treves being for once in agreement, the latter led the way, and presently the three stood on the broad stone plateau which afforded a truly striking panorama of the Rhine. The July sun sinking in the west transformed the river into a crimson flood, and at that height the cool evening breeze was delicious. Cologne stood with one hand on the parapet, and gazed entranced at the scene, but the practical Mayence paid no attention whatever to it.

"Your troublesome guest, Treves, has one more request to make, which is that you order his flag hoisted to the top of that pole."

Treves at once departed to give this command, while Cologne, with clouded brow, turned from his appreciation of the view.

"My Lord," he said, "you have requested the raising of a signal."

"Yes," was the reply.

"A signal which calls your men from the Lahn to the landing at Stolzenfels?"

"Yes," repeated Mayence.

"My Lord, I have kept my promise not only to the letter, but in the spirit as well. My troops are marching peaceably away, and will reach their barracks some time to-morrow. Although I exacted no promise from you, you implied there was a truce between us, and that your army, like my company, was not to be called into action of any kind."

"Your understanding of our pact is concisely stated, even though my share in that pact remained unspoken. A truce, did you say? Is it not more than that? I hoped that my seconding of the nomination you proposed proved me in complete accord with your views."

"I am not in effect your prisoner, then?"

"Surely not; so contrary to the fact is such an assumption that I implore you to accept my hospitality. The signal, which I see is now at the mast-head, calls for one barge only, and that contains no soldier, merely a captain and his ten stout rowers, whom you may at this moment, if you turn round, see emerging from the mouth of the Lahn. I present to you, and to the Countess von Sayn, my Schloss of Martinsburg for as long as you may require it. It is well furnished, well provisioned, and attended to by a group of capable servants, who are at your command. I suggest that you cross in my barge, in company with the Countess and her kinsman, the Reverend Father. You agree, I take it, to convoy the lady safely to her temporary restraint in Pfalz. It was her own request, you remember."

"I shall convoy her thither."

"I am trusting to you entirely. The distance is but thirteen leagues, and

734

can be accomplished easily in a day. Once on the other side of the river she may despatch her kinsman, or some more trustworthy messenger, to her own Castle, and thus summon the two waiting-women who will share her seclusion."

"Is it your intention, my Lord, that her imprisonment shall—?"

The Archbishop of Mayence held up his thin hand with a gesture of deprecation.

"I use no word so harsh as 'imprisonment.' The penance, if you wish so to characterize it, is rather in the nature of a retreat, giving her needed opportunity for reflection, and, I hope, for regret."

"Nevertheless, my Lord, your action seems to me unnecessarily severe. How long do you propose to detain her?"

"I am pained to hear you term it severity, for her treatment will be of the mildest description. I thought you would understand that no other course was open to me. So far as I am personally concerned, she might have said what pleased her, with no adverse consequences, but she flouted the highest Court of the realm, and such contempt cannot be overlooked. As for the duration of her discipline, it will continue until the new Emperor is married, after which celebration the Countess is free to go whither she pleases. I shall myself call at Pfalz four days from now, that I may be satisfied the lady enjoys every comfort the Castle affords."

"And also, perhaps, to be certain she is there immured."

Mayence's thin lips indulged in a wry smile.

"I need no such assurance," he said, "since my Lord of Cologne has pledged his word to see that the order of the Court is carried out."

The conversation was here interrupted by the return of Treves. Already the great barge was half-way across the river. The surging, swift current swept it some distance below Stolzenfels, and the rowers, five a side, were working strenuously to force it into slower waters. Lord, lady, and monk crossed over to the mouth of the Lahn, and the barge returned immediately to convey across horses and escort.

As the valley of the Lahn opened out it presented a picture of quiet sylvan beauty, apparently uninhabited by any living thing. The Archbishop of Cologne rose, and, shading his eyes from the still radiant sun, gazed intently up the little river. No floating craft was anywhere in sight. He turned to the captain.

"Where is the flotilla from Mayence?" he asked.

"Flotilla, my Lord?"

"Yes; a hundred barges sailed down from Mayence in the darkness either last night or the night before, taking harbor here in the Lahn."

"My Lord, even one barge, manned as this is, could not have journeyed such a distance in so short a time, and, indeed, for a flotilla to attempt the voyage, except in daylight, would have been impossible. No barges have come down the Rhine for months, and had they ventured the little Lahn is too shallow to harbor them."

"Thank you, captain. I appear to be ignorant both of the history and the geography of this district. If I were to ask you and your stout rowers to take me down through the swiftest part of the river to Coblentz, how soon would we reach that town?"

"Very speedily, my Lord, but I could undertake no such voyage except at the command of my master. He is not one to be disobeyed."

"I quite credit that," said Cologne, sitting down again, the momentary desire to recall his marching troops, that had arisen when he saw the empty Lahn, dying down when he realized how effectually he had been outwitted.

When the horses were brought across, Father Ambrose, at the request of the Countess, rode back to Sayn, and sent forward the two waiting-women whom she required, and so well did he accomplish his task that they arrived at Schloss Martinsburg before ten of the clock that night. At an early hour next morning the little procession began its journey up the Rhine, his Lordship and the Countess in front; the six horsemen bringing up the rear.

736

The lady was in a mood of deep dejection; the regret which Mayence had anticipated as result of imprisonment already enveloped her. It was only too evident that the Archbishop of Cologne was bitterly disappointed, for he rode silently by her side making no attempt at conversation. They rested for several hours during midday, arriving at Caub before the red sun set, and now the Countess saw her pinnacled prison lying like an anchored ship in midstream.

At Caub they were met by a bearded, truculent-looking ruffian, who introduced himself to the Archbishop as the Pfalzgraf von Stahleck.

"You take us rather by surprise, Prince of Cologne," he said. "It is true that my overlord, the Archbishop of Mayence, called upon me several days ago while descending the Rhine in his ten-oared barge, and said there was a remote chance that a prisoner might shortly be given into my care. This had often happened before, for my Castle covers some gruesome cells that extend under the river,—cells with secret entrances not easily come by should any one search the Castle. It is sometimes convenient that a prisoner of State should be immured in one of them when the Archbishop has no room in his own Schloss Ehrenfels, so I paid little attention, and merely said the prisoner would receive a welcome on arrival. This morning there came one of the Archbishop's men from Stolzenfels, and both my wife and myself were astonished to learn that the prisoner would be here this evening under your escort, my Lord, and that it was a woman we were to harbor. Further, she was to be given the best suite of rooms we had in the Castle, and to be treated with all respect as a person of rank. Now, this apartment is in no state of readiness to receive such a lady, much less to house one of the dignity of your Lordship."

"It does not matter for me," replied the Archbishop. "Being, as I may say, part soldier, the bed and board of an inn is quite acceptable upon occasion."

"Oh no, your Highness, such a hardship is not to be thought of. The Castle of Gutenfels, standing above us, is comfortable as any on the Rhine. Its owner, the Count Palatine, is fellow-Elector of yours, and a very close friend of my overlord of Mayence, and I am told they vote together whenever my overlord needs his assistance."

"That is true," commented Cologne.

"My overlord sent word that anything I needed for the accommodation of her ladyship, he recognizing that my warning had been short, I should requisition from the Count Palatine, so at midday I went up to call upon him, not saying anything, of course, about State prisoners, male or female. The moment he heard that you, my Lord, were visiting this neighborhood, he begged me to tender to you, and to all your companions or following, the hospitality of his Castle for so long as you might honor him with your presence."

"The Count Palatine is very gracious, and I shall be glad to accept shelter and refreshment."

"He would have been here to greet your Highness, but I was unable to inform him at what hour you would arrive, so I waited for you myself, and will be pleased to guide you to the gates of Gutenfels."

The conversation was interrupted by a great clatter of galloping horses, descending the hill with reckless speed, and at its foot swinging round into the main street of the town.

"Ha!" cried the amateur jailer, "here is the Count Palatine himself;" and thus it is our fate to meet the fourth Elector of the Empire, who, added to the three Archbishops, formed a quorum so potent that it could elect or depose an Emperor at will.

The cavalry of the Count Palatine was composed of fifty fully-armed men, and their gallop through the town roused the echoes of that ancient bailiwick, which, together with the Castle, belonged to the Palatinate. The powerful noble extended a cordial welcome to his fellow-Elector, and together they mounted to the Castle of Gutenfels.

At dinner that night the Count Palatine proved an amiable host. Under his geniality the charming Countess von Sayn gradually recovered her lost good spirits, and forgot she was on her way to prison. After all, she was young, naturally joyous, and loved interesting company, especially that of the two Electors, who were well informed, and had seen much of the world. The Archbishop also shook off some of his somberness; indeed, all of it as the flagons flowed. Being asked his preference in wine, he replied that yesterday he had been regaled with a very excellent sample of Oberweseler.

"That is from this neighborhood," replied the Count. "Oberwesel lies but a very short distance below, on the opposite side of the river, but we contend that our beverage of Caub is at least equal, and sometimes superior. You shall try a good vintage of both. How did you come by Oberweseler so far north as Stolzenfels?"

"Simply because I was so forward, counting on the good nature of my friend of Treves, that I stipulated for Oberweseler."

"Ah! I am anxious to know why."

"For reasons of history, not of the palate. A fair English Princess was guest of Stolzenfels long ago, and this wine was served to her."

"In that case," returned the Count, "I also shall fall back on history, and first order brimming tankards of old Caub. Really, Madam," he said, turning to Hildegunde, "we should have had Royalty here to meet you, instead of two old wine-bibbers like his Highness and myself."

The girl looked startled at this mention of Royalty, bringing to her mind the turbulent events of yesterday. Nevertheless, with great composure, she smiled at her enthusiastic host.

"Still," went on the Count, "if we are not royal ourselves, 'tis a degree we are empowered to confer, and, indeed, may be very shortly called upon to bestow. That is true from what I hear, is it not, your Highness?"

"Yes," replied the Archbishop gravely.

"Well, as I was about to say, this Castle belonged to the Falkensteins, and was sold by them to the Palatinate. Rumor, legend, history, call it what you like, asserts that the most beautiful woman ever born on the Rhine was Countess Beatrice of Falkenstein. But when I drink to the toast I am about to offer I shall, Madam," he smiled at Hildegunde, "assert that the legend no longer holds, a contention I am prepared to maintain by mortal combat. Know then that the Earl of Cornwall, who was elected King of Germany in 1257, met Beatrice of Falkenstein in this Castle. The meeting was brought about by the Electors themselves, who, stupid matchmakers, attempted to coerce each into a marriage with the other. Beatrice refused to marry a foreigner.

"The Chronicles are a little vague about the most interesting part of the negotiations, but minutely plain about the outcome. In some manner the Earl and Beatrice met, and he became instantly enamored of her. This is the portion so deplorably slurred by these old monkish writers. I need hardly tell you that the Earl himself succeeded where the seven Electors failed. Beatrice became Cornwall's wife and Queen of Germany, and they lived happily ever afterwards.

"I give you the toast!" cried the chivalrous Count Palatine, rising. "To the cherished memory of the Royal lovers of Gutenfels!"

The Archbishop's eyes twinkled as he looked across the table at Hildegunde.

"This seems to be a time of Royal betrothals," he said, raising his flagon.

"'Seems' is the right word, Guardian," replied the Countess.

Then she sipped the ancient wine of Caub.

Next morning Hildegunde was early afoot. Notwithstanding her trouble of mind, she had slept well, and awakened with the birds, so great is the influence of youth and health. During her last conscious moments the night before, as she lay in the stately bed of the most noble room the Castle contained, she bitterly accused herself for the disastrous failure of the previous day. The Archbishop of Cologne had given her good counsel that was not followed, and his disappointment with the result, generously as he endeavored to conceal it, was doubtless the deeper because undiscussed. Thinking of coming captivity, a dream of grim Pfalz was expected, but instead the girl's spirit wandered through the sweet seclusion of Nonnenwerth, living again that happy, earlier time, free from politics and the tramp of armed men.

In the morning the porter, at her behest, withdrew bolt, bar, and chain, allowing exit into the fresh, cool air, and skirting the Castle, she arrived at a broad terrace which fronted it. A fleecy mist extending from shore to shore concealed the waters of the Rhine, and partially obliterated the little village of Caub at the foot of the hill. Where she stood the air was crystal clear, and she seemed to be looking out on a broad snow-field of purest white. Beyond Caub its surface was pierced by the dozen sharp pinnacles of her future prison, looking like a bed of spikes, upon which one might imagine a giant martyr impaled by the verdict of a cruel Archbishop.

Gazing upon this nightmare Castle, whose tusks alone were revealed, the girl formulated the resolution but faintly suggested the night before. On her release should ensue an abandonment of the world, and the adoption of a nun's veil in the convent opposite Drachenfels, an island exchanged for an island; turmoil for peace.

At breakfast she met again the jovial Count Palatine, and her more sober guardian, who both complimented her on the results of her beauty rest, the one with great gallantry, the other with more reserve, as befitted a Churchman. The Archbishop seemed old and haggard in the morning light, and it was not difficult to guess that no beauty sleep had soothed his pillow. It wrung the girl's heart to look at him, and again she accused herself for lack of all tact and discretion, wishing that her guardian took his disappointment more vengefully, setting her to some detested task that she might willingly perform.

The hospitable Count, eager that they should stop at least another night under his roof, pressed his invitation upon them, and the Archbishop gave a tacit consent.

"If the Countess is not too tired," said Cologne, "I propose that she accompany me on a little journey I have in view farther up the river. We will return here in the evening."

"I should be delighted," cried Hildegunde, "for all sense of fatigue has been swept away by a most restful night."

The good-natured Count left them to their own devices, and shortly afterwards guardian and ward rode together down the steep declivity to the river. The mist was already driven away, except a wisp here and there clinging to the gray surface of the water, trailing along as if drawn by the current, for the air was motionless, and there was promise of a sultry day. They proceeded in silence until a bend in the Rhine shut Caub and its sinister water-prison out of sight, and then it was the girl who spoke.

"Guardian," she said, "have I offended you beyond forgiveness?"

A gentle smile came to his lips as he gazed upon her with affection.

"You have not offended me at all, my dear," he said, "but I am grieved at thwarting circumstance."

"I have been thinking over circumstances too, and hold myself solely to blame for their baffling opposition. I will submit without demur to whatever length of imprisonment may please, and, if possible, soften the Archbishop of Mayence. After my release I shall ask your consent that I may forthwith join the Sisterhood at Nonnenwerth. I wish to divide my wealth equally between yourself and the convent."

The Archbishop shook his head.

"I could not accept such donation."

"Why not? The former Archbishop of Cologne accepted Linz from my ancestress Matilda."

"That was intended to be but a temporary loan."

"Well; call my benefaction temporary if you like, to be kept until I call for it, but meanwhile to be used at your discretion."

"It is quite impossible," said the Archbishop firmly.

"Does that mean you will not allow me to adopt the religious life?"

"It means, my child, that I should not feel justified in permitting this renunciation of the world until you knew more of what you were giving up."

"I know enough already."

"You think so, but your experience of it is too recent for us to expect unbiased judgment this morning. I should insist on a year, at least, and preferably two years, part of that time to be spent in Frankfort and in Cologne. I anticipate a great improvement in Frankfort when the new Emperor comes to the throne. If at the end of two years you are still of the same mind, I shall offer no further opposition."

"I shall never change my intention."

"Perhaps not. I am told that the determination of a woman is irrevocable, so a little delay does not much matter. Meanwhile, another problem passes my comprehension. I have thought and thought about it, and am convinced there is a misunderstanding somewhere, which possibly will be cleared away too late. I am quite certain that Father Ambrose did not meet Prince Roland in Frankfort."

"Do you, then, dispute the word of Father Ambrose?" asked the girl, quickly checking the accent of indignation that arose in her voice, for humility was to be her rôle ever after.

"Father Ambrose is at once both the gentlest and most truthful of men. He has undoubtedly seen somebody rob a merchant in Frankfort. He has undoubtedly been imprisoned among wine-casks; but that this thief and this jailer was Roland is incredible to me who know the young man, and physically impossible, for Prince Roland at that time was himself a prisoner, as, indeed, he is to-day. Prince Roland cannot be liberated from Ehrenfels without an order signed by Mayence, Treves, and myself. I alone have not the power to encompass his freedom, and Mayence is equally powerless although he is owner of the Castle. Some scoundrel is walking the streets of Frankfort pretending to be Roland."

"In that case, my Lord, he would not deny his identity when accosted on the bridge."

"A very clever point, my dear, but it does not overcome my difficulty.

743

There might be a dozen reasons why the rascal would not incriminate himself to any stranger who thus took him by surprise. However, it is useless to argue the question, for I persuade you as little as you persuade me. The practical thing is to fathom the misunderstanding, and remove it. Will you assist me in this?"

"Willingly, if I can, Guardian."

"Very well. I must first inform you that your imprisonment is likely to be very short. You are to know that the harmony supposed to exist in Stolzenfels is largely mythical: I left behind me the seeds of discord. I proposed that the glum niece of Treves, whom you met at our historic lunch, should be the future Empress. This nomination was seconded by Mayence himself, and received with unconcealed joy by my brother of Treves."

"Then for once the Court was unanimous? I think your choice an admirable one."

"The Archbishop of Mayence does not agree with you, my dear."

"Then why did he second your nomination?"

"Because he is so much more clever than Treves, who a few minutes later would have been the seconder."

"Why should his Lordship of Mayence think one thing and act another?"

"Why is he always doing it? No one can guess what Mayence really thinks, if he is judged by what he says. Were Treves' niece to become Empress, her uncle would speedily realize his power, and Mayence would lose his leadership. Could Mayence to-day secretly promote you to the position of Empress, he would gladly do so."

"But won't he at once look for some one else?"

"Certainly. That choice is now occupying his mind. His seconding of the nomination was merely a ruse to gain time, but if he proposes any one else he will find both Treves and myself against him. His only hope of circumventing the ambition of Treves is that something may happen, causing you to change your mind concerning Prince Roland."

"You forget, Guardian," protested the girl, "that his Lordship of Mayence said he would not permit me to marry Prince Roland after the way I had spoken and acted."

"He said that, my dear, under the influence of great resentment against you, but Mayence never allows resentment or any other feeling to stand in the way of his own interests. If you wrote him a contrite letter regretting your defiance of him, and expressing your willingness to bow to his wishes, I am very sure he would welcome the communication as a happy solution of the quandary in which he finds himself."

"You wish me to do this, Guardian?" she asked wistfully.

"Not until you are satisfied that Prince Roland is innocent of the charges you make against him."

"How can I receive such assurance?"

"Ah, now you come to the object of this apparently purposeless journey. I have had much experience in the world you are so anxious to renounce, and although I have seen the wicked prosper for a time, yet my faith has never been shaken in an overruling Providence, and what happened last night set me thinking so deeply that daylight stole in upon my meditations."

"Oh, my poor Guardian, I knew you had not slept, and all because of a worthless creature like myself, and a wicked creature, too, for I did not see the hand of Providence so visible to you."

"Surely, my dear, a moment's thought would reveal it to you. Remember how we came almost to the door of the prison, when a temporary reprieve was handed to us by that coarse reprobate, the Pfalzgraf. Your suite of rooms was not yet ready, and thus we found bestowed upon us another free day; a day of untrammeled liberty, quite unlooked for. Now, much may be done in a day. An Empire has been lost and won within a few hours. With this gift came a revelation. That wine-blotched Pfalzgraf would have shown no consideration for you: to him a prisoner is a prisoner, to be cast anywhere, lock the door, and have done, but a wholesome fear had been instilled into him by his overlord. The Archbishop of Mayence had taken thought for your comfort, ordering that the best rooms in the Castle should be placed at your disposal. Hence, after all that had passed, his Lordship felt no malignancy against you, and I dare say would have been glad to rescind the order for your imprisonment, were it not that he would never admit defeat."

"Oh, Guardian, what an imagination is yours! I am sure his Lordship of Mayence will never forgive me."

"His Lordship of Mayence, my dear, is in a dilemma from which no one except yourself can extricate him."

"His own cleverness will extricate him."

"Perhaps. Still, I'm not troubling about him. My thoughts are much too selfish for that. I wish you to lift me from my uncertainty."

"You mean about Prince Roland? I shall do whatever you ask of me."

"I place no command, but I proffer a suggestion."

"It shall be a command, nevertheless."

"We have left your own prison far behind, and are approaching that of Prince Roland. To the door of that detaining Castle I propose to lead you. I am forbidden by my compact with the other Electors to see Prince Roland or to hold any communication with him. The custodian of the Castle, who knows me well, will not refuse any request I make, even if I ask to see the young man himself. He will therefore not hesitate to admit you when I require him to do so. To take away any taint of surreptitiousness about my action, interfering, as one might say, with another man's house, I shall this evening write to the Archbishop of Mayence, tell him exactly what I have done, and why."

"Do you intend, then, that I should see Prince Roland and talk with him?"

"Yes."

"My dear Guardian!" cried the girl, her face flushing red, "what on earth can I say to him? How am I to excuse my intrusion?"

"A prisoner, I fancy, does not resent intrusion, especially if the intruder is—" The old man smiled as he looked at the girl, whose blush grew deeper and deeper; then, seeing her confusion, he added: "There are many things to say. Introduce yourself as the ward of his Lordship of Cologne; reveal that your guardian has confided to you that Prince Roland is to be the future Emperor; ask for some assurance from him that the property descending to you from your ancestors shall not be molested; or perhaps, better still, with the same introduction, tell him the story of Father Ambrose. Add that this has disquieted you: demand the truth, hearken to what the youth says for himself, thank him, and withdraw. It needs no long conversation, though I am prepared to hear that he wished to lengthen your stay. I am certain that five minutes face to face with him will completely overturn all Father Ambrose has said to his disparagement, and a few simple words from him will probably dispel the whole mystery. If someone is personating him in Frankfort it is more than likely he knows who it is."

They traveled a generous furlong together in silence, the girl's head bowed and her brow troubled. At last, as if with an effort, she cleared doubt away, and raised her head.

"I will do it," she said decisively.

The Archbishop heaved a deep sigh of relief. He knew now he was out of the wood.

"Is this Assmannshausen we are coming to?" she asked, as if to hint that the subject on which they had talked so earnestly was finally done with.

"No; this is Lorch, and that is the Castle of Nollich standing above it."

"I hope," said the girl, with a sigh of weariness, "that no English Princess about to marry an Emperor lodged there, or no Englishman who was to become an Emperor—"

The Archbishop interrupted the plaint with a hearty laugh, the first he had enjoyed for several days.

"The English seem an interfering race," she went on. "I wish they would attend to their own affairs."

"Nollich is uncontaminated," said the Archbishop, "though in olden days a reckless knight on horseback rode up to secure his lady-love, and I believe rode down again with her, and his route is still called the Devil's Ladder."

"Did the marriage turn out so badly?"

"No; I believe they lived happily ever after; but the ascent was so cliff-like that mountain sprites are supposed to have given their assistance."

"How much farther is Assmannshausen?"

"Less than two leagues. We will stop there and refresh ourselves. Are you tired?"

"Oh no; not in the least. I merely wish the ordeal was past."

"You are a brave girl, Hildegunde."

"I am anything but that, Guardian. Still, do not fear I shall flinch."

After partaking of the midday meal at Assmannshausen, the Countess proposed that they should leave their horses in the stable, and walk the short third of a league to Ehrenfels, and to this her guardian agreed.

He found more difficulty with the custodian than had been expected. The man objected, trembling. Without a written order from his master he dare not allow any one to visit the prisoner. He would be delighted to oblige his Lordship of Cologne, but he was merely a poor wretch who had no option in the matter.

"Very well," said Cologne. "I have just come from your master, who is stopping with my brother Treves at Stolzenfels. If you persist I must then request lodgings from you until such time as a speedy messenger can bring your master hither. This journey may cause him great inconvenience, and should such be the case, I fear you will fare ill with him."

"That may be, my Lord, but I must do my duty."

"Are you sure you have already done it on all occasions?" asked the Archbishop severely.

The man's face became ghastly in its pallor.

"I don't know what you mean, my Lord."

"Then I will quickly tell you what I mean. It is rumored that Prince Roland has been seen on the streets of Frankfort."

"How—how could that be, my Lord?"

"That is exactly what I wish to know. I believe the Prince is not in your custody."

"I assure you, my Lord," said the now thoroughly frightened man, "that his Highness is in his room."

"Very well; then conduct this lady thither. Although she does not know the Prince, a relative of hers who does asserts that he met his Highness in Frankfort. I said this was impossible if you had done that duty you prate so much about. The lady merely wishes to ask him for some explanation of this affair, so make your choice. Shall she go up with you now, or must I send for the other two Archbishops?"

There was but one comforting phrase in this remark, namely, that the lady did not know the Prince. Still, it was a dreadful risk, yet the custodian hesitated no longer. He took down a bunch of keys, and asked the Countess to follow him. Ascending the stair, he unlocked the door, and stood aside for the Countess to pass through.

Some one with wildly tousled hair sat sprawling in a chair; arms on the table, and head sunk forward down upon them. A full tankard of wine within his reach, and a flagon had been overset, sluicing the table with its contents, which still fell drip, drip, drip, to the floor.

The young man raised his head, aroused by the harsh unlocking of the door, and with the crash it made as his father flung it hard against the stone wall for the purpose of giving him warning, but the youth was in no condition to profit by this thoughtfulness, nor to understand the signals his father made from behind the frightened girl. He clutched wildly at the overturned flagon, and with an oath cried:

"Bring me more wine, you old—"

Staggering to his feet, he threw the flagon wide, then slipped on the spilled wine and fell heavily to the floor, roaring defiance at the world.

The panic-stricken girl shrank back, crying to the jailer:

"Let me out! Close the door quickly, and lock it!" an order obeyed with alacrity.

When Hildegunde emerged to the court her guardian asked no question. The horror in her face told all.

"I am sorry, my Lord," said the cringing custodian, "but his Highness is drunk."

"Does this—does this happen often?"

"Alas! yes, my Lord."

"Poor lad, poor lad! The sins of the fathers shall be visited on the children to the third and fourth generation. Hildegunde, forgive me. Let us away and forget it all."

The next morning the Countess began her imprisonment in Pfalz.

XV. JOURNEYS END IN LOVERS' MEETING

Roland slept until the sun was about an hour high over the western hills. He found the captain waiting patiently for him to awake, and then that useful martinet instantly set his crew at tying up the bales which had been torn open, placing them once more in the hold. He was about to do the same with the weapons captured from Furstenberg, but Greusel stepped forward, and asked him to put pikes, battle-axes, and the long swords into the cabin.

Roland nodded his approval, saying:

"They may prove useful instruments in case of an attack on the barge. Our own swords are just a trifle short for adding interest to an assault."

When once more the hatches were down, and the deck clear, supper was served. Shortly after sunset, Roland told the captain to cast off, directing him to keep to the eastern shore, passing between what might be called the marine Castle of Pfalz and the village of Caub, with the strictest silence he could enjoin upon his crew. Pfalz stands upon a rock in the Rhine, a short distance up the river from Caub, while above that village on the hill behind are situated the strong, square towers of Gutenfels.

"Don't you intend to pay a call upon Pfalzgrafenstein?" asked Ebearhard. "It is notoriously the most pestilent robber's nest between Mayence and Cologne."

"No," said Roland. "On this occasion Pfalz shall escape. You see, Ebearhard, on our first trip down the Rhine it is not my intention to fight if I can avoid conflict. The plan which proved successful with the four castles we have visited is impossible so far as Pfalz is concerned. If we attempted to enter this waterschloss by stealth, we would be discovered by those levying contributions on the barge. There is no cover to conceal us, so I shall give Pfalz the go-by, and also Gutenfels, because the latter is not a robber castle, but is owned by the Count Palatine, a true gentleman and no thief. The next object of our attentions will be Schonburg, on the western side of the river, near Oberwesel."

As the grotesque, hexagonal bulk of the Pfalz, with its numerous jutting corners and turrets, and over all the pentagonal tower, appeared dimly in the center of the Rhine, under the clear stars, the captain ordered his men to lie flat on the deck, himself following their example. Roland and his company were already seated in the cabin, and the great barge, lying so low in the water as to be almost invisible with its black paint, floated noiseless as a dream down the swift current.

Without the slightest warning came a shock, and every man on the lockers was flung to the floor of the cabin, with cries of dismay, for too well they recognized the preliminary to their disasters of the night before. Roland sprang up on deck, and found the boat swinging round broadside to the current, which had swept it so near to the Castle that at first it seemed to have struck against one of the outlying rocks. The fantastic form of the Pfalz hung over them, looking like some weird building seen in a nightmare, its sharp, pointed pinnacles outlined against the starlit sky.

The captain, muttering sonorous German oaths, ordered his men to the sweeps, but Roland saw at once that they were too close to the ledge of rock for any chance of escape. He hurried down into the cabin.

"Every man his sword, and follow me as silently as possible!"

Up on deck again, Roland said to the captain:

"Let your rowers help the chain to bring the barge alongside, but when the robbers appear, pretend to be getting away, although you must instantly obey them when ordered to cease your efforts."

The prow of the boat ground against the solid rock, jammed in between the stout chain and the low cliff. Roland was the first to spring ashore, and the rest nimbly followed him. With every motion of the barge the bell inside the Castle rang, and now they could hear the bestirring of the garrison, and clashing of metal, although the single door of the Pfalz had not yet been opened. This door stood six feet above the plateau of rock, and could be entered or quitted only by means of a ladder.

Roland led his men to a place of effective concealment along the western wall of the Pfalz, only just in time, for as he peered round the corner, his men standing back against the wall to the rear, he saw the flash of torches from the now-open door, and the placing of a stout ladder at a steep angle between the threshold and the floor of rock below. Most of the garrison, however, did not wait for this convenience, but leaped impetuously from doorway to rock. Others slid down the ladder, and all rushed headlong towards the barge, which made its presence known by the grinding of its side against the rock, and also by the despairing orders of the captain, and the hurrying footsteps of his men on deck.

More leisurely down the ladder came two officers, followed by one whom Roland recognized as lord of the Castle, Pfalzgraf Hermann von Stahleck, a namesake and relative of the Laughing Baron of Furstenberg, and quite as ruthless a robber as he.

"Cease your efforts at the prow," shouted the Pfalzgraf to the captain when he had descended the ladder, "and concentrate your force at the stern, swinging your boat round broadside on to the landing."

The captain obeyed, and presently the boat lay in such position as the nobleman desired. Now there was a great commotion as, at a word from the Pfalzgraf, the garrison fell on the barge, and began to wrench off the hatches, a task which they well knew how to perform.

"Follow as quietly as possible," whispered Roland to the two lieutenants behind him, who, under their breath, passed on word to the men. Roland ran nimbly up the ladder. No guard was set where none had ever been needed before. Greusel was the last to ascend, then the ladder was pulled up, and the massive door swung shut, bolted and chained.

The invaders found torches stuck here and there along the wall, and the picturesque courtyard, with its irregular balconies and stairways, seemed, in the flickering light, more spacious than was actually the case.

Although for the moment in safety, Roland experienced a sense of imprisonment as he gazed round the narrow limits of this enclosure. He had endeavored to count the number of men who followed the Pfalzgraf, but their impetuosity in seeking the barge prevented an accurate estimate, although he knew there were more than double the force that obeyed him, and therefore it would be suicidal to lead his untrained coterie against the seasoned warriors of Stahleck.

He ordered Greusel to take with him six men, and search the Castle, bringing into the courtyard whomsoever they might find; also to discover whether any window existed that looked out upon the eastern landing-place. The remainder of his men he grouped at the door, under command of Ebearhard.

"I fear, Ebearhard," he said, "that I boasted prematurely in thinking good luck would attend me now that I lead what appears to be an obedient following. Here we are in a trap, and unless we can escape through rat-holes, I admit that I fail to see for the moment how we are to get safely afloat again."

"We are in better fettle than the Pfalzgraf and his men outside," returned Ebearhard, "because this fortress is doubtless well supplied with provisions, and is considered impregnable, while the Pfalzgraf's impetuous chaps, who did not know enough to stay in comfortable quarters when they had them, are without shelter and without food. You have certainly done the best you could in the circumstances, and for those circumstances you are free of blame, since, not being a wizard, you could scarcely know of the chain."

"Indeed, Ebearhard, it is just in that respect I blame myself, neglecting your own good example, who discovered the chain at Furstenberg. This trap is a new invention, and, so far as I know, has never before been attempted on the Rhine. I might have remembered that Stahleck here is cousin to the Red Margrave, who likely has told him of the device. Indeed, the chances are that Stahleck himself was the contriver of the chain, for he seems a man of much more craft and intelligence than that huge, laughing animal farther up the river. I should have ordered the captain to tie up against the eastern bank, and then sent some men in a small boat to learn if the way was clear. No, Ebearhard, I blame myself for this muddle, and, through anxiety to pass the Pfalz, I have landed myself and my men within its walls. I must pace this courtyard for a time, and ponder what next to do. Go you, Ebearhard, with the men to the door. Allow no talking or noise. Listen intently, and report to me if you hear anything. You see, Ebearhard, the devil of it is that Stahleck, like his cousin with Cologne, swears allegiance to the Archbishop of Mayence, and here am I, after destroying the fief of one Archbishop, securely snared in the fief of another. I fear their Lordships' next meeting with me will not pass off so amicably as did the last."

"Next meeting?" cried Ebearhard in astonishment; "have you ever met the Archbishops?"

Roland gasped, realizing that his absorption in one subject had nearly caused him to betray his momentous secret.

"Ah, I remember," continued Ebearhard. "It was on account of the Archbishop's presence in Bonn that you returned from that town when first you journeyed up the Rhine."

"Yes," said Roland, with relief.

"It seems to me," went on Ebearhard consolingly, "that even if we may not leave the Castle, at least the Pfalzgraf cannot penetrate into the stronghold, therefore we are safe enough."

"Not so, Ebearhard," replied his chief. "The Pfalzgraf has the barge, remember, and it can carry his whole force to Caub or elsewhere, returning with ample provisions and siege instruments that will batter in the door despite all we can do. Nevertheless, let us keep up our hearts. Get you to the gate, Ebearhard. I must have time to think before Greusel returns."

Alone, with bent head, he paced back and forwards across the courtyard under the wavering light of the torches. Very speedily he concluded that no plan could be formed until Greusel made his report regarding the intricacies of the Castle.

"My luck is against me! My luck is against me!" he said aloud to himself, as if the sound of his own voice might suggest some way out of the difficulty.

"Luck always turns against a thief and a marauder," said a sweet and

755

clear voice behind him; "and how can it be otherwise, when the gallows-tree stands at the end of his journey."

Roland stopped in his walk, and turned abruptly towards the sound. He saw standing there, just descended from the stairway at her back, one quite evidently a lady; not more than eighteen, perhaps, but nevertheless with a flash of defiance in her somber eyes, which were bent fearlessly upon him. The two tirewomen accompanying her shrank timorously to the background, palpably panic-stricken, and ready to faint with fright.

"Ah, Madam, how came you here?" cried Roland, ignoring her insulting words, too much surprised by her beauty of face and form to think of aught else.

"I came here, because your bully upstairs hammered at my door and bade me open, which I would not do, defying him to break it down if he had the power. It so happened that he possessed the power, and used it."

"I deeply regret that you should have been disturbed, Madam. My lieutenant erred through over-zeal, and I ask your pardon for the offense."

The girl laughed.

"Why, sir, you are the politest of pirates, but, indeed, your lieutenant seems a harsh man. Without even removing his bonnet, he commanded me to betake myself to the courtyard and report to his chief, which obediently I have done."

"I did not guess that women inhabited this robber's nest. My lieutenant is searching for men in hiding, so please accept my assurance that you will suffer no further annoyance. You are surely not alone in this house?"

"Oh no. Her ladyship the Pfalzgraf's wife, and her entourage, have sought shelter in another part of the Castle, and presently they will all troop down here, prisoners to your most ungallant subordinate; that is, should their doors prove no stouter than mine, or if your furious men have not dislocated their shoulders."

"How came you to be absent from her ladyship's party?"

"Because, urbane pirate captain, I am an unwilling prisoner in this stronghold, being an obstreperous person, who refused to obey my superiors; those set in authority over me. Consequently am I immured in this dismal dungeon of the water-rats, and thus, youthful pirate, I welcome even so red-handed an outlaw as yourself."

"Then are we in like case, my lady of midnight beauty, for I, too, am a prisoner in Pfalzgrafenstein, and, when you came, was cogitating some plan of escape. Therefore, rebellious maiden, the sword of this red-handed freebooter is most completely at your service," and the speaker once more doffed his bonnet with a gallant sweep that caused the plume to kiss the flagstones at his feet, and he bowed low to the brave girl who had shown no fear of him.

XVI. MY LADY SCATTERS THE FREEBOOTERS AND CAPTURES THEIR CHIEF

Greusel appeared on one of the balconies, and called down to his leader.

"There are," he said, "a number of women in the western rooms of the Castle. They have bolted their doors, but tell me that the rooms contain the Pfalzgravine von Stahleck and other noble ladies, with their tirewomen. What am I to do?"

"Place a guard in the corridor, Greusel, to make sure that these ladies communicate with no one outside the fortress."

"I thought it well," explained Greusel, "not to break in the doors without definite instructions from you to that effect."

"Quite right. Tell the ladies we will not molest them."

"You molested me!" cried the handsome girl in the courtyard, her dark eyes flashing in the glow of the torches.

"This person," said the unemotional Greusel, betraying no eye for beauty, "called us every uncomplimentary name she could think of. We were the scum of the earth, according to her account."

The girl laughed scornfully.

"But I would not have dislodged her," continued Greusel, unperturbed, "had she not said there was a window in her room, which is on the eastern side of the Castle, overlooking the operations of the Pfalzgraf on the barge, and she proclaimed her determination to warn Stahleck that his Castle was filled with freebooters, as soon as she could make her voice heard above the din at the landing. Therefore I broke in the door, ordering her and the tirewomen to descend to the courtyard. On examining her room I find there is no such window as she described, and she could not communicate with the Count, so I advise that you send her back again."

Once more the young lady laughed, and exclaimed:

"I could not break down the door for myself, so compelled you and your clods to do it. I am immured here; a reluctant captive. You will not have me sent back to my cell, I hope, Commander?"

"No; if you are really my fellow-prisoner, and not one of the enemy."

"She may be deluding you also," warned Greusel.

"I will take the risk of that," replied Roland, smiling at the girl, who smiled back at him. She had a will of her own, but seemed sensitively responsive to fair treatment.

"Are there any men-servants?" asked Roland.

"Only three, and they are tottering with age," replied Greusel, "more frightened than the women themselves. Nevertheless, one of the retainers is important, being, as he told me, keeper of the treasure-house. I relieved him of his keys, and find that the strong-room is well supplied with bags of gold. 'Twill be the richest haul yet, excepting our two barrels of coin from—"

"Hush, hush!" cried Roland. "Mention no names. Did you discover any other exit excepting the door by which we entered?"

"No; but at the northern end there is a window through which a man of ordinary size might pass. It is, however, high above the rocks, and I discern floating in the tide a fleet of small boats."

"Ah," said Roland, "that is important."

"Taken in conjunction with the gold, most amiable robber," suggested the girl.

"Taken in conjunction with the gold," repeated Roland, smiling again; and adding, "Taken also in conjunction with a lady who, if I understand her, wishes to escape from the Pfalz."

"You are right," agreed the young girl archly. "Do I receive a share of the money?"

"Yes; if you join our band."

"Oh!" she cried, with a pout of feigned disappointment, "I thought you had already accepted me as a member. And what am I to call my new overlord, who acquires wealth so successfully that he does not wish the amount mentioned, or the place from which it was taken specified?"

"My name is Roland. Will you consent to a fair exchange?"

"I am called Hilda by my friends."

"Then, Hilda," said the young man, looking at her with admiration, "I welcome you as one of my lieutenants."

"One, indeed!" she exclaimed, with affected indignation. "I shall be first lieutenant or nothing."

"Up to this moment Herr Joseph Greusel, who so unceremoniously made your acquaintance, has been my chief lieutenant, but I willingly depose him, and give you his place."

"Do you hear that, Joseph?" Hilda called up to the man leaning over the balcony.

The deposed one made a grimace, but no reply.

"Set your guard, and come down, Greusel."

Presently Greusel appeared in the courtyard, followed by four men.

"I have left two on guard," he said.

"Right. What have you done with the servants?"

"Tied them up in a hard knot. I found a loft full of ropes."

"Right again. Take your four men, and stand guard at the door. Send Ebearhard to me."

Before Ebearhard arrived, Roland turned to the girl.

"Retire to your room," he said, "and bid your women gather together whatever you wish to carry with you."

"I'd rather stay where I am," protested Hilda, "being anxious to hear what your plans are. I confess I don't know how you can emerge from this Castle in safety."

"Fräulein Hilda, the first duty of a chief lieutenant is obedience."

"Refusing that, what will you do?"

"I shall call two of my men, cause you to be transported to your room, and order them to see that you do not leave it again."

"Remaining here when you have departed?"

"That, of course."

"You will take the gold, however."

"Certainly; the gold obeys me; doing what I ask of it."

For a few moments the girl stood there, gazing defiance at him, but although a slight smile hovered about his lips, she realized in some subtle way—woman's intuition, perhaps—that he meant what he said. Her eyes lowered, and an expression of pique came into her pretty face; then she breathed a long sigh.

"I shall go to my room," she said very quietly.

"I will call upon you the moment I have given some instructions to my third lieutenant."

"You need not trouble," she replied haughtily, speaking, however, as mildly as himself. "I remain a prisoner of the Pfalzgraf von Stahleck, who, though a distinguished pillager like yourself, nevertheless possesses some instincts of a gentleman."

With that, the young woman retired slowly up the stairway, and disappeared, followed by her two servants.

"Ebearhard," said Roland, when that official appeared, "Greusel has discovered a window to the north through which yourself and a number of your men can get down to the rocks with the aid of a cord, and he tells me there is a loft full of ropes. A flotilla of boats is tied up at the lower end of the Castle. He has visited the treasury, and finds it well supplied with bags of coin. I intend to effect a junction between those bags and that flotilla. Our position here is quite untenable, for there is probably some secret entrance to this Castle that we know nothing of. There are also a number of women within whom we cannot coerce, and must not starve. Truth to tell, I fear them more than I do the ruffians outside. Have any of the men-at-arms discovered that we pulled up the ladder and closed the door?"

"I think not, for in such case they would return from their pillages as quickly as did the Red Margrave when he found his house was ablaze. My opinion is that they are making a clean job of looting the barge."

"If that is so, our barrels of gold are gone, rendering it the more necessary that we should carry away every kreuzer our friend Stahleck possesses. Call, therefore, every man except one from the door. Greusel has the keys, and will lead you to the treasury. Hoist the bags to the north window. While your men are doing this, rive a stout rope so that you may all speedily descend to the rocks, except as many as are necessary to lower the bags. When this is accomplished, Greusel is to report to me from the balcony, and then descend, taking with him the man on guard at the door. Apportion men and bags in all the boats but one. That one I shall take charge of. Put Greusel in command of the flotilla, and tell him to convey his fleet as quietly as possible to the eastern shore; then paddle up in slack water until he is, say, a third of a league above Pfalz. There he must await my skiff. You will stand by that skiff until I join you. I shall likely be accompanied by three women, so retain the largest and most comfortable of the small boats."

Ebearhard raised his eyebrows at the mention of the women, but said nothing.

Roland went in person to the room occupied by the young woman, and knocked at her door, whereupon it was opened very promptly.

"Madam," he said, "there is opportunity for escape if you care to avail yourself of it."

The girl had been seated when he entered, but now she rose, speaking in a voice that was rather tremulous.

"Sir, I was wrong to disobey you when you had treated me so kindly. I shall therefore punish myself by remaining where I am."

"In that case, Madam, you will punish me as well; and, indeed, I deserve it, forgetting as I did for the moment that I addressed a lady. If you will give me the pleasure of escorting you, I shall conduct you in safety to whatever place of refuge you wish to reach."

"Sir, you are most courteous, but I fear my intended destination might take you farther afield than would be convenient for you."

"My time is my own, and nothing could afford me greater gratification than the assurance of your security. Tell me your destination."

"It is the Convent of Nonnenwerth, situated on an island larger than this, near Rolandseck."

"I shall be happy to convoy you thither."

"Again I thank you. It is my desire to join the Sisterhood there."

"Not to become a nun?" cried Roland, an intonation of disappointment in his voice.

"Yes; although to this determination my guardian is opposed."

"Alas," said Roland, with a sigh, "I confess myself in agreement with him so far as your taking the veil is concerned. Still, imprisonment seems an unduly harsh alternative."

The girl's seriousness fled, and she smiled at him.

"As you have had some experience of my obstinacy, and proposed an even harsher remedy than that—"

"Ah, you forget," interrupted Roland, "that I apologized for my lack of manners. I hope during our journey to Nonnenwerth I may earn complete forgiveness."

"Oh, you are forgiven already, which is magnanimous of me, when you recollect that the fault was wholly my own. I will join you in the courtyard at once if I may."

"Very well. I shall be down there after I have given final instructions to my men."

Roland arrived at the north window, and saw that the flotilla had already departed. He could discern Ebearhard standing with his hand on the prow of the remaining boat, so pulled up the rope, untied it from the ring to which it was fastened, and threw it down to his lieutenant.

"A rope is always useful," he whispered, "and we will puzzle the good Pfalzgraf regarding our exit."

In the courtyard he found the three women awaiting him. Quietly he drew back the heavy bolts, and undid the stout chains. Holding the door slightly ajar, he peered out at the scene on the landing, brightly illuminated by numerous torches which the servants held aloft.

The men-at-arms were enjoying themselves hugely, and the great heap of bales already on the rocks showed that they resolved not to leave even one package on the barge. The fact that they stood in the light prevented their seeing the exit of the quartette from the Castle, even had any been on the outlook.

Roland swung the door wide, placed the ladder in exactly the same position it had formerly occupied, assisted the three women to the ground, and then led them round the western side of the Castle through the darkness to Ebearhard and his skiff. Dipping their paddles with great caution, they kept well out of the torchlight radius.

As they left the shadow of the Castle, and came within sight of the party on the landing, they were somewhat startled by a lusty cheer.

"Ah," said Ebearhard, "they have discovered our barrels of gold."

"'Tis very likely," replied Roland.

"Still," added Ebearhard consolingly, "I think we have made a good exchange. There appears to be more money in Stahleck's bags than in our two barrels."

"By the Three Kings!" cried Roland, staring upstream, "the barge is getting away. They have looted her completely, and are giving her a parting salute. The robbers evidently bear no malice against our popular captain. Hear them inviting him to call again!"

They listened to the rattle of the big chain. It was more amenable than that at Furstenberg, confirming Roland in his belief that Stahleck was the inventor of the device. They saw half a dozen men paying out a rope, while the first section of the chain sank, leaving a passage-way for the barge. Silhouetted against the torchlight, the boatmen were getting ready with their sweeps, prepared to dip them into the water as soon as the vessel got clear of the rocky island.

"We will paddle alongside before they begin to row," said Roland; and Captain Blumenfels was gently hailed from the river, much to his astonishment.

"Make for the eastern bank, captain," whispered Roland, "and keep a lookout ahead for a number of small boats like this."

Presently, rowing up the river strenuously, close to the shore, the barge came upon the flotilla. Here Roland bade Hilda remain where she was, and leaving Ebearhard in charge of the skiff, he clambered up on the barge, ordering Greusel to range his boats alongside and fling aboard the treasure.

"Well, captain, did his Excellency of Pfalz leave you anything at all?"

"Not a rag," replied the captain. "The barge is empty as a drum."

"In that case there is nothing for it but a speedy return to Frankfort. I do not regret the cloth, which has been paid for over and over again, but I am mercenary enough to grudge Stahleck our two barrels of gold."

"Oh, as to the gold," replied the captain gravely, "I took the liberty of reversing your plan at Lorch."

"What plan?"

"Your honor poured gold into wine barrels, but I poured the red wine of Lorch into the gold barrels, and threw the empty cask overboard. Perhaps you know that the Pfalzgraf grows excellent white wine round his Castle of Stahleck, and despises the red wine of Lorch and Assmannshausen. He tasted the wine, which had not been improved by being poured into the dirty gold barrels, spat it out with an oath, and said we were welcome to keep it. He has also promised to send me a cask of good white wine to Frankfort."

"Captain, despite your quiet, unassuming manner, you are the most ingenious of men."

"Indeed, I but copied your honor's ingenuity."

"However it happened, you saved the gold, and that action alone will make a rich man of you, for you must accept my third share of the money."

By this time the bags had been heaved aboard. Greusel followed them, and stood ready to receive further orders.

"You will all make for Frankfort," said Roland, "keeping close as possible to this side of the river. No man is to be allowed ashore until you reach the capital. Captain, are there provisions enough aboard for the voyage?"

"Yes, your honor."

"Very well. Put every available person at the oars, and get past Furstenberg before daybreak. My men, who have not had an opportunity to distinguish themselves as warriors, will take their turn at the sweeps. You and Ebearhard," he continued, turning to Greusel, "will employ the time in counting the money and making a fair division. With regard to the two barrels, the captain will receive my third share, and also be one of us in the apportionment of the gold we secured to-night. It was through his thoughtfulness that the barrels were saved. Whatever portion you find me entitled to, place in the keeping of the merchant, Herr Goebel. And now I shall tie four bags to my belt for emergencies."

766

"Are you not coming with us, Roland?" asked Greusel anxiously.

"No. Urgent business requires my presence in the neighborhood of Bonn, but I shall meet you in the Kaiser cellar before a month is out."

Saying this, he shook hands with the captain and Greusel, and descended into the small boat, bidding farewell to Ebearhard.

"Urge them," were his last words, "to get well out of sight of Pfalz and Furstenberg before the day breaks, and as for the small boats, turn them loose; present them as a peace-offering to the Rhine."

In the darkness Prince Roland allowed his frail barque to float down the stream, using his paddle merely to keep it toward the east, so to avoid the chain. He found himself accompanied by a silent, spectral fleet; the empty boats that his men had sent adrift. To all appearance the little squadron lay motionless, while the dim Castle of Pfalz, with its score of pointed turrets piercing a less dark sky, seemed like a great ship moving slowly up the Rhine. When it had disappeared to the south, Roland ventured to speak, in a low voice.

"Madam," he said, "tell your women so to arrange what extra apparel you have brought to form a couch, where you may recline, and sleep for the rest of the night."

"Captain Roland," she replied, her gentle little laugh floating with so musical a cadence athwart the waters that he found himself regretting such a sweet voice should be kept from the world by the unappreciative walls of a convent,—"Captain Roland, I was never more awake than I am at this moment. Life has somehow become unexpectedly interesting. I experience the deliciously guilty feeling of belonging to a stealthy society of banditti. Do not, I beg of you, deprive me of that pleasure by asking me to sleep."

"In the morning, Madam, there will be little opportunity for rest. We must put all the distance we can between ourselves and the Pfalzgraf von Stahleck. I expect you to ride far and fast to-morrow."

"Do you intend, then, to abandon this boat?"

"I must, Madam. The river has been long so empty that this flotilla, which I cannot shake off, being unaccustomed to oars or paddle, will attract attention from both sides of the Rhine, and when the darkness lifts we are almost certain to be stopped. The boats will be recognized as belonging to the Pfalzgraf, and I wish to sever all connection between this night's work and my own future."

"What, then, do you propose?"

"As soon as day breaks we will come to land, and allow our boat to float away with the rest. Can you walk?"

"I love walking," cried the girl with enthusiasm. "I ask your pity for myself, immured in that windowless dungeon, situated on a tiny point of rock; I, who have roamed the hills and explored the valleys of my own land on foot, breathing the air of freedom with delight. Let me, therefore, I beg of you, remain awake that I may taste the pleasure of anticipation in my thoughts; or is such a wish disobedience on the part of your first lieutenant? I do not mean it so, and will quietly cry myself to sleep if you insist."

"Indeed, Hilda," said Roland, laughing, and abandoning the more formal title of "madam," "I am no such tyrant as you suppose. Besides, your office of first lieutenant has lapsed, because our men have all gone south, while we travel north."

"Then may I talk with you?"

"Nothing would please me better. I was thinking of your own welfare, and not of my desire, when I counseled slumber."

"Oh, I assure you I slept very well during the first part of the night, for, there being nothing else to do, I went to bed early, and was quite unconscious until the dreadful ringing of that alarm bell, which set the whole Castle astir."

"Why were you imprisoned?"

"Because—because," she replied haltingly, "I had chosen the religious life, the which my guardian opposed. He appeared to think that some experience of the rigors of the convent might make me less eager to immure

768

myself in a nunnery, which, like Pfalz Castle, is also on a restricted island."

"Then his remedy has proved unavailing?"

"Quite. The Sisters will be very good to me, for I shall enrich their convent with my wealth. 'Twill be vastly different from incarceration in Pfalz."

"Hilda, I doubt that. Captivity is captivity, under whatever name you term it. I cannot understand why one who spoke so enthusiastically just now of hills and valleys and liberty should take the irrevocable step which you propose; a step that will rob you forever of those joys."

The girl remained silent, and he went on, speaking earnestly:

"I think in one respect you are like myself. You love the murmur of the trees, and the song of the running stream."

"I do, I do," she whispered, as if to herself.

"The air that blows around the mountain-top inspires you, and you cannot view the hills on the horizon without wishing to explore them, and learn what is on the other side."

There was light enough for him to see that the girl's head sank into her open hand.

"You, I take it, have never been restricted by discipline."

Her head came up quickly.

"You think that because of what I said in the courtyard?"

"No; my mind was running towards the future rather than to the past. The rigor of strict rules would prove as irksome to you as would a cage to a free bird of the forest."

"I fear you are in the right," she said with a sigh; and then, impatiently, "Oh, you do not understand the situation, and I cannot explain! The convent is merely a retreat for me; the lesser of two evils presented."

"You spoke of your land. Where is that land?"

"Do you know Schloss Sayn?" she asked.

"Sayn? Sayn?" he repeated. "Where have I heard that name before, and recently too? I thought I knew every castle on the Rhine, but I do not remember Sayn."

The girl laughed.

"You will find no fellow-craftsman there, Pirate Roland, if ever you visit it. The Schloss is not on the Rhine, and, perhaps on that account, rather than because of its owner's honesty, is free from the taint you suggest. It stands high in the valley of the Saynbach, more than half a league from this river."

"Ah, that accounts for my ignorance. I never saw Sayn Castle, although I seem to have heard of it. Are you its owner?"

"Yes; I told you I was wealthy."

"Where is the Schloss situated?"

"Below Coblentz, on the eastern side of the river."

"Then why not let me take you there instead of to the convent?"

"Willingly, if you had brought your barge-load of armed men, but in Sayn Castle I am helpless, commanding a peaceful retinue of servants who, although devoted to me, are useless when it comes to defense."

"I cannot account for it," said Roland in meditative tone, "but the thought of that convent becomes more and more distasteful. You will be free of your guardian, no doubt, but you merely exchange one whom you know for another whom you don't, and that other a member of your own sex."

"Do you disparage my sex, then?"

"No; but I cannot imagine any man being discourteous to you. Surely every gentleman with a sword by his side should spring at once to your defense."

The girl laughed.

"Ah, Captain Roland, you are very young, and, I fear, inexperienced, despite your filibustering. However, this lovely, still, summer night, with its warm, velvety darkness, was made for pleasant thoughts. Enough about myself. Let me hear something of you. Did you come up the river or down, with your barge?"

"We came down."

"How long since you adopted a career of crime? You do not seem to be a hardened villain."

"Believe me," protested Roland earnestly, "I am not, and I do not admit that my career is one of crime."

"Indeed," said the girl, laughing again, "I am not so gullible as you think. I could almost fancy that you were the incendiary of Furstenberg Castle."

"What!" exclaimed Roland in consternation. "How came you to learn of its destruction?"

"There!" cried the girl gleefully, "you have all but confessed. You are as startled as if I had said: 'I arrest you in the name of the Emperor!'"

"Who told you that Furstenberg Castle was burned?" demanded the young man sternly.

"Yesterday morning there came swiftly down the river, with no less than twelve oarsmen, a long, thin boat, traveling like the wind. It did not pause at Pfalz, but the man standing in the stern hailed the Castle, and shouted to the Pfalzgraf that Furstenberg had been burned by the outlaws of the Hunsruck. He was on his way to Bonn to inform the Archbishop of Cologne, and he carried also Imperial news for his Lordship: tidings that the Emperor is dead."

"Dead!" breathed Roland in horror, scarcely above his breath. "The Emperor dead! I wonder if that can be true."

"Little matter whether it is true or no," said the girl indifferently. "He doubtless passed away in a drunken sleep, and I am told his drunken son will be elected in his place."

"Madam!" said Roland harshly, awakened from his stupor by her words,

771

"I must inform your ignorance that the Emperor's son is not a drunkard, and, indeed, scarcely touches wine at all, being a most strenuous opposer to its misuse. How can one so fair, and, as I believed, so honest, repeat such unfounded slander?"

"Are you a partisan of his?"

"I come from Frankfort; have seen the Prince, and know I speak the truth."

"Ah, well," replied the girl lightly, "you and I will not quarrel over his Highness. I accept your amendment, and will never more bear false witness against him. After all, it makes slight difference one way or the other. An Emperor goes, and an Emperor is elected in his place as powerless as his predecessor. 'Tis the Archbishops who rule."

"You seem well versed in politics, Madam."

The girl leaned forward to him.

"Do not 'madam' me, I beg of you, Roland. I dare say rumor has prejudiced me against the young man, but I have promised not to speak slightingly of him again. I wish this veil of darkness was lifted, that I might see your face, to note the effect of anger. Do you know, I am disappointed in you, Roland? You spoke in such level tones in the courtyard that I thought anger was foreign to your nature."

"I am not angry," said Roland gruffly, "but I detest malicious gossip."

"Oh, so do I, so do I! I spoke thoughtlessly. I will kneel to the new Emperor and beg his pardon, if you insist."

Roland remained silent, and for a time they floated thus down the river, she trailing her fingers in the water, which made a pleasant ripple against them, looking up at him now and then. Perceptibly the darkness was thinning. One seemed to smell morning in the air. A bird piped dreamily in the forest at intervals, as if only half-awakened. The two women reclining in the prow were sound asleep.

Roland picked up the paddle, and with a strong, sweeping stroke turned the head of the boat towards the land. Now she could see his lowering brow, and if the sight pleased her, 'twas not manifested in her next remark.

She took her hand from the water, drew herself up proudly, and said:

"I shall not apologize to you again, and I hate your blameless Prince!"

"Madam, I ask for no apology, and whether you hate or like the Prince matters nothing to me, or, I dare say, to him, either."

"Cannot you even allow a woman her privilege of the last word?" she cried indignantly.

Roland's brow cleared, and a smile came to his lips, as he remained silent, thus bestowing upon her the prerogative she seemed to crave. Hilda lay back in the prow of the boat between her sleeping women, with hands clasped behind her head, and her eyes closed. More and more the light increased, and sturdily with his paddle Roland propelled the boat towards the shore, bringing it alongside the low bank at last. He sprang out on the turf, and with the paddle in one hand held the boat to land with the other.

"We are now," he said, "a short distance above St. Goarhausen, where I hope to purchase horses. Will you kindly disembark?"

The girl, without moving, or opening her eyes, said quietly:

"Please throw the paddle into the boat again. I shall make for Nonnenwerth in this craft, which is more comfortable than a saddle."

The paddle came rattling down upon the bottom of the skiff. Roland stooped, and before she knew what he was about, took Hilda in his arms, lifted her ashore, and laid her carefully on the grass.

"Come," he cried to the newly-awakened serving-women, "tumble out of that without further delay," and they obeyed him in haste.

He stepped into the skiff, flung their belongings on the sward, turned the prow to the west, and, leaping ashore, bestowed a kick upon the boat that impelled it like an arrow far out into the stream.

Hilda was standing on her feet now, speechless with indignation.

"Come along," urged Roland cheerfully, "breakfast awaits us when we earn it;" but seeing that she made no move, the frown furrowed his brow again.

"Madam," he said, "I tell you frankly that to be thwarted by petulance annoys me. It happens that time is of the utmost importance until we are much farther from Pfalz. If you think that the ownership of wealth and a castle gives you the right to flout a plain, ordinary man, you take a mistaken view of things. I care nothing for your castle, or for your wealth. You may be a lady of title for aught I know, but even that does not impress me. We must not stand here like two quarrelsome children. I will conduct you to the Adler Inn at St. Goarhausen, where I know from experience you will be taken care of. I shall then purchase four horses, and return to the inn after you have breakfasted. Three of these horses are at your disposal, also the fourth and myself, if you will condescend to make use of us. If not, I shall ask you to accept what money you need for your journey, so that you may travel north unmolested, while I take my way in the other direction."

"How can I repay the money," she demanded, "if I do not know who and what you are?"

"I shall send for it, either to your Castle of Sayn, or the Convent of Nonnenwerth. You need be under no obligation to me."

"But," cried the girl with a sob, "I am already under obligation to you; an obligation which I cannot repay."

"Oh yes, you can."

"How?"

"By coming with me, who will persuade you, as readily as you did with your guardian, who coerced you."

"I am an ungrateful simpleton," she murmured. "Of course your way is the right one, and I am quite helpless if you desert me."

"There," cried Roland, with enthusiasm, "you have more than repaid whatever you may owe."

After breakfasting at St. Goarhausen and purchasing the horses, they journeyed down the rough road that extended along the right bank of the Rhine. Roland and Hilda rode side by side, the other two following some distance to the rear. The young man maintained a gloomy silence, and the girl, misapprehending his thoughts, remained silent also, with downcast eyes, seeing nothing of the beautiful scenery they were passing. Every now and then Roland cast a sidelong glance at her, and his melancholy deepened as he remembered how heedlessly he had pledged his word to the three Archbishops regarding his marriage.

"I see," she said at last, "that I have offended you more seriously than I feared."

"No, no," he assured her. "There is a burden that I cannot cast from my mind."

"May I know what it is?"

"I dare not tell you, Hilda. I have been a fool. I am in the position of a man who must break his oath and live dishonored, or keep it, and remain for ever unhappy. Which would you do were you in my place?"

"Once given, I should keep my oath," she replied promptly, "unless those who accepted it would release me."

Roland shook his head.

"They will not release me," he said dolefully.

Again they rode together in silence, content to be near each other, despite the young man's alternations of elation and despair. 'Twas, all in all, a long summer's day of sweet unhappiness for each.

One of Roland's reasons for choosing the right bank of the Rhine was to avoid the important city of Coblentz, with its inevitable questioning, and it was late afternoon when they saw this town on the farther shore, passing it without hindrance.

"You will rest this night," she said, "in my Castle of Sayn, and then, as

775

time is pressing, to-morrow you must return. We have met no interference even by this dangerous route, and I shall make my way alone without fear to Nonnenwerth, for I know you are anxious to be in Frankfort once more."

"I swear to you, Hilda, that if, without breaking my oath, I should never see Frankfort again, I would be the most joyous of men."

"Does your oath relate to Frankfort?"

"My oath relates to a woman," he said shortly.

"Ah," she breathed, "then you must keep it," and so they fell into silence and unhappiness again.

She had talked of security on the road they traversed, but turning a corner north of Vallandar they speedily found that a Rhine road is never safe.

Both reined in their horses as if moved by the same impulse, but to retreat now would simply draw pursuit upon them. Mounted on a splendid white charger, gorgeous with trappings, glittering with silver and gold, rode a dignified man in the outdoor habit of a general in times of peace.

Following him came an escort of twoscore horsemen; they in the full panoply of war; and behind them, on foot, in procession extending like a gigantic snake down the Rhine road, an army of at least three thousand men, the setting sun flashing fire from the points of their spears. Here and there, down the line, floated above them silken flags, and Roland recognized the device on the foremost one.

"God!" he shouted in dismay. "The Archbishop of Cologne!"

The girl uttered a little frightened cry, and edged her horse nearer to that of her escort.

"My guardian! My guardian!" she breathed. "I shall be rearrested!"

Seeing them standing as if stricken to stone, two horsemen detached themselves from the cavalry and galloped forward.

"Make way there, you fools!" cried the leader. "Get ye to the side; into the river; where you like; out of the path of my Lord the Archbishop."

Nevertheless Roland stood his ground, and dared even to frown at the officers of his Lordship.

"Stand aside you," he commanded in a tone of mastery, "and do not venture to intrude between the Archbishop and me."

The rider knew that no man who valued his head would dare use such language in the very presence of the Archbishop, unless he were the highest in the land. His dignified Lordship looked up to see the cause of this interruption, and of these angry words.

First came into his face an expression of amazement, then a smile melted the stern lips as he looked on Roland and recognized him. The impetuous horsemen faded away to the background. There was no answering smile on Roland's face. He reached out and clasped the hand of the girl.

"Now, by the Three Kings!" he whispered, "I shall break my oath."

Hilda glanced up at him, frightened by his vehemence, wincing under his iron grasp.

An unexpected sound interrupted the tension. The Archbishop had come to a stand, and "Halt! Halt! Halt!" rang out the word along the line of men, whose feet ceased to stir the dust of the road. The unexpected sound was that of hearty laughter from the dignified and mighty Prince of the Church.

"Forgive me, your Highness!" he cried, "but I laugh to think of the countenances of my somber brothers, Treves and Mayence, when they learn how sturdily you have kept your word with them. By the true Cross, Prince Roland, although we wished you to marry her, we had no thought that you would break into the Castle of Pfalz to win her hand. Ah, dear, what a pity 'tis we grow old! The impetuousness of youth outweighs the calculated wisdom of the three greatest prelates outside Rome. Judging by your fair face (and I have always held it to be beautiful, remember), you, Hildegunde Lauretta Priscilla Agnes, Countess of Sayn, are not moving northward to Nonnenwerth. I always insisted that the Saalhof at Frankfort was a more cheerful edifice than any nunnery on the Rhine, yet you never turned upon me such a glance of confidence as I see you bestow on your future Emperor."

"I hope, my Lord and Guardian," cried the girl, "that I have met you in time to deflect your course to my Castle of Sayn."

"Sweet Countess, I thank you for the invitation. My men can go on to their camp in the stronghold of my brother of Mayence, Schloss Martinsburg, and I shall gladly return with you to the hospitable hearth of Sayn. Indeed," said the Archbishop, lowering his voice, "I shall feel safer there than in enjoying the hospitality I had intended to accept."

"Are you not surprised to meet me?" asked the lady, with a laugh, adjusting words and manner to the new situation, which she more quickly comprehended than did her companion, who glanced with bewilderment from Countess to prelate, and back again.

The Archbishop waved his hand.

"Nothing you could do would surprise me, since your interview with the Court of Archbishops. I am on my way to Frankfort." Then, more seriously, to Prince Roland: "You heard of your father's death?"

"I learned it only this morning, my Lord. I shall return to Frankfort when I am assured that this gentlewoman is in a place of safety."

"Ah, Countess, there will be no lack of safety now! But will you not ease an old man's conscience by admitting he was in the right?"

The Countess looked up at Roland with a smile.

"Yes, dear Guardian," she said. "You were in the right."

XVII. "FOR THE EMPRESS, AND NOT FOR THE EMPIRE"

While the long line of troops stood at salute in single file, the Archbishop turned his horse to the north and rode past his regiments, followed by the Countess and Roland. His Lordship was accompanied to the end of the ranks by his general, who received final instructions regarding the march.

"You will encamp for the night not at Schloss Martinsburg, as I had intended, but a league or two up the Lahn. To-morrow morning continue your march along the Lahn as far as Limburg, and there await my arrival. We will enter Frankfort by the north gate instead of from the west."

The Archbishop sat on his horse for some minutes, watching the departing force, then called Roland to his right hand, and Hildegunde to his left, and thus the three set out on the short journey to Sayn.

"Your Highness," began the Archbishop, "I find myself in a position of some embarrassment. I think explanations are due to me from you both. Here I ride between two escaped prisoners, and I travel away from, instead of towards, their respective dungeons. My plain duty, on encountering you, was to place you in custody of a sufficient guard, marching you separately the one to Pfalz and the other to Ehrenfels. Having accomplished this I should report the case to my two colleagues, yet here am I actually compounding a misdemeanor, and assisting prisoners to escape."

"My Lord," spoke up Roland, "I am quite satisfied that my own imprisonment has been illegal, therefore I make no apology for circumventing it. Before entering upon any explanation, I ask enlightenment regarding the detention of my lady of Sayn. Am I right in surmising that she, like myself, was placed under arrest by the three Archbishops?"

"Yes, your Highness."

"On what charge?"

"High treason."

"Against whom?"

There was a pause, during which the Archbishop did not reply.

"I need not have asked such a question," resumed the Prince, "for high treason can relate only to the monarch. In what measure has her ladyship encroached upon the prerogative of the Emperor?"

"Your Highness forgets that there is such a thing as treason against the State."

"Are not members of the nobility privileged in this matter?"

"They cannot be, for the State is greater than any individual."

"I shall make a note of that, my Lord of Cologne. I believe you are in the right, and I hope so. During my lonely incarceration," the Prince laughed a little, "I have studied the condition of the State, arriving at the conclusion that the greatest traitors in our land are the three Archbishops, who, arrogating to themselves power that should belong to the Crown, did not use that power for suppressing those other treason-mongers, the Barons of the Rhine."

"What would you have us do with them?"

"You should disarm them. You should exact restitution of their illegally-won wealth. You should open the Rhine to honest commerce."

"That is easy to enunciate, and difficult to perform. If the Castles were disarmed, especially those on the left bank, a great injustice would be done that might lead to the extinction of many noble families. Why, the forests of Germany are filled with desperate outlaws, who respect neither life nor property. I myself have suffered but recently from their depredations. In broad daylight an irresistible band of these ruffians descended upon and captured the supposed impregnable Castle of Rheinstein, shamefully maltreating Baron Hugo von Hohenfels, tying him motionless, and nearly strangling him with stout ropes, after which the scoundrels robbed him of every stiver he possessed. The following midnight but one they descended on Furstenberg, a fief of my own, and not contenting themselves with robbery, brought red ruin on the Margrave by burning his Castle to the ground."

"My Lord, red ruin and the Red Margrave were made for each other. It was the justice of God that they should meet." The young man raised aloft his swordarm, shaking his clenched fist at the sky. "That hand held the torch that fired Furstenberg. The Castle was taken and burned by three sword makers from Frankfort, who never saw the Hunsruck or the outlaws thereof."

The Archbishop reined in his horse, and looked at the excited young man with amazement.

"You fired Furstenberg?"

"Yes; and effectively, my Lord. I shall rebuild it for you, but the Red Margrave I shall hang, as my predecessor Rudolph did his ancestor."

An expression of sternness hardened the Archbishop's face.

"Sir," he said, "I regret to hear you speak like this, and your safety lies in the fact that I do not believe a word of it. Even so, such wild words fill me with displeasure. I beg to remind you that the Election of an Emperor has not yet taken place, and I, for one, am likely to reconsider my decision. Still, as I said, I do not believe a word of your absurd tale."

"I believe every syllable of it!" cried the Countess with enthusiasm, "and glory that there is a mind brave enough, and a hand obedient to it, to smoke out a robber and a murderer."

The tension this astonishing revelation caused was relieved by a laugh from the Archbishop.

"My dear Hildegunde, you are forgetting your own ancestors. I venture that no woman of the House of Sayn talked thus when the Emperor Rudolph marched Count von Sayn to the scaffold. You would probably sing another song if asked to restore the millions amassed by Henry III. of Sayn and his successors; all accumulated by robbery as cruel as any that the Red Margrave has perpetrated."

"My Lord," said the Countess proudly, "you had no need to ask that question, for you knew the answer to it before you spoke. Every thaler I control shall be handed over to Prince Roland, to be used for the regeneration

781

of his country."

Again the Archbishop laughed.

"Surely I knew that, my dear, and I should not have said what I did. I suppose you will not allow me to vote against his Highness at the coming Election."

"Indeed, you shall vote enthusiastically for him, because you know in your own heart he is the man Germany needs."

"Was there ever such a change of front?" cried the Archbishop. "Why, my dear, the charges you so hotly made against his Highness are as nothing to what he has himself confessed; yet now he is the savior of Germany, when previously—Ah, well, I must not play the tale-bearer."

"Prince Roland," cried the girl, "my kinsman, Father Ambrose, said he met you in Frankfort, although now I believe him to have been mistaken."

"Oh no; I encountered the good Father on the bridge."

"There now!" exclaimed the Archbishop, "what do you say to that, my lady?"

She seemed perplexed by the admission, but quickly replied to his Lordship:

"'Twas you said that could not be, as he was a close prisoner in Ehrenfels." She continued, addressing the Prince: "Father Ambrose asserted that you were a companion of drinkers and brawlers in a low wine cellar of Frankfort."

"Quite true; a score of them."

The girl became more and more perplexed.

"Did you imprison Father Ambrose?"

"Yes; in the lowest wine cellar, but only for a day or two. I am very sorry, Madam, but it was a stern necessity of war. He was meddling with affairs he knew nothing of, and there was no time for explanations. He, a man of peace, would not have sanctioned what there was to do even if I had explained."

"He says," continued the girl, "that he saw you rob a merchant of a bag of gold."

"That is untrue!" cried the Prince.

"My dear Hildegunde, what is the robbing of a bag of gold from a merchant when he admits having stolen gold by the castle full?"

"I robbed no merchant," protested the Prince. "How could Father Ambrose make such a statement?"

"He mounted an outside stairway on the Fahrgasse, and through lighted windows on the opposite side saw you place the point of your sword at the throat of an unarmed merchant, and take from him a bag of gold."

Roland, whose brow had been knitted into an angry frown, now threw back his head and laughed joyously.

"Oh, that was a mere frolic," he alleged.

It was the girl's turn to frown.

"When you took stolen treasure from thievish Barons and Margraves protected by scores of armed men, with the object of breaking their power, for the relief of commerce, I admired you, but to say that the despoiling of a helpless merchant is a frolic—"

"No, no, my dear, you do not understand," eagerly corrected the Prince, unconscious of the affectionate phrase that caused a flush to rise in the cheeks of his listener. "The merchant was, and is, my partner; a blameless man, Herr Goebel, who came near to being hanged on my behalf when these Archbishops took me captive. I sought from him a thousand thalers; he insisted on learning my plans for opening the Rhine, and still would not give the money until, reluctantly, I was obliged to confess myself son of the Emperor. This he could not credit, stipulating that before giving the money I must produce for him a safe-conduct, signed by the Emperor, and verified by the Great Seal of the Empire. This document I obtained at dire personal risk, through the aid of my mother. Here it is."

He thrust his hand into his doublet, and produced the parchment in question, delivering it to the lady, who, however, did not unfold it, but kept her eyes fixed upon him.

"This distrust annoyed me; it should not have done so, for he was merely acting in the cautious manner natural to a merchant. With a boyishness I now regret, I put my sword to his throat, demanding the money, which I received. I took only half of it, for my mother had given me five hundred thalers. Oh, no; I did not rob my friend Goebel, but merely tried to teach him that lack of faith is a dangerous thing."

If the old man who listened could have exchanged confidences with the young woman who listened, he would have learned they shared the same thought, which was that the young Prince spoke so straight-forwardly neither doubted him for a moment. The old man, it is true, felt that his talk was rather reckless of consequences, but, on the other hand, this in itself was complimentary, for, as he remembered, the Prince had been cautious enough when catechized by the three Archbishops together.

"I have often read," said Cologne, with a smile, "pathetic accounts of prisoners, who in extreme loneliness carved their names over and over again on stone as hard as the jailer's heart, but your Highness seems rather to have enjoyed yourself while so cruelly interned. May I further beg of you to enlighten us concerning a somewhat bibulous youth who at the present moment is enjoying, in every sense of the word, the hospitality of Ehrenfels Castle?"

It was now the Archbishop's turn to astonish the Prince.

"You knew of my device, then?"

"'Knew' is a little too strong. 'Suspect' more nearly fits the case. You won over your jailer, and some one else took your place as prisoner."

"Yes; a young man to whom I owe small thanks, and with whom I have an account to settle. He is son of the custodian, and thinks he has us both under his thumb, Heinrich drinks as if he were a fish or a Baron, but I shall cure him of that habit before it becomes firmly established."

"Am I correct in assuming that you found your liberty only after your interview with the three Electors?"

"Oh, bless you, no! I was free months before that time. Indeed, it is only since then that my substitute is practically useless. Heinrich might have passed for me at a pinch, but only because neither you nor your colleagues had seen me. I have kept him under lock and key ever since, because I dare not allow him abroad until the Election has taken place."

"I see. A very wise precaution. Well, your Highness, I shall say nothing of what you tell me; furthermore, I still promise you my vote; that is, if you will obey my orders until you are elected Emperor. I foresee we are not going to have the easy time with you that was anticipated, but this concerns Mayence and Treves, rather than myself, for I have no ambition to rule by proxy. And now, my lady of Sayn, when we journeyed southward that day from Gutenfels Castle I gave you some information regarding the mind of Mayence. You remember, perhaps, what I said about his quandary. I rather suspect that he admires you, notwithstanding your defiance of him; but there is nothing remarkable in that, for we all appreciate you, old and young. I, too, carry a document of safe-conduct, like Prince Roland here, although I see that his Highness has placed his safety in your hands."

The old man smiled, and Hildegunde found herself still carrying the parchment Roland had given her. For a moment she was confused, then smiled also, and offered it back; but the Prince shook his head. The Archbishop went on:

"Mayence sent down to me your written release, signed by himself and Treves. He asked me to attach a signature, and liberate you on my way to Frankfort, which I intended to do had this impetuous young man not forestalled me. By the way, Highness, how did you happen to meet Countess von Sayn in Pfalz?"

"We will tell you about that later, Guardian," said Hildegunde, before Roland could speak. "What instructions did his Lordship of Mayence give concerning me?"

"He asked me to bring you to my palace in Frankfort, and subtly expressed the hope you had changed your mind."

"You may assure him I have," said the Countess, again speaking rapidly; "but let us leave all details of that for the moment. I am then to go with you to the capital?"

"Yes; to-morrow morning."

"To remain until the coronation?"

"Certainly; if such is your wish. But do you not see something very significant in my brother Mayence's change of plan, for you know he did not intend to release you until after that event?"

"Yes, yes," replied the Countess breathlessly. "I see it quite clearly, but do not wish to discuss the matter at the present moment."

"Very well. I intended to enter Frankfort from the west, but meeting you so unexpectedly, I have deflected my troops up the Lahn to Limburg, at which town we will join them to-morrow night, thus following Father Ambrose's route to the capital."

"Ah, that will be very interesting. Prince Roland, you accompany us, I hope?"

"Of a surety," replied the young man confidently.

"No," quietly said the Archbishop.

"Why not?"

"Because I say no."

The young man almost an Emperor drew himself up proudly, and his lips pressed together into a firm line of determination.

"Does your Highness so quickly forget your promise?"

"What promise?" asked the Prince, scowling.

"In consideration of my keeping silence touching your recent outrageous career of fire and slaughter, and the enslavement of Heinrich, you promised to obey me until you became Emperor."

"I intend to obey all reasonable requests, but I very much desire to accompany the Countess from her Castle to the capital, I have never seen Limburg, or taken that route to Frankfort."

"It is a charming old city," replied the Archbishop dryly, "which you can visit any time at the expense of a day's ride. Meanwhile, I shall escort the Countess thither, and endeavor to entertain her with pleasing and instructive conversation during the journey."

The Prince continued to frown, yet bit his lip and repressed an angry retort.

"But," protested the girl, "would it not be much safer for his Highness to enter the city of Frankfort protected by your army?"

The Archbishop laughed a little.

"My dear Hildegunde, the presence of Prince Roland causes you to overlook a vast difference in the status of you both, but surely the exercise of a little imagination should present to you the true aspect of affairs. You are a free woman, and I hold the document by which you regained your liberty. Do not be deluded, therefore, by the apparent fact that his Highness can raise a clenched fist aloft and defy the heavens. It is not so. He wears fetters on his ankles, and manacles round his wrists. Roland is a prisoner, and must straightway immure himself. Your Highness, before us stands the stately Castle of Sayn, where presently you shall refresh yourself, and be furnished with an untired charger, on which to ride all night, that you may reach the gates of Ehrenfels early to-morrow morning. Once there, place the wine-loving Heinrich out of harm in the deepest dungeon, and take his place as prisoner. It is arranged that the three Archbishops personally escort you to Frankfort in the barge of Mayence, which will land you at the water-steps of the Royal Palace. If it were known that I had been even an hour in your company your chances of reaching the throne would be seriously jeopardized."

"Surely such haste is unnecessary," cried the girl. "He can set out to-morrow in one direction while we go in another. He traveled all last night, and for most part of it was paddling a boat containing four people; has ridden almost since daylight, and now to journey on horseback throughout the night is too much for human endurance."

The grave smile of the Archbishop shone upon her anxiety.

"For lack of a nail the shoe was lost," he said, "and you know the remainder of the warning. If Prince Roland cares to risk an Empire for a night's rest, I withdraw my objection."

The Prince suddenly wheeled his horse, and coming briskly round to the side of the girl, placed a hand on hers.

"A decision, Countess!" he cried. "Give me your decision. I shall always obey you!"

"Oh, the rashness of youth!" murmured the Archbishop.

The girl looked up at the young man, and he caught his breath and clasped her hand more tightly as he gazed into the depths of her glorious eyes.

"You must go," she sighed.

"Yes, alas!"

He raised her unresisting hand to his lips, and again turned his horse.

"You will obey?" asked the Archbishop.

"I will obey, my Lord."

He flashed from its scabbard, into the rays of the setting sun, the sword he had made, and elevating the hilt to his forehead, saluted the Archbishop.

"I shall see you at Ehrenfels, my Lord."

"Ah, do not go thus. Come to the Castle for an hour's rest at least."

The young man whirled his sword around, and caught it by the blade, touching the hilt with his lips as if it were a cross.

"I thank God," said he, "that I can willingly keep my oath."

788

Then, looking at the girl—"For the Empress, and not for the Empire!" he cried.

The sword seemed to drop into the scabbard of its own accord, as Roland set spurs to his steed and away.

XVIII. THE SWORD MAKER AT BAY

The heir-presumptive to the throne reached Frankfort very quietly in the Archbishop's barge, and was landed after nightfall at the water-steps of the Imperial Palace. The funeral of the Emperor took place almost as if it were a private ceremonial. Grave trouble had been anticipated, and the route of the procession for the short distance between Palace and Cathedral was thickly lined on either side by the troops of the three Archbishops. This precaution proved unnecessary. The dispirited citizens cared nothing for their late nominal ruler, and they manifested their undisguised hatred of the real rulers, the Archbishops, by keeping indoors while their soldiers marched the streets.

The condition of the capital was unique. It suffered from a famine of money rather than a famine of food. Frankfort starved in the midst of plenty. Never had the earth been more fruitful than during this year, and the coming autumn promised a harvest that would fill the granaries to overflowing, yet no one brought in food to Frankfort, for the common people had not the money to buy. The working population depended entirely upon the merchants and manufacturers, and with the collapse of mercantile business thousands were thrown out of employment, and this penniless mob was augmented by the speedy cessation of all manufacturing.

After the futile bread riots earlier in the year, put down so drastically by the Archbishops, the population of the city greatly diminished, and the country round about swarmed with homeless wanderers, who at least were sure of something to eat, but being city-bred, and consequently useless for agricultural employment, they gradually joined into groups and marauding bands, greatly to the menace of the provinces they traversed. Indeed, rumor had it that the robberies from certain castles on the Rhine, and the burning of Furstenberg, were the work of these free companies, consequently a sense of uneasiness permeated the Empire, whose rulers, great and small, began to foresee that a continuance of this state of things meant disaster to the rich as well as misery to the poor. Charity, spasmodic and unorganized, proved wholly unable to cope with the disaster that had befallen the capital city.

When darkness set in on the third night after Roland's return to Frankfort, he made his way out into the unlighted streets, acting with caution until certain he was not followed, then betook himself to the Palace belonging to the Archbishop of Cologne.

The porter at first refused him entrance, and Roland, not wishing to make himself known, declared he had an appointment with his Lordship. Trusting that the underling could not read, he presented his parchment safe-conduct, asking him to give that to his Lordship, with a message that the bearer awaited his pleasure. The suspicious servant, seeing the Grand Seal of the Empire upon the document, at once conducted Roland to a room on the ground floor, then departed with the manuscript to find his master.

The Archbishop returned with him, the Imperial scroll in his hand, and a distinctly perceptible frown on his brow. When the servant withdrew, closing the door, the prelate said:

"Highness, this is a very dangerous procedure on your part."

"Why, my Lord?"

"Because you are certain to have been followed."

"What matter for that?" asked the young man. "I am quite unknown in Frankfort."

"Prince Roland," said the Archbishop gravely, "until your Election is actually accomplished, you would be wise to do nothing that might arouse the suspicion of Mayence. This house is watched night and day, and all who come and go are noted. I dare say that within fifteen minutes Mayence will know you have visited me."

"My dear Archbishop, they cannot note an unknown man. The uneasiness of Frankfort has already taken hold of me, and therefore I saw to it that I was not followed."

"If you were not followed when you came, you will certainly be followed as you return."

"In that case, my Lord, the spies will track me to the innocent home of Herr Goebel, the merchant, in the Fahrgasse."

"They will shadow you when you leave his house."

"Then their industry will be rewarded by an enjoyable terminus; in other words, the drinking cellar of the Rheingold."

"Be assured, your Highness, that ultimately you will be traced to the Royal Palace."

"Again not so, my Lord. They will be led across the bridge into the mechanics' quarter of Sachsenhausen, and if the watch continues, they must make a night of it, for I shall enter my humble room there and go to bed."

"I see you have it all planned out," commented the discomfited Archbishop.

The young man laughed.

"I anticipate an interesting life, my Lord, because it is my habit to think before I act, and I notice that this apparently baffles the Electors. The truth is that you three are so subtle, and so much afraid of one another, so on the alert lest you be taken by surprise, that a straightforward action on my part throws all intrigue out of gear. Now, I'll warrant you cannot guess why I came here to-night."

"Oh, I know the reason very well."

"Do you? That astonishes me. What is the reason?"

"You came to see the Countess von Sayn."

"Ah, is the lady within? Why, of course, she must be. I remember now, she was to accompany you to Frankfort, and it naturally follows she is your guest."

"She is my guest, your Highness, and one reason why you cannot see her is because at this moment the lady converses with the Count Palatine, who has just arrived from Gutenfels. As the Countess and myself enjoyed his hospitality not long ago in that stronghold, I have invited him to be my guest until the coronation ceremonies are completed."

"My Lord, I regret that your hospitality halts when it reaches your future Emperor. Why may I not be introduced to the Count Palatine?"

"Such introduction must not take place except in the presence of the other Electors. I am very anxious, as you may perceive, that nothing shall be done to jeopardize your own prospects. We have arrived, your Highness, at a critical moment. History relates that more than one candidate has come to the very steps of the throne, only to be rejected at the last moment. I am too sincere a friend to risk such an outcome in your own case."

"Then you think it injudicious of me to see the Countess until after the Election?"

"I not only think it injudicious, your Highness, but I intend to prevent a meeting."

Again the young man laughed.

"'Tis blessed then that I came for no such purpose; otherwise I might be deeply disappointed."

"For what purpose did you come, Highness?"

"The Imperial Palace, my Lord, belongs no more to my mother. If she or I continue there to reside, we seem to be taking for granted that I shall be elected Emperor; an assumption unfair to the seven Electors, whose choice should be untrammeled by even a hint of influence. I beg of you, therefore, my Lord, to extend your hospitality to my mother. I have spoken to her on this subject, and she will gladly be your guest, happy, I am sure, to forsake that gloomy abode."

"I am honored, your Highness, by the opportunity you give me. I shall wait upon the Empress to-morrow at whatever hour it is convenient for her Majesty to receive me."

"You are most kind. I suggested that she should name an hour, and midday was chosen."

The Archbishop bowed profoundly. The young man rose, and held out his hand, which the Archbishop took with cordiality. The Prince looked very straight-forwardly at his host, and the latter thought he detected a twinkle in his eye, as he said with decision:

"To-morrow I shall formally notify my Lord of Mayence that the Empress has chosen your Palace as her place of residence until after the coronation, and I shall request his Lordship to crave your permission that I may call here every day to see my mother."

Again Cologne bowed, and made no further protest, although Roland seemingly expected one, but as it did not come, the Prince continued:

"Here is my address in Sachsenhausen, should you wish a communication to reach me in haste; and kindly command your porter not to parley when I again demand speech with your Lordship. Good-night. I thank you, my Lord, for your courtesy," and the energetic youth disappeared before the slow-thinking Archbishop could call up words with which to reply.

Cologne did not immediately rejoin his guests, but stood a very figure of perplexity, muttering to himself:

"If our friend Mayence thinks that youngster is to be molded like soft clay, he is very much mistaken. I hope Roland will not cause him to feel the iron hand too soon. I wonder why Mayence is delaying the Election? Can it be that already he distrusts his choice, or is it the question of a wife?"

Meanwhile the front door of the Archbishop's Palace had clanged shut, and Roland strode across the square careless or unconscious of spies, looking neither to the right nor to the left. He made his way speedily to the Fahrgasse, walking down that thoroughfare until he came to Herr Goebel's door, where he knocked, and was admitted. Ushered into the room where he had parted from the merchant, he found Herr Goebel seated at his table as if he had never left it. The merchant, with a cry of delight, greeted the young man.

"Well, Herr Goebel, you see I have been a successful trafficker. Your bales of goods are all in Castle Pfalz, and I trust the barge returned safely to you with the money."

"It did indeed, your Highness."

"Has the coin been counted?"

"Yes; and it totals an enormous, almost unbelievable, sum, which I have set down here to the last stiver."

"That is brave news. Have any demands been made on you for its partition?"

"No, your Highness."

"Now, Herr Goebel, I have determined that all that money, which is in effect stolen property, shall go to the feeding of Frankfort's poor. Buying provender shrewdly, how long would this treasure keep hunger away from the gates of Frankfort?"

"That requires some calculation, your Highness."

"A month?"

"Surely so."

"Two months, perhaps?"

"'Tis likely; but I deal in cloth, not in food, and therefore cannot speak definitely without computation and the advice of those expert in the matter."

"Very well, Herr Goebel; get your computations made as soon as possible. Call together your merchants' guild, and ask its members—By the way," said Roland, suddenly checking himself, "give to me in writing the amount of gold I have sent you."

The unsuspecting merchant did so, and Roland's eyes opened with astonishment when he glanced at the total. He then placed the paper in the wallet he carried.

"You were perhaps about to suggest that a committee be appointed," ventured the merchant.

"Yes; a small but capable committee, of which you shall be chairman and treasurer. But first you will ask the merchants to subscribe, out of their known wealth, a sum equaling the gold I filched from the Barons."

The merchant's face fell, and took on a doleful expression.

"The times, your Highness, have long been very bad, none of us making money—"

The Prince held up his hand, and the merchant ceased his plaint.

"If I can strip a Baron of his wealth," he said, "I will not waste words over the fleecing of merchants. This contribution is to be given in the name of the three Archbishops, whose heavy hands came down on you after the late insurrection. The Archbishops have now nine thousand troops in Frankfort. If given leave, they will collect the sum three times over within a very few hours; so you, as chairman of the committee, may decide whether the fund shall be a voluntary contribution or an impost gathered by soldiery: it matters nothing to me. Have it proclaimed throughout the city that owing to the graciousness of the three Archbishops starvation is now at an end in Frankfort."

"Highness, with your permission, and all due deference, it seems rather unjust that we should contribute the cash and lose the credit."

"Yes, Herr Goebel; this is a very unjust world, as doubtless many of the starving people thought when they recollected that a few hundred of you possessed vast wealth while they were penniless. Nevertheless, there are good times ahead for all of us. Let me suggest that this money which I sent to you may prove sufficient and so the subscriptions of the merchants can be returned to them; that is, if the relief fund is honestly administered. So set to work early to-morrow with energy. You merchants have had a long vacation. I think the Rhine will be open before many weeks are past, and then you can turn to your money-making, but our first duty is to feed the hungry. Good-night, Herr Goebel."

He left the merchant as dazed as was the Archbishop. Once again outside he made directly for the wine cellar of the Rheingold. On reaching the steps he heard a roar of talk, lightened now and then by the sound of laughter. He paused a moment before descending. It was evident that the company was enjoying itself, and Roland soliloquized somewhat sadly:

"I am the disturbing element in that group. They seem to agree famously when by themselves. Ah, well, no matter. They will soon be rid of me!"

When Roland descended the stair, the proprietor greeted him with joy.

"I have missed you, Herr Roland," he said, "so you may imagine how much the guild has regretted your absence."

"Yes; I hear them bemoaning their fate."

The inn-keeper laughed.

"How many are here to-night?"

"There is a full house, Sir Roland."

"Really? Are Kurzbold and Gensbein within?"

"Oh, yes; and there is no scarcity of money, thanks to you, I understand."

"Rather, our thanks are for ever due to you, Herr Host, for sustaining us so long when we were penniless. We shall never forget that," and so with a semi-military salute to the gratified cellar-man, Roland pushed open the door and entered the banqueting room of the iron-workers' guild. An instant silence fell on the group.

"Good evening to you, gentlemen," said the Prince, taking off his hat, and with a twist of his shoulders flinging the cloak from them.

Instantly arose a great cheer, and Greusel, who occupied the chair at the head of the table, strode forward, took Roland's hat and cloak, and hung them up. After that he attempted to lead their Captain to the seat of honor.

"No, no, my dear lieutenant," said Roland, placing his hand affectionately on the other's shoulder, "a better man than I occupies the chair, and shall never be displaced by me."

The others, now on their feet, with the exception of Kurzbold and Gensbein, vociferously demanded that Roland take the chair. Smilingly he shook his head, and holding up his hand for silence, addressed them.

"Take your seats, comrades; and, Greusel, if you force me to give a command, I order you into that chair without further protest."

Greusel, with evident reluctance, obeyed.

"Truth to tell, brothers, I have but a few moments to stop. I merely dropped in to enjoy a sip of wine with you, and to offer a proposal that, within five minutes, will make me the most unpopular man in this room, therefore you see my wisdom in refusing a chair from which I should be very promptly ejected."

One of the members poured a tankard full of wine from a flagon, and handed it to Roland, who, saluting the company, drank.

"You did not divide the money, Greusel?"

"No, Roland. We gave each man five hundred thalers, to keep as best he might. We then concealed the rest of the gold between the bottom of the boat and its inner planking. Ebearhard and I construed your orders somewhat liberally, conceiving it was your desire to get our treasure and ourselves safely into Frankfort."

"Quite right," corroborated Roland.

"When morning came upon us, we soon discovered that the whole country was aroused, because of the destruction of Furstenberg and the looting of Sonneck. No one knew where the next raid would strike, and therefore the whole country-side was in a turmoil. Now, the only fact known to the despoiled was that a long black barge had appeared in front of the Castle while the attack was made from behind. We realized that it would be impossible for us to go up the river except in darkness, so in case of a search we concealed the treasure where it was not likely to be come at, and each day lay quiet at an unfrequented part of the river, rowing all night. Not until we reached the Main did we venture on a daylight voyage. It was agreed among us unanimously that the money should be placed in Herr Goebel's keeping until you returned."

"That was all excellently done," commented Roland. "I have just been to see Herr Goebel, and was surprised to learn how much we had actually taken. And now I ask you to make a great sacrifice. This city is starving. If we give that gold to its relief, the merchants of Frankfort will contribute an equal amount. I do not know how long such a total will keep the wolves from the doors of Frankfort; probably for six months. I shall learn definitely to-morrow." Here Roland outlined his plan of relief, which was received in silence.

Kurzbold spoke up.

"I should like to know how much the total is?"

"That is a matter with which you have nothing to do," growled Greusel; then, turning to Roland, who had not yet taken a seat, he said: "So far as my share is concerned, I agree."

"I agree," added Ebearhard; and so it went down along each side of the table until eighteen had spoken.

Kurzbold rose with a smile on his face.

"I don't know how it is, ex-Captain, that the moment you come among us there seems to arise a spirit of disputation."

"Curiously enough, Herr Kurzbold, that same thought arose in my mind as I listened to your hilarity before I entered. I beg to add, for your satisfaction, that this is my last visit to the guild, and never again shall I disturb its harmony."

"There is no lack of harmony," cried Ebearhard, laughing, as he rose. "The agreement has been practically unanimous—quite unanimous in fact, among those entitled to share in the great treasure. I believe Herr Kurzbold has a claim, if it has not been forfeited, to the loot of Rheinstein."

"Now, even the genial Ebearhard," continued Kurzbold, "although his words are blameless, speaks with a certain tone of acerbity, while my friend Greusel has become gruff as a bear."

"You need not labor that point, Herr Kurzbold," said Roland. "I have resigned."

"I just wished to remark," Kurzbold went on, "that I rose for the purpose of stating I had some slight share in something; stolen property; honor among thieves, you know. Are my rights to this share disputed?"

"No," said the chairman shortly.

"Very well," concluded Kurzbold, "as I am graciously permitted to speak in the august presence of our ex-Captain, I desire to say that whatever my share happens to be, I bestow it gladly, nay, exultantly, upon the poor of Frankfort."

With that Kurzbold sat down, and there was first a roar of laughter, followed by a clapping of hands. Gensbein rose, and said briefly:

"I do as Kurzbold does."

"Now," said Roland, "I want a number of volunteers to start out into the country early to-morrow morning, Greusel, you, as chairman, will designate the routes. Each man is to penetrate as far as he can along the main roads, asking the farmers to bring everything in the shape of food they have to sell. Tell them a vast sum has been collected, and that their cartloads will be bought entire the moment they enter the city. There will be no waiting for their money. Prompt payment, and everything eatable purchased immediately. Greusel, I put on you the hardest task. Penetrate into the forest south of the Main, and tell the charcoal-burners and woodmen to bring in material for kitchen fires. How many will volunteer?"

Every man rose. Roland thanked them. "I shall now divulge a secret, and you will see that when it was told to me I remembered your interests. It has been my privilege to meet, since I saw you, more than one man who is a ruler in this Empire."

"Did they tell you who is to be the new Emperor?" cried one.

"That is known only to the Electors. But what I was about to say is this. There are to be established by the Government ironworks on a scale hitherto unknown in any land. I believe, and did my best to inculcate that belief in others, that we are on the verge of an age of iron, and, knowing your skill, I am privileged to offer each of you the superintendency of a department, with compensation never before given so lavishly in Germany. I am also induced to believe that the new Emperor will bestow a title on each of you who desire such honor, so that there can be no question of your right to wear a sword. Greusel, you must receive reports from each of our food scouts, and I shall be glad to know the outcome, if you take the trouble to call upon me any hour after nine o'clock at night, at my old room in Sachsenhausen. And now, good-night, and good-luck to you all."

Roland went over the bridge, and so reached his room on the other side. He glanced around several times to satisfy himself he was not spied upon, and laughed at the apprehension of the Archbishop. Entering his room, he lit a lamp, took off his cloak and flung it on the bed, then unbuckled his sword-belt and hung it and the weapon on a peg, placing his cloak above them. He was startled by a loud knock at the door, and stood for a moment astonished, until it was repeated with the stern warning:

"Open in the name of the Archbishop!"

The young man strode forward, drew back the bolt, and flung open the door. An officer, with two soldiers behind him, came across the threshold, and at the side-motion of the officer's head a soldier closed and bolted the door. Roland experienced a momentary thrill of indignation at this rude intrusion, then he remembered he was a mechanic, and that his line must be the humble and deferential.

"You came to-night from the Imperial Palace. What were you doing there?"

"I was trying to gain admission, sir."

"For what purpose?"

"I wished," said Roland, rapidly outlining his defense in his own mind,

"I wished to see some high officer; some one of your own position, sir, but was not so fortunate as to succeed. I could not pass the sentries without a permit, which I did not then possess, but hope to acquire to-morrow."

"Again I ask, for what purpose?"

"For a purpose which causes me delight in meeting your excellency."

"I am no excellency. Come to the point! For what purpose?"

"To show the officer a sword of such superior quality that a man armed with it, and given a certain amount of skill, stands impregnable."

"Do you mean to tell me you went to the Royal Palace for the purpose of selling a second-hand sword?"

"Oh, no, my lord."

"Do not be so free with your titles. Call me Lieutenant."

"Well, Lieutenant, sir; I hope to get orders for a hundred, or perhaps a thousand of these weapons."

"Where did you go after leaving the Palace?"

"I went to the residence of that great Prince of the Church, the Archbishop of Cologne."

"Ah! You did not succeed in seeing his Lordship, I suppose?"

"Pardon me, Lieutenant, but I did. His Lordship is keenly interested in both weapons and armor."

"Did he give you an order for swords?"

"No, Lieutenant; he seems to be a very cautious man. He asked me to visit him in Cologne, or if I could not do that, to see his general, now in Frankfort. You understand, Lieutenant, the presence of the three Archbishops with their armies offers me a great opportunity, by which I hope to profit."

The officer looked at him with a puzzled expression on his face.

"Where next did you go?"

"I went to the house of a merchant in the Fahrgasse."

"Ah, that tale doesn't hold! Merchants are not allowed to wear swords."

"No, Lieutenant, but a merchant on occasion can supply capital that will enable a skilled workman to accept a large contract. If I should see the general of his Lordship to-morrow, and he gave me an order for, say, two thousand swords, I have not enough money to buy the metal, and I could not ask for payment until I delivered the weapons."

"Did the merchant agree to capitalize you?"

"He, too, was a cautious man, Lieutenant. He wished first to see the contract, and know who stood responsible for payment."

"Wise man," commented the officer; "and so, disheartened, I suppose, you returned here?"

"No, Lieutenant; the day has been warm, and I have traveled a good deal. I went from the merchant's house to the Rheingold tavern, there to drink a tankard of wine with my comrades, a score of men who have formed what they call the ironworkers' guild. I drank a tankard with them, and then came direct here, where I arrived but a few moments ago."

The officer was more and more puzzled. Despite this young man's deferential manner, his language was scarcely that of a mechanic, yet this certainly was his own room, and he had told the absolute truth about his wanderings, as one who has nothing to fear.

The Lieutenant stood for a space of time with eyes to the floor, as silent as the soldiers behind him. Suddenly he looked up.

"Show me the sword. I'll tell you where it's made!"

If he expected hesitation he was mistaken. Roland gave a joyful cry, swept aside the cloak, whisked forth the sword, flung it up, and caught it by the blade, then with a low bow handed it to the officer, who flashed it through the air, bent the blade between finger and thumb, then took it near the lamp and scrutinized it with the eye of an expert.

803

"A good weapon, my friend. Where was it made? I have never seen one like it."

"It was made by my own hands here in Frankfort. Of course I go first to those who know least about the matter, but if I can get an introduction to his Lordship of Mayence, his officers will know a sword when they see it; and I hope to-night fortune, in leading you to my door, has brought me an officer of Mayence."

The Lieutenant looked at him, and for the first time smiled. He handed back the weapon, signed to his men to unbolt the door, which they did, stepping out; then he said:

"I bid you good-night. Your answers have been satisfactory, but I set you down not as a mechanic, but a very excellent merchant of swords."

"Lieutenant," said Roland, "you do not flatter me." He raised his weapon in military salute. "I am no merchant, but a sword maker."

XIX. THE BETROTHAL IN THE GARDEN

Next morning Prince Roland sent a letter to the Archbishop of Mayence informing him that the Empress had taken up her abode in the Palace of her old friend, the Lord of Cologne, giving the reasons for this move and his own desertion of the Imperial Palace, and asking permission to call upon his mother each day. The messenger brought back a prompt reply, which commended the delicacy of his motives in leaving the Royal Palace, but added that, so far as the three Archbishops were concerned, the Saalhof was still at their disposal: of course Prince Roland's movements were quite untrammeled, and again, so far as concerned the three Archbishops, he was at liberty to visit whom he pleased, as often as he liked.

While waiting for the return of his messenger, Roland called upon Herr Goebel, and told him that twenty emissaries had gone forth in every direction from Frankfort to inform the farming community that a market had been opened in the city, and in exchange learned what the merchant had already done towards furthering the necessary organization.

"Oh, by the way, Herr Goebel," he cried, suddenly recollecting, "just write out and sign a document to this effect: 'I promise Herr Roland, sword maker of Sachsenhausen, to supply him with the capital necessary for carrying out his contract with his Lordship the Archbishop of Cologne.'"

Without demur the merchant indited the document, signed it, and gave it to the Prince.

"If any emissary of Mayence pays you a domiciliary visit, Herr Goebel, asking questions about me, carefully conceal my real status, and reply that I am an honest, skillful sword maker, anxious to revive the iron-working industry, and for this reason, being yourself solicitous for the welfare of Frankfort, you are risking some money."

In the afternoon Roland walked to the Palace of Cologne and boldly entered, with no attempt at secrecy, the doorkeeper on this occasion offering no impediment to his progress. He learned that the Empress, much fatigued, had retired to her room and must not be disturbed; that the Archbishop was consulting with the Count Palatine, while the Countess von Sayn was walking in the garden. Roland passed with some haste through the Palace, and emerged into the grounds behind it: grounds delightfully umbrageous, and of an extent surprisingly large, surrounded by a very high wall of stone, so solidly built that it might successfully stand a siege.

Roland found the girl sauntering very slowly along one of the most secluded alleys, whose gravel-path lay deeply in the shade caused by the thick foliage of over-hanging trees, which made a cool, green tunnel of the walk. Her head was slightly bowed in thought, her beautiful face pathetic in its weariness, and the young man realized, with a pang of sympathy, that she was still to all intents and purposes a prisoner, with no companions but venerable people. She could not, and indeed did not attempt to suppress an exclamation of delight at seeing him, stretching out both hands in greeting, and her countenance cleared as if by magic.

"I was thinking of you!" she cried, without a trace of coquetry.

"I judged your thoughts to be rather gloomy," he said, with a laugh, in which she joined.

"Gloomy only because I could see or hear nothing of you."

"Did you know I came yesterday?"

"No. Why did you not ask to see me?"

"I was informed you were entertaining the Count Palatine."

"Ah, yes. He is a delightful old man. I like him better and better as time goes on. My guardian and I were guests of his at Gutenfels just before I occupied the marine prison of Pfalz."

"So your guardian told me."

They were now walking side by side in this secluded, thickly-wooded avenue, just wide enough for two, running in a straight line from wall to wall

806

the whole length of the property, in the part most remote from the house.

"Nothing disastrous has happened to you?" she asked. "I have had miserable forebodings."

"No; I am living a most commonplace life, quite uneventful."

"But why, why does the Archbishop of Mayence delay the Election?"

"I did not know he was doing so."

"Oh, my guardian is very anxious about it. Such postponement, I understand, never happened before. The State is without a head."

"Has your guardian spoken to Mayence about it?"

"Yes; and has been met by the most icy politeness. Mayence wishes this Election to take place with a full conclave of the seven Electors, three of whom have not yet arrived. But my guardian says they never arrive, and take no interest in Imperial matters. He pointed out to Mayence that a quorum of the Court is already in Frankfort, but his Lordship of the Upper Rhine merely protests that they must not force an Election, all of which my guardian thinks is a mere hiding of some design on the part of Mayence."

Prince Roland meditated on this for a few moments, then, as if shaking off his doubts, he said:

"It never occurs to one Archbishop that either of the others may be speaking the truth. There is so much mistrust among them that they nullify all united action, which accounts for the prostrate state of this city, the capital of one of the most prosperous countries under the sun. So far as I can see, taken individually, they are upright, trustworthy men. Now, to give you an instance. Your guardian last night was simply panic-stricken at my audacity in visiting him. He said I must not come again, refusing me permission to see you; he told you nothing of my conference with him: he felt certain I was being tracked by spies, and could not be made to understand that my presence here was of no consequence one way or another."

"Then why are you here now?"

"I am just coming to that. I asked your guardian to invite my mother as his guest. Have you met her yet?"

"No; they told me the Empress was too tired to receive any one. I am to be introduced at dinner to-night."

"Well, this morning I wrote to the Archbishop of Mayence, telling him of my interview with your guardian, the reason for it, and the results. His reply came promptly by return." Roland produced the document. "Just read that, and see whether you detect anything sinister in it."

She read the letter thoughtfully.

"That is honest enough on the surface."

"On the surface, yes; but why not below the surface as well? That is a frank assent to a frank request. I think that if the Archbishops would treat each other with open candor they would save themselves a good deal of anxiety."

"Perhaps," said the girl, very quietly.

"You are not convinced?"

"I don't know what to think." Then she looked up at him quickly. "Were you followed last night?"

"Ah!" ejaculated Roland, laughing a little "apparently not, so far as I could see, but the night was very dark." Then he related to her the incidents succeeding the return to his room, while she listened with breathless eagerness. "The Lieutenant," he concluded, "did not deny that he was in the service of Mayence when I hinted as much, but, on the other hand, he did not admit it. Of course, I knew by his uniform to whom he belonged. He conducted my examination with military abruptness, but skillfully and with increasing courtesy, although I proclaimed myself a mechanic."

"You a mechanic!" she said incredulously. "Do you think he believed it?"

"I see you doubt my histrionic ability, but when next he waits upon me I shall produce documentary evidence of my status, and, what is more, I'll take to my workshop."

"Do you possess a workshop?" cried the girl in amazement.

"Do I? Why, I am partner with a man named Greusel, and we own a workshop together. A gruff, clumsy individual, as you would think, but who, nevertheless, with his delicate hammer, would beat you out in metal a brooch finer than that you are wearing."

"Do you mean Joseph?"

"Yes," replied Roland, astonished. "What do you know of him?"

"Have you forgotten so soon? It was his stalwart shoulders that burst in my door at Pfalz, and you yourself told me his name was Joseph Greusel. Were all those marauders you commanded honest mechanics?"

"Every man of them."

"Then you must be the villain of the piece who led those worthy ironworkers astray?"

Roland laughed heartily.

"That is quite true," he said. "Have I fallen in your estimation?"

"No; to me you appeared as a rescuer. Besides, I come of a race of ruffians, and doubtless on that account take a more lenient view of your villainy than may be the case with others."

The young man stopped in his walk, and seized her hands again, which she allowed him to possess unresisting.

"Hilda," he said solemnly, "your guardian thought the Archbishop of Mayence had relented, and would withdraw his opposition to our marriage. Has Mayence said anything to corroborate that estimate?"

"Nothing."

"Has your guardian broached the subject to him?"

"Yes; but the attitude of my Lord of Mayence was quite inscrutable. Personally I think my guardian wrong in his surmise. The Archbishop of

Treves murmured that Mayence never forgives. I am certain I offended him too deeply for pardon. He wishes the future Empress to be a pliable creature who will influence her husband according to his Lordship's desires, but, as I have boasted several times, I belong to the House of Sayn."

"Hilda, will you marry me in spite of the Archbishops?"

"Roland, will you forego kingship for my sake?"

"Yes; a thousand times yes!"

"You said 'For the Empress; not for the Empire,' but if I am no Empress, you will as cheerfully wed me?"

"Yes."

"Then I say yes!"

He caught her in his arms, and they floated into the heaven of their first kiss, an ecstatic melting together. Suddenly she drew away from him.

"There is some one coming," she whispered.

"Nothing matters now," said Roland breathlessly. "There is no one in the world to-day but you and me."

Hildegunde drew her hands down her cheeks, as if to brush away their tell-tale color and their warmth.

"'Tis like," said Roland, "that you marry a poor man."

"Nothing matters now," she repeated, laughing tremulously. "I am said to be the richest woman in Germany. I shall build you a forge and enlist myself your apprentice. We will paint over the door 'Herr Roland and wife; sword makers.'"

Two men appeared at the end of the alley, and stood still; the one with a frown on his brow, the other with a smile on his lips.

"Oh!" whispered the Countess, panic striking from her face the color that her palms had failed to remove, "the Archbishop and the Count Palatine!"

810

His Lordship strode forward, followed more leisurely by the smiling Count.

"Prince Roland," said Cologne, "I had not expected this after our conference of last night."

"I fail to understand why, my Lord, when my parting words were 'Tell your porter to let me in without parley.' That surely indicated an intention on my part to visit the Palace."

"Your Highness knows that so far as I am concerned you are very welcome, and always shall be so, but at this juncture there are others to consider."

Roland interrupted.

"Read this letter, my Lord, and you will learn that I am here with the full concurrence of that generous Prince of the Church, Mayence."

Cologne, with knitted brow, scrutinized the communication.

"Your Highness is most courageous, but, if I may be permitted, just a trifle too clever."

"My Highness is not clever at all, but merely meets a situation as it arises."

"Prince Roland," said the Countess, her head raised proudly, "may I introduce to you my friend, and almost my neighbor, the Count Palatine of the Rhine?"

"Ah, pardon me," murmured the Archbishop, covered with confusion, but the jovial Count swept away all embarrassment by his hearty greeting.

"Prince Roland, I am delighted with the honor her ladyship accords me."

"And I, my Lord, am exceedingly gratified to meet the Count Palatine again."

"Again?" cried the Count in astonishment, "If ever we had encountered one another, your Highness, I certainly should not have been the one to forget the privilege."

The Prince laughed.

"It is true, nevertheless. My Lord Count, there is a namesake of mine in the precincts of your strong Castle of Gutenfels; a namesake who does more honor to the title than I do myself."

The Count Palatine threw back his head, and the forest garden echoed with boisterous laughter.

"You mean my black charger, Prince Roland!" he shouted. "A noble horse indeed. How knew you of him? If your Highness cares for horses allow me to present him to you."

"Never, my Lord Count. You are too fond of him yourself, and I have always had an affectionate feeling towards you for your love of that animal, which, indeed, hardly exceeds my own. I grasped his bridle-rein, and held the stirrup while you mounted."

"How is that possible?" asked the astonished Count.

"I cared for Prince Roland nearly a month, receiving generous wages, and, what I valued more, your own commendation, for you saw I was as fond of horses as you were."

"Good heavens! Were you that youth who came so mysteriously, and disappeared without warning?"

"Yes," laughed the Prince. "I know Gutenfels nearly as well as you do. I was a spy, studying the art of war and methods of fortification. I stopped in various capacities at nearly all the famous Castles of the Rhine, and this knowledge recently came in—"

"Your Highness, your Highness!" pleaded the Archbishop. "I implore you to remember that the Count Palatine is an Elector of the Empire, and, as I told last night, we are facing a crisis. Until that crisis is passed you will add to my already great anxiety by any lack of reticence on your part."

"By the Three Kings!" cried the Count, "this youth, if I may venture to call him so, has bound me to him with bands stronger than chain armor. I shall vote for him whoever falters."

"His Highness," said the Archbishop, with a propitiatory smile, "has been listening to the Eastern tales which our ancestors brought from the Crusades, and I fear has filled his head with fancies."

"Really, Archbishop, you misjudge me," said the young man; "I am the most practical person in the Empire. You interrupted my boasting to her ladyship of my handiwork. I would have you know I am a capable mechanic and a sword maker. What think you of that, my Lord?" he asked, drawing forth his weapon, and handing it to Cologne.

"An excellent blade indeed," said the latter, balancing it in his hand.

"Very well, my Lord, I made it and tempered it unassisted. I beg you to re-enter your palace, and write me out an order for a thousand of these weapons."

"If your Highness really wishes me to do this, and there is no concealed humorism in your request which I am too dull to fathom, you must accompany me to my study and dictate the document I am to indite. I shall wait till you bid farewell to the Countess."

A glance of mutual understanding flashed between the girl and himself, then Roland raised her hand to his lips, and although the onlookers saw the gallant salutation, they knew nothing of the gentle pressure with which the fingers exchanged their confidences.

"Madam," said the Prince, "it will be my pleasure and duty to wait upon my mother to-morrow. May I look forward to the happiness of presenting you to her?"

"I thank you," said the Countess simply, with a glance of appeal at her guardian. That good man sighed, then led the way into the house.

XX. THE MYSTERY OF THE FOREST

Roland left the palace with a sense of elation he had never before experienced, but this received a check as he saw standing in the middle of the square the Lieutenant of the night before. His first impulse was to avoid the officer, yet almost instinctively he turned and walked directly to him, which apparently nonplussed the brave emissary of Mayence.

"Good afternoon to you, sir," began Roland, as if overjoyed to see him. "Will you permit me to speak to you, sir?"

"Well?" said the Lieutenant curtly.

"My forge, which has been black and cold for many a long day, will soon be alight and warm again. What think you of this?" He handed to the Lieutenant his order for a thousand swords, and the officer made a mental note of the commission as an interesting point in armament that would be appreciated by his chief.

"You did not inform me last night who was the merchant you hoped would finance your enterprise."

"Hoped?" echoed Roland, his eyes sparkling. "'Tis more than hope, Herr Lieutenant. His name is Goebel, and he is one of the richest and chiefest traffickers of Frankfort. Why, my fortune is made! Read this, written in his own hand. I got it from him before midday, on my mere word that I was certain of an order from his Lordship."

"You are indeed much to be envied," said the Lieutenant coldly, returning the two documents.

"Ah, but I am just at the beginning. If you would favor me by smoothing the way to his Lordship, the Archbishop of Mayence, I in return—"

"Out upon you for a base-born, profit-mongering churl! Do you think that I, an officer, would demean myself by partnering a bagman!"

The Lieutenant turned on his heel, strode away and left him. Roland pursued his way with bowed head, as though stricken by the rebuff. Nearing the bridge, he saw a crowd around an empty cart, standing by which a man in rough clothing was cursing most vociferously.

At first he thought there had been an accident, but most of the people were laughing loudly; so, halting in the outskirts, he asked the cause of the commotion.

"'Tis but a fool farmer," said a man, "who came from the country with his load of vegetables. 'Tis safer to enter a lion's den unarmed than to come into Frankfort with food while people are starving. He has been plundered to the last leaf."

Roland shouldered his way through the crowd, and touched the frantic man on the shoulder.

"What was the value of your load?" he said.

"A misbegotten liar told me this morning that a market had opened in Frankfort, and that there was money to be had. No sooner am I in the town than everything I brought in is stolen."

"Yes, yes; I know all about that. My question is, How much is your merchandise worth?"

"Worth? Thirty thalers I expected to get, and now—"

"Thirty thalers," interrupted the Prince. "Here is your money. Get you gone, and tell your neighbors there is prompt payment for all the provender they can bring in."

The man calmed down as if a bucket of water had been thrown on him. He counted the payment with miserly care, testing each coin between his teeth, then mounted his cart without a word of thanks, and, to the disappointment of the gathering mob, drove away. Roland, seething with anger, walked directly to the house of Herr Goebel, and found that placid old burgher seated at his table.

"Ten thousand curses on your indolence!" he cried. "Where are your committee, and the emissaries empowered to carry out this scheme of relief I have ordered?"

"Committee? Emissaries?" cried the astonished man. "There has been no time!"

"Time, you thick-headed fool! I'll time you by hanging you to your own front door. There has been time for me to send my men out into the country; time for a farmer to come in with a cartload of produce, and be robbed here under your very nose! Maledictions on you, you sit here, well fed, and cry there is no time! If I had not paid the yeoman he would have gone back into the country crying we were all thieves here in Frankfort. Now listen to me. I drew my sword once upon you in jest. Should I draw it a second time it will be to penetrate your lazy carcass by running you through. If within two hours there is not a paymaster at every gate in Frankfort to buy and pay for each cartload of produce as it comes, and also a number of guides to tell that farmer where to deliver his goods, I'll give your town over to the military, and order the sacking of every merchant's house within its walls."

"It shall be done; it shall be done; it shall be done!" breathed the merchant, trembling as he rose, and he kept repeating the phrase with the iteration of a parrot.

"You owe me thirty thalers," said the Prince calming down; "the first payment out of the relief fund. Give me the money."

With quivering hands Herr Goebel, seeing no humor in the application, handed over the money, which the Prince slipped into his wallet.

Dusk had fallen when at last he reached his room in Sachsenhausen, and there he found awaiting him Joseph Greusel, in semi-darkness and in total gloom.

"Your housekeeper let me in," said the visitor.

"Good! I did not expect you back so soon. Have the others returned?"

"I do not know. I came direct here. I carry very ominous news, Roland, of impending disaster in Frankfort."

"Greater than at present oppresses it?"

"Civil war, fire, and bloodshed. Close the door, Roland; I am tired out, and I do not wish to be overheard."

The Prince obeyed the request, locking the door. Going to a cupboard, he produced a generous flagon of wine and a tankard, setting the same on a small table before Greusel, then he threw himself down in the one armchair the room possessed. Greusel filled the tankard, and emptied it without drawing breath. He plunged directly into his narrative.

"I had penetrated less than half a league into the forest when I was stopped by an armed man who stepped out from behind a tree. He wore the uniform of Mayence, and proclaimed me a prisoner. I explained my mission, but this had no effect upon him. He asked if I would go with him quietly, or compel him to call assistance. Being helpless, I said I would go quietly. Notwithstanding this, he bound my wrists behind me, then with a strip of cloth blindfolded me. Taking me by the arm, he led me through the forest for a distance impossible to calculate. I think, however, we walked not more than ten minutes. There was a stop and a whispered parley; a pause of a few minutes, and a further conference, which I partially heard. The commander before whom I must be taken was not ready to receive me. I should be placed in a tent, and a guard set over me.

"This was done. I asked that the cord, which hurt my wrists, might be removed, but instead, my ankles were tied together, and I sat there on the ground, leaning against a pole at the back of the tent. Here my conductor left me, and I heard him give orders to those without to maintain a strict watch, but to hold no communication with me.

"I imagine that the tent I occupied stood back to back with the tent of the commander, for after some time I heard the sound of voices, and it seemed to me voices of two men in authority. They had come to the back part of their tent, as if to speak confidentially, and their voices were low, yet I could hear them quite distinctly, being separated from them merely by two thicknesses of cloth. What I learned was this. There is concealed in the forest, within half an hour's quick march of the southern gate, a force of seven thousand soldiers. These soldiers belong to the Archbishop of Mayence, who commands an additional three thousand within the walls of Frankfort. Mayence holds the southern gate, as Treves holds the western and Cologne the northern. You see at once what that implies. Mayence can pour his troops into Frankfort, say, at midnight, and in the morning he has ten thousand soldiers as compared with the three thousand each commanded by the Archbishops of Treves and Cologne. That means civil war, and the complete crushing of the two northern Archbishops."

"I think you take too serious a view of the matter," commented Roland. "Mayence is undoubtedly a subtle man, who takes every precaution that he shall have his own way. The reason that there will be no civil war is this. I happen to know on very excellent authority that so far as the Electoral Court goes, Mayence is paramount. He does not need to conquer Cologne and Treves by force, because he is already supreme by his genius for intrigue. He is a born ruler, and his methods are all those of diplomacy as against those of arms. I dare say if occasion demanded it he would strike quick and strike effectually, but occasion does not demand. I am rather sure of my facts, and I know that the three Archbishops, together with the Count Palatine of the Rhine, are in agreement to elect my namesake, Prince Roland, Emperor of Germany."

"Yes," said Greusel, "I heard that rumor, and it is generally believed in Frankfort. Rumor, however, as usual, speaks falsely."

The Prince smiled at his pessimistic colleague, for that colleague was talking to the man who knew; nevertheless, he listened patiently, for of course he could not yet reveal himself to his somber lieutenant, who continued his narrative:

"The two men spoke of the unfortunate Prince, who is, I understand, still a prisoner in Ehrenfels."

Here Roland laughed outright.

"My dear Greusel, you are entirely mistaken. The Prince was never really a prisoner, and is at this moment in Frankfort, as free to do what he likes as

I am."

"I am sorry," said Greusel, "that you do not grasp the seriousness of the situation, but I have not yet come to the vital part of it, although I thought the very fact that seven thousand men threatened Frankfort would impress you."

"It does, Greusel," said Roland, remembering the distrust in which both the Countess and her guardian held Mayence, and also the close watch his Lordship was keeping over Frankfort, as evidenced by the domiciliary visit paid to himself by an officer of that potentate. "Go on, Greusel," he said more soberly, "I shall not interrupt you again."

"I gathered that Prince Roland actually had been chosen, but complications arose which I do not altogether understand. These complications relate to a woman, or two women; both of them equally objectionable to the Archbishop of Mayence. One of these two women was to marry the new Emperor, but rather than have this happen, Mayence determined that another than Prince Roland should be elected, the reason being that Mayence feared one Empress would be entirely under the influence of Cologne, if chosen, and the other under the influence of Treves. So his subtle Lordship is deluding both of these Electors. Cologne has been asked to bring to Frankfort the woman he controls, therefore he harbors the illusion that Mayence is reconciled to her. Treves also has been requested to bring the lady who is his relative; thus she, too, is in Frankfort, and Treves blindly believes Mayence is favorable to her cause.

"As a matter of fact Mayence will have neither, but has resolved to spring upon the Electoral Court at the last moment the name of the Grand Duke Karl of Hesse, a middle-aged man already married, and entirely under the dominance of his Lordship of Mayence."

"Pardon me, Greusel, I must interrupt, in spite of my disclaimer. What you say sounds very ingenious, but it cannot be carried out. Treves, Cologne, and the Count Palatine are already pledged to vote for Prince Roland, so is Mayence himself, and to change front at the last moment would be to forswear himself, and act as traitor to his colleagues. Now, he cannot afford to lose even one vote, and I believe that the Archbishop of Cologne will vote for Prince Roland through thick and thin. I think the same of the Count Palatine. Treves, of course, is always doubtful and wavering, but you see that the negative vote of the Archbishop of Cologne would render Mayence powerless and an Election impossible."

"Doubtless what you say is true, and now you have put your finger on the danger spot. Why has the Election been delayed beyond all precedent?"

"That I do not know," replied Roland.

"Then I will tell you. The Archbishop of Mayence has sent peremptory orders to the other three Electors, who are reported to be careless so far as Imperial affairs are concerned, and quite indifferent regarding the personality of the future Emperor. No one of these three Electors, however, dares offend so powerful a man as Mayence. If the Archbishop can overawe his colleagues nominally equal to him in position, each commanding an army, how think you can three small nobles, with no soldiers at their beck, withstand his requests, suavely given, no doubt, but with an iron menace behind them?"

"True, true," muttered Roland.

"Two of these nobles have already arrived, and are housed with the Archbishop of Mayence. The third is expected here within three days; four days at the farthest. Mayence will immediately convene the Electoral Court, when the Count Palatine, with the two Archbishops, may be astonished to find that for the first time in history, the whole seven are present in the Wahlzimmer. Mayence will ask Cologne to make the nomination, and he will put forward the name of Prince Roland. On a vote being taken the Prince will be in a minority of one. Mayence then shows his hand, nominating the Grand Duke Karl, who will be elected by a majority of one. Then may ensue a commotion in the Wahlzimmer, and accusations of bad faith, but remember that Cologne and Treves are taken completely by surprise. They cannot communicate with their commanders, for the three thousand troops which Mayence already has within Frankfort will have quietly surrounded the Town Hall that contains the Election Chamber, and Mayence's seven thousand men from the forest are pouring through the southern gate into the city, making straight for the Romer. Meanwhile the Grand Duke Karl, a man well known to the populace of Frankfort, appears on the balcony of the Kaisersaal, and is loudly acclaimed the new Emperor."

"Ah, Greusel, forgive my attitude of doubt. It is all as plain now as the Cathedral tower. Still, there will be no civil war. Treves and Cologne will gather up their troops and go home, once more defeated by a man cleverer and more unscrupulous than both of them put together. They are but infants in his hands."

"Have you any suggestion to make?" asked Greusel.

"No; there is nothing to be done. You see, the young Prince has no following. He is quite unknown in Frankfort. His name can arouse no enthusiasm, and, all in all, that strikes me as a very good thing. The Grand Duke Karl is popular, and I believe he will make a very good Emperor."

"You mean, Roland, that the Archbishop of Mayence will make a very good ruler, for he will be the real king."

"Well, after all, Joseph, there is much to be said in favor of Mayence. He is a man who knows what he wants, and, what is more, gets it, and that, after all is the main thing in life. If any one could sway the Archbishop so that he put his great talents to the benefit of his country, instead of thinking only of himself, what a triumph of influence that would be! By the Three Kings, I'd like to do it! I admire him. If I found opportunity and could persuade him to join us in the relief of Frankfort, and in opening the Rhine to commerce, we would give these inane merchants a lesson in organization."

Greusel rose from his chair, poured out another tankard full from the flagon, and drank it off.

"I must go down now and meet the guild," he said. "I have eaten nothing all day, and am as hungry as a wolf from the Taunus."

"Oh, how did you escape, by the way?"

"I didn't escape. I was led blindfolded into a tent, where my bandage was removed, and here a man in ordinary dress questioned me concerning my object in entering the forest. I told him exactly the truth, and explained what we were trying to do in Frankfort. I dare say I looked honest and rather stupid. He asked when I set out; in what direction I came; questioning me with a great affectation of indifference; wanted to know if I had met many persons, and I told him quite truthfully I met no one but the man I understood was a forester; a keeper, I supposed."

"'There are a number of us,' he said, 'hunting the wild boar, and we do not wish the animal life of these woods to be disturbed. We shall not be here longer than a week, but I advise you to seek another spot for what timber you require.'

"He asked me, finally, if any one in Frankfort knew I had come to the forest, and I answered that the guild of twenty knew, and that we were all to meet to-night at the Rheingold tavern to report. He pondered for a while on this statement, and I suppose reached the conclusion that if I did not return to Frankfort, this score of men might set out in the morning to search for me, it being well known that the forest is dangerous on account of wild boars. So, as if it were of no consequence, he blindfolded me again, apologizing privately for doing so, saying it was quite unnecessary in the first instance, but as the guard had done so, he did not wish to censure him by implication.

"I answered that it did not matter at all, but desired him to order my wrists released, which was done."

"I must say," commented Roland, "that the Archbishop of Mayence is well served by his officers. Your examiner was a wise man."

"Yes," replied Greusel, "but nevertheless, I am telling my story here in Frankfort."

"No difference for that, because, as I have said, we can do nothing. Still, it is a blessing your examiner could not guess what you overheard in the other tent. He let you go thinking you had seen and learned nothing, and in doing so warded off a search party to-morrow."

XXI. A SECRET MARRIAGE

Blessed is he that expects nothing, for he shall not be disappointed. Roland walked with Greusel across the bridge and through the streets to the entrance of the Rheingold, and there stopped.

"I shall not go down with you," he said. "You have given me much to think of, and I am in no mood for a hilarious meeting. Indeed, I fear I should but damp the enthusiasm of the lads. Continue your good work to-morrow, and report to me at my room."

With this Roland bade Greusel good-night and turned away. He walked very slowly as far as the bridge, and there, resting his arms on the parapet, looked down at the dark water. He was astonished to realize how little he cared about giving up the Emperorship, and he recalled, with a glow of delight, his recent talk in the garden with Hildegunde, and her assurance that she lacked all ambition to become the first lady in the land so long as they two spent their lives together.

The bells of Frankfort tolling the hour of ten aroused him from his reverie, and brought down his thoughts from delicious dreams of romance to realms of reality. The precious minutes were passing over his head swiftly as the drops of water beneath his feet. There was little use of feeding Frankfort if it must be given over to fire and slaughter.

With a chill of apprehension he reviewed the cold treachery of Mayence, willing to levy the horrors of civil war upon an already stricken city so long as his own selfish purposes were attained.

"And yet," he said to himself, "there must be good in the man. I wish I knew his history. Perhaps he had to fight for every step he has risen in the world. Perhaps he has been baffled and defeated by deception; overcome by chicanery until his faith died within him. My faith would die within me were it not that when I meet a Mayence I encounter also the virtue of a Cologne, and the bluff honesty of a Count Palatine. How marvelous is this world, where the trickery of a Kurzbold and a Gensbein is canceled by the faithfulness unto death of a Greusel and an Ebearhard! Thus doth good balance evil, and then—and then, how Heaven beams upon earth in the angel glance of a good woman. God guide me aright! God guide me aright!" he repeated fervently, "and suppress in me all anger and uncharitableness."

He walked rapidly across the bridge into Sachsenhausen, past his room at the street corner, and on to the monastery of the Benedictines, whose little chapel stood open night and day for the prayers of those in trouble or in sadness, habited only by one of the elder brothers, who gave, if it were needed, advice, encouragement, or spiritual comfort. Removing his hat, the Prince entered into the silence on tiptoe, and kneeling before the altar, prayed devoutly for direction, asking the Almighty to turn the thoughts of His servant, Mayence, into channels that flowed towards peace and the relief of this unhappy city.

As he rose to his feet a weight lifted from his shoulders, and the buoyancy of youth drove away the depression that temporarily overcame him on hearing of the army threatening Frankfort. His plans were honest, his methods conciliatory, and the path now seemed clear before him. The monk in charge, who had been kneeling in a dark corner near the door, now came forward to intercept him.

"Will your Highness deny me in the chapel as you did upon the bridge?"

Roland stopped. In the gloom he had not recognized the ghostly Father.

"No, Father Ambrose, and I do now what I should have done then. I pray your blessing on the enterprise before me."

"My son, it is willingly given, the more willingly that I may atone in part my forgetting of the Holy Words: 'Judge not, that ye be not judged.' I grievously misjudged you, as I learn from both the Archbishop and my kinswoman. I ask your forgiveness."

"I shall forgive you, Father Ambrose, if you make full, not partial atonement. The consequences of your mistake have proved drastic and far-reaching. The least of these consequences is that it has cost me the

Emperorship."

"Oh," moaned the good man, "mea culpa, mea culpa! No penance put upon me can compensate for that disaster."

"You blame yourself overmuch, good Father. The penance I have to impose will leave me deeply in your debt. Now, to come from the least to the greatest of these results, so far as I am concerned, my marriage with your kinswoman, whom I love devotedly, is in jeopardy. Through her conviction that I was a thief, she braved the Archbishop of Mayence, who imprisoned her, and now his Lordship has determined that the Grand Duke Karl of Hesse shall be Emperor. Thus we arrive at the most important outcome of your error. Between the overwhelming forces of Mayence and the insufficient troops of Cologne and Treves there may ensue a conflict causing the streets of Frankfort to flow with blood."

The pious man groaned dismally.

"I have a plan which will prevent this. The day after to-morrow I shall renounce all claim to the throne; but being selfish, like the rest, I refuse to renounce all claim to the woman the Archbishops themselves chose as my wife, neither shall I allow the case to be made further the plaything of circumstance. Your kinswoman, no later ago than this afternoon, confessed her love for me and her complete disregard of any position I may hold in this realm. Now, Father Ambrose, I ask you several questions. Is it in consonance with the rules of the Church that a marriage be solemnized in this chapel?"

"Yes."

"Are you entitled to perform the ceremony?"

"Yes."

"Is it possible this ceremony can be performed to-morrow?"

"Yes."

"Will you therefore attend to the necessary preliminaries, of which I am vastly ignorant, and say at what hour the Countess and I may present ourselves in this chapel?"

"The Archbishop of Cologne is guardian to her ladyship. Will you bring me his sanction?"

"Ah, Father Ambrose, there is just the point. So far as concerns himself I doubt not that the Archbishop is the most unambitious of men, but to the marriage of his ward with a sword maker I fear he would refuse consent which he would gladly give to a marriage with an Emperor."

The monk hung his head, and pondered on the proposition. At last he said:

"Why not ask my Lord the Archbishop?"

"I dare not venture. Too much is at stake. She might be carried away to any castle in Germany. Remember that Cologne has already acquiesced in her imprisonment, and but that the iron chain of the Pfalzgraf brought me to her prison door—The iron chain, do I say? 'Twas the hand of God that directed me to her, and now, with the help of Him who guided me, not all the Archbishops in Christendom shall prevent our marriage. No, Father Ambrose, pile on yourself all the futile penances you can adopt. They are useless, for they do not remedy the wrong you have committed. And now, good-night to your Reverence!"

The young man strode towards the door.

"My son," said the quiet voice of the priest, "when you were on your knees just now did you pray for remission from anger?"

Roland whirled round.

"Mea culpa, as you said just now. Father Ambrose, I ask your pardon. I made an unfair use of your mistake to coerce you. You were quite right in relating what your own eyes saw here in Frankfort, and although the inference drawn was wrong, you were not to blame for that. I recognize your scruples, but nevertheless protest that already I possess the sanction of the Archbishop, which has never been withdrawn."

"Prince Roland, if you bring hither the Countess von Sayn to-morrow afternoon, when the bells strike three, I will marry you, and gladly accept whatever penances ensue. I fear the monk's robe has not crushed out all the impulses of the Sayn blood. In my case, perhaps, it has only covered them. And now, good-night, and God's blessing fall upon you and her you are to marry."

Roland went directly from the chapel to his own room, where he slept the sleep of one who has made up his mind. Nevertheless, it was not a dreamless sleep, for throughout the night he seemed to hear the tramp of armed men marching upon unconscious Frankfort, and this sound was so persistent, that at last he woke, yet still it continued. Springing up in alarm, and flinging wide the wooden shutters of his window, he was amazed to see that the sun was already high, while the sound that disturbed him was caused by a procession of heavy-footed horses, dragging over the cobble-stones carts well-laden with farm produce.

Having dressed and finished breakfast, he wrote a letter to the Archbishop of Mayence:

"My LORD ARCHBISHOP,—There are some important proposals which I wish to make to the Electors, and as it is an unwritten rule that I should not communicate with them separately, I beg of you to convene a meeting to-morrow, in the Wahlzimmer, at the hour of midday. Perhaps it is permissible to add, for your own information, that while my major proposition has to do with the relief of Frankfort, the minor suggestions I shall make will have the effect of clearing away obstacles that at present obstruct your path, and I venture to think that what I say will meet with your warmest approval."

It was so necessary that this communication should reach the Archbishop as soon as possible that Roland became his own messenger, and himself delivered the document at the Archbishop's Palace. As he turned away he was startled by a hand being placed on his shoulder with a weight suggesting an action of arrest rather than a greeting of friendship. He turned quickly, and saw the Lieutenant who had so discourteously used him in the square. There was, however, no menace in the officer's countenance.

"Still thrusting your sword at people?"

"Yes, Lieutenant, and very harmlessly. 'Tis a bloodless combat I wage with the sword. I praise its construction, and leave to superiors like yourself, sir, the proving of its quality."

"You are an energetic young man, and we of Mayence admire competence whether shown by mechanic or noble. Was the letter you handed in just now addressed to his Lordship?"

"Yes, Lieutenant."

"'Twill be quite without effect."

"It grieves me to hear you say so, sir."

"Take my advice, and make no effort to see the Archbishop until after the Election. I judge you to be a sane young fellow, for whom I confess a liking. You are the only man in Frankfort who has unhesitatingly told me the exact truth, and I have not yet recovered from my amazement. Now, when you return to your frugal room in Sachsenhausen you do not attempt to reach it by mounting the stairs with one step?"

"Naturally not, Lieutenant."

"Very well. When the Emperor is proclaimed, come you to me. I'll introduce you to my superior, and he, if impressed with your weapon, will take you a step higher, and thus you will mount until you come to an officer who may give you an astonishing order."

"I thank you, Lieutenant, and hope later to avail myself of your kindness."

The Lieutenant slapped him on the shoulder, and wished him good-luck. As Roland pushed his way through the crowd, he said to himself, with a sigh:

"I regret not being Emperor, if only for the sake of young fellows like that."

Frankfort was transformed as if a magician had waved his wand over it. The streets swarmed with people. Farmers' vehicles of every description added to the confusion, and Roland frowned as he noticed how badly organized had been the preparations for coping with this sudden influx of food, but he also saw that the men of Mayence had taken a hand in the matter, and were rapidly bringing method out of chaos. The uniforms of Cologne or Treves were seldom seen, while the quiet but firm soldiers of Mayence were everywhere ordering to their homes those already served, and clearing the way for the empty-handed.

At last Roland reached the Palace of Cologne, through a square thronged with people. Within he found his mother and the Countess, seated in a room whose windows overlooked the square, watching the stirring scene presented to them. Having saluted his mother, he greeted the girl with a quiet pressure of the hand.

"What is the cause of all this commotion?" asked the Empress.

Roland tapped his breast.

"I am the cause, mother," and he related the history of the relief committee, and if appreciation carries with it gratification, his was the advantage of knowing that the two women agreed he was the most wonderful of men.

"But indeed, mother," continued Roland, "I selfishly rob you of the credit. The beginning of all this was really your gift to me of five hundred thalers, that time I came to crave your assistance in procuring me this document I still carry, and without your thalers and the parchment, this never could have happened. So you see they have increased like the loaves and fishes of Holy Writ, and thus feed the multitude."

Her Majesty arose, smiling.

"Ah, Roland," she said, kissing him, "you always gave your mother more credit than she deserved. It wrung my heart at the time that I was so scant of money." Then, pleading fatigue, the Empress left the room.

"Hilda!" cried the young man, "when you and I discuss things, those things become true. Yesterday we agreed that the Imperial throne was not so enviable a seat as a chair by the domestic hearth. To-day I propose to secure the chair at the hearth, and to-morrow I shall freely give up the Imperial throne."

The girl uttered an exclamation that seemed partly concurrence and partly dismay, but she spoke no word, gazing at him intently as he strode up and down the room, and listening with eagerness. Walking backwards and forwards, looking like an enthusiastic boy, he very graphically detailed the situation as he had learned it from Greusel.

"Now you see, my dear, any opposition to the Archbishop of Mayence means a conflict, and supposing in that conflict our friends were to win, the victory would be scarcely less disastrous than defeat. I at once made up my mind, fortified by my knowledge of your opinion on the subject, that for all the kingships in the world I could not be the cause of civil dissension."

"That is a just and noble decision," she said, speaking for the first time.

Then, standing before her, the young man in more moderate tone related what had happened and what had been said in the chapel of the Benedictine Fathers. She looked up at him, earnest face aglow, during the first part of his recital, and now and then the sunshine of a smile flickered at the corners of her mouth as she recognized her kinsman in her lover's repetition of his words, but when it came to the question of a marriage, her eyes sank to the floor, and remained there.

"Well, Hilda," he said at last, "have you the courage to go with me, all unadvised, all unchaperoned, to the chapel this afternoon at three o'clock?"

She rose slowly, still without looking at him, placed her hands on his shoulders, then slipped them round his neck, laying her cheek beside his.

"It requires no courage, Roland," she whispered, "to go anywhere if you are with me. I need to call up my courage only when I think with a shudder of our being separated."

Some minutes elapsed before conversation was resumed.

"Where is the Archbishop?" asked Roland, in belated manner remembering his host.

"He and the Count Palatine went out together about an hour since. I think they were somewhat disturbed at the unusual commotion, and desired to know what it meant. Do you want to consult my guardian after all?"

"Not unless you desire me to do so?"

"I wish only what you wish, Roland."

"I am glad his Lordship is absent. Let us to the garden, Hilda, and discover a quiet exit if we can."

A stout door was found in the wall to the rear, almost concealed with shrubbery. The bolts were strong, and rusted in, but the prowess of Roland overcame them, and he drew the door partially open. It looked out upon a narrow alley with another high wall opposite. Roland looked up and down the lane, and saw it was completely deserted.

"This will do excellently," he said, shoving the door shut again, but without thrusting the bolts into position. He took her two hands in his.

"Dearest, noblest, sweetest of girls! I must now leave you. Await me here at half-past one. I go out by this door, for it is necessary I should know exactly where the alley joins a main street. It would be rather embarrassing if you were standing here, and Father Ambrose looking for us in the chapel, while I was frantically searching for and not finding the lane."

Some time in advance of the hour set, the impatient young man kept the appointment he had made, and when the Countess appeared exactly on the minute, he held open the door for her, then, drawing it shut behind him, they were both out in the city of Frankfort together. Roland's high spirits were such that he could scarcely refrain from dancing along at her side.

"I'd like to take your hand," he said, "and swing it, and show you the sights of the city, as if we were two young people in from the country."

"I am a country girl, please to remember," said the Countess. "I know nothing of Frankfort, or, indeed, of any other large town."

"I am glad of that, for there is much to see in Frankfort. We will make for the Cathedral, that beautiful red building, splendid and grand, where we should have been married with great and useless ceremony if I had been crowned Emperor. But I am sure the simple chapel in the working town of Sachsenhausen better suits a sword maker and his bride."

Now they came out into the busy street, which seemed more thronged than ever. In making their way to the Cathedral, the mob became so dense that progression was difficult. The current seemed setting in one direction, and it carried them along with it. Hildegunde took the young man's arm, and clung close to him.

"They are driving us, whether we will or no, towards our old enemy, the Archbishop of Mayence. That is his Palace facing the square. There is some sort of demonstration going on," cried Roland, as cheer after cheer ascended to the heavens. "How grim and silent the Palace appears, all shuttered as if it were a house of the dead! Somehow it reminds me of Mayence himself. I had pictured him occupying a house of gloom like that."

"Do you think we are in any danger?" asked the girl. "The people seem very boisterous."

"Oh, no danger at all. This mob is in the greatest good-humor. Listen to their heart-stirring cheers! The people have been fed; that is the reason of it."

"Is that why they cheer? It sounds to me like an ovation to the Archbishop! Listen to them: 'Long live Mayence! God bless the Archbishop!' There is no terror in those shouts."

Nevertheless his Lordship of Mayence had taken every precaution. The shutters of his Palace were tightly closed, and along the whole front of the edifice a double line of soldiers was ranged under the silent command of their officers. They stood still and stiffly as stone-graven statues in front of a Cathedral. The cheers rang unceasingly. Then, suddenly, as if the sinister Palace opened one eye, shutters were turned away from a great window giving upon the portico above the door. The window itself was then thrown wide. Cheering ceased, and in the new silence, from out the darkness there stepped with great dignity an old man, gorgeous in his long robes of office, and surmounting that splendid intellectual head rested the mitered hat of an Archbishop. After the momentary silence the cheers seemed to storm the very door of the sky itself, but the old man moved no muscle, and no color tinged his wan face.

"By the Kings," whispered Roland, during a temporary lull, "what a man! There stands power embodied, and yet I venture 'tis his first taste of popularity. I am glad we have seen this sight, both mob and master. How quick are the people to understand who is the real ruler of Germany! I wish he were my friend!"

Slowly the Archbishop raised his open hands, holding them for a moment in benediction over the vast assemblage. Once more the cheers died away, and every head was bowed, then the Archbishop was in his place no longer. Unseen hands closed the windows, and a moment later the shutters blinded it. The multitude began to dissolve, and the two wanderers found their way become clearer and clearer.

Together they entered the empty, red Cathedral, and together knelt down in a secluded corner. After some minutes passed thus Roland remembered that the hour of two had struck while they were gazing at the Archbishop. Gently he touched the hand of his companion. They rose, and walked slowly through the great church.

"There," he whispered, "is where the Emperor is crowned. The Archbishop of Mayence always performs that ceremony, so, after all, there is some justification for his self-assumed leadership."

Again out into the sunshine they walked to the Fahrgasse, and then to the bridge, where the Countess paused with an expression of delight at the beauty of the waterside city, glorified by the westering sun. Crossing the river, and going down the Bruckenstrasse of Sachsenhausen, Roland said:

"Referring to people who are not Emperors, that is my room at the corner, where I lived when supposed to be in prison."

"Is that where you made your swords?" she asked.

"No; Greusel's workshop and mine is farther along that side street. It is a grimy shop of no importance, but here, on the other side, we have an edifice that counts. That low building is the Benedictine monastery, and this is its little chapel."

The Countess made no comment, but stood looking at it for a few moments until her thoughts were interrupted by the solemn tones of a bell striking three. Roland went up the steps, and held open the door while she passed in, then, removing his hat, he followed her.

XXII. LONG LIVE THEIR MAJESTIES

The most anxious man in all Frankfort was not to be found among the mighty who ruled the Empire, or among the merchants who trafficked therein, or among the people who starved when there was no traffic. The most anxious man was a small, fussy individual of great importance in his own estimation, cringing to those above him, denouncing those beneath; Herr Durnberg, Master of the Romer, in other words, the Keeper of the Town Hall. The great masters whom this little master served were imperious and unreasonable. They gave him too little information regarding their intentions, yet if he failed in his strict duty towards them, they would crush him as ruthlessly as if he were a wasp.

Unhappy Durnberg! Every morning he expected the Electoral Court to be convened that day, and every evening he was disappointed. It was his first duty to lay out upon the table in that great room, the Kaisersaal, a banquet, to be partaken of by the newly-made Emperor, and by the seven potentates who elected him. It was also his duty to provide two huge tanks of wine, one containing the ruby liquor pressed out at Assmannshausen; the other the straw-colored beverage that had made Hochheim famous. These tanks were connected by pipes with the plain, unassuming fountain standing opposite the Town Hall in that square called the Romerberg. The moment an election took place Herr Durnberg turned off the flow of water from the fountain, and turned on the flow of wine, thus for an hour and a half there poured from the northward pointing spout of the fountain the rich red wine of Assmannshausen, and from the southern spout the delicate white wine of Hochheim. Now, wine will keep for a long time, but a dinner will not, so the distracted Durnberg prepared banquet after banquet for which there were no consumers.

At last, thought Herr Durnberg, his vigilance was about to be rewarded. There came up the broad, winding stair, to the landing on which opened the great doors of the Kaisersaal, two joyous-looking young people, evidently lovers, and with the hilt of his sword the youth knocked against the stout panels of the door. It was Herr Durnberg himself who opened, and he said haughtily—

"The Romer is closed, and will not be free to strangers until after the Election."

"We enter, nevertheless. I am Prince Roland, here to meet the Court of Electors, who convene at midday in the adjoining Wahlzimmer. You, Romermeister, will announce to their august Lordships that I am here, and, when their will is expressed, summon me to audience with them."

Herr Durnberg bowed almost to the polished floor, and flinging open both doors, retreated backwards, still bent double as he implored them to enter. Locking the doors, for the Electors would reach the Wahlzimmer through a private way, to be used by none but themselves, the bustling Durnberg produced two chairs, which he set by the windows in the front, and again running the risk of falling on his nose, bowed his distinguished visitors to seats where they might entertain themselves by watching the enormous crowd that filled the Romerberg from end to end, for every man in Frankfort knew an Election was impending, and it was after the banquet, when the wine began to flow in the fountain, that the new Emperor exhibited himself to his people by stepping from the Kaisersaal out upon the balcony in front of it.

"Do you feel any shyness about meeting this formidable conclave? Remember you have at least two good friends among them."

The girl placed her hand in his, and looked affectionately upon him.

"When you are with me, Roland, I am afraid of nothing."

"I should not ask you to pass through this ordeal were it not for your guardian. His astonishment at the announcement of our marriage will be so honest and unacted that even the suspicious Mayence cannot accuse him of connivance in what we have done. Of course, the strength of my position is that I have but carried out the formal request of their three Lordships; a request which has never been rescinded."

Before she could reply the hour of twelve rang forth. The deferential Herr Durnberg entered from the Wahlzimmer, and softly approached them.

"Your Highness," he said, "my Lords, the Electors, request your presence in the Wahlzimmer."

"How many are there, Romer-meister?"

"There are four, your Highness; the three Archbishops and the Count Palatine."

"Ah," breathed Roland, relieved that Mayence had not called up his reserve, and assured now that the seventh Elector had not arrived. With a glance of encouragement at his wife, Roland passed into the presence.

Herr Durnberg, anxious about the outcome, showed an inclination to close the door and remain inside, but a very definite gesture from Mayence wafted the good man to outer regions.

Mayence opened the proceedings.

"Yesterday I received a communication from your Highness, requesting me to convene this Court. I am as ignorant as my colleagues regarding the subjects to be placed before us. I therefore announce to you that we are prepared to listen."

"I thank you, my Lord of Mayence," began the Prince very quietly. "When first I had the honor of meeting your three Lordships in the Castle of Ehrenfels, I signed certain documents, and came to an agreement with you upon other verbal requests. I am not yet a man of large experience, but at that time, although comparatively few days have elapsed, I was a mere boy, trusting in the good faith of the whole world, knowing nothing of its chicanery. Since then I have been through a bitter school, learning bitter lessons, but I am nevertheless encouraged, in that for every man of treachery and deceit I meet two who are trustworthy."

"Pardon me," said Mayence suavely, "I did not understand that the discourse you proposed was to be a sermon. If your theme is a lecture on morality, I beg to remind you that this Wahlzimmer is a place of business, and what you say is better suited to a chapel or even a church, than to the Election Chamber of the Empire."

"I am sorry, my Lord," said Roland humbly, "if my introduction does not meet your approval. I assure you that the very opposite was my intention. My purpose is to show you why a change has come over me, and in order—"

"Once more I regret interrupting, but the reason for whatever change has occurred can be of little interest to any one but yourself. You begin by making vague charges of dishonesty, treachery, and what-not, against some person or persons unknown. May I ask you to be definite?"

"Is it your Lordship's wish that I should mention names?"

Cologne showed signs of uneasiness; Treves looked in bewilderment from one to another of his colleagues; the Count Palatine sat deeply interested, his elbows on the table, massive chin supported by huge hands.

"Your Highness is the best judge whether names should be mentioned or not," said Mayence, quite calmly, as if his withers were unwrung. "But you must see that if you hint at conspiracy and bafflement, certain inferences are likely to be drawn. Since the time you speak of there has been no opportunity for you to meet your fellow-men, therefore these inferences are apt to take the color that reference is made to one or the other of the three personages you did meet. I therefore counsel you either to abstain from innuendo or explain explicitly what you mean."

"I the more willingly bow to your Lordship's decision because it is characterized by that wisdom which accompanies every word your Lordship utters. I shall therefore designate good men and bad."

Mayence gazed at the young man in amazement, but merely said:

"Proceed, sir, on your perilous road."

"I am the head of a gang of freebooters. When this company left Frankfort under my command we appeared to be all of one mind. My gang consisted entirely of ironworkers, well-set-up young fellows in splendid physical condition, yet before I was gone a day on our journey I found myself confronted by mutiny. A man named Kurzbold was the leader of this rebellion; a treacherous hound, whom I sentenced to death. The two who stood by me were Greusel and Ebearhard, therefore I told you that when I met one villain I encountered two trustworthy men."

"When did this happen?" asked Mayence. "And what was the object of your freebooting expedition?"

"High Heaven!" cried the Archbishop of Cologne, unable longer to restrain his impatience when he saw the fatal trend of the Prince's confession, "what madness has overcome you? Can you not see the effect of these disturbing disclosures?"

The Prince smiled, and answered first the last question.

"'Tis an honest confession, my Lord, of what may be considered a dishonest practice. It is information that should be within your knowledge before you sit down to elect an Emperor.

"When did this happen, my Lord of Mayence?" he continued, turning to the chairman. "It happened when you thought I was your prisoner in Ehrenfels. Never for a day did you hold me there. I roamed the country at my pleasure. I examined leisurely and effectively the defenses of nearly every castle on the Rhine from the town of Bonn to your own city of Mayence. The object of our expedition, you ask? It was to loot the stolen treasure of the robber castles, and incidentally it resulted in the destruction by fire of Furstenberg. The marauding excursion ended at Pfalz, where I lightened the Pfalzgraf of his wealth, and liberated the Countess von Sayn, unlawfully imprisoned within that fortress."

"By the Three Kings!" cried the Count Palatine, bringing his huge fist down on the table like the blow of a sledge hammer, "you are a man, and I glory that it is my privilege to vote for you."

"I agree with my brother of Cologne," said Treves, speaking for the first time, "that this young man does not properly weigh the inevitable result of his terrible words. I vote, of course, with my Lord of Mayence, but such a vote will be most reluctantly given for a self-confessed burglar and incendiary."

"Be not too hasty, gentlemen," counseled Mayence. "We are not met here to cast votes. Your Highness, I complained a moment ago of lack of interest in your recital; I beg to withdraw that plea. After having heard you I agree that the Countess was unjustly imprisoned. She was accurate in her estimate of your character."

"I think not, my Lord, I do not regard myself as burglar, incendiary, thief, or robber. I call myself rather a restorer of stolen property. I shed no blood, which in itself is a remarkable feature of action so drastic as mine. The incendiarism was merely incidental, forced upon me by the fact that the Red Margrave tied up eighteen of my men, whom he proposed presently to hang. I diverted his attention from this execution by the first method that occurred to me, namely, the firing of his Castle. In my letter to you yesterday, my Lord, I promised to clear away certain obstacles from your path. I therefore remove one, by saying that an object of this conference is my own renunciation of the Emperorship, thus while I thank my Lord Count for his proffered franchise, I quiet the mind of my Lord of Treves by assuring him his defection has no terror for me. And now, my Lord of Mayence, will you listen carefully to my suggestion?"

"Prince Roland," replied his Lordship, almost with geniality, "I have never heard so graphic a narrator in my life. Proceed, I beg of you."

"When our band of cut-purses set out from Frankfort, they supposed the gold was to be shared equally among us. Mutiny taught me to use the arts of diplomacy, which I despise. I hoped to attain such influence over them that they would agree to abjure wealth for the benefit of Frankfort. I am happy to say that I accomplished my object, so that yesterday and to-day you have witnessed the results of my efforts; the relief of a starving city. I merely removed the wealth of robbers to benefit those whom they robbed. Knowing the dangerous feeling actuating this town against your Lordships, I caused proclamation to be made crediting this relief to the Archbishops.

"My Lord of Mayence, when yesterday I saw you appear on your own balcony, the most stern, the most dignified figure I ever beheld; when I heard the ringing cheers that greeted you; when I realized, as never before, the majesty of your genius, I cursed the stupid decree of Fate that denied me your friendship. What could we not have accomplished together for the Fatherland? I, with my youth and energy, under the tutelage of your wisdom and experience. You tasted there, probably for the first time in your life, the intoxicating cup of popularity, yet it affected you no more than if you had drunk of the fountain in the Romerberg.

"Now, my Lords, here is what I ask of you, and it will show how much I would have depended upon you had I been chosen to the position at first proposed to me. I request you, my Lord of Treves, to remove your three thousand troops to the other side of the Rhine."

"I shall do nothing of the sort," blurted Treves, amazed at the absurd proposal.

Roland went on, unheeding:

"I ask you, my Lord of Cologne, to march your troops to Assmannshausen."

"You indeed babble like the boy you said you were!" cried the indignant Cologne. "You show no grasp of statesmanship."

A faint smile quivered on the thin lips of Mayence at his colleagues' ill-disguised fear at leaving him the man in possession so far as Frankfort was concerned. The naive proposal which angered his two brethren merely amused Mayence. This young man's absurdity was an intellectual treat. Roland smiled in sympathy as he turned towards him, but his next words banished all expression of pleasure from the face of Mayence.

"I hope to succeed better with you, my Lord. Of course I recognize I have no standing with this Court since my refusal of the gift you intended to bestow. I ask you to draft into this city seven thousand men;" then after a pause: *"the seven thousand will not have far to march, my Lord."*

He caught an expression almost of fear in the Archbishop's eyes, which were quickly veiled, but his Lordship's tone was as unwavering as ever when he asked:

"What do you mean by that?"

"I mean that the city of Mayence is nearer to Frankfort than either Cologne or Treves."

"Your geographical point is undeniable. What am I to do with my ten thousand once they are here?"

"My Lord, I admire the rigid discipline of your men, and estimate from that the genius of organization possessed by your officers; a genius imparted, I believe, by you. No one knows better than I the state of confusion which this effort at relief has brought upon the city. I suggest that your capable officers divide this city into cantons, proclaim martial law, and deliver to every inhabitant rations of food as if each man, woman, and child were a member of your army. Meanwhile the merchants should be relieved of a task for which they have proved their incapacity, and turn their attention to commerce. This relief at best must be temporary. The vital task is to open the Rhine. The merchants will load every barge on the river with goods, and this flotilla the armies of Treves and Cologne will escort in safety to the latter city. In passing they will deliver an ultimatum to every castle, demanding a contribution in gold towards the further relief of Frankfort, until commerce readjusts itself, and assuring each nobleman that if this commerce is molested, his castle shall be forfeited, and himself imprisoned or hanged."

"Quite an effective plan, I think, your Highness, to which I willingly agree, if you can assure me of the support of my two colleagues, which I regret to say has already been refused."

His Lordship looked from one to another, but neither withdrew his declaration.

"Prince Roland," continued Mayence, "we seem to have reached a deadlock, and I fear its cause is that distrust of one human being toward another that you deplored a while ago. I confess myself, however, so pleased with the trend of your mind as exhibited in your conversation with us, that I am desirous to know what further proposals you care to make, now that our mutual good intentions have led us into an impasse."

"Willingly, my Lord. I propose that you at once proceed to the Election of an Emperor, for the delay in his choosing has already caused an anxiety and a tension dangerous to the peace of this country."

"Ah, that is easier said than done, your Highness. Having yourself eliminated the one on whom we were agreed, it seems to me you should at least suggest a substitute."

"Again willingly, my Lord. You should choose some quiet, conservative man, and, if possible, one well known to the citizens of Frankfort, and held in good esteem by the people everywhere. He should be a man of middle age—" Mayence's eyes began to close again, and his lips to tighten—"and if he had some experience in government, that would be all to the good. One already married is preferable to a bachelor, for then no delicate considerations regarding a woman can arise, as, I need not remind your Lordship, have arisen in my own case. A man of common sense should be selected, who would not make rash experiments with the ideals of the German people, as a younger and less balanced person might be tempted to do. That he should be a good Churchman goes without saying—"

"A truce, a truce!" cried Mayence sternly. "Again we are running into a moral catalogue impossible of embodiment. Is there any such man in your mind, or are you merely treating us to a counsel of perfection?"

"Notwithstanding my pessimism," said Roland, "I still think so well of my countrymen as to believe there are many such. Not to make any recommendation to those so much better qualified to judge than I, but merely to give a sample, I mention the Grand Duke Karl of Hesse, who fulfills every requirement I have named."

For what seemed to the onlookers a tense period of suspense, the old man seated and the young man standing gazed intently at one another. Mayence knew at once that in some manner unknown to him the Prince had fathomed his intentions; that his Highness alone knew why the Election had been delayed, yet the Prince conveyed this knowledge directly to the person most concerned, in the very presence of those whom Mayence desired to keep ignorant, without giving them the slightest hint anent the actual state of affairs.

The favorable opinion which the Archbishop had originally formed of Roland in Ehrenfels during this conference became greatly augmented. Even the most austere of men is more or less susceptible to flattery, and yet in flattering him Roland had managed to convey his own sincerity in this laudation.

"We will suppose the Grand Duke Karl elected," Mayence said at last. "What then?"

"Why then, my Lord, the three differing bodies of troops at present occupying Frankfort would be withdrawn, and the danger line crossed over to the right side."

Mayence now asked a question that in his own mind was crucial. Once more he would tempt the young man to state plainly what he actually knew.

"Can your Highness give us any reason why you fear danger from the presence of troops commanded by three friendly men like my colleagues and myself?"

"My fear is that the hands of one or the other of you may be forced, and I can perhaps explain my apprehension better by citing an incident to which I have already alluded. I had not the slightest intention of burning Castle Furstenberg, but suddenly my hand was forced. I was responsible for the safety of my men. I hesitated not for one instant to fire the Castle. Of the peaceful intentions of my Lords the Archbishops there can be no question, but at any moment a street brawl between the soldiers, say, of Cologne and Treves, may bring on a crisis that can only be quelled by bloodshed. Do you see my point?"

"Yes, your Highness, I do, and your point is well taken. I repose such confidence in our future Emperor that voluntarily I shall withdraw my troops from Frankfort at once. Furthermore, I shall open the Rhine, by sending along its banks the ultimatum you propose, not supported by my army, but supported by the name of the Archbishop of Mayence, and I shall be interested to know what Baron on the Rhine dare flout that title. Will you accept my aid, Prince Roland?"

"I accept it, my Lord, with deep gratitude, knowing that it will prove effective."

His Lordship rose in his place.

"I said this was not an Electoral Court. I rise to announce my mistake. We Electors here gathered together form a majority. I propose to you the name of Prince Roland, son of our late Emperor."

"My Lord, my Lord!" cried Roland, raising his hand, "you do not know all."

"Patient Heaven!" cried the irritated Archbishop, "you make too much of us as father confessors. Do not tell us now you have been guilty of assassination!"

"No, my Lord, but you should know that I have married the Lady Hildegunde, Countess von Sayn, whom you have already rejected as Empress."

"Well, if you have accepted the dame, the balance is redressed. I am not sure but you made an excellent choice."

It was now the turn of the amazed Archbishop of Cologne to rise to his feet.

"What his Highness says is impossible. The Lady von Sayn has been in my care ever since she entered Frankfort, and I pledge my word she has never left my Palace!"

"We were married yesterday at three o'clock, in the chapel of the Benedictine Fathers, and in the presence of four of them. We left your Palace, my Lord, by a door which you may discover in the wall of your garden, near the summer-house, and my wife is present in the adjoining room to implore your forgiveness."

Cologne collapsed into his chair, and drew a hand across his bewildered brow. The situation appeared to amuse Mayence.

"I wish your Highness had withheld this information until I was sure that my brother of Treves will vote with me, as he promised. My Lord of Treves, you heard my proposition. May I count on your concurrence?"

Treves' house of cards fell so suddenly to the ground that under the compelling eyes of Mayence he could do no more than stammer his acquiescence.

"I vote for the Prince," he said in tones barely audible.

"And you, my Lord of Cologne?"

"Aye," said Cologne gruffly.

"The Count Palatine?"

"Yes," thundered the latter. "A choice that meets my full approval, and I speak now for the Empress as well as the Emperor."

"Durnberg!" cried Mayence, raising his voice.

The doors were instantly opened, and the cringing Romer-meister appeared.

"Is the banquet prepared?"

"Ready to lay on the table, my Lord."

"The wine for the fountains?"

"Needs but the turning of the tap, my Lord."

"Order up the banquet, turn the tap; and as the new Emperor is unknown to the people, cause heralds with trumpets to set out and proclaim the Election of Prince Roland of Frankfort."

"Yes, my Lord."

The Archbishop of Mayence led the way out into the grand Kaisersaal, and the new Empress rose from her chair, standing there, her face white as the costume she wore. Mayence advanced to her, bending his gray head over the hand he took in his own.

"Your Majesty," he said gravely, and this was her first hint of the outcome,

"I congratulate you upon your marriage, as I have already congratulated your husband."

"My Lord Archbishop," she said in uncertain voice, "you cannot blame me for obeying you."

"I think my poor commands would have been futile were it not for the assistance lent me by his Majesty."

The salutations of the others were drowned by the cheers of the great assemblage in the Romerberg. The red wine and white had begun to flow, and the people knew what had happened. In the intervals between the clangor of the trumpets, they heard that a Prince of their own town had been elected, so all eyes turned to the Romer, and cries of "The Emperor! The Emperor!" issued from every throat. The multitude felt that a new day was dawning.

"I believe," said Mayence, "that hitherto only the Emperor has appeared on the balcony, but to-day I suggest a precedent. Let Emperor and Empress appear before the people."

He motioned to Herr Durnberg, and the latter flung open the tall windows; then Roland taking his wife's hand, stepped out upon the balcony.

THE END

About Author

Robert Barr (16 September 1849 – 21 October 1912) was a Scottish-Canadian short story writer and novelist.

Early years in Canada

Robert Barr was born in Barony, Lanark, Scotland to Robert Barr and Jane Watson. In 1854, he emigrated with his parents to Upper Canada at the age of four years old. His family settled on a farm near the village of Muirkirk. Barr assisted his father with his job as a carpenter, and developed a sound work ethic. Robert Barr then worked as a steel smelter for a number of years before he was educated at Toronto Normal School in 1873 to train as a teacher.

After graduating Toronto Normal School, Barr became a teacher, and eventually headmaster/principal of the Central School of Windsor, Ontario in 1874. While Barr worked as head master of the Central School of Windsor, Ontario, he began to contribute short stories—often based on personal experiences, and recorded his work. On August 1876, when he was 27, Robert Barr married Ontario-born Eva Bennett, who was 21. According to the 1891 England Census, the couple appears to have had three children, Laura, William, and Andrew.

In 1876, Barr quit his teaching position to become a staff member of publication, and later on became the news editor for the Detroit Free Press. Barr wrote for this newspaper under the pseudonym, "Luke Sharp." The idea for this pseudonym was inspired during his morning commute to work when Barr saw a sign that read "Luke Sharp, Undertaker." In 1881, Barr left Canada to return to England in order to start a new weekly version of "The Detroit Free Press Magazine."

London years

In 1881 Barr decided to "vamoose the ranch", as he called the process of immigration in search of literary fame outside of Canada, and relocated to London to continue to write/establish the weekly English edition of the Detroit Free Press. During the 1890s, he broadened his literary works, and started writing novels from the popular crime genre. In 1892 he founded the magazine The Idler, choosing Jerome K. Jerome as his collaborator (wanting, as Jerome said, "a popular name"). He retired from its co-editorship in 1895.

In London of the 1890s Barr became a more prolific author—publishing a book a year—and was familiar with many of the best-selling authors of his day, including :Arnold Bennett, Horatio Gilbert Parker, Joseph Conrad, Bret Harte, Rudyard Kipling, H. Rider Haggard, H. G. Wells, and George Robert Gissing. Barr was well-spoken, well-cultured due to travel, and considered a "socializer."

Because most of Barr's literary output was of the crime genre, his works were highly in vogue. As Sherlock Holmes stories were becoming well-known, Barr wrote and published in the Idler the first Holmes parody, "The Adventures of "Sherlaw Kombs" (1892), a spoof that was continued a decade later in another Barr story, "The Adventure of the Second Swag" (1904). Despite those jibes at the growing Holmes phenomenon, Barr remained on very good terms with its creator Arthur Conan Doyle. In Memories and Adventures, a serial memoir published 1923–24, Doyle described him as "a volcanic Anglo—or rather Scot-American, with a violent manner, a wealth of strong adjectives, and one of the kindest natures underneath it all".

In 1904, Robert Barr completed an unfinished novel for Methuen & Co. by the recently deceased American author Stephen Crane entitled The O'Ruddy, a romance.Despite his reservations at taking on the project, Barr reluctantly finished the last eight chapters due to his longstanding friendship with Crane and his common-law wife, Cora, the war correspondent and bordello owner.

Death

The 1911 census places Robert Barr, "a writer of fiction," at Hillhead, Woldingham, Surrey, a small village southeast of London, living with his wife, Eva, their son William, and two female servants. At this home, the author died from heart disease on 21 October 1912.

Writing Style

Barr's volumes of short stories were often written with an ironic twist in the story with a witty, appealing narrator telling the story. Barr's other works also include numerous fiction and non-fiction contributions to periodicals. A few of his mystery stories and stories of the supernatural were put in anthologies, and a few novels have been republished. His writings have also attracted scholarly attention. His narrative personae also featured moral and editorial interpolations within their tales. Barr's achievements were recognized by an honorary degree from the University of Michigan in 1900.

His protagonists were journalists, princes, detectives, deserving commercial and social climbers, financiers, the new woman of bright wit and aggressive accomplishment, and lords. Often, his characters were stereotypical and romanticized.

Barr wrote fiction in an episode-like format. He developed this style when working as an editor for the newspaper Detroit Press. Barr developed his skill with the anecdote and vignette; often only the central character serves to link the nearly self-contained chapters of the novels. (Source: Wikipedia)

NOTABLE WORKS

In a Steamer Chair and Other Stories (Thirteen short stories by one of the most famous writers in his day -1892)

"The Face And The Mask" (1894) consists of twenty-four delightful short stories.

In the Midst of Alarms (1894, 1900, 1912), a story of the attempted Fenian invasion of Canada in 1866.

From Whose Bourne (1896) Novel in which the main character, William Brenton, searches for truth to set his wife free.

One Day's Courtship (1896)

Revenge! (Collection of 20 short stories, Alfred Hitchcock-like style, thriller with a surprise ending)

The Strong Arm

A Woman Intervenes (1896), a story of love, finance, and American journalism.

Tekla: A Romance of Love and War (1898)

Jennie Baxter, Journalist (1899)

The Unchanging East (1900)

The Victors (1901)

A Prince of Good Fellows (1902)

Over The Border: A Romance (1903)

The O'Ruddy, A Romance, with Stephen Crane (1903)

A Chicago Princess (1904)

The Speculations of John Steele (1905)

The Tempestuous Petticoat (1905–12)

A Rock in the Baltic (1906)

The Triumphs of Eugène Valmont (1906)

The Measure of the Rule (1907)

Stranleigh's Millions (1909)

The Sword Maker (Medieval action/adventure novel, genre: Historical Fiction-1910)

The Palace of Logs (1912)

"The Ambassadors Pigeons" (1899)

"And the Rigor of the Game" (1892)

"Converted" (1896)

"Count Conrad's Courtship" (1896)

"The Count's Apology" (1896)

"A Deal on Change " (1896)

"The Exposure of Lord Stanford" (1896)

"Gentlemen: The King!"

"The Hour-Glass" (1899)

"An invitation" (1892)

" A Ladies Man"

"The Long Ladder" (1899)

"Mrs. Tremain" (1892)

" Transformation" (1896)

"The Understudy" (1896)

" The Vengeance of the Dead" (1896)

"The Bromley Gibbert's Story" (1896)

" Out of Thun" (1896)

"The Shadow of Greenback" (1896)

"Flight of the Red Dog" (fiction)

"Lord Stranleigh Abroad" (1913)

"One Day's Courtship and the Herald's of Fame" (1896)

"Cardillac"

"Dr. Barr's Tales"

"The Triumphs of Eugene Valmont"

CPSIA information can be obtained
at www.ICGtesting.com
Printed in the USA
LVHW090346140720
660560LV00013B/620